**PRAISE FOR THE FIREKEEPER NOVELS
OF JANE LINDSKOLD**

"What do you get when you mix lost magic and feral children with dynastic politics, wolf social dynamics, treason, and overambitious, social-climbing parents? You get Jane Lindskold's new novel, *Through Wolf's Eyes*, and another stay-up-to-finish-the-last-page read."

—David Weber

"Her characters live—they're real, but they are *different*. And the world they live in lingers in the mind; heroic, squalid, exotic, everyday. I was convinced that it went on by itself when I turned the last page. Bravo!"

—S. M. Stirling on *Through Wolf's Eyes*

"One thing I like about Jane Lindskold's books is that she plays fair with her readers. It doesn't matter that she's writing a series; each book will stand on its own and be a satisfying read for all that it adds depth and texture to what went before."

—Charles de Lint on *Wolf's Head, Wolf's Heart*

"Exciting!"

—*Publishers Weekly* (starred review) on *Wolf Captured*

WOLF'S
BLOOD

TOR BOOKS BY JANE LINDSKOLD

❧

WOLF'S BLOOD

JANE LINDSKOLD

A TOM DOHERTY ASSOCIATES BOOK
NEW YORK

This is a work of fiction. All of the characters, organizations, and events portrayed in this novel are either products of the author's imagination or are used fictitiously.

WOLF'S BLOOD

Copyright © 2007 by Jane Lindskold

All rights reserved, including the right to reproduce this book, or portions thereof, in any form.

Edited by Teresa Nielsen Hayden

Map by James Sinclair based on an original drawing by James Moore

A Tor Book
Published by Tom Doherty Associates, LLC
175 Fifth Avenue
New York, NY 10010

www.tor.com

Tor® is a registered trademark of Tom Doherty Associates, LLC.

ISBN-13: 978-0-7653-5374-0
ISBN-10: 0-7653-5374-1

First Edition: March 2007
First Mass Market Edition: January 2008

Printed in the United States of America

0 9 8 7 6 5 4 3 2 1

For Jim, as ever, as always . . .

ACKNOWLEDGMENTS

Firekeeper, the wolves, and I have had a good run, and for us all, I'd like to thank those who cleared the trail along the way.

My husband, Jim Moore, serves as my sounding board while the book is being written, as my first reader when I have a manuscript, and as a patient soul throughout the project. He also draws my maps—a challenge in and of itself.

My agent, Kay McCauley, has run with my enthusiasms and kept me going when I faltered.

The folks at Tor have been invaluable, especially my editors, Teresa and Patrick Nielsen Hayden, and my publisher, Tom Doherty.

Julie Bell's artwork has given the book covers a distinctive look, and lured many people who don't usually read fantasy into Firekeeper's world.

The "wild canine people," including the staff of Wild Spirit Wolf Sanctuary, Ellie and Roger Daisley, and Phyllis White, have been of great help supplying facts, permitting contact with various animals, and even letting a wolf pup pee in my lap!

Finally, I'd like to acknowledge the many readers who have contacted me, whether at signings and conventions or through the mail. You have my deepest thanks for taking the time to share your enthusiasm for Firekeeper's story. You know who you are! Thanks!

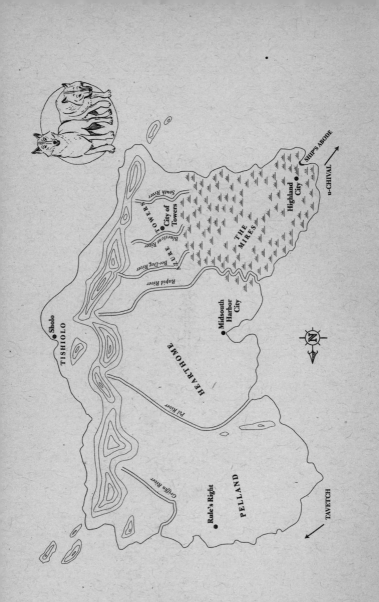

BOOK
ONE

I

FIREKEEPER STOOD, FEET planted slightly apart, head held high, and looked from her past into her future.

She was a woman of indeterminate age, certainly no longer a child, but beyond that certain estimation placing her age would have been a challenge. Life lived in all the tempers changing seasons could hold had browned fair skin and faded brown hair, but her eyes were bright, her teeth white and strong.

Her attire showed hard use. She was clad in worn leather trousers laced below the knee, and a battered cotton shirt that might once have been dyed pale green. Her feet were bare. A long hunting knife from whose hilt a garnet shone a muted dark red was belted at her waist. A bow was slung over her shoulder, along with a quiver containing a handful of arrows.

Dozens of scars, silvery white against the tanned skin, again testified to a hard life, yet there was a quickness to Firekeeper's motions, a fluidity and power that spoke of youth and youth's vigor. This contrasted vividly with something in her dark, dark eyes, something that hinted at challenges and sorrows young bones and muscles should not have known, but that had scarred as deeply as any tooth or claw.

"Blind Seer, how many years have gone by since you and I crossed the Iron Mountains into the east?"

Firekeeper spoke a language most humans would not have even realized was being spoken, much less understood, and the one to whom she spoke was no human but rather a grey wolf the size of a small pony, albeit much leaner in build. Blind Seer did not look at Firekeeper when she spoke, his piercingly blue eyes focused, as were her own, on some middle distance.

"Six springs into spring again," came the wolf's reply. "Six rounding of does' sides and budding of new antlers on proud bucks, six springs where fat puppies stumbled from the dens in which their mothers had hidden them to face the proud inspection of their packs. Six, if you count this spring, and this I do most sincerely."

Firekeeper huffed agreement through her nose, a movement of air that spoke volumes to the wolf.

"Is it spring, then, that makes me restless?"

"Don't blame spring, sweet Firekeeper. Spring has done nothing but be spring. You know who is to blame, who has been whispering in your ear. I have heard what you say in your dreams, and although you have not told me, I know who has returned to haunt you."

"I have always had nightmares," Firekeeper replied, not quite admitting to the truth of the wolf's statement.

"Always," Blind Seer agreed. "As long as I have known you, as long as any of my pack have known you—and we took you in and made you our own when you were but a small child—as long ago as that and maybe before, you have had nightmares, but this is something different, and you know it and I know it. Will you deny what is as plain as sunlight on a cloudless day?"

Firekeeper sighed and buried her hand in the thick fur of Blind Seer's scruff. "I cannot, nor will I, at least not to you. Three nights running and three more before that, the Meddler has come into my dreams. He talks most seriously, and the matters he raises are grave and seem to make sense, but I fear to be guided by him."

Blind Seer's hackles rose. Firekeeper felt the stiff guard hairs of his coat prickle against her skin.

"The Meddler earned that name for a reason, dear heart," the wolf said in a rumbling growl. "He also earned the ill reputation that goes with that name, as we know all too well. His meddling has caused considerable trouble, not just for us, although we have seen our share, but—if we are to believe the tales Harjeedian tells—for generations so long past that even their bones have returned to the soil."

Firekeeper nodded agreement that held the faintest trace of reluctance. The wolf tilted back his head to gaze upon her face.

"Will you tell me what the Meddler has said when he comes into your dreams?"

Firekeeper hesitated, knowing her delay was a trifle longer than would be polite. Had she been speaking with a human, her delay might have been taken as weighing the wisdom of speaking seriously about dreams. However, the wolf—who knew her mood from her scent—was not to be so easily fooled. She felt her skin heat with a blush.

In response to that blush, Firekeeper was aware of the rumble of Blind Seer's growl, inaudible to her ears but felt through her fingertips. Blind Seer had heard the sweet edge of the Meddler's tongue, and he knew the Meddler had an intense interest in Firekeeper. This interest might have flattered Blind Seer, for wolves are not immune to more highly prizing that which another desires, but the bond between Firekeeper and Blind Seer was sufficiently unique that the wolf was threatened rather than flattered.

But while Firekeeper did not precisely return the Meddler's interest, still she experienced her own peculiar fascination with him. The fascination was not—or so she told herself—that which a female feels for a mate. How could it be? The Meddler was not even alive. His body had been slain centuries before Firekeeper had been born, but his spirit, entrapped in a prison constructed for that purpose, had persisted.

Firekeeper told herself that she was interested in the Meddler because he possessed knowledge that no one else did. But Blind Seer read her scent—so much more honest than her thoughts—and was threatened by a potential rival.

"I will tell you," Firekeeper said at last, "but dreams are strange, and sometimes I have trouble recalling their logic."

"Some trouble," Blind Seer agreed, "but not too much trouble, else you would not be so restless. Tell what you can. I will listen."

Firekeeper sat next to the wolf, flinging her arm over his shoulders. He, in turn, settled onto his haunches. Blind Seer was large enough that in this attitude Firekeeper's head now leaned against his own. She sat this way for several long breaths, taking comfort from their proximity.

"The Meddler says," she began, the words tumbling out like water spilling over a beaver's dam, "at great length, supporting his case with many cogent arguments, that I must seek the source of the Fire Plague."

"The source of the Fire Plague?" Blind Seer asked. "What purpose would be served in finding the source of the Fire Plague?"

"Not just the source," Firekeeper amended. "The source and, with the source, the cure."

"Why does the Meddler care?" Blind Seer said. "If anyone is immune to the Fire Plague, it is he. Nor did he take particular care to warn us of the Fire Plague when we crossed to where we would be vulnerable to it. Why should he care now?"

"I asked the Meddler why he didn't warn us," Firekeeper said, glad to prove that she did not listen to the Meddler with unquestioning obedience. "He claims that he did not know the Fire Plague still lived in the Old World. He says that such things fade and die. Over a hundred years have passed since the Fire Plague first appeared—and he was already entrapped then, and so only knew of it in the abstract. The Meddler claims he did not know for certain where the Setting Sun gateway would take us. Nor did he worry unduly that it might take us to the Old World. He thought the Fire Plague likely dead or aged beyond ability to harm us. Remember, he knew nothing of how the Old World had fared since his imprisonment. He had difficulty enough contacting the New."

"Perhaps this is true," Blind Seer admitted grudgingly. "After all, even for one such as him, knowing what is happening across a great ocean might be difficult."

"The Meddler says that such knowing is perhaps not quite impossible," Firekeeper said, "but close enough to impossible."

"I am pleased that the Meddler does not claim his knowing what happens far away is impossible," Blind Seer said, "for I have seen him at home in places I would have termed impossible if I had not been there myself. I would trust him less than I do were he to claim something impossible."

"And you do not trust him very much," Firekeeper said.

"Less even than that," Blind Seer replied. "Has the Meddler told you why it is so important that the source of the Fire Plague be found—beyond, of course, that this is the way to find a cure. Why is a cure necessary all of a sudden?"

"Did you enjoy your experience when you were seized with the Plague?"

The blue-eyed wolf stiffened, even seemed to stop breathing. What had happened to him when the Fire Plague had seized hold of him and nearly killed him was a matter Blind Seer steadfastly refused to discuss. Like Firekeeper's perverse interest in the Meddler, it was one of several things that had driven a wedge between the pair, although to any watching them woman and wolf would seem as close as ever.

"The Fire Plague is not something to enjoy," Blind Seer finally replied, "only to survive."

"I would go a bit further," Firekeeper said, "and say the Fire Plague is something I would wish upon no one—not even an enemy. How then can we wish it upon our friends?"

"I do not."

"The Meddler says that if a cure is not found, then we are as good as wishing the Fire Plague upon our friends. Thus far we have been fortunate. The Plague has not reappeared in the New World, but we know now that those who were born in the New World are not immune. How long will our luck hold? How long before the Fire Plague crosses as we have crossed?"

"We have taken care," Blind Seer protested, "that none actively ill return from the Old World to the New until the sickness has run its course."

"Someday we will judge wrong," Firekeeper said. "Even if we do not, what of those who wish to come from the New World to the Nexus Islands? You know as well as I do that our allies have held those islands thus far only through constant vigilance. How long before weariness or boredom or even betrayal leads to a disaster? We cannot recruit further support from the Old World. If we are to hold the Nexus Islands, we must bring reinforcements from the New World."

"We can bring those who lack the magical talents upon which the Fire Plague feeds."

Firekeeper pulled back so she could look Blind Seer in the face—the locking of her gaze with his own a gesture of challenge among wolves as it was not among humans.

"And can we be sure to know in advance who possesses magical talents and who does not? It seems to me that there are those in whom the talents are so deeply buried that even they do not know the talents are there."

Blind Seer glowered at her, blue eyes narrowing to slits, ears pinning back, and fangs revealed in a snarl. He held that threat for a moment, but Firekeeper did not break his gaze. After a long moment the wolf shook himself calm.

"True. Such does happen. What if we recruit one or more of the maimalodalum to help inspect our candidates in advance? The maimalodalum have the ability to sense magic—even magic that is very faint. They could review potential candidates, and turn away those who would be endangered."

"There are few maimalodalum," Firekeeper said, "and those few are isolated on Misheemnekuru, and do not wish their presence to be known to the world. It is possible we might recruit one or even two, but this would only be a stopgap. In the end, we would still need a cure—or expose our allies to the Fire Plague."

"And the Meddler assures you that to find a cure, you must find the source of the Fire Plague. How does he know that? It seems to me that when the Meddler wishes to do so, he knows a great deal—and when it is convenient, he claims ignorance. Which do we believe, his ignorance or his wisdom?"

"I believe neither," Firekeeper said, "but I can see the sense in what he says. Surely nothing comes from nothing. If you want to stop a stream you must block its source. If the does are killed there will be no more fawns. So it will be with the Fire Plague . . . I hope."

"So he has convinced you to go hunting for the source of the Fire Plague?"

"He is trying to do so."

"A hunt that would take you into the Old World."

"I think so."

"Where you speak none of the languages."

Firekeeper raised her chin in defiance.

"Where there are no Royal Beasts to help you."

Firekeeper held her silence.

"Where, if we are to believe those we met on the Nexus Islands, there are places where magic is—if possible—hated even more fiercely than it is in our homeland. And you will go there, searching for a cure to the very disease or curse or whatever it is that broke the power of magic, that broke the power that was used to dominate and destroy humans and Beasts alike in the Old World and the New."

Firekeeper inclined her head in the smallest of nods.

"Yes. That is what I am considering doing. Will you come with me?"

Blind Seer huffed his breath out in a long sigh. "Of course. Where else would I be but at your side?"

❧

DERIAN CARTER COULDN'T make himself go home. Sitting in the front room of the stable master's house—what had become his house on the Nexus Islands—he tried to explain how he felt to the young woman seated across the room from him.

"Isende, look at me," Derian said, a pleading note in his voice. "Look at what the Plague—what querinalo—has done to me."

"I am looking at you," she replied. Isende tucked a lock of hair behind one ear as if to emphasize that nothing was blocking her vision. "I see a tall young man with broad shoulders, red hair, and very nice eyes."

"Red hair that grows like a mane," Derian said, reaching up and tugging. "By all my ancestors, I have a forelock! My ears are pointed and hairy and I can wriggle them. My eyes—those 'nice eyes' used to be hazel. Now they're brown—and the irises are weird. They blot out more of the whites. My finger and toenails are hard now. I need a farrier's kit to clip them."

"And you can eat grass," Isende said, "and talk to horses. Derian, the moon has shown all aspects of her face five or six times since you had querinalo. I thought you were adjusting to what happened to you. You went to see your friend when she had her baby. When are you going to visit your family? I know you miss them. I've seen the fat letters that go out with just about every post. Spring is going to open up the ports to shipping. With the gate, you're less than a moonspan from the harbor at u-Bishinti. If you left now, you could be home to Hawk Haven by midsummer at the latest. If you delay too long, winter will close the ports again."

"You have no idea how my people feel about magic," Derian replied. "I mean, your people dislike how magic was used and abused by the Old Country rulers, but you don't hate magic for itself. Magic is one of your deities. You see her face when you look up at the moon. It's not that way at home. Having a talent wasn't too bad, especially since my talent was one of those that could pretty much be concealed. After all, I am a livery stable owner's son. When I think about it, I'm not even sure I knew I had a talent until people started pointing out the obvious to me."

"I grew up," Isende said, her tones dreamy, "with people thinking I was a freak. Looking a bit different didn't matter much in Gak, because so many different peoples fled there during the chaos, and after a few generations there were some odd combinations. So having this weird hair that is brown underneath and sort of golden on top wasn't too much different. Lots of people had skin like mine, browner than yours, but not as brown as the Liglim have, but even in Gak I was a freak nonetheless, and for the same reason you think you are. Magic. My brother and I could sense what each other was feeling, almost read each other's minds in a way. When we were really little, if one of us got cut, the other would get a red mark in the same area."

"Really?"

"That's what one of our nurses told us, anyhow," Isende said. "By the time I have really clear memories, that wasn't happening anymore, but there were times Tiniel fell down and I swore I could feel my own knees aching. If he was scared, I knew it. If he was unhappy, I wanted to cry."

"But that's over now," Derian said. He was aware that his tone sounded like he was looking for reassurance.

"That's over now," Isende said. "Querinalo burned away the connection in exchange for letting us live. We paid a price. You paid a price. Querinalo turned your flesh and bones into wax. If we're to believe what those who've survived the disease say, your own will resculpted your body into the shape it now holds. Is that what's driving you crazy? Is the fact that you think you're to blame for what happened making you run from your family?"

Derian found he couldn't answer directly. His next words came out all muddled and confused—much like his thoughts.

"You should have seen the look on Elise's and Doc's faces," he said. "When we heard that the baby had come, but early, and that neither Elise nor the little girl were doing well and they might both die, Firekeeper insisted that we go and see them. I didn't need her pushing. Doc's lost one wife already to childbirth, and Elise's family . . . Well, the history of their women surviving childbirth isn't good."

"I remember what you told me about Elise," Isende said, "and I'm not likely to forget your going. You've only been back a few days. So you went."

"So I went," Derian said. "Would you believe me if I told you that I was so worried about Elise and Doc that I didn't even think about what they'd think when they got a good look at me?"

"If you say so."

"Honestly. That's how it was. When some of the ospreys relayed the news from u-Bishinti, Firekeeper jumped to her feet and was casting around for Ynamynet or Enigma or someone who could open the gate. Eshinarvash offered to come along and carry me so we wouldn't be slowed."

"It was the middle of the night," Isende said, "so most of us were asleep. All we knew was that you were gone the next morning. Plik explained what he could, and that you'd be back. There was an uproar, let me tell you."

Derian ignored her, and went on with his story as if in telling it he might understand his own reaction better. "Well, we were moving at a pretty good clip. Firekeeper and Blind Seer can pace a horse, especially at night. Eshinarvash has good night vision for a horse, but he's still careful that he doesn't wrench something. When it got dark, we decided to stop. Firekeeper suggested that maybe I'd prefer we camp somewhere a little isolated. I said that, given how Blind Seer upsets both humans and livestock, this was a good idea."

"And Firekeeper said something rude?" Isende's hands tightened around the armrests of her chair. "She can be impossibly blunt."

"No." Derian's ears flickered back, almost as a horse's would to express annoyance, then resumed their normal position. "Actually, she was very gentle. She said something about the humans maybe not being ready to see a maimalodalu. I was about to remind her Plik wasn't with us—and then I realized she meant me."

"That's an interesting comparison when you think about it," Isende said. "I mean, the translation is flawed—you didn't start out as a beast, so you can't be beast-souled—but you've the same sort of combination of human and animal traits that Plik does."

Derian forced a laugh. "Are you telling me I look like a raccoon?"

Isende's grin was genuine. "Not in the least, but just like Plik is a mixture of raccoon and human, you're a mixture of human and horse—and far more human than horse. Honestly, Derian, except maybe for the ears, I'm not sure anyone would notice the difference."

"Elise sure did," Derian said, wincing at the memory. "And Doc. I think my eyes got to them more than anything else.

They really don't look human. Too much brown. Too little white. You can't hide that under a broad-brimmed hat."

"Smoked glasses," Isende said promptly. "Like some sailors wear at sea to protect their eyes."

"You have an answer for everything," Derian said, and this time his smile was more honest.

"I see you tearing yourself up," Isende said. "You talk about your family all the time. You obviously miss them."

"I lived with them until I was nineteen," Derian said. "Then I went on the road with Earl Kestrel, and sometimes I don't think I've been home since. I don't feel like I have a home anymore."

"And you want one," Isende said. "I know how you feel. When our father died, there was just me and Tiniel, and Tin, well, he went a little . . ."

She looked very uncomfortable, and Derian struggled to save her from having to talk about her brother. The current relationship between the twins was far from good, and Derian would have had to be a whole lot more self-absorbed than he was to miss the tension. He tried to spare Isende the need to speak about past events by reviewing them himself.

"At first Tiniel wanted your family made a part of Gak's voting council," Derian said. "Then when that proposal was refused, he suggested you go out and reclaim your ancestral stronghold."

"And then we found the gate, and, well . . ." Isende shrugged. Her gaze dropped as if she sought omens in the patterns of the wood grain of the floorboards. "Here we are, two more of the reluctant, responsible residents of the Nexus Islands. You're afraid to go home—and I don't have a home to go back to."

Derian leaned forward, wanting to offer comfort, but not quite sure what to say. He didn't think Isende would want his pity, but what might she want? She couldn't want anything from him. Hadn't she just about said she thought he was like Plik, a sort of unique monstrosity? He started to reach out and at least give her a brotherly pat, but then he remembered Tiniel and froze, and when he did so he caught sight of those heavily horned nails at the ends of each of his fingers, and his impulse died within him.

The silence was getting distinctly uncomfortable. Derian didn't know whether he wanted Isende to leave or whether he wanted her to stay until he could make her smile again.

Poor return for Isende's friendship and sympathy, Derian Carter, he chided himself, *making the poor girl feel miserable and alone. Say something! Anything! Otherwise, she's going to walk out of here, and leave you by yourself feeling like something Eshinarvash leaves on the stable floor.*

"I . . ." he was starting when the howl of a wolf, the note falling from high to low, broke the stillness of the afternoon.

"Firekeeper," he said, feeling such relief that he didn't even mind when he realized that his right ear had automatically swiveled to track the sound. "Back from the mainland."

Plik had been the first to start referring to the New World as the "mainland," a habit evolved from his own life prior to coming to the Nexus Islands when he, along with the small community of maimalodalum, had lived on Center Island at the heart of Misheemnekuru. The other residents from the New World—Derian, Plik, Eshinarvash, Truth, and Harjeedian—had adopted the custom with alacrity.

As Harjeedian had said, showing far more vulnerable humanity than Derian had thought possible, "Calling the New World our mainland gives us roots, a sense that there is something to which we are connected."

And the New World residents all needed that feeling of connectedness. While Firekeeper, Blind Seer, and assorted Wise Beasts tended to commute back and forth between the Nexus Islands and the mainland, the other five had opted for more or less permanent residence on the Nexus Islands. They were needed there, for although the Old World residents had thus far honored the agreement they had made following their defeat the previous autumn, none of the New Worlders were so naïve as to believe they would continue to do so without supervision.

It all comes down to querinalo, Derian thought. *If there was no querinalo, we could instate rotating shifts here, like an army in the field or a crew aboard a ship, but because of querinalo we dare not. None of us who has lived through that horrible fever could risk inflicting it on another—and since we cannot tell for certain who will catch it and who will not . . .*

The thought continued on like a cart wheel rolling down a well-worn rut in a dirt road, but this time the wheel hit a rock and went bouncing off down the embankment.

I don't want to go home—I just can't bear the idea of how my folks would look at me—but I don't want to stay here for-ever and ever and ever.

Each "ever" sounded like the clash of an iron wheel rim against rock, and on the last clash, Firekeeper burst through the front door. Overall, the wolf-woman had improved a great deal about remembering little social courtesies like knocking on doors, but when she was excited, social graces went out the window.

Or rather, Derian thought with mild amusement, *Firekeeper would come through the window if the door wouldn't open.*

Isende looked less horrified than she might at the sight of the lithe, lean young woman and the enormous wolf now bursting through the door.

But then, Isende has known Firekeeper for moonspans now, long enough to be catty about her manners—or lack thereof. And maybe having your brother live in the back of your head most of your life gives you a bit of flexibility about the conventions.

The thought teased Derian as the beginning of something interesting, but before he could pursue it, Firekeeper flung herself down on his hearth rug and said, "Derian, I need to talk to you."

Isende rose, her posture every bit as polite and proper as Firekeeper's had not been.

"I should be going," she began, but the words were hardly out of her mouth before Firekeeper was flapping her hand in an indication that Isende should resume her place.

"No. Is not to say I have a secret to talk. You would be good to hear this, too."

Derian sighed. As always, when she was away from human

conversation for more than a few days, Firekeeper's syntax went to pieces.

Probably out of courtesy to Isende, Firekeeper had been speaking in Liglimosh, the dominant language of the southern nation of Liglim and many of the bordering city-states—including Gak, where Isende and her brother Tiniel had been born. Had Derian been the only one present, Firekeeper doubtless would have spoken Pellish, the language of Hawk Haven and Bright Bay, allied kingdoms that had been founded by the same Old World nation.

The odd thing was that Derian had noticed how Firekeeper was perfectly capable of proper grammar and syntax, but she seemed to reserve these for either those times she must translate for others, or those rare occasions that she wanted to make absolutely certain she was not misunderstood.

I suppose I should be glad Firekeeper is bilingual—at least after a fashion. Trilingual, if I count whatever it is she speaks to the Beasts. When I met her, all she could speak was Beast talk, and I'm still not convinced that counts. Less than ever, since we discovered that while I can now understand Eshinarvash and the other Wise Horses I can't "speak horse" back at them, nor can I speak any Beast language at all. There's so much I don't understand. . . .

These thoughts passed through Derian's mind in the time it took Firekeeper to convince Isende that she was entirely welcome.

"Derian," Firekeeper said when they were all settled. "I think I need to go and find where querinalo comes from. It is dangerous, to us, to our homes. We need to find it, so we can end it."

The effort the wolf-woman made to insure that she could not be misunderstood made Derian perfectly certain that she was serious.

"And how are you going to find where querinalo comes from?" he asked, trying not to sound like he was humoring her. "Does querinalo have a scent by which you can track it?"

"It has a scent," Firekeeper said, "if not one I can use to

track. I was thinking you could track for me—you and Harjee-dian and Ynamynet and all the rest."

"What?"

"Like Lady Melina find the Dragon of Despair," Fire-keeper said. "She find it, so Toriovico tell us later, through old stories. There must be stories from the time before queri-nalo came. Maybe even there are stories about how it began. The New World does not have them, because we always told that it come from the Old World, but the Old World must have stories."

Derian felt some doubt, but Isende was nodding.

"Firekeeper could be right," she said. "If not stories, then histories, records that tell where querinalo first appeared and how it spread. Was it like a bout of late-summer spots, spreading from person to person, or did it come in waves, like the sneezing fits that come with the blooming of certain flowers?"

"Would there be records like that?" Derian asked. "My un-derstanding is that the upheavals and chaos that happened in the New World after querinalo took hold were nothing to what happened in the Old World. In the New World the abandoned colonies had to make do without their rulers and the support of the Old World, but if those tales Urgana likes to tell are representative it seems to me that the Old World fell apart completely."

"But not all at once," Isende insisted. "There was more structure in place in the Old World. As Urgana tells it, the rulers did their best to conceal what was happening. There must be records, archives, something . . ."

"But how do we find those?" Derian asked. "If they're any-where, they're in the Old World, and we're here on the Nexus Islands."

"Nexus," Isende said thoughtfully. "Crossroads. Meeting point. A neutral ground between areas that otherwise were ri-vals. And after the collapse, the Nexus Islands were abandoned for a long, long while. They've only been reinhabited for ten years or so, and many of the old buildings are still untouched."

Derian stared at her. "Are you saying the answers might be right here?"

Isende grinned at him. "We won't know unless we look, will we?"

II

A GREAT DEAL had changed in the not quite five moonspans since Firekeeper and her allies had taken control of the Nexus Islands.

Buildings served different purposes. Almost every resident had been relocated to a different dwelling. The menagerie cages had been torn down. A vegetable garden was planned for that particular location.

One thing remained the same. Ynamynet the Once Dead remained the preeminent spellcaster on the Nexus Island. She was no longer the only one, as she had been when the agreement between the residents of the Nexus Islands had been made. However, there was no doubt in anyone's mind that Ynamynet was the most important.

Even so, when Firekeeper knocked on the door of the building that served as both Ynamynet's home and office, the sorcerer answered the door herself. Of medium height, her thick, light brown hair braided long down her back, one hand still holding a damp cloth, Ynamynet did not at this moment look much like a powerful wielder of magic.

Firekeeper glimpsed the retreating form of the little girl fleeing down the hallway toward the back of the house, caught the scent of strawberry jam, and guessed that they had interrupted the sorcerer immersed in one of her other identities, that of mother to a lively little girl everyone called Sunshine.

Ynamynet's neutral expression changed to one of surprise

when she saw who her callers were. She motioned them inside with her damp cloth.

"Firekeeper, Blind Seer . . . I didn't know you had returned. Counselor Derian, Isende . . . Please come inside. Everyone keeps saying that spring is here, but I for one find the weather still rather cold."

The human callers accepted Ynamynet's invitation with alacrity, for the winds coming off the oceans were indeed chilly. Firekeeper and Blind Seer followed without the same impetus. Neither of them found the weather anything other than invigorating.

Ynamynet left them in a sunny front room, promising to return. Soft-voiced conversation in a language Firekeeper didn't know followed by a muted clattering of pots and plates hinted at possible refreshments. A squeal of protest indicated that Sunshine was having her face scrubbed, but when Ynamynet returned, her expression was tranquil and a touch more composed than it had been when they had arrived.

"I apologize for calling unannounced," Derian began, "but Firekeeper has a question for you."

"And Firekeeper will not be kept waiting," Ynamynet said with a smile. She had brought a fur-trimmed robe with her, and pulled it on as she arrayed herself in a chair she moved to where it would be in the sun coming through the window. Firekeeper found herself sweating just looking at her, but Ynamynet looked comfortable.

There was no real annoyance in Ynamynet's tone, just a statement of fact: Firekeeper was one who could not be kept waiting. Firekeeper felt pleased. Wolves value their privileges highly. Besides, she approved of Ynamynet. The woman was brave and devoted. If she had a tendency toward—not treachery . . . that wouldn't be a fair description. There is no treachery when a mother bird feigns a broken wing to protect her fledglings.

"Is important," Firekeeper assured their host. "We want to know what is said about where querinalo came from."

Ynamynet glanced at Derian as if waiting for clarification, and when the young man added nothing, frowned slightly.

"Where querinalo came from? I don't know. It has been a bane—that's what we called it in my homeland, 'the Bane' or 'the sorcerer's bane'—for something like a hundred and fifty years. It wiped out the sorcerers who once ruled the Old World and the New. Apparently, it then left the New World alone, but the Bane continues to kill and mutilate residents of the Old World to this very day."

"But you not know where it come from?" Firekeeper asked. "Not even in stories?"

"You mean like the stories the Liglim tell? About how the Bane was sent as divine retribution against those who abused the gifts of magic?"

Firekeeper inclined her head in acknowledgment.

"No." Ynamynet's tone was bitter. "I have no such stories, and my family was descended from the very sorcerers who once ruled our land and many others."

Derian spoke very gently. "What about enemies? I have heard some say that the Plague might not have been a disease at all, but rather a magical curse. Could someone have created a curse and then that curse have gotten out of hand?"

Ynamynet regained her composure. "I suppose that's possible, although it seems idiotic to me that someone would create a curse that might backwash so horribly."

"Still," Isende said softly, "you admit it's possible."

"Anything's possible," Ynamynet replied. "Including deities capable of such incredible cruelty. I know you New Worlders don't think highly of what the sorcerer monarchs did. All you remember are the tales of their cruelty and abuse. You forget the wonderful things they did as well."

She motioned to the lantern that waited on the table to be lit when evening came.

"They had lights that didn't smoke or smell. They could travel vast distances in moments. They could heal wounds with a touch. Some say they could even defy old age and death. I'm sure that many of them were perfectly good and just rulers, but no one ever remembers those who rule over them with any fondness—especially when those rulers are forced to be strict. Right now Sunshine thinks I'm an absolute tyrant because I won't let her eat all the jam she wants and then run about sticky afterwards."

"I can see," Blind Seer said to Firekeeper, *"why Ynamynet would prefer to remember her ancestors in such a light, but I have heard many tales of the abuses perpetrated by those Once Dead who reigned on these islands only a few moonspans ago, enough to give lie to those summershine dreams."*

Firekeeper reached out and pulled loose a clump of shedding fur from one of his shoulders.

"I agree, dear heart, but we will not get what we want by reminding Ynamynet of what she prefers to forget."

"Nor will we if you drop clumps of shed fur on her carpet," Blind Seer reproved. *"Leave grooming for now. You have asserted your precedence enough already."*

Derian spoke to Ynamynet. "So you, personally, have no information about the coming of querinalo. Do you think anyone else among the Old World community might? Your husband, Skea, comes from another people than your own. What about him? We'd even like to hear stories that might be dismissed as legends. Sometimes there's a good deal of truth hidden underneath."

"Querinalo is not something about which Skea and I have talked much," Ynamynet said. "We both passed through the Bane long before we met. Would you like me to ask among the other Old World residents here who might have stories to share?"

"That would be helpful," Derian said.

"I will do that, then," Ynamynet said.

She half rose, indicating the interview was ended. Isende spoke before they were quite dismissed.

"What about records? Are there any archives here on the Islands that might contain information about the coming of querinalo?"

Ynamynet frowned. "Possibly. Although I lived here a good many years before your coming, I can't claim to know everything that's here. My interests tended to be in the active practice of magic, not in history. Urgana might know. She long made herself useful by doing research for various projects. Why don't you speak to her?"

"We'll do that," Derian promised. "Thank you for seeing us on such short notice."

Ynamynet looked tired, as if suddenly aware that she had been less than the ideal hostess. ·

"I'm sorry I couldn't help more. The Bane was a shadow over my entire life. I sat and watched it burn my brother, Kiriel, alive when I was only six. I've feared it and hated it all my life. Will you tell me why you're so interested in it?"

Firekeeper could hear the fear Ynamynet was trying to conceal. She realized that Ynamynet thought they might be seeking to learn about querinalo in order to somehow use it. Such behavior would have been quite in line with the practices of the Once Dead, many of whom had sought magic for the power it would bring them. What was querinalo if not a terrible power?

Firekeeper rose to her feet in one fluid motion and touched Ynamynet on the arm. The woman's skin was cold as ice.

"We seek querinalo to kill it," Firekeeper said. "So that once and for ever it will never hunt another—so that little ones like your Sunshine will be safe from the fear that even now makes your blood so cold."

Ynamynet gaped at her, and a warmth Firekeeper had never before seen lit her eyes from within and brought color to her pale skin.

"Do that," Ynamynet promised, "and I will be your slave."

Firekeeper shook her head. "I would not have that. But I will find querinalo and I will kill it dead, even so. I promise."

❦

URGANA TURNED OUT to be the wrong person to ask for help. The older woman belonged to what had been, before the coming of the New Worlders had led to a major restructuring of the social order, the so-called "Never Lived." This was the

term given by the Once Dead—those who had survived querinalo with their magical ability intact—to those who had been
born with no inherent magical ability at all.

Those who had—like Plik or Ynamynet's husband, Skea—
once possessed some ability but had sacrificed it in order to
survive querinalo were categorized with the unflattering term
"Twice Dead," for they had died twice, once in suffering
querinalo, once in the death of their magical ability. However,
the Twice Dead possessed more status than the Never Lived,
because at least they had fought, and by not dying achieved a
victory of sorts.

Because of her former low status, Urgana was usually
among the most cooperative of the Old World residents with
the new rulers of the Nexus Islands. Although lacking magical
ability herself, Urgana had been part of the group that had first
rediscovered and later colonized the Nexus Islands, because
of her refusal to abandon her sister, Ellabrana. When the first
signs of querinalo manifested—and with them confirmation
that Ellabrana had magical abilities—Ellabrana had been cast
out by her family. Urgana had protested against this cruel
treatment, and had been exiled herself. This sister had died
before the New World conquest of the Nexus Islands, prey to
some seasonal illness far less spectacular than querinalo.

After nursing Ellabrana through querinalo, Urgana had
learned of a poor but well-run monarchy where rumor
claimed the ruler welcomed those who had survived querinalo. The two sisters had gone there, and had indeed been
welcomed, but the price of that welcome was that Ellabrana
put her magical abilities at the ruler's disposal.

Urgana was a natural storyteller, and many times over the
past winter she had entertained the weirdly isolated island community with tales of her adventures in those days. Derian had
listened to the stories with something of the same uneasy pleasure with which he had listened to his grandmother tell scary
tales of the days when the Old Country rulers had dominated
the lands now known as Hawk Haven. Perhaps his own uneasiness had made him miss a hidden element of those stories: Urgana herself regretted her participation in the use of magic.

"I didn't have much choice then," Urgana explained when Derian, Firekeeper, and Blind Seer came to call on her on the morning following their interview with Ynamynet. "My sister had survived querinalo, but you know how weak it leaves you. We needed a refuge. We could never go home."

Firekeeper, who had not been present for most of the winter storytelling circles, spoke from where she sat on the floor next to Blind Seer.

"I don't understand this," she said. "You had done nothing wrong, and your sister . . . Ellabrana had no more choice in how magic touched her than a wolf does on where the white will fall in his coat. Why were they so fierce against you?"

Rather than looking relieved at Firekeeper's support of what had, after all, been Urgana's own conclusion all those years ago, Urgana drew herself up stiff and even prim in her chair. She was of the same race as the New World's Liglim, with warm brown skin and straight black hair, in her case streaked with silver. Her eyes were a darker brown than her skin, and more oval-shaped than Firekeeper or Derian's. Like all her people, she had high cheekbones.

Derian, who had become something of an expert on Liglimese concepts of beauty during the time he had resided in Liglim, thought Urgana might have been considered lovely once. Now, however, her brown skin was lined with the marks of a life lived—at best—as a sort of privileged slave. The pinch marks around her mouth, deeply graven from a lifetime of not being free to say what she felt, were indented tightly now, so that her mouth almost seemed stitched shut.

"Perhaps Ellabrana and I should have listened to our parents. This was not rebelling, say, as a girl might when presented with a betrothal she does not desire. In resisting the banishment decreed against Ellabrana, we were resisting the will of the deities, as presented by the disdum who serve the Divine Five and make their will known to those of us who serve merely through our worship."

Once Derian would have found this last statement incomprehensible. His own people practiced a complex form of ancestor worship. The family shrine was the heart of every household. Indeed, Derian had carried duplicates of the key elements with which to furnish his own shrine with him when he had left Hawk Haven to take a post as assistant to the ambassador to the Liglimom. When he had gone to visit Elise and Doc, these had been among the few things he had brought back with him—although he had wondered if his ancestors would still consider a monster one of the line they were bound to guide and protect.

Firekeeper's religion—if she had any at all—was that of the Royal Wolves who had raised her. As she never spoke of it, what she believed, if anything, remained a mystery even to Derian, who was her closest human friend.

Arriving in Liglim, where the entire society was structured around the worship of the five elements—Earth, Air, Fire, Water, and Magic—and where the rulers were selected by interpretation of omens believed to be sent by these deities, had been rather shocking to both Derian and Firekeeper. Now, however, enough time had passed that they both accepted the practices of the Liglim as normal enough that meeting one of that people who did not honor the Five would have been shocking rather than otherwise.

So they accepted Urgana's religiously based explanation with composure, and waited for her to elucidate.

"You know that Magic is one of our deities," Urgana began. "The child of Water."

When they nodded, Urgana went on.

"Magic had a very odd birth, for she was born because of Water's envy of Fire, from Water's desire to impress Earth and Air with his own creativity. However, Water was not completely successful. As he brought Magic forth, she broke into many pieces. The largest of these remains in our sky, and we see her as the moon. However, although much of Magic remained intact, numerous fragments were lost. Many fell to Earth, and whatever they touched became imbued with Magic."

Derian nodded. He'd heard several versions of the tale, and the basics remained the same. He thought Urgana was leaving a bit out—that faithful Water had a pretty good reason to envy sulking Fire—but as he tried to remember the details, Urgana's version of the tale took a twist Derian had not heard before.

"Now, since the impulse behind Magic's creation was Water's envy, Magic was tainted by that envy. Water and Fire both were born out of the love between Earth and Air, and their desire to create something from that love. Of all the deities, only Magic was created for less than ideal reasons, and so Magic remains the easiest of the elemental gifts to abuse."

Derian could see Firekeeper starting to fidget, so he didn't ask any of the questions that occurred to him. For one, it seemed to him that Fire had been less than an ideal child to his loving parents, but then maybe Urgana's people, the u-Chivalum, had a different version of Fire's story than did the Liglim.

"When Ellabrana developed querinalo," Urgana said, "I could not believe that she would abuse her gift. Indeed, she did not do so . . . at least not directly. However, to survive, we needed a home, and not only our own family, but all our homeland was turned against us. I've told you how we sought refuge with what seemed to us an enlightened ruler. I've also told you how we learned too late that there was a price for his patronage. He had discovered a gate in his land. He wanted that gate open and operational.

"Ellabrana had a gift for sensing stone, and that gift was recruited to assist in learning how the gate worked. I will not bore you with the tedium of those researches, but how I wish they had never ended. I should have known that our joy on the day we finally made the gate operational was tainted. Indeed, the omens showed this was so, for instead of going to another prosperous land, the gate took us here, to the Nexus Islands.

"You see this place as it is now, and it is a bleak enough land. Wind and water are not kind neighbors, not when they thrive virtually unchecked as they do here. However, in the years since I first stepped through the gate and saw this place, let me assure you that much has been improved. What we saw were ruins, buildings deserted with broken windows and sagging doors. We nearly gave up hope. Even our patron doubted the wisdom of pursuing his ambitions. Then someone found an inscription, and we realized that we had come to a place none of us had completely believed existed, a nexus of gates, a myriad of doors to a myriad of lands. Do you know who found that cursed inscription and realized its significance?"

Blind Seer lifted his head as if he would speak, but Firekeeper remained silent.

At last Derian said, "It was you, wasn't it?"

"That's right. I am the one who showed an ambitious man, long thwarted in his goals, that he had before him the doors to a host of incontestable invasions."

❦

FIREKEEPER SYMPATHIZED WITH the pain she heard in Urgana's voice. Hadn't she felt something similar when shortly after her coming east, humans from Hawk Haven had attempted to colonize the lands west of the Iron Mountains? She had blamed herself because her appearance, ten years after the last known expedition west had been assumed lost without any survivors, had given some the impression that the western lands were not as dangerous as had been believed.

Those who had believed this had been wrong, but nonetheless, Firekeeper had blamed herself for the pain and suffering that had resulted both to humans and to beasts.

"You is not to blame," Firekeeper said, "for how others think."

Urgana looked at her blankly. "I could have kept my mouth shut. Perhaps someone else would have understood what we had found, but at least it would not have been me. Instead, out of a desire to be valued for myself, rather than merely tolerated because of Ellabrana's gifts, I spoke out. Wars followed on the heels of my pride, and the deities turned their backs on those of us who had dared support the magic they had denied humanity. Eventually, when our patron's enemies finally defeated him, we were pressed into even deeper exile. The Once Dead who set themselves to rule over us were the harsh rulers we deserved."

"I've wondered about that," Derian said. "Your sister was Once Dead, wasn't she?"

Urgana nodded. Firekeeper thought that for all Urgana's complaints there was some shadow of the old pride there still, but it was a pride on which guilt followed firmly at the heels.

"She was. Her gift was for working stone, for sensing the life within it."

Urgana might have expected them to question this idea that rocks could hold life, but Derian and Firekeeper had seen too much to doubt. They'd even seen something that might be called living rock, but neither of them said anything for fear they would divert Urgana from her explanation.

"Ellabrana's power did not extend to the type of spellcasting Ynamynet can do. It was more in the line of a talent. Some of the Once Dead pressed her to try and learn more, but Ellabrana resisted, saying she had no sense for spells. We never discussed it, but I have wondered if, like me, Ellabrana felt guilty over what we had become."

"So Ellabrana was Once Dead, but she was not part of the ruling power structure?" Derian said.

"That's right. She took her turn guarding the gates. I think she loved them in a strange way. Otherwise, she devoted her energies to helping restore the ruined buildings here. The ones who had lived here before us—the ones who had shut down the facility when they realized they were in danger of being stranded when the last one who could work the gate spells died—they closed and locked many of the buildings, but even so, the weather found its way inside. Many of the structures remained sound outside, but inside the shell, ceilings had collapsed, walls had crumpled. Ellabrana could often tell if a floor was safe to walk upon or whether the supporting pillars were damaged. Things like that . . ."

Urgana paused and wiped a tear from the corner of one eye without seeming to notice.

"Later, when rebuilding began, Ellabrana did a great deal. She could convince mortar to dry more evenly or seal a crack in a foundation stone. Her handiwork is all around us."

"And you?" Firekeeper asked. "Did you build, too?"

Urgana began to shake her head, then nodded.

"I did some building, but the Once Dead who ruled—let me call them the Spell Wielders, as they did themselves, marking themselves out as special even among the Once Dead—the Spell Wielders made plain that they accepted me here on sufferance. If I did not make myself useful, then they would make me useful, and for them, the greatest use to which any of the non-magical could be turned was as a source of blood for their disgusting spells."

Firekeeper felt her lips drawn back from her teeth in a snarl of revulsion. Beside her, Blind Seer shook with a belly-deep growl.

Urgana did not need to be told the reaction was not directed toward her. She even relaxed as she had not since she had admitted her perceived guilt in helping discover the function of the Nexus Islands.

"So I made myself of use," Urgana continued, "even though the use they had for me was disgusting to me."

Derian frowned. "They didn't . . ."

Urgana reached out and gave his hand a motherly pat. "It's not what you're thinking, young man, although I won't say that I didn't deal with that, as well, especially when I was younger and more attractive. No, what they wanted from me was my skills as a researcher. By this time, I could read half a dozen languages, and make my way fairly well in several more. I've rather quickly glossed over just how many years of research and experimentation went on before we opened that very first gate, but I was a young woman when we started, and seeing grey in my hair before I first stepped on the Nexus Islands."

"Is research so bad?" Firekeeper asked.

The wolf-woman thought she knew what Urgana meant, but also knew that she could ask such questions and not be thought stupid. No one was ever quite sure just how much of human culture and motivations she understood. There were times, indeed, that Firekeeper knew Blind Seer was more sophisticated in his comprehension than she was.

Urgana shook her head. "Child, research in itself is not wrong, but when you know as I did that the research will be turned to destruction or exploitation of the weak, then there is no joy in the work. Perhaps if I had believed, as some of the Spell Wielders truly did, that the world would be improved with a return to the old ways, then I might have gone about my work with a lighter heart, but I knew that what I did was in defiance of Divine Retribution, that I was working against the will of the deities. I will not deny that there were times I thought of ending my life, but then Ellabrana would have felt guilty, and by the time Ellabrana had gone to the Divine Five, my sensibilities had been dulled."

"So you will not help us," Firekeeper said, "not even when I tell you that we have no wish to conquest or fight. All we wish to know is where querinalo came from."

"Querinalo came from the deities," Urgana said firmly. "That is all I know, and all I need to know. If I had remembered this when I was a brash young woman, then perhaps today I would not be a lonely old woman making my home on an island whose purpose I doubt and despise—but which is my home because I have no other."

THEY LEFT URGANA shortly thereafter and retired to Derian's house near the stable. The morning had become afternoon, and a patio that took advantage of the pale spring sunlight was comfortable enough for them all to take their meal out-of-doors. There they were joined by Eshinarvash, the Wise Horse, who resided in the stable because he found it comfortable, but on whose stall door there was no lock or latch.

Eshinarvash was a glorious animal. Even Firekeeper, who thought wolves the most beautiful creatures ever to grace the earth, agreed with this assessment. Eshinarvash was what the Liglim called a "paint," black upon white, or perhaps white upon black, the contrast in wild splashes that made even his mane and tail parti-colored.

Eshinarvash, along with the jaguar Truth, had been among the very few Wise Beasts who had chosen to take up something like a permanent residence on the Nexus Islands. No one knew why Truth had stayed, because Truth was, if anything, harder to understand than ever before. No one doubted that Eshinarvash had stayed as comfort and companion to Derian.

Over the meal, they had related their failure with Urgana to Eshinarvash, and now the Wise Horse responded. It was an odd conversation in a way, for Firekeeper was accustomed to the need to translate for Derian when the Beasts spoke, but when Eshinarvash spoke there was no such need.

"Urgana and I are of the same religion, although there are differences between the way the New and Old Worlds follow the Divine Will. Our deities are kind deities, I think, at least in contrast to some of the tales I have heard the Old World residents relate. However, perhaps because the deities have given us so many omens by which to guide our decisions, our tradition holds that they are less than tolerant of defiance."

Firekeeper thought fleetingly of the Meddler, of whom Harjeedian the aridisdu could not speak without horror—and this when the Meddler had been so helpful . . . well, at least helpful at times.

Blind Seer said, *"Eshinarvash, do you believe that querinalo—what my people called the Fire Plague, what the people of New Kelvin called the 'Burning Time'—do you believe that it is indeed as the Liglim term it 'divine retribution'?"*

"Do I believe querinalo is indeed 'divine retribution'?" Eshinarvash said, phrasing his reply so that Derian would know a question had been asked. "Blind Seer, that is a question for an aridisdu, not for a simple worshipper like myself."

"Still, I would hear your answer," Blind Seer persisted. *"Harjeedian is the only aridisdu here, and he is too aware of his position for me to fully trust his answer."*

"Indeed, Harjeedian is all of u-Liall in himself," Eshinarvash said, referring to the five-person governing body of Liglim with a snort of laughter. "Such a role might shape the ruling of a less self-important individual than Harjeedian. Very well. I will give you what answer I have arrived at for myself.

"Did the deities send Divine Retribution down upon us as the tales tell? Certainly there is a part of me that wishes to believe this is so. Remember, according to how the tale is told in the New World, Divine Retribution was a direct result of how the Old World sorcerers abused the Wise Beasts, the yarimaimalom.

"However, there is a part of me—and you wolves will understand this, being of a pack, as I am of a herd—that is uncomfortable with the idea that the deities might reach out and punish all the herd, guilty and not, for the transgressions of a few. True, querinalo strikes only those who have magical ability, but as Urgana's experience shows, the blow strikes even those who are without talent. I did not experience querinalo, but I watched over those who did, and I saw the suffering that came with it—and I know the suffering I experienced for not being able to help those I cared about.

"When I think of this, then I find myself wondering if the deities did create querinalo and set it to gallop among us. Truly it saved the New World, but it ruined the Old World. To believe that the deities would destroy one set of worshippers to save another makes me uncomfortable. Moreover, querinalo did not only touch those who follow our creed. It killed many who had never given their wills to the guidance of the deities."

"So is it their retribution or not?" Blind Seer pressed.

"I do not know if querinalo is divine retribution as such," Eshinarvash said. "I do know that when it appeared, the deities did not stop its spread, nor did they give omens that indicated we should do so. If they did not create it to punish the wrongdoers, well, then, they certainly did not provide guidance on how to stop it. Therefore, if querinalo is not their retribution, perhaps it is their will."

Blind Seer grumbled something, and cracked down so hard on the bone he had been chewing that it broke in two.

"I had hoped," the wolf said, *"that in your explanation I would find something we could use to turn Urgana to our way of thinking. There may be other ways to learn what we need. There are many here who may have tales, and Ynamynet has promised to ask among them, but there is no doubt that Urgana with her ability to read so many languages, and to find trails where Firekeeper and I would only smell dry paper, would have been useful."*

Firekeeper felt that if she had proper ears, they would have pricked in excitement as a new course of action came to her.

"The answer may be here nonetheless. Let us talk with Harjeedian. He is an aridisdu, and Urgana regularly goes to him for counsel. If we can convince him of the rightness of what we would do, then perhaps he can convince Urgana."

"And if his thinking is as confused as mine?" Eshinarvash asked.

"Then there are omens," Firekeeper said. "Truth is a great seer, and if she saw omens indicating that the deities might favor our hunt, then surely Harjeedian and Urgana would obey."

"Truth is honest in those omens she gives," Blind Seer warned. *"Since she wrestled Amhyn—or believes she did—when querinalo seized her, she is more devout than ever. What if her omens are not what we wish?"*

Firekeeper shrugged. "Then we are no worse off than we are now, and may need to hunt stories more slowly."

She leapt to her feet, feeling her body one clean line of purpose. "Harjeedian will be at the gates at this time. I saw him there earlier, and the watch runs until dusk. Let's go find him, and maybe with him we will find Truth."

III

"BLOCKED? I FEAR I do not understand."

The words were spoken politely, but the speaker put into his tone that which made quite clear that "fear" was not his dominant emotion. Irritation sizzling on the verge of explosive anger was closer to what the young man sitting in the chair at the end of the high table projected, as well he knew.

Although Bryessidan, King of the Mires, was not much past

twenty-five, already his temper had graven deep lines between his eyebrows. The edges of his mouth bore deep creases from pressing his lips tightly shut over his immediate response. The lines gave a fierce character to features that were otherwise not particularly remarkable. Bryessidan shared the same slight build, brown hair, long brown eyes, and golden brown skin that set the majority of the Mires' dwellers apart from the other residents of the continent-spanning realm once known as Pelland. Without his regalia—and his distinctive royal glower—Bryessidan could have blended into any crowd.

Even though Bryessidan had long ago learned that acting as prompted by his temper was not the best response to most situations, still he felt that keeping the reminder that he might do so visibly present was a wise tactic.

Certainly, being known for a short temper was better than revealing the insecurity that lay under the king's surface confidence. A king might be many things, but insecure was not one of these. An insecure king was a weak king, and a weak king was soon a king in name only—and often not even that.

Bryessidan had inherited his throne from his father, who had, in turn, inherited it from his own father, who had—quite frankly—stolen it. The man from whom Grandfather had stolen the throne on which Bryessidan now sat had made the mistake of being insecure. He had confided a great many things to a very few people, and one of those people had . . . well, what was reported to have been done varied with the point of view of the one who told the tale.

Grandfather's enemies said that Grandfather had violated those confidences, and used them to undermine the sovereign he should have supported. Grandfather's supporters had said that Grandfather had wisely revealed that the sovereign he served was less than fit for his post. In return for this courage and forthrightness, he had been elevated by a grateful people to rulership over them.

With which version of the truth was closer to reality, Bryessidan did not trouble himself. The lesson he took from his grandfather's elevation to king was to never show insecurity—not even to one's nearest and dearest.

The lesson Bryessidan took from his father's long reign was more complicated. Bryessidan's father had not been content merely to maintain the holdings he had inherited. King Veztressidan had been determined to strengthen and, if at all possible, expand his kingdom. He faced one difficulty in this goal—the geographical positioning of the land which he ruled.

The Kingdom of the Mires was aptly, if somewhat deceptively, named. Bordered on one edge by the sea, and on two others by expansive marsh and swampland, the kingdom was a great deal more than merely mires. Within those bordering wetlands were a large amount of good, well-watered farmland and some mineral resources, the whole inhabited by a hardy, strong-willed people.

Regular tidal action meant that the wetlands did not breed disease as Bryessidan had been told was typical in many other areas where swamps dominated. What diseases there were, his people had long ago grown strong against. Moreover, the wetlands were home to a wide variety of plants that were rarely found elsewhere, plants valuable for their use as spices, medicinals, and dyes.

But for all these fine aspects, the Kingdom of the Mires possessed only one land route that might be used for transporting armies. Although the ocean-side border possessed some good harbors, the dominant winds and currents made sailing in other than a few predictable directions quite difficult.

So King Veztressidan, Bryessidan's father, had ventured out with his armies along the land route, and even met with a few initial victories in the borderlands of Hearthome. But those victories had not been easy to keep, much less to extend.

Neighbors of Hearthome came to her assistance. They could see that if Veztressidan were permitted to hold on to his new conquests, he would soon be looking beyond those borders to their own kingdoms. Within a few bloody years, the armies of Veztressidan were beaten back into the Mires and sealed there like a bug in a bottle.

That the bug was bottled, rather than being completely squashed, was again due to the marshes and mires that bor-

dered the kingdom. Veztressidan's people might be inured to
the local illnesses, but the armies of the would-be invaders
were not. Moreover, although Veztressidan had been able to
send out scouting and spying forces through the marshes
themselves, the would-be invaders could not do the same.
Therefore, they left the bug in the bottle, called themselves
merciful, called Veztressidan defeated and broken.

But Veztressidan was not so easily convinced to relinquish
his ambitions. He looked about him, and sought another way
out of his bottle. He believed he had discovered it in a resource
his opponents not only ignored, but openly avoided—even destroyed. In short, he found it in the small but definite reappear-
ance of magical ability over the last couple of generations.

Perhaps because the resources of the wetlands could be
harvested only by those who had both skill and willingness,
the residents of the Kingdom of the Mires had never been
abused by sorcerers who had ruled before the coming of the
Sorcerers' Bane. The coming of the Bane had been seen as an
opportunity for restructuring the local government, rather
than the liberation it was celebrated as in so many other lands.

Indeed, there were those who mourned the days when sorcery had ruled the world, for then the Kingdom of the Mires
had not been so isolated by her geography. Then, even the
poorest of her people benefitted, if secondhand, from the
wealth and luxury that their own labors, transported by sorcery, had brought to the mire dwellers.

So King Veztressidan did not find much resistance among
his counselors when he decreed that those of his subjects who
survived the Bane as Once Dead were to come to him at his
court. When the first of those survivors to arrive found themselves welcomed and given employment in the castle itself,
the word spread and others came.

Not long after, King Veztressidan had decreed that the word
of his generous hospitality was to be spread discreetly and
carefully outside his own borders. So it was that those who
found themselves unwelcome elsewhere sought sanctuary
within the Kingdom of the Mires.

Bryessidan did not remember his father's first efforts as

warlord, for these had happened before he was born. He did remember the coming of the Once Dead and the Twice Dead, for during his boyhood what had been a trickle became something of a flood. He remembered the strangely colored, strangely clàd figures who frequented certain areas of the castle. He remembered the efforts to open the magical gate in what had been a walled-up, nearly forgotten building. He remembered when the gate had been opened, and the Nexus Islands discovered. He remembered when his father had once again ventured into war—a more successful war this time—war that made the Kingdom of the Mires a land with borders that extended beyond the mires . . .

And Bryessidan remembered when some ten years ago all that glory collapsed. This had happened when the neighboring lands became suspicious of the source of Veztressidan's success, when the sorcerers Veztressidan had trusted turned against him rather than face annihilation. In the end, after all the treaties were signed, the sorcerers claimed the Nexus Islands for their own and began to charge tariff for the use of their gates.

Once again, the bug was back in its bottle.

Veztressidan accepted this resolution, as he had accepted so much else, with the point of his enemies' swords against his throat. These enemies, however, did not destroy Veztressidan. They were wise enough to see that there was no going back, that magic was once again a power in the world. Moreover, the Spell Wielders would only agree not to turn their power to war if their old patron—for whom Bryessidan reluctantly had to admit they must have felt some gratitude—was spared and his kingdom with him.

And so the situation had stood within the kingdom Bryessidan had inherited upon his father's death eighteen moonspans before.

Bryessidan had no such ambitions as his father or grandfather, only a desire to hold the lands he had inherited and to keep them prosperous. Now, however, the chief among the Once Dead who worked the gates from the Mires side stood before the king, confessing that the gates had been blocked to prevent free use, and the first spring shipments of plants sensitive to decay and rot could not be sent as planned.

"Something has happened on the Nexus Islands," the Once Dead said. In appearance he was as average a mire dweller as Bryessidan himself, but as the king's throne set him apart, so did the Once Dead's elaborately embroidered robes and close-fitting bejeweled cap. "Something has rearranged everything since last we contacted them."

"And when was this?"

"Last autumn. We sent a final shipment, and a final payment, including an installment to reserve service for this spring. Most of our shipping needs come in the warm months, when the goods will not bear the heat. The Nexus Islands charge high fees for their services, and we only use them when the cost balances the need."

Bryessidan knew this, but he did not chide the man for repetition. He was grateful, as the man's nervous babble gave him opportunity to think.

"Rearranged," Bryessidan repeated. "Explain yourself, but first be seated."

After all, I have made my point. No need to keep the man standing, especially when I need his goodwill.

The Once Dead took his place in the chair to the king's right, adjusting his robes fussily as he did so, taking care that the heavily embroidered fabric fell in graceful folds. He claimed that his family had practiced sorcery in these lands before the Bane. As he took care not to even hint that his family had ruled here, and as his given name, Amelo Soapwort, was as common as mud, Bryessidan felt no threat from him.

A swamp healer elevated to king's counselor, Bryessidan thought. *My father and I have done Amelo Soapwort honor enough for him to serve us well.*

A minor attendant quietly filled goblets with thrice-boiled water and thimble-sized cups with honey mead, then withdrew to waiting silence. A sip of mead seemed to settle Amelo, and he began his report with more composure than he had shown since requesting a private audience with the king.

"As Your Majesty may recall," Amelo began, "any contact with the Nexus Islands begins with the sending of an emissary through the gates to make arrangements for the transport. Earlier today I performed the appropriate rituals and made my passage.

"From the moment I passed through the fiery spaces that separate the gates and set foot in the terminus on the Nexus Island side, I realized something was amiss. For one, the exit point was surrounded by a cage of sorts, the bars of which were crafted from iron."

"A cage?" Bryessidan asked. "How so?"

"With three sides and a roof," Amelo sketched the proportions in the air, "crafted so that one might take a few steps from the portal, but go no further. It was anchored with bolts into the stone wall that surrounds the gate."

"So you were imprisoned?"

"I was imprisoned," Amelo agreed, "and hardly had I appreciated this when a voice spoke to me from beyond the cage. I recognized it as that of one Skea, a Twice Dead. You may recall him. Before the Nexus Islands became independent, Skea served for a time as one of your father's bodyguards."

"I remember Skea," Bryessidan said, "a big man, with skin the blue-black of a moonless night. A trustworthy man, until our enemies forced a choice. Even then I think Skea would have stood with my father to the last, but Skea had fallen in love with one of those who chose the Nexus Islands."

"You remember well," Amelo said. His tone was not in the least fawning and so Bryessidan felt the compliment all the more. "Skea spoke to me, calling me by name. He said to me, 'Do you remember how ten years ago choices were forced upon those of us who served King Veztressidan?' I allowed that those were not days any one of us who had lived through them would ever forget.

"Skea then said, 'This past autumn brought changes here to the Nexus Islands, changes at least as marked. I must apologize, but for the time being, the gates may not be used for transit of goods or people.' "

"He said that?" Bryessidan said in astonishment. "That implies that the Nexus Islands have been invaded, and that someone more powerful than the Spell Wielders now rules."

Amelo nodded. "So I thought as well, my king. I did not question Skea to prove his claim, for in the shadows beyond him I could see someone moving. Although this person took care to remain out of my clear line of sight, I do not think he—or she, I could not tell—was any I knew."

"Interesting," Bryessidan said. "I believe you were fairly well acquainted with most who dwelled on the Nexus Islands."

"I was," Amelo Soapwort agreed, and took another tiny sip of mead.

"Finish your tale," Bryessidan said. "I will hold my questions."

Amelo nodded. "What remains is brief enough. I challenged Skea, reminding him of the advance we had paid on services, pleading with him to remember that the goods we sought to transport are sensitive to the passage of time, reminding him that medicinals are not mere luxury goods but save lives and heal illnesses. But Skea remained firm. He apologized and promised that when the Nexus Islands again resumed business, our payment would be remembered. Then he offered me refreshment, and politely asked if I would need help working the spells needed to take me home again."

Bryessidan kept his promise not to interrupt again, but his question must have been written on his features, for Amelo answered it.

"Food and drink were brought to me, and even a cushion so I might sit in cramped comfort, but never was I permitted to leave the cage. Skea stayed with me all the time, and conversed in a very general fashion. I asked after his wife, Ynamynet, and their little girl. He allowed that they were well, but when I asked about anyone else it was as if he did not hear my words. I might have remained longer, hoping that someone else who was more talkative might come, but I remembered Skea of old and knew he could outlast me. Therefore, I returned and begged audience of you."

"You did well," Bryessidan said, and for the first time he

sipped his own mead. "So your sense is that the Nexus Islands have been conquered. I thought that was impossible. Certainly, they were easily held against invasion in my father's day."

The king managed to say this last without letting his bitterness show, for although Amelo had remained in service with the Kingdom of the Mires, in another sense he and all his associates in sorcery had betrayed that kingdom.

"Invasion would explain Skea's words," Amelo said, "but so would some sort of reorganization from within. I find significant that Skea came and spoke with me. He is Twice Dead, remember. Might the Twice Dead have taken rulership over the Once Dead? Many of the Spell Wielders treated those without power very harshly."

"And if the Spell Wielders have somehow been overthrown by the Twice Dead," Bryessidan said, thinking aloud, "perhaps with the assistance of the Never Lived, then the Once Dead who still breathed might refuse to work the gates. Or, perhaps, do you think they killed them all?"

"Skea spoke of his wife, Ynamynet, as if she still lived," Amelo reminded him. "I suppose he could have lied. However, I also remember the figure I glimpsed. I said I knew most of those on the Nexus Islands, but that is not completely true. Those I knew were the Once Dead and some of the Twice Dead, especially those who came from this kingdom. I knew very few of the Never Lived, only those who assisted us with our sorcery and research. Over the ten years since the Nexus Islands separated from the Kingdom of the Mires, new people have come to live there."

"Yes. Those islands became the new refuge for those with magical abilities," Bryessidan said, not attempting to hide the bitterness in his tone, "as once this kingdom was."

Amelo Soapwort, wisely, did not comment.

Bryessidan felt his temper kindling at memories of old wrongs, and spoke aloud, although whether to calm his anger or to kindle it further, even he did not know for certain.

"Ironic if those who ruled the Nexus Islands have been overthrown as once my father was. Do you think they let in too many misfits? That is how my father was betrayed, or so many say. Once the secret of the gates was rediscovered, and once the old maps of the Nexus Islands had been deciphered, then my father had a back door into any land. He used those doors well, slipping in spies and those less than satisfied with their current rulers. Amazing how a few within can do as much damage as many without. Amazing that my father did not realize that the same trick could be played on him."

Amelo said nothing, perhaps secure in the devotion of his long service both before and after the previous king's fall, perhaps wise enough to know the value of silence.

"The gates," Bryessidan said, "are too useful once one knows of them."

"Too useful, my king?"

"Too useful to destroy," Bryessidan said. "Even the small hint of their power tasted by those who would overthrow my father was too much. A few words, a little blood, marks upon the stone, and suddenly one is a moonspan's travel distant—or across a mountain range that is otherwise impassible—or across a stormy sea. My father's ambitions were local, for he knew he needed his borders secured, but had he succeeded here, he could have had it all . . ."

"There is one more thing," Amelo said with quiet firmness. "One more thing than blood and words and the gate itself. Someone with magical power must work the spells. The gates are not like a broken-down old horse, able to be ridden by any. Nor can they be compared to a fine sailing ship, for those can be sailed by any who study the craft. The gates take that study, yes, but one might study all his life and never learn to work the gates unless the natural ability to work spells is there."

Bryessidan nodded. "And that is why we must deal with these Nexus Islands as if they are a kingdom of their own. To spare our homeland a long and bloody war, to spare our people being conquered, my father agreed to negotiate with those who would otherwise conquer him. The Once Dead stood with us knowing they could not win a war when the nations of the world had once again learned to fear the power of magic. They were wiser than that."

Amelo smiled wryly. "Thank you, my king. You forget one

other reason we stood by King Veztressidan. We had reason to be grateful to your father. Enough of us remembered his old kindnesses that we could see the wisdom in making the terms for the Mires' surrender as favorable as they could be."

"And from those negotiations you gained a kingdom for yourselves," Bryessidan grumbled. "And a new profession of sorts: transportation for all those who wished to keep their newly awakened gates alive and working."

"As you yourself said, my king, the gates are too useful to be destroyed."

"I know. I know."

Bryessidan put his head in his hands, and thought about shipments of herbs that if delivered would put wealth in his coffers and if undelivered would be so much slime for the compost bins.

"We must deal with the problem of the herb shipments immediately," he said, sitting upright again. He turned to the attendant who had stood silent all this time. "Send me the minister of the navies and find someone who knows the state of the roads. I want someone skilled in herb lore as well. Perhaps something can be done to preserve these specimens with some of their potency intact."

"I can assist with that last, my king," Amelo said.

"Return then to counsel me," Bryessidan said, "but first alert your associates among the Once Dead here in the Mires as to what you saw."

Amelo rose smoothly. "I agree, my lord. We cannot forget that the gates work both ways. Right now we cannot enter their land, but they can enter ours—and those of our friends."

"Or of our enemies," Bryessidan said, thinking of old betrayals. "Make haste."

❧

"SO WE'RE WONDERING," Derian said to the aridisdu Harjeedian as he concluded his long account, "if you could possibly convince Urgana to work with us as a researcher."

"So that Firekeeper may follow this mad impulse to go chasing after the source of an illness that first appeared over a century ago," Harjeedian said.

The aridisdu had listened to Derian's report in flattering silence, his dark eyes over his almost impossibly high cheekbones as watchful and impassive as those of one of the snakes from his own Serpent Temple.

Harjeedian no longer habitually tended one of those snakes, as he had on the voyage where Derian had first come to know him. That was considered unnecessary, for the presence of the Wise Beasts, the yarimaimalom, made the divining of omens that was part of an aridisdu's role within the complicated theology of the Liglimom more direct—if, as some theologians had argued, more suspect.

However, physically, Harjeedian was little changed from the man Derian had first met over two years ago. He still wore his straight, shining black hair combed from a center part and cut just above his shoulders. He still wore the emblem of the Serpent Temple embroidered on the loose trousers and shirt that were the national attire of the Liglimom. He was still one of the most arrogantly composed people Derian had ever known—and Derian had known kings and queens and those who were as kings and queens, although their titles differed.

And he might have been my brother-in-law, joined to my ancestry, Derian thought. *Perhaps Rahniseeta did me a favor when she dumped me in favor of a crown—or maybe the ancestors didn't want to be obligated to look after Harjeedian. But why lie to myself? Harjeedian may be annoying, but in his way he's honest and reliable.*

"Would you try and convince Urgana to assist us?" Derian pressed.

Harjeedian turned his gaze to where Firekeeper sat perched on a windowsill where she could look out at the several hills that dominated this island—grounds dominated in turn by the looming stone wedges that held the gates.

"I would like to know more about what awakened Firekeeper's sudden interest in querinalo," Harjeedian said. "I claim no divine inspiration in my suspicions, but I admit to suspicions that Firekeeper's impulse is not entirely her own."

Derian might have hedged, knowing Harjeedian's strongly negative feelings about the Meddler, but Firekeeper did not hesitate.

"Do you ask if someone put idea in my head?" she said, turning to face them. "I could answer like a human and say, 'Oh, no, no one *put* the idea in my head.'"

Derian noted the slight emphasis on the word "put" and saw that Harjeedian did as well.

"And I would be human honest, for no one put any idea in my head," Firekeeper said, speaking with unusual precision. "But I will be wolf honest and tell you what you could smell if you had a nose. No one put the idea in my head, but, yes, someone spoke to me about that idea, and yes, that one is the Meddler, and before you say anything, I tell you this. Blind Seer like this no more than you do—maybe less—but he will run with me and perhaps so keep me from foolishness."

Harjeedian's eyes, narrow above those high cheekbones, blinked with slow deliberateness, as a snake might blink.

"Wolf honest," he repeated. "Direct. Clear. Forthright. What a low opinion you have of humanity, Firekeeper, but still you wish our help."

"I have no low opinion of humanity," Firekeeper snorted. "Only of human words and how they is used to tell not the truth. Now, much of what Derian has telled you is what the Meddler has speaked . . ."

"Spoken," Derian said.

"With me about querinalo. Will you help?"

Harjeedian frowned thoughtfully. "All the disdum's teachings warn against getting trapped in the Meddler's games. You remember the stories I have told you?"

"And the ones Plik telled, too," Firekeeper said. "Must we defy good sense because it comes from the Meddler? When he gave you help you needed, you did not refuse."

"True," Harjeedian said, "and I have prayed over my choices since then. Had we not accepted the Meddler's help, then perhaps we would not be here and in this situation."

"Had we not accepted the Meddler's help," Firekeeper said, "some would be dead, and I would be one."

"I didn't say the problem was without complication," Harjeedian said, "nor that I am not glad that you are alive when otherwise you might be dead. I am only stating that our current complexities are a direct result of accepting the Meddler's help—for if you had died, I doubt we would have continued our search for the twins beyond that point, or if we had done so that we would have succeeded as we did."

Firekeeper puffed air out through her nose, but otherwise did not comment.

Harjeedian went on. "Moreover, when one considers that the entire problem of the twins seems to have been of the Meddler's origination . . ."

Firekeeper waved a hand through the air, brushing away Harjeedian's words as she might flies.

"And if I had died in a fire when my human parent did, then I would not be here. Now is what matters, not how we get to now."

"I cannot wholly agree," Harjeedian said, "but I will concede that querinalo is something that influences how we act in the here and now. You say you wish to find out where it came from so that we might learn how to eliminate it. You give good reasons for why we should wish to eliminate it as well. And you want Urgana's help in finding where you should search."

"Yes."

The word was more a grunt from deep in Firekeeper's throat.

Harjeedian sighed. "I cannot answer you 'yes' or 'no' so simply. Derian has faithfully reported what Urgana said, and I, too, share her concern that the illness our local associates have taught us to call 'querinalo' is indeed, as my people call it, Divine Retribution. How can I lightly go against Divine Will and seek to remove what they may have sent—or if not sent, permitted to reshape the world? Urgana balks at assisting you. I might be able to convince her otherwise, but I must be certain that I do so in adherence to the will of the Divine Five, not because I wish to demonstrate my secular power over the small group here that looks to me for guidance."

"Will you pray, then?" Derian asked. "Ask your deities for omens?"

Harjeedian almost grinned. "But those upon whom I rely for omens are Firekeeper's friends—some might say her kinfolk. I would need to be very careful in a matter so closely related to her will and mine. I am not saying the yarimaimalom would deliberately deceive me, but one of the first lessons taught to either branch of the disdum is to take care when reading omens for oneself. Better to have another do it for you."

Derian saw Firekeeper tense, and asked quickly, seeking to deflect an argument, "Then you will ask the temple in Gak to divine for you? I am certain you could do this without revealing overmuch of our strange situation."

Harjeedian shook his head. "For a matter of this importance, where I seek to decide how to act on what can be considered a matter of doctrine, I must consult the central temple in u-Nahal, back in u-Seeheera. Best I consult them in person, but given our situation here—and how small our group is to command so many—I will begin by sending a written account."

Derian frowned. When their small group had taken command of the Nexus Islands nearly five moonspans before, all had agreed that the best course of action was to keep the very existence of the place a secret. As far as he knew, everyone had kept that promise, but he thought it might be wisest to remind Harjeedian.

"Can you ask your superiors for guidance without giving away exactly why we feel it may be essential to know the source of querinalo? Can you tell them what you must without revealing that we have encountered the Plague afresh? Hard as it is for any of us to recall given it has so reshaped our lives, but most of the New World has no idea that querinalo still exists and still has power to touch those with magical ability."

"I would do my best," Harjeedian said. "I still agree that the Nexus Islands and what they contain are a secret better kept by us few. We won't be able to do so forever. Thus far

winter weather has helped us, that and the aid of the yarimaimalom, for they make it impossible for anyone to pass
undetected through the lands surrounding the New World
gate at the Setting Sun stronghold. How long can we keep the
secret?"

"I think," Firekeeper said, "we can keep for a long time, for
no one can go from here without yarimaimalom see, and no
one can come to here without the same."

Derian felt troubled, for Firekeeper was touching on matters he had tried not to consider. Matters of loyalty, to friends,
to nations, to family. He put those thoughts from him once
again. They were not as pressing as this immediate matter.

"So you must ask your superiors for guidance before you will
ask Urgana to assist Firekeeper in her research?" Derian asked.

"I fear that is my best choice," Harjeedian said. "Unless the
deities send other omens, I think consulting my superiors is
my only responsible choice."

"I suppose we can begin other research," Derian began. He
glanced at Firekeeper to see her reaction to Harjeedian's decision, and found her staring fixedly out the window.

"Someone is coming from the gates," she said. "Skea, and
moving quickly. He goes to your house, Derian."

"From the gates?" Derian said. "Oh, Horse! Not again!"

"The gates," Firekeeper repeated, "and he seems very unhappy to me."

IV

 FIREKEEPER AND BLIND Seer caught up with Skea
as he was turning away from thumping on the door of
Derian's little house by the stable.

"Derian come," Firekeeper said. "Harjeedian, too.
We go inside?"

"I think that would be best," Skea said. "Derian will be here quickly? I've sent someone to get Ynamynet. I'd rather tell this all at once, and I asked her to meet us here."

Firekeeper understood the reason Skea had called for Ynamynet and fully approved. Between them, Derian and Ynamynet had somehow become the informal rulers of the community. Harjeedian, for all his formal training in leadership, did not have Derian's advantage in the eyes of the Old World residents who made up the larger part of the population. Harjeedian was not Once Dead, and for all they had been abused by the Spell Wielders, the local community was conditioned to respect those who had defeated querinalo and kept their magical abilities intact.

Then, too, Derian had a good way of running things. He didn't push people around, but listened and weighed their suggestions. When the word spread—and Firekeeper had contributed a great deal to the spreading—that Derian had been counselor to King Tedric of Hawk Haven, as well as a duly appointed ambassador, people simply assumed that the young man had been given a great deal of diplomatic training.

The fact was, Derian had turned the skills he had for handling horses—patience and an awareness that you can manipulate something many times your size—to the handling of people. That Harjeedian had chosen to support Derian rather than set himself up as a rival authority had only helped.

"Derian is just coming from there," Firekeeper said, tossing her head to indicate the building where Harjeedian had his suite.

Unlike Derian, who liked the privacy of a house of his own, Harjeedian had opted for taking over a ground-floor suite in the large building that had been the headquarters and administrative center of the Spell Wielders. Firekeeper knew that in Liglim Harjeedian had lived in common with the disdum of the Serpent Temple, and she guessed that the aridisdu would have felt isolated in a private house. Moreover, the building possessed empty rooms enough that Harjeedian and some of his fellow worshippers were creating a small temple in which to worship their deities.

There was a final advantage to Harjeedian taking up his quarters in the big building. There were gates in the basement, all still partially buried beneath dirt and rubble, and none currently functioning, but Harjeedian's quarters "just happened" to contain one of the entrances to that basement, and the aridisdu periodically checked to make certain no one was tampering with those gates.

Derian and Harjeedian arrived almost as soon as Skea and Firekeeper had taken seats. Soon after, three others arrived: Ynamynet, Tiniel, and, lastly, padding a few paces behind, the Wise Jaguar Truth.

Tiniel, the twin brother of Isende, looked less like his sister than he had when Firekeeper had first met the pair. Then both had been carrying extra weight, a result of their living semi-imprisoned. This, combined with their rather baggy attire, had smoothed out the gender differences between them.

Then, too, there had been matters of grooming. Both had worn their hair loose and the conditions of their imprisonment were not such that they bothered with the finer points of grooming. Since the reorganization, however, Tiniel had taken to wearing his hair in imitation of Derian, pulling the golden brown locks back into a queue tied with a ribbon. This change emphasized the masculine sharpness of his features in contrast to his sister's rounder lines. Certainly anyone seeing them would know they were siblings, but no longer could one be mistaken for the other.

But Firekeeper thought that something else had contributed to divergence between the pair, something more subtle and yet far more important than any other change. This was that Isende and Tiniel were no longer a pair, no longer a partnership, as had been the case most of their lives. This partnership had led them to challenge their government and then seek their ancestral estate together. It had persisted until querinalo had severed the intangible bond that had joined them, a bond that had persisted even after the hands that had been joined at their birth had been separated by surgery.

Firekeeper thought that while Tiniel missed that bond, Isende most definitely did not. The wolf-woman wondered how much of the edgy temper and bitterness she smelled from the young man came from this, and how much was simply an aspect of his character.

But the entrance of the jaguar Truth pushed Firekeeper's speculations about Tiniel completely from her mind.

"Did Skea call for you, too?" Firekeeper asked.

"Ahmyn showed me all my best futures came from my being here at this time," the jaguar replied. *"Thus I am here."*

Once Firekeeper would have dismissed such statements as merely an expression of the jaguar's arrogant nature. After all, what was more arrogant than to claim that a deity would guide one's decisions? Later, she might have tried to explain Truth's statement as an aggrandizement of what otherwise might be explained as a magical talent, for there was no doubt that Truth had the ability to see something of the way one choice or another might affect the future.

Now, however, Firekeeper had decided that accepting Truth's claims was much more reasonable than wasting energy attempting to deny them, for, along with Derian, Truth was the most changed by her battle with querinalo. While Derian blamed his condition on a sudden realization within the course of the fever that he did not wish to live without his inborn talent, Truth's explanation was much stranger. She claimed that she had been willing to surrender to the fever, but that Fire—or Ahmyn in Liglimosh—had confronted her, challenged her, called her a coward, and that to Truth's own surprise the jaguar had found herself giving battle for a life she believed she no longer valued.

The end result of that battle was not only that Truth lived, but that she was transformed. The physical transformation was the most dramatic. Truth had fought with Fire, and that fire had burned her formerly golden coat to a charcoal black. Where black spots had once stood against the gold, now irregular reddish orange markings like tongues of flame took their place. Most startling, however, was the change to Truth's eyes. These were now a strange, translucent white in which pale blue pupils stood out in eerie contrast, but they were certainly not blind. Truth now saw more than ever before.

The jaguar had confessed this change only after irregularities in her physical actions had given her away. She would move to avoid things or people that were not present. More seriously, Truth froze completely when the conflicting visions offered her too many courses of action. Whereas before her battle with Ahymn, Truth had been able to summon visions at need, now she lived in the midst of them and dealt, as well, or as poorly, as she might.

Her battle with Ahmyn had only raised Truth's importance in the view of those who followed the faith of the Liglim, and her surviving querinalo as "Once Dead" had given her status among the Old World residents of the Nexus Islands.

Really, Firekeeper thought without animosity, *there is some veracity to the claim that cats always land on their feet.*

That neither Skea nor Ynamynet questioned the jaguar's appearance said a great deal about the many changes on the Nexus Islands. Certainly there had been Wise Beasts there before the New World contingent had arrived, but they had been captives in close-fitting cages, often tortured or brutalized at the whim of the Once Dead.

Ynamynet, the only surviving Spell Wielder, had sworn she had had no part in tormenting the yarimaimalom. Her oath would have meant nothing, however, had the Wise Beasts not supported her claim.

Firekeeper recalled what Enigma, a puma who was now something like Ynamynet's apprentice, had said: "Ynamynet was not kind. She partook in rites that used our abilities—but she never initiated them nor delighted in our captivity as some others did. I am even willing to allow that she might have been as much in fear of those who were her rulers as we were, and have acted as she did rather than face the penalties that would have been visited not upon her, but upon her kitten and her mate if she had refused."

So Truth and Blind Seer returned Ynamynet's greeting as politely as they would that of any human, then all turned their ears to what Skea had to report.

He began with military efficiency. "I was taking my watch on the gateway hill and saw that the gate from the Kingdom of the Mires was sending. You New Worlders may not recall the name, but certainly you recall our tales of how there was one kingdom that gave sanctuary to those with magical ability. This was the Kingdom of the Mires.

"Like several other lands that possessed active gates," Skea went on, "the Kingdom of the Mires continued to work with us after we had taken command here. I won't say their king liked having to pay for services that had been his to command shortly before, but for all his ambitions toward conquest, Veztressidan was a good ruler, and did not see why his people should suffer any more than they must following the failure of his venture. Therefore, I went over to the gate with some feeling I knew who might be coming through."

Ynamynet had been listening intently; now she looked at Skea. "Amelo? Amelo Soapwort? I'd forgotten the time had come for the early-spring shipment of medical herbs from the Mires. Was the cage in place?"

"The cage was in place," Skea assured her. "I went in and spoke with Amelo. Tiniel was there and can testify to what went on. In fact, given that Amelo was by way of being a friend, perhaps it would better if Tiniel continued this account."

The young man nodded. "I can do that. I hung back as we had agreed was best in these cases, but I heard everything."

He went on to report the conversation between the two men in admirable detail.

"Finally," Tiniel concluded, "this Amelo Soapwort realized he could do nothing really but go back. He managed the spell, but I think the iron in the cage bars inhibited him a little. He didn't like drawing his own blood again so soon after the first time either. Still, I think he should have been able to transport himself safely back to the Kingdom of the Mires."

"We expected iron to inhibit," Ynamynet said thoughtfully. "How many transits does that make now?"

Firekeeper didn't think the Once Dead could have forgotten, not if Firekeeper could remember, but humans were notorious for asking questions for which they already knew the answers.

"Five," she said. "Two not so close, then three more recently. Four we send away. One we keep."

"It's spring," Ynamynet explained unnecessarily. "Winter is not a popular time for transits because what trade there is can easily be handled on snow-packed roads. For someone to wish to pay our tariffs in winter, they must be facing a grave emergency. Early spring, though, when the seas are still wild and the roads wet, has always been a popular time—especially as more southern lands know they can get a good price in the north where winter will stretch on longer."

"So we can expect the frequency to increase," Derian said. "We've done our best to secure the gates, and so far our precautions have worked."

Blind Seer said, *"Firekeeper, speak for me. Tell them that those precautions will only work as long as those who come through have no warning of what they will encounter. Remind them that next time instead of this unarmed man, the one to come through might have a bow or some other means of putting at risk the lives of those who stand gate watch."*

Firekeeper translated for the wolf, and saw the others look grave. Skea nodded.

"I had a similar thought. The Kingdom of the Mires is well known for its medical lore. Had Amelo possessed some weapon coated with a poison and offered the antidote only on grounds we do business, things could have gone very differently."

Tiniel added, "And you went right up to the cage, Skea. He wouldn't have needed a bow. He could have reached out and stuck you with a pin."

There was something taunting in Tiniel's tone, something Firekeeper did not think was wise, given how large Skea was, and how skilled in human-style fighting. Skea, however, did not take offense.

"You're right, Tiniel, and Blind Seer is right, too. In our immediate need to secure against magical attack or against the possibility that someone might make transit through the gate and then wander about undetected . . ."

"As we did," Blind Seer said, with a hint of a brag in his words, well aware no one but Firekeeper and Truth could understand him.

Skea went on without being aware of the interruption, "We

overlooked more normal precautions. I'll put those into action directly."

"I agree," Derian said. "Let's get the word out among those who stand watch, to all the Nexans for that matter."

Ynamynet rose. "I wonder what is going to happen when our former client nations start comparing notes?"

Firekeeper shrugged. "They learn that we is very fair and no one gets more than anyone?"

Ynamynet's expression remained thoughtful. She looked at Truth, but the jaguar offered no prophecies.

"I hope that is all that happens," Ynamynet said. "Is that all you have to report, Skea? Not that it's not a lot, but I need to get the word out about our increased danger."

"That's it," Skea confirmed. He looked sheepish, not in the least a usual expression for him. "For some reason seeing Amelo bothered me more than the couple of other contacts we have had. Maybe it was because he was from the Mires, and the Mires was once our home."

Firekeeper admired him for his openness, especially since that openness might invite suspicion of how much they could trust him.

"Then, if no one else has any business, we'll be off," Ynamynet said.

"By all means go," Derian said. "Thank you, Skea, and you, too, Tiniel, for bringing this to our attention."

Skea and Ynamynet left together, talking intently. Firekeeper might have worried that they were conspiring, but if they were, there was little enough she could do. In any case, she and her allies would find out soon enough. Firekeeper knew that many of the wingéd folk, the ravens, crows, and seagulls who could thrive on the relatively barren island even in winter, continued to spy on the Old Worlders. The ravens in particular had been fooled once by human trickery masquerading as meekness, and were not likely to forget that lesson.

Firekeeper turned back to listen as Harjeedian took his leave.

"I am not needed to brief the gate watchers," he said. "Instead, I will go and speak with Urgana."

"What?" Derian asked. "You mean about Firekeeper's request?"

Tiniel, who had not been part of their earlier discussion, looked puzzled. Firekeeper found this interesting. Isende had known something of their plans, but clearly Isende had not told her brother.

"Precisely," the aridisdu said. He looked over at Truth, but the jaguar did not warn him away from his projected course. "When we spoke before, I said I would need an omen to guide me in my decision. Moments later, Skea gives us this report."

"How is omen?" Firekeeper asked.

"You tell me that we may need to bring in reinforcements someday, but that we cannot because we cannot risk exposing anyone new to querinalo. Moments later, we are reminded that despite our precautions we are still vulnerable. That is omen enough for me, and Truth does not gainsay it."

Truth said, *"Tell him for me. Truth does not gainsay it."*

Firekeeper did so, and Harjeedian nodded.

"So I go and I will do my best to convince Urgana to aid us. I cannot promise, for I will not order her against her better judgment, but I can be persuasive if I try."

Blind Seer panted silent laughter. *"Oh, yes. We remember. Indeed, you can be nearly as persuasive as the Meddler."*

❦

THAT EVENING, KING Bryessidan told his wife over their private dinner table what Amelo Soapwort had discovered. He told himself that this confession came not from weakness but from political sensibility. He would need his wife's cooperation if he was to carry out his current plan.

Despite the songs the minstrels loved to sing, kings did not marry for love, especially kings of kingdoms whose neighbors had not forgotten former warlike impulses, and who wanted to remind the heir apparent not to follow in his father's footsteps.

Soon after being bottled in for the second time, King Veztressidan found himself politely besieged with offers from his erstwhile enemies to provide a wife for his then fifteen-year-old son and sole heir. Many young ladies, and many not so young, had visited the Kingdom of the Mires, straining royal hospitality with the need to properly entertain them.

Of this, too, did the conquerors approve, for they felt the resources expended on gifts and banquets would not be available for other, more martial ventures.

Bryessidan acted as he was expected to do, grateful that his father did not betroth him to a stranger. Veztressidan did, however, make quite clear that the choice of a bride was not to be Bryessidan's own, but did say that, if it were at all within his power, Bryessidan would not be wed to someone he despised.

"After all," Veztressidan had said, dripping a little more of the very fine brandy one suitor had brought with her into his cup, "if this marriage is to encourage mutual respect and unity of purpose . . ."

Bryessidan had grinned. Those phrases kept recurring in formal speeches of introduction, to the point that the Mires' court wondered if all the foreigners crafted their speeches over one table.

"Well, if there is to be anything like respect and accord," Veztressiddan had said, "you must at least tolerate the woman."

And so, for accord, Bryessidan had been married a moon-span after his seventeenth birthday to a woman two years older than himself. Gidji, whose surname translated as Daughter of the Hammer, came from a people who were as tall, big-built, and fair as the people of the Mires were slim, fine-boned, and brown.

Gidji was a princess of high standing among the Tavetch. The only reason she had not been married before was that her affianced husband had been killed shortly before what would have been their wedding day. Custom required that even princesses wait a year after such a tragedy before forming another alliance, especially when the deceased was well born and well placed, and his family might be offended if his memory was discarded too lightly.

Indeed, Gidji being given into a foreign marriage was considered prudent by her family for more than one reason. Not only would it secure them the much desired eyes and ears within the court of the Mires, but it would assure that the family of Gidji's former betrothed did not find reason to object to her marrying into any other family than their own—a thing that Gidji's royal parents, seeing how presumptuous their would-be in-laws had become as soon as the betrothal had been announced, were eager to avoid.

Bryessidan did not learn all of this until after he and Gidji were wed, of course. At the time he met her, all he knew was that she was two years older than him, and had a tragic past. From observation he garnered that she was tall enough to look him in the eyes when they danced, even if his boots had heels and her slippers were as flat as possible. He liked the look of her shining golden hair, and found her sky-blue eyes rather interesting. Mires folk had, almost to a one, brown eyes, though green or hazel did surface occasionally.

He also knew that Gidji had opinions, and wasn't afraid to voice them, but since that was a quality shared by most of those women sent to court him—after all, what use would a timid mouse be to a land that was hoping the new princess and someday queen would continue to think kindly of her birth land?—this did not bother him in the least.

Married at seventeen, Bryessidan was the proud father of a daughter at eighteen. Although the crown of the Mires had passed from father to father to father since Grandfather had stolen it, there was no direct ruling that the heir must be a son. Still, almost everyone agreed a son would be a good idea. Bryessidan and Gidji managed this before he was twenty, and another two children after that. As far as politics were concerned, the marriage was a roaring success.

What had happened almost despite Bryessidan was that the marriage was a personal success as well. Gidji was the first person to tell him to his face that his temper was atrocious. He'd lost it with her once, soon after their marriage, over some minor thing. King Veztressidan had summoned Bryessidan to a private audience and given him a thorough dressing-down.

"The only thing I've asked from you as my son and heir," Veztressidan had said, "is to marry and make that marriage work. I find you a pretty girl about whom the poets are already writing songs, a smart girl, who is clever enough to see that her value as your wife is higher both here and at home than it would ever be if she had married in her own land, then I learn you were yelling at her like she was some chambermaid who had misplaced your pillow."

Bryessidan took the rebuke without a word. The one person he never, ever lost his temper with was his father. Nor did he try and find out who had reported him. He was well aware that the weather had been fine, and the windows open.

He also took the rebuke without a word because Gidji had already made perfectly clear that she would not tolerate his raising his voice to her.

"I am your wife," she had said, her voice low, level, and yet leaving no doubt why she was a fit Daughter of the Hammer, "but not your slave. If you wish me faithful and devoted, treat me well. If not, I'll cuckold you so that you'll never be sure if your children are your own, and assure that you are a laughingstock in your own court. Do you understand me?"

Bryessidan did. He also remembered the lesson of how his grandfather had come to power, and that a king could not be weak.

He remembered that his marriage had been meant to secure his throne, not to threaten it, and for the first time in his adult life he was ashamed of his temper, not proud of it. He realized he had been proud of the fear his temper generated, but now he saw that had not been fear of him, it had been fear because as the king's son he was, to a degree, untouchable.

This didn't mean Bryessidan conquered his rages all at once, but he no longer saw them as making him distinct and powerful. He recognized the fear that underlay them. The fear of seeming weak.

"And so, Gidji," Bryessidan concluded, bringing his full attention to the present, "although I have arranged the means by which our shipments may yet go through, still, this is not a problem we can lightly ignore."

"No," Queen Gidji agreed, toying with her spring chicken poached in wine. "We cannot. Have efforts been made to secure our gates on this side?"

Bryessidan nodded. "Amelo sent me a note reporting that precautions similar to those he had observed on the Nexus Islands were being put in place on our gates. Since you were born in another land, I wished to consult you on the best way we might go about inquiring whether any of the others who use the gates have encountered similar difficulties."

"That would be a good thing to know," Gidji agreed. "For one, it would give us an idea how long the new regime has been in power. For another, it would reassure any who might have found themselves blocked that we are not in collusion with those who are creating the obstacle."

Bryessidan had been so absorbed in contemplating the insult to himself and his goals that Gidji's second point had not occurred to him. However, it was so obvious once pointed out that he did not think he could admit to the oversight without seeming weak.

"True," he said, "although I am not certain if any words of mine would reassure, given that I still labor beneath the shadow of my father's reputation and ambitions."

Gidji smiled. "True. Since you became king, I have had letters and gifts from people I had not heard from since our first child was born. I think they are fishing to see if your new power has given you martial ambitions."

"And you have reassured them," Bryessidan said.

"I have only told what I know," Gidji said. "Is there something more of which I should be aware?"

Bryessidan shook his head. "There is nothing more. This problem with the gates is the first great challenge to occur since my father's death. I wish to deal with it in a fashion that will achieve two things: first, to renew our access to facilities that are ours to use by right of treaty; second, to do so without arousing the suspicions of my father's enemies that I have become their enemy."

"You will have my help in this," Gidji promised, "and that

of my birth land as well, if I have any say. May I report with all honesty that you have no part in this interruption of the gates' services?"

"Except for being inconvenienced myself," Bryessidan agreed.

"And you have no impulse toward conquest?"

"None," Bryessidan replied, then with a sudden return of his anger added, "Although if my way continues to be thwarted, I might have an impulse toward reclaiming the Nexus Islands. Apparently, we are not safe with them in any other hands than our own."

"Not safe?"

"We have been assuming that whatever problems occurred there were internal, but what if they are not? Every land that has an active gate employs a small contingent of Once Dead to operate it. What if the invaders come from the Nexus Islands themselves? We have always assumed that the large number of Once Dead on the Nexus Islands would make conquering the Islands impossible. That was their own claim, and they showed with convincing force that they could support it. What if they were wrong?"

"What if, indeed?" Gidji mused. "You are right. This is a difficult matter. Perhaps it will resolve itself within a few days, but we must take precautions and make preparations in case it will not. I will begin considering how best to approach our associates."

"And I," said Bryessidan, "will inspect our own gate. I have Amelo's word that it has been secured, but for too long have I trusted our own Once Dead and their associates. Time for a few of my own guards to be stationed in the gatehouse. I will tell Amelo that they are there to make sure he and the other Once Dead are safe."

Gidji pushed her plate from her, appetite for action replacing that for food.

"Then we act!" she said.

"Oh, no," Bryessidan answered, pushing back his chair in turn. "We are merely reacting. We are not the aggressors. Remember that, my queen. The Kingdom of the Mires is cowed, quelled, and obedient to the common will. Never would we be aggressive."

"Unless driven to it, of course," Gidji said.

"Unless driven to it," Bryessidan agreed.

V

THE NEXT DAY, Harjeedian reported that he had finally managed to convince Urgana to speak with him. The older woman had proven surprisingly stubborn, saying that her mind was made up and she did not wish her faith troubled further. However, Harjeedian was at least as persistent, and had managed to convince Urgana that she owed him the chance to discuss a matter so close to the heart of their united creed.

Given the prickly situation, Harjeedian did not wish to be accompanied on his visit to Urgana.

"Our discussion will be largely theological," he said, "and would quite possibly bore you."

"And you'd like to keep from reminding her that there is the least secular interest in the matter," Derian said with a slight grin.

There were times Derian had trouble accepting his new role as one of the local governmental heads—if the uneasy alliance they had formed with the Old World residents of the Nexus Islands could even be termed a government—but he knew that Urgana would see him as such.

Derian knew that in his turn, Harjeedian had difficulty in accepting a government where matters of religion and of rulership were so distinctly separated. In Liglim, the disdum were also the rulers, and if the omens showed that someone from outside the disdum was to be appointed to a ruling position, then they also automatically were viewed to be part of the disdum. Such had been the case with Harjeedian's sister Rahniseeta, and her agreement to become junjaldisdu, the supreme representative of divine Water, had begun with her breaking her engagement to Derian.

Derian could think about those events without a twinge, now. Well, almost without a twinge. Especially if he thought about how the people of Hawk Haven were not so different from the Liglim in the matter of religion and government. The Hawk Havenese might turn to their ancestors for supernatural guidance, rather than to the omens supplied by elemental deities, but each Hawk Havenese included the ancestors of the royal family, from Zoranà the Great forward, among those from whom they sought guidance.

The situation in the Nexus Islands was quite different. The Once Dead and their associates who had sought refuge in the Kingdom of the Mires had been from many different lands, with many different religious customs. Bound by the immediate demands of survival, they had accepted the king of the Mires' decree that they tolerate religious differences. Ten years of near isolation on the Nexus Islands had changed this practice only slightly. Although it was never stated as such, the Spell Wielders had become the new deities, decreeing death for infractions, and extracting their tribute in living blood.

Sometimes Derian wondered what the next permutation would be. As the New Year approached—at least the New Year as it was counted in his own land, where the new year began with the coming of the planting season—he had suggested that some sort of celebration was in order.

Immediately, he had been informed that there were at least three different starting dates for the new year according to calendars brought from their homelands by those who now lived on the Nexus Islands. Moreover, the Nexans had their own calendar, one that dated the new year from their holding the islands separate from the rulership of any other land.

In the name of convenience and general accord, the new year was now celebrated in what Derian would call Hummingbird Moon. Derian had quickly agreed that he had no problem with following local custom, but now he regularly burned incense in his ancestral shrine, and prayed for guidance to help him avoid stirring up any other such wrangles.

But for today Derian dismissed both thoughts of future religious conflicts and Harjeedian's conference with Urgana from his mind. The several days he and Firekeeper had been away to see Doc, Elise, and the new baby had been time enough for any number of small problems to develop, problems that, for some reason, he was the only one anyone thought could find a solution.

First, however, he needed to get up to the gates and see for himself that Skea was putting the promised security precautions into place.

As much as Derian wanted to trust Skea and Ynamynet—and they had shown no sign of being untrustworthy to this point—still there was no need to be careless.

And very many reasons indeed to be careful.

❧

A GIFT TO a wise raven named Lovable of rough beads made from broken glass brought Firekeeper and Blind Seer the information that Harjeedian was likely to be some days bringing Urgana around to his theological position.

"And Ynamynet says that no one has come forward with tales to tell," Firekeeper said mournfully to Blind Seer, watching the black and glitter that was Lovable and her prize winging off toward the sun. "Here I am, all wild for a hunt, and no game in sight."

"We might catch the scent another way," Blind Seer suggested, raising his head from his paws.

"Tell!"

"I have been considering," Blind Seer said, well pleased with her eagerness, "other ways we might research this matter. Human tales are well and good enough, but there are others who have ears and eyes and memories—and these others have an advantage the humans do not. If the tales we have of the Fire Plague are true, our own people were not touched by it."

Firekeeper grinned at him, her dark, dark eyes shining with pleasure. "You are wise, sweet hunter. I wonder though, might not the local yarimaimalom share the same prejudices as do Urgana and Harjeedian? Many of them share the same beliefs as the Liglimom."

"Possible," Blind Seer agreed. "Very possible, but here we are in lands far enough south that Liglim's influence is not so strong among either humans or beasts. If we run farther west, we may find those who, like our own pack, have never heard the merest whisper of this faith."

"A run sounds good in any case," Firekeeper said. "Spring warmth comes to the southern lands sooner than to our own forests. Where our home pack ranges, nights are still cold and the new leaves only testing their welcome, but when we returned last from the mainland, I noticed that the birds were already spring mad, and the season well advanced."

"Then we go?" Blind Seer said, rising and stretching, nose tip to tail tip.

"As soon as we tell Derian," Firekeeper said, "and find who is available to work the gate."

They found Derian easily enough, but had to wait until he settled an argument between two humans over who had the rights to some furnishings discovered in a ruin they had been laboring to clear away.

Derian welcomed them, listened as Firekeeper explained where they were going, and nodded.

"Good thinking. The note Harjeedian sent to me earlier agrees with Lovable's assessment. He adds that he thinks Urgana can be convinced, but only if handled gently and given time to meditate between discussions. I spoke with Ynamynet earlier, and she added that her feeling was that a few who might have tales are waiting to see how Urgana is treated."

The redhead shoved a hand through his thick hair, pushing his forelock back, though it flopped over his forehead immediately after.

"I don't blame them for not trusting us," he said, "but having you elsewhere, rather than providing a visible reminder that this is more than a theoretical discussion, won't hurt either."

Firekeeper nodded.

"Who is gate opener?" she asked. "So I find."

Derian glanced at a list tacked to his wall.

"Kalyndra."

"We be back in some days," Firekeeper promised, and gave Derian a quick hug.

Derian hugged her back. "You'll need to tell the gatekeepers something more solid than that, so they know when to check for you."

"Three days?" Firekeeper hazarded.

"Three should be enough," Blind Seer agreed, *"at least for us to make a start."*

"Three days," Firekeeper repeated. "To make a start."

Blind Seer gave Derian a long, stretching bow, and Derian reached out and tugged the scruff of the wolf's neck.

"Keep her out of trouble," Derian said.

"And me, him," Firekeeper said.

KALYNDRA WAS ONE of the very small number of new permanent residents to be added to the community on the Nexus Islands. She had appeared one day through a gate that connected the Nexus Islands to a land called Tey-yo.

Even if the maps of the gate complex had not supplied this information, the New Worlder conquerors—as they still very much were at this point—would have guessed, for Kalyndra had raven-wing glossy, blue-black skin even darker than Skea's, and Tey-yo was the land that Skea and the few Nexus Islanders who shared his coloring had identified as their homeland.

Unlike many of the active gates, which connected lands that were relatively close geographically, Tey-yo was so far south that Skea claimed even the stars made different patterns in the night sky. Back in the days when King Veztressidan was beginning to lose his wars, the gate to Tey-yo had been opened in the hope that reinforcements for his army and magical corps might be recruited from there, from peoples who had no alliances with those Veztressidan had made his enemies.

In Tey-yo, King Veztressidan's efforts to recruit had met with limited success, for the gate had been built in a city set high on a plateau where the weather was comparatively cool. Without magic to ease the passage up and down from that plateau, most of the inhabitants had moved away. Those who had not had descended into savagery. Only within the last fifty or so years, as the violence of querinalo's fevers ebbed, had people begun to return. These were mostly the magically talented and their kin, exiled from their families when their abilities became evident. Therefore, the community there was small.

Skea had been the son of a pair of those who had come to reclaim the city. He had been born on the plateau, and had joined in battle with the things that dwelt in the green tangled ruins from the time he could walk. Later, when he was a man grown, Skea and some others had gone from the city of the plateau into the service of King Veztressidan, who welcomed Twice Dead along with Once, eager for any augmentation to his forces. There they traded their services for supplies to help the kindred they left behind.

When Kalyndra arrived on the Nexus Islands, a moonspan and more had passed since the conquest had been completed, time enough for stories to be shared and personal histories to be known. Therefore, when the gate to Tey-yo shone with the swimming shadow that indicated the gate was coming alive, Skea was alerted. The muscular Twice Dead had stood impassively as a single form made its transit.

Blind Seer had turned to Firekeeper and commented, "Skea's face is calm, and his limbs relaxed, but his sweat reeks of apprehension. Have a hand to your Fang, dear heart. I do not think an enemy comes, but there is something more here than Skea is saying."

First through the gate was the woman they now knew as Kalyndra. The composed, well-groomed woman who now turned in grave welcome as the wolves entered the center of the gate complex was far improved from when they had first met her. Now she stood sleek and tall, the thick, wooly hair that fell to her waist twisted into hanks ornamented with fat beads and loops of copper wire, the heavy white robe she wore pristine. Then she had seemed some strange beast, her hair a mane, her skin sheened with blood where it was not matted with filth.

She had been alone, but not alone, for she bore in her arms a man sorely wounded, a man who would die within hours of the transit, a man who, they soon learned, was Skea's father—as Kalyndra was Skea's mother.

Two more came through soon after. One was a boy child, the other a young man stumbling sick with what anyone with a nose immediately knew was the onset of querinalo.

All was chaos for a long while then. The gate's shimmering surface had fallen cold and dead after the second transit. With wounded to tend, no one considered the possibility that this might be the front line of an invasion.

None but for Firekeeper and Blind Seer, who had learned to respect human cunning. The pair kept watch through the day and the long night that followed. Only the next day did they learn how slim was the likelihood of anyone coming through that gate ever again.

Kalyndra told the tale, although her skin was ashen and her eyes were red with grief for the husband who had died in her arms only hours before.

The settlement on the plateau had been attacked and overwhelmed. The attack did not come from the savages or from the strange creatures who still lurked in the ruins, despite the best efforts of over thirty years spent attempting to eliminate them. The attack came from the peoples who inhabited the towns and villages in the jungles surrounding the base of the plateau, people with whom the plateau dwellers had traded and who they thought were their friends.

But a man possessed of nothing but two interlinked qualities had come to the region, a man who would have been nothing but for those two qualities. One was a charisma so blinding that Kalyndra said many thought it was a talent. The other was a belief that his star-ordained role was to unite the scattered villages and make from them one people again.

This man knew that in order to overcome the factions and feuds that had grown up among the various villages—most of which were nothing more than extended families—he must find something for them to hate and fear more than they hated and feared each other. He found this in the city on the plateau, and the still vivid memories of the sorcerers who had ruled before querinalo.

"Nearly overnight he could convert a village to his cause," Kalyndra said, "and as his horde of followers grew, others joined. I am certain not all believed in his cause or his vision. I believe that he will not long outlive us, but for those of us who lived on the plateau, unwarned, not anticipating treachery, there was no defending ourselves."

Firekeeper had not understood much of what Kalyndra had said about how exactly her people had been destroyed. Too many of the words Kalyndra used were unfamiliar, and although Skea did his best to translate into Liglimosh, that language was not his first, and he frequently was less than clear.

What was clear beyond a doubt was that Kalyndra and the other two could not return to their home. Watch was kept upon the gate to Tey-yo, but no one else came through. When, a hand of days later, Ynamynet insisted on opening the gate so that Skea and a few others might pass through and rescue any survivors, the gate did not come alive, no matter how loudly she said her chants or how much blood was poured in the cut-stone channels.

"Broken from the other side," Ynamynet said, her manner as cool as ever, but her eyes nonetheless bright with tears. She knew many of those people, for the gates had meant that she and Skea had been frequent visitors to the city on the plateau, where they had found a welcome they would never find in her homeland.

Firekeeper knew Ynamynet had tried to open the gate, repeatedly over the days that had followed, only resigning herself to failure when Kalyndra herself took her daughter-in-law aside and chided her for spending energy on the dead that was needed for the living.

So Kalyndra had taken up residence on the Nexus Islands, moving into the house adjoining the one in which her son and his family lived. She was Once Dead, trained in sorcery and spells, but the death and destruction she had experienced had killed any ambition she might once have had. Before long, she was trusted enough to be given a watch stand near the gates, one of three who had the power to awaken the artifacts for use. The young man who had been carried through also had known the spells, but querinalo had stripped him of his magic, while preserving him alive to mourn his people.

Kalyndra had learned to speak a little Liglimosh, even before the destruction of her home had driven her to find sanctuary on the Nexus Islands, for the language had been one of those adopted in common by the residents of the Islands. Since her coming, she had learned a bit more, but the notes of her native language accented it so that Firekeeper often had a bit of trouble understanding her.

Fortunately, today's business did not require a great deal of conversation.

"Going back to your forests, Lady Firekeeper?" Kalyndra said.

Firekeeper nodded. "Going there. Will come back in three days. Not today in count. Three days after this one."

"About what time?" Kalyndra asked.

Firekeeper frowned. When alone, she and Blind Seer kept wolf's hours, avoiding the heat of the day, traveling when it pleased them.

Blind Seer suggested, *"Tell her dawn of the fourth day. That will give us a little more time without inconveniencing them."*

Firekeeper translated this, and Kalyndra seemed to understand.

"Someone will come and wait for you," she promised. "Probably Enigma. He's not bothered so much by weather."

Firekeeper understood this. The gate into the New World, the only one they had opened thus far, had its end point in a ruined stronghold that had once belonged, as humans saw things—and technically still belonged—to Tiniel and Isende, the last remnants of the family who had been given the land by other humans.

In reality, the stronghold belonged to the bats that roosted in its rafters and the little creatures who laired beneath the broken floorboards. It was a place much open to weather, as humans saw things, but Enigma was not human. Enigma was a puma, one who had demonstrated repeatedly in the past few moonspans that if someone set up the basic forms he could work spells as easily as any sorcerer.

Assured that they would be able to find their way back to the Nexus Islands, Firekeeper and Blind Seer watched as Kalyndra made the now familiar traceries. The only difficult part for them was supplying the blood to power the spell, but that they must do. There was one new, nearly inviolable law on the Nexus Islands: No one would work magic or benefit from it without supplying at least part of the blood necessary to make the spell work.

Nodding their thanks to Kalyndra, Firekeeper and Blind Seer walked side by side into the shimmering stone. They emerged into weather much warmer than that they had left behind. This was evident even in the relatively cool shadiness of the interior courtyard of which the gate was one wall.

This courtyard was much changed since Firekeeper and Blind Seer had first seen it. The vegetative detritus that had accumulated over the many years that the stronghold had stood empty had been swept away, the vines trimmed to order. The gnarled apple tree had been shaped and pruned, and was now coming into both leaf and flower. The well had been cleaned and a solid oak cover built. A new rope and bucket waited for use.

Firekeeper pushed back the well cover and pulled a bucket of fresh, crystalline water. She and Blind Seer drank lightly, for one does not travel comfortably with water splashing about inside.

The tending to this little courtyard had been done for more than cosmetic reasons. The garden beds had been planted with a variety of perennial herbs, plants that would flourish in this protected space in the relatively mild weather of the southlands, but which were much more difficult to grow on the colder, windswept Nexus Islands. The repaired well provided a backup for the sometimes brackish springs on the Nexus Islands.

Ynamynet and the others who had moved to the Nexus Islands after the parting from the Kingdom of the Mires had rapidly learned one thing about their new home. The rocky islands would support life, but only just. A bad storm that tainted the wells or stripped the carefully tended garden beds could mean disaster. Reliable connections to other areas assured survival.

Firekeeper used the surplus water from the bucket to water the herb bed, remembering as she did so Holly Gardener, the first person to teach her how food could be reliably grown. In her younger life, Firekeeper had known starvation often enough to find garden lore more wonderful than any magic. To the surprise of many of the Nexus Islanders, all of whom thought of the wolf-woman first as the stranger who had challenged their powerful rulers—and had won—Firekeeper had been among those who spent hours weeding to prepare this courtyard for spring gardening.

When they were done inspecting the gardens, the two wolves went out through the stronghold. The large building was still mostly in ruins, but here and there efforts had been made to strengthen chancy floorboards or shore up roof timbers. More importantly, at least when preserving the secret of this place was considered, Ynamynet had taken time to reinforce the illusions that hid the stronghold within the seeming of a grove of trees.

The horrid bracken beasts that had guarded the copse were gone now, their role as defenders assumed by various yarimaimalom who had shared the island dwellers' desire that the gate's secret not be casually learned. However, the blood-briar vines still grew freely, taking occasional toll from Cousinkind, but never from the yarimaimalom now that they knew the danger the innocent-appearing vines offered.

Firekeeper and Blind Seer carefully avoided the blood briars, exchanged news with the lynx and the crows who were watching over the copse that day. Then, with afternoon giving way to the long shadows that heralded evening, they considered where they would go.

"Onion and Half-Ear both," Blind Seer said, speaking of two of the local wolf pack, "share too much of the Liglim's beliefs to be any more help to us than was Eshinarvash or the other yarimaimalom. I was thinking we should run west, angling south when the land will not let us go west, and see what other Beasts we might encounter. If we are lucky, we may find some who are more Royal than Wise in their outlook."

Firekeeper nodded, thinking how odd it was that the rough term she had invented when first trying to explain to Derian that the wolves who had reared her were something more than the wolves he had known east of the Iron Mountains should have become a means now of differentiating wolf from wolf. The "Royal" wolves were no such thing, but at that time her vocabulary had not included many words to indicate the abstract concept of exceptional ability.

The Liglim had done better, for their use of the word "yari," or "wise," indicated the thing that most separated beasts like Blind Seer or Eshinarvash from their Cousin-kind, the intelligence that let them bridge the gap between themselves and other bloods, whether those moved on two legs or four or, as in the case of some of the sea beasts, on none at all.

And I, Firekeeper thought, as so often before, *am a two-legged wolf, uncrippled, yet crippled. Still, the evening is fair and fine, and the western way is open. I am no broody bird. Let me run.*

She matched thought to action, stretching limbs that somehow always felt cramped on the Nexus Islands where she was too aware both of people and of ocean bordering around, though the islands themselves were not so small. Blind Seer felt her wish, reading it in the first intake of breath, the first lifting of bare foot from damp soil. Such was much of the language of the beasts, an awareness of things that humans had learned to forget, forgetting so they could learn many other things, things so peculiar that Firekeeper often wondered if knowing them was worth the exchange.

Firekeeper and Blind Seer ran through the evening and into the night, stopping from time to time to visit with various friends. They were yet within the range they had run through-out the winter, an area of meadows and woodlands with good hunting, and not overpopulated.

Usually, they would ask for stories about the coming of the Fire Plague, but as Blind Seer had expected, the tales they were told were so heavily colored by the theology of the Liglimom as to add nothing to their understanding. When the sun rose high and hot, the pair lay up in a thicket. Firekeeper made a small fire and set a duck packed round with wet mud to slowly bake while she and Blind Seer drowsed. Later, the greasy meat went well with the raw greens she dug from the verges of a snowmelt-chilled brook.

They moved on again with the long shadows through the new-leafed forest where the songbirds squabbled their territo-rial claims or sang defiant love songs. The ground underfoot was damp and soft, pleasant against Firekeeper's bare feet af-ter the rock and sand of the Nexus Islands. Rains just past had awakened little flowers in every hollow: white and pale pink, mostly, not needing the gaudier hues of late summer to attract the attention of slow-moving, newly awakened butterflies.

Now the pair were in lands they did not know as well, but when they chanced upon one of the woodland's inhabitants they found news of them had come before. There was no won-der in this. The Beasts are at least as curious as humans. Blind Seer by himself, a wolf from far, far to the north and west, would have been interesting all in himself. Firekeeper was the rich marrow that made the bone worth cracking.

Moreover, the tales told of them told as well that strangers, strange though they were, Blind Seer and Firekeeper both were proven friends of the local Beasts, friends even to the eaters of leaves and grass who otherwise might have shied away lest they find themselves prey.

So the pair did not need to seek the inhabitants of the regions they crossed. Many sought them out. Wingéd folk came first, feeling safe in the high branches of trees. Then came the local wolves, glad to welcome these far-ranging kin, and even trusting them with the location of their dens, where the little puppies still huddled beneath the earth, mewling for their mother's milk, not yet strong enough to be trusted out in the sun.

None of these wolf packs were large, consisting perhaps of a mated pair, some of their pups from earlier litters, maybe an outlier come seeking variety, perhaps an elder too old to lead but not too old to teach. Usually there would be no more than six or so adults of varying ages.

Firekeeper had been astonished by how humans—even those who claimed to admire wolves—envisioned wolf packs as traveling, ravening hordes. She supposed the humans were imposing their own way of living all heaped up upon each other in towns and cities upon their images of wolves. If wolves lived in such large groups they would strip the land in short order—as humans would do, if they did not grow food both from the ground and on the hoof.

When the game animals gathered, then more than one pack might come and share the hunting—Firekeeper supposed some such sight might have given humans the source of their tales—but most of the time wolf packs were smaller. Come summer, when the hunting was easier, the pack might even fragment for a time, rejoining when winter approached and the kill would come more easily with the joining of six or seven hunters.

So in their night of running, Firekeeper and Blind Seer crossed the territories of several packs and visited with them. These western wolves were more like the ones Firekeeper and Blind Seer had known from their homeland. Some had heard the beliefs of the Liglim, but they had not adopted them for their own, as the Wise Wolves did.

The local wolves were pleased to hear tales from along the trail the pair had run—and not just the trail of the last few days, but of all of Firekeeper and Blind Seer's wanderings. They were even more pleased to counter with their own stories, for wolves delight in besting each other.

In this mood of friendly competition, Firekeeper would have come right out and asked for tales from the days before the Fire Plague, tales that might give hint as to where the plague first arose. However, Blind Seer wished to be more indirect, and she followed his lead. In years she was the older, but wolves do not spend a full two hands and more of years simply growing to maturity. Although only eight years old, Blind Seer was in many ways her elder.

Firekeeper also never forgot that Blind Seer's keen nose shouted to him things that she heard only as whispers. If he sensed reason for caution, she would walk softly, watching where he set his paws, and taking care to break not even a twig.

But when they had left the second pack behind them and were alone in open country, Firekeeper could hold her question no longer.

"Blind Seer, why do you not simply ask what it is we want to know? You did when we were farther east, but now you dance around the question like the pack cutting a slow runner from the herd."

"Farther east I asked more openly, and now I do regret it. I think rumor of our interest has run before us."

Firekeeper started to ask how he knew, but Blind Seer snapped at the air—or perhaps merely at the gnats that were worrying his eyes.

"Hear me out," he said. "Remember how the tales we heard when we were small went back and back, reaching to stories that must have had their source in the days before human ships ever touched the shores?"

"I do."

"Do you remember when our mother told us the story of the songbirds? How she was unhappy to share with us such a dark tale, one that spoke so poorly of our kind?"

"I do."

"When I herded the tales to the days when humans came, preparing to ask our question, I scented an odor I had not caught since that day. A sour odor of troubled bowels and uneasy stomach. At first I did not make the connection, but memory brought it to me. Then I noted that the One Male who was then our host was shedding rather more than the season might merit, and the One Female had slid back into her den, although to that point she had been eager enough to meet us."

"I remember. I thought the puppies must have wakened, although I had heard nothing."

"Their whimpers came after. I decided to hold my question, and when I let the One Male take our talk elsewhere, the sour smells ebbed."

"And the One Female returned to see us off," Firekeeper added.

"The same happened at this last pack," Blind Seer said. "Similar scents, this time from the Ones and the elder who we were told had been a One in his time."

"So something is being hidden from us," Firekeeper said.

"I think so."

"Something is being hidden from us," Firekeeper repeated with growing anger. "Again."

VI

 TINIEL SAT WITH his sketch pad in the little cottage he had once shared with his sister and wondered when his self-esteem had fallen so low that he was grateful because a raccoon wanted to share a meal with him.

Not that Plik was just any raccoon, or even really a raccoon at all. Plik was of the maimalodalum, the beast-souled, a weird hybrid of human and yarimaimalom originating in the days when magic had been the rule by which events were governed.

To casual inspection, Plik was more raccoon than otherwise. Height was the greatest divider, but a boar raccoon raised on its hind legs was taller than many humans realized. Therefore, it was not lack of height that made Plik stand out, but rather the shape of his mouth, a quality that let him speak human languages with an ease no raccoon could manage. Facial features blended human and raccoon harmoniously, fur and mask and bushy eyebrows complemented each other to the point that if the tip of Plik's nose had not possessed the blackened tip of the raccoon, this would have seemed odd rather than otherwise.

But Tiniel was too familiar with Plik to dwell long on his physical uniqueness. What kept nagging at the young man was that Plik was sitting across the table from him rather than the person who should be there, the person who had always been there until slightly under five moonspans ago.

Isende. Tiniel's sister. His twin. His other half.

One of the first things to happen following the conquest of the Nexus Islands by the New Worlders had been the reorganization of who resided where. Not only were quarters needed for those who had arrived from the New World, but after what Firekeeper had termed—in what everyone was assured was meant to be humor—"the Battle of the Basement," having unpredictable elements continue to reside in the large building that had formerly served as both group residence and headquarters had not been deemed a good idea.

Now only Harjeedian lived in the large building, Harjeedian and a rotating contingent of Wise Beasts, who seemed to enjoy the aridisdu's respectful company, even if, unlike Firekeeper, he could not speak their language.

Tiniel had thought the relocation of the inhabitants, many of whom took over the more opulent quarters that had been used by the Once Dead, a good thing. What he had not expected was that Isende would be among those to choose a new place for herself. Now she lived across the island from him in a suite of rooms near Rhul and Saeta, a couple with a seemingly inexhaustible supply of small children.

Now Tiniel saw his sister only at the dining hall where all the Islanders took their meals in common. Limited supplies made common meals necessary. Even when they did meet, Isende usually had one or more of her small neighbors in tow. Tiniel found it impossible to have a constructive conversation when Isende was constantly interrupting to wipe something off someone's face or to answer some idiotic question.

This didn't bother him nearly as much as his suspicion that Isende wanted things this way.

So Tiniel found himself making excuses to avoid the dining hall whenever possible. Breakfast was the easiest meal to manage, for other than porridge, the meal consisted of bread, cheese, and a garnish of some sort—usually, these days, of pickled onions. Those on cookhouse duty didn't care if you carried your portion away, only that you brought back the bowl.

Not long after Tiniel instituted the custom of eating alone, a tap at the door announced Plik, his own meal in a basket over his arm.

"May I join you?" Plik said, walking in before Tiniel could say anything. "I saw what you were doing, and thought it a good idea. I am still unaccustomed to living among so many, and the clamor of the dining hall in the morning is more than I care for. Still, company over breakfast is nice."

Wordlessly, Tiniel folded away his current drawing and waved Plik over to the small table where for many moon-spans he and Isende had taken their meals. Then the little cottage had been more a prison than anything else, but Tiniel found himself reflecting back upon those days with increasing nostalgia.

Plik continued to join Tiniel for breakfast daily, and although initially Tiniel had been inclined to feel that his perfectly good protest against Isende's neglect was being attenuated, he couldn't think of a way to dismiss the maimalodalu without being rude. Not only was Plik a popular member of the community—something of a cross between everyone's grandfather and, especially to the children, a rather cuddly toy—Plik was also Tiniel's closest neighbor. There were two small cottages within the blood-briar hedge, and now that they need not serve as prisons, they made good housing for one or two people, as long as their needs were simple.

Plik resided in the smaller of the two cottages, Tiniel the larger. No one protested one young man having so much space, partly because there was ample better housing, and partly because no one really cared to live surrounded by blood briar. Tiniel, perversely, found himself becoming almost fond of the queer, blood-sucking plant, for it assured him of the privacy he craved.

Or didn't crave. There were times, as now, as he sat chatting with Plik about when they could hope for fresh food from the mainland, that Tiniel craved easy companionship. He had never really been alone, because there had always been Isende, yet in other ways Tiniel felt he had always been alone, precisely because his intimacy with Isende had made other friendships unnecessary.

And then Plik said a word that increasingly made the blood pound in Tiniel's head, a single word, a name: Derian.

Tiniel was no fool. He hadn't missed how Isende had taken to Derian. He'd seen how her gaze followed the tall redhead whenever they were in the same room. He'd noticed how she made excuses to visit Derian, often going alone to that ostler's cottage near the stable. Sometimes she had one of the brats along. Lately, more often she didn't.

Tiniel's only comfort in this betrayal was that he didn't think Derian had noticed Isende's interest in him. The man had come through querinalo Once Dead, but couldn't stop whining about how his transformation set him apart.

Tiniel had felt a surge of hope when Derian had galloped off to Liglim to see his friend's new baby. Derian was important in Liglim. Maybe the ambassador who was his boss would insist he stay. Maybe Derian would even take the time to go all the way to his northern homeland, but Derian had come trotting back to the Nexus Island, all the more agitated about how his family would react to his altered self.

"Derian was wondering if you wanted to take charge of the supply run into Gak," Plik was saying when Tiniel cleared the pounding from his head well enough to listen.

"Doesn't Harjeedian usually do that?" Tiniel asked.

Tiniel hadn't been back to his home city-state since he and Isende had left more than a year and a half before, and he hadn't much desire to go there now. Gak was the scene of the first of his monumental failures—the failure to achieve his father's dream of having their family accepted as a separate clan, with voting rights in the city council.

"Usually," Plik agreed, "but Harjeedian is deeply involved with trying to convince Urgana to undertake some necessary research. He has told Derian that he thinks it best if he doesn't leave."

Derian, again, Tiniel thought. *How had Derian ever become leader when all he's done is follow. . . .* A new thought interrupted this familiar one.

"Would Isende be coming with me?" he asked, suddenly happy.

"Probably not," Plik said. "After all, the story Harjeedian has been telling in Gak is that you two have managed to make at least a small success of your venture to reclaim your ancestral holdings. It would hardly make sense for both of you to leave."

Tiniel nodded. "Still, with you people out here—I mean there—helping, we both could leave for a few days, right?"

"Derian thinks," Plik said, and Tiniel did his best to hide a wince, "that it would be best if we start downplaying our still being here. After all, both he and Harjeedian have fairly important posts back in Liglim. It's one thing to assume that they might stay to help you and Isende through a bad winter when you were ill, but it might raise questions if they were to remain."

"Are they leaving then?" Tiniel asked, his heart dancing with hope.

"Oh, no," Plik said in a tone Tiniel realized was meant to be reassuring. "Don't worry about that. Rather, you will take over the trips into Gak, and let it be assumed the others have moved on. If anyone suggests they come out and assist you— although I don't think that likely, since there's ample land for the taking closer to Gak—you can state you're fine as you are. They'd believe that."

They'd believe it, Tiniel thought, *because they'd want to believe it. They let us go easily enough, didn't they, and the two of us hardly more than children.*

He didn't admit even to himself that there was no legal way

short of imprisonment that he and Isende could have been held in Gak. After all, there was no law against ambition—or idiocy.

"Maybe Derian and Harjeedian should go," Tiniel said, "with me, I mean. Then they could be seen as leaving the area. If they wanted to double back then . . ."

Plik wrinkled his nose. "We discussed that, actually, but Derian is adamant that no one needs to get a good look at him as he is now, and Harjeedian has his business with Urgana. That leaves you or Isende. I certainly can't go, and Firekeeper—even if she were in the area—would be impossible. Can you see her doing trade?"

"And none of the Old Worlders can go," Tiniel said, trying to sound reasonable. "Even the ones who look like they could be from one of the city-states would give themselves away over and over."

"There has been talk," Plik said, and Tiniel found himself wondering when all these talks had been held, and why he hadn't been invited, then realized that likely he could have been present, but that he'd been avoiding everything but his assigned duties, "that maybe later this summer you could take one or two of the others along. The Old Country Liglimom—they don't call themselves that, but you know what I mean—might be accepted as people sent from the north by Harjeedian."

"That's an idea," Tiniel agreed, "but I still wish Derian or Harjeedian would go on this trip. I'm no merchant."

Plik spoke on, reassuring Tiniel that this had also been discussed, and that Harjeedian had promised to provide price guidelines, and Derian would give tutoring on bartering.

Tiniel let the words flow over him like water over rocks. He was thinking about leaving. Leaving and maybe not coming back, but that would mean leaving Isende. Losing her. Maybe losing her to Derian.

He wouldn't stand for that.

"I'll think about making the trip," Tiniel said, trying to sound brave but apprehensive, "but I'm not sure. I'd feel a lot better if Isende came with me. Women are taught a lot more about barter and trade."

Plik nodded, scraping his bowl with the edge of his spoon. "Would you like to tell the others, or shall I?"

"I'll tell them," Tiniel said, "but I'll speak with Isende first."

And when I do, he thought, *I'll show her where her loyalties should lie. I'll show her!*

❧

HARJEEDIAN SUCCEEDED IN convincing Urgana to attempt at least a little research on the very day that, if Derian had understood Kalyndra's somewhat confused reckoning, Firekeeper and Blind Seer were due to return to the Nexus Islands.

"Urgana has a natural inquisitiveness," Harjeedian said, "and after we had talked for some time, I realized that this curiosity could either help or hinder me."

Derian, accustomed to Harjeedian's habit of making speeches, made an encouraging sound in his throat.

Harjeedian went on. "Urgana had mentioned her fear that her pride, her dislike of being viewed as a lesser entity, simply because she did not possess magical talent, had been the reason she had bragged before King Veztressidan."

"And thereby let him know what function the Nexus Islands served," Derian said, not quite prompting.

"Exactly. I realized that I needed to show her that such pride was natural, and that denying the gifts the deities had given her would be wrong. From that point, Urgana began to yield, but not without," Harjeedian mimed wiping sweat from his brow, "considerable further discussion."

"So she will help us," Derian said.

"She is already at work," Harjeedian said. "The archived material was stored on the upper floors of the building in which I am currently residing. I took her there and left her—not, however, before requesting that Bitter and Lovable do me the favor of circumspectly watching her, and intervening if Urgana should begin to do anything untoward."

"Like starting to destroy old documents?" Derian hazarded.

"Precisely."

The two Wise Ravens were among the yarimaimalom to make the Nexus Islands more or less their permanent base of operation. Ravens were not picky eaters, and they seemed to enjoy watching humans. Also, although Bitter had mostly recovered from the punishing injuries he had taken from the blood-briar vines some moonspans before, still he was not as strong a flier as once he had been. Being able to hitch a ride, especially on a windy day, on the back or shoulder of a friend was a great advantage.

The ravens also had begun to talk what everyone simply called "human." Even Cousin ravens could learn to mimic some human words, and the Wise Ravens were intelligent enough to understand human speech—as long as it was in a language they knew—perfectly well. The jump to acquiring a few useful words was not a great one, and Derian wondered that more Wise Ravens had not done so. The Liglimom were almost pathetic in their eagerness to understand what the beasts might tell them, so surely they would have welcomed this.

Eshinarvash had translated the raven's reply: "They say that although they are clever beyond what words can explain . . ." Here the horse paused and shook his parti-colored mane in comment. "They cannot manage many of the words that are used for more complex terminology. Words that indicate simple affirmative and negative and the like are hardly an improvement over the divination equipment currently used. Moreover, Lovable adds that the boards are fun to play with."

The raven bobbed up and down, croaking "Pretty! Pretty!" in passable Pellish.

Although the bulk of what the ravens spoke was Liglimosh, where a word was too complex—and Liglimosh had an alarming tendency, at least to Derian's way of thinking, of stringing words together to make more complex words—they used Pellish instead. Occasionally, they borrowed from one of the other languages in use in the community, forcing everyone to learn a bit here and there.

And reminding us all, Derian thought, *how clever they are, and that they—if not the rest of us—seem to have learned enough that no one is safe from our feathered eavesdroppers. Well, it could be worse.*

Firekeeper and Blind Seer returned in late afternoon, Firekeeper with a freshly slaughtered deer slung over her shoulders, Blind Seer with rounded sides that testified wordlessly that he would not be joining in the venison that evening.

However, even when she had scrubbed off the deer's blood, and dressed in some of the clean clothing Derian kept for her in his house, Firekeeper did not become talkative. Even the news that Urgana was already immersed in some journals dating back to about the time querinalo was thought to have first appeared did not cheer the wolf-woman.

When Firekeeper came to sit on the sheltered patio behind his house in the evening, Derian decided her being there was an invitation to press for details.

"What's bothering you, Firekeeper?"

Firekeeper didn't pretend she didn't understand his question.

"We not learn anything when we go," she said. "Nothing."

Derian knew how impatient the wolf-woman could be, and so said soothingly, "But it was a long shot anyhow. We knew that. Your people don't keep written records. Anyhow it seems that querinalo didn't affect them back then."

Something in how Blind Seer raised his head made Derian anticipate the question Firekeeper obediently translated.

"Blind Seer say, 'I wonder why this changed.' "

Derian shrugged. "I don't know, but certainly if you find the source of querinalo, you'll find the answer to that question."

"I wonder," Firekeeper said. She looked at Blind Seer, then up and about, clearly making sure no one—not even a bird—was close enough to overhear. "Derian, I tell you we learn nothing, but I not think this is because there is nothing to know. I think it is because there is something to know, but no one wishes to tell us."

Briefly, she sketched their encounters with the various wolf packs, and the fearful evasiveness Blind Seer had scented.

"We not so good at knowing if other Beasts, not just

wolves, is hiding something, too," she concluded, "because they is not our people and we not have the same . . ."

She flapped her hands, searching for a word. "Knowing? Information? Knowing of little things that tell much, like you know I am unhappy when many others not see."

Derian nodded. "I understand. You and Blind Seer can talk to all the beasts, but you're going to understand the subtleties of what a wolf says better than you would, say, a bear."

Firekeeper nodded. "Is that. Am not sure they had anything to tell for real. Might just be a tale such as the Ones teach only to other Ones. I have told you about this before."

Derian nodded again. "I remember. I also remember how upset you were last time you learned some of these Ones' stories. Are you sure you want to know?"

"If is only way to get trail," Firekeeper said simply, "must."

"I see your point. Are you planning on running off all the way back to where your birth pack lives?"

"Was thinking," Firekeeper admitted, "but is very long run back—all the way Hawk Haven, but more to west."

Blind Seer panted in what Derian knew was laughter, and Firekeeper added, translating what he had said, "And not just run, but maybe boat, and I not do too good on boats."

Derian grinned. Firekeeper was one of the worst sailors he had ever met, tormented by seasickness so extreme that only through the use of some medicine Harjeedian had supplied had she survived their long voyage south.

"Well," Derian said, "don't go running off too fast. Maybe Urgana will find something. Maybe one of the other residents will start telling stories now that Urgana's cooperation will have given them courage."

"I not run," Firekeeper promised, "but somehow my fur prickles. I think that we will need this answer, and that if the hunt is too long, we not have it in time."

AMELO SOAPWORT HURRIED into Bryessidan's private office, all but waving a pair of tiny pieces of paper gripped between the thumb and forefinger of his right hand.

"News, Your Majesty. News about the gates. These came in by carrier pigeon just a short time ago."

Bryessidan knew that the carrier pigeons were tended by a Once Dead with a strong talent for understanding the birds—and with little else to recommend him. In the usual course of things, the man doubtless would have cooed over the birds, checking their every wing and tail feather before thinking to forward the messages they carried. That Amelo had the messages meant that he had somehow managed to stir the man to action.

"I have read them," Amelo said, "and the report is neither good nor otherwise."

Bryessidan held up a hand for silence and spread the thin strips of paper on his desk, weighting each end with whatever was convenient. The first was from Hearthome, the nation directly to the west of the Mires, the land his father had briefly conquered and that now served as gatekeeper against the Mires' ambitions.

"Had not used gate. After missive arrived tried. Were turned back. Vexing."

It was a measure indeed of how vexing Hearthome must have found being blocked that they had sent this cryptic message by carrier pigeon. A fuller letter could have been sent nearly as swiftly by messenger, as Bryessidan's own missive had been sent.

"I think we can expect a follow-up from Hearthome by tomorrow morning, afternoon at the latest," Bryessidan said, "that is, unless there is some suspicion as to our involvement . . ."

Amelo nodded. "That is always a possibility, but not one I would take too seriously. Hearthome knows better than any other nation the state of our national policy."

Bryessidan mentally interpreted this as "Hearthome is best suited to have numerous spies on our borders, and, indeed, to see whatever goes in and out via the roads."

He nodded, and read the message written on the second

strip of paper. This one came from Pelland, a land to the distant northwest.

"Gate functional but blocked. Have tried twice. Been warned against third attempt. Very upsetting, especially in light of severe winter illnesses. Must make arrangements soon. Rider en route."

"Pelland seems mostly concerned with restocking their supplies," Bryessidan commented.

"And the best thing Your Majesty can do," Amelo said, "is reassure them in advance of their messenger's arrival that we do not plan to use this gate malfunction as a reason for renegotiating last autumn's trade agreement."

"I know that," Bryessidan said testily. "Although there are sufficient grounds for doing so. Part of the price agreed upon was based on using the gates for shipping, and thus saving ourselves a great deal of preparation and packing."

Amelo nodded. As the sorcerer in charge of the gates, he knew this, of course, but unlike the king, he could not say so. Bryessidan did not apologize. To do so would be to show weakness, but he did try and moderate his tone.

"These are from two of our nearer neighbors," the king said. "I expect more reports will come in fairly rapidly."

"Probably nothing more until daylight," Amelo said. "The birds will roost with dusk."

"Well, I sincerely appreciate your initiative in making certain I received these as promptly as possible," Bryessidan said. "In turn, be assured I will keep you fully aware of any other developments."

Amelo bowed respectful thanks.

"If I may return to my more usual post," he said.

"Do. On your way out," Bryessidan said, "tell my clerk I will need the minister for trade. He may as well know what we're facing."

BRYESSIDAN DIDN'T ARRIVE at the dinner table until the soup had been cleared away. He apologized to Gidji, who replied simply.

"As penalty for your rudeness, I insist on being given a full explanation."

Bryessidan knew that there were rulers who used every meal as an excuse to curry favor with some noble or important person or other. He reserved only the midday meal for such, saying that to be too frequently available would be to cheapen the honor.

In truth, he had come to need the evening meal as a time when he could talk freely to Gidji about whatever the business of the day had been. Talking to her let him organize his thoughts, clarify issues. Nor was she simply an echo chamber, giving him back the lilt of his own voice, slightly distorted. She had her own opinions, and wasn't in the least shy about offering them.

Now he sketched an outline, beginning with Amelo's arrival with the messages, and ending with the exhaustive meeting with Chelm Charlock, the minister for international trade.

"Before the gates," Bryessidan concluded, "we simply could not ship a good many of the herbal preparations we make. They were too fragile, too perishable. After my father ceased to keep the gates a secret—and needed to find a way to rebuild our economy—someone realized that hurdle had been overcome. The Mires has done well, even has thrived. However, there is a problem I never anticipated."

"People have come to depend on what the Mires provides," Gidji said. "What we offer is not a luxury good, no frivolous thing of gold or silver. We offer life itself. No wonder people grow nervous at the thought of doing without our goods."

Bryessidan had never ceased to be warmed whenever Gidji referred to the Mires as "we" rather than "you," but he hid his pleasure lest she think she had found a soft spot.

"Correct."

"And we need the gates to transport what we have to offer at its fullest potency."

"That is what we have found."

Gidji, Queen of the Mires, Daughter of the Hammer, frowned thoughtfully, lowering her chin onto a platform made from her folded hands. "So what these people who have taken over the gates have done is to conspire to rob thousands of people of life."

"I suppose it could be seen that way," Bryessidan said, rather startled by the thought.

"I think it is a very good way to see the situation," Gidji went on, "for it permits us to be seen in the very best of light, while making these faceless ones the enemy."

"Enemy? You speak as if we stood on the verge of war."

Gidji nodded. "Medicines and culinary herbs from the Mires. Gold that Tishiolo requires to pay its troops, gold for which they have been trading the white pollen of their high-land flowers and for which a good portion of Pelland has developed quite a fondness. Gems that the disdum of u-Chival have come to rely upon for adorning that temple they are building—the temple into which they have channeled a frightening amount of their resources, and which must be dedicated this summer, at least according to their own religious traditions."

Bryessidan said nothing, and Gidji went on, her tone still vague and thoughtful.

"I guess that Amelo has some idea of what has been passing through the Nexus Islands these last ten years. We are not the only land for whom the gates have provided a convenience that has rapidly become a necessity. I suspect that some of those who share those crossroads with us will suffer more greatly than we will. They will be looking for someone to blame. Who better to suspect than the Kingdom of the Mires, that home of treachery and haven to sorcerers?"

Bryessidan's heart was pounding so hard that his head ached. He had known war all his childhood, and had no desire to pass that legacy on to his own children. Had his father and grandfather's ability passed to him? Could he lead his land in war as he had in defeat?

"So we need another to be the enemy," he said, pleased that his voice came out level. "I understand you all too well. Those to whom the gates are now closed will tell each other: 'The Mires must be involved. Not so long ago, the Spell Wielders were sworn to Veztressidan. What old promises, old alliances has his son brought to bear so they turn against us?' Yes, my queen, my counselor, we may well need an enemy on whom to turn the wrath we might otherwise face."

Gidji nodded. "And in any case it would be very nice to have the gates working for us again. After all, I promised my parents I would come and bring the children for a visit."

VII

FIREKEEPER WAS ASSURED that the best thing she could do to help Urgana with her research was stay away. She knew this, of course, and for the first time in her life really thought seriously about the advantages to be gained from learning to read.

What language though? Pellish, as used in Hawk Haven? New Kelvinese? Whatever it was the peoples of Stonehold and Waterland spoke? Liglimosh? And if she chose Liglimosh, which form? She understood there was an old form of the language as well as the one currently in use. That was why Harjeedian was closeted with Urgana, because he could read that archaic tongue more easily than she, and it was closer to what some of the records were written in.

Firekeeper sighed, and postponed the decision to learn to read once again. Instead, a day or so after her return from the mainland, she went looking for Derian. He was talking with Tiniel. The two men's voices were raised loudly enough that Firekeeper didn't have any trouble overhearing.

They were discussing the much needed supply trip into Gak. Tiniel had been told he was the best person to take charge of such a trip, but rather than being pleased, he was balking. Blind Seer's nose told him why.

"He reeks like a young buck at rutting time when he knows a rival stag is beyond his ability to challenge. Frustration. Anger. Even a bit of fear."

"Does Tiniel then wish to be One in Derian's place?" Firekeeper asked.

"One at least where Isende is concerned," Blind Seer replied, curling his lip. "This anger of his is as foolish as a pup chasing his tail. Derian has no idea that the woman is sniffing after him."

"Derian," Firekeeper said, with more compassion than most of her human friends would have credited her with, "has bruised his feelings on the rock of Rahniseeta's duty to her deities. Isende would need to beat Derian about the head and shoulders to make him see that she admires him, horse's ears and all."

"Sometimes," Blind Seer said, leaning against Firekeeper to take any sting from his words, "the one who loves is first to see a danger of losing the beloved."

"Never here," Firekeeper said fiercely, knowing the blue-eyed wolf needed reassurance. "Never here."

Blind Seer mouthed her arm affectionately, and the two wolves listened to the conversation inside Derian's house for a while longer. They were more comfortable together since their run to speak with the mainland Beasts. Learning that once again secrets were being kept from them had renewed their awareness that when it came to a fight each could count on the other.

"They speak of us," Blind Seer said after a while, "as escort for Tiniel."

"Perhaps," Firekeeper said. "I like our plan for what we do next better. Let us see what Derian thinks. Tiniel is coming out now," Firekeeper added after a few more words were exchanged within. "Do we let him see us?"

"I think so," Blind Seer said, "but perhaps not that we have been here so long. If we walk as if we are just arriving . . ."

They did this. Plik would not have been fooled, and not just because his nose would have told him they had been in the area longer than their location and attitude would admit. Elise would not have been fooled, because she knew Firekeeper, but Tiniel, immersed in his own feelings, was hardly of a mind to note the coincidence of their timely arrival.

Neglecting to knock, Firekeeper led the way into Derian's front room. Once he would not have heard their coming, but his horse's ears heard better, and one swiveled independently to track their coming.

"How many times," Derian said, "must I remind you to knock?"

"The door was open," Firekeeper said, "when Tiniel go. What is there to knock on?"

"The frame," Derian said.

He looked very tired, and Firekeeper thought that running a human pack must be more difficult than being One of a wolf pack. She had rather enjoyed her own year as One of a pack on Misheemnekuru. Sometimes she dreamed of those green islands, her heart twisting with longing.

"I have an idea," Firekeeper said. "For helping with Urgana search."

"I have an idea, too," Derian said, "for a solution to more immediate problems. You go first."

Firekeeper nodded. "Here, in this place, I am no good. Why not Blind Seer and I run to Misheemnekuru and ask the maimalodalum to do what Urgana do here? Harjeedian can write paper telling them why they should do this in keeping with deities and Divine Retribution and all those things."

Derian considered. "That might work, but why do you need to make the run?"

Firekeeper blinked. "To bring message, and convince if can."

"If we're going to have Harjeedian write out an message, why not simply send a letter containing our request?"

Firekeeper felt stupid. Blind Seer sniggered. She had a feeling the wolf had already thought of this, but had known how much she wanted to run, to do something, and so had forborne from comment.

"A letter has another advantage," Derian said, thoughtfully.

"Arguing with a letter is impossible. Let's see . . . Why would we want to know about when Divine Retribution first occurred? We don't want to tell them we've encountered it, even in a less potent form. We certainly aren't ready to tell them about the gates."

Blind Seer said, *"The maimalodalum have long kept vigil against the return of the Old World rulers. What if we said that we had encountered omens that that return might be coming, and sought to understand the illness or curse that had sent them away?"*

Firekeeper translated.

"That has potential," Derian said. "Another thing, something we should have considered earlier. If we don't tell the maimalodalum that we have encountered querinalo, then they don't need to know we are attempting to find a means to resist it. This means that they should not have the same qualms as Urgana. Therefore, Harjeedian's theological expertise will not be necessary."

"Maybe so," Firekeeper admitted. "And omens is thing the Liglimom—and in this the maimalodalum think like Liglimom—omens is thing in which they put much belief."

"I'll consult Plik as to the best approach," Derian said. "After all, the maimalodalum are his people. He may have better suggestions as to how to most easily learn what we need. Meanwhile, if you're in need of a run, I have a good one for you."

Quickly, Derian explained the need to make a trip into Gak, concluding, "Tiniel has been resisting. I think he wants Isende to go with him, but she thinks it would be wiser if one of them remains here. Otherwise, how can they maintain the pretense that they have succeeded in making something of the old stronghold? Farms aren't left alone, even for a day."

Firekeeper had listened to enough other discussions to know that Derian and Harjeedian had decided to minimize awareness of the northerners' continued residency lest that start speculation on what there could be in the isolated stronghold to keep them there. She didn't think this an unnecessary precaution at all. When it came to twisting the mind around useless questions, she had yet to meet any creatures as adept as humans.

Derian went on, "I think we finally have Tiniel convinced that making the supply run is his duty. In fact, once I pointed out to him that this would be his opportunity to strut before those who had scorned him, he was almost eager. We're going to send two of the Old World Liglim along to help with the animals and loading and unloading and such. They're to keep to the background, and, if asked, Tiniel is to represent them as non-religious associates of Harjeedian."

"Is wise, to let go?" Firekeeper asked.

"We're going to need to do so sometime," Derian said. "You're not the only one to find these islands confining, my friend. Remember, most of those who came to live here did so with the understanding that they could come and go to any of the lands where there was an active gate. Until we figure out how to restore trade through the Nexus Islands without inviting either invasion or betrayal, they're stuck with either staying on the islands or visiting the area around the Setting Sun stronghold. Humans are a bit like horses or wolves. They need the company of their own kind. This is a start, a promise."

"Is company here on island," Firekeeper pointed out.

"True, but the same faces day in and out . . . that can be hard for people who are accustomed to having access to many different peoples and places."

Firekeeper didn't argue. Wolves were indeed social creatures. Warmer weather and easier hunting invited mingling and socializing. Often the packs that rejoined when autumn shifted into winter were markedly different from those who had parted for the summer.

Blind Seer said, *"Ask Derian if we will be expected to help with the trading?"*

Firekeeper did, and Derian shook his head, broadly, as a horse would.

"Not in the least. Tiniel is going to get some coaching, and we'll just need to hope he doesn't spend too freely. Your job will be to make certain that he and the others get through safely, and that no one decides not to come back. One reason for sending those who share kinship with the Liglim is that they will respect you and Blind Seer."

Firekeeper nodded. The Liglimom certainly did respect animals, taking omens from the actions of even dumb cousins. When their Old World rulers had come to the New World and discovered the Wise Beasts, the foundations of the religious practices upon which they based both their lives and their government had been adapted and the contributions of the Wise Beasts had been greatly honored.

Judging from Urgana's reaction when she had learned that some of the Spell Wielders had been abusing the yarimaimalom, this respect had passed into the Old World traditions before contact between the lands had been severed.

Idly, Firekeeper wondered if any of the yarimaimalom had journeyed to the Old World, and what had happened to them if they had done so.

Derian was speaking. "So tell me you'll go, and don't make me talk you around to my point of view. I've done enough of that with Tiniel."

Firekeeper considered, tilting her head to one side. As much as she would rather go to Liglim and then to Misheemnekuru, Derian's arguments were all good ones. She didn't think the maimalodalum would be able to get her to tell about the gates or about querinalo, but what if she slipped up and said something that gave them a hint?

"I go," she said. "I go with Tiniel, and get supplies."

Derian smiled. "Thank you. That is a genuine relief."

Firekeeper shrugged. "Is what you say. Wolves is pack. We go and help with this hunting."

"Do what you can to hurry Tiniel along," Derian said. "In the seven or eight days since Skea told us about that Amelo Soapwort, the gates are suddenly getting more use, and not just the gate to the Kingdom of the Mires, gates from other lands as well."

Firekeeper nodded. "I hear about this when I come back from mainland."

Derian sighed. "Harjeedian and I have checked the records, and spring is one of the times that gates have always seen the most use. I should have thought of it—carter's son that I am.

Winter is actually a good time for hauling, especially once snow falls and the roads are packed for easy sledding. Spring comes and brings rains that turn the roads to mud."

Firekeeper thought of their second trip to New Kelvin, when the toll roads had been frozen. She had seen how easily even kegs of wine and heavy chunks of building stone had been moved then, the draft horses hardly raising a sweat. Spring, though, that season of wet and mud, was indeed a difficult time for travel, at least human-style travel. She would need to remember this when they were escorting Tiniel and not roam too far lest a wagon needed to be lifted from a rut.

Derian straightened, perhaps hearing a note of frustration in his voice. "So far our defenses have worked fine. None of the Once Dead has made it through, and most have struggled even to work the spell to take them back to their home. We don't need to worry about them coming through and working some dire enchantment on our guards."

Firekeeper nodded. She'd seen for herself how those guards took extra care to stand clear of the cages around the gates. Skea's instructions were not being ignored.

Derian grinned. "Enigma, however, apparently decided our current forces were not sufficient. He took it upon himself to go recruit a few more yarimaimalom to stand watch here. Don't mistake me. I'm grateful. Beasts are infinitely more useful after dark than humans are, but having them here does put a strain on the supplies. Chaker Torn says that if he had the means to repair his nets and lines, he could do more fishing. That would help, at least with feeding the great cats and the eagles. We still need hay to tide us over until we can cut the meadows around the stronghold. At least half a moonspan should pass before we can cut, and then the hay should dry or we'll be risking the horses getting colic."

He went on, planning aloud to cover these contingencies and more, the wolf-woman half forgotten except as a friendly ear.

Firekeeper looked at her friend, feeling something like pity for him, but that wolves never pitied the One, only respected and admired him. So much to think about, so much to have ready. Spring was hardly unfolding her leaves, and Derian was looking ahead to winter.

She offered the only comfort, the only promise of support she could give.

"I make sure Tiniel come back here with all quickness."

"Don't hurt him," Derian said. "We need his help, and he's not a bad fellow when one gets past the sulking. He's just confused and out of his element. As if this is any of our element," he added, his voice soft.

"We not hurt Tiniel," Firekeeper promised.

"Why should we?" Blind Seer said, panting laughter. *"Sometimes howls will drive the deer more surely than any number of nips on the flank. All we need to do to hurry Tiniel home is remind him that Isende is here with Derian."*

THEY DIDN'T DEPART for Gak until several days later. Tiniel's skills at bartering were limited, because in the days when he and Isende could feel each other's moods, they had developed an elaborate system where Isende would stand where the merchant could not see she was watching, and then she would judge whether Tiniel was really offering too little, or whether the merchant was just hoping to get more. Without that crutch, Tiniel's abilities were limited.

As little as Tiniel liked being coached by Derian, he seemed to like less the idea of seeming a fool. Then there were complexities Firekeeper couldn't quite follow having to do with the fact that the Nexans had decided that it would be unwise for Tiniel to have too much coin with which to make his purchases—not because anyone thought he would steal it, but because Tiniel and Isende had spent most of their personal fortune to outfit their initial, catastrophic (although no one in Gak was to know this) venture to their ancestral landholding.

Therefore, although the Nexans actually had a moderate fortune laid by, Tiniel must instead learn how to barter furs, items that could reasonably have been scavenged from the stronghold's ruins, and the like. This was augmented with a certain amount of Liglimese coin (the dominant currency in the city-states), which could be assumed to have been supplied by Harjeedian. It was all very confusing.

Firekeeper didn't mind the delay. She spent the time chasing down the horses that had been fattening on the mainland's spring grass, and learning how to harness them properly to the wagons. The horses had gone half wild ever since they had been permitted to roam under Eshinarvash's supervision, and she quite enjoyed reminding them of their place.

Once on the road, Firekeeper and Blind Seer were forced to keep human hours, but this was hardly a trial in the spring coolness. The local ravens and crows fed their curiosity by tracking the wagons, and their conversation was always interesting and sometimes even informative. Blind Seer had regrown the thickness of his coat over the winter, and was now shedding. Firekeeper kept a bag of the mats she pulled loose. Isende had indicated an interest in learning if she could spin wolf-wool into a usable yarn.

With the trails—one could hardly call them roads—muddy, and the wagons heavily (although not punishingly) laden, travel was slow. Firekeeper and Blind Seer took jaunts off into the forests, acquainting themselves with the denizens who were moving back into the area now that the worst of the Spell Wielders' traps were gone.

From time to time a raven's call would announce that one of the wagons had stuck or that Tiniel and his two assistants were in some trouble from which they couldn't extract themselves. Firekeeper and Blind Seer would come loping back, and solve the problem. It was all very good for the wolfwoman's sense of self-worth.

But one night, a day out from Gak, the colorful chaos of her dreams slid into something more.

Firekeeper is running, chasing a bright-feathered blue jay that is screaming creative invective at her.

"Stupid! Stupid! Only a wolf would walk when she could fly!"

"How can I fly, stupid bird? I don't have wings."

"Do so! Do so! Just won't look and find them!"

Firekeeper considers this with mounting confusion. She swims nearly as well as an otter. Running, she can pace a deer—at least for a short burst. She has climbed trees to where the squirrels keep their secret hoards, but never has she been able to fly.

"Stupid! Stupid!"

The jay dives into a dense growth of maple, spring-thick but close to the ground. Firekeeper dives in after, knowing the very leaves that hide the bird will keep it from easily launching itself skyward once more.

With the logical illogic of dreams, she finds herself in a pavilion-style tent, the green-dyed canvas filtering the sunlight as the leaves would do. There is no jay, and with the swift change of focus and pure absence of memory that only dreams hold, Firekeeper no longer seeks it.

Instead, she sits cross-legged on the soft moss that carpets the inside of the tent, and speaks to the man who lounges with comfortable insolence across from her. He is well-made after the human fashion, all but his head, which is that of a wolf. His clothing is blue, knee-britches, shirt, stockings, and waistcoat after the style of Hawk Haven. Fleetingly, the color makes Firekeeper think of birds, but she doesn't wonder why.

"Meddler," she says. "I thought you were seeking the way to your homeland."

"Firekeeper," he replies, "I am, but does this mean I cannot come and visit with a friend?"

Firekeeper bristles just a little at this, genuinely bristles, the hackles on her neck rising, for suddenly she is no longer a human, but a wolf, her fur thick and alive as the hair of a human is never alive. She looks at the Meddler through wolf's eyes and from a wolf's perspective, and does not find this in the least strange.

"Friend?" she says. "I wish I knew for sure. The tales told

of you, Meddler, all have the same conclusion. Perhaps it is safer to be your enemy than to be your friend."

The Meddler laughs. "Be my enemy, then, if that reassures you, Firekeeper. Certainly, Blind Seer would prefer you felt so, but friend or enemy, it is good to see you."

Firekeeper lets her ears prick forward and her hackles settle.

"What new gambit have you come to convince me is wise and good?" she asks.

"Gambit?" The Meddler looked slightly hurt. "I only wondered why you take this long road to Gak when you could reach the town in moments."

"A gate," she says. "You think we should open a gate."

The Meddler smiles winningly. "It would be so much easier."

"There is no gate in Gak," Firekeeper says. "The gate that served the area near Gak is the one in the twins' stronghold. All the records agree."

"Gak . . ." The Meddler waves a dismissive hand. "That is nothing. I was thinking of other places, places you would much rather go. Misheemnekuru, for example. There is a gate there. The Liglimom thought placing a gate where their commoners could easily access it would be unwise. It's on Misheemnekuru, right near where your friends the maimalodalum now reside."

"We had surmised as much," Firekeeper sniffs dismissively. "The maimalodalum live where the Liglimom built their greatest temples, dedicated to the deities in whose name they did the sacrifices that powered their spells."

"Do you want to know where the gate is in Hawk Haven?" the Meddler teases. "I know where it is. . . ."

Firekeeper pretends not to hear. She does want to know where that gate is. Not a day has passed since she and Blind Seer returned from speaking to the local beasts that she has not considered why the Beasts might have refused to speak with her about the coming of querinalo. Certainly, her parents could be convinced to speak to her. Shining Coat and Rip are guardians of the pass through the Iron Mountains. She suspects there are few secrets they do not know.

But Shining Coat and Rip are a long way north. Moreover, a broad expanse of water slices into the land between the southernmost reaches of the land on which Hawk Haven is, and the land of the Liglim. Firekeeper knows the overland journey could be made, but she also knows it would take months, maybe years. The only one she knows who has made that journey is dead now, and cannot advise her as to routes. Moreover, when he made his journey, he was not in any hurry.

As much as she hates to admit it, Firekeeper feels a growing sense of urgency whenever she contemplates the mystery of querinalo, and where it originated—and, most importantly, how it might be ended.

She lifts her head from where she let it rest on her paws while she thought, and looks at the Meddler. She knows now with perfect clarity of thought that he has pulled her from dreams into some other reality in which they might talk. Had this been a dream, he would probably have vanished entirely, or turned into something else—a flower or a pond. But there he sits, a man clad in blue-jay blue, his head that of an amber-eyed wolf.

"Do you know where querinalo began?" she asks.

"I don't," he says. "I've been trying to find out, but the trail is old and dry. The scents I have caught are elusive."

"So you are looking as well," she says. "This is not just something you set me on for your amusement."

"Ask Truth," the Meddler says, "if the future holds much amusement. Then see if you think of me as friend or enemy. Now, curl up and get some sleep. The easy days are almost over for you. You'll need your rest."

Firekeeper knows that in this at least, the Meddler speaks truth. Whether or not the maimalodalum send her word to come to them, she will be heading away from the Nexus Islands. A nagging sense of urgency will press her forth, even if nothing else does.

"I will speak with Truth," Firekeeper says, curling on her side and burying her nose in her belly fur. "Although speaking with her is as maddening as a dream."

The Meddler laughs softly. "Sleep well, Firekeeper. Peaceful dreams."

And Firekeeper did sleep, and in her dreams she ran, wolf and wolf with Blind Seer. The feeling was so strong and so true that she believed she would remain a wolf when she wakened, but when dawn came and the little camp roused, the fur in which she buried her nose was Blind Seer's, not her own.

She had to fight down a very unwolfish impulse to weep.

VIII

THE EMISSARIES STARTED arriving a few days after the written missives from their rulers. They spurred their mounts to be as swift as the wings of the carrier pigeons, guided by some gut instinct that in this circumstance the written word could never prove sufficient.

Gazes must meet. Gestures be noted. Posture, dress, composure must all be analyzed.

On one level, King Bryessidan of the Mires was relieved. He hadn't looked forward to drafting replies to all those letters, to remembering the appropriate etiquette for dealing with these different peoples.

On another level he was alarmed. Where was he to put all these people? Certainly, the various nations maintained embassies, but those were often little more than large private homes. The overflow had to go somewhere. What entertainment would they expect? The last time the Mires had hosted such a large gathering of notables had been for Bryessidan's own coronation, and that had been laboriously planned in advance, King Veztressidan not being one of those monarchs who persisted in the illusion that he would live forever and ever.

First to come was a small contingent from Hearthome, the nation that commanded the only land route into the Kingdom of the Mires. Being gatekeeper to the land that had tried to conquer it in living memory had made Hearthome inclined to view the Mires rather as a man might view a particularly spirited horse that now answers obediently to his hand on the rein.

It helped that King Veztressidan had never been a cruel conqueror. Rather, his delight in ruling Hearthome had been so obvious the residents had felt their own worth all the more strongly. Upon Veztressidan's death, Hearthome had suggested that they would not hold the crimes of the father against the son—especially as the son had shown no tendency to follow his father's inclinations.

Now, though, the emissary who arrived and made his formal compliments looked as if he was wondering if the horse had broken training and planned to throw the rider. Bryessidan did his best to say all the polite things, but alone with Gidji, he allowed himself to rage at the unfairness of it all.

Next to arrive was a contingent from Azure Towers. Azure Towers shared the Mires' only other land border. Indeed, the rivers that emptied into the Mires passed through the Azure Towers uplands before draining into the wetlands. Veztressidan had coveted Azure Towers for control of those all-important waters. Back in Bryessidan's grandfather's day, there had been a nasty situation regarding an ambitious plan to dam one of the key rivers, but natural forces had stepped in before raids could escalate into outright war. Heavy rains and flooding had proven the lack of wisdom involved in damming a major river so thoroughly there was no outflow. No one talked about it, but no one had forgotten it either.

Bryessidan listened to the words of the tall woman in her long gown of superfine wool, and heard beneath what she said the question: *"Are you the one building dams this time?"*

He hastened to assure her not, and he hoped she believed him.

Emissaries arrived almost every day thereafter. The continent was not united as Bryessidan had been taught it had been in the days when sorcery had been the true law of the land. Then the Mires and its neighbors had all been one nation, the gates not the means of international commerce, but conveniences, doors between sections of one rambling house.

Gidji's people came as part of what Bryessidan thought of as the second wave: that is, representatives of peoples who were not precisely neighbors, but who had lived close enough to see what Veztressidan's ambitions might mean to them someday in the not too distant future.

Like many of those in the second wave, they came by ship, fighting contrary currents and annoying winds to the security of the harbor nearest to the capital of the Mires. Unlike many of those new arrivals, no mere emissary arrived but King Hurwin the Hammer himself, Gidji's father and, despite his surface affability, a rather terrifying person to Bryessidan.

Tall, broad-shouldered, barrel-chested, ruddy-complected, with fair hair that shone all the brighter where age touched it with silver, King Hurwin stooped to embrace his daughter and grandchildren before bothering with the formalities.

The second-youngest, four-year-old Neysa, chirped, "Grandpapa, you're hard to hug. My face is all bruised!"

King Hurwin laughed, knuckling the child's head with rough affection.

"Does one of my kin bruise so easily? Bruise at the touch of metal? I think not."

He threw back his cloak, and for the first time Bryessidan realized that Hurwin wore breastplate and greaves beneath his tunic.

"Father-in-law," Bryessidan said. "Why are you armored?"

"Would you expect me not be armored," King Hurwin boomed as if they were sharing one great joke, "when I am come to war?"

"War?" Bryessidan took thin comfort from the warmth with which King Hurwin had greeted his grandchildren. "Surely, my people and I have done nothing to bring you to war against us?"

King Hurwin laughed all the more deeply.

"Nothing of the sort. You are my ally and my friend."

"Then this talk of war?"

"Against those cursed Spell Wielders who have closed the

gates against us," King Hurwin said, his tone holding genuine surprise. "Who else?"

Queen Gidji looked at her father, and Bryessidan felt a certain degree of comfort that she looked at least as confused as he felt.

"Papa," she said, "I think we need to talk, but first take off that ridiculous armor. Even if war is necessary, we're not going to join battle right now."

The king did not look in the least abashed. "I think it was a good idea. Cut through lots of unnecessary chatter, as I see it, but it has served its immediate purpose. I will change my attire, but I will never change my resolve. Either the gates must be opened to us and our commerce, or it will be war."

KING HURWIN'S ENTRANCE had been too grand, too loud, and his statements too emphatic for Bryessidan to give more than fleeting, wistful consideration to the idea of swearing those who had been present to secrecy until he himself had heard what King Hurwin had to say. Even if his own attendants and those of the Hammer would agree, too many servants had overheard the exchange, and Bryessidan never forgot that those who served him quite likely spied for those his father's ambition had made his parole officers.

Instead, Bryessidan had messengers sent to each of the embassies, inviting the ambassadors and the newly arrived emissaries from their homelands to a reception and meeting that evening. He had briefly contemplated a formal banquet, but only so much could be done at a few hours' notice, and he was not going to give these varying factions more time to think and brood.

"Right now," Bryessidan said to Gidji, pacing up and down the length of one of the high galleries in the section of the castle that held their private chambers, "everyone is united in one thing: fear of whoever has taken hold of the Nexus Islands. If we give them time to think, if word spreads that your father arrived bellowing about war, we're going to have factions crop up.

"Most of these emissaries," Bryessidan went on, feeling anger flare hot in his cheeks as he remembered, "arrived here to make me nervous, to check the veracity of my report about the gates. I've since learned that at least two gate-holding nations had their own incidents with being blocked, but they chose not to report them. Then I did, and now they have to make themselves look less like the cowardly mudsliders they are."

Gidji smiled and shook her head. "You're right, but saying so won't make the situation one whit better, Bryessidan, King of the Mires. They'll simply say they had reason to be suspect, then look sidelong at you. No. We are better concentrating on those who are our true enemies, these Nexans who have chosen to violate treaties and close the gates against us."

Bryessidan nodded. "I agree. Tonight at the reception, we must keep the focus on the Nexans rather than allowing old resentments to dominate the situation. I've spoken to my minsters, and they all agree."

He was about to say more, but Gidji interrupted him with an imperious gesture.

"You have hardly time to bathe and dress," Gidji said practically. "You can't expect to command this gathering if you are not looking your best."

Bryessidan looked at her. "One question, Gidji. How much did you write your father about our situation?"

"Enough." Her gaze slid sideways and her sky-blue eyes seemed transparent of thought, but Bryessidan knew her strength and cleverness, and did not think she was immune to intrigue.

"Enough that he might realize the suspicion we faced?"

"Enough," Gidji replied, and from her tone, Bryessidan knew that was all she would say. He left for his bath, oddly comforted, and far less angry than he had been before.

BRYESSIDAN SURVEYED THE crowded reception hall from a curtained upper gallery. The initial impression of a sea of rich colors resolved into specific individuals. The king of the Mires made a note of who was talking with whom, of the anxious note that underlay the buzz of conversation, then turned to Gidji.

"Ready, my queen?" he asked, extending his arm to her.

As she placed her hand lightly on his forearm, Bryessidan noted that although her attire was in the green and white of the Mires, her silver cloak clasp was the seahorse that was the emblem of her birth land. The jeweled eyes captured the light and gave it back as emerald sparks.

What is she saying? Bryessidan thought. *Is she declaring that despite her marriage to me, she still considers herself one with her father's people? Or is she providing a reminder—as if any should be needed—that the Mires and Tavetch are joined through our marriage? Or maybe she just wanted her father to see she liked the gift her family sent for her birthday.*

For a moment, Bryessidan considered insisting that Gidji remove the clasp and replace it with something less alarmingly ambiguous. Of course, there was the likelihood that she would refuse. Then what would he do? Refuse to have her in the reception hall? Enter the hall glowering at each other? Either of those reactions would arouse far more comment than a cloak clasp.

Instead, Bryessidan found a smile and a courtly bow.

"You look lovely, my dear. Ready to face the wolves?"

Gidji nodded and raised her head high. "At your side, my lord."

They swept down the broad formal staircase to the sound of a trumpet flourish and a herald bellowing titles that Bryessidan still felt mildly surprised to hear applied to himself rather than his father. Fleetingly, he wondered what Veztressidan would do in this circumstance. Then he put the thought from him. Veztressidan had been many things—including a father loved by his son—but he had not always made the wisest decisions.

Even if diplomacy had been the late king's gift, that would not have mattered. Veztressidan was nothing but ashes in the royal vaults. Bryessidan must deal with this situation on his own, ever his own, no matter how many fawned and promised friendship. He must never forget the lesson King Essidan's accession had taught him: there is weakness in needing others; there is strength in solitude.

A reception line formed almost as soon as Bryessidan's feet touched the floor of the hall. He and Gidji greeted all their guests by name, asking after their journeys, commenting on the weather.

Over and over again, the responses to his polite courtesies were mentions of muddy roads, of seas stormy with spring squalls, of river crossings closed because snowmelt had swollen the rivers, making fords useless and carrying away the bridges.

Bryessidan listened and nodded, hearing the message beneath these banalities: *If the gates had not been closed to us, none of this would have mattered. What are we going to do about it?*

When the endless serpent of the reception line finally trailed off into a thin tail, Bryessidan and Gidji parted, strolling about the room, continuing little conversations. Bryessidan's ministers for trade and the navy were there as well. There also was the head of the Chemists Guild, a lean, leathery lizard-like woman, responsible for maintaining the standards of the potions and philters that made the Mires, if not rich, at least very necessary to those who might otherwise consider taking the land under their "protection."

Notably absent among the king's close advisors was Amelo Soapwort, the Once Dead in charge of keeping the gate. An amazing number of the newly arrived ambassadorial contingents had included in their number one of the Once Dead, usually the one of those who, like Amelo, had been responsible for maintaining that particular nation's gate.

Whether or not to include these in the reception had been a matter of furious debate. Bryessidan had already gathered that while the matter of the various resident Once Dead's loyalty was not precisely in question, still, free discussion of the Nexan situation might be restrained by the presence of those who had—at least until recently—been the Nexans' close associates.

Thus the Once Dead were meeting in a reception of their own, with Amelo as host. Some had questioned whether this might lead to conspiracy, but Bryessidan had taken precautions. He could not stop conspiracy, but he could make certain that if conspiring was being undertaken news of it would come to his ears. Spies were useful, especially spies who could wait table.

After Bryessidan had circulated among his guests, he gave his chief steward a slight nod. The steward struck a polished brass gong.

At the sound, an almost imperceptible ripple spread through the crowded reception hall. Two people from each contingent politely separated themselves from whatever conversation they had been taking part in. Earlier, notes had been sent to each foreign diplomatic contingent requesting that both the resident ambassador and the newly arrived emissary make themselves available for a smaller meeting.

Now these select men and women made their way to a smaller, if still not small, meeting room. Here the housekeeping staff had managed to construct a long table with room enough for everyone to be seated around the board.

Bryessidan took the head, and his father-in-law drifted to the foot. Everyone else was left to mill and find their own seats, thus avoiding any carping over place. The steward had thought this procedure was rather rude and violated protocol, but Bryessidan had retorted that he felt that having all these people invite themselves into his land was rather rude and a violation of protocol. Just because these varied nations had defeated his father ten years before did not mean that the Mires was their land.

Despite—or perhaps because of—the informal seating arrangements, everyone settled quickly. Bryessidan cut the flowery formalities that he knew were usual and moved to the root of the matter.

"Each of you is here for a specific reason," he said. "Either you are the resident ambassador for your land, or you are head of the ambassadorial group recently arrived from your homeland. The matter that brought each of you here is the same.

The gates through the Nexus Islands, gates that we have all come to rely upon, have suddenly been blocked. Passage has been refused. The gates are useless to us. Is this essentially correct?"

A brown-skinned woman with high cheekbones and glossy hair the color of wet ink cleared her throat. Bryessidan recognized her as the resident ambassador from the land of u-Chival to the south. The king inclined his head to her.

"Aridisdu Shervanu, please speak."

Shervanu's voice was musical and spoke the language of the Mires with an accent that was perfectly correct and yet somehow managed to give the impression that each word had several more syllables than were actually spoken.

"Kidisdu Laloreezo has come here to the Kingdom of the Mires because the omens indicated that the closing of the gates heralded difficulties to come for our land. This may indeed be so, but I should like to make it perfectly clear that our land does not rely upon the gate network. That it is useful, we do not deny, but we would not like it thought that we were in any way reliant upon the creations of the sorcery that was crippled by divine will."

Bryessidan had been briefed to expect something like this. The people of u-Chival held very conflicted opinions about the gates. On the one hand, they were a practical people. Therefore, they could not see refusing to use the gates if the gates were present and functioning. On the other hand, ever since the days of what they persisted in viewing as Divine Retribution the people of u-Chival were markedly uncomfortable with the use of sorcery. Every land, every culture had its own explanation for why the fevers had come, but as far as Bryessidan knew, the u-Chivalum were the only culture to outright state that the fever was a condemnation from the divine.

Most nations were more comfortable leaving deities or stars or ancestral judgment out of what was already a complicated issue. Yes, magical ability was now considered questionable almost everywhere—that was why Veztressidan had been able to recruit those with magical talent as easily as he had done—but even when religious reasons were provided as a gloss, the real reason underlying the condemnation of magical ability had been simple. Magic was dreadfully powerful, and very easily abused.

King Bryessidan nodded politely to Aridisdu Shervanu and Kidisdu Laloreezo, acknowledging if not precisely agreeing with their point of view. Personally, he thought the u-Chivalum were as dependent on the gates as anyone else. Weren't they the ones who had been building that expensive temple? Their own land was hot and wet, gems uncommon. The already expensive project would have been prohibitive without the gates through which to bring slabs of marble and other valuables. However, there was no advantage to stating so, not here, not now.

Bryessidan acknowledged Kembrel Speaker, the emissary from Hearthome. Perhaps because Hearthome had been among those Veztressidan had succeeded in conquering—and who had turned conqueror in turn—there was something snide about Kembrel's manner.

"I am not reluctant to admit that my land has found the gates convenient. However, as with our friends from u-Chival, I would not say we *rely* upon them. Our timber, woolens, and metal goods are not as delicate and susceptible to travel damage as are the goods of some lands. We also have several excellent harbors."

Kembrel's warm, understanding smile barely hid a condescending sneer.

Making sure I don't miss that you mean me and my land? Bryessidan thought, but oddly, instead of anger he felt amusement, maybe because the ploy was so transparent.

"And so you are here," Bryessidan asked with smooth politeness, "to assure us that Hearthome will not suffer if the gate network is disabled. We are all very grateful, I am sure."

The emissary's brows lowered, and his tone became nasty.

"I was sent here to gain assurance that the Kingdom of the Mires is not up to her former games. You were so swift to inform us that your access to the gates had been blocked. My queen found herself wondering if this was the assurance of the boy whose ball has broken the window."

"Are your spies then so incompetent," Bryessidan replied sharply, "that you could entertain such suspicions?"

King Hurwin's soft chuckle, answered by those of several other delegates, defused what might have become a shouting match. The honest fact was that Queen Iline was notorious for her spy corps—created, it was said, so she could keep an eye on her horde of ambitious relatives.

The emissary raised his eyebrows as if he deigned not to reply, but Bryessidan saw the flush on his cheeks and knew—and had the satisfaction of knowing everyone else knew as well—that the man knew there was nothing he could say.

Loris Ambler, newly arrived emissary from Azure Towers, the land east of the Mires that also bordered on Hearthome, cleared her throat.

"Invasion remains a matter for discussion," Loris said. Her voice, although pitched no louder than any other, carried in the sudden hush that fell following her first word. "Invasion from the Nexus Islands."

"Ridiculous," said Kembrel of Hearthome. "I'm not denying that the Nexans control the gates, but they lack the means for an invasion."

"What means?" Loris Ambler's voice was silky, and Bryessidan remembered reports speculating that the bandit raids on the border between Hearthome and Azure Towers had very little to do with bandits and a great deal to do with jockeying for position and resources in those border areas.

"Well," Kembrel Speaker replied, "troops for one. Arms and weapons for another."

"You forget," Loris Ambler said, as all the others continued in silence, content to let these two rivals articulate what many had thought, but none had wished to be the first to state, "the Nexans have all the gates at their command, where each of our lands has but one. I see two fairly easy ways that they might acquire what they lack.

"One, they might ally themselves with one land that holds the end point to a gate. You have cast the Mires in this role, but I do not think the Mires would serve the Nexans' needs for the obvious reason that all of us keep rather a close watch, just in case King Bryessidan matches his father in military fervor."

Bryessidan frowned, and Loris Ambler smiled reassuringly as she spoke on.

"However, we have seen not the least indication of renewed military action. Moreover, the Mires are not the best location from which to start a military action. King Veztressidan was some years acquiring the resources he needed—and he had the advantage of stockpiles laid in by his father, and the previous ruler as well. Those stockpiles are depleted, the remnants paid out in retribution following the war.

"If I were a Nexan, I would seek an ally who was known to be restless and ambitious. Perhaps a king—or queen—with a surplus of edgy progeny. I would seek a land where there were ample metal and mineral resources, a good source of timber, and a population that had not been depleted of its soldiery by past wars. Then I would do my very best to cast suspicion elsewhere, so that no one would take too close a look at what comings and goings there might be in my own lands."

This was such an apt description of Hearthome that Bryessidan felt himself studying the uncomfortable emissary more closely. Although quite likely guiltless, both Kembrel and the resident ambassador from Hearthome shifted uncomfortably. Loris Ambler smiled too sweetly and continued her monologue into a room hushed with the doubled silences of personal interest and fear that speaking might draw suspicion to oneself.

"I did say that there were two fairly easy ways the Nexans might acquire what they lack. Alliance with a gate-holding land on the established network is the first. The second is simpler. They could open gates until they located a land where what they need is available. Remember how startled we all were when Veztressidan's armies suddenly swelled by the addition of those dark-skinned peoples? The Tey-yo, I think they were called. Most of us had never seen their like. Some of our lands retained tales of their existence from the days of the sorcerer monarchs, but that's not the same.

"What is to keep the Nexans from doing something similar? I have been to the Nexus Islands on an inspection tour. I know many of you have done the same. Remember all those structures containing gates that had not yet been opened? Remember how the Spell Wielders reported their interest in someday gathering the resources to reconstruct the entire network? Who is to say that in their explorations they have not found some people interested in expansion?"

A chill silence met this announcement; then Bryessidan broke in with what he hoped was the voice of reason.

"I agree that both these scenarios are well reasoned, and quite possible. However, we should remember the limitations of the gates, as well as their powers. To the best of my knowledge, no more than two living creatures at a time may pass through any gate. True, the pause between passages is not long, but even so, I cannot believe more than two or perhaps four could pass before alarm would be cried.

"My father's advantage," Bryessidan continued, hoping his words would be taken for matter-of-fact analysis and not gloating, "was that none of the lands into which he and his allies opened gates were aware of what was happening. In most cases, the gates were in structures that were locked and shuttered. Many had not been opened since the days when querinalo thinned the ranks of the sorcerers, and the gates were sealed until the crisis had passed and business as usual could be resumed. In time, they were forgotten, and the sealed structures were either declared off-limits or their original purpose was forgotten and they were turned to other uses."

King Hurwin gave one of his belly laughs. "The one in my land, as I recall, had been turned into a barn for sheltering dairy cattle in winter. We were unprepared for armed warriors emerging from among the cows."

"Precisely," Bryessidan said, grateful for his father-in-law's support, even while he wondered what price would be extracted for those cheery words. "The Nexans cannot expect to have that advantage. What good would come from recruiting even vast armies if we will see them as they arrive?"

Bryessidan was pleased to see nods of agreement and a certain amount of general relaxation.

Wantoniala, the emissary from far Tishiolo across the eastern mountains, commented, "Certainly my own land has taken precautions to secure our gate. Any invader might find a certain irony that our security is patterned after what our spellcasters observed when balked upon arrival at the Nexus Islands."

Other of the newly arrived emissaries hastened to comment that similar precautions had been taken in their own lands. Bryessidan had noticed that the emissaries were more likely to speak than the resident ambassadors. This made sense, since they were the ones who had been in more recent touch with their rulers and so could answer more appropriately.

Before the discussion could veer off in the direction of which techniques were best, Bryessidan thumped the table to call the meeting back to order.

Predictably, Kembrel Speaker, still stinging over his treatment earlier, was the one to pour vinegar into the sweetened mood.

"Very good," he said, twisting his lips into the sort of smile people make when they've just bitten into a sour apple. "We are safe, just mildly inconvenienced by the gates being shut down. Shall we wait a few days, see what happens? We might send an embassy across, two people at a time, per gate, of course. We might say, 'Excuse me, gentles, but when might we expect gate service to resume? You see, we have perishable goods we need to ship and my wifey wanted to take the children to visit the folks.' "

They do have good spies, don't they? Bryessidan thought wryly.

Kembrel paused, then leaned forward, elbows on the table, almost as if he were about to jump to his feet.

"But haven't we rather overlooked a key resource the Nexans have? One we cannot match by their own design?"

Bryessidan watched as expressions shifted from confusion or neutrality to understanding. Kembrel continued on relentlessly, stating what everyone must be thinking.

"They have a plethora of Once Dead . . . both those with highly specialized talents and spellcasters. After the Veztressidan incident, we were all too glad to be rid of them, to think of them as exiled and dependent. They were for a while, but ten years is a long, long time. Ten years is sufficient time to stockpile resources, to open new gates, to train followers about whom we know little or nothing." •

Laloreezo of u-Chival interrupted before Kembrel could heighten the intensity of his harangue.

"You forget, sir, that we had to make a compromise with the Once Dead. Granting them the Nexus Islands was the only way we could convince them to moderate their alliance with King Veztressidan."

Kembrel nodded. "That's right. It was the best decision at that time, for those situations. I was one of those who signed the agreement. I would not have done so if I had not believed it was the best solution for us all. When battled and beleaguered, one thinks about ending the war promptly, before further loss or damage is incurred."

Or, Bryessidan thought, *before you actually need to commit more than a token force to the field. Your queen was more interested in indignation and reparations than actually encouraging conquest of the Mires. I remember that, and I was hardly more than a boy. I am sure that others here remember much more clearly.*

But if they did remember, no one chose to comment, and Kembrel Speaker continued with loud eloquence, "Visions of what may happen ten years later are not so clear—or more accurately, there are many visions, and you cannot tell which one will come to fruition. At the time, most imagined the Nexans would scrape out a living trading gate service for necessities. That they so often requested goods rather than coin reinforced the impression that they were a threadbare community simply scraping by. I wonder now . . . I wonder . . ."

Skilled rhetorician that he was, Kembrel Speaker did not state exactly what it was he wondered, but left each listener's imagination to color in with his or her own private fears.

Bryessidan spoke with a flat bluntness he hoped would stop the wilder imaginings. "So, you think the Spell Wielders may have found some other way to harm us, some route that does not involve the gates."

"I think it is a possibility we cannot overlook."

Kidisdu Laloreezo spoke, his voice tight and nervous.

"What about the Once Dead who did not join the Nexans, but remained to serve on this side of the gates? Can we trust them? Do you believe we cannot? Is that why they are not part of this meeting, although they might know best what we could expect?"

Bryessidan dammed the flood of questions by raising one hand. "I thought we might sort out less esoteric matters first. I, for one, trust my resident Once Dead as much as I do any of my advisors."

That is, he thought, *not much at all, but no need to tell them that.*

"While we have held our reception, the Once Dead have been holding one of their own. I would not be at all surprised if they have discussed many of the same matters."

In fact, he knew they had, having been given a preliminary report by one of his own spies before calling this more exclusive meeting.

"Shall I call the Once Dead to us so we might ask their opinions?" Bryessidan asked.

There was nervous shuffling, as each man or woman present tried to decide whether summoning the Once Dead would be good policy or an invitation to disaster.

Bryessidan gave a sardonic smile. "How about tomorrow, then? We have already had a long day, and doubtless the report of the Once Dead will be filled with esoterica we would do best to consider with fresh minds and bodies. Perhaps it would be best if we rejoined the larger reception."

There was general agreement to this, and the various emissaries and ambassadors departed, heads low, faces thoughtful, voices murmuring.

Only King Hurwin lingered. "I see you did not swear them to secrecy."

"No reason in extracting a useless promise," Bryessidan said. "My stewards report that most of them brought carrier pigeons, ostensibly to restock the local coveys. One way or another, word will fly, quite literally, with dawn."

"I agree with your decision," King Hurwin said. "Nothing is more divisive than swearing politicians to an oath each sifts through lying teeth."

"So I thought as well," Bryessidan agreed.

"And the Once Dead?"

"And?"

"Do you sincerely trust them?"

"I think we will do best if we treat them as advisors rather than acting as if we anticipate enmity. I cannot forget that each one could have joined the Nexans, but had reason for preferring some mainland alliance."

"True." King Hurwin used heavily muscled forearms to shove himself to his feet. "Let us go join the reception before everyone decides we are conspiring."

Bryessidan laughed. "As if that hasn't been decided already, grandfather of my sons and daughters."

And sage old warrior who arrived speaking of war. I have noticed that for all our talk of peace and compromise, still your prophecy seems all too likely to come true.

IX

TINIEL WAS CERTAIN something important had happened while they'd been away on the trading trip to Gak.

Enigma had been waiting to open the gate for them. Tiniel was positive the puma had said something to Firekeeper. The wolf-woman's dark eyes had narrowed and her posture had undergone a subtle shift, becoming guarded and tense as it had not before.

However, Firekeeper did not offer any explanation and Tiniel was too proud to ask. When he had learned that Firekeeper and Blind Seer would be accompanying the trading party, he hadn't known whether to be offended or relieved. Derian had made clear that Tiniel was in charge of the expedition, that Firekeeper was simply along for what help she could offer.

Tiniel remembered his and Isende's first journey out to the stronghold, how they'd stood long watches night after night out of fear that their fire wouldn't keep the wild animals away, how one night despite their care a couple of raccoons had gotten into the food they'd packed for the trail. How they'd had to dig into the dry meat and flour they'd brought for the winter far earlier than expected, how that would have made for short rations if the yarimaimalom had not undertaken to feed them. Remembering all of this, knowing how much relied upon the supplies he was supposed to get, Tiniel was glad for the protection the wolves would offer.

But Tiniel couldn't get out of his mind the idea that Firekeeper was coming along not only to protect him and the two u-Chivalum who were accompanying him, but also to spy on him, to make certain he wouldn't do or say anything foolish, that he and the others would return.

As if I'd abandon Isende, Tiniel thought scornfully. *As if I'd leave her to Derian. And what do Gak or any of the city-states have to offer me? Isende and I sold everything we had to stock our first expedition. I'm not about to throw myself on the charity of my relatives.*

And thinking this, Tiniel would realize his suspicions that Firekeeper was there to watch him as well as protect him were foolish, but his lack of trust in her—for she was Derian's ally—never left him.

Once they arrived in Gak, Tiniel was very careful to play by the rules established on the Nexus Islands. He said nothing about the gates, told and embroidered upon the tale of his and Isende's struggle to survive. He even praised the efforts of Harjeedian and the others in helping them make preparations for the winter.

The two u-Chivalum were quickly accepted as Liglimom. Their odd accent and twists of phrasing might not have let them pass in Liglim itself, but Gak was far enough from the border that not many Liglimom were seen. Those residents who were descended from former residents of Liglim already found the strictly theocratic Liglimom odd enough to dismiss any further oddities.

Tiniel handled the trading with what he thought was praiseworthy efficiency, but even when alone in some closed room with a merchant, or in a fountain-bedecked courtyard, he did not let a single word slip about any of those things the Nexans had vowed to keep secret. Spring in Gak meant open windows, and open windows meant that nothing said within those rooms was truly secret—at least not from birds, and Tiniel knew that Firekeeper could speak to yarimaimalom birds as easily as she could speak to Blind Seer.

Nor did he particularly wish to tell. His return to Gak was far more pleasant than he had expected, but it also reminded him of the insults he felt had been done to him and his family. His maternal grandmother was kindly condescending. Other relatives hinted delicately at "opportunities" they would make for Tiniel and Isende should they wish to return. After his time first on the Setting Sun land grant, then on the Nexus Islands, those offers sounded remarkably like thinly disguised opportunities to enter indentured servitude. By the time the trading was completed and the wagons were heavily loaded with grain, cooking oil, iron, and other necessary supplies, Tiniel turned the lead horse's head in the direction of what he now realized was "home."

Firekeeper's taciturnity upon their first encounter with Enigma renewed many of Tiniel's earlier insecurities about the motives behind sending him away. Nor were these insecurities helped by the people who were present to greet them on their return. Isende was waiting, which was a pleasure. Kalyndra was also present, doubtless on gate watch. Derian came striding up the hillside. He had probably been notified as soon as Enigma activated the gate on the mainland side. Others arrived soon after, so Tiniel never got a chance to reassure himself that Isende hadn't done anything irreversible while he was away.

The transit made the horses fractious, so they were left on

the mainland under Eshinarvash's care. The Wise Horse had apparently been there for several days, waiting, and, incidentally, fattening noticeably on the spring grazing.

Since bringing the fully loaded wagons through without the horses was impossible (although, annoyingly, Firekeeper proved able to push through a quite heavily loaded wagon) Tiniel wasn't surprised that many people arrived to help reload and haul the bundles. However, he soon realized that many of these people had not been summoned for this particular job. They'd been in the vicinity of the gates all along.

Isende explained as she worked, moving and stacking.

"The gates are suddenly active again. I mean, it's not that Ynamynet and Skea didn't warn us that spring would see the demand for the nexus rising, but this is sort of different. Somebody comes through. Whoever—usually Skea or one of the other Nexans who speaks a couple of languages and who wouldn't be a stranger to the new arrival—explains the gates are out of service for now.

"What's interesting is that usually the gate goes quiet for a couple of hours or sometimes days, then someone else pops through, like he or she's checking out what the first person said. They get the same answer, and because they can't get through the iron barrier, they turn around. Sometimes there's a third check, and then whoever is on watch on our side gets pretty severe with them."

"Pretty severe?" Tiniel asked.

"Usually making clear that if there's any more of this, whoever comes through won't get a chance to go home again. You know the iron barrier makes it hard for the Once Dead to do the return spell anyhow."

Tiniel did. Iron affected spellcasting, although not talents. He didn't know why. Maybe because talents were internal, while spells were an effort to make magic external. What he had possessed—what he and Isende had possessed—had been more in the light of a talent, but Isende had hinted just once (at least once in his hearing) that she thought she might have some hint of a magical ability remaining after her battle with querinalo.

Tiniel had nothing. He often brooded about this, but today the urgency in Isende's voice kept him focused on her words.

"What is really unsettling is that Skea and Wort both swear that some of the more recent of what we've come to think of as scouting transits have been by people coming through the wrong gates."

"You mean they've found a way to link the gates without using the Nexus Islands?" Tiniel asked. "I thought that was impossible."

"We still think it's impossible," Isende assured him, "though that was the first thought lots of people had here, too. What makes more sense is that the various lands that possess gates have been in contact with each other, comparing notes. One of the first of these odd transits was from the gate to the Kingdom of the Mires, and Skea recognized the person making the transit as a Once Dead from Hearthome, the kingdom to the Mires' northern border."

"I see," Tiniel said, shifting a sack of oats. They'd been high on the list of purchases because they could double as both human and horse feed. "They've talked to each other. That makes sense. And they're checking each other's stories while they're about it."

"That's what we think," Isende agreed.

Tiniel hoped that her constant use of "we" meant the Nexans, not her and somebody specific, someone like Derian. He'd never before found the way couples talked about things in the plural disconcerting. After all, he'd always been part of a pair. Lately, however, he found himself listening to Isende's speech for any clue that she might have begun to think of herself as someone else's partner. He wasn't sure, but . . .

"And what are we doing?" Tiniel asked, watching to see if there was anything peculiar in Isende's reaction.

"We've put more watchers on, for one," Isende said, without the least twitch. "There are three basic languages we need to deal with, and happily Skea speaks two of the three well, and the other passably. However, he can't be on watch all the time. Nor can he be two places at once, and there have been a couple of times, recently, that more than one gate has gone off at the same time. Moreover, we're trying . . ."

This time Isende did pause, and Tiniel wondered if more than the weight of her latest burden was the reason, and if he did indeed see a touch of rose beneath her tan.

"We're trying," Isende said, lowering her voice slightly, "to make sure that someone from the mainland is here, to balance. The yarimaimalom help, but only Plik could translate for them when Firekeeper was away and Eshinarvash was on the mainland. Plik can talk directly to the Beasts, then to us, but Eshinarvash can only speak to Derian or to Plik. The entire thing gets complicated, and tiring. We need mainland humans here just to make sure we don't miss anything. There's only you and me and Harjeedian and Derian . . . and Firekeeper, if she's around and paying attention. And I guess Plik counts as more or less human in this, but Plik is already stretched thin doing translations."

Tiniel could believe relying on the translated reports of the yarimaimalom could be difficult and confusing. Beasts perceived things differently than did humans—and not simply because their sensory organs were different. Depending on the species, the various beasts assigned different levels of importance to different actions. A wolf, for example, would automatically notice hierarchical posturing a crow would not. A raven would be sensitive to equipment and attire, especially if there was anything particularly flashy or colorful, but wolves wouldn't notice gear unless it was used against them.

Tiniel also didn't need to have explained to him the reason the mainlanders were concerned about placing too much trust in the Nexans. So far, the Nexans seemed to rather like their new rulers or bosses or whatever it was the small mainland contingent constituted—especially in contrast to the Spell Wielders.

For one thing, none of the mainlanders ever asked for enforced donation of blood to power their spells. For another, Derian and Harjeedian wanted allies, not subjects. However, five moonspans was a short time in which to build trust, especially now that the worst memories of the Spell Wielders' rule had been mitigated.

Tiniel had been a prisoner of the Spell Wielders, had nearly lost his life at their hands, and he wasn't about to forget how dangerous they could be.

"Count me in as a watcher," he said promptly, and was rewarded by the warmth of Isende's smile.

"Thanks," she said. Then she immediately dampened his pleasure by adding, "I'll tell Derian at dinner. He usually eats the same time I do. Unless you're planning on joining us? Then you can tell him yourself."

Tiniel couldn't decide whether the note he heard in her voice was hope that he might break his isolation or hope that he wouldn't—that he would leave her to dine with Derian.

"I hadn't really decided," he said sulkily.

"Join us," Isende urged, and again his heart did that rise and crash. "Everyone will love hearing about your adventures on the mainland. We're starved for news of any sort."

"Right," Tiniel said. "I'll remember that."

A swarm of would-be bearers arrived about then, and opportunity for private conversation vanished. Even as Tiniel answered the questions showered on him from all sides, he noticed an added advantage to be garnered from taking watch up on the gateway hills. The raised elevations gave a great view of most of the island, including most of the residences, most especially Derian's residence.

From here he could keep an eye on Isende's comings and goings, watch over her, just like a brother should. Watch, and wait, and learn.

And, maybe, do.

❧

FIREKEEPER DIDN'T MUCH like unloading and hauling, but she had learned that people noticed if she didn't do her part. Unlike the days on the trail when she and Blind Seer might claim to be hunting or scouting—and thus acting for the good of all—here there was no such excuse to avoid the repetitive labor. Moreover, people didn't admire her for shirking, and Firekeeper was too much wolf to court the disdain of those who she couldn't help but think of as her pack.

But she minimized being part of the shouting, chattering mob for as long as possible by doing her share from the mainland side of the gate. After all, someone had to unload the wagons and shift the heavy bundles to where they could be hauled through the gate.

Only when the last heavy load needed to be pulled through did she cross onto the Nexus Islands. As she had hoped, much of the fuss had died down by then, and what remained was focused on delight in the supplies rather than on those who had brought them.

Firekeeper shifted bundle after bundle onto the donkey cart, and when the last one was loaded, considered her part done. She was about to alert Blind Seer that she was ready to slip away when Derian came over to her.

"Before you go and hide," he said, "I wanted to talk with you."

Firekeeper blew her breath out in a gusty sigh. "The sun is high. I am hot. I hoped to sleep."

"Sleep then," Derian said, half turning away. "I'll tell you about the maimalodalum's message later."

Had Derian been a wolf, Firekeeper would have flung herself against him as if to physically beat the news from him, but humans were not as fond of rough play as wolves, so she restrained herself.

"Tell!" she said, heat forgotten—in truth, it was not so hot, especially here on the Nexus Islands.

Derian grinned. "Wait for me at my house. You can start your resting there, and I'll come when I've finished supervising the stowing of the new goods."

As she followed him to the storehouse buildings—for Firekeeper knew perfectly well that her strength and determination would move the job along more swiftly—Firekeeper fought down a sneaking suspicion that this was precisely what

Derian had had in mind. Even so, she went, Blind Seer padding, laughing, at her side.

Some time later, Firekeeper, Blind Seer, Derian, and Plik gathered in the front room of Derian's house. Some sort of tea brought from Gak had been brewed, but Firekeeper preferred water, even if to her taste it held the slightest touch of salt. Everything did here, where all the land was surrounded by the ocean. Only after she had spent an extended amount of time on the mainland did she notice.

Small talk had been taken care of during the unloading of the supplies. In any case, Derian knew that Firekeeper had little tolerance for such, especially when there was something she wanted to know.

"Plik," he said, "the maimalodalum are your people. Why don't you tell Firekeeper and Blind Seer what they said?"

The short, plump raccoon-man nodded and took from the belt around his waist a slim case made from a bird's bone. He shook out a tightly rolled piece of paper, which he glanced at, although Firekeeper felt certain he had no need to refresh himself as to the contents.

"Hope writes," Plik said, his first word referring to the bird-woman who was one of the leaders of the maimalodalum, "that they may indeed have some old records and journals dating back to the first days when querinalo appeared. Other than that, she says nothing substantial, and expressed interest in knowing why we are suddenly so interested."

He paused, and Firekeeper waited, hearing from the rise and fall of Plik's breath that more was to come.

"Actually, Hope does more than express interest. She refuses to write or say anything more unless we say why we wish to know." Plik raised the bushy brows that were one of the more human features on his face. "I have known Hope all her life. She is not to be convinced otherwise. Indeed, from her phrasing, this is the will of the community at large, not hers alone."

While Firekeeper considered this, Derian added, "The message arrived yesterday. We have been debating whether or not to take the maimalodalum into our confidence."

"And not learn what they know?" Firekeeper asked. She

heard something of a puppy yelp in her voice, but there was no helping it.

Derian glanced over at Plik. "There are three alternatives as we see it. One, we take the maimalodalum into our confidence and hope that they will see things as we do. Two, we refuse, and thereby lose whatever information they may have. Three . . ."

Derian stopped and looked at Plik again, clearly uncomfortable with being the one to voice this third option.

The raccoon-man wrinkled his nose and continued in a thoughtful tone of voice, "Three, we manufacture a tale that will hopefully fulfill their curiosity without giving away that we have encountered querinalo or that the Sorcerers' Bane—as Ynamynet calls it—continues to attack those with magic, even those it may have once left alone."

"Like Beasts," Firekeeper said.

"Like Beasts," Plik agreed.

"What you think we should do?" Firekeeper asked. "Like Derian say, the maimalodalum is your people."

"Said. Are," Derian muttered.

Firekeeper ignored him, and looked at Plik. Beside her on the hearth rug, Blind Seer kept a listening silence.

"I would opt for the truth," Plik said, "and not simply because these are my people and I trust them. What harm would be done by telling them what we have found? They are a small community, and live in near isolation. Even the yari-maimalom do not associate with them overmuch. I cannot believe that Hope or Powerful Tenderness or any of the others would suddenly break that isolation to send word to u-See-heera of our findings. True, we maimalodalum view the Liglimom with a certain distant fondness, but they are not our people. We have no people, other than ourselves."

"I agree that truth would be best," Derian said. "It's either that or pass up potentially valuable information. I cannot imagine constructing a lie that would hold up to the type of penetrating cross-examination that the maimalodalum would give it. I wasn't on Center Island long, but I was there long enough to gain great respect for the maimalodalum."

Firekeeper nodded. "I owe much to the maimalodalum, even from before I know. I do not like lies. Wolves' hearts is true."

"Speaking of Truth," Blind Seer said, *"has anyone asked her opinion on this?"*

"Truth says," Plik replied, his answer translating the question for Derian, "that the matter is too complex for her vision. She did say something about a warrior in armor of silver and brass, but when I asked for clarification she only twitched her tail. Her eyes had that wild look they get when she's seeing too much and can't sort out the visions."

"I'm not really surprised," Derian said. "The question doesn't merely involve confiding in the maimalodalum or not, it involves everything that might happen if we do or if we don't."

Firekeeper nodded. "We tell truth. What they do? Tell us what we want? Refuse, like Urgana tried to refuse until Harjeedian shake her? What they tell us? Useful? Not? No wonder Truth not know. Not even Blind Seer's nose could follow such a tangled trail."

"Speak when you have a nose," Blind Seer replied, but his tail thumped lazily as he did so.

"So we will offer them the truth," Derian said. "Is that agreed?"

Firekeeper nodded.

"They might refuse," Plik reminded them. "As far as religion goes, we maimalodalum are closer in culture to the Liglimom than we are to any other human mind-set. And we have great reason to hate sorcery—especially spellcasting."

Firekeeper shrugged. "We not tell, we learn nothing. We lie and they trip us in the lie, I think this would be far worse. Truth and the risk of truth is best."

"Will you leave immediately?" Derian asked. "The run to u-Seeheera isn't too bad, and from there I'm sure you can arrange to have someone take you to Misheemnekuru. Harjeedian could write you a note. Rahniseeta is the junjaldisdu now, and she owes both you and the maimalodalum a great deal."

"He mentions her without a tremor," Blind Seer noted. *"I wonder if someone else has filled his heart?"*

Plik answered as a beast would, so Derian did not hear, *"Not yet. I think work and worry fill the places sorrow once lived, but I think young Isende would like to help banish sorrow forever."*

Firekeeper ignored the distraction. "I have another thought. Maybe one that make it so Plik can come, too. He could see his people, and give me advice."

Derian straightened. "I know better than to trust you. Whenever your grammar improves, you want something. Spit it out."

Firekeeper ignored Blind Seer's panted laughter and said steadily, "There may be a gate to Misheemnekuru. We could open it, and then Plik would have a way home."

She didn't miss how Plik perked then tensed at her words. The maimalodalum were a close community, and Plik had been away from them for two seasons and more, during which time he had come very close to dying. Firekeeper knew that Plik had no more intended to fall into a semi-permanent exile than she had herself.

When Derian, Firekeeper, and Blind Seer had made their hurried trip to u-Seeheera to see Elise, Doc, and the baby, they had offered to take Plik with them, but the maimalodalu had demurred on the grounds that he would slow them down—a fact only too true. Moreover, like Derian, Plik needed to take care not to be seen, and this made travel difficult, even awkward, for unlike Derian, Plik was not built for speed.

Now here was Firekeeper, suddenly offering the raccoon-man the temptation of his distant homeland as easily reached as if he stepped over a threshold from one room into another. She knew she was being cruel. Blind Seer's blue gaze turned cold and penetrating in her direction, making her think that her partner knew the origin of the suggestion.

Derian, thankfully, was not as sensitive to the wolf's moods as either herself or Plik.

"I wonder if there is a gate to Misheemnekuru?"

"Quite probably," Plik said, his tones artificially level.

"Misheemnekuru was where the Old Country rulers settled first, before the mainland. Even after they had settled the mainland, many kept estates on Misheemnekuru. I would think locating a gate there would be more likely than on the mainland."

"Because the islands were reserved for the elite members of society?" Derian asked.

"For them," Plik agreed, "and for their servants and retinues, of course."

"Have the maimalodalum come across anything that might be a gate?" Derian asked.

"Not that I know of," Plik replied, "but that doesn't mean there isn't one. Center Island is only of moderate size, compared to the majority of the islands that make up Misheemnekuru. My guess is that the gate would have been located on the largest island, where there was a good harbor."

Firekeeper tried to keep her tone casual as she said, "When Blind Seer and I spend a year on Misheemnekuru, we see many ruins in many places. Some is not all fallen into pieces. If a gate was there, it might be able to be used."

Derian nodded. "Possibly, but possibly not. It depends on whether those Plik so lightly refers to as 'servants and retainers' knew of the gate, and if they attempted to destroy it when their masters fell ill. My understanding is that while the Liglimom managed to retain their nation mostly intact after Plague struck—not like in my homeland, where the colony split into two separate kingdoms . . ."

"Hawk Haven and Bright Bay," Firekeeper said impatiently. "Yes."

Derian raised his eyebrows and flicked back his ears in a reprimand that very effectively mingled the horse and the human.

"My understanding," he repeated heavily, "is that while the Liglimom managed to retain their nation mostly intact, the government underwent a revolution from below, with lesser members of the disdum taking the places that had been held by their magically gifted superiors. They might have also taken actions to assure those magically gifted superiors wouldn't return and attempt to reclaim their place."

Firekeeper knew this was quite possible. When Urgana and Ynamynet told tales of the days when the gates had first been being reopened, many of their tales ended in discovering that a hoped-for gate had been blocked or that the non-Nexan end point had been destroyed. Still, she felt a curious certainty that not only would the records show there was a gate on Misheemnekuru, but this gate would be intact.

"Still," the wolf-woman said, trying hard not to sound like a whining pup, "we can check surely. Think how much better we would do with the maimalodalum if Plik can speak, too. I am not so good at speaking."

Blind Seer sniffed. *"The maimalodalum speak after the manner of the Beasts as easily as you do, Firekeeper. Your 'limitations' in Pellish and Liglimosh would not restrain you."*

Firekeeper glowered at him, wondering when her closest friend had become her greatest critic, but there was no fooling herself. She knew. Blind Seer snarled and snapped most when he scented the Meddler's foot on the trail, and in this matter of using gates, the wolf was not mistaken.

"What do you think, Plik?" Derian asked.

"Opening a gate would permit me to travel to Misheemnekuru more easily and without risking detection," Plik said, "but there are complications above and beyond those we have mentioned. For one, remember that Misheemnekuru belongs to the Wise Beasts, the yarimaimalom alone. Firekeeper has permission to travel there, but no other human—not even you and Harjeedian, who have visited there before."

Firekeeper did not sulk at Plik's referring to her as a human. She knew that in this matter many would see her as such—including, before she had earned their respect, the yarimaimalom themselves.

"That means," Plik continued, "that even if we opened the gate, it could not be used by any of the other humans."

Derian nodded. "I know the Nexans don't think I have heard the grumbling about their relative isolation here. They forget how well these donkey-ears of mine hear."

He reached up and touched them. "Even if I didn't have the advantage of good hearing, the wingéd folk give me their reports. Yes. The Nexans feel isolated, more than they ever have done during their ten years of residence on the islands. Opening a gate to Misheemnekuru would provide a reminder that here is one more place they can't go. Still, would it be that much of a problem?"

"I think so," Plik said. "The Nexus Islands are habitable, but they are not a friendly land. They lack the forests of Misheemnekuru. They are rocky, windblown, and, frankly, not what most people would choose as a permanent home. During the winter months, when the 'mainland' surrounding the stronghold was cold, wet, and sodden, no one much thought about the contrast, but now spring is coming. The mainland is becoming green and warm. Enough time has passed that people have adjusted to all the changes."

"And they want to go home, at least for a visit," Derian concluded.

"And if we open a gate to Misheemnekuru, or to Hawk Haven, or even to New Kelvin, there's going to be considerable resentment," Plik said. "They're going to ask, 'Why can they go home, and we can't?' "

"And that's going to bring to the forefront the simple, nasty point that we conquered this place and have chosen to hold it," Derian said. "And that we're holding it because ultimately we don't trust the Old World not to invade the New if the opportunity arises."

Derian turned to Firekeeper, and Firekeeper didn't need to hear his words to know what his reply was going to be.

"I'm sorry, Firekeeper. For a moment, I thought that opening a gate to Misheemnekuru wouldn't be much of a problem, but Plik is right. We would not only be opening a gate to another land, we'd be opening one to all sorts of problems. If you want to hear what the maimalodalum have to report, you're going to need to make the trip yourself, on foot."

"And on boat," Blind Seer said nastily. *"Are you willing to ride on a boat to help your Meddler do his meddling?"*

Plik looked sharply at the two wolves, but did not comment on Blind Seer's words. Firekeeper knew that while the raccoon-man did not hold quite the level of distrust for the

Meddler that Harjeedian did, still, some of his ancestry came from the same roots. Indeed, Plik had been the source of many of the most vivid of the Meddler tales.

She resolved to speak to Plik before leaving. Otherwise, no matter how quickly she ran, Plik could send a message ahead carried by one of the wingéd folk, and she would find more questions waiting her for upon her arrival.

Aloud all she said was "On foot, then on boat. Before I go, I will carry messages for Harjeedian if he wishes. To his temple, to his sister. I think is best if I not try to hide my coming. Someone might see boat crossing waters out to Misheemnekuru, and this would then make questions."

Derian agreed. "You keep saying 'I.' Are you going alone then? I thought Blind Seer would be with you."

Firekeeper glanced at the blue-eyed wolf. *"Do you come with me?"*

"Oh, yes," the wolf replied. *"Someone must take care that the Meddler does not too easily have his way with you."*

"Blind Seer come, too," Firekeeper said, but for the first time since the wolf had crossed the Iron Mountains with her five years before, she did not feel comforted by the knowledge that he would be beside her, close as her shadow.

X

KING BRYESSIDAN ARRANGED that the meeting with the Once Dead would take place midmorning of the day following the general reception.

Tactful inquiries on the part of various members of his staff had made certain that none of the various ambassadorial groups would be offended if asked to keep their contingent to two people. This meant that the meeting might actually provide productive discussion. However, Bryessidan wouldn't count on it. According to his spies, flurries of carrier pigeons had taken off from just about every embassy with the coming of dawn. Probably, those newly arrived emissaries from countries more than a few days' ride distant had been given guidelines on what decisions they could and could not make. However, those such as Tishiolo and u-Chival would doubtless need to await instructions.

Seating for the gathering had been one of those protocol nightmares that demanded a meeting which had gone into the late hours of the night before. The deliberately informal arrangement of the previous night would not work again, since there would certainly be those who would jockey for what they perceived as favorable positions. The seat at the table's foot, where King Hurwin had been the night before, would surely be hotly contested.

Another protocol complication was offered by the attendance of the Once Dead. Were they to be treated as members of the meeting, or as experts offering testimony? Should they be seated with the contingent from the land in which they resided, or in their own group? Each option had its own tactical advantages.

Various suggestions were made and rejected until a very tired junior steward suggested, "Even though we're going to need a larger room, I suggest that we have each group sit where they did last night. From what I can see, no one ended up right next to someone they couldn't stand. No one can complain about being given a seat he or she originally chose."

Bryessidan nodded. "We'll do that. As for the Once Dead, after reviewing all the proposals, I think we'd do best treating them as experts giving testimony. If we seat them as a group, they'll be inclined to view themselves as a separate nation. If we seat them with the nation in which they have residence, then they'll certainly worry about what their sponsor wants. This way, we're treating them as what they are: specialized advisors. This may insult one or two, but right now I'm too tired to care."

He pushed back his chair and rose, only to be interrupted by his own senior steward.

"Your Majesty, we haven't settled the question of whether or not we should take precautions against treachery on the part of the Once Dead."

Bryessidan knew what the man was referring to. The matter had come up earlier and been discussed at great length.

"You mean the fact that we'll have important representatives—and in a few cases rulers—of several allied nations crowded into a relatively small room with a group of potentially dangerous spellcasters."

"Yes, Your Majesty. That's exactly the matter to which I am referring."

"We have no choice but to trust the Once Dead," Bryessidan said. "However, we'll take some polite precautions. Make sure the 'ceremonial' guards that would be present in any case are bearing cold-forged iron weapons rather than steel. We have some in the armory. Dig them out and have them sharpened. They won't hold an edge as well, but the presence of iron will make spellcasting more difficult."

"The Once Dead might sense this and take offense," the junior steward said.

"Right now," Bryessidan said, "I'm too tired to care. Let them. Let everyone get offended and go home and deal with this on their own. They came here. They threw this problem in my lap. They all but accused me of treachery and treaty breaking. It's my turn to risk offending someone. Does anyone have any objections?"

If there were, the gathered stewards and ministers were too aware of their king's mood to raise them.

Bryessidan moved toward the door, pausing to point sharply at four of the figures who had politely risen to their feet.

"You and you and you and you, I hereby command you to go and get some sleep. I'm going to need you alert and clear-thinking by midmorning tomorrow. Assign a couple of your subordinates to deal with those arrangements that will keep them up all night."

He wheeled and looked at the middle-aged woman who was the very effective head of his spy service.

"You make sure my order is obeyed. If I hear that my order

has been disobeyed, there are going to be demotions across the board. Training competent subordinates is part of your job. Understood?"

His glare was met by nods and a few sheepish smiles.

"Good. Thank you for your intelligent contributions. See you in the morning."

❦

DESPITE THE HASTY planning—or perhaps because of it—the meeting the next morning started with minimal problems. A few ambassadors tried to pretend that they hadn't understood that the limitation on the size of their contingents didn't include secretaries or other flunkies. A few protested the separation of the Once Dead from the rest. Others tried to shift seats for some obscure reason or another.

Bryessidan left his stewards to deal with this, knowing they would find following orders easier if he was not present in person for the various diplomats to appeal to.

When the appointed time came, Bryessidan arrived promptly, stood on the most minimal ceremony possible, and opened the meeting by standing. A hush fell instantly, and into that Bryessidan spoke.

"I'm not going to make any speeches. I'm not going to waste time thanking you for being here or telling you how grateful I am. Last night we discussed why we are here and our concerns regarding the current situation. This morning's meeting is an attempt to acquire answers to some of the questions we raised. If there are any other matters you would like to discuss, make a note of them and we will deal with them later, if such proves necessary."

No one offered comment, for which Bryessidan was grateful.

"Steward, have the Once Dead shown in so they might advise us."

A semicircle of chairs had been set on a raised dais at the same end as Bryessidan's own seat, thus avoiding the risk of insulting someone or other by forcing them to turn. Bryessidan shoved his own chair back so that he could face either the dais or the assembled dignitaries with equivalent ease.

The Once Dead filed in, each dressed in the gaudy attire typical of their calling. A few gave the impassive "ceremonial" guard sharp glances, and Bryessidan guessed that these were sensitive enough to the presence of iron that they sensed it, even though weapons were sheathed and spear points held high.

Bryessidan permitted the Once Dead to seat themselves before addressing them.

"Thank you for coming to advise us on this complex matter. In anticipation of making this meeting as efficient as possible, I asked that you appoint one or two of your number who could speak for the whole on general matters. Have you done so?"

Amelo Soapwort rose and said, "Yes, Your Majesty. Rae of Pelland and I have that honor."

Rae of Pelland was a short woman whose age and build were both concealed by her elaborate yellow robes embroidered with a weird sigils worked in a variety of clashing colors.

Bryessidan admired Amelo for his choice of associate. Pelland had once been the name given to the landmass that had now fragmented into four independent nations. Rule's Right, the original capital, had been near the northern edge, and the people there—especially those who resided in the city itself—managed to extract a degree of grudging deference from their neighbors.

In choosing Rae, Amelo had turned that respect to his king's service, or at least so Bryessidan hoped.

"Very good" was all Bryessidan said aloud. He heard rustling among the assembled diplomats, but did not need to turn to see who was reacting. His stewards had made certain a highly polished ornamental shield was placed where it served as an admirable mirror. "Now, I wish you all to understand that Amelo and Rae are not the only members of the Once Dead permitted to speak. Any of them may offer an opinion if they feel some essential point has been overlooked. However, the appointment of official speakers should eliminate the need of speech by those who would be speaking only because they fear that otherwise they might be overlooked."

There was a chuckle at this, from both elements in the room. Bryessidan was pleased to sense a general relaxation of tension. Who knew? A few delegates might even hold their tongues rather than risking being thought blabbermouths. He doubted it, but it was a pleasant idea.

Bryessidan turned to face the delegates. "This gathering has occurred because over the last few moonspans the gates have been blocked. Do we need a summary of those events?"

No one requested such, and Bryessidan continued. "Very well. Could we hear what theories you Once Dead have evolved to explain this altered situation?"

Rae rose.

"Most honored auditors, my associates in the Art and I first wish you to be most assured that not a one of us had any idea that this was about to happen."

Kembrel Speaker of Hearthome interrupted with gruff grumpiness. "I don't see how this could be. I know that use of the gates for trade was limited by expense, but surely it was not limited for you of the Once Dead. You know the spells to make the gates work. What's to stop you?"

Rae gave a very tight little smile. "Honored One, you say 'you of the Once Dead' as if we are one people, of one mind. If you but consider, you will see that this cannot have been so. Even before the Reprieve, we were very different peoples— differences that went beyond nationality to matters far deeper, to considerations of religion, family structures, personal codes of behavior. Before the Reprieve, there was one essential thing that bridged all these differences, one thing we shared. In our homelands, we were considered criminal monsters, sometimes killed outright, other times merely ostracized and forced to wear bands of iron about our wrists and brows."

The bitterness in Rae's tone was undisguised, and Bryessidan saw in his polished shield how many of the delegates shifted uneasily, knowing the fitness of her rebuke, taking it without protest because they needed what the Once Dead could offer.

Not all the Once Dead were comfortable with Rae's expression of bitterness, perhaps fearing retribution at some future date, but for now they held their peace.

As in the days of which Rae speaks, Bryessidan thought, *we are bound by a common need. I must not forget that. This alliance is fragile, barely forged, and repercussions for an unwise word or act may come home to me or my children.*

Rae pretended not to notice the varied reactions, but went on, her attitude part that of a storyteller, part that of a minister giving a report.

"Those conditions drove many of us to take refuge beneath the shield of King Veztressidan. None of us need recap what happened then, or how it ended, but with King Veztressidan's surrender we Once Dead were each forced to make a decision. Should we accept the invitation of one of the suddenly welcoming nations or should we join forces with those who were taking control of the Nexus Islands? All of us here chose for one reason or another not to join the Nexans.

"I will not pretend that we do not have ties to them, ties of friendship or long association or sometimes blood relation. However, so do each of you with people from other lands. Does that mean you think of yourself as 'we diplomats' rather than as members of your homeland? I think not."

Kembrel Speaker looked as if he might bluster, but something—Bryessidan was willing to bet a skillfully placed kick on the ankle from the Hearthome ambassador—made him hold his tongue.

Rae permitted herself a tiny smile. "Ten years is a long time. Ten years transforms an infant into a youth ready to be apprenticed. In ten years, a pup becomes a stiff old dog. In ten years, alliances shift and what were close associations become strained. So it has been for those of us Once Dead who chose not to become residents of the Nexus Islands, in regard to the Nexans themselves. Time and distance played their part, but the primary reason for this estrangement is that over the years the Nexans have come to be ruled by those among them who are . . ."

She glanced over at her associates, and Amelo Soapwort

rose to his feet and said, "Who are, frankly, honestly, and rather frighteningly, those who come closest to the mind-set of the most despotic of the sorcerers who reigned in the days before the coming of the Sorcerer's Bane. They viewed their contracting and surviving the fevers not as a condemnation or punishment or as bad luck, but as a test that they had passed and that showed them to be among the elite."

Amelo sat again. After giving him a nod of thanks, Rae continued.

"You may wonder how all of this is a reply to your question," she said, "but I needed to make clear—at least to some of your number—that far from being free to come and go between the Nexus Islands and our places of residence, we were required to request permission to visit. Even when we did visit, the visits were closely supervised. We were made to feel like invaders, potential spies, and, perhaps worst of all, as inferiors who had shown themselves lacking in ambition and talent by choosing not to live among our fellow practitioners of magic. I cannot answer for all of the Once Dead here, but I know that for the last several years, whenever I wished to visit one of my friends or kinfolk, I preferred to invite them to my home rather than going to theirs. They, for their part, were usually pleased to leave the Nexus Islands for a while. After a time, I stopped inviting them, but made clear that guests were welcome, suspecting that too many invitations from me might mark my friends as somehow suspect."

Aridisdu Shervanu from u-Chival said thoughtfully, "If conditions were as unpleasant as you say, I wonder that any remained."

"I did not say they were unpleasant for the Nexans," Rae corrected politely. "However, I suspect that for some of them the conditions were less than ideal. The hierarchy on the Nexus Islands names Once Dead as superior to Twice Dead, Twice Dead as superior to Never Lived. Moreover, within the Once Dead hierarchy, strict distinctions were made between those who possessed talents, and those who were able to cast spells.

"But you must remember, those who chose to make the Nexus Islands their permanent home had no good memories of life in their birth lands. They had fled persecution, had seen family and neighbors turn against them. Universally, they believed the Reprieve would end, fear would return, and persecutions would begin again."

Uncomfortable shifting among the delegates gave mute testimony as to how close that Reprieve had been to ending in some cases. Bryessidan did not think he and his spies were the only ones taking note. Quite a few of the Once Dead suddenly showed hardened gazes and tightened lips.

Rae pretended not to notice, but went on. "So when the number of visits I received—already rather limited—dwindled, I cannot say I thought much about it. In Pelland, we were focused on various local projects. From discussions with my associates here, the situation was much the same for all of us. Ten years has been long enough that our homes are here, not on a distant island where we have been made feel increasingly unwelcome."

Despite—or perhaps because of—Rae's bitter eloquence, Kembrel Speaker was not satisfied.

"Still, what about scrying? What about other forms of divination? In my homeland, we find them quite useful."

"So I have heard," Rae said dryly. "However, long before we rediscovered those arts, the Nexus Islands were proofed against such magics. Just as the gates remained, dormant but useful, so those protections have remained."

Kembrel nodded and muttered a polite thanks, but he looked uncomfortable. Bryessidan was unsurprised. Kembrel was certain to be reprimanded for letting so casually slip the full extent of his queen's willingness to spy—possibly only on her subjects, but quite likely on her neighbors as well.

Bryessidan noticed that Rae was about to take her seat and said, "I appreciate your clarification of this last essential point, but if we could return to my initial question, what theories have you evolved that might explain why the gates have been closed?"

Rae glanced at Amelo and he twitched his lips in a tight

smile. "If your throat is not too dry, why don't you go on?"

Bryessidan wondered at his advisor's self-effacement, for Amelo was normally quite content to offer his opinions, but Rae's first words made the reason for Amelo's choice clear.

"We believe there has been a radical change in government," Rae said, and a slight change in her intonation made Bryessidan suspect she was reciting from a prepared statement. "This could take one of several forms. The first possibility is that one of the more powerful—and quite probably more ruthless—Spell Wielders has taken complete control. The second is a variation on this, that a small group—no more than two or three—has overthrown the former governing council.

"A third possibility is that the Spell Wielders themselves have met with an uprising among their subjects. As I noted a few moments ago, a strict hierarchy of precedence had been evolving over the last few years. It is completely possible that some of the Twice Dead or Never Lived became frustrated and found a way to overthrow the Once Dead, perhaps leaving a few of the less abusive alive.

"Fourth, and we all think this the most distant possibility, the Nexans have been invaded and overthrown. We know that their policy included investigating other, currently dormant gates, and thereby increasing their own sphere of influence. However, that same policy tended to focus on looking to open gates into lands tangential to their current sphere because trade routes and markets would already exist—and the opportunity to exploit these existing connections was seen as advantageous."

A lean man seated at the end of the row of Once Dead added, "Not to mention such came closer to assuring familiarity with the language or languages spoken in that land. I remember early on—in King Veztressidan's day—gates were opened into lands where we couldn't speak to anyone. We had some real problems then. Being taken for monsters was the least of it."

Bryessidan remembered that Amelo had seen Skea during his interrupted jaunt to the Nexus Islands, and recalled that Skea's people had been one of those met up with during those days.

Loris Ambler of Azure Towers asked politely, "Could you explain why you think this invasion theory unlikely to be correct?"

Rae nodded to Amelo. "Please, take over for me. I need a drink."

Amelo rose. "If the Nexans had opened a gate into a land tangential to one of those with an active gate—as was their policy—then I believe someone would have an inkling that this had been done. Each nation possessing an active gate has managed to get a representative here to the Mires—even though some of you had to travel a fair distance to pay us this honor. Unless someone is withholding vital information about a new gate in your region . . ."

He made a marked show of studying each of the delegates, but none offered any new information, so he went on.

"Which it seems that no one is doing, then we think this is a distant possibility. We have not, however, eliminated it from consideration, as it would provide a valid answer to one of the questions for which we do not have a clear answer."

King Hurwin said, "And that is?"

"Who are the strangers many of us have glimpsed?" Amelo said promptly. "Given that our visits to the Nexus Islands have been less than frequent these last several years, and given that the Nexans do take immigrants—especially from among those who have experienced querinalo—none of us can claim to know everyone there. Equally, inhabitants who went there as children in the company of their parents have had time to grow and change. Still, when we compared experiences, we found that several of us had glimpsed people we did not recognize: a tall Once Dead with red hair, a man whose appearance and attire were similar yet different from that of u-Chival, a young man—some say young woman—of mixed ethnicity. One or two also glimpsed a young woman of apparently Pellish extraction but as she always kept to the shadows, it is uncertain whether she was in fact a stranger or merely a child now grown.

"What is odd," Amelo went on, "is that although one or more of these people have been present when someone is newly arrived, not one of them has come forth to speak with us."

Kidisdu Laloreezo asked, "Have all of you been spoken to by the same people?"

"By overlappings of the same small group," Amelo said. "Some of you may know them yourselves: Skea the Twice Dead; Ynamynet the Once Dead; Zebel, a Twice Dead who, despite having no magical ability, holds a great deal of honor among the Nexans for his healing abilities; Frostweed the Once Dead, and Wort the Never Lived."

"Always just these?" Kidisdu Laloreezo asked.

"Yes. Those recent crossings were rather momentous for all of us, so we were not likely to forget who greeted us. Moreover, as most of you here know, while these days I have had the pleasure to host some of my associates from other lands, we have tested both the gate here in the Mires and sent Once Dead out to check the gates in Hearthome and Azure Towers, since these could be reached in a few days' travel. In each case, we were blocked. In each case, those who sent us back were from this same group."

"One of the theories that you presented," King Bryessidan said, "was that there could have been a coup among the Once Dead. Can you tell us how many of the Once Dead you have seen?"

"Leaving out the red-haired man none of us recognized," Amelo replied promptly, "two. Ynamynet and Frostweed. Ynamynet is a spellcaster of some ability, but not a member of the upper hierarchy. Frostweed is not even a spellcaster."

"And, as I recall," Bryessidan went on, "Skea is Ynamynet's husband."

"Yes."

"I find it very interesting that these two are represented among those—shall we term them 'greeters'? I wonder if there has indeed been a coup from within, led perhaps by Skea and Ynamynet."

Amelo glanced at the other Once Dead, and Rae rose. "That, King Bryessidan, is the theory which we favor. Ynamynet and Skea are quite likely conspirators against the extant power structure. Skea could rally both the Twice Dead and Never Lived to him. Ynamynet would know how to foil her fellow spellcasters. We even arrived at a reason they might so act."

"Oh?" Bryessidan's question was echoed by several other delegates.

Amelo resumed the role of speaker. "Skea and Ynamynet have a small daughter, born and reared on the Nexus Islands. If they perceived some danger to Sunshine, they might well act to prevent it."

"Danger?" Again the question took the form of a general murmur.

Amelo colored beneath his gardener's tan. "One of the most common things for a Once Dead to lose to querinalo's fever is the ability to bear children. Sunshine is a child of a Once Dead and a Twice Dead. The likelihood, therefore, that she will develop magical potential is quite high. Moreover, my recollection was that she was a winning child, intelligent and energetic."

Bryessidan, father of four children himself, felt a sudden flaring of fellow feeling toward Ynamynet and Skea. He knew how he would feel if anyone tried to take his children from him. He knew very well, for the likelihood that one or more would spend some years abroad as fosterlings was quite high, but at least no one would be able to take them from him without his consent.

"You think then," Bryessidan said, "that someone might have decided that Sunshine would be better off fostered by another parent or parents?"

"It is not an unlikely possibility," Amelo said. "As Rae noted earlier, there was a group among the Nexan spellcasters who were becoming increasingly autocratic. They regularly demanded tributes of blood from the Twice Dead and Never Lived, blood that they used in their spells and magical experimentation. To go from taking blood to taking a living child is not a great step."

Amelo must have known his statement would fuel a negative reaction against all spellcasters—that is, all the Once Dead currently present—but he folded his arms across his chest and glowered at the assembled delegates, as if challenging any one of them to state that he and his associates had ever been guilty of such a heinous transgression.

After a long moment of uncomfortable silence, King Hurwin asked, "Have you seen any other Once Dead?"

"We have," Amelo replied. "Frostweed who is one of those you term 'greeters' is Once Dead, possessed of a talent for making plants grow. However, what we have not seen are any other spellcasters. Ynamynet is the only one."

"And the spellcasters," Kembrel of Hearthome said in the tones of one who is making very sure that he understands subtle distinctions, "are the segment of the Once Dead who had risen to rulership."

"That is correct," Amelo said.

"More and more," Kembrel said almost grudgingly, "this sounds like an internal coup."

"But why," asked Loris of Azure Towers, "would they close the gates?"

King Hurwin snorted. "That should be obvious. They are consolidating their position. Doubtless when the gates reopen we will be told that something nasty happened to the Spell Wielders—a new form of querinalo, perhaps, that targeted spellcasters. They will present themselves as having all the most altruistic motivations you can imagine for closing the gates."

"Possible, quite possible," Bryessidan agreed. He turned to face the Once Dead. "Do you have anything to add?"

"Regarding the situation on the Nexus Islands," Amelo said, "we do not. However, I would like your permission to make a statement, a statement for each and every Once Dead—not only those of us gathered here, but those who remained to attend to their duties elsewhere."

Bryessidan glanced around the table at the gathered delegates, as if requesting their permission. In truth, he really didn't care if they wanted to hear what Amelo said or not. He wanted to hear, and certainly that should count for something in his own kingdom.

"Go ahead, Amelo."

The Once Dead shifted from foot to foot, showing an uneasiness he had not before. Then he cleared his throat and spoke in a voice that rang like a bell.

"We have been exiles before. All of us know what it is like to be hunted and feared. Even the younger members of our community, those who have come to age and talent since the Reprieve, know, because we have told them of our experiences. We have told them of watching those close to us suffer and die. We have told them of waiting to see whether the Sorcerer's Bane would come to us in turn, of having the horrible suffering of that illness—and I assure all of you here who have never felt that fever's heat, querinalo is truly horrid—increased by the knowledge that even if we lived, we would be ostracized for life.

"We have no desire to be exiles again, to face that isolation and ostracism. Many of us have children now. If we do not have children, we have apprentices or protégés. We can no longer think only of ourselves alone, but must think of their future as well. Therefore, we wish to assure you of our continued loyalty and support in whatever course of action you choose to adopt.

"We will even volunteer to accept limitations on our ability to use magic. Iron distorts our powers, in many cases makes them unusable. I will not pretend that wearing iron is pleasant. For me the sensation is one of dizziness, verging on vertigo, but I would suffer that rather than face the greater suffering of seeing the Reprieve ended. In this, as I said at the onset, I speak for my associates as well."

Amelo bowed his head to indicate that he had finished, but he remained standing. Bryessidan scanned the row of seated Once Dead and found that the expression on each face mirrored Amelo's own. Resignation touched with fear was there, but pride dominated. This was not the pride of arrogance or assumed superiority, but rather the pure pride that comes from willing self-sacrifice and clear resolve.

"Thank you, Amelo," Bryessidan said, and was surprised to hear a note of tenderness in his voice. He cleared his throat. "Thank you all, not only for this offer, but for making it so freely. Please, bide a moment more while I speak to my associates."

Bryessidan turned and faced the gathered delegates.

"We have heard a great deal this morning. We have learned things that merit careful meditation and discussion. Therefore, I suggest that we adjourn this meeting and meet again tomorrow or perhaps even the next day, when we will have had opportunity to think about what we have learned. Then, we may be better situated to decide if any further action needs to be taken in this matter of the closing of the gates to us by the Nexus Islanders. Does this meet with your approval?"

Delegates glanced at their partners, exchanged a few murmured words, but Bryessidan knew they would agree.

After a formal thanks was offered to the Once Dead, the meeting was adjourned. Many delegates stopped to speak with Bryessidan before they left, usually about something trivial or to thank him for his continued hospitality. Bryessidan heard these words for what they were: apologies for ever doubting his motivations. He took them for what they were: empty air.

As soon as he could get away, Bryessidan mounted the stairs to his private apartments, let his valets strip him of his formal garb. As he was cleaned and refreshed, Bryessidan thought of the words with which his father-in-law had greeted him, and wondered how the older man had known. Then he went to where his children were gathered at play, or, in the case of the older two, pretending to study.

They swarmed to him, reassured by his presence as by nothing else, and as Bryessidan let himself relax in noisy babble, he found himself thinking again about Skea and Ynamynet, and wondering if they had indeed contrived at murder and revolution to keep their little girl safe.

He thought, too, how sad it was that if Hurwin proved prophet, he and his people were likely to be at war against these loving parents sometime in the not too distant future.

XI

FIREKEEPER AND BLIND Seer left for Misheemnekuru the second evening after their talk with Derian and Plik. They would have left sooner, but both Harjeedian and Derian wanted to review in some detail all the things Firekeeper must say—and more importantly, must not say.

Aware of the importance of her mission, Firekeeper had listened carefully. She had learned there was more than one kind of hunt—and that in matters of diplomacy the cost of failure could be paid in lives rather than by a hungry belly.

Even with traveling from twilight through early morning, the trip took a good number of days. Unlike a human, Firekeeper did not count them off, nor worry. She knew that she and Blind Seer were moving as quickly as was reasonable, and also that news that had kept for over a hundred years would not spoil for a few days more. Nonetheless, she found herself waking each morning plagued by a strange sense of urgency, and wondered what the Meddler might have been whispering into her dreams.

The wolves arrived in the vicinity of u-Seeheera, the capital city of Liglim, well before nightfall. They chose to lie up in the forests that bordered the city rather than causing a stir by walking the streets in broad daylight. In u-Seeheera, the fuss would not be caused by the sight of an enormous wolf walking the streets at a human's side. The Liglimom had a close— uniquely so, as far as Firekeeper knew—relationship with the Wise Beasts. The yarimaimalom were both welcomed and honored in their cities—indeed, even in their homes.

The stir Firekeeper and Blind Seer would have created would have been for themselves. They had spent time in u-Seeheera, first as captives, later, after a fashion, as guests. They had been of some service to the Liglimom at that time.

Although the average person had no idea exactly what the wolves had done, rumors and whisperings enough had been exchanged that the sight of the two would have been seen as some sort of omen.

Of course, the Liglimom saw omens in nearly everything, but Firekeeper didn't care to be the source of a new one.

While the wolves napped in a shady thicket, a broadwinged raven dipped over their resting place, before gliding in and landing on a tree limb well out of their reach.

"A message arrived several days ago that you were to be expected," the raven said.

"Kind of you to seek us out," Firekeeper said lazily.

She thought she knew this raven from the time she and Blind Seer had lived on Misheemnekuru. Wolves and ravens often keep company, and unlike the land-dwelling residents of the Sanctuary Islands, the wingéd folk went between the places regularly.

"I thought so," the raven agreed.

"We have hunted together," Blind Seer said, his more sensitive nose clarifying Firekeeper's subjective impressions. "You were a year beyond hatching, and already possessed of a powerful voice. 'Shouter' they called you then."

"'Shouter' they call me still," the raven said, bobbing a bit to express his pleasure. "I have come to the mainland to learn a bit more about humans. Over and over again my elders have told me that what I thought I had learned about humans while hunting with Firekeeper was useless."

"At least for understanding humans," Firekeeper agreed, laughing.

"I have some information for you," Shouter said.

This did not sunrise Firekeeper in the least. She'd expected this from the moment the raven had arrived, but had known better than to press. Ravens were chatty folk, and refusing them the opportunity to talk only made them sulk.

"We would like to know it," she said politely.

"If you still wish to go to Misheemnekuru," Shouter went on, "a boat will be waiting for you—is waiting for you—at the Temple of Water in the harbor. A crew will be ready at your need."

"Have they been waiting all this time?" Firekeeper asked in some alarm. She enjoyed her privileges—no wolf did not—but she also knew humans could become very unpleasant if asked to wait on someone else's leisure.

"Only since earlier this afternoon when the omens," Shouter puffed his feathers in a fashion that made clear he had contributed to those omens, "indicated that the boat requested by the junjaldisdu Rahniseeta in response to a letter written by her brother, the aridisdu Harjeedian, might be needed."

Firekeeper did not ask how any had known they were coming. She and Blind Seer had hidden their trail from human notice, but had made no effort to do so from that of the Beasts. She wondered if such would even be possible.

"We thank you," Blind Seer said. "Would you do us the favor of carrying a small message to those who wait? We would like to sail after dark—if the omens and the tides will permit."

"I would carry such a message," Shouter said, "but I cannot speak to humans as Firekeeper can, and the aridisdu on duty might not take omens from a land bird such as myself."

"I am sure you would manage," Firekeeper said, "but Blind Seer and I have worked out something that should serve."

She was rather proud of herself for this. Blind Seer was always pestering her to learn to read and write, and, frankly, she had not been the best of students. However, during her first visit to Misheemnekuru, she had learned a few simple written signs so that she could reassure Derian that she was well when circumstances had forced them apart.

Since then she had learned a few more, including signs indicating the numbers for one through nine. Now she plucked a broad leaf from a nearby tree and with a sharp stick etched the back with moon and stars (indicating night or darkness) and a boat. Dark lines appeared clear in contrast against the pale leaf back. She signed the missive with a rough outline of a human hand with a wolf's paw beside it, a sign that had become her and Blind Seer's signature.

"There," she said, extending the leaf to Shouter. "Hold that by the stem and the writing will not be marred. Those who read it will know they need not stand ready until after dark. If for some reason they cannot sail then, perhaps you can tell us."

"Where will you be?" Shouter asked, accepting the leaf. "Still here?

"When twilight comes, we are going to the Bright Haven embassy," Firekeeper said. "Fewer humans are about then, and we would like to see our friends."

"Then I will know where to look," Shouter said.

They chatted for a while more. Shouter shared the most recent gossip about their mutual friends on Misheemnekuru. Firekeeper did not doubt that he had gathered news as soon as he heard they were coming, as a squirrel hoarded nuts for winter. Then the raven flapped down toward the Temple of Water.

The wolves, hearing a change in the hum of the city noise, and knowing that they could move through the parks without exciting much notice, went down to the large building near the harbor that housed the Bright Haven embassy.

The wolves' appearance at the front entrance excited only a little excitement, and that was the excitement of welcome, rather than that of surprise. Derian had written ahead, letting the occupants know to expect them, and within moments the pair were admitted and a runner sent to find if Lady Archer or Sir Jared were present.

Firekeeper's relation to the peculiar entity that called itself Bright Haven was almost as odd as the kingdom itself. Technically, Bright Haven did not yet exist, would not exist until the deaths of both of the current reigning monarchs of Bright Bay and Hawk Haven. These were rival nations, splinters of the same Old World colony, that had fought each other for decades after the Plague had sent those who had governed either into death or back to the Old World.

The rivals had finally become allies some four years before, and were gradually accustoming their residents to trade old angers for new friendships. This was not as impossible as it might seem, for the lands shared a common language and similar customs. Some associations, such as trade guilds, had often conducted business as if the two governments had never split. The policy of these allied lands was to start the merging gradually, even before the deaths of the current monarchs, and this embassy to Liglim was one of the boldest declarations that Bright Haven was the nation—Hawk Haven and Bright Bay were the fictions.

From the start of her association with humans, Firekeeper had been considered a citizen of Hawk Haven—at least by the humans. She was the sole survivor of a small settlement started by Prince Barden, the youngest son of the current king, Tedric. Her precise parentage had been unknown to her, for she remembered nothing of her life before becoming a wolf. Nor did she particularly care.

If some of the humans wanted to believe that Firekeeper might be the daughter of Prince Barden and his wife, Eirene—records showed there had been a daughter—then that was fine with Firekeeper. If Earl Kestrel of the Northwoods wanted to adopt her as his daughter and name her "Lady Blysse," that was fine, too. What mattered to the wolf-woman was whether they tried to imprison her or otherwise restrict her choice of action. After a few had tried to coerce her, Firekeeper had shown that winning her friendship worked far better than any coercion.

So, these days humans probably thought of her as a citizen of this new Bright Haven. Firekeeper didn't mind this newest designation, for that meant that she and Blind Seer could easily go visit those humans who meant the most to them both. Derian certainly came first, but after him, Lady Archer and Sir Jared were among those given highest preference.

The Liglimom had been generous when giving Bright Haven a place to situate an embassy, turning over a large building near the harbor. That this same building had once served as an informal prison for the very first northerners to set foot in Liglim for over a hundred years did not matter to the new residents. What mattered was that they held the keys to the heavy gates, and that the four wings built around a large central courtyard gave ample room for both offices and private residences.

Not long before, the huge building would have seemed intimidating to Firekeeper, but after living among the semi-ruined structures on the Nexus Islands, it seemed about right.

Firekeeper knew in which wing Doc and Elise had their quarters, and was looking in that direction when the runner returned, Doc walking briskly beside him.

Sir Jared Surcliffe—or Doc, as he preferred to be called—was a slightly built man who shared the distinctive hawk-like nose of his cousin Earl Kestrel. This relatively small build and the nose were all but a certain familial fondness that Doc shared with his cousin. In terms of temper and ambition, Doc was the earl's antithesis.

Yet, Firekeeper thought as she stepped forward and gave Doc a fierce embrace, that wasn't true either. Where Earl Kestrel was ambitious for his family and his name, aware that his was the lowest ranked of the seven Great Houses of Hawk Haven, Doc's ambitions were more personal. Among these had been to do something to make him worthy of the lovely and intelligent heir to the Archer Barony.

Despite his relation to House Kestrel, within Hawk Haven's strict hierarchical structure, Doc was not considered noble-born. Nor was he one to trade on relationships. Firekeeper had met Doc—along with Derian—as one of the members of the expedition Earl Kestrel had mounted in hopes of finding Prince Barden alive. The position had not been a mere sinecure. Doc was one of the best physicians and surgeons Firekeeper had met, his studies of the medical arts enhanced by a magical talent that permitted him to speed healing or to sustain the strength in an injured body.

As a member of his cousin's entourage, Doc had reencountered Elise Archer, whom he had met when both were hardly more than children. A romance had flowered, but had taken—at least by Firekeeper's wolfish sense of these things—a long time to be acknowledged by the participants. Even more time had passed before the romance had borne fruit, but now, padding beside Doc toward the quarters he and Elise shared, Firekeeper could hear that fruit shrieking protest at some indignity.

"Nothing wrong with her lungs," Doc said indulgently, but with a certain pride as well.

Firekeeper understood the reason for this. Little Elexa had been born early, and her early cries had been weak and feeble. Firekeeper thought that she, too, might hear music in these cries were she the child's parent, but for now she wished that she, like Blind Seer, had ears she could flatten to deaden some of the sound.

The cries ebbed as they approached and Blind Seer commented, *"The pup was hungry. I smell milk."*

And when they entered the front room of the suite, Elise did indeed hold the infant to her breast. Her beatific smile of maternal pleasure warmed with welcome as they entered.

"I'll give you a hug as soon as Elexa is done nursing," Elise promised.

When Firekeeper had first met her, Elise had been a young woman with sea-green eyes and fair hair, her ripening body verging on beauty—at least as humans measured these things. Now the strain of her difficult pregnancy and the numerous duties she had attended to as long as she could had diminished that youthful flush, revealing an underlying strength and tenacity of character that in no way made her less attractive— at least to Firekeeper's way of thinking.

Elise looked down at the suckling infant. "Elexa couldn't seem to decide if she was hungry or simply bored, but I think she's made up her mind."

"Think so, too," Firekeeper agreed.

The wolf-woman settled on the hearth rug, Blind Seer beside her. Doc took a chair from which he could see both his wife and his guests, then realized he had been remiss as a host.

"Can I get you some water or tea? We have both here already. The kitchens are closed, but I can raid the pantry. There was a good chicken stew for dinner tonight."

Firekeeper shook her head. She was familiar with Liglimom cooking and usually found the spices got in the way of her pleasure in her meat.

"We eat," she said, "before. Thank you."

"Besides," Blind Seer said, *"you of all people don't want to eat before getting on a boat."*

Doc and Elise didn't quite share Derian's sensitivity to

when Blind Seer was talking, but they couldn't miss the punch Firekeeper gave to the wolf's shoulder.

"What did he say?" Elise asked.

"We go on boat later," Firekeeper said, "to Misheem-nekuru. After dark is full."

"Probably better, then," Doc agreed, "that you don't have anything to eat. Do I need to mix you anything?"

"Harjeedian give me powder to put in water," Firekeeper said, patting her waistband. "But if you have here, then I have this for come back."

"Return voyage," Elise said. "Honestly, Firekeeper, your Pellish is getting worse."

"My Liglimosh is getting much better," Firekeeper said in that language. "It is the human tongue I use most often lately."

"Nice," Elise said. Then she grinned. "But I bet you take shortcuts with that, too, when you're not trying to impress someone. Tell us how Derian is. What are you up to there in the south?"

Her tone was casual, a friend asking after a mutual friend, but to Firekeeper, who knew Elise well, and who had been trained to hear the different inflections in a robin's song, there was a false note. Was it only that Elise was still unsettled by Derian's changed appearance, or was there something more?

She decided not to let on that she'd noticed anything, but she saw from the twitch of Blind Seer's ear that he, too, had noticed the odd note in Elise's voice.

Firekeeper told what truth she could about their life on the Nexus Islands, but really there wasn't much she could say without giving away what she had promised to keep secret. Derian had gone south with Firekeeper last autumn, on the trail of something Firekeeper and Blind Seer had discovered when assisting the jaguar Truth. His role then had been to keep Firekeeper out of trouble, but here she was, and he remained south.

Elexa finished nursing, and Elise handed the drowsy infant to Doc while she tidied herself and drew up the bodice of her housedress. Doc, meanwhile, draped a cloth over his shoulder and patted the infant on the back until it burped and drooled.

Firekeeper pretended to be distracted by these domestic details, and let her account fade into silence. In truth, she was rather fascinated. No one ever bothered to burp wolf pups, although their mothers often licked their bellies. Maybe a similar purpose was served.

"Firekeeper," Elise said, her tone a touch more crisp, that of the assistant to the ambassador she had been since Derian's departure, "I know you're not telling us everything. I should be accustomed to that by now. What has me bothered is how secretive Derian has become. What is he doing in the city-states?"

"*Hiding,*" Blind Seer suggested. "*Hiding because of what the 'curse' did to him.*"

Firekeeper laid her hand on the wolf's shoulder in mute thanks for his counsel.

"Hiding. He not think looking like a horse is very good."

Elise nodded, glancing at Doc. Clearly Blind Seer's proposal was one they had already considered.

"He can't hide forever," Elise said. "What about his family?"

"He write them," Firekeeper said. "Now that the yarimaimalom and the Royal wingéd folk is a little friends, messages can go to Hawk Haven."

"But writing won't hold them forever," Elise persisted. "They're going to want to see him. The seas won't be open forever either. You know that summer is the best time for long voyages."

Fleetingly, Firekeeper thought of the gates, how they could eliminate the need for worrying about weather or ships. If the gate in Hawk Haven still existed, Derian could be home in a few strides, and back to the Nexus Islands in time to share dinner at the common table.

"I not think he sail this summer," Firekeeper said. "Young humans, like young wolves, often disperse to find their strength. Surely his parents understand this."

"You can talk well when you choose," Doc said. "That was almost poetic. Firekeeper, Derian's parents are only part of the situation—or rather, they're related in a fashion you can't possibly guess. Lately, Ambassador Sailor has been dropping broad hints that Derian should be here, doing his job. Only the fact that Harjeedian has also not returned has kept the ambassador from getting quite indignant over the matter."

"Why need Derian?" Firekeeper asked, genuinely confused. "He have you, Elise. When we here before I see others with northern features."

"He needs Derian because Derian is one of the few who speak Liglimosh well," Elise explained. "The language gap keeps us relying on translators far more than we'd like. If Fairwind knew you were as fluent as I've just learned, he might try and keep you here to help."

Firekeeper's eyes widened in horror, and Elise laughed.

She went on more seriously. "Derian also understands the local culture and religion as well as any of us do, and far better than most of us."

"And," Doc said, "the Liglimom owe Derian a favor or two. We don't know exactly what went on here last year, but one of u-Liall died suddenly, and apparently a fair number of well-placed people were disgraced. Derian is still spoken of with a certain respect and even fondness—and not merely by Junjaldisdu Rahniseeta."

"Because," Firekeeper said pointedly, "he not talk about favors he do then."

"And because he did them," Doc agreed. "You have a good reputation, too, but clearly they see you more as one of the yarimaimalom than as a citizen of Bright Haven. You just aren't the same type of playing piece on the diplomatic board."

Firekeeper was trying to decide if she liked this or not when Elise cleared her throat and lowered her voice.

"Firekeeper, Ambassador Fairwind has been making quiet inquiries about what Harjeedian and the rest of you have been about in the city-states. He thinks I don't know, but it's pretty easy for me to find things like this out."

Firekeeper tried hard not to stiffen. Had anyone learned about the Nexus Islands? She had thought they were safe from spies, but many of the yarimaimalom viewed themselves as part of the Liglim community rather than of the wild. An eagle or raven might have seen a great deal, and if they then took the time to communicate to an aridisdu . . . The process was laborious and prone to error, but a wealth of information might be shared in that way.

Blind Seer licked her hand and Firekeeper remembered to speak.

"What questions Fairwind Sailor ask?" Firekeeper said as casually as she could.

"Enough to learn that you and your group passed through the city-states last year, visiting several, inquiring about certain emblems."

"So," Firekeeper shrugged. "You knew we is going to do this."

"We did," Elise agreed. "But what Fairwind finds interesting is that apparently in the city-state of Gak, you found what you sought, information that led you to go after a pair of twins, brother and sister, missing for a year even then."

Firekeeper shrugged again. "I think we tell you this when we come to see baby."

"You did," Elise agreed, "but what Ambassador Sailor finds even more interesting is that no sign of you or your group has been seen further south or east than Gak. However, a few times Harjeedian has gone into Gak for supplies or to speak with local theologians."

"And so this troubles ambassador?" Firekeeper asked.

"It troubles the ambassador," Doc said, taking up the thread when the urgency in Elise's voice made the baby start to fuss, "because—not knowing anything about the curse Derian encountered—he thinks that Derian has abandoned his post. When Fairwind learned one of the twins in question was a young lady, and apparently a young lady of property, the ambassador decided that Derian has decided to settle down with her and raise horses or something."

"Closer to the truth than he knows," Blind Seer said, *"at least Derian would be raising foals if Isende could get him to notice how she lifts her tail at him."*

Firekeeper swatted him, and shook her head, deciding to try misdirection.

"Derian not do that. Isende like him, sure, but he not see this. I think his heart still sore from Rahniseeta."

Elise was not to be distracted.

"Firekeeper, we can't tell the ambassador that without telling him about how Derian was cursed, and I doubt he'd believe that unless he saw the evidence himself."

"Derian not want that!" Firekeeper said. "He nearly hide for days after you see him he so upset that you think him strange."

"I hoped we hadn't hurt his feelings," Elise said. Her sea-green eyes narrowed in pain. "But I won't deny that his appearance was a shock. However, how we reacted to Derian's new appearance isn't the most important thing."

"What is?"

"Firekeeper, I think you'll understand this. Derian's actions reflect not only on him, but on Hawk Haven, and even on his birth family. If Ambassador Sailor decides that Derian is shirking, he may decide that Hawk Haven is also shirking."

"You here!"

"I know, but Fairwind was a ship's captain, and he thinks in terms of chains of command and assigned posts."

"King Tedric know Derian is good," Firekeeper said.

"King Tedric is an old man. More and more he leaves the responsibilities of ruling to Sapphire and Shad. My mother thinks he's preparing them for his death."

Firekeeper winced at this. She knew the old king couldn't live forever—and she respected, even loved him. Far more rapidly than many humans, King Tedric had accepted her for what she was, and his favor was one of the reasons—in addition to her own fierce disapproval of the idea—that no one had tried to lay more than a veneer of civilization on her.

Doc patted Firekeeper on the shoulder.

"I know. We don't like the idea either, but the reality is that Derian cannot hide forever, not without hurting his country at a sensitive time, not without hurting his family. Can you explain this to him?"

"I try," Firekeeper said. "You try, too. Write this for me, and I carry it when I go back."

"Deal," Doc said. "Now. How long until you catch your boat?"

Firekeeper shrugged. "I tell sailors I come after dark. I stay a little more. Is not too dark, too long."

"Then I'll mix you something to help with the seasickness," Doc said, "and you can tell us what brings you all the way to Misheemnekuru."

Firekeeper and Blind Seer had expected some such question, and had come up with a suitable explanation in advance.

"Is almost like when we come to you," Firekeeper said. "When we live on Misheemnekuru, we have a small pack. Message come to us from Dark Death—that is now One Male of that pack—that the new puppies is born, but is not too strong. We go to see them, and maybe to see if help is in our hands."

The young parents' sympathetic response made Firekeeper feel quite guilty. Immediately, she was pressed to describe what was wrong, and when—quite reasonably—she could not explain, Doc and Elise began coming up with possible illnesses on their own. When Firekeeper and Blind Seer departed to meet their boat, Firekeeper had quite a heavy sack containing a variety of possible treatments slung over one shoulder.

She wished she could confide in these good friends the true reason for her trip, but that would mean telling too much else—including revealing the existence of the maimalodalum. Therefore, she must keep her promised silence.

Firekeeper hugged her friends and Blind Seer wriggled in the very puppy-like fashion he reserved for those he liked best.

"Come and visit when you get back," Elise said. "Let us know how the puppies are."

"I try," Firekeeper said. "I try."

A SMALL SAILBOAT was waiting in the appointed place, and the crew greeted Firekeeper with respect and Blind Seer with something closer to awe. Once again, Firekeeper was reminded of the deep respect with which the Liglimom viewed the Wise Beasts, a respect that kept the Sanctuary Islands as an area free from humans, other than a small outpost at one tip of one of the outer islands.

The boat set course for the lights that marked the outpost, but when they neared the islands, a dull thud shook the hull.

"What was that?" one of the sailors asked.

Blind Seer answered, *"Tell him that there are Wise Seals in the water. If one of the crew will come to the bow with a light, the seals will guide them to a safe place where we may be dropped off, closer to our destination."*

Firekeeper translated the gist of this, and the sailors obediently did as they were told. Well before the medication she had taken before leaving Doc and Elise could wear off, the wolves were leaping ashore.

"Thank you," Firekeeper said. "The seals will guide you again to open water."

The sailor in the bow grinned, his teeth catching the light, so that he seemed all smile. "Tell them we are honored to accept their guidance. Will you be able to get back to the mainland?"

"If no other way," Firekeeper said, "I will go to the outpost and most politely request for someone to give me a boat ride."

"That's all right then," the sailor said.

Firekeeper nodded, turning away from the lantern, and letting her gaze adjust to the darkness. In a moment she could distinguish the darker shadows that were tree trunks. In a moment more, she could see clearly.

To the sailors watching from the boat, it seemed that she merely shook her hair from her eyes, then stepped with perfect sureness into the absolute darkness of the island's interior.

XII

FOLLOWING HIS FATHER-IN-LAW'S advice, King Bryessidan did not schedule a follow-up meeting until several days following the one at which the Once Dead had testified.

"Give them time to think over what they've learned," the older king said. He was bouncing two-year-old Vahon on his foot as he talked. "Give them time to talk to each other, for the ones closer to their homelands to send messages and maybe get answers. Let the allies make sure they're still friends, and those who hate each other have time to remember why. Let them plot."

"Why?"

"For one thing, it will save a great deal of time when we all gather around a table again. Right now, they don't know what they want. When we meet again, they'll have a better idea."

Bryessidan looked at the other man, decided that he might as well think of him as an ally. For one thing, if he didn't, Gidji was quite likely to make life unbearable for him; for another, the old king had done nothing to deserve distrust.

Bryessidan found a smile. "And I suppose that's exactly what we're doing. You and I. Allies talking to each other, trying to decide what we want."

King Hurwin slipped Vahon off his foot, and four-year-old Neysa raced to take her brother's place. The king adjusted his bouncing rhythm to the heavier load before speaking.

"Do you know what you want, Bryessidan?"

"I want these people to leave here knowing I'm not conspiring to break the terms of my father's surrender. I want them to leave the Mires alone."

"I think you have achieved that. I think you have even achieved more. Before this the Mires was rather like a thief released from jail, time served, but trust unrestored. You've gone a long way to show that you will honor treaties. That's something everyone worries about when a new ruler takes over."

"They certainly don't treat me like they trust me," Bryessidan said, but when he thought over the events of the last several days, and of the days before that, to the time when he first began receiving answers to his letter about the blocked gate, he did see a difference. "No. They don't treat me like they trust me, but they treat me like an equal who must be dealt with on equal terms. Before—you're right—I was aware of people watching me sideways. I never really realized why. If I thought about it at all, I thought they were waiting for me to do something war-like."

"Some were," King Hurwin agreed. "Some were waiting for you to show what your own policies were—policies separate from those you inherited from your father. You have done this now. You notified them of the change in your gate rather than waiting. You have conducted these meetings admirably. So I think you can say you have achieved your first goal. What now?"

Bryessidan looked at the man dandling the giggling little girl on his foot and remembered that for all his amiable mien, this was Gidji's father, and a warrior king who regularly contended with the rougher elements in his own distant land. This was no gentle grandpapa, but a skilled ruler. He would not be wise to answer too quickly, too easily.

"What now for you?" Bryessidan said. "Your first words to me were of war. I have not forgotten. At the time, I thought that the war might be in defense of the Mires against those who thought I had ambitions to see if I could win on a battlefield where my father failed. Now, however, I wonder."

"Wonder?" King Hurwin's tone was ingenuous, but his eyes narrowed and his shoulders were tight.

"I wonder who you think we should be at war against."

King Hurwin slid Neysa from his foot, and sent her and her siblings away with a promise that he would play with them later. The children pouted, just a little, but they were true princes and princesses, aware of the responsibilities that went with their titles.

"Do you like having a gate in your land, Bryessidan?" King Hurwin asked.

Bryessidan's gaze met that of his father-in-law.

Changing the subject? he thought. *No. Not really. I think you're holding out on me, old man, for all your talk of allies. Still, I'll play along. Maybe you'll give something away.*

He answered the question.

"Having a gate is useful. I think all of us who have access to one have found that out. The problem is, all of us are only just now realizing how much we have come to rely on those gates. It's an odd reliance, too. We really didn't use them that often, but knowing they were there to use—it changed how we planned, it added an option that, even if we didn't employ it, was there."

"The Mires," King Hurwin said, "are less isolated than my own land. For us the gate was a lifeline to distant shores. Before, winter storms might keep us walled in for moonspans on end. It's like you say . . . We didn't change our lives greatly. We still stored food for those long periods when the weather would keep us secluded. We still planned tasks to be completed when neither land nor sea welcomed us. The difference was that the isolation was no longer absolute. It was the difference between being locked in a room and having a key, and being locked in without the means of opening the door. One is security. The other is imprisonment. I don't like being imprisoned."

Bryessidan nodded. "Yes. I can see that you would not. So you would like to get those gates opened again, to have the network operating as before. What if the Nexans refuse?"

"Then I say we give them no choice."

❀

FIREKEEPER AND BLIND Seer got their bearings fairly quickly after the boat pulled away from shore, assisted to no small extent by the young wolf who came barreling out of the shrubbery and hit Blind Seer along flank and shoulder, biting at his ear in an enthusiastic greeting.

The older wolf knocked the new arrival back and rolled him over, biting the loose skin on his throat and shaking him fiercely. The younger wolf went limp in surrender, but couldn't stop his hindquarters wriggling in joyful welcome.

As soon as Blind Seer released him, the young wolf bounded over to Firekeeper, his greeting less physically exuberant, but no less joyful.

"Firekeeper! Firekeeper! Blind Seer!" he howled.

"Rascal!" Firekeeper howled in reply. She grabbed him and hugged him hard. "You're filling out nicely. Strong bones under that baggy fur. The winter's eating was good then?"

"Good," Rascal agreed, "for winter. Dark Death and Moon Frost won territory for us on one of the islands bordering Center Island—not too far from where the building collapsed. Do you remember?"

Firekeeper shuddered. "I hope I never forget. That is not a lesson to learn twice."

"So Dark Death tells it," Rascal agreed. "We sing the story to the little pups as well."

"Then you still run with that pack?" Blind Seer asked.

Rascal was Moon Frost's younger brother. It was not unusual for a younger wolf to run with his parents or an older sibling until he himself found a mate. Some never did form packs of their own, preferring the secondary role.

"For this last winter," Rascal said. "The puppies were never too strong, and my speed and strength were much appreciated."

"Did Moon Frost whelp again this spring?" Firekeeper asked.

"No. She felt she was not strong enough, and, as I said, last year's two needed all our care."

By now the trio had begun moving inland, Firekeeper and Blind Seer following Rascal's guidance with an automatic acceptance that this was his place to lead, theirs to follow.

"The pups lived through the winter?" Blind Seer asked.

"Both," Rascal said, with pride, "and both show signs that this summer—if they avoid the snakes, bad food, storms, and all the rest—they will outgrow their weakness."

"And the rest of the pack?"

"We will meet with them soon enough," Rascal said. "You are to rest with us until evening. Then the tide will be low enough to permit the crossing to Center Island."

Neither Firekeeper nor Blind Seer asked why the seals had not simply guided the sailboat directly to Center Island. The yarimaimalom fiercely guarded their right to hold Misheemnekuru as their own, permitting no humans to visit there. Letting the sailboat touch shore at another place than the designated outpost had already been a huge concession, a courtesy granted the visitors in thanks for the role they had played in protecting the islands two years before—and perhaps a small kindness shown to Firekeeper's seasickness. However, letting the sailors take the vessels into the waterways that ran between the islands, letting them thus scout the interior, would have been more than even courtesy could permit.

In a short time, they met up with Dark Death, Moon Frost, and their two pups. All four resembled each other rather more than wolves, even wolves of one pack, usually did. Inbreeding had been a serious problem for the wolves of Misheemnekuru at one time, and Firekeeper had been astonished to learn that the wolves knew their lineages in detail, as might a human. Another difference was that although the packs of Misheemnekuru were led by a mated pair, the pups the female bore were not necessarily fathered by her "mate." Sometimes, the best combination for strong pups was not the best to lead a pack.

Firekeeper glanced sidelong at Blind Seer. There had been a time she had thought he might have chosen to run with Moon Frost. Certainly, the sleek female had made her interest obvious—even obnoxious. When Firekeeper had learned that Moon Frost was carrying pups, she had even wondered if Blind Seer might have taken up the local custom, but she had never asked. When the pups had been born, weak, sickly, and showing all the signs of the inbreeding that sometimes plagued the island packs, she had felt angry with herself for being reassured, and had done her best to make sure those pups were well fed and well cared for.

The meeting of the newcomers with their former pack mates was warm and enthusiastic, a whirling of fur and flashing of fangs that would have convinced an untutored human that the wolves were trying to kill each other—or at least reestablishing some sense of hierarchy. When the greeting was done, Firekeeper had a thin slice running down one arm, and bruises and scrapes over her torso. She flung herself down on the relatively soft carpet of leaves, and let the two pups—tall wolflings now—inspect her and remind themselves that her scent was familiar.

"You wintered well," Firekeeper said. "To show fat so early in the season is a good sign indeed."

Dark Death thumped behind his ear with one hind leg, bringing away a great tuft of wooly fur from his undercoat.

"The weather was mild, and the deer and elk stayed fat," he said. "And with Rascal's tutoring, the pups learned to be of help when taking prey larger than a rabbit."

Moon Frost panted laughter. "Although we did eat a lot of rabbits. Three adults and two younglings are not much for taking big game. We missed you and your bow."

Firekeeper didn't doubt they had. That good, long year they had all run together, unencumbered by pups, exploring the length and breadth of Misheemnekuru, had been a fat year for them all. They had hunted as wolves hunt, but when the prey was clever, often Firekeeper's arrows made the difference.

Stories were told then, some of friends Firekeeper and Blind Seer had not seen for a time, some of victorious hunts, more of the times when the deer leapt, escaped, and the pack went hungry, but had learned something so that next time that same leap and twist meant a broken neck and good eating for all. In turn, Firekeeper and Blind Seer told of Bitter and Lovable, of the jaguar Truth, for each of these were known here, and missed.

But even as she told how Lovable still gloried in hoarding anything that caught the light—and of the time she had tried to keep dewdrops—or repeated one of Bitter's dry jests, Firekeeper was reminded of everything they could not say. Thus, for all the warmth of this homecoming, she felt lonely, and snuggled a little closer against Blind Seer's flank.

They slept when the day grew hot—although here the weather was neither as hot as the lands near the Setting Sun stronghold, nor as cool and windblown as in the Nexus Islands. Raven calls, harsh and friendly, woke them when afternoon was feeling the delicious threads of evening coolness.

Escorted by the ravens, the entire pack headed to the place where, when the tide was low and the currents not too strong, wolves could easily swim between this island and Center Island. Here Blind Seer and Firekeeper parted from their friends.

"We are welcome on Center Island," Dark Death said, "but spring hunting is thin hunting, and there are wolves enough on that island. Sing the moon tonight. From ear to ear, throat to throat, the song will carry and all Misheemnekuru will recall the many reasons we have to give you both welcome."

Firekeeper nodded. "We will sing, but first we must speak with the maimalodalum."

"One of their kin went with you last year," Moon Frost remembered. "Is he well?"

"Well enough," Firekeeper said.

Blind Seer had already begun wading into the water.

"The tide will rise while you chatter, dear heart," he called back. "Has talking with ravens turned you into one?"

For answer, Firekeeper splashed into the shallows beside him, feeling the tug of the current, and how the salt water stung the fresh scrapes on her skin. There were times she truly wished for the protection offered by a thick fur coat, even if fur would be uncomfortable come summer.

Wading ashore on the farther bank, Firekeeper turned to wave to the watching wolves. Beside her, Blind Seer shook, showering her throughly with salt water and bits of shed fur. Rascal yipped in amusement, although Firekeeper didn't think the joke was that good. If Blind Seer had waited until she had dried off, that might have been funny.

She bent at the waist to press the worst of the wet from her hair, then squeezed the rather tattered cotton of her shirt. On inspection, the shirt wasn't worth saving, and she took it off.

Wringing the worst of the water from it, she bound it around her waist.

"Why are you saving that?" Blind Seer asked as they trotted up the trail.

"The maimalodalum might have some use for it," Firekeeper said. "It is woven fabric, and that takes work to make."

Blind Seer huffed his agreement. A few moments later, a twitch of an ear and a slightly lifted muzzle told Firekeeper the blue-eyed wolf had spotted something. She looked but saw nothing but the clusters of evening shadows, bluish grey and faded tan beneath the spreading spring foliage.

"Wolf," Blind Seer said softly. "Tenacity or Integrity, I think, but they are downwind and the scent is faint."

Firekeeper nodded. Tenacity and Integrity led the local pack, but they were not kin to Blind Seer and Firekeeper as were the pack the pair had just left. It would be natural for them to wait and watch before offering greeting.

Within a few paces, Firekeeper saw a low-slung branch swaying where no wind could move it. Then Tenacity stepped forth. His head—too broad between the ears, and too heavy for his neck—was momentarily held high in greeting, while his ears pricked in welcome.

"We heard of your coming," he said. "I am here to give you leave to hunt in our territory, then I return to my mate. We have pups this year, and they are nearly new whelped so she stays with them. It falls to me to lead the hunt without her."

"Thank you for your welcome," Firekeeper said. "If our business with the maimalodalum permits, perhaps we may join your hunting."

Tenacity's tail, like his head, heavier than his body should bear, moved in a slow arc. Wolves do not wag their tails like dogs do, nor hold them high, but they do use them to express their moods.

"You and Blind Seer are mighty hunters and would be welcome. Sing and we will hear."

The wolf vanished into the underbrush as silently as he had come, and Firekeeper looked after him, wondering if the pups

Integrity had borne were his, or some other's. Like her mate, Integrity showed the marks of the long-ago inbreeding. In her this showed in the form of extra toes upon her feet, oversized ears, and a ragged coat. Yet the pair's last litter had seemed healthy, arguing that they had not mated, for surely that would have passed on the traits they both carried.

Firekeeper shook the puzzle from her, deciding that Elise's new baby was making her far too interested in other people's matings, but her free hand brushed against Blind Seer's back, refusing to let her deny the wellspring of her thoughts.

Here and there bird or beast greeted them as they climbed the long slope that led to the ruined temples wherein now dwelled the maimalodalum. When Firekeeper had first seen this place, there had been five towers, but only four structures still remained that could be called towers. The fifth was a heap of rubble, and Firekeeper glanced over at it, remembering. Then she shook herself, for those memories were not pleasant, nor could she see anything to be gained by cultivating them.

Far more pleasant and useful was gazing on the strange forms and features of those who had gathered to welcome them. Slightly to the fore stood the pair Firekeeper and Blind Seer knew best: Powerful Tenderness and Hope.

In appearance, Powerful Tenderness was a frightening figure, one whose name fit only after one had been given opportunity to learn what a strong and gentle creature he was. Firekeeper had yet to decide whether Powerful Tenderness more resembled a very hairy man or a bear standing on its hind legs, yet this alone would not have made him frightening. Rather it was the cold gaze of snake's eyes from his furred face, the forked tongue that slipped from between his very human lips whenever he spoke, the heavy claws that tipped both hands and feet that made Powerful Tenderness a creature from nightmare.

Hope was more pleasing to the eye. Her essentially human form was covered with blue-grey feathers, short and downy on her torso, longer on her arms, as if those arms had tried to turn into wings but stopped partway in the process. Her eyes were bright, round bird's eyes, and her nose short and thin.

Behind them stood in a loose semicircle other of the maimalodalum. Looking at them, Firekeeper realized that she knew these better than ever before. Having been close to Plik for these many moonspans, she had heard him mention most of them, and knew more of their qualities.

The one who blended the features of a vixen and a human with touches of something less definable was called Surf Hands, and not because of any deformity. Rather, she was as nimble with her long-fingered hands as waves sliding up and down a sandy shore. She was the weaver among the group, not the only one, but the one best at making fine textiles. Knowing now what she was seeing, Firekeeper recognized what must be Surf Hands' work worn by most of those gathered, even if just in the form of a narrow scarf or shawl. Seeing this, the wolf-woman realized that she and Blind Seer were being honored, for the maimalodalum had brought out their best.

The boar-headed one was called, as was one of Firekeeper's first human friends, Gardener. Eschewing plow or hoe, he tilled the small gardens in which the maimalodalum grew many of their food crops with his nose, just as a wild boar would do. Because of him, the community had vegetables throughout the year.

Firekeeper smelled the interesting scents of roasting tubers, and once again knew honor done where she once would have not, for Plik had told her how spring was a thin time for the maimalodalum, as would be expected among a people who voluntarily restricted themselves to a small island. That a great banquet had been prepared showed how welcome the newcomers were.

Powerful Tenderness motioned Firekeeper and Blind Seer to the star-shaped Tower of Air.

"The sea winds grow brisk," he said, his voice coming deep from his broad bear's chest. "And although I recall you both claim not to mind cold, still, why shouldn't we be comfortable when there is comfort so near?"

Firekeeper grinned. "Why not? I smell good things, and am ashamed that in our haste we have come empty-handed."

Hope said in her high, clear voice, "You come with news,

and, as the message that came before you hinted, with tales to spice the meat. Empty-handed, perhaps, but hardly without gifts."

"How is Plik?" Surf Hands asked. "Tell him I miss his sheddings. His undercoat made for good wool."

She laughed then, a sound like a fox's bark, shrill and short, so Firekeeper wasn't sure if she was joking or not.

"Plik is well enough," Blind Seer said. "He has had his misadventures, as have we all, but you can be assured that no matter how terrifying a tale we tell, Plik will live at the end. He remains a valued counselor to us all."

"And the others?" Hope asked. "Derian and Harjeedian both went with you. They remain in the south still. So do Bitter and Lovable. What keeps you there?"

"Plik wrote that you found twins who were the source of the figurines," Powerful Tenderness said. "But very little else. Even the ospreys who have carried Plik's messages seem to know little enough."

Amid this shower of questions, they had entered the Tower of Air. On the inside, the structure showed much better repair than the exterior might have led one to imagine, for the maimalodalum did not wish for any—say a sailor blown off course, or someone with intentions less pure—to see the towers and wonder at their good repair when most other buildings on Misheemnekuru were overgrown with vines or collapsed to ruin.

There were windows piercing the thick stone walls, but these were not the sole source of light. Instead, after the fashion of the Old World sorcerers, blocks had been set into the walls, enchanted to take in magic and give back light. These still worked, but Firekeeper wondered for how much longer. Sky-Dreaming-Earth-Bound, who had fed the blocks their power, was dead now. She wondered if the maimalodalum had found someone else who could feed the blocks, wondered, too, if Enigma might be able to learn the spell, but how to explain the puma's new gifts?

With a flash of relief, Firekeeper recalled that soon the maimalodalum would be among the few who shared the secrets she and Blind Seer guarded. Eagerness to tell and so disperse the burden almost made her less than attentive to the food being carried into the heart of the common circle. However, although wolves may not be the neatest of eaters, there is not a one among them who is not enthusiastic about food, and Firekeeper's earliest training saved her from discourtesy.

Over the meal, the conversation was kept general, so that Firekeeper and Blind Seer could fill their bellies before the food grew cold. Later, when the empty platters had been carried away, and no one but the hungriest did anything more than nibble, Hope directed the conversation to what everyone had been too polite to say.

"Plik wrote saying that you desired to learn whatever you could about the days when Divine Retribution first appeared among the Old Country rulers. We said we would tell you what we knew, but that first we must know why you wished to know. His next letter gave us reason to believe you would fulfill our curiosity. Are you rested enough to begin?"

Firekeeper nodded. "It is simple enough. We believe—we know—that we have encountered the Fire Plague. It lives, although perhaps it is not as strong as when it was young and hungry for its meat. Still, for reasons you will hear, I do not wish the Fire Plague to have free run again. I hope that in finding what I can about how it began, I can find how it may be controlled or perhaps ended."

The maimalodalum began peppering them with questions, most of which Firekeeper and Blind Seer had heard before and so easily answered. Without hesitation they spoke openly and honestly of what they had discovered, even to the finding of the gates, and the situation on the Nexus Islands.

The telling led to debate over the wisdom of Firekeeper's proposed course of action. Firekeeper watched as the sky she glimpsed through the tower chamber's high windows shaded from blue to silver to grey and finally to night black. The light within the chamber washed away the paler glow of the stars.

At last Hope said, "Are there any other questions?"

None of the gathered maimalodalum spoke, so Hope asked,

"Does anyone object to my telling Firekeeper and Blind Seer what little we have learned?"

This time the silence was so complete that it rang as loudly as a shout. When Hope moved her head, examining each furred or feathered or scaled face for possible objections, Firekeeper could hear her feathers brush against each other.

Hope began without further preamble. "As you know, these towers suffered somewhat less from the general looting and destruction that followed the fall of the Old Country rulers. One reason was because they were located on Misheemnekuru. Other than servants, none of the 'common' population lived on this island—and most of these were shipped back to the mainland before their employers departed. Another reason was that these towers were regarded as temples, and therefore were sacred to the deities.

"Lastly," Hope gave a thin smile, "we—or rather our ancestors—arrived and did our best to preserve what was here. There was hope then that we might find among the written texts some means of amending what had been done to us. That hope was disappointed, but there were other things among the writings that made them worth preserving. Among the written material we have preserved were letters and journals. Some of these had already been read by someone or other among our community. There's an odd fascination to reading other people's letters . . . but you wouldn't know about that.

"In any case, we already had some idea where to look for the information you wanted before Plik's letter arrived. Although early spring is a busy time, just about everyone found time to go through the stacks and bundles. I'm going to summarize for you what we learned."

Firekeeper had done her best not to fidget during this long introduction, for she knew that Hope was beginning this way to forestall later questions. Still, when she leaned forward slightly as if that shift in posture might make her hear better, Hope's next words were underscored with a trace of amused laughter.

"We did not learn a great deal, but what we did learn was significant. First, the origin of the Fire Plague—to use a less judgmental term than Divine Retribution—seems to have been here, in the New World. Now that you have told us about the gates—things whose origin we suspected from our readings, but about which we were not sure—we are less certain even about that deduction."

Blind Seer interrupted. "If you read about the gates, how could you doubt their existence?"

Hope's chirruping sound mingled annoyance and appreciation. "The gates were never mentioned in detail. As you know, there was an agreement among the Old World sorcerers who came to the New World to assure that any who had any spell-casting ability would be trained in the New World. In this way, they could control the spread of knowledge about their own abilities—and perhaps place some sort of restriction on those they taught, so that their secrets would not become general. This conspiracy of silence extended to not mentioning any details about the tools or procedures they used."

Powerful Tenderness cleared his throat, a great rumble like distant thunder. "There's another reason, Blind Seer. The journals in particular were written to supplement the writer's own memory. Why would they have written details about what was, for them, a routine procedure? Would Derian Carter outline how he traveled between u-Bishinti and u-Seeheera? No. At most he might note that he rode or walked. More usually he would say something like, 'I went to u-Seeheera today.' No one writes details of the usual; only the unusual is worth mentioning."

"I will need to take your word on that," Blind Seer said, panting laughter, "having never written a single word in all my life."

Firekeeper thought, *Derian might well mention details of such a journey, if only to record which horse he rode, but I understand what Powerful Tenderness means. Now . . . let them continue the chase before I die from holding my breath!*

Hope went on, "However, even with what you have told us about how the gates work, still I think the Fire Plague must have originated in the New World. Why else would the Old World rulers have done their best to return to the Old World if they did not think they would be safer there?"

Gardener grunted, "Possibly because they had kept their most powerful magics there, and so hoped to find a cure. Still, I agree. I rooted through many letters, and all of what I read gave me the impression that the Fire Plague originated here."

"The other thing we learned," Hope said, "is that the Plague seems to have occurred all at once. It reappeared in waves, but those waves were unrelated to region or area."

Firekeeper tilted her head to one side. "I don't understand. Is this important?"

"It could be," Powerful Tenderness replied. "Sickness does not usually occur all at once. Usually it spreads from person to person, like to like. Some sicknesses will only affect those closely related—say seagulls only. Others might harm all fish eaters. Still others all birds. Others, all creatures that live near water. It is often by looking at how a sickness spreads that the source of that sickness can be found."

Firekeeper nodded. "I see. If only seagulls grow sick, then you might try and see what they eat that no other seabirds eat. If all seabirds grow sick, but not the seals or whales, then you might look for a cause to be found in sea air, not sea water."

"Very good," Powerful Tenderness said. "But as far as we can tell, the Fire Plague struck in distinct waves. First to be taken ill were spellcasters. Next to become ill were those with a strong talent. Then fell those with weaker talents, but other than those waves, there is no pattern to show how the Plague was spread. We have a letter written from someone in New Kelvin that notes when his teacher fell ill. The date matches the time when a journal written here on this very island notes someone of a similar ability falling ill, yet New Kelvin and Center Island are moonspans' journey apart."

"Not so far," Blind Seer reminded, "when one remembers the gates. Those two might have dined together on the Nexus Islands and been poisoned at the same time."

"We thought of that," Hope said, "and did our best to make lists whenever places and dates were mentioned. There was some crossover, but not enough to allay our feeling that this lack of a pattern is in itself a pattern."

WOLF'S BLOOD / 179

Firekeeper bent her head humbly. "If I could read, I would ask to see these writings to see if there was some fresh trail I might find. However, I am—as Blind Seer often reminds me—a fool in these things."

"I read a little," Blind Seer said, not so much surprising Firekeeper as confirming something she had long suspected, "but I doubt I read the languages I would need."

"Many of the documents are in an older form of Liglimosh," Hope said. "Have you mastered that?"

"Only a few signs," Blind Seer said, "and those the ones closest to the modern form."

This did surprise Firekeeper. Both she and Blind Seer had initially experienced some difficulty in grasping human representational art. She remembered how much trouble she had experienced when she had been first shown a map. Now she understood a great deal more, and could even enjoy a painting or mosaic, but she had not thought that Blind Seer had progressed so far beyond her.

Hope continued to speak to Blind Seer. "I suspect then that you would have difficulty making sense of these documents. Our notes, however, are in the modern language, and you are welcome to review them."

"I can only do so if someone else will turn the pages," the wolf said. "My paws lack the dexterity to turn paper or unroll hides."

"I would be happy to assist," Surf Hands said. "I can set up a small loom in the scriptorium."

Firekeeper felt distinctly useless, a sensation that was not made in the least better by her awareness that she had herself alone to blame.

"Someone," she said, then remembered that she had told them about the Meddler, "the Meddler, suggested that the Fire Plague stank to him of a curse, rather than a real illness. Could this explain why it occurred in such an odd fashion?"

"We know little more about curses," Powerful Tenderness said, "than we do about gates. What we do know tends to come to us through old tales about those who had been cursed. While these may hold a germ of the truth, they don't tell us much about the making of curses. Could you ask the Meddler to tell you more?"

Firekeeper did her best not to look at Blind Seer, but her gaze slipped to where he sat beside her, and she saw his ears flicker back before he righted them into an attitude expressing curiosity, nothing more.

"I can try," she said, knowing her words danced on the edge of a lie. "The Meddler is more likely to speak to me than me to him. Still, if we speak, I could ask him."

The reality was that Firekeeper suspected that she could speak to the Meddler as often as she cared, but that she had been avoiding doing so. Now the possibility of calling on him tantalized her, making her heart beat strangely fast.

"The Meddler might tell us something useful," Powerful Tenderness said. "Ask if the opportunity arises."

Hope sighed and stretched. "You wolves are night creatures, but many of us have been up since dawn. Blind Seer's inspection of the notes would best be done in daylight. Does anyone object to our parting ways until morning?"

No one did.

Firekeeper and Blind Seer departed for the forest to find Tenacity and Integrity and renew their acquaintance with that pack. Neither spoke to the other as they slipped among the trees, although the silence that hung between them was stiff with things that needed saying.

XIII

WHEN KING BRYESSIDAN reconvened the meeting, the mood of the delegates had undergone a subtle shift. He made a small speech of welcome, then smiled in what he hoped would be taken as a self-deprecating fashion.

"For no other reason than that we have all met here, in my kingdom, I have taken it upon myself to head these meetings. Rumblings have come to my ears that some here believe that I have an agenda of my own that I am subtly seeking to promote. I assure you that I do not, but to support my claim I will, without further ado, let one of you raise the first topic for discussion."

Actually, there had been no such "rumblings." If anything, what Bryessidan's spies had told him was being said of him was distinctly complimentary. However, Bryessidan wished to keep these chancy allies—allied first against his kingdom, as he must never forget—off balance. What better way to do that than putting each of them in the position of suddenly needing to choose against the very different but very real advantages offered by acting rather than reacting.

There was a long stretch of silence, long enough that it was becoming uncomfortable, before Kembrel Speaker from Hearthome broke it.

"Very well." He rose, cleared his throat, then said again, "Very well."

This time, he seemed to have decided what to say.

"Each of us is here because we have a gate in our lands. A door. A passage. Years have passed since King Veztressidan used what were then forgotten gates to further his ambitions. Indeed, enough years have passed that we are accustomed to thinking of those passages as going *from* our lands rather than *into* our lands. What my associate and I wish to ask is how might we control these passages?"

Kembrel seated himself heavily, trying not to look too pleased with himself for having the courage to speak first . . . even if what he had said was so obvious as to verge on the banal.

No one spoke; then Amelo Soapwort, who, along with Rae of Pelland, had been requested to attend, looked at King Bryessidan for permission to respond.

When Bryessidan nodded, Amelo rose, shook down the sleeves of his robe, and said in tones of measured politeness, "As my associates and I have found to our dismay, controlling the gates is all too simple. Bars of iron forming a cage across the entry will enable one to make the transit but not to leave the area—except by returning back through the gate itself. From our early experiments with attempting to open gates we learned that if a gate is walled up so that the portal is completely covered, then the person attempting the transit is bounced back to his or her point of origin."

Amelo was only partway through his speech when Kembrel Speaker began shaking his head.

"I said 'control,' honored Once Dead, not block or restrict."

Amelo looked down his nose at the man. "The gates are ultimately controlled by possession of the Nexus Islands, honored emissary."

"Yes." Kembrel rose again, rubbing his hands together like a workman eliminating the dust and grime of a day's labor. "That is what I thought. Without the Nexus Islands, the gates are merely disadvantages to us all. They allow those we now no longer have the least reason to trust access to our lands, but refuse us advantage from those same gates."

Kidisdu Laloreezo from u-Chival rose. "Surely the gates will be opened for service again. The Nexus Islands are habitable, but they are not in the least hospitable. Surely whoever rules there will wish to reestablish trade—and quickly, too, before we all find other alternatives to the services they offer."

Chetuk Meadows of Pelland said, "My land is, as you know, renowned for the fertility of our fields. However, as you also know, we are not so blessed in metals. Over the last several years, we have been trading with Azure Towers and Tishiolo for some of what we lack. Each time, we have paid our gate fee in grain and other foodstuffs. I have been consulting with Rae, the Once Dead who accompanied me from my homeland, and we conclude that, unless the Nexans have been trading away much of what they received from us, they will not lack for food for years to come."

Bryessidan raised his voice slightly. "Does anyone among you know of such trade? No? Interesting. So the Nexans are likely well-supplied with foodstuffs, unless, of course, whatever catastrophe led to their change in governments also led to this being destroyed."

"Unlikely," someone muttered farther down the table, and heads inclined in agreement.

"There is the question of how long can they wait without risking our taking our business elsewhere," said Kidisdu Laloreezo.

. Kembrel Speaker waved his hand dismissively.

"We may find alternatives," he said, "but I think we all agree that the Nexans offer a unique service, one that we have paid for even though the tariff was high. I do not think they will be overworried about losing our business."

"True," Kidisdu Laloreezo agreed. "Although they may lose it nonetheless."

"That is their risk," King Hurwin said briskly. "I think, however, that Kembrel Speaker is correct in stating that we cannot use this as a means to judge whether or not they will reopen the gates with any speed. Tell me, Kembrel, are you stating that the only way we can be safe is if we have control of the gates?"

"We can have safety in other ways," Kembrel said almost scornfully, "but as Amelo Soapwort has pointed out, these involve our either resigning to using the gates at the Nexans' behest or giving the gates up entirely."

Bryessidan said as mildly as he could, rather enjoying the role of peaceable facilitator, "Does anyone have any alternatives to those Amelo has suggested?"

No one spoke, but everyone looked at Kembrel. He only sat and looked at his steepled fingers.

"What my dear neighbor is suggesting," said Loris Ambler of Azure Towers in a snide tone, "is that we somehow attempt to take control of the Nexus Islands. Easy to suggest, but rather hard to achieve. It is rather difficult to invade a land whose only border with your own is a patch of stone only wide enough to admit two people or so abreast."

"You must admit," Kembrel said smoothly, not bothering to rise, continuing to study his fingertips as if he was talking to them rather than to the assembled dignitaries, "there would be advantages. We could eliminate—or at least greatly reduce—the tariffs. We could establish free and prosperous trade between our lands. I admit, a cartload or two at a time is not a great deal, but it does add up over time. And most of us would choose to ship items more profitable than grain. I will say it, if none of you will. I dislike the current situation. Waiting would only make it worse. I wish to act."

His queen, ever impatient, wishes him to act. No wonder he won't look up from his fingertips. Hearthome already has a bad reputation for looking over its borders. He must know that in suggesting this he is reminding us all of that.

"Prettily stated," Loris Ambler said, proving that people will speak tactlessly from dislike where they would never from fear. "But how do you propose we do this? Sling bridges across a gorge where never before there were bridges? Seek to suborn the locals? Take advantage of a little-used mountain pass?"

All of these were things Queen Iline had attempted over the years. All had eventually failed, but not without considerable loss of life and property on the Azure Towers side.

"You know full well none of these things would work," Kembrel Speaker said sharply. "I thought we might use the gates themselves. A coordinated crossing from each of our gates into their central area would be disconcerting in the least. If, as we suspect, the Nexans are short of spellcasters, our allied forces could gain the upper hand."

Amelo spoke: "May I remind you that we cannot cast spells when we are in such close proximity to iron? Or rather, we can, but the results are unreliable."

"Then send one spellcaster and one strong soldier with the means of breaking through the iron cages," Kembrel Speaker said. "We could practice, and time the maneuver so that a second wave—small admittedly, but potent—could follow."

"It might work," Amelo said reluctantly. "However, we have no idea how large their forces are."

"Not overly, if what you and the other Once Dead have reported is based in fact," Kembrel Speaker said. He was no longer looking at his fingertips, but was leaning forward, his eyes shining. "Think of it. We could time arrivals so that they are staggered. I have talked to the Once Dead from my own land and he says that all the operational gates are not in one building. If we draw attention to one area, then send more though to gates in another area . . ."

Voices rose now around the table, a hungry babble of men and women suddenly fixed on the idea of breaking the Nexans' hold on the gates. Bryessidan watched them, wondering just when they had all decided that invasion was the only solution to the problem. The rapidity with which possible tactics were being presented made fairly certain that the idea had been in many minds long before Kembrel Speaker had brought it to his lips.

And I had thoughts too, Bryessidan thought, *at least from when my father-in-law stepped from his ship and maybe even before.*

But he said nothing, preferring that the others feel they must convince him to join them. Who knew what favors they would barter? Perhaps this would be the means by which the Mires would return to equality among the nations.

Eventually, someone did raise the question of whether it was right to invade a land that had done nothing more than close its borders—"And what may be a temporary closing at that. I cannot say that the ruler I represent would care for having his ability to restrict access to his lands so limited."

"This is a different situation," Kembrel Speaker said eagerly. "The Nexus Islands only exist as a 'nation,' if you can dignify them with that term, precisely because they agreed to grant access to the gates—and that means to their land. If they had explained there was a problem of some sort—a plague perhaps that they did not wish to spread—then I am sure we would all understand, and, indeed, be doing our best to provide them with medical aid and support.

"This is a different matter. Not only has the treaty by which the Nexus Islands gained their independence been violated, but all the Once Dead who have attempted to use the gates report that they have not glimpsed those who until recently ruled there. These are the very people with whom we made our treaties ten years ago. What we are contemplating is not invasion, but rather an inspection to assure ourselves that our allies are well, and that the treaty to which all our varied nations were signatory has not been violated by some less than scrupulous band of individuals."

Despite himself, Bryessidan was impressed. He never would have come up with anything like that way of thinking about the matter. Kembrel Speaker must have a mind like a nest of hibernating snakes, all twists and coils.

Reassured that they were not contemplating anything as heinous as invasion of a peaceful power, the gathered dignitaries continued debating possible means of achieving their goal.

At last, after the discussion was becoming repetitive, King Hurwin said in a voice that carried through the chatter like a hot knife through butter, "I believe I know where the Nexus Islands are—physically. I think we can sail there."

Silence fell.

Bryessidan stared at the older man. Anger kindled, hot coals deep in his belly, anger at himself as much as at King Hurwin.

Fool! he thought. *You knew Hurwin was playing his own game all along.*

Chairs creaked as dignitaries leaned forward to better see the man who sat at what to Bryessidan suddenly seemed like the table's head, rather than its foot.

Then Chetuk Meadows of Pelland said, "Are you suggesting a two-front attack? Through the gates and by sea as well?"

"Where are the Nexus Islands?" Kembrel Speaker added, a touch snappishly. Clearly, he was not thrilled to have been manipulated so neatly into introducing the question of invading the Nexus Islands only to be upstaged by another.

"How long to reach them?" Wantoniola of Tishiolo asked.

"I remember tales that the oceans surrounding the Nexus Islands were alive with sea monsters," Kidisdu Laloreezo put in, "so that the only way to safely reach them was through the gates."

King Hurwin waited out the flurry of questions, then said conversationally, "If the maps I have found are accurate, the

Nexus Islands are to the north. In Tavetch's libraries my archivists found ship's logs. From these I have gathered that for much of the year sailing to the Nexus Islands is nearly impossible. However, for a few moonspans in summer, the winds and currents permit passage."

Hurwin looked over at Chetuk Meadows. "I think your suggestion of a two-front attack would be wisest. Unless we are willing to use this summer to explore and delay our attack until next summer, there is no way we can test the information I have found. A fleet would need to sail provisioned for a return voyage, just in case the seaways have changed. As for how long the voyage took? That can only be estimated. If we decided to take this course of action, further study of the maps and logs in my archives—and perhaps in other archives as well—would be wise."

Kidisdu Laloreezo raised his voice. "And sea monsters? The water dragons that were said to make the seas around the Nexus Islands impassable?"

King Hurwin shrugged. "I have sailed since I was a child, and although I have seen many wondrous things, I have never seen anything that could be termed a sea dragon—or a sea monster either. I have seen whales, sharks, seals, walrus, and any number of aquatic creatures, but nothing that could be called a dragon—although any creature is a monster when it is trying to sink your boat."

As we will be monsters to the Nexans, Bryessidan thought. *As they have made themselves monsters to us.*

Rae of Pelland spoke for the first time that meeting. "I have made some small study of creatures that seem to have been common in the days when the sorcerers ruled. King Hurwin says he has never seen a sea dragon. However, we have ample evidence that in the days before querinalo there were flying dragons. They were not precisely common, but the sorcerers apparently used them as steeds. Although not a one remains today—at least that I have found—I have seen and handled tack and trappings far too large for any horse. There are other remnants as well: dragon tooth and scale used in armor and ornament. Paintings done apparently from life."

"But there are none left now," Bryessidan prompted.

Rae looked at him as if she thought he blamed her for the absence of dragons.

"There may be thousands," she said coolly, "but although I have sought them, I have never found them, nor have I spoken to anyone living now who has seen one—although there are old men and women who say that their parents claimed to have done so when they themselves were children."

Bryessidan waved a hand in something like apology for his abruptness. "What I am attempting to ask is this: What do you think happened to these dragons, and do you think the same things happened to the dragons or sea monsters that were said to inhabit the seas surrounding the Nexus Islands?"

Rae shifted her posture, standing tall with her hands clasped within the flowing fabric of her embroidered yellow sleeves.

"There are many theories as to what happened to the dragons," she said. "One is that they, like the sorcerers of old, contracted querinalo and died from it. This is persuasive for many reasons. Dragons must have possessed some form of inherent magic. How else could a creature so large manage to fly—and to fly bearing the weight of one or more humans as well? Querinalo—especially in its earliest manifestation—was known to attack with a ferocity directly proportionate to the magical ability of the victim.

"Another theory, and one that is persuasive for other reasons, is that the dragons were not precisely natural creatures. This proposes that they were created or summoned by means of magic. When the sorcerers died, the dragons died with their creators or vanished back to wherever they had been summoned from.

"Both of these theories account for why dragons—and various other beasts that were known only through their association with sorcerers—have not been seen since querinalo moved us into the modern age."

"So," Bryessidan said, "if dragons vanished either because they caught querinalo and died or because they were creations of the sorcerers who once ruled these lands, then do you think it likely that we will find them inhabiting the seas surrounding the Nexus Islands?"

Rae pursed her lips. "The tales told regarding the Nexus Islands pointedly state that the sea monsters—or dragons in some versions of the tale—were put there to guard the islands from invasion. Most creatures do not stay put once whatever held them is gone, so, even if the sea monsters survived querinalo, they should have dispersed to their native waters in the interim. The likelihood of finding a sea monster in those particular waters seems no higher than of finding them anywhere else, and—as King Hurwin stated earlier—even those who have sailed the oceans their entire life have no evidence (beyond the occasional wild tale) to prove they have seen actual sea monsters."

"I wish we knew more," Wantoniola of Tishiolo said. "Planning a battle against opponents whose numbers we do not know, whose defenses we cannot spy out in advance is bad enough. To do so within such a narrow time frame—that is, if we are to send a fleet rather than merely press through the gates—is worse."

"Still," Loris Ambler of Azure Towers said thoughtfully, "there is potential for success—even without a fleet, and if we could get a fleet there, then success would be assured.

"If a fleet is to be assembled and provisioned," King Hurwin said, "and reach the Nexus Islands while the winds and currents are favorable, then we must act quickly. Those of you who represent others must take counsel with them and learn whether they will agree to join us in this bold venture. I believe some of the Once Dead may be able to facilitate communication, but their abilities are limited, am I correct?"

Amelo Soapwort rose. "Some of the Once Dead can talk mind-to-mind, but only to others who already possess this talent, and only if they have already met and established a linkage."

"Some help then," King Hurwin said, "but nothing like the gates for speedy trading of information. I suggest we take a vote now—not whether or not to go ahead with this matter, but whether to consider bringing the matter before those who must make the final decision."

Ambassadors and emissaries looked at each other. Bryessidan thought that they must have discussed this matter earlier. Really King Hurwin wasn't asking much, just that they agree to bring the matter up with their superiors.

King Hurwin looked at Bryessidan. "Will you call for a vote?"

Bryessidan knew the power of coercion involved in a show of hands, so he did not wait for someone to suggest a secret ballot.

"Who is for breaking up this assembly in order that the emissaries may return to their homelands and put the question of whether or not a joint attempt should be made to pass into the Nexus Islands—by force if necessary—and discover the reason for the current interruption of service?"

He heard numerous quills skittering across paper and knew his wording was being taken down. He was pleased to think he had sounded very polished, especially given how little time he had been given to prepare.

As the quills ceased their motion, hands rose around the table. Bryessidan counted aloud.

"Very good," he said. "We are unanimous."

"Now," King Hurwin said, "I would like to suggest another vote—that other than the most elementary preparations, we all agree not to act until we know who is with us and who is not. Many of the plans discussed involved using the gates, and I fear that premature probing may give away what element of surprise we possess."

Bryessidan gritted his teeth, once again feeling that head and foot of the table had been reversed. Quills skittered, and then King Hurwin said sharply, seeing Bryessidan was not going to serve as his echo, "Well? Are we agreed or not?"

Again hands raised, but Bryessidan noted that the agreement was more tentative. Only the fact that no one apparently wished to be seen as disagreeing kept the vote moving.

"Unanimous," King Hurwin said. "Very good."

Very good for us, Bryessidan thought as he rose to dismiss his guests, *but not nearly so good for the Nexans, not nearly so good for them at all.*

❧

BLIND SEER PROVED less able to read the notes taken by the various maimalodalum than he had hoped. Although the wolf had come to comprehend an astonishing amount about how various signs stood for sounds, and how these sounds in turn fit together to represent words, his wolf's eyes were not made to focus for long at such a close distance.

Then there were the idiosyncrasies in the different handwriting styles used by the varying maimalodalum. Some of these resulted from the peculiar shapes of their hands. Hope's writing really did resemble bird tracks, while Powerful Tenderness's massive fists could not handle the delicate quills the bird-woman preferred. He wrote with the burned tips of sticks, his characters jagged and bold.

Within a short time, it became evident that having the various scribes read their notes to Firekeeper and Blind Seer would be far more efficient than the pair attempting to decipher them on their own.

Embarrassed by her lack of literacy, Firekeeper sat with unwonted patience through the long sessions. Although copies of the notes were being made for them to carry back to the Nexus Islands, Firekeeper had been shamed and felt her only chance to redeem herself would be to find something of significance among the varied texts that the maimalodalum themselves had missed.

She had her opportunity on the second day. The materials Hope and Powerful Tenderness had read to them on the first day had been more than enough to confirm the maimalodulum's conclusion that the Fire Plague had originated in the New World, and that it had dealt its damage in waves. By the second day, Firekeeper was beginning to despair that the archives would contain anything more of significance when Surf Hands, whose turn it was to read to them, picked up a nearly flat journal, the yellowing pages of which were fastened between wooden boards covered in something that cracked and flaked under even the fox-woman's delicate touch.

Blind Seer sniffed some of the flaking matter and sneezed. Surf Hands laughed.

"It is a fabric of some sort, but not one I know. Here we have cotton, linen, and various fleeces but . . . If I did not know it was impossible, I would say spider silk was woven to make this cloth."

"Perhaps the Old World sorcerers did make cloth from spider webs," Blind Seer said, sneezing again.

Firekeeper lifted a large flake of the material to the light. That told her little more than that it was indeed woven material. Impulsively, she dropped it onto the tip of her tongue. Sometimes taste proved far wiser than her other senses.

The main sensation was sour, but there was a hint of something else, something familiar. In a moment, she placed it.

"Silk!" she said. "Very old and nearly perished, but the taste is there."

"Silk?" Surf Hands asked, twitching her ears to indicate curiosity.

"It is a fiber that comes from New Kelvin," Firekeeper said. "As far as I know, the New Kelvinese are the only people in all the New World to know the secret of its making. It comes from insects. Some say the silk comes from spiders, but Grateful Peace—he is a New Kelvinese friend of ours—says that the actual source is the cocoon of a special worm."

"Worm?"

"More like a caterpillar," Firekeeper said, "or so Peace says."

Blind Seer sniffed cautiously, then licked a few of the dry fragments. "Silk. It might be. When did you eat silk, Little Two-legs?"

The affectionate use of her baby name warmed Firekeeper. She reached out and touched the blue-eyed wolf lightly between his shoulders.

"Long ago. There was some formal reception, and I was

trying to lace my gown. The laces, when I held them in my teeth, tasted like a younger version of these flakes."

Blind Seer huffed laughter. "I remember, now. The laces had to be completely replaced. Earl Kestrel was greatly annoyed."

They turned their attention to Surf Hands.

"Whose book is this? Does it say?"

"This book was written by Bhaharahma, a young man from Liglim. When he showed a talent for spellcasting, he was sent from his home to a place called u-Chival in the Old World for further testing, then to someplace else for his actual education. Much of this journal is quite interesting, but is useless in regard to our needs—all but here, at the end. Then Bhaharahma writes about how his mentor—whom Bhaharahma had accompanied to Center Island when the first phase of his education was completed—fell ill. Later, he writes a little about his own illness."

"Read," Firekeeper said. "Please, read!"

Surf Hands complied. Initially, the account was depressingly familiar: the high fevers, the hallucinations, the sense that the very ability to do magic was being burned away. There was an important difference, however. From the start, Bhaharahma had held little hope his mentor would survive.

"Perhaps if I can get him back to u-Chival, they can save him. The Mires in Pelland would be best, but I have heard they are turning people away. Too many of their own have fallen ill for them to have resources to spare. When Orumvantu arrived yesterday, he reported that nearly all the faculty at Azure Towers is ill. Those who are not ill are already dead."

Bhaharahma's mentor's fever raged so hot that the gatekeepers would not let him be moved through the gate lest the heat of the transition finish the fever's work. Once or twice in the past someone had died during the transition, and apparently the consequences were horrific, often rendering the gate completely unusable. With the Old Country rulers already beginning their retreat from the New World, no one wanted to risk a gate being ruined.

Bhaharahma's own decline began with nightmares, dreams

haunted by an exotic figure who danced elaborate figures and twisted his own flesh into thin strands of silk or wire that he then tossed out to cut into the convolutions of Bhaharahma's brain, where they emerged burning. In some dreams, the dancer's form became that of a fantastical mountain sheep. Its huge horns glittered like cut crystal or broken ice. Its absurdly delicate hooves were pure gold.

Haunted by the vividness of these nightmares, Bhaharahma shared them with the young woman who sat vigil with him over his dying mentor. To Bhaharahma's surprise, not only did the young woman admit to having similar dreams, but his mentor, who had not spoken a coherent word for over a day, screamed out, "He dances on the backs of my eyes! I can hear him laughing even now! The light from his horns! It burns! It burns!"

He collapsed, coughing as if the words had choked him, and soon thereafter died.

Bhaharahma wrote little after this, and little of what he wrote made any sense at all, but Firekeeper had heard enough to give her hope. When Surf Hands shut the journal, Firekeeper spoke, her voice tight with restrained excitement.

"Something in that," she said, "sounded familiar."

Blind Seer huffed agreement. "Somewhere, someone told us a tale that featured just such a creature. Was it Queen Elexa?"

Firekeeper shook her head. "We heard it in New Kelvin. Grateful Peace may have been the teller."

"Tale?" interrupted Surf Hands. "Of what?"

"Of the figure this young man mentions," Firekeeper clarified, "the mountain sheep."

"That was just the beginning of hallucination," Surf Hands protested.

"Sometimes madness holds terrifying sanity," Blind Seer said. "Firekeeper, you remember this other tale more clearly than I do. What was it?"

"It was in reference to how Toriovico became Healed One of New Kelvin," Firekeeper said. "You remember how he was not the firstborn son of the Healed One. He had a brother who died. Vanviko was his name."

"Yes. I remember some of this now," Blind Seer said. "Go on."

"Vanviko died in a hunting accident," Firekeeper said, "but it was a curious hunting. A wanderer from the northern mountains came to Dragon's Breath. He won himself a meal in the Healed One's hall in return for telling tales of his journeys. One tale he told was how he had been in the mountains not too many days past, and had seen a marvelous creature."

"Not a mountain sheep with crystal horns and hooves of gold?" Surf Hands interrupted in disbelief.

"The very same," Firekeeper said. "Vanviko resolved to go hunting this beast. He and his companions went out into the snowy hills, but rather than finding good hunting, they met with disaster. As I recall the tale, there was an avalanche. Vanviko and several of his companions were killed, their bodies buried beneath the snow. Had one of the hunters not been the heir apparent to the Healed One, perhaps the bodies would have remained until spring, but Vanviko's death must be confirmed. The next day, a group went forth again, but this time armed with shovels, not with bows and spears. As the story was told to me, the laborers felt themselves watched, and looking up into the heights above, they glimpsed the mountain sheep, safe on a ledge well out of reach. They heard it laugh as they dug after the bodies of the slain, and some claimed the bleating mockery held a note that was almost human."

Surf Hands shuddered. "Could it be a coincidence?"

"A twisting trail that doubles back on itself if so," Blind Seer said. "If you see rabbit tracks, you do not expect to hunt elk."

"True," Surf Hands admitted. "But is this somehow connected to your search?"

Firekeeper drew her Fang and began methodically honing the already sharp blade.

"I think so," she said. "When I first heard that tale, I thought that Vanviko went hunting the mountain sheep because it was winter and he was bored. Human tales are full of such stories. Men and women go forth to kill not because they are hungry, but because they are bored or because they seek a challenge—or sometimes because they wish to find trouble before that trouble comes hunting them. But I wonder if Vanviko or his father the Healed One had heard tell of this strange mountain sheep before. Might others have had such dreams, and those dreams been recorded in the lore of New Kelvin?"

"The trail is even more clearly marked than that," Blind Seer said. "Remember why the Healed One bears that strange title? In all of New Kelvin, the First Healed One was the only sorcerer to survive what they call the Burning Times. What if he recorded what he had seen in his hallucinations? What if he even attached some significance to those visions? If so, he would have told his successor, and so on down the generations. Perhaps Vanviko did not go on an idle hunt, but went bravely chasing something his ancestor had seen."

"I certainly would like to ask questions of a hallucination made flesh," Firekeeper said, rising to her feet and slipping her Fang back into its sheath. "Indeed, perhaps that is precisely what we must do."

"Do you go to New Kelvin next?" Surf Hands asked.

Firekeeper shook her head. "The archives on the Nexus Islands may have yielded more information. In any case, Derian and the others deserve to hear what we have learned. May I ask you and yours to recheck the records for any other references to this mountain sheep? I do not know if I will be able to come myself, but perhaps one of the wingéd folk would serve as courier."

Surf Hands barked a sharp fox-laugh. "Try and stop us from looking," she said. "We have a fresh scent, and that always prompts the appetite. Besides, what had seemed a tangle of threads now is looking more and more like a bit of fabric—tattered, true, but worth darning."

Firekeeper grinned. "I thank you. Now, to give our thanks to the others, and start a long run."

Blind Seer rose and shook. "I don't much care for them, I'll admit it, but I am beginning to feel a longing for the ease of travel offered by those gates. The moon's full face will have markedly waned before we can be to the Nexus Islands. I begrudge the time."

Firekeeper felt her smile vanish. "And we have known that ease of travel for only a little while. I wonder how those in the Old World who have known it for ten years and more are feeling now that we deny it. The Meddler may have set me on this trail, but I think it is a necessary one."

Blind Seer shook again. "Must I keep admitting things I dislike? For here again, dear heart, I think you are right."

XIV

DERIAN CARTER STOOD staring out to sea, marveling how the waters of early spring appeared so much more inviting than those he had so often studied during autumn and winter. The frothing, foaming waves looked warmer, somehow, dancing under the brighter sunlight of the longer days.

Impulsively, he trotted down the rise to a sheltered bit of rocky beach. There, not giving himself time to think, Derian stripped off shoes, socks, shirt, and trousers. Then, clad only in his undergarments, he dove into the waves.

Derian was skilled at the shallow dive, learned when splashing in the waters of the Flin, the river that ran alongside the city of Eagle's Nest. Despite his trust that his skill would not have gone sour, at first Derian thought he had somehow managed to hit bottom. Then he realized that the solidity he felt was the water, icy cold hitting him like something solid, seeming to seize his limbs while paradoxically making his brain fizz and tingle.

He rolled, feeling the waves lift and drop him. These ocean

waters were much more lively than the rivers in which he had learned to swim, but he was far stronger than that boy had been. Confidently, Derian broke from the current's pull, swimming a few strokes overhand, feeling his blood come alive against the cold, then turned and let the waves carry him back to shore.

He half swam, half stumbled onto the rocky slope of the shore, laughing at his own dripping impulsiveness. A long time seemed to have gone by since he had let himself do anything so ridiculous. It felt good, and he shook like a wet dog, letting the water stream from him and dapple the rocks. He was gathering his clothing to him when he heard a sound that would have seemed strange anywhere else: the rise and fall of wolves howling beneath the noonday sun.

"Firekeeper!" he said aloud, but he didn't bother to call in return. He'd already seen one of the seagulls overhead break from the shrieking flock that always seemed to ride the winds over the island and knew that one of the Wise Gulls had gone to tell Firekeeper where she might find whoever it was she sought.

Him, probably. If he wanted a chance to rinse the salt from his skin, he'd better be ready to do it with an audience.

But Firekeeper was more mannerly than Derian expected, and he had time to bathe and dress in clean clothing before she came knocking—actually knocking!—on his door.

"Fox Hair," she said, giving him one of her rough hugs by way of greeting.

"You're not growling," he said, "and you're not grumpy. Therefore, I'm guessing you learned something useful. That means the maimalodalum decided to help, am I right?"

Firekeeper nodded, her dark eyes shining.

"Almost as direct as a wolf," she said approvingly. "Yes. The maimalodalum were not the happiest about what we tell them, but they were not the unhappiest either. They are not a people to waste time wishing that what is could be made what is not."

"I think Harjeedian and Urgana have made some progress as well," Derian said. "Knowing how much you love giving reports, how about we check if they're free? Then you can share your information."

Firekeeper nodded. "Good and good. Also, I bring letters for you and for Harjeedian. And to tell that the baby Elexa is now crying as she should and there is hope she will be strong."

Derian felt his cheeks ache with the force of his grin.

"Letters and a healthy baby. Wonderful!"

He accepted the precious letter from his family in Hawk Haven, savoring its weight. He glanced at the cover sheet. He had suggested to his mother—his most usual correspondent—that she start each letter with a cover sheet that would provide a quick status report on each member of the family. After he had reassured himself that his parents, his sister, brother, and various relatives had been well when the letter had been sent, Derian put the packet down, promising himself that he would savor the contents at his leisure.

Firekeeper had stood patiently through this inspection. Whatever her flaws, she understood the importance of family, and wouldn't have interrupted his reassuring himself that all was well for anything less than an announcement of imminent attack.

They left his house, and Firekeeper told him how healthy Elise had looked, and how the baby had screamed, and how Doc seemed sleek and contented.

Perhaps Harjeedian had heard the wolves' howl earlier. Perhaps someone else had alerted him as to their return, but the aridisdu met them on the ground floor of the large building in which he made his home, and where, conveniently, many of the documents they had needed to study had been archived.

After welcoming the travelers, and congratulating them on their safe return, Harjeedian gratefully accepted the packet they had brought for him. Like Derian, he checked to make sure that neither the letter from his sister nor any of the ones from his associates in the Serpent Temple contained any bad news; then he gave them his full attention.

"Urgana insisted on making tea. Shall we sit in the kitchen?"

No one objected, and Derian found himself thinking how much he preferred this informal Harjeedian to the self-contained and ritualistic man he had first known. Of course, the situation was vastly different, but even a few moonspans ago Harjeedian would not have held a meeting over a kitchen table. Perhaps the periodic intrusions through the gates had unsettled the aridisdu as much as they had Derian himself, making formalities—and the sense of separation they created—much less inviting.

Urgana was pouring boiling water into a teapot when they entered. The scent of mint made the insides of Derian's nostrils tingle. Firekeeper accepted a glass of well-water, and Blind Seer a bowl of the same. Then the wolf-woman launched into her account.

Derian listened, asking questions, and demanding clarifications when Firekeeper's sketchy manner of speech made her meaning less than perfectly clear. She spoke mostly Liglimosh, probably because that was the language of the maimalodalum, but from time to time she employed a term or phrase in Pellish.

The early parts of her report met with nods from Harjeedian and Urgana. Clearly, they were not surprised to learn the fashion in which querinalo had manifested, or to hear confirmation of the old tales that the disease had taken the strongest first, moving on to the weaker practitioners only later. However, when Firekeeper began to tell of the strange reference to the mountain sheep, the two researchers listened intently.

"Wait," Harjeedian said, raising one hand slightly as if he might stop the words physically. "I think there is more to this sheep than you are saying. You speak as if this is something about which we already know."

Like Firekeeper, Derian had heard the tales of Vanviko's death. Now the wolf-woman turned to him. She must have seen that he remembered, for she sighed in relief.

"You tell," she said. "My tongue is thick."

Derian grinned, rather liking the turn of phrase.

"I know Harjeedian has heard about New Kelvin," he began, "but what do you know, Urgana?"

"I know that of all the northern New World countries, they

are the only one that welcomes magic, rather than shunning it," she said. "That has something to do with the man who ruled them first, after querinalo. Wasn't he a spellcaster himself?"

"That's what their legends say," Derian agreed. "The First Healed One was so ill that he couldn't be moved when the rest of his people fled the New World. They expected him to die, as so many others had, but he managed to survive querinalo. Even though his power was gone, they called him the Healed One. As the only living spellcaster, somehow he managed to retain an element of prestige. I guess he must have been a good ruler, because no one threw him out."

Firekeeper snorted. "I think they fear the return of the others—the Old World rulers—and when they realize these not come back, is too late. This Healed One is One in fact not just name."

Derian looked down his nose at the wolf-woman. "I thought you said your tongue was thick. Are you telling this story or am I?"

"You," Firekeeper said, making herself small for a moment. "You do better."

"For whatever reason," Derian said, "the Healed One of New Kelvin continued to reign, and because of precedents he set, New Kelvin is the only one of what you call the 'northern' lands not to be openly antagonistic to magic."

"Do they have spellcasters there?" Urgana asked, leaning forward in her chair, her expression mingling interest and apprehension.

"Not that we saw," Derian said. "In fact, they didn't seem to know a whole lot more about how to make magic work than we did—and certainly a lot less than we here know now."

"Ah," Urgana said, allowing herself to relax against the chair back, her relief evident.

"Where was I?" Derian said.

"You were explaining where this mountain sheep fits into the lore of New Kelvin," Harjeedian replied.

"Right," Derian nodded. "Actually, the events hardly qualify as 'lore.' They're from contemporary history. Toriovico, the current ruler of New Kelvin, was not the heir apparent. His much older brother was, but this brother—Vanviko—was killed in an avalanche when hunting."

Harjeedian frowned. "Hunting a mountain sheep, I suppose."

"That is correct," Derian said. "A mountain sheep with hooves of gold and horns that sparkled like diamond, or so the story goes. Interestingly, the hunt didn't happen by chance. A wanderer who had come to court brought the story with him."

Firekeeper said, "Blind Seer and me, we wonder. Maybe this Vanviko go hunting not because is winter and he is bored, but because he has heard of this sheep before. The first Healed One, he had querinalo. Did he—like this mentor who Surf Hands tell us about—did he also see the sheep?"

"A very good question," Harjeedian said. "It is not one to which Urgana and I have found an answer, but we have learned a few other things that might be useful."

He looked at Urgana and the older woman nodded, then smiled mysteriously. "And with a little further labor, we may even be able to give your sheep a name."

Derian stiffened, but Firekeeper bounced where she sat. Blind Seer's ears canted forward and he tilted his head to one side in such obvious query that Firekeeper's next words were hardly necessary.

"Tell! Do tell! Blind Seer and me both ask."

"Blind Seer and I," Derian muttered automatically.

Harjeedian permitted himself a single, thin-lipped smile, but clearly he was not going to be rushed.

"First, our own work confirms what the maimalodalum said about how querinalo manifested. Perhaps it did not strike each group all at once, as their smaller sample seemed to show, but the occurrences were closely grouped. Within a few days, traffic through the Nexus Islands increased considerably— and all in one direction. There is not one logged account of a person ill with querinalo—obviously it is not mentioned by that name, but the indications are clear enough—originating in the Old World. They all come from the New World."

"The records are that detailed?" Derian asked, ignoring

Firekeeper's evident impatience at being told something she felt she already knew.

"Yes," Harjeedian said. "Apparently, the gatekeepers routinely kept records of why a transit was being made, of goods being shipped, and the like. Sick people fell into the category of goods being shipped, so not only was this noted, but the type of illness or injury was routinely noted as well."

"And they shipped them through?" Derian said. "No effort was made to quarantine them?"

Harjeedian gave a dry laugh. "Where? Other of the islands in this archipelago were inhabited then, but still this is not the most hospitable of lands. Urgana found cross references in various journals, and apparently those who operated the gates and coordinated the facilities wanted the ill off these islands as soon as possible."

Firekeeper had stopped her impatient fidgeting, and now she frowned.

"Harjeedian, was querinalo in Old World, too? On Nexus Islands, too?"

Harjeedian nodded approval, as if Firekeeper was a student who had shown particular insight into a complex problem.

"Very good. From what we can tell, querinalo both was and was not in the Old World at this time. Wait. This is not as nonsensical as it seems."

Firekeeper, who had been about to protest, fell into perfect, listening stillness.

"We found a record kept by one of the less powerful residents of the gate facility. She was not a spellcaster, not even talented. She simply resided here with her husband who was among those who worked the gates. This woman—her name was Fael—notes the following."

He inclined his head toward Urgana, and the woman began to read aloud in a voice lighter and somehow younger than her own natural speaking voice.

"'When the first of those with the New World fever came through the gates for passage home, none of those who were contacted in their homelands seemed to have heard of the disease—no more than had we here at the nexus. Within a day or two, however, word came to us that the disease was being found in the Old World as well. Curiously, it appears to have manifested without there being any contact with those brought from the New World.

" 'Questions have been raised as to whether the sickness might be being carried by some other than humans. Birds travel great distances, ignoring elements of the terrain that would slow human travel. However, there has been no report of mass illness among any of the creatures of air or field. Previously, when a sickness is shared by those of varied bloods, there is some evidence.

" 'The fever has touched its first victim here on the Nexus Islands. Victims, I should say, but one touches my heart so closely that when I see him, I must struggle to remember that he is not the only one so affected. Even as I write this, my dear husband, my Klart, tosses and turns on his pallet. We are long out of ice, and even towels dipped in seawater do nothing to lower his fevers.' "

Urgana skipped a few pages and continued reading, " 'Klart is dead. Yet in the midst of this horror, I find that something can touch me. Those who kept the gates closed all ways into the New World as soon as the first case of the fever manifested here, in this way hoping to halt the spread. Now we have clear proof that the fever will touch even those who have had not contact with land, or with the infection. One of the ships that patrols our seas and keeps peace with the sea dragons came into harbor. They had been gone from before the first sick one came through the gate, yet their windmaster is dead. He fell ill the very day Klart did, and nearly at the same hour.' "

Urgana put down the journal, and spoke in her own voice. "Because Fael herself did not contract querinalo, she goes into some detail about what happened next. I will summarize. The last of those who could operate the gates—a weakly talented spellcaster, a child hardly awakened to her power—opened the gates time and time after, so that some of the inhabitants could escape. Others took to ship, even though the weather made setting sail a chancy proposition, because there was no way that all could leave through the gates with the young spellcaster growing more and more feverish with every transition.

"Fael herself seems to have intended to leave by ship. She wanted some record of what happened here to remain, and she left this journal in the library. On the last few pages, she has done her best to mark where the dead were buried—buried, that is, before the situation became so uncontrolled that the dead were no longer being buried. She marks her husband's grave in particular."

Derian glanced at the writing in the book. "Pellish. No wonder she wanted the grave remembered. This Klart would have become an ancestor, and be due what respect could be given him. It must have been hard for Fael to leave without the proper ceremonies celebrating the transition. She probably hoped to come back someday and do them, or to send some-one to do them for her."

He set the book back on the table. "So, what is the significance of the mountain sheep?"

In answer, Harjeedian rose from the kitchen table and motioned them toward the door.

"There is a book in the library I wish to consult before offering my opinion."

Without comment, Firekeeper and Blind Seer rose, falling back to let Harjeedian and Urgana lead the way. Derian followed in bemused silence.

The rooms that served as library and archives occupied all of one long side of the building. They had clearly been built for this purpose, lined with tall, wide windows. In some places, the original glass remained in place, having defied who knew how many years of storms and hurricanes. Derian suspected that the glass itself might have been enchanted to give it greater strength.

That was something he was coming to learn about the Old World sorcerers. The tales he had been told as a boy had high-lighted the terrible and destructive things of which they were capable. How they could pull lightning from the skies, or make the marrow in the bones of a living person heat, so that the victim died from his skeleton collapsing around him, or how they had drunk blood from cups made from the skulls of those who thwarted them.

But those stories had left out the numerous practical uses to which magic could be turned. Lighting. Heating. Strengthening glass or metal. Summoning wind or rain. Easy transportation. Other comforts Derian could only just barely imagine. Without those aspects, the temptation magic offered was limited—the power only a bully or despot might crave. When one saw the myriad practical uses to which the same power might be turned, then truly did magic become seductive.

The library also had magical lighting, blocks set into the walls and ceiling that glowed bright without glare. These, Urgana had told them, had been in place, but without power, when she and her allies had arrived ten years or so before. Later, they had been repowered by one of the Once Dead for whose deaths Derian and his allies had been—if indirectly—responsible.

And someday, perhaps not too long from now, he thought, *we will need to decide whether we, too, cannot do without these little comforts, and whether we will accept the price we must pay—in blood—to obtain them.*

But maybe he would be gone by then, back to being a horse carter's son and sometime advisor to royalty. Derian reached up and touched his elongated ears and knew that unless a miracle happened, this would never be so. The Nexus Islands, or some place like them, where he would be accepted despite his strangeness, would be his only home for the rest of his life.

Harjeedian motioned them all to take seats at one of the long, wide tables set down the middle of the room. It was some measure of how seriously Firekeeper was taking all of this that she not only accepted a seat for herself, but also pulled out one of the heavy wooden chairs for Blind Seer. The wolf leapt lightly up and seated himself, head and chest rising well above the table's polished surface.

While the others were settling themselves, Harjeedian went and inspected the shelves, finally pulling down a pair of fat volumes. One of these he set in front of Urgana.

"It will take us a minute or so to find what we are seeking," he said, carefully turning the brittle pages as he spoke. "These books are codices of the heraldic emblems associated with specific spellcasters and other highly magically talented people. As best we can tell, these emblems were only assigned to those who had received formal training in some aspect of the magical arts. A local gardener with a green thumb, let us say, who never stirred from her local plot would not have been assigned such an emblem, not even if she was so talented that she could make a tree grow from a seed to a fruiting plant within a single day."

"So the emblems," Derian said, "indicate initiation to some organization: a guild or sodality or something like that."

"That is what we think," Harjeedian said. "As with so many of the texts preserved here, the problem is that no one bothers to put down in writing what 'everyone' already knows."

Firekeeper said, "Blind Seer ask, 'All the pictures he see on the page have animals. Did all the sorcerers choose animals as their emblems?'"

Urgana looked over at the wolf, slightly startled, for although all of the Nexans had become accustomed to treating the Wise Beasts as something like equals, very few of those beasts showed any interest in printed matter—and those who did were usually avians. However, she answered with an ease that reminded Derian that her heritage, unlike his own, had long accepted the idea of animals having thoughts to communicate.

"No, Blind Seer, all the sorcerers did not choose animal emblems." She indicated the floor-to-ceiling series of shelves from which Harjeedian had taken the two volumes. "That entire series of volumes lists emblems. Some use natural features like sunbeams or storm clouds. Others use tools or articles of attire. Some use symbols whose meaning are a mystery to us. The volumes, however, are arranged by category. These two that Harjeedian pulled for us to inspect concentrate on larger herbivores: horses, various types of cattle, sheep, and goats."

She had not stopped turning the pages as she spoke, and Derian thought that was why Firekeeper did not fidget. Certainly, the wolf-woman was not bored. She was strung as tightly as a bowstring. Next to her, Blind Seer—even sitting bolt-upright as he was—looked relaxed by contrast.

"The emblems," Urgana continued, "are detailed one to a page, with basic details about the person to whom the emblem has been assigned given in several languages beneath the picture."

"Heraldry," Derian said. "Good. Did you notice this mountain sheep Firekeeper mentioned?"

"Not in particular," Harjeedian said, "but it sounds like the type of emblem that would be recorded here."

"What if is not emblem but is person?" Firekeeper asked. "Vanviko story is about person, sheep that laughs, not emblem."

"Still," Harjeedian said, never pausing in his rhythmic page turning, "I would be willing to bet . . ."

Silence but for the chuffing noise of stiff pages being turned came to occupy the room. Once or twice Harjeedian or Urgana would pause, but always after reading the text beneath the drawing, they would go back to turning pages.

Derian found himself wondering if the emblem would be there. Perhaps the mountain sheep was just some very odd Royal Beast or maimalodalum. Perhaps if it was a heraldic emblem, it belonged to some more conventional heraldry, a royal family or warrior clan. But then hadn't all the rulers in the Old World been sorcerers?

He was musing over this point when Urgana gave a small, sharp cry, almost as if she were in pain, but when Derian half rose from his seat to go to her aid, he found she was smiling with thinly veiled triumph. Here for a moment was the proud young woman whose skills as a researcher had given her value to sorcerers and kings.

"You have!" Firekeeper said. "Hold up! Show!"

Urgana did so. There on the page, painted in colors still brilliant despite the passage of over a century, was a stylized rendering of the very creature they sought. There was a mountain sheep, filled with the arrogant glory very few herbivores share with those that prey upon them. The curling horns glittered with imprisoned rainbows, their natural ridges sharpened and faceted. The hooves, poised to balance the creature at the edge of a rocky crevice, were shining gold. The eyes held an expression that was strangely knowing.

"This emblem belonged to a man named Virim. His nationality seems to have been mixed, with his father from Pelland, and his mother from Tishiolo. His date of birth is given in one of the older classifications. Give me a moment . . ."

She did some calculations with her fingertip against the glossy surface of the table, frowned, did them once more, and then rubbed the entire thing out.

"I must have done one of the conversions wrong. For these dates to be right, Virim would have had to be over a hundred and sixty when Divine Retribution struck. Never mind. That's not important. What is interesting, is that these notes seem to indicate that Virim had close ties with the New World. There is a note that he was educated at Azure Towers, which is where those from the New World who developed magical abilities were educated."

"Do the notes say anything else about this Virim?" Derian asked. "Where he lived? Who were his teachers? Anything? I'm wondering if Bhaharahma's mentor might have known this Virim."

"A few names are listed, but neither Bhaharahma's nor that of his mentor," Urgana said, "so finding a link between them—even if there is one—may not be so easy. Still, there may be more details in the notes Firekeeper brought back with her from Misheemnekuru."

"We'll examine those records, of course," Harjeedian said, "and look through the library here for other references to this Virim. Until now, we have been searching blind, afraid to neglect anything lest we overlook something essential. This will help narrow our search a great deal."

"There may be no need to undertake such extensive research, Harjeedian," said a strong, male voice, speaking from off to one side of the room. "I know who Virim is, and I would be more than happy to share with you everything I know."

Derian turned his head, knowing already who he would see. There, leaning against a shelf loaded with books, his form almost but not quite solid, was the Meddler.

XV

KING BRYESSIDAN OF the Mires stared out a high window at the moon. That orb had been waxing when the decision had been made to seriously consider some sort of invasion of the Nexus Islands. Now it had passed full and was nightly waning. Twelve days had passed since that fateful meeting, and in twelve days a certain number of things had been decided.

Hearthome and Azure Towers, the two lands physically closest to the Kingdom of the Mires, had sent word that they would join in the venture. Queen Iline of Hearthome had even offered to have her land serve as a base of operations. There were reasons to consider accepting that offer. For one, Hearthome was more centrally located. For another, it possessed better roads and better harbors than did the Mires, but Bryessidan found himself oddly uncertain about giving up the marginal command that had been his—even though he remained uncertain about whether he was actually in favor of the planned invasion.

For planned it now was, even if no other land chose to join them. Four nations had agreed to join in the venture: the Mires, Tavetch, Azure Towers, and Hearthome. Bryessidan firmly expected Pelland to join as well. Not to do so would be to forever relinquish claims to supremacy the rulers of Pelland had held since the days of the Sorcerer's Bane.

He was less certain about u-Chival and Tishiolo, but four nations—probably five—were enough. So it would be war.

Bryessidan felt a hand on his shoulder and turned, already knowing who would be there. Gidji smiled at him.

"Want to tell me what has you so serious?"

He didn't attempt to evade. If he went to war, she would need to rule the Mires as regent.

"War. Whether I should try and insist that the invasion is coordinated from here."

"As opposed to Hearthome?"

He nodded.

"Let Hearthome coordinate it," Gidji said immediately. "They do have the better location, and that means they will be the ones who need to invite the armies and navies of other nations within their borders."

Bryessidan stared at her. Wonder at her brilliance mingled with self-derision at his own lack of insight.

I was so caught up in my own self-importance, my own concern regarding the prominence I might lose that I never thought about the possible cost to the Mires.

He kissed her lightly, astonishing Gidji, for he usually took care not to mingle affection and matters of state. Her sky-blue eyes momentarily widened with delight.

"That," Bryessidan said with deliberation, "is a matter I had failed to take into consideration. I wonder if Queen Iline regrets her offer?"

"Probably not," Gidji said. "Remember, she is constantly concerned about conflicting factions within her own land. Having foreigners for the factions to worry about will slow their internal intriguing. If her offer is accepted, I wouldn't be surprised to hear that some of the most troublesome have been 'honored' with incredibly time-consuming and laborious tasks."

Bryessidan grinned. "I think you are almost certainly correct. I will consult with my ministers, but unless one of them has a telling reason why Queen Iline's offer should not be accepted, I believe a courier will be heading to Hearthome before the sun sets tomorrow."

Gidji said, "I would not mind attending that meeting."

Bryessidan nodded. "By all means. If I find myself involved in war, you will be regent. You must know all the details."

"Then you plan to lead our forces yourself?" Gidji said.

"I had thought to do so," Bryessidan said. "I will not go to sea with the fleet. That would put me too out of touch, but if we were able to break through via the gates . . . Well, I've actually been to the Nexus Islands. Admittedly, it was a long time ago, but that's more than most of those who will be fighting for the Mires can claim."

"A good point," Gidji said, thoughtfully. "Actually, it is a claim most of our allies could not make either. Even those of us who have used the gates have not been beyond the gate facility. The Once Dead did not welcome tourists."

"I know," Bryessidan said, "but when the Nexus Islands were in my father's control I did visit them repeatedly. Much will have changed, but some things will not have done so."

Gidji nodded. "Has there been any discussion of who would command the invasion? My father will command the fleet, of that I have no doubt, but what about the land forces?"

Bryessidan shook his head. "I don't think anyone has considered. If we do manage an invasion via the gates, the forces will need to originate from numerous points. The more gates that come active all at once, the more fronts the Nexans will need to cover."

"Yes," Gidji agreed, "but once the gates have been breached and the forces are flowing through, then someone will need to coordinate them. Four or five or six separate armies, arriving two by two and waiting for their commanders, is a recipe for disaster, but if one brave leader is willing to go through with the first or second wave and coordinate the troops as they arrive, then success would be assured."

Newly humbled by the blindness into which his pride had almost led him, Bryessidan could not feel certain that she was recommending him.

Almost hesitantly he asked, "And do you have a recommendation for that commander?"

Gidji met his eyes squarely. "I would recommend you. As you say, you know something of the terrain. You were reared amid your father's wars and their aftermath. I do not think you will spend lives lightly. You know the rewards of war, but you also know its costs."

Bryessidan did his best to hide how his heart had swollen to the bounds of his breast with her praise.

"There will be others who wish the honor," he said.

"Show them it is no honor," she countered. "Show them the danger involved. I have looked at the old maps of the complex. Also, I remember what I have seen the times I have passed through. Although the gates are centered on one part of the island, they are not all in one structure. Rather, they are scattered among numerous structures, each of which has its own walls. This separate but joined element of the construction is what we are counting on to make the invasion possible, but it is also the element that might defeat us. Whoever commands the land forces must first find a way to join them up."

Bryessidan turned away from the window and began pacing back and forth along the length of the room. Conflicting desires warred within him. He wanted the honor and prestige of command, yet he feared that he was not equal to the task.

"You say that your father will be appointed to lead the sea forces," he said, "and I agree. Perhaps that will work against my winning command of the land forces. Our lands are already closely allied. Might not the others—Hearthome, Azure Towers, Pelland, the rest—feel we already have our share of honor?"

"Not if you keep them from thinking that way. If the matter comes up, point out the honor Hearthome has already secured. Quietly remind those from Azure Towers that their old opponent bears watching. Queen Anitra is probably already thinking that Iline's offer is meant to mask some move to weaken Azure Towers. As for Pelland . . . I think if handled correctly they will be content with empty praise paid to their greatness. There is a decadence in that land."

Bryessidan remembered how Pelland was said to import a great deal of a drug refined from flowers grown in the highlands of Tishiolo. The drug stimulated thought, but at the cost of dulled energy and will to act. He paced faster, thinking out loud.

"The disdum of u-Chival are not likely to join in this venture," he said, "but even if they do, their aversion to magic will make them unwilling to have one of their own serve as general."

"True," Gidji said. "Offer to have one of the aridisdum serve to read omens for the venture, and their sense of honor and respect will be served."

"I will bring this up when I meet with my ministers," Bryessidan said. "If they agree, do you think I should make my offer in the same letter in which I accept Queen Iline's offer to make Hearthome our base of operations?"

Gidji shook her head. "I think not. Better that someone else nominate you. My father would be possible, but even better would be someone else."

"We could approach Queen Anitra of Azure Towers," Bryessidan said. "If accompanied by a quiet offer of aid should Hearthome overreach itself, she should be delighted to have her emissary make the suggestion."

"Not to mention," Gidji said, "that the very fact that you are offering the Mires' aid should intensify any paranoia she is feeling about Hearthome's intent. I had thought to suggest one of the u-Chivalum, but this is even better."

Bryessidan rubbed his hands together.

"Then it is settled. I was scheduled to meet with my ministers tomorrow morning on more routine matters. I believe some of those must wait until later. This is more important, and more time-sensitive."

"Time-sensitive?" Gidji asked. "I suppose for locking Queen Iline into her offer, but for the matter of command . . . Bull Moon is waning. Horse Moon has yet to show her face. My father seemed to think a fleet could not safely sail until Lion Moon, and that comes later still."

"And before that fleet sails," Bryessidan said, "my position must be secure. Once the ships leave, then communication between land and sea will be difficult, if not impossible. We cannot waste what contact we will have on political wrangling."

"True," Gidji said.

Bryessidan looked at his wife and knew that she, like him, was suddenly realizing the import of the plans they had laid with such enthusiasm. Dreams were one thing, but the reality could well mean his death and her struggling to hold a land that was not hers by birth until their daughter, now only seven, came of age. The struggle would be heightened by the fact that the grandson of Essidan's claim was hardly based on long tenure or divine appointment, but on a coup that might inspire others to try something similar.

"I can step back," he said, hardly believing the weakness he was allowing himself to show. "Someone else can have formal command. I will earn sufficient honor commanding for the Mires."

"Honor among our own, yes," Gidji said softly, "but honor enough to restore the Mires to the place from which your father let her slip? Honor enough to make clear that the Mires no longer lives on the sufferance of her neighbors? Bryessidan, if the Nexus Islands have indeed fallen into the hands of those who bear no gratitude to the memory of the Reprieve, then the Mires will need all the respect and honor—and fear—you can win for her. Otherwise, even the alliance with my birth land will not be enough to keep the Mires from being swallowed by her neighbors."

Bryessidan stared at her. "You care about the Mires?"

"It is my homeland, now," Gidji said fiercely. "It is where my child will rule someday. More than that, it is a good place, with good people who do not deserve to live on the sufferance of others. Yes, I care! By your ancestors and the stars that dart and wheel in the heavens, I swear that my dream is to have the Mires once again the equal of her peers, a land from which my children can go out into the world with the strong reputation of their father's deeds to stand as a shield between them and their grandfather's failure. Is that vow enough for you?"

Bryessidan gave her a bow as deep and low as he would give to any ruler in the land.

"I think," he said, "I am only beginning to realize the honor done to me when you consented to be my wife. I am humbled, and I will strive to make your dreams a reality."

Gidji looked at him, and he thought he saw her blink back a tear. Then she forced a smile, and was all practicality once more.

"Then, you had better get a good night's sleep before the meeting with your ministers tomorrow."

"As you command, my queen," Bryessidan said, offering

her another bow before sweeping her into his embrace. "As ever you command."

✤

WHEN THE MEDDLER spoke, Urgana's high, shrill shriek of surprise was the only reply—the only audible reply, that is. Firekeeper felt Blind Seer's hackles rise, the soft fur brushing against her arm. Ominously, the wolf did not growl, did not move from his seat. A hunting wolf howls when the sound might terrify the prey, but strikes from silence when the noise would only serve to warn the intended victim.

Firekeeper placed her left hand squarely at the base of Blind Seer's neck, reminding him of her presence—and hopefully reassuring him that she remained where she should be, beside him.

Firekeeper knew the Meddler appeared differently to all who saw him manifest. Doubtless, when Harjeedian rose to address the new arrival, he thought he was addressing a man of his own race, and probably about his own age. The Meddler always sought to seem likable, or so it seemed from the various ways he had appeared to her and her friends over time.

To Firekeeper, at this time, in this place, he manifested as he had several times before, as a lean, muscular human with the head of a wolf. She wondered how Blind Seer saw him, but decided not to ask—not now, maybe not ever.

"Meddler," Harjeedian said, his voice stiff, his intonation formal, "you have been watching us?"

"Not for long," the Meddler said, shifting slightly, as a real human would, relaxing into a comfortable slouch against the bookcase. "Let us say I have put little markers in place so that I would be alerted when certain events occurred. One of these was when Firekeeper returned from her journey to Misheemnekuru. Since I started her on what has proven to be a rather arduous course of action, I thought it was only polite to come and hear her report. I would have listened without comment, but when I realized I could spare you all a great deal of labor, well . . . Here I am."

He smiled a bright, warm, all-embracing smile meant to show them all what a good fellow he was. In Firekeeper's case, that meant it was the smile of a lesser-ranking wolf—although not a least wolf—reminding the Ones what a good and useful hunter he was. She could not help react to it, but noted that beside her, Blind Seer's hackles continued to rise around her hand.

The Meddler turned now to Urgana, and Firekeeper could see his legendary charm was having almost as hard a time with her as with the blue-eyed wolf. No wonder. Urgana came from the same general cultural heritage as did Harjeedian, and in their shared lore, the Meddler was regarded as a very dangerous person indeed.

"For example," the Meddler said, "I could have saved you, dear lady, a certain amount of doubt regarding your skill in calculating dates. Virim is indeed at least as old as those dates seem to show—and he may be a great deal older."

"How?" Firekeeper asked, her tone challenging. "How?"

"You don't think that the great sorcerers of old went about strengthening things like window glass against breakage and paper against mold and rot without thinking about how decay might affect their own bodies, did you?"

Actually, Firekeeper had not, and judging from the expressions on Derian's and Harjeedian's faces, neither of them had thought much about it either. Urgana, however, was nodding thoughtfully.

"I should have considered that," she said, not giving the Meddler credit, but rather being critical of herself. "I heard such stories when I was a girl. Indeed, several of the Once Dead here on the Nexus Islands were beginning to talk of re-discovering such spells once they held a secure position and had wealth to spare."

"Oh, they would have found there was far more involved than a spell," the Meddler said. "A series of detailed and highly complex rituals were involved, and even then they didn't always take. The person who hoped to extend his or her life might die instead, or suffer some rather nasty side effects. However, the procedure worked frequently enough that those who could manage it often took advantage. Virim was one such."

"Ah" was all Urgana could manage in reply.

Harjeedian spoke into the thoughtful silence that followed.

"So it seems you do know the sorcerer of whom we speak. Is there anything else that you would care to tell us?"

"Certainly," the Meddler said. "For one thing, I believe—although I do not know for certain, and I certainly do not know how it was done—that he is a likely candidate for the originator of querinalo. It quite fits in with his personality."

"Oh?" Derian prompted. "He liked killing people?"

"Not really," the Meddler said. "Virim was a conflicted and contested person. Urgana read to you how Virim seemed to have ties to both the Old and New Worlds. This was so. He was born in the New World, but his parents were both firmly ensconced in the Old World, born of highly ranking families of prestigious magical heritage.

"Now, all of you know the strange fact that until the coming of colonists from the Old World, there do not appear to have been any humans at all in the New World. The New World was the domain of beasts, both those similar to what had been known in the Old World—although often with variations as you might expect given the distance between the landmasses—and those who were markedly different from those usual animals, often being more intelligent, sometimes markedly larger in size, and, finally, gifted with magical talents. That the New World had its own inhabitants who claimed it for their own did not trouble those who came to colonize. Nor did the fact that these inhabitants were physically different have much to do with the colonizers' attitude. I think you've heard enough tales about how life was in the Old World before querinalo to know that the Old World rulers weren't particularly thoughtful or considerate toward any who crossed their will.

"Virim was the son of two who came to colonize the New World. Over time, he grew to feel that the New World should not be ruled by the Old. From what I recall, he had a liking and sympathy for the Royal Beasts. After some nasty clashes, the colonizing groups made treaties and agreements with the Royal Beasts—or Wise Beasts, whatever you want to call them. I'll call them 'Royal' in honor of Firekeeper's chosen nomenclature, and because, honestly, I think that name reflects how Virim himself saw them."

"As Royal?" Derian asked. "I don't quite follow."

The Meddler grinned. "I think you just might, Derian Carter. Virim saw them as noble, as mighty, as stronger, wiser, better—and this is important—not only than the other beasts, those Firekeeper so affectionately calls the 'Cousins,' but than humans."

Firekeeper tightened her fingers in Blind Seer's scruff, thinking not so long before, she would have agreed with this view. Over time, however, she had grown to accept that at least some humans were as fine as any Beast, and that there were some Beasts—she recalled a particularly annoying young wolf called Northwest—who were worse than most humans.

The Meddler continued. "As I think your own histories tell, there came a time when the Old World colonists—specifically, those in charge—decided that they were firmly enough entrenched in their new holdings that they need no longer avoid the territory held by the Royal Beasts. New war broke out, but this time the Royal Beasts found themselves at a disadvantage. The humans had larger population bases. The first of the gates were in place and so reinforcements could be brought in more easily. The humans now knew the land, if not as well as the Royal Beasts, at least well enough to take advantage of terrain as they had not been able to in those earlier encounters.

"Eventually, the Royal Beasts retreated rather than suffer complete slaughter. The boundary became the mountains to the west. Not only did the mountains provide a natural barrier, they also contained a high enough amount of iron ore that they caused spells to behave in an unpredictable fashion. This meant that they could not be surmounted by magic.

"In any case, why should anyone bother? Now the lands

east of the mountains, a considerable amount of new territory, were exclusively under human control. Moreover, although the losses had not been enough to force a retreat, the humans had not come through the battles with the Royal Beasts unscathed. The time had come to settle in, to claim new territories, and—and this cannot be overlooked if you are to understand Virim—to fight among themselves."

Harjeedian frowned thoughtfully. "I believe I understand better than I would have a few years ago. The Old World sorcerers did not cooperate easily. While they had a common opponent, they would have done so, but when that opponent retreated, then they would return to old feuds."

"Good," the Meddler said. "Now, consider what happens when you have men and women of that temperament, and at least some of these men and women have found the means to extend their natural life spans. Their sons and daughters—for they did have children—see no end to parental authority. There will be no inheritance coming to them, no openings at the top. Therefore, either they must make those openings, or they must find new places to assert themselves."

"Ugly," Derian said.

Firekeeper wondered if he was thinking of the battles a few years ago when the throne of Hawk Haven had been considered open. That would have been nothing to what the Meddler described, for at least in that battle families had stood together—or mostly so—rather than tearing into each other.

The Meddler waited, studying their expressions in perfect silence.

Finally, Firekeeper said, "But this Virim was different? He thought the New World should be for Royal Beasts and Cousins, not for humans?"

"That is what he said," the Meddler agreed, "not at first, because at first he was a young man, not in a position to speak out in such a fashion. Later, however, when he was an older man and a new onslaught west began to be discussed, then Virim spoke out."

Derian said, "This wouldn't happen to be shortly before the Plague occurred, would it?"

The Meddler shook his head. "Not shortly, not if by that you mean by time as measured by the turning of the moon. Shortly, however, if you mean within a few years before the Plague. Virim spoke first. His speeches made a difference initially."

Harjeedian raised a finger. "Pause a moment, Meddler. From what you told us before, you were imprisoned for many, many years before the Plague was released. How is it that you know of this, then?"

The Meddler grinned. "Because it was before I was imprisoned, of course. As I said, at first Virim was successful. He was not the only one against expansion further west. There were a few who were opposed because they were idealists and wished to honor the treaties with the Royal Beasts. There were those who were opposed because they had troubles in either their homelands or in the colonies they already held, and they did not have the resources to spare . . ."

"And didn't want anyone getting ahead of them," Derian said.

"Right," the Meddler agreed. "There were those who were opposed because they were still developing those lands they already held, and did not wish to divert resources. Virim had many allies in those early years. My guess is that as time passed, all but the idealists dropped away, and, sadly, even idealists change their ideals."

"And you are guessing," Derian said, "that at some point Virim decided he must win—even if that meant taking drastic action, even if that meant something like the Plague."

"There are some telling elements," the Meddler said, "above and beyond the vision to which Firekeeper and Blind Seer found reference. For one, although the Plague fastened onto anyone with magical ability, it spared the Royal Beasts, many of whom have some talent. For another, it began in the New World, forcing a retreat from those lands, leaving the human population weak enough that, should the Royal Beasts choose, they could probably wipe out the remaining humans, even today when the human population has done a very fine job of recovering."

Firekeeper stirred at this, thinking of arguments she had heard. There were those among the Royal Beasts—maybe even among the Wise Beasts—who desired the elimination of humans from the New World. However, thus far they had not been pressed to act. If threatened, the varying bloods that made up the Royal Beasts might indeed ally for a time, and then humans would find out how vulnerable they were.

And where would I stand? she thought. *Could I, like this Virim, wipe out my own kind—whether Beasts or humans— favor one over the other?*

She shivered at the thought, and Blind Seer turned his head to lick her arm in comfort.

"So we must hunt out more on this Virim," she said aloud. "Where did he lair? Who were his kin? Meddler, you say he was very old, even when Plague come. Could he be alive even now?"

The Meddler shrugged. "I don't know. I wonder if he might have died, perhaps a generation or so back."

Urgana looked at the Meddler sharply. "When those with magical ability began to survive."

"When, although they didn't know it," Derian added softly, "querinalo began to prey on the beasts who had once been immune. Interesting. So Virim may be dead. Perhaps Firekeeper does not need to look for him, then. Within another generation or two, querinalo may unravel all by itself, fade away into a terrible memory."

Firekeeper shook her head. "I wish, but no. We need for now. If querinalo sometime go away, then good, but what for now, what for keeping of Nexus Islands. Did you forget this? Did you forget the people who look through gates at us?"

Derian shook his head ruefully. "I think that for a moment I may have done so. I'd like to forget, but you're right. If we're to hold the Nexus Islands, to keep them from being taken and used to invade the New World . . ."

"Or to facilitate invasion in the Old World," Urgana cut in. "Don't forget. That has been done before, and would be again."

Derian nodded. "For whatever reason, we need to hold these islands or destroy the gates, and I'm reluctant to destroy the gates. They're very useful, and, as we discussed before, we don't have any guarantee that there aren't unconnected gates that might be used."

"Or newly created," Urgana put in again. "You forget. The knowledge is there. If querinalo is indeed losing its fangs, then each year will see more and more powerful Once Dead surviving. Someday, they might not even need to 'die' to keep their power."

Blind Seer said softly, *"She has never had querinalo or she would never say it has lost its fangs. Still, I can almost see the nightmare rising in her eyes. I wonder if Virim was so wrong. Perhaps we need to find the source of querinalo and rather than destroying it, make it live and bite and kill once more."*

He spoke with such ferocity that Firekeeper could not even think of a reply. Instead, she moved closer to him, hating the arms of the chairs that kept her from fully embracing him.

She had forgotten that the Meddler understood Blind Seer's speech as easily as he did various human tongues. When she looked at the translucent figure he was studying the blue-eyed wolf with interest.

"Blind Seer, you understand Virim's impulses more intimately than I could ever," he said, and the humans, none of whom had understood Blind Seer's words, or even known he was speaking, looked puzzled. Firekeeper did not choose to enlighten them.

Blind Seer did not deign to reply, but stared through the Meddler as if he were not there.

Harjeedian was wise enough to know when not to ask questions. Instead, he cleared his throat.

"I agree with Derian that we need to try and hold these islands, to leave the gates intact for as long as possible. I also agree with Firekeeper that in order to do so, we need reinforcements, and to bring in reinforcements, we need to be able to counter querinalo. That means continuing on our given course."

Everyone—even Blind Seer—nodded.

"Urgana and I will do library research," Harjeedian said. "Derian, will you speak with Ynamynet? Tell her what we have learned here, and ask them to pursue oral history. I can't believe that no one but Bhaharahma's small group saw this vision if it is indeed significantly connected to querinalo."

He paused, eyes narrowing as he considered a thought. "I don't suppose any of you who suffered querinalo saw a similar vision?"

Derian shook his head. "The closest I came to a vision was one in which I talked to the Meddler, Truth, and Blind Seer."

Firekeeper shook her head. "Not even that."

Blind Seer raised a paw and hit the table with it so that there would be not the least doubt he was speaking.

"I did," he said.

He looked at Firekeeper.

"Speak for me, as I speak," he said.

She nodded and began translating word for word as Blind Seer spoke, dreading what he would say, but knowing that if she did not give the wolf a voice, the Meddler would not be able to resist doing so. Given how he felt about the Meddler, Blind Seer might never forgive her.

"I saw this figure," Blind Seer said. *"I saw this golden-hoofed, diamond-horned mountain sheep. It taunted me and I chased it. In one mad dream, I believe I even killed it."*

XVI

BEFORE ANY OF the select group gathered in the archive room could ask a question, Blind Seer leapt down from the chair and bolted from the room.

"What was that about?" Derian asked. "He was really upset. I don't think I've ever seen Blind Seer upset—not that way."

Firekeeper looked over to where the Meddler stood. He was markedly translucent now, the characters printed on the spines of the books behind him distinct enough to read—if Fire-keeper could have read.

The Meddler smiled at her, a wolf's grin, showing many teeth, as much threat as anything.

"Virim," he said, his voice a howling whisper. "Virim, after all these years. Astonishing."

But Firekeeper wasn't listening. Roughly, she knocked the chair in which she had been sitting to the floor. It fell with a thud against the carpet, but the seasoned hardwood didn't crack.

"Firekeeper," Derian said, "what's going on?"

"You hear much as me," she said, calling the words after her as she fled out the door into the fading light of day.

Had they been among the forests of the mainland, Fire-keeper might never have found Blind Seer, but this was an island, an island on which Blind Seer could never outdistance her. She stood poised on the front porch of the headquarters building, scanning for sign of which way Blind Seer might have run. She found it in the black wings of a raven, soaring high, dipping like the winking of a human's eye. There then, down below.

Firekeeper bolted in that direction, ignoring the curious looks many of the Nexans shot in her direction. None, how-ever, tried to stop her. They probably thought she and Blind Seer were playing some game.

No game, Firekeeper thought. *This is deadly serious, al-though I have no idea why Blind Seer is so upset.*

At long last she found the blue-eyed wolf down on a length of pebble-strewn beach, snapping at the waves as they crashed down onto the shore. He was soaking wet.

He ran without knowing where he ran, Firekeeper thought. *Unless the waves slapped him back, he might have run until he dropped.*

Firekeeper slowed her pace, trotting to Blind Seer's side, trying to make her pace say that she expected to be welcome, although in fact she was not certain at all. Glancing up, she saw the distant black spot of the raven against the sky and knew they were watched, but the distance was so great they might as well have been alone.

Good. Solitude was what they must have if she were to pry some explanation from Blind Seer.

"Hey," she said, coming and dropping onto the course, damp sand, choosing a patch not too heavily strewn with pebbles.

Blind Seer did not acknowledge her except to heave out his breath in a manner that meant, "You're here. What of it?" It was a very un-wolf-like attitude, for wolves are more rough and rambunctious in their greetings than otherwise.

Firekeeper remembered another time, another island, but then she had been the one nearly lost to something that had come from dreams. Blind Seer had sought her. She wasn't going to leave him now, no matter how little he seemed to care about her presence.

She scooted closer, brushing pebbles away with her hand, pitching a few of the larger ones toward the water. They hit in silence, the sound of the waves overwhelming the small plops of their landing.

"You're wet," she said, reaching out and brushing Blind Seer's scruff with her hand.

He gave no reply, not even to shake her away.

"You're upset. You've been upset, one way or another, since querinalo came to you. Maybe even before."

No reply.

Firekeeper reached to rub Blind Seer's ear along the long guard hairs. It was one of his favorite caresses, and normally he would have leaned into it, but today she might as well have been stroking stone. Wet furry stone, but no more yielding.

She kept talking. The world was reduced to this little stretch of ocean-washed beach, to the crash of the waves, to the silent wolf beside her.

"I've noticed, but I haven't even tried to bring it up. I'd like to say I don't know why, but I do, at least a little. I thought if I asked you questions, you might ask me questions. I wasn't sure I wanted to hear those questions, so I didn't invite them. Does that make any sense?"

No reply, not even a twitch of a tail or a flicker of an ear, but unless Blind Seer had somehow been rendered deaf, there was no way he didn't hear her. She kept talking.

"Querinalo was different for me. Different than it was for you, for Derian, for Plik, for anyone I've talked to who has been through it. It confirmed that I had some sort of magical talent, but I've suspected that for a long time. Hazel Healer suggested some talent might explain why I could speak to Beasts so easily. Remember? Later, when Questioner told me about my human parents, well, that seemed to fit, too."

She bit her lip, remembering, then forced herself to go on.

"When the fevers hit me, I was focused on you. You'd gone down first, and you'd gone down hard, far harder than anyone else, harder even than Derian. For a while, I don't think I even knew what I was feeling was in my own body, I'd become so wrapped up in your pain. Later, I realized that I was also sick, but in me there is something that stands like a wall between me and whatever weird magic it is I have. Do you know what that is?"

Blind Seer did not respond.

"It's the same insane circular thinking that nearly got me killed that time on Center Island in Misheemnekuru. Heart and soul and mind, but not body, never body, I believe myself to be a wolf. Wolf is who I am, what I am, how I think, how I act, how I believe. But if it is the working of some talent that makes me able to talk to my people, makes me able to think like them, then I am not a wolf, I am a human with a talent. I cannot believe this. Therefore, I have no talent. Querinalo feeds on talent, on magical ability, but it cannot find that fuel in me.

"Derian, when given a choice between keeping his talent and letting it be burned away realized that without his talent he would not be who he has always been. He realized that without that extra sense for horses, he would not be himself. He diverted the fires of querinalo, and those fires made him into what he is now: man and horse both. In his soul, though, for all his body looks strange, he is a man still. In my soul, for all I look human, I am more wolf. I denied my talents, and in denying them, I gave them shelter."

She wanted desperately to ask Blind Seer what had been his experience, what was it he had seen, what was it he had fled from, but thus far he had not yet indicated in the slightest fashion that he was aware of her. If she were to ask him now, he would simply maintain the barrier of silence that separated them, never mind that her hand was on his head, and her skin and clothing were damp with the ocean waters spread by his fur.

She must keep talking, even if in that talking she addressed issues of which they had never spoken, issues of which she did not want to speak, for to speak of them would be to admit something disgusting about herself.

"Did I ever tell you how the Meddler looks to me when he appears?"

This won her an ear-flicker, a victory of sorts, but as the ear had been moving to flatten in anger Firekeeper wasn't precisely encouraged.

"He looks like a man blended with a wolf. He looks like something from what I once dreamed, long ago, on Misheemnekuru. All but for one thing, in my dream that figure had blue eyes, that figure was you."

Blind Seer hadn't moved, but there was something new in his posture, a stiffness that hadn't been there before. Before he had been somewhere else, hardly hearing her voice. Now he was acutely focused on her, his mood as tense and brittle as glass.

Firekeeper went on. "I don't know if the Meddler can read our minds, or whether our minds somehow read him and make him into someone attractive, someone we will want to trust."

She couldn't say more. She couldn't admit that she had found the Meddler weirdly attractive. Wolves were faithful in their pairings. She did not want to admit infidelity, even in the most random thought, to this wolf, who, had things been different, would certainly have been her mate as well as her partner.

Nor did she want to speak of that attraction aloud, for she could never be sure when the Meddler might be listening, and she didn't know to what advantage he might turn such an open confession.

So Firekeeper held her breath, hoping Blind Seer's now brittle silence would break, and she would not need to confess her own perfidious nature, bringing him back, perhaps only to drive him away.

She sat frozen into motionlessness, no longer even moving the fingers of the hand that had scratched along the edge of Blind Seer's ear. Thus she felt him shudder and draw breath deeply, and thus she heard the words he spoke, although they came forth faintly.

"Trust? Am I really the image of trust for you, Firekeeper?"

She said nothing, but let her fingers stir against his ear so he would know she listened.

Blind Seer leaned slightly into her, a light, wolfish embrace.

"Trust. How can you trust me when I cannot trust myself? You have let yourself be tempted by one who thrives on temptation. How can you blame yourself for stumbling where so many others have fallen? Me, though, my sins are far more grave."

"Sins?" Firekeeper said. "Where there is no religion, can there be sin? Have you been among the yarimaimalom so much that you have taken on their religion?"

"Religion?" Blind Seer shivered his skin. "Not their religion, but even where there is not religion there can be belief. You and I were reared to believe certain things were what certain things should be. How could you torment yourself for being drawn to the Meddler's temptation if you did not believe that somehow the promises you have made to me should make you immune?"

Firekeeper tensed. "Was I then so obvious?"

"Not in how you treated him," Blind Seer said, a trace of his usual good humor thawing the lines of his body, "but in how you strove not to treat him. He made me so angry, not with anything he ever did—for how could a creature that lacks a body do anything?—but how he made you feel about yourself."

Firekeeper sighed, let herself relax. Somehow they had come to sit as they had so many times before: she close beside the wolf, her arm around him, he leaning into her. Within this closeness, Firekeeper could feel the knotted muscles that testified that Blind Seer was not relieved of whatever had driven him from the archive room, but at least he was no longer fleeing from her.

"You have something to tell," she said, hoping she was not overbold. "Tell me what rasps beneath your breath. What sin did querinalo make you think you had committed?"

"You said you trusted me, Firekeeper," Blind Seer said. "I am terrified you will not trust me if I tell you what sort of abomination I know myself to be."

She could smell his terror, and the scent raised an answering terror within her own breast, but she forced her breathing to be calm.

"Tell," she said. "Not telling has driven us apart. Can telling make that worse?"

She knew it might, but she could not believe there was anything about Blind Seer that she might not embrace. She had already been forced to accept that he housed some magical talent within him. Such talents were not unknown among either the Royal Beasts or the Wise. What talent could Blind Seer have discovered that would make her trust him less?

"You tell me that we were walking together when the fever seized me," Blind Seer began.

Firekeeper recognized the need to slowly stalk up on what was bothering him, and did not remind Blind Seer as she might have one of the talkative humans that since she was the one who had told him of course she knew.

"I remember none of that," Blind Seer went on. "I remember the end of our battle with the Once Dead. I remember some of the organizational meetings immediately following. I remember talking to the yarimaimalom, enlisting their continued aid. Those memories grow less and less real whenever I examine them, as if I do not really remember, but remember being told, and from that construct some sort of reality.

"What I remember more sharply is being in a deep forest,

like but unlike the one in which I was born. I knew this forest intimately, yet some part of me also knew that I had never been in it before. For a time I ran though the forest, chasing the deer, dodging the elk, frolicking with pack mates forgotten until that time—or perhaps never known.

"Then I came upon a hilltop, and there I met three others: the jaguar Truth, the human Derian, and whatever it is the Meddler is. We talked for a time, and the question of how might we preserve our lives arose. Things were said that you have heard already—about the trades one might make, about the choices.

"Despite what seemed like moonspans of running, at this point I was no closer to knowing what it was within me that had attracted querinalo's fire. All I knew was that where my body lay was pain, while here in these green woods I was without pain, without confusion.

"The Meddler's words troubled me, especially his simple view that querinalo could only be defeated either by letting it have what it wanted or giving it something in return. It seemed to me those were—forgive me, beloved—very human solutions. A wolf surrenders only to those he trusts. I certainly did not trust this fire that was trying to devour me alive. Nor did the other solution suit my nature. Derian might contemplate trade, but humans have built entire societies around various kinds of trade.

"Wolves share in a strange fashion, but wolves do not trade. Never has one wolf said to another, 'I will give you this elk's lung for that bit of kidney.' We grab. We struggle. We take. Even when we feed our pups there is a bit of the same, for although we give to them, they must learn to take from each other or be ill prepared for the life they will live.

"So I thought these solutions were human solutions, not a wolf's solutions, and I resolved to fight the pain and hunt what it was that was hunting me. I ran from that hilltop, and forgot everything but my desire and my resolve. I would hunt. I would live. I would win—or I would die."

Firekeeper raised a hand and scratched lightly between Blind Seer's ears, moving herself slightly away from him as she did so. Heat was radiating from him, an indication of the tension he was hiding so well. He panted slightly to cool himself as he continued his account.

"Nose to the ground, I sought the scent of querinalo. At first, I could find no trace, and began to despair. Then I thought to seek my own scent. If I backtracked my trail, which I rationalized was the trail of my own journey through this illness, then I would find the root.

"It is not easy to track oneself, for learning to dismiss one's own scent is one of the first things a tracker learns, but soon I found it. The trail was a long one, and a weary one, but at last I reached my goal."

Firekeeper recalled the long hours she had sat sleepless at Blind Seer's side, watching as his paws grew cut and bloody although they moved against nothing but air, and she thought she had some idea just how arduous that journey must have been.

"I came to a place where a wolf just like me—a wolf who was me—both lay upon the ground and was suspended in the air. This wolf was intact, yet somehow I could see every element within it and knew its workings with an intellectual awareness I had never felt before. Intertwined with the organs and muscle, with the blood and brains and guts, was something I must call a bluish liquid, although it was neither blue, nor liquid, nor in any way like these things. Still, this is as close as I can reach with words.

"This blue liquid was what querinalo fed upon. I leaned closer and sniffed, trying to understand the nature of this thing within me, trying to learn what it might do. I will not pretend that I had not thought what talents might be useful to me. What if I had the ability within me to heal others as Doc does? That would be wonderful. I would not care to divine the future as Truth does, but what if I had a latent ability to find fresh water? That would also be useful. I considered that I might have a special sensitivity for humans, as Derian does for horses, and you do for beasts. This would be useful, and it would also explain why I am so impossibly drawn to you."

He licked the side of Firekeeper's face, so the human would not feel insulted. She grasped his scruff and rattled him gently.

"Which did you find?"

"None of these, and yet . . ." Blind Seer moved restlessly. "Neither did I sense that these were not there. I was trying to reason my way through this when I first heard the sheep laughing from somewhere behind me."

Firekeeper let her eyes fall shut. Such was the intensity in Blind Seer's tone that she felt as if she saw what had happened coming to life behind her closed lids.

THE LAUGHTER BLENDED the sound of human derision with a flat, ovine bleat. Blind Seer wheeled lightly, head raised, fangs bared, ears flattened against his skull. He had no expectations as to what he would see, but even without expectations he was astonished.

Safe on the craggy rise of rock behind him was a mountain sheep, but it was no mountain sheep like any of those he had seen before. The disproportionately tiny hooves on which it balanced its shaggy-coated weight shone like polished gold. The heavy, curving horn on its proudly carried head gave back iridescent rainbow sparkles in the clear morning light.

"Why are you laughing?" Blind Seer growled.

"What are you hunting?" the sheep replied.

"I hunt myself and what is in myself, so that I will know whether what is in me is worth preserving."

The sheep did not seem to need further explanation.

"And?" it said. "What did you find?"

"I found something and nothing," Blind Seer said. "I see that what I knew was there was there indeed, but I am no closer to knowing whether it is that which I should preserve, or that which I should let be destroyed."

The mountain sheep gave another mocking, bleating laugh.

"Are you saying that there is anything about you not worth preserving? Are you saying there is that which is you that is not worth fighting to keep?"

Blind Seer considered this, sitting and thumping at one ear with a hind leg.

"If my tail was trapped beneath a rock," he said at last, "and there was no moving that rock, I would be a fool to die for the sake of my tail. If I were fighting a puma, and that puma hooked me by a ear, I would be a fool to let the puma draw me into her grasp when by tearing the ear I could break free and get away. What if this thing within me is as an ear or a tail? Something I would dislike losing, but that if I lost I could preserve my life? Wouldn't I be a fool to struggle to keep it?"

"And what if it is as a paw or a leg?" the mountain sheep asked. "What of that?"

"A strong wolf can survive without a paw, or even without a leg," Blind Seer said boldly, "as long as the severing is clean and no infection takes hold."

"Two legs or two paws?" the sheep prompted. "What then?"

"Then," Blind Seer admitted, "even a strong wolf might do better to give over to death. It would be very hard to run and hunt without two legs or two paws. But that is not the question. The question is whether this thing I have seen within me is as a tail or an ear, or whether it is more vital than that."

"I think you know," the mountain sheep said. "I think you know and do not want to know. What do you say to that, wolf?"

"I say I have no idea what you mean," Blind Seer growled.

"Truly blind in refusing to see," the sheep taunted. "You shame yourself."

Blind Seer lunged for the sheep, but lost his footing on the sliding shale. The mountain sheep danced lightly in the crevice, casting shadows with the rainbows from its curving horns.

"You will know when you accept what your nose has already told you," the mountain sheep said. "Or in the name of old favors and new games, I will tell you—but only if you can catch me."

Blind Seer's paws were already sore, the pads bloody, but in reply he lunged upward. This time he landed on the ledge where the mountain sheep had balanced, but the mountain sheep had already bounded to the next and higher ledge. Howling, refusing to consider the bloody streaks his paws left on the rock, Blind Seer gathered himself and leapt. This time his jaws clamped down on a few stray strands of wool, but the mountain sheep was gone.

Blind Seer struggled after, into terrain for which a wolf was not well suited, and which was challenging even for the agile golden hooves of the mountain sheep. That other had given off laughing now. Blind Seer had the satisfaction of smelling the raw stink of its fear.

We must come to a meadow. We must come to some flat ground, the wolf thought, panting as he climbed. *Or we will come to some place so flat and so high that this creature can no longer flee. Then I will have it cornered and caught, and the answers it holds will be mine.*

And gradually, perhaps fearing that indeed it would become trapped, the mountain sheep ceased seeking higher and ever higher crags, leading them instead to a highland meadow like nothing Blind Seer had ever seen, even in dreams. The grass was thick, and running through it was as difficult as breaking trail through snow.

Wherever fell the rainbow light from the mountain sheep's horns flowers grew among the grass. Most were tiny, delicate things, but their perfume muddled the wolf's nose, slowing his tracking as the grass tangled his feet.

But Blind Seer pushed on, gathering himself and leaping as if he were a pup again, mousing with his litter mates in that tall spring grass. At least here the ground did not cut his sore pads, and if the flower scent muddled his nose, it could not blind his eyes.

He drove the sheep as his pack might drive an injured elk, darting back and forth, choosing a direction where the grass seemed less high, and clouds over the sun diminished the rainbows from the curving horns. In time his nose brought him news: the mountain sheep was growing both weary and afraid.

The mountain sheep wheeled at a place where the terrain favored neither wolf nor sheep. Its horns no longer dazzled, but were iron and ice. Its hooves still shone with the dull glimmer of gold, but here among the thick grass their agility counted for less than where they might bound from rock to rock. Still, although he had gained some advantage, Blind Seer did not give way to prideful carelessness.

Watching for the least motion, he challenged the sheep.

"Are you caught then? Tell me what I want to know and I will let you live."

"Tell you what you want to know?" the sheep echoed. "Or tell you what is right and true? These may not be the same."

Blind Seer acknowledged the truth in this. "Tell me what is right and true. Tell me the nature of this thing in me."

The mountain sheep danced nervously on those golden hooves.

"And what if you do not care for the answer? You already know it, and if you ran to that knowing as you have run after me, then you would already have made your choice."

"If I already know the answer," Blind Seer replied, trying to be reasonable, "then my comprehension has slid over it as even the sharpest gaze may slide over a fawn who lies still in the shadow-dappled sunlight."

"One who is hungry enough," the mountain sheep said, "does not miss the signs. Are you hungry enough?"

"How can I be hungry for a meal that I did not know existed until sickness drove me to this place? You set the challenge, sheep. Keep your part or I will hunt you until the option to flee no longer remains."

The mountain sheep curled down its head so that the curve of its horns stood between it and Blind Seer.

"Take care, wolf. You have no pack here to worry my flanks while you go for my throat. You are alone. In any case, who is to say I would talk more readily if you were to harm me?"

"You set the terms of this hunt," Blind Seer asserted again. "Speak or run."

For a long moment, Blind Seer thought the mountain sheep would indeed run, and he bunched tired muscles that he might spring while the sheep was turning. The clouds gathered more tightly, bringing the coolness the wolf craved, deadening the shine in the mountain sheep's horns until they resembled dull iron.

"Very well," the mountain sheep said. "The answer is 'yes.'"

"Yes?" Blind Seer was befuddled, but not so much that he lowered his guard. "Yes?"

"When you looked at the vision of yourself and saw the power coursing through it, you wondered whether it might be for healing or for divining or for any number of things. The answer is 'yes.' The power is there for all that, and for abilities you have not even imagined."

Blind Seer wanted to growl, but he was too sharp a hunter, had learned too much the years he had spent wandering with Firekeeper to not understand where this trail was heading. Still, he tried to believe for a moment longer that he was not what this strange creature was telling him.

"I have several talents," he said, "including those for healing and divining."

"You have one talent," the mountain sheep said, "and you know full well what it can do. You know it is not alien even to your people who strive so hard to deny it. Had you remained safely in the forests west of the Iron Mountains, you might never have known of it. However, you lacked the sense to stay home. Now the choice is yours. Is this a tail to gnaw off to preserve the whole? Or is this a heart, a belly, something you cannot live without? What is the answer, wolf? What is the answer, spellcaster?"

And with another mocking laugh, the mountain sheep wheeled and leapt. It was yet in mid-leap when Blind Seer caught it. He knocked it back and onto its side. While the mountain sheep kicked and flailed, trying to get those enormous, heavy horns into play, Blind Seer bit into its flank, ripped into its throat, and without pause or mercy slew it, reddening the thick green grass with the gushing, then ebbing flood of its life's blood.

"SPELLCASTER," FIREKEEPER ECHOED softly, trying to keep from shivering and failing. "So that was the talent that hid silently within you?"

"Spellcasting," the blue-eyed wolf echoed, trying to pull away from her, but she would not let him. "No simple talent.

No innocent ability, but the ugly ability to channel my will and another's life into the shape of my desire."

Firekeeper stared at him. She knew spellcasting was possible for Beasts. The puma Enigma had already revealed this was so, but finding such a force lurking within Blind Seer made him as strange to her as if he had suddenly become a mole or mouse.

She didn't know how to ask, and he did not offer, so silently between them loomed the question.

Had Blind Seer let querinalo burn the taint of sorcery from him or did it yet lurk within him? Was it as dead as Plik's ability to sense magic or did it remain, strengthened and fortified by his desire to continue being that which he had not known he was until fate in the form of Firekeeper's ever-present, insatiable curiosity had brought them to where the hidden springs must rise to the surface to be dammed or to burble forth?

XVII

FIREKEEPER WAS FINALLY leaving the Nexus Islands! It was all Tiniel could do not to dance a quick bouncing happy dance when Plik came trotting up the gateway hillside to share the news. Even so, he traced the steps in his imagination.

"She's leaving?" he said, hoping the joy in his voice would sound like astonishment. "Just like that?"

Plik nodded. "The clincher was the letter that came in today from Misheemnekuru. Some information my fellow maimalodalum found filled in the gaps in the research Harjeedian and Urgana's team have been doing. They've narrowed the possible location of Virim's fastness, and there's no longer any reason for her to delay. The only questions left are how she will get there, and who will accompany her."

Tiniel's imaginary dance stopped in mid-figure.

"How she will get there? Who will accompany her? I thought she'd go as she always does, on her own two feet. And I thought that at least Blind Seer and Derian would go with her. Don't they always?"

Plik gave a sorrowful shake of his head.

"Perhaps not this time," the maimalodalu said. "There is to be a public meeting to discuss matters. The yarimaimalom have agreed to take over the gate watch so that all the permanent residents of the Nexus Islands can be present."

"But what if something happens?" Tiniel stammered. "What about communication?"

"We've already arranged that if something happens, one of the wingéd folk will fly down to the meeting hall. Happily, all of those who can translate for them will be present."

Tiniel heard a soft, rough-voiced cough and saw the puma Enigma padding up. He noticed that other of the yarimaimalom—including a motley flock of raptors quite unlike what would usually be found in nature—had gathered and were perched on various of the gate structures. He had to admit the facility was probably better-guarded than usual.

"Enigma says that you should get moving," Plik translated. "He'll take charge here. Skea has already headed to the headquarters building."

"The meeting is now?" Tiniel said.

"Patience—at least when she is hot on the scent of something she desires—is not one of Firekeeper's virtues," Plik said with a squeak of laughter. "More importantly, Truth prophesied that the omens for success were best if we met immediately."

Tiniel turned and followed Plik down the hill. He had thought about refusing to attend, but when he had looked down toward the headquarters building he had seen what looked like the entirety of the Nexus Islands' human population—children down to infants included—streaming toward the building. He didn't want to draw comment by being the only one to refuse to attend. He might look odd—or odder than he did already.

Following his return from Gak, Tiniel had really tried to integrate himself more into the human society of the island. He'd made himself attend at least one meal a day in the common hall, and had faithfully taken watch stands on the gateway hill. However, no matter how hard he tried, he didn't seem to be able to feel part of the slowly integrating community. He didn't care to dandle other people's babies as Isende did. Small talk about the weather or the results of some card or dice game didn't interest him.

Although he could speak—at least a little—several languages learned since he arrived on the Nexus Islands, Tiniel's only written language was city-state-influenced Liglimosh. His and Isende's father hadn't taught them much of his own language beyond a few words that Skea and Kalyndra had tentatively identified as coming from a language spoken far to the west of their own birth land. That put Tiniel out of the running for the exclusive group that now assisted Harjeedian and Urgana in a mixture of further research and new organization of the library and archives.

Local politics—hardly more than town meetings—were something Tiniel might have found interesting, given that he had studied a great deal about how governments should be run in anticipation of joining the senate in Gak, but he kept away because in those meetings he would have been forced to associate with Derian. Worse, in those meetings Tiniel would have had to watch what Derian himself seemed unaware of—the increasingly admiring, even adoring looks that Isende lavished upon the tall, horse-faced horse's ass of a redhead.

Tiniel couldn't figure out quite why he was so bothered by Derian's apparent immunity to Isende's charms. After all, he didn't like the other man, so why should he want him to notice his sister? Tiniel told himself it was because Derian's thickheadedness was an insult to Isende, but sometimes late at night he wondered if it was because Derian's lack of attention to Isende robbed Tiniel of an excuse to get into a fight with the other man.

And now Firekeeper's leaving, Tiniel thought, hope flaring in him anew. *No matter what Plik says, surely Derian will go with her. She's hardly competent anywhere in civilization. She barely speaks her own language, much less Liglimosh. He's fluent in two languages, and has a smattering of that New Kelvinese. Certainly, he'll go. Plik's probably just indulging in wishful thinking.*

Lately, the large hall in the headquarters building had been kept clear, used for dances or dramatic performances, even as a playground for the small children, for the weather on the Nexus Islands did not always invite outdoor games. Now, however, it was furnished much as it had been in the days when the Once Dead ruled. Rising tiers of seats were arrayed about the edges, providing ample seating for the entire community, even allowing for the various yarimaimalom who were attending.

A long table had been set up front and center, and a small knot of people were seated there, including Derian, Ynamynet, and Wort. Wort had once been among those set to guard Isende and Tiniel. Now he had become the quartermaster, managing the Nexus Islands' limited supplies.

Off to one end of the long table, pen and ink in hand, sat Frostweed, one of the few Once Dead to survive that strange battle when the Once Dead's own magic had turned against them. Firekeeper and Blind Seer were sprawled on the floor to one side of the head table, part but not part of this ruling cabal.

No translators were provided, for unlike at the meeting some moonspans ago at which the current Nexan government had been formed, a marked effort had been made to make sure that everyone present shared at least one language. Liglimosh had been chosen, because all the New Worlders, and many of the Old World residents, already spoke or understood at least some. All those who didn't speak it already had been teamed with one or more who did, and progress had been astonishingly good, fueled by the awareness that in a very real sense the Nexans now had only each other.

Tiniel located Isende with almost supernatural ease. She was seated down front, off to one side, helping tend—as usual—her neighbor's small children. She was bouncing one small, round-cheeked creature of indeterminate gender on her knee, probably crooning something sweet in its ear, but Tiniel noticed her gaze was fixed on the front table where, oblivious of her adoration, Derian was going over some final notes with Ynamynet.

Soon after Tiniel and Plik settled down, the last arrivals trickled in and the large doors were closed. As best as Tiniel could tell from an informal census, no one was missing, not even the head of the kitchens, who rarely left the heated, steamy rooms back of the common cafeteria, or the tall, gnarled Tavetchian who nearly lived on the small vessel from which he checked the traps and lines he had strung around the island.

Ynamynet rose from her seat, and the buzzing chatter in the room stilled.

"Most of you know why this meeting was called," she said with her usual cool bluntness. "A moonspan and a half ago, it was decided that we needed to learn what we could about querinalo in the hope of finding a way to defeat it. After many, many days of researching, and several long trips between here and our new allies on Misheemnekuru, we have gathered the information we need to begin the next stage of our search."

She continued, summarizing what had been learned about the mysterious figure known only as Virim, and their suppositions as to his motivations in creating querinalo. She did not, Tiniel noticed, mention the Meddler or that he had contributed several of the bits of information that had strung the entire complicated web together. Tiniel didn't blame her—or even Derian—for leaving the Meddler out of the picture. Events were complicated enough without trying to explain the contributions of a ghost whose antecedents were, to say the least, untrustworthy.

Besides, Tiniel was all too aware that he had been one of the Meddler's playing pieces, and he was just as glad that particular matter didn't come up for discussion.

"Within the last few hours," Ynamynet continued, "we have received information that makes us fairly certain that a search if not for Virim himself, at least for where he once resided, might be successfully undertaken. We have found several mentions of a fastness in the mountains of the far, far north in the New World. We now think that we have sufficient information that someone might be able to locate it. There is just one problem. Derian?"

The tall redhead rose. Behind him and to one side Wort started unrolling what Tiniel realized was a piece of canvas on which a rough map had been painted with broad brushstrokes of dark brown ink.

Derian took a pointer from the table, and, looking very self-conscious, began to indicate areas on the map.

"Right. This map shows the New World, so the Nexus Islands aren't on it. This here is the location of the Setting Sun stronghold, where our one gate to the New World is. Here is Gak. Here is the river that acts as the border between Liglim and the city-states."

He moved the pointer up a bit north, tracing the coastline. "Here is u-Vreeheera, one of the major Liglimom cities. Here is u-Seeheera, their capital city. Out here, in the bay, sort of flanking both, is Misheemnekuru, where our allies the maimalodalum dwell. Everyone with me?"

Heads nodded, a light wind blowing through a field of multi-hued flowers. A few voices spoke encouragement.

"Good." Derian turned back to the map and placed his pointer on the location of the Setting Sun stronghold again. "Before I go any further, I want to talk a little about distances. See how short this line is?"

Murmurs of agreement.

"That's the distance between the stronghold and Gak. Even without wagons or horses to slow down progress, covering that distance takes a couple of days. From Gak to the border takes about a quarter of a moonspan. From Gak to u-Seeheera, even if the travelers in question are Firekeeper and Blind Seer, who don't bother with baggage or gear, the journey takes four or five days. Let me stress that travel time is based on not stopping for long hunts, just eating what they could scrounge along the trail. They didn't sleep much either. A more reasonable estimate would be eight or even ten days for more usual travelers."

There was a small titter of laughter at this last comment, but most of the Nexans looked appropriately serious. A few nodded, or whispered comments to their closer neighbors.

Derian waited for this information to sink in. When the small conversations around the room had stilled, he moved the pointer again.

"See this broad, deep inlet? That's what divides the northern lands where I was born from these southern lands. That inlet is a large part of why there was so little communication between these parts of the New World after the coming of querinalo. It's rough and hosts nasty weather patterns. Crossing it isn't easy. Better is crossing out here, on the main ocean."

Again the pointer moved. This time it touched on the northern mainland.

"Here are the northern lands: Stonehold here; across the Fox River are Bright Bay and Hawk Haven—lands that in a few years will join to become the kingdom of Bright Haven, ancestors willing. Here, even further north, is Waterland, down east by the ocean. Lastly, there is New Kelvin in the middle-northeastern uplands."

Derian swept his pointer in a great swath across the expanse of canvas, emphasizing the distance involved. It was vast. Tiniel thought he knew where this discussion was headed, even before Derian put his pointer on the map again, indicating an area to the west of New Kelvin, west of a jagged barrier of mountains.

"Out here, somewhere, probably in the western foothills of these mountains, is where our research indicates that Virim established his base, a fastness guarded by mountains on one flank, and by wild lands which may even have been inhospitable to the Royal Beasts. I have told you something of the time involved traveling between the Setting Sun stronghold and u-Seeheera."

He indicated the map again, and Tiniel had to grudgingly admit that the setup had been well done. In contrast, the distance looked minuscule.

"Traveling from the south to the north across the divide provided by the inlet can take a moonspan or more by sea—and that is if a ship is ready. We know that the journey can be done by land—or at least that it was done some fifteen years ago. We also know that the person who made that journey was gone for years, for he frequently had to backtrack in order to find a clear passage. Even after the inlet has been crossed, the journey is not over. Even for Firekeeper and Blind Seer six or seven moonspans, quite possibly more, would pass before they would be in the right general vicinity to begin their search.

"You know that winter comes earlier the further north you go. You may also know that the cold winter weather grows more vicious in the highlands. Here and now we are in late spring. It is hard to imagine how quickly winter will come there—or maybe for those of you who have seen how quickly the warm weather leaves these islands it is not."

Derian shrugged and put down his pointer.

"I'm not much of a speaker, but I've done my best to show you the problem. What we wanted all of you to do here today is start working on a solution. The problem is distance and the time it takes to cover distance. The problem is how much longer do we wait to find out if we can eliminate querinalo from our lives. The problem is, the fastest solution to both these problems creates new problems. I can see from the expressions on many of your faces that you're ahead of me, but I'll ask the question anyhow. Do we open a gate or gates to speed Firekeeper and Blind Seer on their way?"

There was no shocked outburst, no shouting to be heard. Derian was absolutely right, Tiniel thought bitterly. Even before he asked his question, most of the adults present had already asked it of themselves.

Xaha, the dark-skinned refugee from Tey-yo, asked, "What gate and where?"

Ynamynet rose and Derian slid into his seat.

"The gate to New Kelvin, most probably," Ynamynet said.

"It would be the closest to where Firekeeper and Blind Seer need to go. We have located the entry point on this side, but we will not know until we try if the gate remains intact."

Ynamynet glanced down at Derian, and he nodded for her to continue.

"The likelihood is," she said, "that it will be. Almost unique among the colonies, the New Kelvinese did not move to actively destroy magical artifacts."

Tiniel was surprised to find himself on his feet and hear his voice asking, "Will just Firekeeper and Blind Seer go? I mean, are they the best people to do this? I mean, she can't even read. What is she supposed to do when she gets to this Virim's stronghold or whatever?"

Firekeeper stirred from where she sat on the floor alongside Blind Seer, but she did not protest against the justness of Tiniel's comments.

Ynamynet looked at Derian, and they changed places.

"There has been some discussion of this matter," Derian admitted. "However, given the recent activity of the gates, we are reluctant to remove any more of our strength from the Nexus Islands than is absolutely necessary."

Derian did not clarify exactly what he meant by "our" and Tiniel glimpsed a flicker of an ironic smile on Ynamynet's face before she schooled herself to neutrally polite listening once more.

Derian continued, "Firekeeper and Blind Seer will be going as preliminary scouts. Blind Seer actually reads somewhat better than Firekeeper does."

He grinned over at his friend, and she wrinkled her nose at him in an expression of mock disgust. Blind Seer beat the ground with his tail in amusement.

"Blind Seer wouldn't be able to translate documents written in a language strange to him, or even in an archaic form of a modern language, but he can arrive at conclusions that may help them either to select documents to bring back, or to at least advise who might be best to send on a second journey."

Tiniel nodded stiffly, and even remembered to thank Derian

before he sat down. He hardly heard what was being discussed around him: arrangements for returning through the gate, how Firekeeper planned to deal with the situation if she were detected by the New Kelvinese, the likelihood that Virim's stronghold might still be occupied. He needed all his willpower to keep his disappointment from showing.

Firekeeper was going away, but Derian wasn't. Derian even had the gall to announce that he had arranged for the government of Liglim—who apparently owed Derian a favor or two—to soothe the ruffled feelings of the Bright Haven ambassador, who had apparently been rather annoyed that his assistant had not returned to his post.

This revelation crashed Tiniel's hopes that Derian would be called back to his duties, and leave the southlands, and Tiniel's too trusting sister, alone.

By the time the meeting had ended, a vote had been passed to reawaken the gate into New Kelvin. Tiniel thought he had voted in favor. After all, Firekeeper might get herself into some mess that only Derian could get her out of. However, as the crowd streamed from the meeting hall, everyone chattering to whoever was near about the possibilities that were opening to them, Tiniel walked alone and in silence.

Never before had he felt so isolated, so imprisoned, so eager to do something, anything, to restore him to the feeling that he had control over his life.

❧❧❧

"REMEMBER," DERIAN SAID to Firekeeper, as they watched the preliminary stages of the ritual that would open the new gate, "from what we saw the first time this gate was opened, it came out somewhere underground. It's possible that you're going to be somewhere in that maze of tunnels beneath Dragon's Breath. You know what to do if that's the case."

Firekeeper looked at her oldest human friend with affectionate exasperation.

"If possible, get out, no one wiser. If must see people, ask for Peace or Citrine. If no them, then ask for Toriovico, the Healed One."

"Right," Derian said. "Don't hurt anyone. Diplomatic relations between Hawk Haven and New Kelvin are solid these days. You may dismiss your connection to House Kestrel and King Tedric, but if you're caught skulking in sewers or have to be hauled out of some pit trap, you could do some real damage."

Firekeeper nodded. "Spy."

"That's right. You'd likely be taken for a spy. We know better than most that Toriovico is not an absolute monarch. He needs the goodwill of . . ."

Firekeeper let the words drift over her ears, heard but not really registered. She didn't think anyone would catch her and Blind Seer, but she also wasn't going to risk causing trouble for Hawk Haven, or for Derian and the Nexans.

"You remember the arrangements for getting you back here?" Derian prompted.

"One time each day, same time," Firekeeper said, "someone here will open gate and check if we need trip back."

Derian heard the exasperation in her voice and had the grace to look sheepish.

"Sorry. I admit, I'm worried. I'm sending you off on the trail of something as insubstantial as a curse. Who knows whether it's a waste of time and effort? Worse, what if it isn't? What if you find someone still alive there? What type of power might an immortal sorcerer have accumulated in the past hundred or so years?"

Firekeeper grinned and touched her Fang.

"Iron should still bite and hard. In forge here they make iron heads for my arrows. Most important, I not forget this. I have not forgotten how Once Dead almost defeat themselves, not us them. I will not forget what we hunt is an strong old one, not a weak one. But think . . . Can it really live all this time?"

Did Blind Seer already kill him in a dream? Might we simply find what we want waiting?

She didn't say any of this, but she wanted to reassure Derian.

"Too, we go where my people are. Not all love me as my pack do, is true, but still, Blind Seer and I are of them, and they should help us."

"That's true," Derian said, relaxing some. "You managed well enough on Misheemnekuru, and then again here, and these yarimaimalom are not the ones who raised you. I'll try and remember that when I wake up in a cold sweat for worry."

Firekeeper stood on her toes and kissed him on one cheek. Blind Seer gave Derian a sloppy lick, standing on his hind legs to do so. That broke the tension.

"Get out of here, both of you!" Derian laughed.

Firekeeper nicked Blind Seer's ear, then her own wrist. When the blood from these wounds had been smeared on the gate, Kalyndra began to sing—not just chant as Ynamynet usually did, but sing—the spell that would open the portal. When the rock shimmered and changed character, the wolves strode forward.

They did not look back.

WHEN THEY EMERGED on the other side of the gate, they paused to get their bearings. The one earlier transition that had been performed to test the gate had told them very little.

When Firekeeper had come across with Ynamynet, the area in which they had emerged had been completely dark, so dark that the normally poised Once Dead had reached out and touched Firekeeper on the arm, clearly to reassure herself that the wolf-woman was there. Her hand felt like ice, but other than this sign of fear, Ynamynet had waited with absolute patience until Firekeeper had touched her lips to her ear and given her report.

"No scent, other than ours. Closedness with sulfur taint. Underground, surely. Dragon's Breath probably."

Ynamynet, thoroughly briefed before this as to the basics of New Kelvinese geography, had asked for no explanation, only nodded. Firekeeper had felt the motion.

"Scout?" the wolf-woman had asked. "Or back?"

"Scout a little," had been Ynamynet's reply, "but don't lose me."

Firekeeper had scouted, but despite her excellent night vision, she could not see where there was no light at all. After stubbing her bare toes a few times—and swallowing the squeak of pain—she had made her way back to Ynamynet.

"Without light, I learn nothing but that I think we are alone."

"Make a small light," Ynamynet said. "I'll need it to get us back in any case."

Firekeeper had carried a hot coal, candle, and shielded candle lantern. When she kindled a light, the single candle flame seemed impossibly bright. It showed that they were in a spacious subterranean chamber, carved from the living rock. The gate dominated one wall. No other furnishings remained.

In mutual agreement, the Once Dead and the wolf-woman resisted the impulse to scout further. Ynamynet remembered all too well other openings of old gates, done in the days when King Veztressidan was still in power, and she had told Firekeeper tales of times when all that had seemed empty and peaceful had not been so.

Better Firekeeper return with Blind Seer, and hopefully make their departure from this place and New Kelvin, no one the wiser for the invasion.

A full day had passed before they had returned. Now, once again Firekeeper stood in the subterranean chamber deep beneath the capital city of New Kelvin. Even before she felt Blind Seer stiffen at her side, she was aware something had changed.

For one, there was light. Faint light. Either from a dim source or at a distance, but unmistakably light. For another, Firekeeper could smell at least one, probably more than one, person. The New Kelvinese practiced elaborate facial adornment, and the scent of the cosmetics was unmistakable.

Firekeeper slid her Fang from its sheath and held it lightly balanced in her hand. She did not want to kill anyone, but she had no proof that whoever had made the light felt the same.

"Blind Seer," she asked. *"What is there?"*

A human voice spoke before the wolf could reply.

"I do not think I had really believed the legends," it said, speaking Pellish in familiar measured tones. "But apparently one can pass through solid stone."

Firekeeper swallowed an impulse to yip in recognition. The voice belonged to one who had been enemy, then friend, and who might well, in the years that had passed since she had seen him last, be enemy again.

The light had come closer, and she blinked, but did not shield her eyes from its relative brilliance. In it she beheld a slender, elegant man dressed in long-sleeved robes that did not quite conceal that his right arm had been amputated. His bone-white hair had receded so far that all that remained was a long white braid down his back. Round spectacles did not hide several bluish green tattoos on his face, nor were they intended to do so, for such ornaments were not only common, but highly respectable among the New Kelvinese.

Beside Grateful Peace stood someone Firekeeper might not have recognized, for the years passing had changed a round-cheeked child into a girl on the verge of being a woman. Citrine, formerly Shield, now the adopted daughter of Grateful Peace and probably carrying some other name Firekeeper had never learned, stood beside her adopted father. She showed promise of someday matching her sister Princess Sapphire for height and strength. Right now she seemed all arms and legs. Her reddish gold hair was dressed after an elaborate New Kelvinese fashion, and she wore New Kelvinese robes. A tiny stylized figure of some sort was tattooed on her right temple in blue almost the same color as her eyes. Her smile was as warm and enthusiastic as when Firekeeper had first met her as a girl of eight, unhaunted by the madness and sorrow that had still scored her when they had parted.

Reassured by that smile and the fact that no one was calling for guards, Firekeeper decided to match Grateful Peace's casual tone.

"Is not solid stone," she said, "or is, but when spell is done, stone opens to gate."

"Not much more articulate," Grateful Peace replied, "but

still accurate in your own fashion. So this is a magical gate, then. I thought as much when I inspected it earlier, and compared what I saw with what I had read in old books. Do you come from Hawk Haven in this unorthodox fashion?"

Firekeeper shook her head, but chose not to clarify further until she was certain Grateful Peace remained a friend. Given the possibility that she might need to explain how she had come to New Kelvin, Derian and Ynamynet had worked out between them what they thought was safe for her to say.

"Perhaps from that land to the far south," Peace continued imperturbably. "Liglim, correct? We have had reports, you see. There is even some talk of sending an embassy of our own."

Firekeeper blinked, deciding to take refuge from a direct answer in pretending not to understand.

Peace glanced past her, and she realized that his seemingly casual conversation had been intended to keep her from insisting they move on while he waited to see if she and Blind Seer were the forerunners of an invading force.

"No one else coming through?" he asked.

Firekeeper shook her head. "Just me and Blind Seer."

"Is that the whole truth? You see," Peace smiled, "I have the means of knowing when the gate is used. I would dislike learning you had lied to me."

"Tell him," Blind Seer said.

"Tomorrow, near this time," Firekeeper said. "Someone will come to check for us and see if we need to go back. That one will go no further than here to see, then back."

"So you cannot work this gate yourself?"

Firekeeper shook her head. "No. Is something only one with training can do."

"And somewhere you have found someone who can open the old gates," Grateful Peace said. "Interesting indeed. May I invite you to join me for a meal?"

Firekeeper now knew when what sounded like an invitation was in reality an order.

"We come," she said, and tried to look pleased. It wasn't that difficult. Citrine was standing with her hands decorously folded in front of her, but her smile hadn't diminished and there was a hint of a bounce beneath the skirts of her long robe.

"I smell no threat from either of them," Blind Seer reported. *"Both smell of pleasure and a bit of astonishment. I would guess that although Peace knew the gate was in use, he did not know who had used it. He is happy to find a friend, not an enemy."*

"Is he armed?" Firekeeper asked.

"Both he and Citrine carry weapons beneath those full sleeves. I smell the oil used to season the metal. There is the stink of hardened leather as well. I would guess they each wear something to protect their vitals."

Firekeeper smiled. She was pleased that the intervening years had not diminished in any way Grateful Peace's guile, and that father seemed to be teaching some of the same skills to daughter. Citrine had been reared to be defenseless, and many had taken advantage of that. There were reasons for Citrine's smile beyond her pleasure at seeing old friends.

That pleasure was real enough. As Grateful Peace led the way through the tunnels via a route he promised would take them up directly into his own quarters in Thendulla Lypella—the exclusive complex on the northern edge of Dragon's Breath—Citrine dropped her formality and hurried to give both Firekeeper and Blind Seer hugs.

Her embrace confirmed the presence of armor and weapon, but Firekeeper felt no threat. Her own Fang had returned to its Mouth almost without her being aware. If Blind Seer did not smell threat, there was no threat to fear.

"You are taller," Firekeeper said, hearing herself sounding like every idiot human she had ever encountered.

"Did you expect her to get smaller?" Blind Seer sniggered.

Firekeeper ignored him, and Citrine merely straightened a bit in pride.

"I'm not as tall as Sapphire, yet, but I'm taller than Ruby or Opal," she said proudly.

"Then you see Sapphire?" Firekeeper asked.

"Last autumn," Citrine said. "She went to Plum Orchard,

and we crossed to meet her. She was showing off Sun. He's a little boy now, not a baby, and talking so almost everyone can understand him."

Firekeeper smiled. "I not see since Prince Sun he was infant in wraps. Derian say from letters he hear Sun do well, but time goes so far."

Citrine froze in midstep. "Have you seen Elise? She's at the embassy in Liglim, too, right? How is she? She and Doc got married you know. Sapphire sends letters, to us here, telling us things, but we haven't heard much yet this spring. The White Water is still chancy for crossing, and the interior roads slow things further."

Firekeeper had forgotten how long news took to travel without yarimaimalom willing to serve as couriers.

"I have secret," the wolf-woman said. "Can you keep? Peace, too?"

Grateful Peace had been undoing some locks on a heavy iron gate. "Unless it affects the safety of New Kelvin, I can keep a secret."

Firekeeper grinned. "No such. Elise and Doc have baby girl. She is very small still. Called Elexa, for the queen."

Citrine lifted her long skirts and did a frolicking dance in the corridor. Grateful Peace was more formal, but he looked equally pleased.

"Elexa," Citrine said. "That's good. Grand Duchess Rosene can't be annoyed at the baby not being named for her—even if it is her first granddaughter—if the baby is named for the queen. She'll probably praise Elise for her political sense."

Firekeeper had almost forgotten the touchy politics of Hawk Haven's ruling families in the years she had been away. After the small-town simplicity of the Nexus Islands, and the regimented hierarchy of the Liglimom, they seemed more chaotic than ever.

Peace seemed to sense Firekeeper's sudden dismay, and gestured them through the newly opened gate. On the other side was a small foyer leading into a long flight of steep stairs cut directly into the rock.

"Enough chatter now, Citrine. Run ahead and make certain

none of the servants are about and in a position to gossip. In fact, send any who are about home early. We can make do for ourselves and our guests."

Citrine responded with an alacrity that told Firekeeper that she was accustomed to such commands. Grateful Peace locked the gate behind them and gestured up the stairs.

"Please," he said, "follow me. I believe you have much to tell me, and I believe I have a piece or two of information that will interest you as well."

XVIII

FIREKEEPER ACCEPTED WATER and the dish of highland strawberries Citrine brought in for her. There was a shallow dish of water for Blind Seer, as well, but Citrine's expression as she turned to her adopted father was unhappy.

"There is no raw meat," she said, "only cooked. If I go to the market and buy raw meat, especially after sending the servants away . . . I only had to dismiss the cook, and she was glad enough to go, but still, it may raise questions."

Grateful Peace inclined his head in approval. "Well thought. Even though no one saw our visitors arrive, someone might wonder."

Remembering the elaborate spy networks in New Kelvin, Firekeeper knew what the pair were discussing. Again she was pleased by this evidence that Citrine was receiving a good—if rather odd by the standards of her class and culture—education.

She hastened to reassure them. "We are fed, well fed before leaving."

"Then I think we can dispense with supplying a meal, Citrine," Grateful Peace said.

The girl took a seat from which she could watch both Grateful Peace and the two wolves. She had brought strawberries for herself and Grateful Peace, and now offered a small pitcher of cream. Firekeeper accepted, for although they had cattle on the Nexus Islands, most of the cream was reserved for cooking.

"Berries is very good," she said. "Sweet. There are none like these where I come from."

"Would you like to tell me where that is?" Grateful Peace said. "I am no longer a member of the Dragon's Three, nor do I hold any official position. This dwelling and the other privileges I enjoy are the Healed One's reward to me for performing a task few know even exists."

Firekeeper hid a shiver. She knew what that task was, and the cost exacted from Grateful Peace for performing it.

"Before you sympathize too much," Blind Seer said dryly, *"notice that he has not said he would keep whatever you told him in confidence. He has only implied that this would be so. Get a promise, and make him tell you how he knew the gate was being used before being too free with what we can tell, otherwise we will have no teeth left when the time comes for us to bite."*

Firekeeper laid her hand on the wolf's shoulder in mute thanks for his counsel, and smiled.

"Is good that Healed One treat you so well," she said. "That means he is good One, and that he knows a well-fed hunter remains strong for the next hunt. I like Toriovico, and I think he be more interested than disturbed in what I can say. Still, I think I must ask that you and Citrine promise not to say or to write or in any way give sniff or scent or howl of what Blind Seer and I tell."

Grateful Peace beamed, an expression so unfamiliar to Firekeeper that she found herself blinking in astonishment.

"Wherever you have been since you were stolen away from Hawk Haven, you have learned a great deal about diplomacy. No more leap for the throat of the problem, I see."

Firekeeper nodded. "I have learned that not all problems are solved by this way. Some are better served by hunting around the edges."

"I am pleased," Grateful Peace said. "Your more impulsive ventures have not always been kind to you or your allies."

Firekeeper nodded. "Is true. Am glad you is pleased, but still you and Citrine have not give me your word not to tell."

Grateful Peace considered. "As long as you do not tell me something that will immediately weaken the security of New Kelvin . . ."

"Or Bright Haven," Citrine piped in.

"Then we will listen and keep what you tell us to ourselves. We will not relate it in speech or writing or in any other form of communication known to human or Beast, and we will take care not to be overheard or detected in matters related to whatever you choose to confide."

Firekeeper glanced at Blind Seer.

"Seems reasonable," the wolf replied. *"Offer him a morsel to tease his appetite, then ask him how he came to know about the gate."*

"I accept your words," Firekeeper said formally. "You ask from where we come. We come from an island that is a place where a long time ago the Old World sorcerers made many gates. Place is in Old World, but far from other places in Old World, so is only place in Old World we have been."

Remembering how the New Kelvinese remained among the few residents of the New World to recall the Old with any longing, she stopped there, thinking this was enough.

"How did you come to this island of gates?" Peace asked.

Firekeeper shook her head. "Our question, now. Like you, Blind Seer and I promise not to speak of anything you tell us unless it touches those we is promised to protect."

Grateful Peace nodded. "Fair enough. Tell me, was this time the first the gate had been activated?"

"Once before," Firekeeper replied, not liking this answering her question with another question, but thinking Peace might have a reason beyond merely attempting to gain something more before giving anything away. "Just to test."

"That is what I thought," Grateful Peace said. "How did I know? The dragon told me."

Firekeeper looked at the thaumaturge in horror. She knew

the price the dragon Peace held bound had extracted for its services. It seemed a high price to pay for so little.

Grateful Peace correctly assessed her expression, and hastened to reassure her.

"No, I haven't started spending what years remain to me lightly," he said. "Would you be surprised if I told you that in some odd way I think the dragon has come to like me?"

"Yes. Is not a liking creature, from what I remember."

Grateful Peace nodded. "True, but what you encountered was the monster unbound after long, long years of isolation. There was a reason that those few legends that recalled it named it 'the Dragon of Despair.' However, more apt was the name we learned later, 'the Despairing Dragon.' I cannot say that the creature is anything like a comfortable, easy force to have linked to me, and it still extracts the price it made me offer. However, it volunteers bits of knowledge from time to time."

"I wonder why?" Blind Seer asked.

Firekeeper repeated the question aloud.

Grateful Peace considered. "I believe I amuse it, now. Initially, I believe there was some malice involved."

Firekeeper glanced over at Citrine, wondering how much the girl knew of all this, but the still rounded features were placid, unguarded, and yet gave nothing away.

Grateful Peace went on. "I doubt you will ever forget the terms by which the dragon was bound."

Firekeeper had not, having nearly offered herself as the one who would hold the other side of that bargain.

"The cost," Peace said, "even for holding the dragon is high, but if one wishes to draw on the dragon's powers, the price is higher still. Melina, Consolor to the Healed One, thought she had found a way to use the dragon, and yet to avoid paying the price."

Again Firekeeper glanced at Citrine. The girl gave her a reassuring smile.

"It's okay, Firekeeper. You've been away a long time. I really have learned to accept my mother for what she was. What Peace is saying isn't hurting me."

Firekeeper relaxed. One thing she thought was good about being a wolf is that no one ever thought ill of friend for being concerned about friend.

Peace smiled at his adopted daughter. "Citrine makes me very proud. But, I was speaking of the dragon. I sincerely believe the dragon did not expect me to leave it alone. It expected that some time or another, the temptation to draw upon its powers to make myself more feared or influential would arise. I did not, even when demonstrating the force I had at my command would have made my life easier, for many were displeased to see one they had seen branded a traitor now so high in the Healed One's favor. Many did not trust my honesty and fidelity to my native land."

Citrine interrupted. "It didn't help that he adopted me, either. They thought he was doing something political. They couldn't forget that my sister is queen of Hawk Haven."

"They still don't forget," Peace said fondly, "but I think they have grown more accustomed to the idea."

Firekeeper nodded. "Is like me. No one forget I am wolf, but now everyone is so used to this that they would think stranger if I suddenly was not wolf."

"Correct," Peace said. "In any case, when the dragon realized I was not going to draw on its powers, it tried tempting me with what you might call free tastes or samples of what it could do. I continued to resist. In time I think the dragon came to respect my restraint. I think it also came to realize that I was not using its powers not only because of the price I would pay, but also—and more importantly—because I respected it as a creature of free will, one who should not be treated as a tool. So while we are not friends, I think in a strange fashion we have become allies.

"When the dragon informed me that a gate long dormant beneath Thendulla Lypella had been used, I thanked it. I located the gate from old maps and a few hints the dragon granted me. A short while ago, the dragon hinted that the gate was going to be used again, and I hurried down to greet whoever or whatever should come forth."

Firekeeper considered the length of the ritual used to open

the gate, and thought that if the dragon informed Peace just when the ritual began, the timing would work.

"What you do if not me, or someone harmless like me?" she asked.

"I would never insult you and Blind Seer by referring to either of you as harmless," Peace said with a dry chuckle. "But I understand your question. There are barriers built into the tunnels along there. The previous day I had inspected them, and done some minor repairs to make certain they would still function. That was one reason why we stood where we did. If something less inclined to be friendly had come through that portal, the barriers would have been lowered immediately."

"You not tell Toriovico, the Healed One, of the gate?"

Peace smiled. "I did not. I prefer not to mention my moderated relationship with the dragon, and although I might have come up with an elaborate explanation that would suit the situation, I prefer not to lie to my monarch. I did, however, leave a full explanation locked away where it would be found if I vanished, thereby fulfilling my responsibilities to my ruler."

Firekeeper nodded. "Good. Gates are dangerous, once someone knows how to open. Now, I answer you."

As briefly as she could, although with inevitable interruptions and requests for clarification, Firekeeper gave a true account of how they had found the first gate, where it had led them, and what they had done to secure their hold. For now, she said nothing of the Meddler, nor of querinalo, nor did she give a very precise idea where the Setting Sun stronghold might be found. The New Kelvinese were not a seagoing people, but the Waterlanders to the east were almost as home at sea as on land, and their services could quite possibly be bought with such interesting information.

Firekeeper didn't think either Grateful Peace or the Healed One would invade a land so far from their own, but she wasn't taking any chances.

Her throat was dry and she was very tired of talking when she finished her account. However, she knew Grateful Peace too well to think he had not noticed the gaps in her tale. She waited for his questions, and was surprised when he neglected to examine her evasions and instead came to the present moment.

"And what brings you here?" he asked. "Is there something in New Kelvin you need or desire?"

"Not New Kelvin," Firekeeper said. "I not think. West of mountains, but New Kelvin was closest to start. Save moonspans and moonspans of walking."

"I see, and what would you have done if the gate had been somewhere more public?"

Firekeeper smiled. "We think this, but gates not usually public. Old World rulers prefer to be like shadows, come and go, no one but their own know how, especially to here in New World where they wish to keep colonists not so knowing how they do what they do."

"There is an element of sense in that," Grateful Peace agreed. "Wonder and awe can control a population as or more easily than force. Some would have known the secret, but their rulers would certainly have made certain that they were either in no position to tell, or had ample incentive not to tell. But I stray from the point. Why are you so interested in this nameless place to the northwest?"

Firekeeper's allies had agreed that on this point, as on so many others, some version of the truth was preferable.

"There is a sickness in the Old World," she said. "Harjeedian and others have looked much at old papers and things, and they think this sickness may have come from the New World first, but be worse for people of Old World."

She paused, struggling for the correct words. The concept was not an easy one to explain given her limited vocabulary. Happily, Peace seemed to understand her already.

"I see," he said. "We in New Kelvin know something of this. Waterland's climate is very different from our own, for all that we share a border. Their land is wet, and in summer there are many miasmas and fevers that do not occur here. We have observed that while those born in Waterland are not necessarily immune to these sicknesses, what makes them merely feverish can kill one of our people."

Firekeeper nodded. "This sickness is like that. Harjeedian

think that in northwest we may learn what we need to make medicine or treatment. I am not the one who will make this, but Blind Seer and I go first, because we can scout more easily."

"So I might find other visitors coming through the tunnels?" Grateful Peace asked. "That could be difficult."

"That," Firekeeper said, "is for you to think. Are other ways to go, only more slow. Blind Seer and me not even need go back by gate if you not think so is good. We would send message slow way. Maybe people die because is slow, but still scouting is done."

Grateful Peace did not react at all to the image of people dying, but the Firekeeper had not expected him to do so. He was too skilled at hiding his true thoughts and feelings. All Firekeeper had intended was to plant a seed of potential sympathy.

Instead he said thoughtfully, almost idly, "What happens if I refuse to let you leave here?"

Firekeeper grinned, but it was a wolf's grin and held no warmth, only the promise of a fight. She had this speech prepared and polished.

"We think of this, because although we think gate will not be seed, we cannot be sure. If I not come back, then checking would be done. You know the Royal Beasts watch human cities. I am to leave word with one of these when I go from here. They will pass on that word. If Blind Seer and I vanish without word, then time will go and in time—maybe long time, but not so long as things of politics are made—then letter will go to Hawk Haven and Bright Bay and Earl Kestrel and others.

"Letters will say that Firekeeper who is also Lady Blysse go into New Kelvin, and has not been seed for a long time since. Questions would be asked, many, and Earl Kestrel at least would probably not want New Kelvinese things to come into Kestrel lands. Might be a little problem, might be start of bigger problems. Also Liglimom like me, too, very much, and might not want to be friends with little land, far away that is not good to their friend."

Grateful Peace nodded. "Very well thought out, but you would still be imprisoned—or dead."

Firekeeper shrugged. "I am wolf. I hunt for my pack. In hunt of elk, I might be kicked and killed. I am not human to wait forever because someday, sometime I might be killed."

The Illuminator actually looked approving. "Very good. Very well planned. And I somehow doubt that the threats you have mentioned would be the only dangers we would risk if the last place you were seen was our land. As you say, the Royal Beasts watch human cities, and they like you even more than these Liglimom do. Yes. Ample reason to let you go on your way—if I had ever intended otherwise."

Firekeeper let him see her relax, but in truth she had not thought the threat was a real one. By now, having had a chance to sort through the odors of cosmetics and perfumes, Blind Seer would have scented a change in mood. Humans gave themselves away by forgetting that just because they did not use their sense of smell did not mean that others were not aware of changes in body odor.

Citrine had attended to this exchange in alert, listening silence, rising only to refill water glasses and attend to other little domestic courtesies. Now she turned to Grateful Peace.

"So you will not tell the Healed One, Father?"

"I have heard nothing that makes me feel that Firekeeper or these Nexans are a threat to New Kelvin."

"Good," Citrine said. "I just wanted to make sure."

"We have some time yet until dark," Grateful Peace said, addressing Firekeeper again, "and from what I recall, you and Blind Seer would be more comfortable departing after dark. I can arrange to get you out of the city. I will even entrust you with a way that will enable you to return and locate the nearest tunnel without alerting the guards."

"Thank you."

Firekeeper waited. She could hear from Grateful Peace's breathing that he had more to say.

"However, I think I would like an introduction to those who will be making what you say will be a daily check for you through the gate. Are you willing to wait until the appropriate time tomorrow?"

Firekeeper hesitated. Now that she had the scent in her nostrils, she was reluctant to slow, but Peace's suggestion was a good one.

"If we wait," she said, "you hide us?"

"Certainly," Grateful Peace said. "Citrine and I do not keep full-time servants. I was too long a spy master not to assume that others would not eventually find a way to use even my most trusted of servants against me. This room is private in any case. You and Blind Seer should be comfortable here."

Firekeeper looked at Blind Seer.

"Like you, I am eager to be off, but Peace's suggestion is a wise one. Let us wait. We might even ask him to show us maps of the area we will be traveling through. Those we examined on the Nexus Islands were far from current."

Firekeeper felt cheered at the thought the time would not be wasted. She asked Grateful Peace if they might look at some of his maps, and he agreed with alacrity.

"Your having this knowledge is to my people's advantage as well," he said with one of his rare smiles. "I would not like to have any stumble upon you unawares. The experience would be, at the least, frightening."

Firekeeper grinned at the compliment.

"I would like to make you a small gift as well," Grateful Peace said. "From what you have said, the Once Dead are hampered by the presence of iron, even as our own legends tell. I know you are carrying some iron with you, but I would like to give you some more."

Firekeeper pursed her lips thoughtfully.

"Iron is very heavy," she said, "but would be good, too. I not want to take too much from Nexus Islands. They need what they have."

"What I had in mind," Grateful Peace said, "was a small coil or two of iron wire. You could break off pieces to use as needed—for binding, for example, or to lay along the shaft of an arrow if you ran short of iron arrowheads."

Firekeeper liked the idea. "Let me see, please. If I can break, is worth carrying."

Citrine scampered off and came back with the wire almost immediately.

"We keep some in the kitchen," she explained.

Firekeeper discovered that with a little effort she could break the wire, and accepted the gift with gratitude.

"This be useful," she said, "whether this Virim and his pack are across the Iron Mountains or whether only their den is there. Thank you."

Grateful Peace nodded, and offered her an oiled canvas bag in which to carry the wire.

"Good," Firekeeper said, securing it onto her belt. "Now, may we see the maps?"

WHAT SHOULD HAVE been a simple matter was complicated some when the Once Dead who came through the gate proved to be Enigma, rather than either Ynamynet or Kalyndra.

Firekeeper could understand the sense in the choice. Of the Once Dead who could operate the gate, Enigma was the best equipped to defend himself, and would know immediately from scent trails not only who was about at the present time, but what had happened during the interval.

Firekeeper and Blind Seer explained the situation to the puma, and Enigma agreed to return and check if someone else was willing to cross and speak with Peace.

Under the fascinated gazes of Grateful Peace and Citrine, Enigma transitioned through the gate. Firekeeper had thought that Derian might be among those who came back, but when the stone face shimmered and shifted, only Ynamynet came through.

Her Pellish was limited but serviceable and after formal introductions were completed she said, "Derian sends his greetings, but he is unwell. He has suffered from this very disease for which we search for a cure, and although he is over the worst, it flares up unpredictably."

Grateful Peace glanced at Firekeeper. "You didn't mention this."

Firekeeper shrugged. "Is true. Derian have had. I have had. Is nasty illness, but we live."

"Perhaps because you are from the New World originally," Peace speculated. "Very interesting indeed."

Firekeeper stood by patiently while Grateful Peace and Ynamynet negotiated the terms upon which Peace agreed to permit the gate to be used.

"I have no problem," he said, "with your checking for Firekeeper and Blind Seer, especially since there is apparently no other way of letting them return through the gate. However, as we have explained already, I will know if the gate is used more than once a day. I may even be able to tell how many make the crossing. Please do not abuse my trust."

"I wonder if he will really be able to do so," Blind Seer said. *"The dragon is capricious enough to suddenly stop offering that information."*

"If it did," Firekeeper replied, hiding an impulse to laugh, *"then I think Peace would 'just happen' to be down here at the proper time each day. He might in any case. He is not one to trust lightly."*

"True," the wolf agreed.

"Those terms are fine with us," Ynamynet agreed. "Enigma will most likely be the one who makes the transition. Lack of light does not inconvenience him as it does a human."

"Very good," Peace agreed. "But if you alter who makes the transition, I will not be disturbed. One transition a day, shall we say at noon?"

"Noon where we are," Ynamynet agreed. "From what Derian has told us, navigation is nearly a lost art in the New World, but we have indications that depending on where you are on the earth's surface, noon will occur at different times."

"Interesting," Grateful Peace said, "and something I can believe. After all, the sun moves, so how can it be in the same place at all times? Noon your time then. That will suit me. After a few such transitions, I am sure I will work out where that falls in relation to our local time."

Soon after, Ynamynet made her departure. Grateful Peace watched the gate's surface return to dull stone with absorbed attention.

"I wish I could try that," he said.

"Then wish and hope we find cure for sickness," Firekeeper said. "I not wish for an old man like you or child like Citrine to risk being sick. Was hard enough for the young and strong."

Citrine looked indignant, but Grateful Peace did not.

"The difference between the young who think they are strong," Blind Seer said, *"and the old is that the old have the good sense to know that they are not strong. Peace will not try and cross that border—nor will he be eager to have others do so."*

Firekeeper nodded. Then she turned to Peace.

"We go now?"

Peace nodded. "Follow us. We will take you out of the city without your ever needing to go above ground. The way is not easy, but I trust you will remember it."

"We do what we can," Firekeeper said. Then she grinned, a human grin filled with laughter. "But I think that not matter so much. I not think you show us a door, and not make sure you know who use it and when."

Grateful Peace gave her an answering smile.

"That may indeed be true. That may indeed be true."

BOOK
TWO

XIX

DERIAN FOUND THAT the days passed very slowly once Firekeeper and Blind Seer departed from the Nexus Islands in the early days of Horse Moon.

As all of the members of the Nexus Islands' ruling council had feared, opening the New Kelvin gate had awakened an almost universal longing for the now unreachable places that all but a few of the most completely exiled of the islands' residents thought of as "home."

Even those who had resided almost exclusively on the Nexus Islands in the years since the fall of King Veztressidan felt this restlessness to some degree. Never before had they been so completely and totally isolated. There had always been visitors to inspect and gossip about, often mail or packages from friends and family based elsewhere. Home the Nexus Islands had become, but now they increasingly felt like a prison.

Derian thought he had come to terms with his own semi-voluntary exile, but the opening of the gate into New Kelvin, and his awareness that Grateful Peace and Citrine were now close enough to talk to, should he choose, awakened all his restlessness and longing.

While not a close friend, Grateful Peace was someone Derian had grown to like and respect. Citrine, however, was someone Derian had known since she was a child of eight. They had traveled together, lived under the same roof, and shared an almost familial intimacy. Perhaps most important of all, Citrine was from his own land. She would speak Pellish without an accent and would know exactly what he meant if he talked about celebrating the Festival of the Horse, even to the taste of a certain oatmeal and raisin cake made at that time of the year and no other.

The fact that Firekeeper had departed near the beginning of Horse Moon didn't help Derian's sudden longing to be out and away. He'd been given to the Horse Society before he could remember, and as the heir apparent to a prominent carter's establishment, he had been involved in the festivities since before he could walk.

With nothing but routine chores and administration to distract him, Derian found himself thinking about what he'd be doing if he were back in Eagle's Nest. There would be parades, and feasts and dances, for all of which he would be as much host as guest. There would be girls eager for his company, for everyone knew that a Horse man was lucky at that time of year.

Along with the other New World residents, he took a regular patrol up on the gateway hills, and he found that his wandering route took him a bit more frequently than was absolutely necessary past the gate that—if it still worked—would take him to Hawk Haven. It would probably take him right to Eagle's Nest, if they were correctly translating the unintentionally cryptic descriptions left by those who had made the gates.

I could slip through, he thought. *The moon will be full soon, and the festivities would be at their height then. I might even go unnoticed—or relatively so. Lots of people wear costumes to the parades and dances. They might just think mine was better than most.*

Derian allowed his mind to wander through such fantasies as his feet wandered in and out among the silent buildings, checking each to make sure it remained empty, with no sign of the glow that began before each transition, and lingered for a time thereafter. He enjoyed imaginary walks through the streets of the city that had been his home until he'd left with Earl Kestrel's expedition to the west of the Iron Mountains, and had never really returned.

He danced near the central fountain plaza and led the parade up to the assembly square by Eagle's Nest Castle. He ate cake and drank quantities of good ale, both the last of winter's brew and the first of the spring's. He flirted with girls he had known, and with a few he had only admired. The details of these imaginary liaisons kept him quite absorbed, imagining, then perfecting every thing he might say.

But there were two places he could not make his imaginary feet turn their steps: Prancing Steed Stables, outside the eastern edge of Eagle's Nest, and the house his parents owned, within the walls of the city itself. He tried a few times, but could never get beyond the expressions of shock and surprise on the faces of his parents and younger brother and sister.

Damita had a serious suitor now, although their mother wasn't sure Dami was actually ready to marry. Would that young man want a horse for a brother-in-law? Might the sight of Derian create a situation that Dami would blame him over for the rest of their lives? Brock had been horse-crazy when Derian had left Hawk Haven, and from the neatly detailed lists of horses he included as his contribution to the family correspondence, he still was. Even so, would he like having a brother who looked like a cross between a horse with a shiny chestnut coat and a man? And Colby and Vernita had always been so proud of him. How could he disappoint them?

He laughed, and heard the sound echo harshly from the interior of the gate building he was then inspecting.

When I was engaged to Rahniseeta, I was worried about bringing home a beautiful bride who looked a bit different than we did, and who had some strange ideas about deities. What would I give to have that as my only problem!

He was so engrossed in his thoughts that he didn't see the figure standing near the center hub to one of the circular configurations of gates until it moved.

"Who's there?" he said, reaching for his sword.

The figure stepped forward out of the shadows.

"Derian, it's me. Isende."

Derian slid the blade back into its sheath.

"Sorry. I was woolgathering. Anything wrong?"

"Why, no. I'm making the routine check."

Periodic checks were part of the security precautions. They

had been designed so that even if the humans and yarimaimalom who took various watch shifts were somehow all overcome without being able to give warning—something the Nexans could not rule out, given the possible abilities of the Once Dead—then the hourly checks would make certain that an unwelcome visitor would have only a short time in which to act.

"Right."

Derian looked around. Evening had passed into twilight while he paced and dreamed. He regularly took a watch that started after the evening meal because his altered vision handled the shift better than his human eyes had ever done. He couldn't see in the dark, but while he would never be as good at it as Firekeeper was, he was learning how to make his eyes understand and interpret what he was seeing.

"So you don't need anything?" Isende asked, falling into step beside him when he began his patrol once more.

"No. I ate before coming up here, and brought water."

"Oh." The young woman paused, then said rather too quickly, "Do you mind if I walk with you for a while? Verul is taking over the hourly checks, and, well, you look like you could use company."

"If you really want to," Derian said. Then, his own imagined conversations with various young ladies fresh in his mind, he realized how ungracious he sounded. "I mean, I would very much enjoy your company, but you've already had a long day."

"No longer than yours," Isende said, reminding him how true that was. They'd eaten breakfast at the same table in the communal dining hall. She'd been bouncing one of the toddlers, explaining to it why it shouldn't spit out its milk, because milk wasn't easy to get on the Nexus Islands.

Derian asked after the child in question, but even as he listened to Isende's reply he found himself thinking.

She was there at breakfast. Lunch, too. And she dropped by midday to give me the report from Harjeedian's archivists. I didn't see her midafternoon, but that's when I was napping so I'd be fresh for tonight. Now that I think about it, Isende has been around a lot.

The need to reply to a question of Isende's about fodder and when another trip into Gak might be necessary forced Derian to put this intriguing train of thought aside, but it stayed with him, tingling below his thoughts.

Verul arrived to make the hourly check astonishingly soon thereafter, and when he seemed to show up only minutes after that, Derian realized how much he was enjoying talking to Isende. He was sorry when she took her leave after Verul's second check, but his step remained light, and his thoughts for the rest of the evening were not filled with longing for his unattainable home.

DERIAN'S LATE SHIFT meant that he slept in the next morning, but the kitchens always kept some food by for those who were on night duty. Derian wondered if it was a coincidence that Isende was making herself useful in the kitchens when he arrived, teaching a couple of children how to shell fresh peas.

He took his meal at a corner table in the kitchen itself, making the excuse that they'd already tidied and mopped the main room. He didn't comment, and neither did anyone else, that his more usual pattern would have been to take his food back to his own house and eat there while reviewing whatever problems had cropped up in the meantime.

The kitchen staff was pleased to have him there, and bent his ear about spices and suchlike they would like from Gak, if trade could not be started elsewhere. Isende got drawn into the conversation fairly naturally, as while Derian had some idea what could be purchased in Hawk Haven, he had little idea what was available in Gak.

After he had scraped his porridge bowl clean, and eaten a stack of griddle cakes and cheese, it seemed the most natural thing in the world that Isende and her miniature followers come with him to his house so they could consult over a supply list.

He thought he caught the head cook grinning in her reflection on the bottom of a polished pan, but he decided he must have been mistaken, for when he turned to bid the staff a polite good morning, that good woman was completely absorbed in boning fish.

* * *

BUT SEVERAL DAYS later, after Isende came up and kept him company during another of his evening patrols, and it had seemed natural to return the favor during one of hers that happened to fall when he was able to make an opening in his schedule, Derian realized that not only did Isende seem to be making excuses to spend time with him, but that he was glad that she was doing so.

Derian had always been a healthy young man, and he'd had his share of sweethearts, sometimes more than one at a time. He'd nursed a fancy for Elise for a time, before deciding that he'd much rather see her with Doc. He'd even had a few brief thoughts regarding Firekeeper, but not only was she simply too strange, he had been among the first to realize that her feelings for Blind Seer went beyond brotherly.

Nonetheless, despite much time on the road, and even some time in captivity, Derian had managed a romantic tryst or two, and even managed to become engaged to Rahniseeta. Usually, he had a pretty fair idea what to do when a girl started paying him attention—especially if he liked the girl and the attention.

This time, however, when Derian contemplated kisses in quiet corners, and what that might lead to, he found himself panicked. Isende surely noticed the change in his formerly relaxed and affable mood, but because nothing had been said between them—at least about possible feelings for each other, although it seemed they had talked about everything else under the sun, moon, and stars—she really could say nothing.

However, a time or two, Derian noticed her looking confused, and even hurt.

I've got to talk to someone, he thought in desperation, *before I do something completely stupid and drive her away before I've even gathered her in. But who would I talk to? Elise is too far away. I can't leave for half a moonspan just to get her views on romance. Harjeedian? Never. Especially not with having been engaged to his sister. Wort? I don't know. Those Old Worlders have some odd views on things. . . .*

The sight of a short, round, furred figure making his way down the path that led to the pair of cottages some distance from the main complex solved Derian's problem.

He was out the door of his house and galloping down the path before he could think himself out of his idea.

"Plik!" he called. "Do you have a moment or three to talk with me?"

The raccoon-man turned and smiled. "I am just back from taking a turn in the archives, and there is nothing that I would enjoy more than a chat with a friend. Would you come to my house, or shall I step into yours?"

Derian thought for a moment, remembered that he had read the watch list earlier (denying to himself all the while that he was checking to see when Isende was next taking a stand), and recalled that Tiniel was currently on duty.

"Your place," Derian said. "If we try to talk in mine, sure as horses make little brown apples, that will be the moment two people get into an argument only I can resolve."

Plik gave one of his little chortling laughs, like the rest of him, part animal, part man.

"That does seem to happen," he said, "and was one of the reasons that on Misheemnekuru I preferred to make my bed in one of several convenient hollow trees. Someone really had to want me to interrupt my rest."

Once they were in the cottage, even before Plik finished putting a kettle on the arm and stoking up the banked coals on the hearth, Derian started talking, certain that someone would interrupt otherwise.

"It's Isende," he said, almost stammering. "I think . . . That is, I think I've noticed . . . I'm almost sure that she likes me."

Plik looked solemnly up from where he knelt by the fire.

"You are a likable person, Derian."

Then he grinned, and with a hot blush Derian knew that he had indeed seen the head cook grinning. How long had everyone but himself been aware of Isende's interest?

Plik took mercy on his guest. "Yes. I think Isende likes you—is 'interested' in you, as I have heard it said. The first question is, do you return the interest, or are you looking for me to help you escape from an unwanted complication?"

"I'm interested," Derian admitted, feeling relief at the admission. "But I'm wondering if it is wise for me to be interested."

Plik tilted his head to one side inquiringly, reminding Derian rather oddly of Firekeeper.

"Wise? Wisdom and matters of the heart rarely march in step."

"I know," Derian said. "But this situation is different. I mean, we're on this island, and I'm . . . well, what I am."

"Let's start with that second point," Plik said. "You are referring to your current, somewhat equine, appearance."

Derian resisted an urge to glower at the raccoon-man. After all, he *had* introduced the subject. Instead, he forced himself to nod.

"Very well," Plik said. "Isende met you before querinalo reshaped you, correct?"

"A few days before," Derian agreed.

"And so she has been offered an opportunity to compare versions. My feeling is, if the alteration doesn't bother her, then you should not trouble yourself."

"But I'm a freak!" Derian colored as he realized to whom he had said those words, but Plik did not take offense.

"Because humans do not change over time," Plik said. "Because even if you had remained as you were, you would not have altered in any way."

"No, because I look like I'm part horse," Derian said.

"Still, wouldn't you agree that physical appearance is the most shallow reason for choosing a life-partner? If this had not happened, wouldn't you have expected your wife to continue to remain loyal to you if, for example, you became bald? This is something I understand often happens to men from your land. Over time your skin would become etched with permanent lines. What hair you kept might turn grey. However, you would not expect your wife to leave you because of this, and I hope you would not leave your wife for such insignificant reasons."

Derian frowned. "Of course I wouldn't, but this transformation is different. I am socially unacceptable. Who knows what may have happened to my ability to father children."

"Have you discussed this with Isende?"

Derian felt himself blushing. "Not that last part, but a bit about how I'm not sure I can go home again. We've talked about that."

"And would this latter problem change if you did not become involved with a young woman—any young woman? Would allowing yourself an attachment make it harder to go home?"

"I don't think so."

"Then I think the matter is irrelevant to the current situation. Isende has no living parents whose permission she must ask. Indeed, I have the impression that even before we encountered them she and Tiniel had cut themselves off from their living kin in Gak. So, let us dismiss the matter of your appearance for a time, shall we? It is certainly something Isende could not have missed. If she has continued to show interest in you—as she has done—then she must have arrived at some agreement within herself regarding it."

Plik poured hot water over tea leaves and brought the pot back to the table. Going to a small cabinet to one side of the room, he took out a sealed jar that held some rather hard cookies.

"They're fine if you dunk them first in your tea," Plik said. "Otherwise, I have been told they break teeth. Now, let us talk about why you think that being on an island might be an element in a potential relationship with Isende."

Derian nodded. "What if she's only interested in me because there are so few available men?"

"That's hardly true," Plik said. "I can think of five or six unattached men who are of an age for Isende to be interested in them. If one raises the age limit, there are even more. True, few of these are from the New World, but given that Isende's culture and yours are not at all alike, I cannot believe she is drawn to you simply because you remind her of home. If she was seeking that, Harjeedian would be a better candidate for her affections."

Derian had to admit this was true.

"A more serious matter," Plik went on, "would be if you fear that Isende is only interested in you because of your relative prominence in the local community."

Derian hadn't wanted to bring this up. It sounded too much like bragging, but the idea had occurred to him.

Plik went on, "This may be part of your appeal, but I think I detected some interest in you even before you acquired your role as informal mayor. Indeed, even in the early days of our meeting, she seemed interested in you."

"A hero to the rescue," Derian said, "one who rather inconveniently turns into his horse."

Plik swatted Derian's hand, dunked a cookie into a newly poured cup of tea, and said, "I thought we agreed that was not an issue. What is an issue is whether you wish to encourage Isende, or to put her off. I suggest you make your choice relatively soon. Her interest in you is more and more apparent, and over the last several days you have seemed to return it. As you noted, this is an island, and since there is very little to talk about, people pay an inordinate amount of attention to each other's lives."

"I know," Derian said. "Half of what I do is straighten out mistakes regarding who is getting what from whom and why someone else should get what that one has. And I've heard gossip about other people. I guess I thought I'd been discreet enough that no one had noticed."

"You have been, mostly," Plik assured him, "but Isende has been watching you with hero worship in her eyes for quite a while now. You didn't need to do much to raise speculation."

Derian sighed. "So I do need to make a decision, soon, or that girl is going to feel a fool—and have nowhere to hide her head."

"Don't start up with her out of some misplaced pity," Plik scolded. "That would be worse."

"I know," Derian said. "I know. It's just it's hard enough to believe any nice young woman could be interested in me, without worrying about conducting a relationship in public."

Plik smiled. "Why not start by talking openly with Isende?

Tell her your concerns. Find out what she thinks. Then move on from there. You might learn things about her you don't even suspect."

Derian looked suspiciously at the twinkling eyes framed in the raccoon mask. "You haven't talked to her already, have you?"

Plik looked completely innocent. "Me? I'm more likely to talk to her brother. He is my closest neighbor. But as odd as you persist in seeing the maimalodalum—or creatures like yourself—I think we are all quite alike under our skins. Where romance enters the picture, the human heart beats very strongly."

Derian dunked a cookie, and as he bit into it he found himself thinking of Firekeeper and her impossible love for a creature who didn't even come close to matching her in shape or species. Now that he thought about it, he—especially if Isende was interested—had it easy.

⚜

BRYESSIDAN COULD HARDLY believe Horse Moon was galloping past the full, and that Lion Moon—and with it the launching of the fleet under the command of King Hurwin—was padding swiftly forward. The fleet would not finish grouping for at least a moonspan. Some estimates held that departure would not be possible until sometime in early Bear Moon—but that was hardly any time for the amount of work that still needed to be done.

The Kingdom of the Mires was supplying fewer troops than many of her neighbors; the restrictions enacted after King Veztressidan's defeat meant that the Mires did not have a standing army, only a smaller force meant to deal with domestic problems. However, most of the healers who would sail with the fleet were coming from the Mires, as were boxes and bales of powders, tinctures, and ointments to treat both shipboard illnesses and battlefield injuries.

Then there was the influx of seagoing traffic through the Mires' own harbors. Since Hearthome was providing the launch point for the fleet, her harbors were crowded with ships receiving crews, equipment, and, in many cases, final outfittings or repairs in suddenly overworked dockyards. Therefore, many of the smaller ships bringing supplies were coming into the Mires' harbors, where goods and troops were off-loaded and sent overland into Hearthome.

Meanwhile, the lack of a standing army meant that the Mires was hard-pressed to supply the armed force they had agreed to have ready to send through their gate in no less than two moonspans, and quite probably less.

Timing could not be exact. The old ship's logs and maps King Hurwin had found had been exhaustively analyzed, the material in them compared to similar material in records archived in seaboard lands such as the Mires, Hearthome, and u-Chival. When differing points of origin were taken into account, the records seemed to agree that the voyage to the Nexus Islands would take no less than half a moonspan, and possibly as much as a full moonspan.

Bryessidan had been to sea, but always as a passenger, never in command of a vessel. Without Gidji's help, all the talk of tides, currents, predominant winds, calms, and other, less comprehensible things would have sent him into a temper. As it was, he listened with what patience he could, taking copious notes, and counting on Gidji to explain the details to him later.

And those "laters" were becoming harder and harder to find. Their regular private meals had become intermittent, for in addition to advising her husband, Queen Gidji was taking over more and more of the routine jobs of rulership, both in preparation for the regency, and to free the king to deal with all the new problems arising from the planned project.

There were times Bryessidan wished the newly allied lands could all sit down, admit this had been a bad idea, and go back to their previous lives. Then something would happen—like a sudden outbreak of the summer spots in Pelland—and an outcry would arise for some medication only the Mires could supply, and Bryessidan would curse the Nexans for breaking their treaty, closing off the gates, and leaving all those people to suffer and, quite possibly, die for lack of herbs that now must be prepared as medication in advance of shipping lest they lose their virtue in the journey overland.

We need those gates, he found himself thinking over and over again. *The Nexans have no right to shut us off from them!*

Bryessidan found himself almost longing for the midpoint of Lion Moon, for then the fleet would be launched, and there could be no more calls for just a few more boxes of powdered willow, no more ships crowding his harbors with supplies for the fleet. Then he could give his full attention to training his army, and reassuring them—and himself—that they were equal to anything they would encounter on the other side of the gate.

He wished he believed it. Ever since invasion had been agreed upon, the gates had been allowed to lie dormant. The hope was that the Nexans would relax the vigilance that had been so evident during earlier transitions.

Some of Bryessidan's allies had even wondered if the Nexans would reinstate use of the gates before the invasion. Of these, some thought that this would negate the need for an invasion. Others, however, drunk on the prospect of controlling those gates, thought that the best course of action would be to continue the invasion as planned, to send through a few shipments of goods as before, as a distraction, but with the intention that when the ships were in position the invasion would go forward as planned.

That's something we'll need to resolve before the fleet departs, Bryessidan thought as he moved to don the heavy leather armor he wore for practice with his troops. *Once the fleet has gone, changing plans is going to be difficult.*

Surmounting the communication problem had been one of the biggest hurdles. In the days before the Sorcerer's Bane, long-distance magical communication had been routine, if never simple. However, although some of the old spells still existed they did not seem to work. Amelo Soapwort said that the Once Dead had been working on the problem for years, and had come to the conclusion that the spells might have relied upon a talent that was gone forever—or at least had yet to resurface.

The best magical communication that could be managed now was over a range about the equivalent to a day's steady march by a lightly armored soldier. This was useful on land, but would be useless once the fleet headed out toward the Nexus Islands. Amelo and his associates had started an ambitious program to make certain that at least one Once Dead in every gate-transition group would know the spell and be ready to use it to facilitate communication between teams.

That plan, however admirable it might seem, had raised an entirely new problem. How do you arm and armor a force without resorting to the very iron that would interfere with the use of magic for communication and defense and, of course, to operate the gates themselves?

Although the heat at which iron was treated to make steel did something so that the metal did not interfere with the use of magic to the same extent, still, in quantity it continued to have a deleterious effect on the Once Dead's ability to use their varied powers. Spellcasters suffered the most, probably because their ability was the least internalized, and spellcasters were the ones whose abilities would be the most useful.

Once again, Bryessidan found himself and his more senior advisors in high demand. King Veztressidan had been forced to find solutions to these problems and others like them back when he had attempted to reunite—or conquer, it was all a matter of point of view—the continent. Now the same people who a matter of moonspans before had viewed Bryessidan askance because of their apprehension that he would be inclined to repeat his father's venture were trying to find a tactful way to ask Bryessidan to share what had been learned at that time.

"And some don't even bother to be tactful," Bryessidan complained to Gidji during one of their rare private meetings. "Queen Iline of Hearthome had the gall to write and inform me that it was my duty as a member of the allied forces to ride to Hearthome immediately upon receipt of her letter and allow myself to be grilled. Oh, and I was to bring with me Amelo, and any of my father's sorcerers who were available so that they could share what I—who after all had been rather young at the time—might not know."

"I assume you didn't agree," Gidji said, smiling slightly as she cut into a pastry stuffed with a finely chopped blend of duck and spring cress.

"I did not," Bryessidan said. "And you'll be impressed to know that I didn't even call her ambassador in and tell him what a presumptuous twit I thought his mistress was being. And let me tell you, I was tempted to do so. I kept having this sense, reading between the lines of that letter as it were, that Queen Iline was informing me I had better do as she wished, because I owed obedience to the other nations since they had not wiped out the Mires ten years ago."

"More like eleven, now," Gidji said. "Or close enough. Yes, I am pleased. I think that one of the unanticipated side effects of this venture is going to be that Queen Iline's people are going to insist that she name an heir. Already people are saying that the son who is generaling Hearthome's gate force deserves the honor as reward for his patriotism. That is making Azure Towers very unhappy. Queen Anitra has had enough problems with Hearthome without seeing a war leader named heir apparent to her enemy's throne. Behind the scenes, Anitra has factions who favor an end to Iline's perpetual harrying of Azure Towers agitating for a less military-minded heir."

"And how does this affect us?" Bryessidan asked.

"When we come out of this conflict," Gidji said, "not only will our gate be reactivated, but we will have a standing military once more. Queen Anitra will support our keeping that force intact, because she can use her support of our need for a standing military to emphasize the threat she sees in Hearthome."

"Ah . . ." Bryessidan said. "I'm afraid I've been thinking so much about immediate problems, I hadn't considered any of this. For weeks, I haven't thought beyond our taking the Nexus Islands."

Gidji smiled. "You may have not, but there are those who are already thinking to those days. There are even those who say that this alliance is the beginning of a reunited Pelland—the continent as it was, not the kingdom that has claimed the name. Interesting, isn't it? Your father's dream may come true."

"My father's dream was that he rule all Pelland."

"He or his son," Gidji replied. "Come, my dear, think. Queen Anitra has named no heir apparent, and her people are happy enough with her that they have not agitated for her to do so. She might accept the Mire's protection at first—later she might find it wise to make you or one of our children heir apparent."

Bryessidan started to speak, but Gidji stayed him with a raised hand.

"Queen Iline's children are so accustomed to squabbling over who will win Hearthome's throne that they view each other as enemies. When Iline sails across the seas to her final port, they might be convinced to accept another solution, that of inviting an outsider to take the throne, especially since inviting another to rule would mean none of them would need to bow to brother or sister.

"Pelland has become decadent. Half the court—or so I hear from my brother, who visited there recently as aide to our father—is suffering from withdrawal because they no longer have ample supply of the white pollen from Tishiolo. Do you think they will stop craving it once the gates are reopened, and acquisition becomes simple once more?"

Bryessidan nodded slowly, seeing the vision laid out before him. He heard his voice speak with dreamy thoughtfulness.

"I believe the king of Pelland has a daughter not too far apart in age from our elder son. We might arrange a marriage there. The throne would become ours without need of conquest, especially if the girl shares her people's addiction."

"My father would support the idea," Gidji said. "He thinks well of our son, and of you, while his recent experiences with Pelland have lowered his never too high opinion of that people."

A servant knocked, and when Bryessidan called permission to enter, the servant asked if he might come in and clear away the plates.

"Also, Your Majesties, several messages have been delivered while you were dining. Also, the nanny asked me to pass on the word that Prince Vahon has fallen and is likely to need his knee stitched. He is crying for his mother—or father."

Queen Gidji pushed back her chair and rose.

"Rolf, have my messages sent to me at the night nursery."

She curtsied to Bryessidan. "Your Majesty, if I might have your leave to attend upon the prince?"

Bryessidan grinned at her, hearing affection where once he would only have heard mockery.

"You are free to go, my queen, and be assured that I will think deeply over what you have told me. There is great wisdom in your words."

After she had left, even as he was leafing through the sheaf of messages Rolf had handed him, Bryessidan couldn't help but think about Gidji's lovely vision of the future.

My father's dream fulfilled. I had never realized how I ached to vindicate him until Gidji spoke of it. I had thought to come out of this coming war only with what we had held before, and a bit more because the Once Dead of the Nexus Islands would no longer be so free to dictate terms to us. But Gidji is right. Pelland could be reunited. I am young yet. Rather than merely King of the Mires, I might go to the Ancestors as Emperor of Pelland, and ruler of who knows what other lands besides? The gates go many places. My father told me that. Many, many places, and the New World was said to be very, very rich.

XX

THE MOON HAD turned her face full around since Firekeeper and Blind Seer had left the Nexus Islands. Then it had been a quarter of the way to full, curved but not yet filled in. Now it showed that same face again.

"What is it the humans call this moon?" she asked Blind Seer idly as they eased their way through scrub growth and tangle. "The last one was Horse. I remember that because Derian placed much importance on the name. I can't remember this one."

"Puma," Blind Seer said. "I don't know why. Maybe because a puma would be quite happy to chase a horse."

They laughed, and continued on in the steady, distance-eating trot they had adapted for their purposes. Although not a run, it was faster than most humans walked, and they could maintain it for the greater part of the day without tiring. Sometimes the unevenness of the terrain demanded slower. Sometimes a verdant meadow invited them to run, but mostly they moved at this one steady pace.

Beneath the waxing moon and the waning, Firekeeper and Blind Seer had moved west from New Kelvin. Their overnight stop with Grateful Peace and Citrine—although it been an unwelcome delay then—had proven very useful. Peace's maps had shown them what roads would take them most directly north, and he had written on a piece of oiled cloth the symbols that would mark the signs the New Kelvinese had erected where roads crossed, so they would not take the wrong route. His maps had shown some of the mountain passes as well, but, like most human maps, they faded to fanciful conjecture the farther west they went.

Firekeeper remembered with some satisfaction how complimentary Peace had been regarding her increased ability both to read and to see the usefulness in written signs. Citrine had been pleased, too, so much so that Firekeeper had felt she must confess that Blind Seer was more skilled than she. Wolves bragged, but only when the brag was worth fighting over.

They had left New Kelvin's marked roads behind them before the moon's face turned dark. As Puma Moon waxed, they were finding their way through mountain passes, huddling together to sleep in the daytime, moving at night, for the nights this far north and at great heights were cold and one might fall asleep and never awaken.

During their journey, they had seen many Cousins, but few

Royal Beasts. Those that they had met up with seemed not to know them, or even the tales Firekeeper knew were told farther to the south. Because of this, Firekeeper felt that she and Blind Seer had come to a land as strange as Liglim or even the Nexus Islands.

She was not so vain that she expected everyone they met to know them, but wolves were social creatures and enjoyed howling stories far and wide. Wolves loved tales of the strange. Firekeeper well knew how very strange she was, and how strange Blind Seer was for having chosen her company when he might have led a pack on his own.

True, those Beasts they had encountered thus far—most notably a very bad-temperered wolverine, and some pumas—had been of solitary kind. True, the more social Beasts would have moved their herds and packs to areas away from this cruel high country. This was the season when calves and pups and fawns tottered about, equal parts unsteady step and curious spirit. Even the wingéd folk would be occupied more with feeding their voracious nestlings than in scouting the area.

Even so, Firekeeper wondered if she and Blind Seer were being avoided, and if so, were they being avoided because their reputation had preceded them even in these northern highlands or because it had not, and so she was taken as human, and humans were to be avoided if at all possible.

The latter thought was distasteful in the extreme, and Firekeeper did not speak it aloud. To do so would be to admit her insecurities at a time when she and Blind Seer were being very careful with each other. He had not spoken further of his experiences beneath querinalo's fever, and she had not pressed him, not really knowing what answer she wanted from him. Blind Seer with the power to make magic work for him would not be the Blind Seer she knew—or would he be, for that power must have been in him all along? Firekeeper puzzled over this as they moved farther and farther west, as their trail gradually began to slope downward, as the air began to smell of green growth and wet, and the nights become less cold.

* * *

DURING A MOONSPAN'S long, hard travel, Firekeeper had developed some conjectures as to what she and Blind Seer might expect to find when they arrived in the general vicinity of where Virim had made his lair.

She and Blind Seer had made a study of ruins during their time on Misheemnekuru. Their residence on the Nexus Islands had added to their knowledge, so now the pair were as adept at finding human sign as most wolves were at finding that of deer or elk.

Moreover, although querinalo had initially touched human populations over a hundred years before, the Meddler had given them reason to believe that Virim could have lived long after that time, so the indications might be even newer.

Despite Blind Seer's hallucination, Firekeeper did not think that Virim could possibly have survived to the present day. His appearing in Blind Seer's fever dreams was no proof, not when one took into account creatures like the Meddler.

The Meddler had been killed long before querinalo seared the magic from the minds and bodies of those—or the descendants of those—who had made him prisoner. Yet Firekeeper had ample proof that the Meddler had maintained a life of sorts. Then, too, she had seen the strange spaces where lives could hover between living and dying, eventually becoming entrapped so that their bodies died, but their spirits could not move on.

This is what she thought might have happened with Virim. From what they had been able to learn about him, Virim had been a strong-willed individual. A man who could contemplate designing a curse that would wipe out all those who he saw as a threat to his view of what was right and proper would not give in easily to death.

Probably scraps of his spirit had lingered in one of those weird, undefined, indeterminate spaces between life and death, and somehow Blind Seer had drawn those fragments to him.

Probably, Firekeeper thought proudly, *because Blind Seer's way of dealing with querinalo was like nothing Virim had ever seen. Most of his victims have been human, and humans are as*

*self-absorbed as baby birds. Among the yarimaimalom who
crossed to the Nexus Islands, only one that I know of shares
Blind Seer's ability for spellcasting. Enigma is a puma, and, if
anything, great cats are worse than humans for turning in to
themselves. Doubtless Enigma's battle was fought—like
Truth's—between himself and some aspect of himself. Only
Blind Seer ran, refusing to let the fires have anything of him, so
only Blind Seer drew the attention of this fragment of Virim.*

It was a good theory, one that covered most of the information. She would have liked to present it to Blind Seer, so the
wolf might worry and shake it, looking for weak points and
flaws. However, Firekeeper could not do this without returning to a matter that, but for the one confession, Blind Seer had
pointedly refused to address.

The wolf was deaf to hints that Firekeeper would like to
know more about the ability he did or no longer had, even to
the point of ignoring the few direct questions Firekeeper had
asked. Finally, she had given up. They had a long way yet to
travel together, and she was not about to alienate her one
ally—and her dearest friend.

Once they had crossed into the western foothills of the
Iron Mountains, Firekeeper and Blind Seer began to scout
for indications of human habitation, past or present. They
found a few. There was a segment of a stone wall, bits of
mortar still clinging to the interior edges of the rock. A stand
of second growth forest, the trees solid and well developed to
any but eyes that saw how they did not fit in with their surroundings, marked where land had been cleared for field or
pasturage.

Once their search intersected the remnants of an old road.
This road had once been big enough to permit a large wagon
passage, and was identifiable by the straight ranks of now
gnarled apple trees planted along its edges. The road was
gone, scrub brush and young trees interrupting its course, and
nothing but birds, bears, and raccoons had harvested the apples for many years past.

"This road is our best sign so far that humans once laired in these western lands," Firekeeper said, "but roads stretch two ways. Which way should we go?"

Blind Seer had been sniffing along the vanished verges, but now his head snapped back, ears pricked, angling to catch what the wind would bring.

Although her own less acute sense had caught no sign of danger, Firekeeper swung her bow around and had it strung, arrow to hand, before she knew what had alerted the wolf.

The small birds, the seed and insect eaters whose spring territorial battles and courtships had been background to their journey, had fallen completely silent. Now a ruckus of disharmonious complaint arose from the dense forests somewhat to the south. Crows and jays led the chorus, but the littler birds joined in, and by this Firekeeper knew that whatever had stirred them to such furor was a solitary creature.

Although the birds did not speak a flexible language as did the Royal Beasts, still, as the notes of the multilayered cry grew more distinct, Firekeeper knew what the birds were saying.

"Hawk! Hawk!" the little birds screamed.

The jays and crows were rougher in their address. The songbirds spoke in panic, but the corvid-kin rejoiced in threat.

Firekeeper expected the cry to die down, for no hawk would remain where the hunting was certain to be poor, but the cries remained loud and, if possible, became more frantic.

"The hawk must have flown directly over some nesting ground," Blind Seer said, "or perhaps has designs on some carrion the crows and jays have marked for their own."

"Any hawk to alarm so many crows and jays," Firekeeper said, "must be of the larger breeds. The kestrels and merlins would not cause such a reaction."

"True," Blind Seer replied, "and this thought has led you somewhere."

"The larger the hawk," Firekeeper said, slipping her arrow back into her quiver, and loosening her bowstring, "the more likely it is to hunt over open ground. Humans also like open ground. Perhaps we would do better to find where this hawk is hunting, and see if there are indications of humans having been there at some time."

"And the largest hawks," Blind Seer agreed, "are Royal-kind. Even if not, better than making our way along a road that might only have existed to make apple picking easier many years ago. This way."

Firekeeper followed, knowing that Blind Seer's hearing would have better isolated the specific direction from sound that to her ears translated only as "over there."

She stayed alert, for although few creatures would challenge a wolf the size of Blind Seer, springtime was kit time, cub time, pup time, fawn time, fledgling time. Even a songbird had been known to find courage when it felt its eggs were threatened. Bears had no fear of wolves, and a she-bear with cubs was something any sane creature knew to avoid. The apple trees with dried and withered fruit clinging to the upper boughs might attract a winter-thin, nursing-thin bear.

But other than the birds, that had by now stilled the frantic level of their cries, Firekeeper saw few creatures. A squirrel scolded them. She glimpsed a palm-sized rabbit too young to have learned fear, but otherwise they might have been alone in the trees.

The light began to brighten, announcing the coming of open spaces. Firekeeper heard a new sound, one the cacophony of crow and jay calls with their under-chorus of songbird screams had drowned out before. It was an eagle's scream, shrill, fierce, and triumphant.

But the little birds yelled "hawk," she thought, and found her feet quickening of their own accord as she ran toward the open spaces where she could see what the sky held. Moved by the same impulse, Blind Seer loped alongside, and the two wolves burst into a highland meadow knee-deep in spring grasses and flowers.

One glance into the sky was enough to explain why the littler birds had cried so loud and so long. Two large raptors dipped and soared in aerial battle. One was the promised "hawk," a splendid peregrine falcon. The other was a golden eagle. The eagle's brown wing feathers were edged along the underside of the wings in deep bands of white that caught the sunlight. In contrast, the underfeathers of the peregrine falcon were barred, so that the white patch beneath the head and along the throat seemed curiously vulnerable, especially in contrast to the dark feathers that hooded the head.

The eagle was in pursuit of the peregrine, and though the eagle was nearly twice the size of the falcon, the peregrine was performing some astonishing maneuvers that made it impossible for the eagle to maintain a position above the falcon long enough to dive into what would surely be a fatal attack.

But the falcon could not continue to avoid the eagle for much longer. The twisting dance of their battle kept both birds from the glides they usually used to rest their wings, but the eagle was larger, and could probably last longer than the falcon.

She—for Firekeeper felt certain the peregrine was a female; among raptors the females were almost always larger than the males, and this was a magnificent bird—seemed to know she could not last much longer. Already her darting moves were covering less space. The eagle was adjusting its own flight to take advantage of its opponent's weakness.

Firekeeper shifted her bow into her hands, stringing the shaft and setting arrow to string. She was not completely certain, for the sky did not provide landmarks by which she might judge the birds' size, but she thought both of the raptors might be Royal. There was an intelligence to their tactics, to how they banked and adjusted. There was also the simple fact that raptors did not usually pursue other raptors without good cause.

The peregrine clutched no prey in her talons the eagle might covet. The fields teemed with rabbits and other small game, the streams with fish. The eagle could not be so hungry as to want the stringy, muscular meat the peregrine would yield. Why then was the eagle so intent going after the smaller bird?

Blind Seer saw what Firekeeper was doing.

"Will you kill the eagle?"

"I will try not," Firekeeper said, "not until we know the quarrel between them, but these are unfair odds, and I have an old fondness for peregrines."

Blind Seer did not stay her hand, but waited, sniffing the air as if trying to puzzle what little scent the drifts of air would carry to him.

Firekeeper pulled back the bowstring and set the arrow, waiting for a moment when the two raptors would be separated in their airborne dance. She released the shaft so that it cut the air between them, and sent another almost as fast as thought in the first arrow's wake.

As she had hoped, her interruption broke the eagle's concentration. It banked and backed, beating its wings hard as it tried to rise above the height an arrow might reach.

Another proof that they are Royal, Firekeeper thought, *and that the eagle at least knows something of human weapons.*

In contrast, the peregrine fell into one of the sharp dives for which her kind, with their angular wings, almost razor-edged in contrast to the eagle's broad-feathered plumage, were known. In that dive and in the way the peregrine neatly soared to take cover beneath the shelter of one of the large trees near the meadow's edge, Firekeeper knew that this was not just any peregrine, but one close to her heart.

Screaming defiance and disappointment, the golden eagle continued its rise, wheeling toward the clouds and then away. Once she was certain her back was safe, Firekeeper spared it no further thought or mind, but pelted through the thick grass to where the peregrine now rested on the outstretched bough of a pale-leafed old oak.

"Elation!" Firekeeper howled, not caring who the midday cry of a wolf might disturb. "Fierce Joy in Flight!"

The falcon shifted foot to foot on the branch, turning her head so that one golden-rimmed brown eye might see those who approached clearly.

"The wolfling," came the peregrine's reply, "not so little Two-legs, and the blue-eyed one beside her as ever. You could not have chosen to show yourselves at a better time."

Firekeeper knew the peregrine of old, and knew, too, that in her own way Elation was as proud as any great cat. Elation's relief must be great indeed if she would greet them with both thanks and a compliment.

Blind Seer looked up at the peregrine and panted a wolfish smile. "I thought I knew who cut the air so fine by her manner of flight, but the winds would not carry me down a scent. It is good to see you again, Elation."

Firekeeper was laughing from pure joy, and unable to reach the peregrine and greet her as wolf would wolf—if Elation would have permitted such liberties—she thumped Blind Seer on his broad back with her fist.

"Did I say an 'old fondness for peregrines'?" she laughed. "Here is that old fondness herself. Elation, what brings you here so far in the north?"

Elation shook her feathers straight, preening one wind-twisted pinion into line.

"I will tell, and in full," she said. "This I promise, but I have flown hard and my gullet is empty. I must hunt or I will not have the strength to fly."

Firekeeper shook her head. "Your battle with the eagle will have frightened everything that knows a falcon's silhouette. Rest. I will backtrack a ways, and find you hot blood and flesh."

"And I," Blind Seer said, "will do the same. Call out, sweet Firekeeper, if you strike first, and I will do the same. I do not fancy Elation's tale is one that should wait."

That Elation did not protest that she was perfectly fit to hunt for herself said more than any speeches. She did raise herself from her exhaustion to offer warning.

"Hunt south of here, east or west as you will, but do not go north. There are things there that would hunt you as the eagle did me."

The few words took such effort that Firekeeper and Blind Seer did not ask for clarification. Instead they split south, keeping out of the open meadow where they might be easily seen, one going a bit east, the other a bit west.

FIREKEEPER FOUND HER prey first, a surly groundhog that knew nothing of the range of bows, nor the sharpness of arrows. She cried her kill to Blind Seer, and when his reply came back, she collected her prey and headed to rejoin Elation.

The peregrine had not moved from her perch, but woke from her drowse when Firekeeper returned. She drifted down on stiffly spread wings, and eagerly accepted the rich liver and heart still steaming with the groundhog's life that Firekeeper cut out for her. Thus revitalized, Elation moved to do her own feeding, and Firekeeper drew back, having too much respect for what that curved beak and sharp talons could do to insist on interfering further.

Blind Seer returned while Elation fed, carrying the arrows Firekeeper had shot in his jaws. Although he had brought nothing to add to their meal, something in the tilt of his ears and the slight rise of fur along his spine told Firekeeper that his hunt had not been completely useless.

She held herself from questioning him when Blind Seer did not offer explanation, sensing he wanted Elation to offer her information untainted by the addition of his own suspicions.

While Elation ate, Firekeeper found herself remembering the many journeys she and Blind Seer had taken in the peregrine falcon's company. Elation had been with them when they had first crossed the Iron Mountains in the company of Earl Kestrel's expedition. Indeed, the falcon had known far more about human customs and speech than had either of the wolves.

When, overwhelmed by her new environment, Firekeeper had been tempted to slip into passivity, Elation's taunts had forced the wolf-woman into action. Later still, Elation had served as high guard and scout during their two journeys into New Kelvin. However, she had been more than a pair of wings and sharp eyes. Without Elation's wisdom and good counsel, Firekeeper knew certain events would have turned out for the worse.

Over the time they had spent together, Elation had also developed a liking for Derian Carter, and she paused in her feeding.

"Where is Fox Hair? When I learned that you were returning north, I thought to find him with you. I hope he still lives."

"He lives," Firekeeper said, fighting down an impulse to ask just how Elation had known about their travel plans. "But he is much changed, and those changes make him very reluctant to travel into human lands."

"Querinalo," Elation replied, saying more with one word than she could have with speeches. "Something has been said of this, but I will admit, I have not completely understood."

She sat straight, and made a small sound indicating satisfaction. Raising one leg, she picked bits of raw flesh from her talons, then groomed and smoothed her feathers.

"Much better," she said, flapping up onto the tree limb again. "My thanks."

Firekeeper indicated to Blind Seer that he was welcome to what remained of the groundhog carcass. Not only didn't she have much taste for falcon-ravaged meat, but she thought making a fire might be unwise until they learned what Elation had to tell. She had thought about suggesting they retreat deeper into the forest, but then realized that she had no idea which direction was safe. In any case, they had been seen. This was as good a place as any to watch for other possible attacks.

"You have been patient," Elation said after she had settled herself onto the bough, "especially for wolves who I remember fondly for many traits, but not particularly for patience."

"We have run more than a few long roads since those days," Blind Seer replied, "and even Little Two-legs has learned that sometimes waiting brings the game to you."

"I have heard something of those roads," Elation said, "as you must have gathered. When you three vanished from Eagle's Nest, humankind may not have noticed, but the Beasts did. The wingéd folk who report on the actions of the humans east of the Iron Mountains had gathered that you intended to travel west. That word was relayed, and those of Royal-kind who had reason to love you were quite pleased. Even those who are less biased were pleased, for they felt that this journey indicated that Firekeeper was taking responsibility for actions they felt she had set in motion."

Firekeeper felt Blind Seer's growl rumble through her arm where it rested over his shoulder, but he did not interrupt. Neither did she. As much as she loved the wolves who had raised her, she would have had to be blind and deaf not to know all the Royal Beasts did not feel as comfortable with her. Oddly, the Wise Beasts of the southlands, because they had never felt themselves the enemies of all humankind had accepted her more easily.

Elation ignored the blue-eyed wolf's growl and went on with her account.

"But you did not arrive, and when messages were sent back we soon realized that not only had you not arrived, you had never departed from Eagle's Nest. Your trails ended at the dancing and celebrations following the naming of young Prince Sun, and not even those with the keenest noses or sharpest eyes could find you."

Firekeeper thought this was no great surprise. If the alarm had not been raised until days after they had been kidnapped, what scent trail they would have left would surely have been obliterated. They had not been permitted sight of sky until they were well out at sea. The Royal Wingéd Folk did keep some track of ships, but they had no reason to watch for a large vessel coming from the far south, a vessel that had stayed out of sight of land. Humans in the New World rarely navigated out of sight of land, but the Liglimom, on their sacred mission, had taken risks.

Moreover, there had been much for the wingéd folk to watch closer to shore, as ships came from ports to the north and south of Hawk Haven bringing guests and supplies to the celebration for the new prince. There was no wonder they had not seen a ship that no one expected to see, carrying passengers they might not have known in their foreign attire.

Even now when Firekeeper had reason to believe that the oceans held their own Royal—or Wise—inhabitants, she knew little about them. Sea otters and seals both she had met, but although these creatures had served as guides in a few critical occasions, they had not told her anything of themselves or how they viewed the land dwellers. For all Firekeeper knew, they—or deeper-dwelling kin such as whales and dolphins— might have witnessed her and Blind Seer's plight, but if so they had chosen to let their fate ride out uninterrupted.

"But we knew you were missing," Elation went on, "and when no one found you dead, and no one found you living, we began to expand the area of our search. You must understand, many of us did this for love for you, or from gratitude for what you had done for us. Others, however, joined the search because from the moment you and Blind Seer crossed the Iron Mountains, you have become unknowable properties, and sometimes the actions you have taken have given reason for alarm. Derian Carter, as your closest human ally, was also one these felt should not be permitted to drop from sight."

Firekeeper thought how she had chosen to make her own interpretation of the orders given to her back in the days when Queen Valora had taken the artifacts from the castle at Silver Whale Cove. She thought how she had argued for the lives of the humans in New Bardenville, even though that settlement threatened to violate the treaty lines that had been drawn between Beast and human since long before the coming of the Plague had drastically set back human colonization efforts.

She could understand why some of the Royal Beasts continued to view her as unknowable, and she felt a perverse pride in this. After all, although she was a wolf, she was no longer a pup. Didn't she have some right to make her own decisions?

"When many had begun to give all three of you both up for dead," Elation continued, "and to offer theories and conjectures how such an unusual trio might vanish without a trace, a pair of fish eagles came from the far south, across the deep inlet that has always divided those heretical lands from our own. When the wingéd folk who held those reaches would have driven them back as they had time and time again, these ospreys shrieked your names and requested parley.

"By then the search for you three missing ones had become common enough knowledge, at least among those who fly long distances, that the ospreys were permitted to land and speak their piece. What they told us, you already know."

Firekeeper nodded.

Blind Seer growled, "And since then communication has been slowly reestablished between Wise and Royal. Is it through this link that news of our journey north came to your attention?"

"Indirectly," Elation replied. "Was this a violation of some trust?"

Blind Seer looked at Firekeeper, and Firekeeper shrugged.

"Not really," she said. "I don't think that we expected any much to care if we went looking for some old ruins."

"Is that what you seek, then?" Elation asked. "Ruins?"

"We seek what was once the lair of a human named Virim," Firekeeper said. "He lived in the days when the Plague was first released into the lands, and although we have heard a few tales that might indicate he lived unduly beyond that time, we will first accept what is the evidence of our ears and eyes . . ."

"And noses," Blind Seer added. "But I think you know more than we do, Elation. What is it you have to tell us?"

"What if I told you," Elation said, "that this Virim and his pack not only live, but live here west of the Iron Mountains, where human kind is said not to be welcome. What if I told you that they maintain their lair not through violence or strong walls, but because the Royal Beasts protect them?"

Firekeeper thought of the golden eagle that had pursued Elation and her heart grew tight within her. Still, she made her lips speak the words she felt in her heart were right.

"I would say I thought you must be mistaken, for how could this be?"

Elation made a sad little crying noise, "But I am not mistaken. What I have told you is the truth, and I have flown here lest you be unwarned and slain by those you think of as kin."

XXI

 "As THE TALE was told to me," Elation said, "and I have no reason to believe that account was wrong, for it was told to me in an effort to keep me from doing precisely what I have done, this is how Virim came to build his nest in this region, and how for over a hundred years the Royal Beasts have guarded him, to his benefit and to their—or should I say 'our'—abiding shame."

"CAN WE BE honest?" Virim said. "There is a war about to begin."

He paused, swallowing a swelling lump of discomfort beneath his breastbone. Over the course of the last few decades, Virim had given any number of speeches. He considered himself a good speaker—even an excellent speaker. However, he had never tried to give a speech to an audience whose reactions he could so little judge. He had been assured that those to whom he spoke would understand him, but still . . .

A raven, a moose, a wolf, a puma, a raccoon, a bear, several raptors, a doe, an elk, a wolverine . . . and these were the animals who had possessed the courage to step forth and face him. He suspected there were others who lingered listening in the shadowed greenness of the surrounding forest. It was an unsettling thought.

The wolf hammered at one ear with a hind foot. An eagle shifted leg to leg. The bear scratched its belly with one forepaw. The doe stepped over to a shrub and bit off a bunch of leaves and stood chewing them, her liquid brown eyes studying him with absent thoughtfulness.

Virim forced himself to remember that humans would fidget as much or more, and continued speaking.

"Perhaps it would be more honest to admit that this war never really ended. Certainly, no treaties were signed, no formal agreements reached—at least in most circumstances. Rather, humans acquired what they wanted—free run of all the lands east of the Iron Mountains—and the Beasts retreated to where they thought they would be safe. I am here today to tell you—as I have already told some of your people—that this respite is ending. Humans are preparing to cross the Iron Mountains in force, and this time a simple geographic barrier will not be enough to stop them."

The raven croaked something that sounded remarkably like "Why?" and Virim chose to take this as a question.

"Why? Because in the decades since humans first came to the New World, they have not merely founded cities, clear-cut forests for farmland, replaced the native animals with ones brought from the Old World. Humans have done more than this. They have established a foothold for their magical powers. They have discovered the means by which they can more easily surmount the difficulties offered to them by the Iron Mountains. In short, they are far more powerful than those your ancestors fought against—and finally fled from."

The Beasts who were his audience studied Virim with unblinking eyes. There was no scratching now, no idle chewing of grass or leaf. Virim had their full attention, and he was surprised at how uncomfortable he found the assorted gazes of their inhuman eyes.

"I have come," Virim went on, "to offer you an alternative to war. I have come to offer myself—and some few humans who think as I do—as your allies."

Again the raven croaked, "Why?," and more confidently Virim replied.

"Because I think what my fellow humans plan to do is wrong. Why? Because unlike many of them I was born in the New World, and strange as it may seem to you, I think of these lands as my home. When I was a boy I showed promise of great magical ability, and because of that I was taken to the Old World to receive my training. My parents explained to me that this was a great honor. My teachers never let me forget the wonders the Old World offered.

"Those teachers took me and my classmates on tours of the great monuments of the Old World. We marveled over prism towers that shot rainbows even when the sky was overcast. We wondered over fountains and falls that ran with fire, as more usual ones run with water. We were permitted to study creatures conjured from magic, and to ride high above the earth on the backs of dragons and griffins. We were lifted so high above the surface of the earth that the most teeming human cities seemed like something a child might build from blocks, that the tilled fields and cropped pastures were but scraps among the greater untamed green."

A falcon with sharp-cut wings, a peregrine, Virim thought, gave a sharp shriek of what Virim thought might be laughter. He abruptly terminated his oratory. Such images might impress a human audience, but he had to remember that such vistas were nothing new to many of the Beasts, and that they would have viewed them under their own power, not dependent upon the ability of another.

He lowered his tone to inflections of humility, and noted that the ears of the wolf and puma twitched to follow his shifted tone.

"Many of my classmates did not see what I saw. They gloried in the power of human deeds, and failed to see how minuscule they were in contrast to what the natural world did so effortlessly. Me? The more I saw what passed for the wonders of the Old World, the more I longed for the simpler glories of the New. I longed to be again where I might hope to know the natural world through those who lived close to it. I longed to be home.

"And to the New World I returned when my time of training had ended. I went not as many of my classmates went, souls awash with bittersweet sorrow at being parted from all that was marvelous. Unlike them, I did not return with a desire to make the New World more and more like the Old. I went hoping to use my abilities to draw closer to those who understood my birth land far better than I ever had done.

"And many of you know that I followed that purpose with all my heart and soul. I sought the Beasts who I knew must still dwell among humanity. I found them first in the wingéd folk, but later, here and there, I found them intermingling with their less gifted cousins. Slowly, with great care, I made a friend here, another there. Never did I tell any human that humanity's former opponents moved freely among us, even nested on our proudest buildings. Repeatedly, I spoke out against exploitation of the New World's resources, against transforming it into a poor copy of the Old.

"But although I made some converts among humanity to my way of thinking, overall, I must admit that I failed. The majority of those with magical ability—and in the Old World and the New alike, these are the ones who rule—saw the New World as a treasure vault to plunder for their own gain. I don't need to tell you that not all the resources they sought were mineral or vegetable. You have seen the horrors they have perpetrated upon the thinking Beasts of the New World.

"I protested, but what good would such protests do against men and women who did not hesitate to mine their own race for blood with which to power their spells? The spellcasters in particular had come to view any who did not share their ability as unworthy of consideration as equals. Why would they extend this courtesy to creatures with whom they did not share even a common race? Their view was that if they could use the Beasts, they would use them. That was the only rationale that made any sense at all."

Virim dragged his hands across his face, feeling the tips of his fingers abrade the skin before anchoring in the tangled length of his beard. It was a good gesture before a human audience, but his animal audience looked unimpressed by this expression of grief and anguish.

He let his hands drop, straightened his shoulders, and raised his voice to more dynamic tones.

"Now time enough has passed that humans desire fresh challenges. Not only has a new generation trained to the magical arts arisen, hot with a desire to prove themselves, but also, through their arts, many of the older generation remain alive and powerful. Some of these wish to expand their abilities and resources. Others wish no more than to exhaust those younger spellcasters by sending them where other rivals—human and Beast—will thin the ranks. Where to find such rivals? Where to find these potent challenges? West of the Iron Mountains, of course. West into what land remains to you and yours."

This time his oratory had some effect. The wolverine and bear both growled. The puma unsheathed a pawful of impressively menacing claws and took a swipe at the trunk of a fallen tree, leaving deep slashes in the wood. The other animals did not react with such overt anger, but Virim sensed it nonetheless. Heartened, he continued.

"But I am here to offer the Beasts an alternative." Virim gestured to the slash marks on the piece of wood. "I will not argue that individually most of you are more than a match for any human."

He paused, cleared his throat, looked apologetic, then wondered if he was wasting effort on such gestures. How well did Beasts read human body language?

"That is, humans are no match unless the human is armed with a bow and arrows. Then even a wolf or puma would be endangered. Several shafts might be needed to fell a bear, but there are many bows, and many, many arrows—not only here in the New World, but in the Old World, ready to be imported at need. And surely your peoples remember that bows and arrows, spears and swords, are only the least of the weapons that humans can muster to their need."

From the rippling of fur and feathers, the gaping of beaks and showing of fangs, the Beasts surely did remember.

"Those weapons have only become more powerful in the years that have passed. In those early days, the spellcasters had limited resources upon which they could draw. I assure you, that is no longer the case. If it comes to battle between you and them, this time there will be no limit; there will be no need to retreat."

Virim paused, and this time, although he could understand nothing of it, he was aware of a sense that conversation was happening around him. Finally, the raven flapped forward a few paces and croaked.

"What?"

"What can we do?" Virim said. The raven made no further comment, but stared at him with bright, intelligent eyes. Virim went on. "I said I had an alternative to offer. My alternative is that you Beasts join forces with me and with those sorcerers I have convinced to see the justice of my cause—of your cause. We will defeat the other sorcerers for you, driving them from the New World entirely, perhaps from the face of the Earth. In return, we ask that you defend us while we do this, for we will be vulnerable. We ask that this protection not only extend during the time that we engage your enemies, but afterwards. We know all too well that when only we few remain, then we will be vulnerable to attack not only from humans, but from the very Beasts whom we have chosen to champion."

The raven raised the feathers on its head into odd little horns, then puffed out the feathers on its neck, making itself into a comical parody of one of the beasts of prey, a wolf, perhaps. Virim didn't know what to make of this display, but he nodded as if he did. Again he had the sense that the Beasts were talking among themselves, even arguing heatedly. He kept his silence, aware that the time for words on his part was past. He had offered himself to the Beasts. Would the Beasts accept him or reject him out of hand?

At last the raven turned its attention back to Virim. It puffed its feathers, especially those on its head, making a variety of grotesque shapes that Virim—for all his love of nature and the natural world—had never known were possible. At last the raven, perhaps frustrated by its limited vocabulary, began bobbing up and down.

Virim thought, *I need to say something. "What?" and "Why?" are hardly sufficient to answer the complicated issue I have raised.*

"You have conferred then?" he asked.

The raven ceased its agitated feather molding and croaked a sound rather like "Yes."

"Will you accept my offer?"

The raven began raising and lowering feathers again. Virim shook himself from fascinated observation with an effort.

"I think I understand. The matter is not that simple. Do you need an opportunity to confer with those you represent?"

"Yes," came the croak, more distinct this time.

"Will one day be enough?"

"No."

"Three days?"

The raven turned and faced the other Beasts. The bear grumbled and scratched. The wolf shook as if ridding itself of excess water.

"No," the raven said to Virim.

"By the next full moon?" That would give these ambassadors nearly a full moonspan to speak with their constituents.

The raven consulted his fellows, then looked at Virim.

"Yes."

"Here?"

"Yes."

"Very good. I will do my best to delay any catastrophe during that time," Virim said, "but I cannot promise."

Humans might have offered him some thanks, but the Beasts did not wait upon such formalities. Almost before Virim finished speaking they had melted one by one into the surrounding forest, the winged ones rising into the air and becoming motes among the blue.

Virim considered what he had done, stroking the tangles from his beard. Then he too returned to his people, feeling some relief that he would be able to speak and to be spoken to in return.

WHEN ELATION FINISHED her narration, Blind Seer said, "And we know what the Beasts replied. They accepted Virim's proposal, and so the Plague was released into the New World and spread into the Old as well."

"But Beasts accepting the aid of humans!" Firekeeper protested. "Accepting the aid of sorcerers! I can't believe it."

"So the buck said when the puma dropped onto his back," Blind Seer retorted. "Belief makes no difference. What has happened, has happened. Only humans believe that refusing to believe in what they know must be true will change reality."

Firekeeper was instantly humbled. "You are right. I don't want to believe it, but Elation would not lie to us."

"Perhaps I believed more easily," Blind Seer said kindly, licking her arm, "because of what my nose showed me when we scouted earlier. I found scent trails for many Beasts, oddly overlapping in ways that do not usually happen in the natural course of events. I also found the scent trails of at least one human as well, so close in time and place to those of the Beasts that they must have been in company. I was disturbed, but not as disturbed as I would have been before we encountered the Liglimom and the yarimaimalom. We cannot deny that there are fruitful partnerships between humans and Beasts."

Elation squawked with something like her usual contemptuous derision. "I would have thought you could have known this without flying days and days to the far south, and meeting with strange peoples. The pair of you is proof enough for these eyes that Beasts and humans can work as one."

Firekeeper was so overwhelmed by all she had learned that she did not even feel the urge to protest that she was wolf, not human. Right now if someone had told her she was a field mouse, she would have checked for a long bare tail trailing behind her before denying the possibility.

"Then the Beasts of a hundred and more years ago made a pact with Virim and his allies, and in return Virim and his allies released the Plague. Very well. I accept that. If that is true, then other things follow. The eagle that chased you, that was no mere rivalry between the rulers of the air, that was something more."

"You see clearly now," Elation agreed. "That was something more indeed. That golden eagle belongs to a flock that has kept the pact with Virim and his followers all these long years and more. Nor are the golden eagles the only ones who do so. As the years passed, Virim lived on and on, living well beyond the usual life span of humankind."

"We have heard that this was an art among the great sorcerers," Firekeeper said, feeling strange that an ability so peculiar could feel now like solid ground. "The Beasts must have been greatly surprised."

"They were," Elation said, "and from what the Mothers of my aerie told when news of your search came to our hearing, those Beasts had learned to live with unpleasant surprises."

"It does not take this nose and these ears," Blind Seer said, "to guess that not all the Royal Beasts were delighted with the pact that had been made in their name."

"Good stalking," Elation agreed. "You have soared true. Less than a full moonspan was time for the Beasts whom Virim had contacted to speak with many who lived near, but certainly not to achieve congress or accord among all the packs and flocks and herds. It was far from enough time to seek those who thrive in isolation. Yet, during the time over which the moon changed her face, something happened that made the northwestern Beasts feel they must accept Virim's offer, even if their fellows did not."

"Humans began their attack," Firekeeper said, as certain as if she had seen it happen.

"True flown," Elation said. "And the attack came through a pass in these northern mountains, so the Beasts in this region felt themselves greatly threatened."

"I wonder," Blind Seer mused, "if Virim's presence had anything to do with prompting that attack?"

"I do not know," Elation said, "but from what I know of humans, I would not deny the possibility—or even overlook the possibility that Virim himself did something to encourage what happened."

Firekeeper nodded, "Either he could have done something to make his pack mates wish to pursue him, or they simply could have been trying to cut him off before he ran free of their reach. The results would have been much the same. The Beasts would have seen themselves threatened as Virim had predicted they would be threatened, and so would have made a pact with him."

Blind Seer shuddered, "And what a pact. Those of their kin who live today must have served Virim and his kind for so long that they must hardly know there is another way to live."

Elation twisted and preened her shoulder feathers. "And not only them. Others have served that cause, if rather more indirectly. That service is why I am here."

Firekeeper stiffened, but she kept her manners polite as she asked, "Having you with us again seemed as natural as sunrise. I almost forgot how very strange it was. You said you had flown here so that we might not be slain by those we think of as kin. I understand, now. You mean these Beasts who have made pact with Virim."

"That is so," Elation said.

Blind Seer's hackles had risen. "But from what you said, about having done so following your own impulse, not all the

Royal Beasts agreed we should be warned. What have we done to earn such enmity?"

"I will not deny," Elation replied, "that there are those among the Royal Beasts who dislike how you and Firekeeper have comported yourselves since you went east. You have become a power in yourselves, one with influence all out of proportion to your numbers. Nor have you proven loyalty to those who reared you. Rather you have shown a disturbing tendency to make decisions for yourselves.

"However, that is not the main reason why, when the Royal Beasts near whom I dwelled received word of what you two intended, that they decided that perhaps the best course of action was no action at all—neither to attempt to warn you about what you might encounter, nor to send any to stop you. Why they decided this, as I saw it as I sat amid those joined in council, was that they feared Virim, and what Virim might do in retaliation."

Neither Firekeeper nor Blind Seer asked what the Beasts had feared. They knew all too well the old legends. Even more, they knew the lingering reality of Old World magic. Moreover, this Virim and those who dwelled with him were no Once Dead; they were not semi-trained, and nor were they seared by querinalo, kept from full use of their dubious gifts. They were the last of the Old World sorcerers themselves, the last remnant of a power that had kept all the world in thrall.

Thinking of this, Firekeeper said very softly. "I can hardly blame the Royal Beasts for their fear, but I am grateful that you, at least, had courage to act against that course. But now that we are warned, what is your intent? Do you hope that your warning will stop us from what we are here to do?"

Elation shrieked a falcon's laugh. "As if I could! No, Firekeeper, I wish you and Blind Seer to do what rumor told us you hoped to do."

"You wish us to find the source of the Plague?" Blind Seer said. "Why should it matter to you?"

Elation slicked her feathers tight and flat. "I care little about the Plague, as such, but I care very much about an Old World sorcerer living this close to where my chicks are finding their wings. I do not consider myself terribly imaginative, but the same ones who told us of your journeys and what you had learned during them told us of the Once Dead, grown into magical power despite the Plague.

"Peregrine are not as territorial as wolves, but even so we do not like others who would take our nests. Virim must know of these budding rivals. I have ridden hot currents of thought, considering what may happen when Virim concludes that these Once Dead have flown too high. Nor am I among those who thinks Virim will continue to honor his treaty with Royalkind forever. We hear that querinalo struck even Beasts who crossed into the Old World. How long before he releases it, or something worse, into the New?"

"So you are with us," Blind Seer said.

"I am with you and above you," Elation assured him. "I am your eyes above the trees. My beak and talons will fight even my own nestlings if that would be needed. What knowledge I have hunted down is yours, but as to what three such as we can do against one such as Virim, even forgetting that he has humans and Beasts alike who serve him, as to this, I can offer no answers."

Firekeeper reached out and scratched Blind Seer between his ears.

"We have learned a great deal about humans," she said thoughtfully, "in the years since we ran with you holding the skies above us. Once I would have thought that we would need to go and dig this Virim from his lair as a wolverine digs after a rabbit. Now, though, now I wonder if the hunting will go both ways."

"Why would Virim hunt you?" Elation asked. "He is safe in his lair. Beasts vowed to his protection roamed this forest, and if he so ordered, they would hunt you as the golden eagle hunted me. You drove off the eagle, but could you drive off a wolf pack? Could you defeat even a single bear?"

Firekeeper shrugged. "Blind Seer and I might fight better than you imagine. I am far stronger than when I first learned to pull a bow, and my arrows drive very deep. Blind Seer has fought some strange battles as well. But I do not think we will find ourselves fighting Virim's lackeys, at least not at first. I think he will wish to observe us."

Elation made a scornful sound, and Firekeeper grinned. Blind Seer scratched at one ear, then addressed the falcon.

"Humans," Blind Seer said pedantically, "as you may have noticed, are equipped with something far more deadly than claws or fangs or talons. They are plagued with curiosity. When this bites into them, they are no better than puppies. A pup will fall into a river giving battle to his reflection—no matter that he is told what will happen. So it is with a human bitten with curiosity. They will risk themselves to satisfy it."

Elation cocked her head, focusing on Firekeeper in amusement. "You do not growl at this assessment as once you might have, Firekeeper."

"I could say," Firekeeper replied, "that this is because I am a wolf, and Blind Seer is not speaking of me, but that would be less than honest. I do not growl because what Blind Seer says is true. I think that curiosity—either that of Virim, or of one of those humans who is allied with him—will cause them to hold their hand from us, at least for a while."

Elation almost cooed, a strange sound from so fierce a falcon. "There is a great deal about which one might be curious in regard to the two of you. Sometimes I forget how very strange the wolf-woman would be to one who has not had the dubious pleasure of observing her firsthand."

Firekeeper ignored the taunt, hearing the affection that underlay it.

"There is that," she agreed. "There is also the fact that Blind Seer and I are widely traveled. I do not know what resources Virim has, but I suspect we have been places where he has not gone, places where even those who know how to use magic to extend their ability to see cannot go."

"The Nexus Islands," Blind Seer mused aloud. "Yes. The Meddler told us that he could not see into them, even though otherwise his vision stretches into strange reaches indeed."

"The Meddler?" Elation said. "I have not heard of this one.

Is it one of these maimalodalum of whom the yarimaimalom speak?"

"I wish the Meddler was so simple to explain," Firekeeper said. "I will tell you another time, but I think that I would rather not speak of him where we might be overheard."

Elation, who had been rucking her feathers in displeasure, smoothed them flat.

"Another thing, then," she said, "about which there might be curiosity."

"Precisely," Firekeeper said.

She did not think any Beast could creep close enough to overhear them without either Blind Seer or Elation noticing, but there was no being certain. And who knew what Virim might be capable of doing? Elation's tale had implied that once Virim had not known how to understand the speech of the Beasts, but in a hundred years and more he surely would have worked to overcome that impediment. Best to be very careful, and if they were overheard? Well, that might be the scent to awaken hungry curiosity.

"And if curiosity is not enough to draw someone to us?" Elation asked.

"Then we still have the option of working our way into their lair," Firekeeper said, "or of forcing them out."

"And if Virim uses magic against us?" Elation asked. "What then? Remember, this is the one whose spell slew those who imagined themselves untouchable."

"He cannot use querinalo against us," Firekeeper said. "We have met that challenge and beaten it flat. As for other magics? I don't know for certain. I carry iron on me, and, if you and Blind Seer permit, I will find a way for you to carry some on you so that you may be somewhat protected against spells. If that is not enough, well . . ."

Blind Seer rose and stretched, giving Firekeeper and Elation a gap-jawed, panting wolf's smile.

"If that is not enough, then we were doomed from before we made this run. If our only choice is to turn around and run back to the Nexus Islands, then tell those who trusted us that we ran because we had heard the buck was large and had a heavy rack, well, I think I'd rather be gored."

Brave words, Firekeeper thought, *from a brave heart. I hope we do not come to regret them.*

XXII

DERIAN WATCHED THE rising moon as he walked his path among the various gate buildings. His senses were keyed to alertness, but not because he had any reason to expect any trouble. Indeed, the gates had remained quiet for so long now that there were those who thought the patrols were a waste of time, that the Old World nations had accepted that the gates were closed to them.

But happily for Derian, Ynamynet was not one of those who felt thus, and as long as she continued to support the watches, Derian knew that they would continue. The Wise Beasts also continued to support the patrols, sending representatives from among their number to join the community. Most of these were from among the wingéd folk, and when Derian had wondered why, Eshinarvash had explained.

"Spring is a busy time for packs and herds. Not only are there young to be raised and guarded, but winter has worn away the last fat and the grass is not so thick—nor the herds so plump—that this is easily rebuilt. Later, when summer makes all plentiful, I would not be surprised to see the wolves and bears and great cats show willing to come here again."

"But the wingéd folk? Don't they have the same needs?"

"Not all," Eshinarvash said. "Many avians go through periods where they are not yet interested in mating and establishing territory. They mob about in flocks with other young birds, learning their limits. Many of those who have risked querinalo to come here are such. The wingéd folk also have another advantage over the rest of us."

"What?"

"They can travel over great distances, even over water, with relatively good speed and little inconvenience. Those who have crossed to the Nexus Islands through the gates have made another stop first—one that explains why none among them has fallen to querinalo."

"They're going to Misheemnekuru," Derian exclaimed. "They're having the maimalodalum inspect them to see if they sense any whiff of a magical talent!"

"That is so," Eshinarvash said. "I believe Plik suggested the course of action to Bitter and Lovable, and they, in turn, have made clear that only those who have been checked first should cross."

"I wish we could do that with humans," Derian said wistfully. "We could use some new recruits, but we can't use the same process, not as long as the maimalodalum choose to remain in isolation."

"Even if the maimalodalum did not," Eshinarvash reminded him with a snort, "they cannot be everywhere at once, and most certainly they cannot come here. That would be too dangerous."

Derian nodded, remembering how Plik had lost his own talent to querinalo.

"So we must rely on Firekeeper finding something out, and so far there is no sign of her or Blind Seer."

"It is far too early," Eshinarvash reminded him. "They are fast travelers, but they have a long way to go."

"I know," Derian said. "I know."

Derian thought all of this over as he paced his route among the gates. It seemed like Firekeeper had been gone forever, but actually hardly more than a moonspan had passed. Enigma made his daily checks, and although sometimes he found Grateful Peace or Citrine bearing some gift or perhaps a note on which they had written some question, the puma had not seen nor smelled either of the wolves.

From time to time, Harjeedian had sought omens as he had

been trained, but they were inconclusive. The jaguar, Truth, had given the aridisdu assurance that his skills were not at fault.

"Firekeeper," she had said through Plik's translation, "has never been one for whom the omen stream runs steady. Even I at my greatest, in my year, could not trace her course with any ease."

Truth would say little more on the matter, other than to offer reassurance that she had seen none of the ripples that would certainly occur if Firekeeper were to die. With this, they were forced to be content.

The moon rose higher, and Derian listened with more and more care, but not, he knew, because he expected any trouble. Isende had continued to join him when the night patrol fell to him, walking with him sometimes for hours.

Sometimes he wondered that they kept finding things to talk about, and he would do his best to prepare something in advance just in case Isende might think he was bored and decide to take her leave early. This never happened, though. Story after story poured out of both of them, ranging between the trivial and the profound with illogical facility.

One night they might begin by discussing childhood games, and end by confessing old fears they had never outgrown. Another night they might start with something profound—such as Derian's never-resolved fear that his family would reject him or Isende's still unrealized hope that some small gem of magical ability had escaped querinalo's fire—and end up making puns in the mishmash of Pellish and Liglimosh, flavored with a heavy salting of five or six other languages, that was becoming the common language of the Nexus Islands.

Derian never knew what would happen, but he knew he'd miss Isende if for some reason she couldn't join him.

And we've done nothing yet but talk, Derian marveled. *Well, talk and hold hands a little. I've thought about kissing her, and about doing a lot more than kissing her, but I can't seem to manage.*

There were good reasons for his reluctance. Derian was fairly certain that Isende wasn't repulsed by his physical form, but strangely enough Derian himself still was. He avoided his reflection, and went out of his way not to look at himself. That was fairly easy to do. With resources rationed, just about everyone dressed and undressed in the dark, but Derian knew he took the matter to extremes. He swam or bathed after dark as well, didn't look at his hands when he was writing, and even avoided his shadow.

This was a great change from his previous self. He'd had his share of lovers, casual and serious, and while he had never been vain about his appearance, he'd been content enough with what he had to offer to not shy from either making or accepting advances.

But Derian's own insecurities were only part of the problem. Another was that even when he was ostensibly alone with Isende, say on one of these patrols, there was always someone near. At night it was usually one of the yarimaimalom; tonight a pair of owls. He didn't think they would be repulsed by human physical interaction, but unlike some of the humans on the Nexus Islands, Derian never forgot that the Beasts were as intelligent and inquisitive—and gossipy—as their human associates.

Then there was Tiniel. The young man had not come out and said directly that he disapproved of Isende's interest in Derian, but his very silence on the subject, and how he avoided any but the most routine contact with Derian, made his feelings quite plain.

From his talks with Isende, Derian knew that she and Tiniel had been almost impossibly close since birth, linked not so much in thought as by an emotional bond. Querinalo had severed this, and while Isende was content, even relieved, by the change, Tiniel still mourned the loss.

So why doesn't Tiniel find himself another confidant? Derian mused, almost angrily. *He's not a bad-looking fellow, and there are some unattached women not too far from his age. If he's not interested in romance, he could at least make a few friends. I think the only person he talks to at all regularly is Plik.*

Footsteps sounded on the graveled path leading up the hillside, and Derian felt his breath catch. He knew those footsteps and felt they matched the excited beating of his heart.

Isende topped the hillside a moment later.

"Looking for me?" Derian asked, trying to sound teasing, and hoping he didn't sound plaintive instead.

"I just might be," Isende replied, orienting on his voice, and making her way toward him.

The moon had risen enough that its waxing crescent made a torch or candle unnecessary, even for Isende's unaltered eyes. Grudgingly, Derian had to admit that one thing that had improved since his transformation was his night vision, and now he enjoyed watching Isende almost skip over to him.

"Any trouble?" she asked, rising on her toes to kiss him lightly on one cheek.

"All quiet," he replied, wishing he could manage the same casual affection. He thought, though, he'd either balk at the last moment or crush her to him and never let go. He'd do better to avoid either.

He settled for reaching out a hand.

"Path's rough here," he said, feeling her slim fingers slip between his. "Let me help."

They walked then, hand in hand, chattering softly, overflown by silent winged owls who kept watch over their human allies—and the gates—with wordless satisfaction.

∞

FIREKEEPER WAS RUNNING, but her paws were touching clouds. The clouds felt good against her pads, for she was footsore and tired.

Stirring up curiosity was proving to be hard work. For the last several days, she, Blind Seer, and Elation had been doing just that. Although they had been very, very aware of eyes watching them from cloudless skies and beneath the thickening greenery of the forest, those eyes had all been those of

Beasts. No one had come forth from the keep built deep into the heavy granite of the foothills, no one they could pounce and pin, and so hold that they might ask questions.

Firekeeper felt hands gripping her shoulders, anchoring firmly in the loose skin, pulling slightly against the fur. The grasp was tight, but not so tight as to restrict movement. She felt weight now, too, now that she thought about it. Weight as if a human sat upon her back, straddling her as humans did horses.

She sniffed with her keen wolf's nose, but even when she cut a circle in the air so that she could catch her own trail she smelled no one. Only one person of her acquaintance had no scent, and by this lack of scent, Firekeeper knew both who rode upon her and that she was dreaming.

"Hey, Meddler," she called, and her voice held a wolf's howl. "Why are you running in my dreams?"

"Because it's the best way to show you a few things you need to know—at least the best way that won't involve upsetting Blind Seer, and you wouldn't want me to do that, would you?"

The Meddler's tone was mocking and sardonic as ever, but Firekeeper didn't let that bother her. She appreciated the courtesy. The great gulf of silence that had separated her from her beloved had closed some over the last moonspan or so, bridged in part by confession and in part by acceptance, but she would be the first to admit this was a shaky bridge, strung on spiderwebs and planked with ice.

"So what do you wish to show me?" Firekeeper asked.

The Meddler tugged at her right ear, steering her as one might a horse by the reins, and Firekeeper growled at the affront.

Instantly, there was no weight on her back, and for a moment Firekeeper thought the Meddler had taken offense and departed. Then she saw a wolf running alongside her, a wolf very like Blind Seer but that his eyes were amber and mocking.

"Several things," the Meddler replied, "and since you seem willing to look, let me be your guide."

He pulled out ahead, breaking trail through the clouds as the Ones did through snowdrifts when the pack ventured forth for a winter hunt.

"There, below. Look," the Meddler said, pausing at a break in the clouds.

Firekeeper looked. Through the white-edged hole she saw the bluish grey of ocean water on a partially overcast day. There were many interruptions on the water. At first they made no sense to her; then she adjusted her perspective, remembering things seen from the high towers of the castle at Silver Whale Cove in Bright Bay.

"Ships," she said. "Many, many ships. Big, too, I think. Bigger than most I have seen. At least as big as the *Fayonejunjal*."

This last was the ship that had come from Liglim north into the vicinity of Hawk Haven, the ship that had carried her and Blind Seer and Derian into captivity.

"Many ships," the Meddler agreed, "and you're right about their size, too. Think yourself closer alongside me."

Normally, Firekeeper would have protested such an odd command, but this time she did not. After all, she was dreaming and so such things were possible.

Details became sharper and the Meddler said, "Look there and there. Tell me what you see?"

Firekeeper did not frown, not precisely. Wolves did not frown as humans did, but she concentrated hard, pricking her ears forward.

"Many humans, dressed oddly, I think, for fishing. Some are clad as sailors, but others . . . they remind me more of soldiers."

"That is correct," the Meddler said. "What you see there is an army being gathered, an army that will travel on those ships."

Firekeeper started to ask where that army might be going, but the Meddler had begun to run again. She loped after, not at all certain what would happen if she were left behind.

Again they ran, and the clouds grew thicker and heavier. Time and again, the Meddler paused and sniffed. Once or twice he dug a little with his forepaws, but always he moved on before Firekeeper could guess what he might be digging after.

At last he seemed satisfied with his hole, for this time he kept digging, piling up the whiteness of the clouds until it heaped to one side.

"There, below. Look," the Meddler said, as he had done before. Then he added, "Tell me what you see."

Firekeeper looked and this time the hole in the clouds showed her a human city. In style of building it was not unlike what she was familiar with from Hawk Haven and Bright Bay. She was surprised to feel a slight pang of homesickness. Humans were moving about in various areas in a fashion that tickled her memory. She thought herself closer, and what she saw made her flatten her ears and tuck her tail down.

"Those are soldiers," she said, "marching as I have seen them do when preparing for war. What is this place? Does this have anything to do with those ships?"

The Meddler laughed and turned to kick cloud stuff back over the hole he had dug.

"That place is called the Kingdom of the Mires. It is one nation among many on a larger piece of land that was once called Pelland."

"Pelland," Firekeeper said. "That is where those who founded the colony of Gildcrest came from. I think I have heard Urgana and other of the Old World Nexans speak of those Mires as well. That is where the king who gave a home to the Once Dead lived."

"Your memory is sharp," the Meddler said, beginning to run again, "even when you are asleep. The Kingdom of the Mires prepares for war again, but this time their target is not their neighboring lands. It is the Nexus Islands. They are offended that the gates are closed to them, and have determined to win them open once more."

He paused at the edge of a mass of clouds and looked down. Running up to join him, Firekeeper did so as well. Below were islands, and even before she thought herself close she knew what islands they must be.

"The Nexus Islands," she said. "They know nothing of what comes for them?"

"Nothing," the Meddler agreed.

He indicated a figure seated on a jutting spit of land facing south. The fur was charcoal dark and blended well with the spray-dashed stone, but there was no mistaking those burning spots for some errant wildflowers.

"Truth suspects something," the Meddler said, "but try as she might, she cannot refine her vision. She watches, and perhaps someone will have the sense to ask her what is it she watches for."

"Derian might," Firekeeper said hopefully. "Derian notices many things."

"Not so many these days," the Meddler said with an indulgent chuckle. "He has found himself a good distraction."

He pricked his ears forward and Firekeeper saw Derian sitting in the sunshine near his house. Isende sat with him, and although both had handwork to keep them busy, Firekeeper was a wolf, and wolves do not need words for explanation.

"He finally noticed!" she howled in pleasure. "I thought she might need to crawl into his bed to get him to see her interest."

"I don't think there has been any bed crawling yet," the Meddler said, "but as you can see, Derian is not quite as alert as he might be to the even odder behavior of already strange jaguars."

"Can't you speak to him as you are to me?" Firekeeper asked. "Couldn't you slide into his dreams?"

The Meddler's tone was gently amused. "I have tried, but Derian's dreams are rather crowded of late. I am having difficulty getting his attention. You . . . You are different, Firekeeper. I have your kiss to link us."

Firekeeper was glad she was a wolf, because her skin would not color and give her away. She remembered that kiss. The Meddler had extracted it from her in payment of a debt, and she still remembered all too acutely how it had felt to be held in human arms and kissed by human lips and tongue.

"Well," she said, determinedly keeping her ears up and tail firm, "keep trying. You touched his thoughts when he had querinalo. Perhaps some link remains."

The Meddler rose from the edge of the clouds and began to run again. Firekeeper gave one more longing glance toward her distant friend, then dashed to join the Meddler.

"I will try," he said, and the words had the weight of a promise. "The problem is that the other times I have been able to send visions—to Derian, to Bitter, to Blind Seer, even to Truth—they were more than halfway to me, pushed by illness or injury into places where visions are more real than those things the senses know. None of them are that way now."

"You contacted Truth before," Firekeeper said. "That is how we came to make your acquaintance."

"Ah, yes," the Meddler agreed, "but then I had created an item to provide the link. I had the means to make a body for myself then. I no longer do."

Firekeeper did not ask why not. She was growing more comfortable with the ways of magic, but she still felt no great desire to know more about such lore than she must.

"Still," she said, "you might reach Truth. She does not like you, but she is more gone into dreams than ever since her battle with Ahmyn."

"And both of those are good reasons," the Meddler replied, "why I should not waste energy trying to contact her. Even if I did reach her, she would be able to dismiss me by viewing me as one of the many distracting visions with which she must live. Still, you give me a thought . . ."

"Tiniel?" Firekeeper said. "Isende?"

"Yes," the Meddler agreed. "I had a link with them both, a link very like that which I had with Truth. I will try, but not now. I have more to show you."

Firekeeper made herself content with this. She was growing tired, and guessed that this dream running took as much toll as—or even more than—the more usual kind.

"You must follow me very carefully now," the Meddler said. "I took you to places where we were not likely to be observed, but there are two places I wish to take you where we will be in some danger."

"Danger?" Firekeeper said. "But this is a dream!"

"You know better than most who walk the earth since querinalo," the Meddler reproved, "that dreams can be very real. Have you forgotten the Dragon?"

"Never," Firekeeper said.

She lowered her tail slightly, conceding the point without groveling.

"What are we hunting?"

"As I said, there are things I wish to show you," the Meddler said. "You have seen the gathering of an army and a navy. You have seen how the Nexans go about their business unconcerned. Now I will show you two things closer to your own mission. Follow me. Hold your questions. Do not think yourself nearer to what I show you unless I signal that it is safe."

Firekeeper indicated her agreement. Wolves followed the commands of the Ones without question. Certainly, in this weird hunt, the Meddler was the One and she the least pup.

When the Meddler paused next and indicated that Firekeeper should look through a parting in the clouds, she immediately recognized their destination as the keep in the rocks which Virim and his followers had made their refuge and their stronghold. There was a strange solidity about the stone from which the keep was made, as if it were harder and denser than the surrounding foothills, than even the precise cliffs and boulders from which it was carved.

The perspective was odd as well. They did not look down upon the keep as they had in the other visions. Rather the Meddler had brought them level with one of the higher towers, a heavy, square structure, blocked about by jagged crenellations. Before this, Firekeeper had seen the tower only from the ground, angles distorted by her need to look up. This view was more as if she were perched high in the boughs of a tree or on some facing range of hills.

After a long moment of silent watching, Firekeeper detected motion from between the crenellations.

Almost instinctively, for so quickly had she adjusted to the Meddler's way of showing her things, Firekeeper began to think herself closer so she might look upon this figure, but she remembered the Meddler's warning and contented herself with this more distant view.

What moved about the top of the tower was a human—that much she could tell—but whether a man or woman, whether old or young, the elaborate robes and headdresses favored by those who used magic made impossible to tell. The human was watchful, moving a few steps, then pausing and taking long looks out into the surrounding forest.

Firekeeper got a good look at the face then, and saw it was beardless: a woman then, or a young man, or a man who chose not to wear a beard. Try as she could, she could not resolve the image any more clearly.

After a time, the figure turned and opened a door, going back inside the tower. Even so, Firekeeper did not speak until the Meddler had led them away and they were among the thick clouds again and the Meddler had reclined in a posture of rest.

"So Virim's keep is still inhabited," Firekeeper said, "as Elation told us, and as our own noses confirmed."

"Disappointed," the Meddler said. "Well, so was I. I wanted to show you why I couldn't tell you more about what goes on within Virim's stronghold."

Firekeeper thought about how heavy and solid the stone had seemed and understood.

"It is blocked to creatures such as you," she said, "as you told me the Nexus Islands were before I gave you passage."

"That is correct," the Meddler said.

"Do you think they sought to block you specifically?" Firekeeper asked.

"I don't think so," the Meddler said. "Remember, Virim was prepared to make all those who practiced magic his enemies. He must have believed querinalo would work as he had planned, but he could not be certain. Were I him, I would have made myself a very secure place to which I could retreat if something went wrong."

"As a mother wolf digs her den in advance of pupping," Firekeeper said. "Yes. That makes sense."

She scratched behind her left ear with her left hind leg, and realized how very tired she was.

"One more thing," she said, trying not to whine. "I think I can follow."

The Meddler rose. "This last place is not far, but once again, I warn you. Stay quiet."

Firekeeper answered by being so, not feeling as if she had breath or thought to waste. The Meddler slowed his pace, leading them not over vast plains of clouds as before, but through towering vistas that reminded Firekeeper of the sky mountains that sailed the air before the coming of a thunderstorm. Here the clouds were not all white, nor so fluffy, but were touched with shades of grey. They rasped against the tired pads of Firekeeper's paws, like ground glass or coarse sand.

Eventually, the Meddler slid through a narrow pass between two very tall, very grey peaks. Firekeeper found herself on a rise that looked down over a sheltered area, a glade among the cloud mountains. This time the Meddler did not look for a gap in the clouds, nor dig to create one, but indicated with a pricking of his ears and the lift of his nose that she should examine the glade.

Firekeeper did and for a long moment saw nothing but clouds. Then she realized that what she had taken for a bit of variegated grey was a creature in the glade, a creature moving in a purposeful fashion among what Firekeeper now saw were books and scrolls.

She resisted the urge to think herself closer, and waited instead with the long patience of the hunter who must be patient or else starve. The creature moved, and Firekeeper separated enough of its soft greyness from the surroundings to be sure it was a wolf. She continued to watch, and when the wolf turned in their direction to consult one of the scrolls, Firekeeper saw a flash of blue and knew who they watched.

Blind Seer was in that sheltered glade, consulting books and scrolls as might Harjeedian or Urgana. He was calm and methodical, but nonetheless, Firekeeper was aware of a tightly strung, tense urgency to the search. Blind Seer was not one to tear about madly, but the care and method with which he unrolled scrolls and turned pages could not disguise that this was a search for something vital.

Firekeeper restrained herself from dashing down into the glade to offer her help. She watched, tension growing into alarm until the Meddler drew her back and away. This time she did not speak, even when they had collapsed on soft clouds that gave way beneath aching bones.

"So," the Meddler said, "you knew him."

"Blind Seer," Firekeeper said.

"He searches for the secret that will unlock what querinalo revealed to him," the Meddler said. For once his tone was free from mockery. Indeed, it was almost gentle. "He seeks to discover how to become a spellcaster."

Firekeeper raised her head and stared dully at the Meddler.

"Then he did not let it burn away?"

The question was useless. She knew the answer. She suspected she had known it from the start. Why else had Blind Seer not boasted of his achievement?

"He did not," the Meddler said. "Your beloved is a sorcerer. By now he knows what he has long suspected. He is no minor talent. Indeed, because Blind Seer dealt with querinalo as no other has ever done, that blue-eyed wolf may hold within him the most latent power of any who has lived since querinalo burned the Old World rulers into dust. However, he is like a pup somehow born to the size and weight and strength of his father. The raw ability is there, but not the coordination to use it."

"What about Enigma?" Firekeeper asked, grasping for anything that would reduce the enormity of this discovery. "He is a Beast. He can cast spells."

"Enigma gave querinalo something else to feed upon," the Meddler replied. "Enigma did not know that he was preserving a talent for spellcasting when he did so, or else he might have not. Cats are difficult for me to understand."

Given that the Meddler had believed he could use Truth, Firekeeper could only agree.

She said nothing else, thinking over all she had learned. War was coming to the Nexus Islands. She needed to discover a cure to querinalo, or no reinforcements could be brought. Without those, the Nexus Islands, and through them the New World, might well be doomed.

That was unchanged. What had changed was that the one she had most trusted, the one who she thought of as her other self, now seemed far too likely to ally himself with the other side.

Virim and his people, after all, had the knowledge and the teaching Blind Seer would need to use his talent.

She had no idea when the Meddler left her. She sat there among the clouds, unthinking, until she slipped from waking dreams into the chill chaos of nightmare.

XXIII

"SO OUR SHIPS have joined the larger fleet," Bryessidan said, addressing Chelm Charlock, his minister for international trade. "That is good news."

Like all of Bryessidan's court, Chelm Charlock had been forced by circumstances to expand beyond his more usual role. With trade via the gates stalled to nothing, Chelm had his assistants developing more conventional routes. Meanwhile, he concentrated on the difficult and time-sensitive task of arranging for sailors, ships, and supplies to join the invasion fleet.

"King Hurwin plans to begin practicing maneuvers while waiting for the rest of the fleet to assemble," Chelm said. "He says it is too early to sail for the Nexus Islands. The fleet would simply encounter foul weather, and would undoubtedly lose ships. This way the fleet will be accustomed to working as a unit long before they leave safe waters."

"And how," Bryessidan asked, "is the fleet performing?"

Chelm glanced at notes he almost certainly did not need before replying.

"The marines Pelland is supplying are, predictably, undertrained and poorly disciplined. Their sailors—drawn mostly, like ours, from a merchant marine—are doing better. The marines from Azure Towers and Hearthome are more skilled fighters, but those from Azure Towers need to be taught to adapt some of their tactics to shipboard."

Bryessidan waved a hand to forestall further reporting on the condition of their allies' troops. They would be King Hurwin's problem.

"And the Mires' contribution?" he said. "You must have heard rumors."

Chelm Charlock shifted a bit anxiously from foot to foot.

"Our marines and sailors are reported to be adequate," he finally said.

Bryessidan smiled sardonically. "Barely so, I am sure. Well, what do they expect when we have not been permitted to maintain a standing army or navy for over ten years?"

He fell silent, brooding over the more serious problem of the land forces. The sailors they had contributed to King Hurwin's fleet were unquestionably skilled at handling their ships. They also possessed some skill with weapons, although their tactics were more geared to defense then offense.

The land forces Bryessidan was to lead through the gate were more of a problem. Despite himself, Bryessidan was beginning to doubt he could be the unifying commander that Gidji believed he could be.

I almost wish, the king of the Mires thought, keeping just enough attention on Chelm Charlock's report that he could nod at appropriate points, *that our situation was different. Gidji would probably make a far better military commander than I. She did not spend the last ten years assuring everyone and anyone that she had no desire to go to war. At least I kept up with my swordplay and archery. I have no reason to feel shame on those points, but what of my soldiers? Most of them are bog farmers and fishers, more accustomed to dealing with wild animals and bad weather than with human opponents— all but those who fought for my father, and even those who were young men then haven't used their skills for a decade.*

On the other hand, if Gidji was to command, then I think the Tavetch would be overrepresented in this action. I have no desire to have my kingdom fall into vassalage even to a friendly ally. No. I must have more faith in my troops—and in myself.

Chelm Charlock departed, leaving a sheaf of documents,

mostly maps showing the new trade routes by which his staff had determined at least some of the Mires' produce might be carried. Bryessidan thanked the minister warmly for his efforts, without which the economy of the Mires would suffer greatly.

Preparing for a war was not an inexpensive option. The guilds were delighted by all the work coming their way. This work, in turn, had stimulated the economy, for both raw materials and able hands were needed. The army and navy, too, had created demands for goods, services, and troops, but even at the "patriotic" pay scale Bryessidan had been forced to instate, the money to pay the troops had to come from somewhere.

Right now that "somewhere" was the royal treasury. Even with what Veztressidan had laid by after his retirement from war, and which Bryessidan had husbanded since, that would not last forever.

And will the Nexus Islands reward us with sufficient plunder to refill our coffers? I know Queen Iline believes this will be the case, but I am less certain. Unless they have opened markets to replace those they have cut themselves off from, they must be living on their supplies. Winter comes early there, and hard. They won't have forgotten that.

Amelo Soapwort was announced next. The liaison for the Once Dead had been given a formal title within Bryessidan's advisory cabinet, mostly to keep the notoriously fractious spell-casters from appointing a new liaison every few days. Amelo still wore his elaborate robes, but he had lost a great deal of weight, and moved both more lightly and more stiffly, the result of the physical training he and the other Once Dead were now required to undergo. Bryessidan was not about to have the entire elaborate invasion plan disintegrate because the Once Dead were not up to the exertion that would be demanded of them.

Bryessidan waved Amelo to a seat, waited while the steward served refreshments, then had the room cleared of all but himself and the Once Dead. Even though they were allies now, he hadn't forgotten Queen Iline's fondness for knowing everyone else's business, nor did he think the other nations would have suddenly become more trusting.

After all, King Hurwin commanded the navy. What if he was to turn it against the land? Who would be a better ally than Bryessidan, Hurwin's son-in-law? Bryessidan was certain that Veztressidan's ambitions had not been forgotten.

"What do you have to report?" Bryessidan asked Amelo.

"A fair amount of progress, Your Majesty," Amelo said with satisfaction. "As you suggested, we have been testing which spellcasters can function best in the presence of iron. As you recalled, tolerance does vary—sometimes considerably.

"What we have learned is that the less versatile the spellcaster, the more likely he or she will be to have some resistance to iron's inhibiting effects," Amelo went on. "We have isolated the three with the greatest resistance, and made certain they learned the gate-opening ritual. Once they had it perfect—although, of course, we cannot test their ability without a working gate—we drilled them in performing spells while in proximity to iron. I feel assured that when the date for the invasion arrives, we will have at least one candidate who can be expected to manage a spell while in close proximity to iron."

"Good," Bryessidan said, "and I sincerely hope that these candidates are being trained in something other than the gate ritual. After all, getting through will not be the problem. Staying alive once we are on enemy territory will be."

"True," Amelo said, "but we do not wish anyone stranded if some element of the plan goes awry. As I said, those spellcasters who are most likely to be able to resist iron are also those who are not as versatile—or usually as strong."

"In an odd way," Bryessidan said, "that makes sense. However, that is only one of our difficulties. How is work going on developing a way in which we might more easily communicate with the other land forces, and with the fleet?"

Amelo looked discouraged. "Not as well, Your Majesty. Mind-to-mind communication is very difficult. Focusing on one thing and one thing only is a necessary element. Very few people can manage to achieve this level of focus immediately after casting a spell."

"But what about all those tales of people being controlled by sorcerers?" Bryessidan asked testily.

"Control does not create the type of communication we would need. In situations where a control spell has been used, the controlled one loses will, sometimes even loses awareness of his or her surroundings. This is not what we need."

"So putting someone under the control of one of the Once Dead and then shipping them out to sea wouldn't help."

"I fear not, Your Majesty. We do have a few possible solutions under way. One involves reading auguries. It is something that our associates in u-Chival rely upon. We are hoping to work something out so that auguries could be cast on a regular basis and when the omens are right we would know that the fleet has arrived within striking distance of the Nexus Islands."

"That has potential," Bryessidan agreed, "but it won't help coordinate the various gate attacks. Right now it looks like picking a date and sending the troops through the various gates at a prescheduled time remains our best option."

"I fear so," Amelo said. "If we had access to the winged mounts our ancestors used, we might be able to set up some sort of information relay, but I would not want to rest such an important coordination on a carrier pigeon."

"What a shame we do not have intelligent birds and beasts such as were said to have been found in the New World," Bryessidan said. "One of those could carry a message."

"But we do not," Amelo replied. "Those intelligent birds and beasts do not seem to have cared to serve our ancestors, nor are there records that any attempts to breed them in captivity were successful. It is possible that some survive in the wild lands, but they would not make themselves known to us."

"I suppose not," Bryessidan admitted. "So we will need to rely upon auguries and a timetable. I had hoped for more, but I suppose this cannot be avoided."

He expected Amelo to rise and take his leave at this point, but the Once Dead remained seated and even looked pleasantly expectant.

"Yes? You have further business with me?"

Amelo all but beamed. "Your Majesty, we have located something that we had thought was lost forever, something that will make your role as commander of the armies of the Mires all the more certain of success. May I have it brought in?"

Bryessidan stared blankly at the Once Dead, then nodded.

Amelo rose and walked briskly to the door. In a moment he had returned with two of the lesser Once Dead, who between them carried a battered wooden chest bound with thick bands of tarnished brass. Bryessidan rose and went to join them.

Amelo bent and opened the chest, revealing something that Bryessidan recognized immediately, but that, like Amelo, he had believed lost or stolen.

"My father's armor," he said, his voice soft with wonder.

He knelt next to the chest and pulled out the breastplate, worked in brass, chased in silver. The white metal against the golden yellow highlighted the elaborately worked details, especially the emblem of the Kingdom of the Mires centered on the upper chest. The other pieces were as beautifully done, each one a work of the metalsmith's art.

"I thought it was lost, a prize of war in someone's armory. Where did you find it?"

Amelo looked pleased.

"I thought it had been lost as well," he admitted. "So did we all. We found it when we were going through a store of special weapons shoved in a back room, weapons made to be carried by those of us who use magic and so cannot bear iron or steel. In the very back, we found this chest."

Bryessidan was holding the helmet now, almost able to imagine his father's eyes staring out from beneath the closed visor.

"The armor was made," Amelo said, "so that your father could walk among the Once Dead and not disrupt their spells. It should enable you the same freedom. The copper in the brass was melded with special alloys so that it would gain in strength without becoming brittle. The shield is in the chest as well."

Bryessidan turned the helmet in his hands. The padding within had perished, victim to the Mires' omnipresent humidity, but the rest seemed sound. He tapped his fingertip against the dome and the metal rang like a muted bell.

"I wonder if the armor would fit me," he mused aloud.

"You are built much like your father," Amelo said. "I think the armor should fit. Perhaps the greaves and gauntlets will need alternation, but since the straps need to be replaced in any case . . ."

He let his words trail off. Bryessidan nodded.

"We have been looking for omens," he said. "Surely this discovery is an omen that the Ancestors favor our venture and arm us for it."

The three Once Dead looked very pleased. One knelt by the chest and rummaged toward the bottom.

"Your father's mace does not seem to be here," he said, "but we will check among the weapons in the armory."

Bryessidan nodded approval. He could carry a sword, but the blade would need to be made from a metal less reliable than steel. Better to do as King Veztressidan had done and carry a weapon that did not rely upon an edge.

"You have been good and faithful servants," he said to the Once Dead. "I am deeply grateful. Know that whoever goes through the gate into the Nexus Islands, I will stand with him, wearing this armor, and assuring his safety with my strong arm and shield."

"Whichever of us makes that journey," Amelo said, "none of us could ask more of our good and faithful lord."

"Leave the armor here," Bryessidan said, "and leave word with my secretary that I wish the best armor maker in the city brought here at once. Then go with my thanks."

The three Once Dead took their leave, and when they were gone, Bryessidan took his father's helmet and placed it upon his own head. When he looked in the polished surface of one of the shields that hung upon the chamber's wall, it seemed to him that his father's eyes did indeed look back at him.

"WHEN BLIND SEER and I first came looking for this Virim," Firekeeper said to Elation and Blind Seer, "what we think we need is very different from what we now know we need."

On the morning following her strange dream journey with the Meddler, Firekeeper had been very tired, but she had insisted on taking the falcon and wolf with her to an open meadow some distance from Virim's keep. This meadow was alongside a river still swollen with snowmelt. The location offered a clear line of sight in all directions, but in addition Firekeeper felt fairly certain that anyone attempting to listen from hiding would be unable to understand what was being said over the noise of the water.

True, the language of the Beasts was not exclusively limited to sound as were human languages. Therefore, someone might be able to spy upon them using other senses. Having considered this, Firekeeper had chosen to give her report in Pellish, feeling that the handicaps her limited vocabulary offered were more than compensated for by the assurance of privacy.

Blind Seer had been amused, and Elation impressed, by her caution. As Firekeeper told of what the Meddler had shown her, the blue-eyed wolf's amusement had vanished, and he had moved to where he could keep his restless gaze upon the meadow as he listened.

Firekeeper told them almost everything, omitting only the final vision, the one of Blind Seer searching among that strange library. She trusted the Meddler more than did Blind Seer, but she was not so trusting that she had forgotten the weird rivalry between the two males. The Meddler had seemed impressed by Blind Seer's vast talent, but Firekeeper did not think that even such compliments would make Blind Seer comfortable with being spied upon.

And would the blue-eyed wolf accept what the Meddler had said as a compliment? Like Firekeeper, Blind Seer had been reared in a culture that abhorred magic. The Meddler had said that Blind Seer was seeking to learn how to use his ability, but until Firekeeper heard this from the wolf himself, she would always remember to take care before accepting the Meddler's interpretation of anything at all.

"You are right, Firekeeper," Blind Seer growled. "We know a great deal more now than we did before we left the Nexus Islands. What I want to know is if the Meddler knew the immediacy of the danger the Nexus Islands faced back when he was prompting us to go on this journey. If so, why didn't he tell us then?"

Firekeeper shrugged. "I not think to ask when Meddler learn what he show me. I not see why it matter now. What matter is that the information we seek is not needed in some vague someday, but probably as soon as this very summer."

"If," Elation said, "reinforcements are going to be needed to hold the Nexus Islands against invasion, and if what the Meddler showed you was a true vision."

Of course, neither of the Beasts could speak Pellish, though they could understand it, but they kept their responses contained, the equivalent of lowered voices. Firekeeper hoped it would be enough.

"When first we come here, we come to scout," Firekeeper said. "Take if we find, but mostly to scout, then go and bring back others who can read and write. Now this is not something we can take time to do. Also, when we leave Nexus Islands, even though Meddler warn us some sorcerers live long times, I think we still expect to find an empty lair. Now we know this lair is not only full, but is well defended. How do we get what we want from that lair, and swiftly?"

Elation shifted restlessly from foot to foot.

"Falcons and wolves both take what they want," she said, "yet I do not see how we three can take—especially when we do not know what it is we wish to seize."

Blind Seer huffed agreement. "The strong take what they desire. The weak surrender what they would rather keep. Before we crossed the Iron Mountains, I would have said that was the way of the world, and the only way. Now, though, perhaps there is another alternative."

"Trade," Firekeeper said softly in Pellish. "We must steal something of theirs, then tell them that to have it back they must give us what we want."

"But what could we have that they want?" Elation asked. "They must have sources for all the usual items I have seen humans trade: food, clothing, and such."

"True," Firekeeper said, "and I be very interested in knowing how they have gotten them. Maybe they stored things a long time ago. But I wonder . . . Maybe they sometimes walk in humans' cities, saying they are from another pack. I wonder how humans would feel?"

"So trade may be a useless option as well," Elation said, wilting a bit on her perch.

Firekeeper shook her head, stilling the motion as soon as she remembered possible watchers.

"There is taking," she continued, "and there is trade, but there is another way we might get what we want. Is a way I like very little, but maybe it is fastest way to find cure for Plague. We could stalk them and hunt them, and when one of them strays—like the one Meddler showed me in vision—then we pounce and take. We give back only when they give us what we want . . . and maybe not until we have proved they gived fair."

Blind Seer's hackles rose. "I have never liked being a hostage. I am not sure I would care to take one. Also, that trick only works when the one taken is of sufficient value."

Firekeeper shrugged. "I not like either, but I like less thinking how we go back to Nexus Islands and find Derian and others dead and rotting, and strangers in their lairs. I think maybe I not feel so bad about taking one of this Virim's pack. Remember. This Virim and his pack are spiders who wove the web that begins this in the days when they make the Plague."

"And so saved our ancestors from conquest and destruction," Elation said. "Spiders, wolves, or wooly snakes, this is no simple web, and untangling it will be no simple task."

Firekeeper slouched back on the grass, leaning on her hands and looking up to the cloud-flecked skies. When she replied, she reverted to Beast talk, tired of trying to explain complex matters in Pellish.

"I have told you what I have seen," she said. "Short of going to the door of the keep and knocking, asking plainly for what we desire, this is all I can think of—that, or doing as we planned from the start, scouting and then returning. Certainly, we have learned a great deal that Derian and the others would like to know."

"Take, trade, ask, or leave," Blind Seer said. "I am loath to leave without more. Could we just ask? I wish I believed that we would walk away from that keep as freely as we might walk toward it. Take or trade are left, but could we take?"

Firekeeper looked at him levelly. "We would need strength to take. Can you think of any strengths we might have that others might not anticipate?"

She was thinking of the magical ability to which Blind Seer had confessed, but she would not speak of it more plainly, not in front of Elation, perhaps not ever. She looked at the blue-eyed wolf, however, hoping he might have some hidden strength to which he might confess.

He remained silent, and although Firekeeper longed to confront him with what she had seen in that last vision, she did not. Instead she leapt to her feet.

"I am hungry," she said. "Will any hunt with me or must I settle for cold fish?"

Blind Seer rose to join her, then froze in midmotion. Firekeeper thought he might have been stung by a bee, but after a brief pause the wolf shook himself.

"Hunt," he said softly. "That we might do. Elation, when did the golden eagle come after you?"

"Shortly before I encountered the two of you," the falcon replied. "I suspect I crossed into lands from which Virim's pets normally keep any but those who share their long-ago trust."

"We are in those lands now," Blind Seer said, "and we know we are watched. So far we have left the watchers be, but what if we hunted them? Firekeeper is skilled at making traps. If we trapped one or two of those who watch us, we might be able to learn something from them, something more about those in the keep, something that might help us to take or trade or even to know what questions to ask."

"I like that," Firekeeper said. "Very much. I think I can construct the traps in such a fashion that those watching will not know what I do. They might even inspect them so as to report to those who hold the other ends of their leashes."

She wanted to howl her delight, to run in joyful circles, but she settled instead for leaping on Blind Seer and pummeling him in a puppyish rush of enthusiasm.

"I am hungry," she said, "but the night's tiredness has left me. Food, fire, camp, and then a bit of misdirection."

She grabbed Blind Seer and hugged him again. He nipped her arm affectionately.

"I smell piglets," he said, "milk-fed and fat."

Firekeeper had a fleeting thought that there were Royal Swine, but dismissed the trepidation that her arrows might find the heart of one of "her" people. If they were that careless, then they deserved to die. That was the way it had always been, and she was very hungry indeed.

FIREKEEPER CONSTRUCTED HER traps in the area she and Blind Seer had chosen for their campsite. Of course, they had no need to make a camp such as humans typically made. The weather was somewhat wet, but both of them were accustomed to either finding shelter from the rain or accepting its caress.

However, although Firekeeper was very good at kindling fires, she preferred not to need to do so from scratch every time. Also there were things that tasted very good if given time to roast among the coals of a buried hearth.

While out hunting, Firekeeper had dug up various edible tubers. Wrapped in wet leaves, these would cook slowly, without burning. She had also shot a duck on the wing. She had packed this in wet mud dug from a stream bank streaked with red clay. Then she had buried the unappetizing-seeming package where the heat from the coals would bake it.

Although the coals were buried, but for a few openings to give the fire the air it needed to survive, errant gusts of wind brought Firekeeper tantalizing hints of her cooking meal. She was well filled from their earlier hunting, but knowing her future needs were provided for was a comforting feeling.

Firekeeper was in a cheerful mood as she prepared a variety of snares. Even before she had met with those in Earl Kestrel's party, she had known a little about making traps. Most of these had been pit traps, or simple snares, mostly made by turning some natural feature of the landscape to her advantage.

In Earl Kestrel's group there had been a man named Race Forester who was a skilled woodsman. He had taught Firekeeper a variety of elegantly simple snares that could be constructed with little more than a knife and materials at hand. He had also taught Firekeeper how to shoot a bow, and these days Firekeeper rarely settled to a meal without thinking fondly of Race.

While Firekeeper constructed snares and bent young saplings to her service, she put Blind Seer to work digging a nice hole that could serve as a pit trap—or a cage. The wolf dug with enthusiasm, the damp soil flying up from under his paws. He would need a good bath when he was done.

"You don't think those who watch us will notice all that dirt flying around?" Elation asked from where she was keeping watch on the surrounding area.

Firekeeper grinned. "Let them. If they do notice what we are doing, perhaps they will think we intend to protect ourselves. Perhaps they will think I need some sheltered place to rest. What of it?"

"What indeed?" Elation replied. "I had forgotten how insane certain wolves could be."

Firekeeper knew that for all Elation's doubts about the wisdom of the wolves' actions, the falcon would remain faithful to her duties as watcher. However, what Firekeeper had not confided in Elation lest she bruise the peregrine's pride was that she actually was counting on someone—Beast or human—being clever enough to find a way to see at least some of what they were doing. For that reason, Firekeeper's snares and traps were constructed with two distinctly different goals in mind.

The first goal was to construct something sufficiently solid to trap or capture any Beast or human foolish enough to trigger the device. Firekeeper hoped this could be done without causing undue damage to the victim. For all that they had chosen to support Virim and his magics, Firekeeper felt no hatred for these northwestern Royal Beasts. They, or rather their ancestors, had made a choice that had preserved all Royal-kind.

Firekeeper had great respect for Royal-kind, and did not think that any of those who spied upon them for Virim and his allies would simply stumble into a trap. Therefore, she had constructed things that would act as alarms, alerting herself, Blind Seer, and Elation that someone was near and vulnerable. With these alarms in place, Firekeeper thought they might be able to take captive one or two who might have some of the information she desired.

These alarms were not as obvious as the bells or gongs humans would use in a similar situation, but were rather dry leaves spread where they might crackle, or twigs and branches that would snap beneath unwary feet. In a few places she cached pebbles loosely gathered in a leaf cup, securing them so they would not fall by chance, but only if jostled. By these contrivances and others, Firekeeper hoped to extend her awareness, to somehow compensate for the pack she and Blind Seer lacked.

When the traps and snares were in place, Firekeeper brushed dirt from her hands with satisfaction.

"One thing more," she said, "to bait these traps."

"Bait?" Elation asked. "Do you really think these traps need bait?"

Blind Seer, still wet from a cleansing swim in the river, did not question, but his ears canted in surprise.

"I have learned many things in my travels," Firekeeper said, "and in the land of the Liglim I learned lore that should make these traps even better than they are already."

While making the snares, Firekeeper had found certain bits of wood that suited her needs, and now she held them up for the falcon's inspection.

"Did you know that while I was in the far southlands I learned to write?" she asked. "But what I learned was no common writing used for merely writing letters or making grocery lists. I learned a special writing, a very powerful writing."

Blind Seer started to pant laughter; then Firekeeper saw him catch himself. Like her, he had not forgotten that they might be being watched. Their hearts were too close for Blind Seer not to have wondered at why Firekeeper was making such a speech, instead of simply getting down to whatever business she intended. Firekeeper knew the wolf had guessed that she spoke for some unseen auditor.

Elation did not know Firekeeper as well, not this Fire-keeper, at least, and she continued to question.

"I am glad that you can write," the peregrine said politely, "but how will writing bait a trap?"

Firekeeper grinned. "Follow and see, but take care to watch for the trip lines."

Elation shrieked something rude at this intimation that she could be anything less than careful, but she also followed. Firekeeper noted that for all her interest in what Firekeeper was doing, Elation did not forget to stay alert. It was good to have such wise and talented friends.

Firekeeper made her way to where she had buried a nice leg-hold snare along a narrow game trail. She had already brushed dirt and leaves to hide the snare, but now she patted a small area smooth. In this smoothed area, she made certain symbols she had learned from the Liglim. They were real symbols, short ways of saying such things as "Keep Away" or "Come Quickly" or "Be Silent." To these she added a few symbols that came from nowhere but cloud patterns in the sky or ripples in the water.

She didn't much like the next part, but she knew enough of human magic that she knew it would be expected. Taking her Fang, she nicked herself lightly on the side of one hand and squeezed out a few drops of blood. These she let fall onto the symbols she had made. She had thought about leaving herself uninjured, using perhaps the blood of some small animal, but had shied from the thought. Even though she was not doing any real magic, Firekeeper felt that killing another for no other reason than to feed a deception would be wrong.

Going to the next large snare, she again smoothed the soil and took out a wooden stylus. This time she chose different symbols, and ornamented the apparent spell with a few smooth pebbles she had found and thought pretty. For her next "spell" Firekeeper used a few gaudy blue-jay feathers as ornament, and so on, sometimes using extra items for ornamentation, sometimes singing a few meaningless phrases in a hodgepodge of the human languages she spoke, always finishing the quasi-ritual by sealing the sigils with a few drops of her own blood.

Blind Seer seemed pleased and even impressed, although Firekeeper could tell that he was less than enchanted with her self-mutilation. Still, he did not stop her, nor did he make any suggestions as to how she might improve on her "bait," and with this Firekeeper had to be content.

Elation had fallen silent for a while, watching Firekeeper's peculiar routine with horrified fascination.

"Is that southern magic?" she asked at last.

"Much of what is there I first learned of in the south," Firekeeper said, careful not to lie, "but as to magic, I think it is my own."

Elation puffed her feathers and looked disgusted, and Firekeeper wished she could reassure the falcon that she had not sunk so low as to practice blood magic. However, there was too much risk they would be overheard. Better to explain later. Better, too, not to risk offending Blind Seer, who was still very touchy on the subject of magic and those who used it.

Firekeeper's hope was that curiosity would draw at least some of Virim's humans into her reach. She fully expected the Royal Beasts to report what they had seen to those within the keep. This report would certainly include the strange "spells" Firekeeper had put on the traps.

Humans were greedy for both knowledge and power, and magic was the quintessence of both. Even if most resisted the temptation to take a closer look, Firekeeper did not think each and every member of that hive of spellcasters could resist the opportunity to examine a new spell. And when they came . . .

Well, then, Firekeeper would be ready for them.

XXIV

"ARE YOU ON night watch again tonight?" Isende asked Derian as they were leaving the dining hall after the midday meal.

All day, Derian had been dreading this question, dreading it as only a few days before he would have waited for it with hopeful anticipation.

"I am," he admitted, "but, Isende, I was wondering if maybe tonight you shouldn't come and walk with me."

She looked up at him, eyes wide with hurt and confusion, touched maybe a bit with anger.

"Have you decided again that I shouldn't be with you?" she asked. "Is this more of that 'I look like a horse' nonsense. It better not be, because I'm just too tired to take it right now."

Derian glanced around, but no one was close enough to have overheard Isende's outburst. The Nexans were viewing his budding courtship of Isende—or hers of him, he really wasn't sure how the matter stood—with gleeful delicacy. There were times—as when a seat next to Isende suddenly appeared in a crowded room, or when the various work schedules miraculously permitted them time together—that Derian felt as if his life was being coordinated by dozens of matchmakers.

He didn't really mind. People were even figuring out how to solve their own problems, or bringing those that needed a neutral moderator to Plik or Harjeedian. For the first time since

Derian and Ynamynet had become the informal mayors of the Nexan community, Derian felt as if he might actually finish one task before another dozen were placed before him.

"No," he said firmly. "This isn't more of that 'I look like a horse nonsense.' It's just, well, you don't look well. You look exhausted, to be honest. I was wondering if it was 'that time' or if you'd caught something from one of Rhul and Saeta's kids."

The hurt and anger left Isende's eyes, and a small smile touched the corners of her mouth.

"I am tired," she admitted. "Maybe I have caught something. The last few nights I haven't been sleeping well."

Derian touched her arm. "Why don't you try and nap now? I saw the children being led off to help Frostweed with the gardens. Surely you can be spared."

Isende shook her head, dismissing the suggestion with unwonted vehemence.

"I've been having some very strange dreams," she admitted, "over the last few nights. It's getting so I don't want to go to sleep."

Derian frowned. Once he would have dismissed this as Isende's imagination running away with her. He would have worried that for all her outward enthusiasm for their growing closeness she actually was plagued by hidden anxieties, and that these were playing out in her sleep. He might have separated himself from her, believing he was doing the only thing a gentleman could when the woman was uncertain.

That was before the Dragon of Despair had haunted Firekeeper's dreams, keeping the wolf-woman so short of sleep she'd done some very dangerous things. That was before querinalo had nearly killed him, and he had roamed places the human mind usually could touch only when the body was dormant. That was before Derian had been forced to realize that the world he had known for the first nineteen or twenty years of his life held but a small sliver of what reality contained.

"Want to talk about it?" he asked. "I need to mend some harness. This sea air isn't kind to leather. You could come and keep me company."

Isende smiled wanly. "I think I'd like that."

Derian fetched the damaged tack, then carried it and his tools out into a sunlit patch near his house. He was too conscious of Isende's reputation to have her sit with him in the tack room or in the house. Better they stay in plain sight.

After all, he thought, *for all Isende's willingness to accept my attentions now, she might change her mind about me. It's the way of things that when one man shows he's interested in a woman, then all the other men who had dismissed her suddenly grow interested. She might change her mind about this horse's face and form if someone more normal paid her court.*

Bringing a blanket and pillow out from his house, Derian encouraged Isende to stretch out in the sun while he seated himself on a folding stool.

"You might find you remember the details of the dreams more easily if you relax," he said. "I know that I often wake up from a dream and think I've forgotten it entirely until I go to bed that night. It's as if the feeling of my bed brings it back to me."

Isende smiled and stretched out drowsily, stretching just a little, not coquettishly, but as an old cat would when it feels the sunlight warm its bones.

"They're strange dreams," she began. "Intense. I mean, it's not like I haven't had intense dreams before, but I don't think I've ever had the same dream over and over again—not without really good reason."

Derian pushed the heavy awl through two pieces of leather with a bit more force than necessary, but he pulled back before he could blunt the tip. Steel tools weren't easy to get right now. Bone needles worked for sewing lighter clothing, but for steel they needed to go into Gak. . . .

He forced himself to give Isende his full attention. She was lying on her back, arm thrown over her eyes. He resisted the urge to bend down far enough to kiss her. He knew someone had to be watching, so he behaved himself.

"What are the dreams about?" he asked.

"Weird things," Isende said. "Things I don't usually dream about. I mean, why should I dream about ships? I've never seen a ship in my entire life. The little fishing boats here were the first oceangoing boats I'd seen. Gak is inland. There isn't even a big lake nearby."

Derian felt a strange thought tingle at the back of his mind, but he didn't articulate the thought. Time enough for speculation when he knew more about Isende's dreams.

"Go on," he said. "Ships? You're sure?"

"I've seen pictures," Isende said, "in the archives here."

"Ships, then," Derian said. "What else?"

"Soldiers. Wearing all sorts of different types of armor, like they're from different lands."

"Ships and soldiers," Derian said. "You haven't been reading one of the history books, have you?"

"No," Isende said. She blushed. "Actually, I've been reading some stories that Urgana tells me originated in Pelland. The book they're in was for teaching languages. I thought . . . well, I thought that maybe I needed to improve my Pellish if someday I might meet your family."

Derian knew he was grinning like an idiot, but since she had her arm over her eyes, he didn't figure he had to hide his delight.

"That's great," he said. "And being multilingual can only help you in the future if the world keeps going in the direction we're seeing. So these stories weren't about wars?"

"No," Isende said. "Simple things, like about how some people from a place called Alkya came to live in the Mires, and how they stayed. That's why the people from the Mires look a little different from the other Pels. Things like that."

"That's interesting," Derian said. "I wonder if that's why that Mires' king was so open to taking in the exiled Once Dead. His land had a tradition of integrating foreigners."

"Maybe," Isende said. "The Mires wasn't a kingdom when the Alkya came to live there. It was just part of Pelland."

"Right," Derian said. "So what you're reading couldn't color your dreams. What about the entertainments? Some of those epic poems Urgana and Verul have been reciting are pretty dramatic."

"Maybe," Isende said, but she didn't sound convinced. "I

can't think why I'd be dreaming about armor and weapons. It's almost like I'm seeing them. That's how good the details are."

Derian nodded and concentrated on stitching, determined not to lead her.

"Anything else?"

"Well, the weirdest thing is that I keep dreaming about Truth—the jaguar, I mean. I'll be looking at these things and then I'll feel fur brush my arm or something warm near me and I'll glance over and there will be Truth."

Derian whistled softly. "Isende . . ."

"I know. I know," she said. "Truth is a seer. I've thought about that. I've wondered if I was having visions, too. I'd been thinking about talking to you about this tonight."

Derian nodded and put down the harness.. Mending it could wait.

"Come on," he said, bending and pulling Isende to her feet. "I think we'd better go talk with Truth. We'll get Plik to translate."

They found the raccoon-man gutting, scaling, and boning fish down near the wharves. His small hands were perfect for the delicate work, and unlike the humans, he was quite happy to snack on the offal. Derian, accustomed to Firekeeper's eating habits, hadn't found this at all repulsive, but most of the Nexans were less open-minded. Therefore, they found Plik alone and were able to explain what they needed without worrying about someone overhearing and starting rumors.

"Dreams of ships and soldiers and Truth," Plik said. "Interesting, and well worth investigating. Have you noticed that Truth has been behaving a bit oddly of late?"

"Odd," Derian said with a shrug. "Maybe, but for Truth what is odd? Ever since her battle with Ahmyn, she has been less connected to reality. The only reason I don't think she has gone insane again is that she shows up for meals with great regularity."

"And for religious services," Isende said. "Harjeedian has been holding services, and Truth is almost always there."

Plik indicated a bucket half filled with fish heads.

"If you would carry that, Derian," he said, "I think we

should bring it along when we go see Truth. She likes raw fish, and eating helps ground her in fewer versions of reality."

Derian obediently picked up the bucket and indicated the buckets containing the already cleaned fish with what he feared was a horse-like toss of his head.

"What about those?"

"We can drop them off at the kitchens on our way to Truth," Plik said. "And if I also happen to mention that I'm taking the heads out to share with a friend, well, I think our privacy will be assured and rumors will be still."

"Good thinking," Derian said.

Isende nodded and picked up two of the buckets of cleaned fish.

"Let's go," she said.

THEY FOUND TRUTH lounging on a jutting spit of rock facing south. Waves crashed and foamed at the base, occasionally splashing them with spray.

Truth's fur pearled with saltwater droplets, silvery against the charcoal grey, but she didn't seem to mind being wet. Derian had learned that, unlike the house cats who had composed most of his experience of felines, jaguars liked water. Truth would swim after fish, and snapping turtles seemed to be her favorite food.

She turned her head before she could have heard or smelled them, doubtless having sensed them coming through one of her visions. Her eyes, once burnt-orange, were now white, the eye slits glowing blue. Their focus was erratic, her gaze flickering after things none of the rest of them could see, for Truth was blessed or cursed with the ability to see all possible futures at all times. Were she not a very strong-willed individual, doubtless this would have driven her insane.

"Truth says," Plik translated, "that she has been expecting us for days now, or perhaps merely hours, but that she is glad we have come. She also hopes we won't mind if she has some fish heads. They smell wonderful."

"They're for the two of you," Derian said magnanimously.

Isende grinned. "I wouldn't deny you the pleasure."

Plik looked concerned. "We should have grabbed something for you from the kitchen when we dropped off the fish."

Derian glanced at Isende and knew she was trying hard to find a polite way of explaining that sitting and eating cake while Plik and Truth munched on fish heads wasn't really an attractive option.

He winked at her, and saw her swallow a grin.

"Actually, we didn't come out here to have a picnic," he said. "Isende has been having some rather disturbing, recurring dreams. We decided that Truth had better hear about them."

Truth dipped her nose into the bucket and came up with a large fish head.

"She says go ahead. She's listening."

Isende complied, her account pretty closely matching what Derian had already heard. He keep his gaze leveled on Truth, and as far as he could tell the jaguar was indeed paying close attention.

"Truth says," Plik began when Isende finished her narrative, "that the omens are quite clear. What Isende has thought were dreams are in fact visions. Moreover, what Isende has spoken about has brought into tighter focus visions Truth herself has been having with increasing frequency over the last several moonspans."

"Visions?" Derian prompted. "Of what?"

"Impending invasion," Plik translated. "The first ones came as soon as the decision was made to close off the gates, but she did not pay them much heed. That was a momentous action, and she saw visions of many things that have not come to pass."

"Such as?" Isende asked in fascination.

"Riots over food. Derian's murder. The gates being surreptitiously opened to clandestine traffic by a cabal of the Once Dead. Derian crowned king. Ynamynet bearing a child with fair skin and red hair. Firekeeper alone on the islands but for a pack of wolves and a flock of seagulls."

Derian held up his hand. "Pull Truth back from that. She's

drifting off. Somebody throw her a fish head. That might bring her around."

Plik dipped his hand into the bucket and came out with a dripping fish head, the offal still trailing behind. Truth shook her head as if gnats were troubling her vision, then bit down hard on the proffered treat. As she chomped, Derian was fairly certain that the blue-white gaze was tightening its focus again.

"I think we understand," Derian said. "Now, Truth, when did the visions of invasion become more frequent, displacing the others?"

"Early this spring," Plik replied promptly, "right about the time, now that she considers it, that we began to have regular requests to use the gates, and that we began consistently refusing them, and putting up safeguards against chance crossings."

"That makes frightening sense," Derian said. "Why didn't Truth say anything earlier?"

Truth's tail lashed, but Plik's translation of her words were mild.

"She was uncertain," he said. "There were still so many options. She has been trying to focus more tightly, but it is difficult to get a clear picture. From this she guesses that the invasion is still in the planning stages, that the armies have not yet marched or the fleet sailed. She has been keeping vigil, and planned to say something when the options narrowed."

"Reasonable," Derian admitted. "But Isende's dreams provided corroboration of a sort."

"Correct," Plik said. "Truth wonders at the origin of those dreams, but fears that they can be relied upon."

Derian knew that Truth shared his own concern that the Meddler was somehow involved. He didn't know why that strange being might try and get them warning, but he did know that the Meddler was interested in Firekeeper, and that by extension he might also be interested in the fate of Firekeeper's friends.

The problem was, the Meddler's interest was not always the safest of things. He had a way of getting those he sought to help in deeper difficulties than if he had just left them alone.

Look at how he'd sent Firekeeper chasing off after a cure

for querinalo. If he hadn't done that, Derian would have Fire-keeper close by. Without her, his ability to coordinate with the yarimaimalom was limited. Plik, for all his verbal talents, was still a fat, round, elderly creature, not at all the vibrant battle leader Firekeeper had shown herself capable of being.

On the other hand, Derian thought, forcing himself to be fair, *if Firekeeper brings a cure for querinalo, or even a way of testing who might be most vulnerable, then we don't need to rely quite so much on the yarimaimalom. We could recruit humans . . . if we dare explain to them what we're fighting against and fighting for.*

His head was beginning to ache, and he rubbed his temples with the heels of his hands.

"Ask Truth," he said to Plik, "if she has read the omens regarding what will happen if I tell what we have learned here—about the possibility of invasion—to the others who live here on the Nexus Islands."

"Truth has attempted to do so," Plik replied, "but much depends on how the matter is presented. Panic and quick surrender are two likely results if the matter is not handled carefully."

"I can see why," Isende interjected. "Only a small proportion of the Old Nexans really view these islands as home. Many of them have no strong desire to defend what is here. It is a refuge, yes, but perhaps not a refuge worth dying for."

Derian frowned. "Do they really think that the same people who once exiled them or their kin would give them sanctuary now? Maybe they do. Still, I can think of a few who will not panic, no matter how bad the news, and they deserve to know that it is highly likely that we face invasion."

Plik nodded. "Ynamynet, Skea, Harjeedian, a few of the others. Why not test reactions on that small group, and see what happens there?"

"I think that's what we're going to need to do," Derian said. "Harjeedian might be able to get Urgana to find something in the archives about the islands' defenses in the old days—back before querinalo, even. I remember hearing about sea dragons. I wonder if they were real?"

"One thing at a time," Isende said. "Talk to Ynamynet and Skea."

"Right," Derian said. "Thank you, Truth. I'll let Isende do the talking for both of you. You keep watching the omens. I think we're going to need whatever you can draw from them."

The jaguar didn't verbalize her thanks, but something in the way she settled back onto her perch on the outcropping of rock told Derian she was pleased.

As he headed toward the house Ynamynet and Skea shared, Derian wondered at how his world had once again transformed. This morning his greatest worry had been how to properly conduct a semi-public courtship he still wasn't quite certain was the correct thing for him to pursue.

Now he was simply glad for the warmth of Isende's hand firmly clasping his own as they hurried to warn allies who not long ago had been bitter enemies that invasion and possibly war were presaged in a young woman's dreams and a crazed jaguar's visions.

❦

AFTER THE SNARES were set, Firekeeper could almost feel the intensity of the observation centered upon them. Birds—usually raptors or corvids—soared close for a look. Wisps of fur caught in the surrounding bracken, footprints of wolf and bear and deer, showed that many had come to take a closer look at this odd thing that Firekeeper had done. Despite this interest, several days passed before one of the watchers let curiosity overweigh caution, and so fell into a trap.

The trap was a snare meant to catch an animal by the leg. Once the animal was caught, the anchor that had held the loop of rope to the ground gave way, permitting the springy strength of a bent sapling to hold the victim clear of the ground. This was not a trap that would have held a bear or even a large deer. Nor was it one that would restrain a human for very long, at least if the human had the presence of mind—and the physical flexibility—to twist and then cut the line that bound it about the leg or ankle.

But Firekeeper had never intended to give her captive the opportunity to work free. Ever since the traps had been set, she had left off ranging through the surrounding forest, instead sleeping for long stretches of time. The sleep was, in fact, welcome, replenishing reserves that had been considerably drained during the moonspan or so since she and Blind Seer had left the Nexus Islands.

She woke immediately when the trap was tripped and the sapling attempted to straighten again. She and Blind Seer were there before the first violent bouncing had ceased, viewing with critical eyes what hung by one leg from the jolting line.

It was a human male, smaller than Derian, who was considered quite tall, perhaps closer to Harjeedian in height and build, but lacking Harjeedian's brown skin and black hair. This man had very fair skin, fairer even than Derian's and without freckles. His hair and beard were pale yellow, almost white, and the eyes that stared at them with mingled indignation and fear were round, and a pale greenish grey.

He wore the long robes that Firekeeper was coming to associate with those who either practiced magic or—as in the case of the thaumaturges of New Kelvin—wished others to believe they did. These were predominantly a blue a few shades darker than Blind Seer's eyes, printed with designs in black and white. The robes would have looked impressive had the man not been hanging upside down. As it was, the skirts hung from his belted waist, falling to almost cover his face.

"He wore good shoes for walking in the forest," Blind Seer commented. *"And I smell oiled metal, so he may carry a blade."*

Firekeeper acknowledged the wolf's warning by drawing her own Fang and making sure the man saw it before she approached him. He stopped flailing some then, and in response the bent sapling bobbed less intensely.

From far above, Firekeeper heard a thin cry from Elation, a

reminder that the falcon was keeping watch above. Blind Seer remained alert to threats from below. They all knew better than to let their guard lapse as humans might. Firekeeper could give her full attention to their captive, knowing her back was being safely watched.

"What you speak?" she asked in Pellish.

The man pressed his lips into a thin, white line. His face was getting pinker from his reversed position, but she didn't think he was in danger of blacking out quite yet.

Firekeeper grinned, and said, "I think Pellish, at least. Now. Hold still."

The man didn't respond, but neither did he grab at the wolf-woman when she stepped closer. Alert to any movement on his part, Firekeeper bent and grabbed both his upper arms. Twisting them behind his back, she bound his wrists, drawing the knots snug, but not cruelly tight.

Next she raised the gathered fabric of his robes. A sheathed knife did hang at his belt, along with a few small pouches. Firekeeper considered the situation, then unbuckled the entire belt, drawing it free in one swift motion as the man's robes tumbled down to swaddle his head and shoulders.

He began to struggle again, and Firekeeper took mercy on him, cutting the loop that had closed around his lower leg and letting him fall the short distance to the ground. Before he could recover himself, she sat on him and twisted lengths of iron wire about his wrists and ankles, making sure the metal touched his bare skin. From what they had learned from Ynamynet and the other Once Dead, if this man had the ability to cast spells, he would now find it difficult to do so.

Her prize secured, Firekeeper got up off the man, grabbed a fistful of robes in the vicinity of his upper chest, and hauled him to his feet. Still tangled in his robes, he stumbled, but Firekeeper used her free hand to clear the tangle of cloth from his head and he managed to retain his balance.

As he did so, Firekeeper studied his face. There was something very odd about the skin. Superficially, it showed very little weathering, very few lines, but even so there was something old about it. She was reminded of tanned and oiled leather, superficially supple, but lacking the glow of life.

She sniffed, and would not have been surprised to find the man smelled musty, but what came to her was the usual odor of male sweat, mingled with a touch of blood and a hint of urine.

Firekeeper released her hold on the man. She didn't think he would try to run, not with Blind Seer right there, not with his hands bound behind him. Still, humans were often reassured by being told what to do.

"Don't move," she said. "I want to talk to you."

The man pressed his lips together again, and for a moment Firekeeper thought he might refuse to speak, or, perhaps, foolishly pretend he didn't understand Pellish. That last would have been pure idiocy. Although he had not replied to anything she had said to him, his reaction had shown he understood. However, humans frequently thought that refusing to vocalize meant that they had not replied. This was no great surprise given how much many humans loved the sound of their own voices.

"What do you want to talk to me about?" the man said. His voice was reedy and nasal. His Pellish held a strange accent, closer to how some of the Nexans had spoken than to how Derian did, but Firekeeper could understand him clearly enough.

"About querinalo," Firekeeper said, adding, in case he did not know the sickness by that name, "the Plague. The Fire Plague. The sickness of the Burning Times. The Sorcerer's Bane. The sickness that killed all the Old World rulers—except for a few."

The man looked at her. "Except for a few. What is it you wish to know?"

"More things than to learn standing here," Firekeeper said. "I take you to my camp. We talk there."

She bent and picked up his belt, eyeing the various little bags and pouches fastened to it. She slid the knife a finger's width or so out of the sheath and saw the warm yellow-brown of bronze. Sharp enough to cut, but not damaging to the abilities of one who would use magic.

"Who are you?" the man said, although Firekeeper suspected he must know. How could he not if the Royal Beasts served these humans? Still, humans loved asking things they already knew.

"Am Firekeeper," she replied. "Also Lady Blysse of House Kestrel and Little Two-legs of the wolves when I was small. And you?"

"I am Bruck," he said.

The name reminded Firekeeper of that of Derian's younger brother, Brock. She wondered if it was the same name, or if this man simply couldn't speak Pellish right.

"Bruck," she repeated. "But not Once Dead, I think."

The man gave an odd smile. "No. I've never been dead, and I've been alive a long, long time."

She had been leading Bruck along a narrow game trail to her camp while they spoke, and he had followed, made docile as anyone sane would be made docile with Blind Seer padding silently behind. Now she motioned for him to take a seat on one side of her dormant fire.

"I tie your hands in front," she said, "if you give promise to be patient while we are talking."

"Are you going to kill me?"

Firekeeper snorted. "How could I talk to you if you is dead? No. I not kill you."

"But what about once I have talked to you? What's to keep you from killing me then?"

Firekeeper gave a slow smile. "I think that people who worry a lot about whether others kill them have maybe done a lot of killing. Maybe I leave your hands behind."

Bruck scowled. "I could sit more easily if they were in front."

"So I think. You be patient while we talk, not think to do something like scoop dirt and try and throw in eyes? I promise it not work, and I would be very angry."

Bruck bit his lip. "I promise I'll be a good prisoner. I can't promise I won't try and get away, though."

Firekeeper shrugged. "Be my job, my and Blind Seer to

keep you, then. Now hold very still. The furred wolf is not the only one with teeth."

She unbound his hands and refastened them in front of him. As she did so, she glanced at his wrists. Tiny blisters, less than those nettles might cause, were rising like a second bracelet. He was sensitive to iron then. But she had thought he would be.

Firekeeper let Bruck make himself comfortable, then ran a loose hobble between his ankles.

"So you not run too easy," she said. "Now, about querinalo. Tell."

Bruck frowned. "In one sense, there is a great deal to tell, in another very little. It might help me if I knew why you wanted to know."

Firekeeper glanced at Blind Seer.

"I don't see how we can keep that back forever," the wolf replied. *"Why not see what he says?"*

"We want to find how to stop it," Firekeeper said. "Cure or ending or whatever. We want no more querinalo in all the world."

"Even if this means the rise of sorcery again?" Bruck countered.

Firekeeper sighed. "Is again rising, in Old World. Querinalo wounds now, sometimes deeply, but does not kill always."

Bruck twitched the corner of his mouth into a half-smile that held no humor at all.

"What if it could be made to kill again?" he asked. "Wouldn't that be better?"

Firekeeper considered. "I have had querinalo. I not wish it even on an enemy. An arrow to the heart is kinder."

"Of course," Bruck said, "you have never had an arrow in your heart."

"And you," Firekeeper growled, "no have had querinalo, I think. But I think you know too much of it."

"Aren't you afraid to keep me here?" Bruck asked. "You don't think my friends will come rescue me?"

"I think your friends might come," Firekeeper said, "but I not think they could rescue you."

She drew a spare knife, one from Liglim that she had kept because it was well balanced for throwing. In a moment, it quivered in the earth next to Bruck's foot.

"An eye is easier," she said. "Softer. If your friends watch, and I am sure that someone watches, they will know this now. You are good to let me show."

Bruck was so fair-skinned that Firekeeper saw the blood drain from his face. She reached out and grabbed him before he fainted.

"This is an odd human," she said to Blind Seer. *"He speaks easily of death and killing, but his own death seems to frighten him too much."*

"Humans can be that way," Blind Seer replied. *"Still, I wish we were a larger pack than we three. My nose tells me that the forest is filled with those who could harm us if they didn't care to preserve this Bruck."*

Firekeeper shrugged in wordless reply. That had always been the risk. She still felt fortunate that they had managed to capture a human, even if it was this fainting Bruck. She had thought they would need to begin with a Beast, and hope a human would come in time.

"It all seemed like a great and noble adventure at the start, you know," Bruck said, his voice thin and wispy with shock. "I don't expect you to believe me, but that's how it seemed."

" 'It'?" Firekeeper asked, tilting her head to one side in a wolfish expression of confusion. "I not understand."

"I didn't make myself very clear, did I?" Bruck pulled himself from Firekeeper's hold, then sat up. "I don't suppose you would let me move to where I could lean against that tree truck. Sitting on the ground this way, not being able to support myself with my hands, is making my muscles ache."

"Not try anything," Firekeeper warned, tapping her Fang. "If promise, then you can lean."

"I do promise," Bruck said, accepting her help in getting to his feet, then shuffling a few steps over to the indicated tree. "You see, I think I want to tell you about it—about our great and noble venture, and what came from it in the end."

XXV

"IT WAS A great and noble venture," Bruck began again, sitting straight, his posture somehow managing to suggest that he was holding up the tree and not the other way around.

Firekeeper settled in to listen. Wolves like stories. Having no writing, that is how they pass along everything that is important and many things that are merely interesting or amusing. Firekeeper listened to Bruck's voice feeling itself into the words as wolf would listen, hearing those words, but never losing awareness of the rhythms of the forest around her.

If this offer to tell a story was all some sort of trick, something meant to distract her from watchfulness, then Bruck would be sadly disappointed.

"Do you know anything of Virim?" Bruck asked. "Of Virim and his great vision?"

"Know some of Virim," Firekeeper said. "Tell of this vision."

Bruck nodded. "Virim decided that he wasn't going to let the New World be destroyed by those who ruled the Old. Virim's creed—if you can call it a creed; his system of belief, rather—was neat and logical, and differed on one key point from those beliefs held by most of those in the Old World. In the Old World, those who ruled believed that because humans and their magic had come to dominate those lands we knew, then they could do the same wherever they went. Is that fairly clear?"

Firekeeper nodded, frustrated that Bruck could talk so much and say so little, yet unwilling to slow this flood of talk. She'd learned that freely speaking humans often said more than they intended.

Bruck went on. "Virim believed that if humans wanted to

dominate those places where there were no other inhabitants than humans and what you would call Cousins, well, that was fine. However, when it came to dominating places where there were already intelligent inhabitants, then he believed they should show some respect for those who had come there first."

"But not if they were humans," Firekeeper said, making sure she understood this, "or Cousins."

"That's right," Bruck said. "Virim was realistic in his thinking. He felt that humans had always competed with other humans, even if, or maybe even especially if, those humans didn't look particularly like them. He thought that humans had done a fairly good job of either dominating, destroying, or avoiding Cousin-kind. However, he thought that the Beasts of the New World fell into a new category and should be respected as such."

Firekeeper blinked.

What else could Beasts be thought of as being? she thought, wishing she could ask Blind Seer, but unwilling to voice anything until she was certain just how much this Bruck understood. *I suppose that humans might have thought of the Royal Beasts as being like another type of humans, just with another shape. That would be very human. Never having lived close to other bloods, never having seen how different wolf is from bear is from puma is from deer, they might well believe that all thinking creatures were merely humans despite their skins and senses and ways of living.*

"When the rulers of the Old World decided that the time had come to push west of the mountains, deeper into the New World, Virim tried to dissuade them. He failed, and decided to take more direct action."

"To make querinalo," Firekeeper said, impatient now. "And we know it worked."

Bruck's smile turned sly. "But isn't knowing how it worked what you have come here to learn? Listen just a little more."

Firekeeper felt a bit ashamed of herself.

"Talk," she said. "Please."

"Querinalo," Bruck said, "is less a disease or illness in the conventional sense than it is a magical curse that mimics the course of a disease."

Firekeeper nodded.

"A curse," Bruck said. "A draining curse, a wasting curse, a curse that would remove the threat to the New World we had sworn to protect. We thought ourselves noble. We thought ourselves virtuous. It was not until the corpses began to accumulate that we realized we were also genocidal."

Firekeeper tilted her head to one side, not knowing that last word. She thought about asking Bruck what it meant, but there was a strange look on his face, and she held her silence.

"Can you believe we thought about killing without thinking about the deaths?" Bruck asked.

Firekeeper nodded. She could indeed. She had seen that years ago, when angry human had fought angry human in a venture they called "war." Only afterward had any seemed to consider that the "enemies" that they had fought were also mothers and fathers, sisters and brothers, nieces and nephews, each one and every one, no matter how poor and how small, beloved by someone.

Bruck must have seen her understanding, for he went on.

"But what we had done was worse than that. We knew we would be draining away. We thought—someone thought, I can't remember just who after all these years—that it would be a pity if all that life, all that energy, went to waste. So something else was added to the curse. We ad . . ."

He froze in midbreath, in midword, bound hands rising to claw at his throat. He made choking sounds, guttural and wet, smothered as if his breath was being squeezed from him.

Horrified, Firekeeper watched as the color began to drain from Bruck's face. Bruck's skin was naturally pale already, but this was different. The living pinkness of his skin was draining away from top to bottom, so his forehead was white in contrast to his nose, then his nose in contrast to lips suddenly white. Even his hair seemed to have less shine.

Firekeeper wanted to help the struggling man, but although she surged to her feet, Fang in hand, she could see nothing at which to strike, although that nothing was strangling Bruck.

She thought it could not be a good thing to have his head lose blood, so she thrust her Fang back into its Mouth. Grabbing Bruck, she turned him so his feet were higher than his head.

Color did not return immediately, but Bruck seemed to breathe a touch easier. She was about to see if she could turn him completely around, perhaps hang his legs over a tree limb, when a low growl warned her back.

"Keep watch," Blind Seer said.

Then the great grey wolf leapt at Bruck, but stopped the merest distance away from the strangling human. By preference, wolves bite for the throat or the belly. Blind Seer's attack did not seem to follow that pattern. Rather than biting and ripping, he was slashing at something, not attempting to take a hold or keep it, but as if he were cutting.

Firekeeper could not tell what manner of creature—if creature it was—was her partner's target, but she could tell that Blind Seer was achieving some sort of success.

Bruck's hands fell onto his chest, and he leaned back on the ground, dragging in breath in ragged gasps. Color was returning to his skin, rising from bottom to top, as it had fallen from top to bottom.

Firekeeper had not forgotten Blind Seer's command that she keep watch, and she did so. Bruck was not going anywhere, not with his feet hobbled. Yet there was a listening silence in the surrounding forest that she did not care for, and she remained alert in case all of this was some sort of feint preceding an attempt to free Bruck.

She spared a glance to where Blind Seer appeared to have battered his invisible opponent to the point that a new form of attack was necessary. He was no longer slashing, but had bitten into something and was shaking it hard, shaking and twisting as if he sought to break bone and sinew.

No blood flowed from whatever wounds he had inflicted on his opponent, but the wolf himself had not been so fortunate. Long narrow weals trailed down his flanks, the fur stripped away as if removed by razors. Blood beaded from these marks, but Firekeeper saw no evidence of punctures.

She longed to learn if her Fang might find a target, when

Blind Seer gave his prey a final violent shake, then sank back on his haunches, battered but without a doubt victorious.

Firekeeper tensed with alertness. Any hunter knew the time to strike was when the prey believed the hunters had been driven back. She spared a glance over at Blind Seer and satisfied herself that his injuries, while doubtless painful, were not severe.

"What was that?" she asked. *"I saw nothing, but you went at it as an arrow does from a bow."*

Blind Seer shook, tiny splatters of blood catching the sunlight as they flew, then began licking his injuries.

"Ask Bruck what it was," he said. *"I think he must know."*

Bruck had clawed about so that he was seated trembling on the ground. His color had returned almost to normal, but his shivering increased as Firekeeper turned her attention on him.

"What was that?" she asked in Pellish.

"That was a warning," Bruck said. "A warning to me that I am talking too much. Your pack mate broke the spell's force. However, I suspect that the iron you wrapped around my wrists and ankles kept the spell from harming me as it might have done."

"Some warning," Firekeeper said, impressed. "It seemed that whatever it was tried to kill you."

"Well," Bruck said with a shrug, "my death would keep me from talking now, wouldn't it?"

Firekeeper glowered at the spellcaster.

"Is not enough," she said. "Who was warning? Was some creature made by spell?"

Bruck looked indecisive, as if having narrowly escaped whatever weird death had been intended for him, he had no desire to risk such again. Firekeeper lowered her hand to where she wore her Fang sheathed at her hip, and Bruck was reminded that there were other dangers than whatever had sent the warning.

"My associates, my pack, if you like that term better . . . those are the ones who were warning me away from telling you too much. They tugged at what binds us to each other, reminding me that I cannot survive separated from them."

"Virim's pack did this?" Firekeeper asked, focusing on what little she had understood in this odd declaration.

Bruck's lips thinned in a grimace so tight that for a moment Firekeeper thought something was attacking him again.

"We were Virim's pack, but some moonspans past, under very strange circumstances, Virim died. Since then what unity that remained among us has dissolved."

Firekeeper fought the urge to glance at Blind Seer. If these spellcasters didn't know that Blind Seer had killed their One, better she did not give the blue-eyed wolf's secret away.

"That is how it often is when the One dies or falls lame," she said. "So those who would be One fight among themselves."

Bruck grimaced again. "Rather say this fight had been going on for many years now. I don't know who finally managed to kill Virim, but there had been those who wanted him gone since long before you were born, long before your parents were born, quite probably."

Firekeeper shrugged. By her best estimate, she was at least twenty now. She had no idea how old her parents had been when they had joined forces with Prince Barden and attempted to colonize the lands west of the Iron Mountains. Twenty at least, probably. Maybe older.

So, Bruck spoke of a conflict that had been brewing for forty years at least? Had Firekeeper not met humans, this would have been difficult for her to comprehend. Wolf battles, for all their brutality, are short and those who live and still bear ill will after them leave and find a new pack. If they are particularly slow in realizing the magnitude of their wrongdoing, they are driven away.

Blind Seer said, *"Ask Bruck if we are safe staying here, or if we need to move. Since his life is in at least as great a danger as our own, I think he will answer honestly."*

Firekeeper translated the question.

Bruck considered. "I think you—we—are as safe here as we would be anywhere in this vicinity. You have trapped this area rather carefully, haven't you?"

Firekeeper grinned, but said nothing.

Bruck sighed. "I know you did. Our spies watched and reported. The order was to remain inside, but I was curious about some of what had been reported, so I slipped out. After all, who were they to give me orders?"

"Who were they?" Firekeeper echoed. "Maybe you tell. Maybe we keep you alive better then. Were these those who shared what you call this 'great and noble venture' thing?"

"All of us were, at one time," Bruck said, "but Virim gave in to a weakness, and that weakness has been both our preservation and our destruction."

Firekeeper glowered, and Bruck raised his bound hands to his face, as if to guard them from a blow.

"Stop frightening him, Firekeeper," Blind Seer said, not entirely unamused. *"You forget how terrifying you can be to those who do not know your impatience rarely goes further than growls."*

Firekeeper didn't think that frightening Bruck was such a bad idea, but she obeyed Blind Seer's direction. She banished the scowl from her face and reached into one of her belt pouches for one of the little jars of soothing ointment she had carried with her.

"Hold out your hands," she said. "I not take iron wire off, but there is no need for you to feel more pain than must. While I put ointment on, you talk."

Reassured, Bruck lowered his hands to where Firekeeper could reach them.

"Where was I? Oh, right. I was about to tell you about Virim's weakness. I told you before how what you call querinalo is generated by a curse that drains away magical power and the life that is intertwined with it. That's the key element to remember. It doesn't destroy the power—except in the sense that the person to whom it originally belonged can no longer use it. It drains it, and what is drained away still exists.

"Now if you drain water away, it either forms a puddle—if the surface isn't porous—or it disperses into the surrounding matter. If you prepare a receptacle for it, then you can collect it and take it elsewhere or use it for something.

"The same can be said to be true of this magical ability and the life that is intertwined with it. It doesn't just vanish. It can be collected. If no effort is made to collect it, then it eventually disperses into the greater energy that surrounds us all. Do you understand?"

Firekeeper nodded. "I think so. Like water—goes or can be kept."

Bruck nodded, reminding Firekeeper for a moment of Harjeedian in one of the aridisdu's more officious moments. She found herself actually liking the spellcaster a little for that familiarity.

"Now, I think that originally Virim intended to let this magical force simply drain away. I don't know if he had the thought himself, or if someone else suggested it to him, but somehow the idea arose that if the freed mana that resulted from querinalo's operation could be collected, it could be used for something else, something very important."

Bruck paused and swallowed hard. "It could be used to prolong the lives and youth of those who had joined in this noble venture. The spells to do so would be difficult, but compared to those we had created when crafting the curse that became querinalo, they were a minor challenge.

"I'm not going to pretend that I was among those who believed that this was a dangerous course of action. I wasn't. I wasn't among those who realized that in benefitting in such an intimate and essential manner from the creation of the curse, we were tainting our effort. I was young and ambitious and possessed of power. I was pretty easily convinced that prolonging my life—and thus extending my ability to serve as a guardian of the innocent Beasts of the New World—was a very good thing. At the worst it was payment, and, as someone pointed out, a good hunter eats what he kills."

Firekeeper, fingertips busy daubing ointment on the leaking sore that now encircled one of Bruck's ankles, couldn't hide a shiver of revulsion. That last justification seemed a perversion of everything she and the wolves who had reared her held dear. She might have voiced her revulsion, but Blind Seer growled.

"The Story of the Songbirds all over again. The shape is different, but the justification all too similar. We are not so unalike, these humans and we Beasts."

And Firekeeper, remembering that tale and the shame of the wolf who had related it to her and Blind Seer long ago, held her tongue. However, she no longer wondered that Bruck's fellows had been willing to kill him rather than let him speak. This was ugliness, a deep rot that corrupted any ideal.

"So that's what we did," Bruck said simply. "Before this plan came up, we had resolved to live out our normal lives in service to the cause. Now that service became the means of enabling us to prolong the cause forever. Forevermore, the New World would be safe from the magics of the old, but a few generations ago, something changed."

Firekeeper looked at Bruck, willing him to raise his eyes to meet her own. He did, and she saw both puzzlement and shame there.

"Querinalo changed. The nature of our curse changed. No longer did it slay outright. Instead it tortured, but permitted the sufferer—if that one was sufficiently devoted to the magic within—to live with some magical ability intact. Believe me when I say I do not know why it changed. I have some suspicions, but I do not know, nor can I claim either credit or blame.

"Something else changed when querinalo changed. Our immortality began to become—it is difficult to explain. None of us began to age, nor did we lose our vitality. Rather it was as if what was resilient within us began to stiffen. Traits of character became not merely habits, but defining elements. I suppose for me that it was fortunate—or unfortunate, given my current situation as your prisoner—that one of my defining traits has always been curiosity. Curiosity is one of the seeds of creativity, so that remained to me as well, but many of my associates were less fortunate.

"Remember that Virim recruited us all because we shared a certain idealism. However, I fear that not much time needs to pass for idealism to become dogmatism. This was the case for many of my associates. They became dogmatic, but not regarding the same things."

Firekeeper wondered what dogs had to do with ideas, but

thought she understood. Dogs, like wolves, were pack animals, but unlike wolves, dogs retained a juvenile desire to follow. So these spellcasters had been Virim's dogs, and when this stiffening happened, they had become even more doglike. It made sense in a way.

"Some few of us, and here I will admit that I was one," Bruck went on, "realized that this loss of resilience was the first indication that other losses threatened us. We would begin to age, to weaken, perhaps to die. When this awareness became general, three ways were suggested to remedy the situation."

"Three?" Firekeeper said. "You not worried you die first?"

Bruck gave a dry laugh. "Querinalo was still granting us sufficient power that we did not need to worry about that. Indeed, some of the most dogmatic among our number refused to admit anything deleterious was happening to us at all. They held that while it seemed true that querinalo was no longer working quite as it had, still nothing all that important had changed. To all the senses, we remained much the ages we had been when the grand project began. As most of us had been relatively youthful to begin with, that meant we were all in quite good condition."

Firekeeper nodded, wishing that Derian were there to explain some of Bruck's more ornate words, but not wishing to show herself vulnerable by asking for explanations. She thought she had gathered enough.

"So three things," she prompted. "What?"

Bruck ticked off on raised fingers. "One was to find what had happened to alter the fiber of our original curse and mend it, returning the curse to what it had been. A second possible course of action was to find a supplementary way of sustaining our lives and youth. Those who favored this course pointed out that even if querinalo was repaired, it no longer had anything like the pool of magically talented to draw upon that had once existed. Something more would be needed in any case.

"The third course of action suggested was that we remember our original goal—which had been to protect the New World from the Old. We had done this, and now our next move should be to accept what was happening. We should use what life remained to us—and that would be many years to come—to reinsert ourselves into the human world. Even with spellcasting reemerging as an art, any one of us should be a match and more for any, even all, of the Once Dead. We should make ourselves this new generation's teachers, trying to educate them so that the arrogance and destructiveness that had dominated in the past would not arise again."

Firekeeper thought of the Once Dead who had reigned on the Nexus Islands before the actions of herself and her allies had broken their power, and wondered if this last course would have had a chance. Surviving querinalo, especially as a spellcaster, seemed to create the very arrogance that these idealists had wanted to prevent.

Blind Seer said, *"Ask Bruck which of these courses Virim favored."*

"I wish I knew for certain," Bruck replied when Firekeeper had translated the wolf's query.

"You not know?" Firekeeper asked.

"I don't think," Bruck said, "that Virim ever really thought about what the consequences of querinalo would be. He knew he wanted to stop the conquest of the New World, but I think that somehow he overlooked the death and destruction his choice would bring to the New and Old Worlds alike."

"And how did your 'pack' react to this lack of certainty on Virim's part?" Blind Seer asked.

"There had always been factions," Bruck responded, looking at Blind Seer as if Firekeeper's voice were the wolf's own. "Now the factions grew more fractioned than ever."

"Even to factions of one," Blind Seer said, *"such as one human letting himself be ruled by his curiosity, although good sense as voiced by all those around him says he should remain within the safe walls of his den with his pack all around him?"*

Firekeeper translated, and Bruck nodded. "Even so."

Blind Seer stood and shook, a motion akin to a human clearing his throat. His next words were for Firekeeper alone.

"Let us call Elation from her high watch. I feel certain we will not have trouble from Bruck's allies for some time yet, and I would speak to you apart from our guest. I am not completely certain he doesn't understand more of our speech than he is letting on."

Firekeeper frowned. *"Will Elation alone be enough?"*

"Enough to scream warning," Blind Seer said, and with this Firekeeper had to agree.

Elation came down at the first short howl.

"I was thinking of landing soon in any case," she said. *"The forest is so still that rabbits are grazing in the open but a glade away. The only motion I have seen from our type has been going in the direction of the keep."*

The wolves explained their need, and Elation concurred.

"Tell him if he stirs in any fashion I don't like," the peregrine said, *"that I will have his eyes for dinner. Flying makes me hungry, but I spared no time for mice and rabbits."*

Firekeeper passed on the warning to Bruck, adding, "And we not be far. We go to check one thing or so. Know, too, that the arrows ready in my quiver have iron heads."

Bruck looked suitably impressed, and Firekeeper felt confident leaving him in Elation's care.

She and Blind Seer went a short distance away and settled themselves so they could share the watch between them without losing sight of each other. It was a thing they did so automatically that the only strangeness Firekeeper felt about the precaution was that she even noticed herself taking it.

"So Little Two-legs, you haven't asked me how I could see and defeat that 'warning' those Bruck angered sent after him."

Firekeeper shrugged. "There hasn't exactly been time for long conversations. I did wonder, though."

"Remember what I told you about back on the Nexus Islands," Blind Seer began, "about my talent?"

Firekeeper nodded.

"I did not tell you what choice I made then," Blind Seer went on.

"I think I guessed," Firekeeper said, speaking her thoughts aloud, "when I remembered that you dreamed you had killed the mountain sheep that was Virim. You kept your magic, didn't you?"

"Do you hate me for that choice?"

"I feel just a little as if I don't know you," Firekeeper admitted. "Magic of that sort seems a thing for humans."

"Such was my first thought as well," Blind Seer said. "I wondered if in fighting as I did to keep an ability I hardly knew was mine, I was somehow becoming less than a wolf. I avoided times when spells must be worked because I now could feel myself reaching out for understanding. I think the ability had been with me all my life, but in the New World there was nothing for it to fasten upon."

"Like waking on a night with neither moon or stars," Firekeeper said, "and reaching to touch to see if your eyes are open or closed because the darkness is so complete."

"Except that until querinalo showed me what lay within me," Blind Seer said, "I was as unaware of what I could sense as a newborn pup who has never opened his eyes and believes that the world is all smells and tastes and sounds."

"That avoiding," Firekeeper said, "that's why you didn't travel by means of the gates unless you absolutely needed to do so. You said you didn't like the sensation of their working, but it was this, wasn't it?"

"That is so. Talents do not trouble me. They are something worked differently by each and every one who has them. They are not spells. After our group took command of the Nexus Islands, Ynamynet was the only spellcaster. Enigma learned to operate the gates, but he has bad memories of Ynamynet's kind, and has not shown a tremendous interest in learning more than how to use the gates and a few minor tricks. There were times I longed to talk with him about what he was feeling, but to do so would have been to admit to an attraction to my own ability, and I could not do so."

Firekeeper did not need to ask Blind Seer why his aversion to his ability should be so much greater than Enigma's. She and Blind Seer belonged to the same culture, one that had much in common with Derian's own in its aversion to magic. On either side of the Iron Mountains, humans and Royal Beasts alike recounted the histories of the uses to which great magics had been turned, and of their even greater abuses. The only difference in these tales was that the Royal Beasts felt themselves separate from such horrors, victims but never perpetrators. How horrible for Blind Seer to find himself one with his nightmares!

Enigma, like many of the yarimaimalom, shared the view of the Liglimom. In their religion, Magic was a goddess. An unpredictable one, and one whose gifts should not be abused, but nonetheless the child of Water, the granddaughter of Earth and Air, niece to equally unpredictable Fire, and in her way more akin to her uncle than her father.

Firekeeper felt a funny surge as these thoughts flickered through her mind. She was Fire's Keeper, or so the Liglimom chose to interpret her name. What if Blind Seer was Magic's? An unsettling thought, but one that brought her odd comfort, putting her once again within that partnership of opposites, male and female, human and wolf that had come to define her relationship with Blind Seer.

"It was a spell they sent after Bruck," she said, "and somehow you could see that spell at work."

Blind Seer relaxed slightly when she articulated what he had done, for there was no disapproval in her words.

"That is so. It was so clear I was startled when I realized you could not see it. The spell tapped something within him, making his life flow away from him, rather than circulate through his body as it should."

"If you say so," Firekeeper laughed. "I have only seen life flow out of a body, never within it."

"I ripped apart the conduit that was draining him," Blind Seer explained. "I did it with my fangs, for I had no idea how to use a spell. I learned two things from this. First, I can affect spells, although I do not know if I can create them. Second, Bruck was right. The spell his fellows sent was inhibited by the iron we bound on him, but . . ."

He paused and Firekeeper could read the mingled uneasiness and delight in his bearing.

"But, Firekeeper, I was not affected by the iron in the least. The same element that causes Bruck's skin to blister does not seem to affect me at all. I don't understand why. There is so much I do not understand."

Firekeeper believed him. The uneasiness she had felt when the Meddler had shown her the dream vision of Blind Seer searching through scrolls ebbed somewhat. She still didn't know how Blind Seer would react if the spellcasters were to offer him an apprenticeship, but she felt certain that he was not planning to abandon her to pursue his new gift.

"We cannot leave Elation for much longer," she said. "Birds need to eat even more frequently than do humans, and she has soared high and long today. Do you have any thoughts as to what we should do next?"

Blind Seer responded immediately. "From what Bruck tells us, this is a pack without a One. Here we are, two Ones such as these humans have never met. I think we know what to do. We make ourselves their Ones, and then we remind them that wolves are obedient to those who rule them."

Firekeeper grinned at him. The thought was pleasantly direct, as familiar as the turning of the seasons.

"A pack without a One," she said. "Yes. I had thought so much about their power I had not considered what Bruck was telling us. If the situation is as he says, we do not face a pack, but a collection of dispersed tail-lickers, each seeking advantage over the others. We will give them the wolf's choice: death or submission."

Her moment of confidence vanished nearly as quickly as it had arisen. There was another side to that simple choice. What if she or Blind Seer were defeated? She knew she could not submit, and she had no great desire to die.

"But can we defeat them, even one or two at a time? These are the last of the great spellcasters, the ones who subdued all the world through their command of fire and lighting and creatures such as none living have seen in over a hundred years."

Blind Seer gaped his jaws in a wolfish grin.

"Remember," he said, "we have iron on our side, iron and the strengths of wolves. Remember that, and the hunting will be sure."

XXVI

WHEN DERIAN AND Ynamynet informed the gathered Nexans that the Islands were probably going to be invaded sometime before the summer had passed, Derian had expected disbelief. After all, what proof did they have but a young woman's dreams and the word of a jaguar known for being unable to sort reality from visions?

But the reliability of the report was accepted without question, and discussion moved immediately to what the Nexans could or should do about the situation.

Later, Derian would realize why the acceptance had come so easily. Unlike New World residents like himself, these people had grown to adulthood surrounded not only by people who could do magic, but by the relics of a magical past. Although in some Old World nations the reaction against magic had been almost as powerfully negative as it had been in the New World, there had been no way to erase physical reminders of what magic could do.

Even in the New World, there were reminders for those who knew where to look, most often in architecture where artifacts ranging from the light blocks built into the walls to the fantastical shapes of some buildings called to mind days when light could be had without smoke or heat, and towers could be raised to stand without visible means of support. Many of the more fantastical buildings had indeed been destroyed, but some, like the religious buildings in Liglim or the strange city within a city of Thendula Lypella in New Kelvin, remained.

In the Old World, where humans had lived for as long as any and all could remember, these architectural reminders were so prevalent that they could not be eliminated short of razing entire cities. Moreover, unlike in the New World, where the benefits of magic were restricted to those who ruled and their close associates, in the Old World magic had touched even the most ordinary of lives in the form of healing or lighting or little domestic comforts.

That routine use of magic had been gone for over a century now, but old people remained who could tell stories of things their own parents or grandparents had known or done.

So, when Isende stood up and reported in a quavering voice about her dream visions of fleets and armies, and Derian stood after her and told what Truth had said, the Nexans did not call them frauds seeking greater control than they already asserted, but politely thanked them and began addressing the situation.

Wort the Never Lived, who had once been a guard and now served the Nexus Islands as quartermaster of sorts, stood. He was a heavyset man with brown skin, wide lips and nose, and a wealth of thick, coarse black hair. He spoke from deep in his chest and his voice carried well throughout the crowded room.

"We have discussed and discussed again our position here as custodians of the Nexus Islands. I do not see how this new information has changed decisions we have made before. We decided to hold this place and control the gates, nor did we think that decision would be popular with those who had come to rely on those gates. Let us continue along the course we have set. Time spent discussing any other choice is time wasted for planning our defense."

Wort resumed his seat, and Derian braced himself for a wave of argument that did not come. Instead, all he saw on the faces of those gathered were varying degrees of agreement. Surprised, he turned to Ynamynet, wondering despite himself if the Once Dead had somehow placed a control on these people.

She met his gaze with a brief smile of understanding, and spoke in a voice loud enough for all to hear.

"No, Derian. I had nothing to do with this sudden accord. Those of us who were born in the Old World know the lands that gave us birth, rejection, and reluctant acceptance. We never thought they would let us hold such a prize as the Nexus Islands without challenge. Our reasons for not wishing to give in without a fight may differ. For some of us it is pride, for others fear, for others a sense that this is the only home we have known for many years. Perhaps it would be most honest to say that our reasons mingle all of these things, but you may feel secure that we from the Old World wish to hold these islands as much as you do, perhaps more. For you the Nexus Islands are an interesting toy, and holding them is a means of protecting your homelands. For us, they are a vital resource, and the only means by which we may hope to walk in our homelands again not as slaves or prisoners, but as people as good as any and better than many."

Derian looked away from Ynamynet and saw that the gathered Nexans did indeed agree with the sentiments Ynamynet had voiced. A few were wiping away tears, but they were tears born of overwhelming emotion, not of sorrow or grief.

"Very well," Derian said. "If we are agreed, then let us decide what we can do. How many adults do we have among us?"

Wort rose. "We have one hundred and nine healthy human adults, if we may count Plik among those."

The short, fat raccoon-man did not bother to rise from his seat on one of the risers. To do so would have only made him shorter.

"You may indeed," Plik said.

Derian looked again to Wort. "And children old enough to be of some help?"

"Twenty or so," Wort said. "I'm less certain about that, but if we count those who might be good for little other than watching the younger children, at least twenty. There are also some invalid adults who could do similar work, or assist in the kitchens and such. However, there are also a handful of chronic invalids who will require care."

Derian nodded. In a different community, there would have been more such invalids or elderly, but the Spell Wielders had not tended to suffer what they considered useless individuals. These had either been sent back to the "mainland" or had been, Derian suspected from rumors he had heard, killed.

Pushing such ugly thoughts from his mind, Derian turned to Plik.

"How about the yarimaimalom? Do you think we can count on their support?"

"Certainly," Plik said without hesitation. "They remember all too well what happened when the Old World last touched the New. However, the amount of yarimaimalom who can actually come to the Nexus Islands is limited because we have no means of knowing who might or might not contract querinalo. The majority of those who would be available will be wingéd folk, useful in many ways, but perhaps not as soldiers."

The ravens Bitter and Lovable were perched along the back of one of the higher risers, and now Bitter gave a series of hoarse croaks.

Plik translated, "Bitter regrets to confirm that my assessment is fairly accurate. We cannot hope that the humans coming here will not have thought to equip themselves with bows and even the most ferocious eagle is not invulnerable to such attacks."

"None of us are," Derian said, remembering with a flash of nostalgia the care Blind Seer and Elation had both taken to make sure they understood the range and limitation of such weapons. "I'll make a note that we should include in our training some lessons about bows and arrows and such. It could prove useful for everyone involved."

"Thanks," croaked Lovable in her hoarse imitation of a human voice. "Good."

Derian looked at Ynamynet. "Any thoughts about our magical resources?"

Ynamynet rose. "We have little enough. Myself, Kalyndra, and Enigma are the only true spellcasters among us. The talents that are available are specialized. I think if we consider carefully, we may be able to find a way to use them to great effect. Your ability to speak with horses, for example, means that in collaboration with one of the Wise Horses you can translate for the yarimaimalom. For this reason, I hope you will not be offended if I state that I do not think you should be general of our forces."

Derian looked at her in astonishment. "Me? I'm trained in sword and bow, true enough, but I'm no soldier. I was going to suggest Skea serve as our general."

Ynamynet looked both pleased and worried, and Derian remembered almost as an afterthought that Skea was her husband, father to her little daughter.

Skea, seated off to one side, rose. "I would accept, but only if I had the support of every adult Nexan. We're going to need to train up an army in a very short time, and that will be neither pleasant nor easy. I can't—we can't—afford a mutiny."

Wort, who might have been considered a rival for Skea, rose.

"I think you'd be better than me, Skea. If I were elected, I would need to train someone to take over this." He hefted the long sheet of paper on which Derian knew he kept a concise record of all their resources. "That would be a demanding job in itself. No. When the invaders come I will take up my weapons and fight as best I can, but I will hardly have time to train, much less to command."

Something similar was said by those of the dozen or so men or women who might have wanted Skea's place in command. One or two did take the opportunity to stress their specialized training in some aspect of the military arts, and Skea gladly made them his officers.

The chief cook waved a plump hand while this was going on, and Ynamynet glanced over at Skea.

"Can you continue to work the military details out after the public meeting?"

Skea nodded, his dark hand busy working a quill across paper. "I can put up some sort of notice in the dining hall."

"Good," Ynamynet said. "Yes, Pishtoolam?"

The chief cook stood. "I realize we must seriously prepare against military invasion, but certainly everyone won't be training as soldiers. There will still be meals to be prepared, just to give one example."

"And laundry to be washed," Ynamynet agreed, "and fish to be caught and herbs to be gathered, and firewood to be cut, and animals to be tended, and all the many, many jobs that are done here on a daily basis. However, there are a variety of tasks that can be ruled less essential, and even more that are going to be necessary."

"Like learning how to use a sword," the cook said hesitantly, obviously trying to show willingness.

"Certainly that," Derian interjected, "although in your case I'd simply hand you one of your kitchen cleavers. I've seen what you can do to bone and meat with one of those."

General laughter responded to this, and Derian went on.

"There are going to be other, less martial skills we'll need to train in. Doctor Zebel . . ."

"Over here," he said.

Derian noted that the doctor's long-jawed face looked tired, as if he was worn out in anticipation of what was to come. Then he remembered that a baby boy had been born the night before. Zebel had probably been woken from a deserved sleep to attend this meeting.

"Doctor, we're going to need to teach as many people as can learn the basics of how to tend a wound. We're also going to need a handful more trained to do tasks more complex than stanching wounds and such. Can you take charge of that?"

"I can," Zebel said. "There are several among us who already have the basic skills, others I think can be taught. I was wondering if some excuse can be found to send someone to Gak almost immediately. I have a supply of medications, and can augment some of these with plants that grow in the meadows near the Setting Sun stronghold, but cloth for bandages, thread for stitching, more alcohol for cleansing . . . I could make a list."

Skea raised his head from contemplating the list he had been making. "And what about weapons? The Spell Wielders had laid in a small armory, but we have nothing like what we'll need if we must face an army."

Derian rubbed a hand across his forehead, feeling a headache coming on. "We'll work on that."

Chaker Torn, who was captain and two-thirds of the crew that manned the fishing vessel that was the Nexus Islands' largest craft, waved for recognition almost as soon as Doctor Zebel sat.

"What about this fleet Isende has dreamed is coming? We have a small number of craft, but nothing that can deal with a fleet of armed vessels."

Ynamynet took this question. "I suspect that the fleet is going to be mostly transportation for those who are going to make landfall. Isende is going to be shown pictures of sailing vessels and she has promised to try and pinpoint what we are seeing. Tell me, is it true that the waters around the Nexus Islands are difficult to navigate?"

"True enough," Chaker responded promptly. "Any ship with a deep draft is going to have a time getting close to shore. They'll need to use landing craft, I would guess."

Ynamynet smiled, but the expression was not particularly nice. In fact, it made Derian's spine creep.

"Chaker, I want you to think about ways you might misdirect these vessels as to where the safe channels lie. I don't know much about such things, but I'm guessing that what the invaders are relying on are old logs and charts from before the Sorcerer's Bane, maybe older than that, even. Certainly, rocks and such may have shifted in all that time. If there is any way we can use that. . . ."

Chaker rubbed the inch or so of bristle that seemed to perpetually adorn his chin and cheeks.

"I might be able to work something," he said, so hesitantly that Derian suspected he had ethical reservations of some sort. "Hard to say, really."

"Just remember," Ynamynet said, "any boat that doesn't make it to shore with its burden of armed and armored marines is one that won't be terrorizing your wife and children."

Chaker stiffened at this, nodded, and took his seat.

Derian saw Harjeedian politely waiting for acknowledgment, and with a glance at Ynamynet to make sure she was finished, called on the aridisdu.

"I realize that archival research is likely to be one of those tasks deemed less important," Harjeedian said, "and while I am fully in agreement with this, I would like to retain a researcher or two—perhaps from among our older residents who would not be physically fighting in any case—to research certain matters that might prove useful."

Derian flicked his ears back in puzzlement, realized what he had done, and said a bit more brusquely than he had intended, "Such as?"

"Such as what defenses the Nexus Islands might have once had in place," Harjeedian said. "From several people, I have heard tales that the waters were said to be populated with sea dragons. If this was true, might they still be there? Might this have been a metaphor for some more mundane form of defense? We of Liglim have had occasional problems with ambitious pirates who think the settlements surrounding our main bay are temptingly defenseless. They learn that underwater chains do unpleasant things to the hulls of ships forced to rely upon narrow channels."

"Interesting thought," Derian said. "What if chains like those are stored somewhere? Even if we couldn't deploy them, we might be about to turn the metal in them to some other purpose. I think some research is in order. Ynamynet?"

"I agree," she said, "especially using those Harjeedian has mentioned."

Harjeedian had remained standing, so Derian asked him, "Something else?"

"I thought I would remind you that while I am not as skilled as Doctor Zebel in medical matters, I do have some solid training in that area. I would like to offer my services in teaching elementary medical techniques, and offer myself to Doctor Zebel as an assistant."

Derian blinked in surprise. As an aridisdu and, quite frankly, as one of the conquerors, Harjeedian had a great deal of status among the Nexus Island community. To have him publicly offer to subordinate himself to one of the conquered in any capacity was a tremendous gesture, and one that should humble any number of those who might even now be contemplating how to jockey for status.

"Thank you, Harjeedian," Derian said. "After this meeting, why don't you speak with Doctor Zebel about how to best arrange your schedules."

Verul, who had been one of the first Nexans Derian had met, back even before Derian had known that there were Nexus Islands, now signaled for attention. Once the ruddy-skinned, fair-haired man had been a bodyguard, equal to Skea in every way. These days he walked with a crutch much of the time, lamed in a fight with Firekeeper. That the wolf-woman had disabled him without taking his life had not made Verul exactly grateful to her. Instead, he resented her reputation among the Nexans, and never missed an opportunity to cast doubt on her prowess.

"I was wondering if anything had been heard from Firekeeper," he said. "We all know she and Blind Seer left here to return to their homeland. I know she said she was going to scout for some information that might enable us to prevent querinalo from attacking any newcomers, but it seems to me she has been gone for quite a long time."

"She's only been gone a bit over a moonspan," Derian protested.

"Still, didn't she take a gate right to where she needed to go?" Verul said.

His tone was guileless and the straight, square lines of his face innocent of malice, but Derian hoped no one was fooled. Probably some did share his curiosity, though. Derian suspected that many of the Nexans had no real idea what was involved in traveling long distances. The gates had spoiled them for that, for even though the gates did not remove all need for travel, they did tend to eliminate awkward, time-consuming tasks like crossing mountain ranges.

Derian schooled his voice to patience. "The gate did not take her 'right where she needed to go.' It took her to a city east of the mountains she would need to cross to reach her destination.

Even if she found a cure almost instantly and returned that minute, I doubt she could be to us for a moonspan or more."

"But you are certain she will return," Verul said.

"Absolutely," Derian replied.

But he wondered, even as the meeting turned to other matters, if when Firekeeper did return would there be anyone to open the gate for her, and if the gate did open, would friends or enemies wait on the other side.

⚜

"I've touched Isende," the Meddler reported with some triumph. "She spoke to Derian, and together they have gone to Truth. The Nexus Islands will not face invasion unwarned."

Firekeeper stretched, paws turning into hands as she awoke from dreams into that strange place wherein the Meddler drew her for their conversations. They were sitting on what might be very thick green moss or rather dense, tinted clouds. The light was indirect, and the mood deceptively restful. Deceptive because although Firekeeper knew her body continued to sleep, this interlude would tire her as if she had not slept at all.

"I have had," she said, "a very long and busy day. We have taken one of Virim's pack, and learned that this pack is not such a pack as we had thought. Now we must find a way to turn this to our advantage."

The Meddler, fully human in this vision, perhaps to match her, nodded. Disappointment touched the shape of his eyes, and Firekeeper thought that he was unhappy that she had not praised him. She considered, decided that he had done something admirable, and that she would be rude to withhold thanks.

"And from what you say, you have had some busy times since last we spoke," she went on. "I am glad you managed to reach Isende. The Nexus Islands should not go unwarned. I only hope that they can hold until Blind Seer and I can return."

"Do you really think two of you would make such a difference?" the Meddler said.

"We would not be two alone," Firekeeper said, "or not for long, not if we could be certain querinalo would not harm those we might convince to help us. That would certainly make a difference."

"Thinking ahead," the Meddler said, and Firekeeper truly could not tell whether she heard mockery or approval in his voice.

"What of it?" she challenged. "Wolves may not be squirrels, but still they know that winter is coming."

"Meaning, I suppose," the Meddler said, "that just because wolves don't store food in advance to get them through the thin months, doesn't mean that they are incapable of advanced preparation."

"That's what I said," Firekeeper retorted.

An odd vision touched her then. She was certain it had been generated by her own imagination, not created by the Meddler.

She saw a world very like the one in which she now lived, only in this world Royal Beasts did not live separately from humans, but rather employed them to do tasks for them. The situation was not at all like that in Liglim, where the relationship between humans and Beasts was religious in nature, but more like the way humans dealt with humans in places like Hawk Haven or New Kelvin.

In her imagination she saw a wolf dragging a freshly slain deer to a human's house. A human came out and examined the deer, exclaiming in awe and appreciation. Then he hung the carcass from a tree, speaking to the wolf as he went about the process of draining the blood and removing the organs as humans did before preparing the meat. Although the wolf could not speak the human's language, it had learned a series of signs that enabled simple communication. Through these an agreement was reached.

The human would keep the deer's hide and some of the organs and bones. The wolf would immediately consume other organs, and enjoy the marrow in some of the thicker bones. The human would then prepare the meat, drying a portion of it and holding it until the wolf returned for it.

Firekeeper thought this would be quite a mutually beneficial situation. Humans were not nearly as good hunters as wolves. Wolves could not preserve food in the fat times for the thin. Yet this would be a different relationship from those that existed between humans and their dogs. For one, the wolf would remain in the wilds. For another, neither would claim mastery over the other. It would be a business partnership, nothing more.

The Meddler looked at her, his amber eyes warm with affection.

"You're dreaming something," he said. "I can't read the details, but I can almost taste them. You're seeing the world inside out and upside down. You do that more than you ever realize. It's one of the things I like about you."

Firekeeper grew guarded. She didn't much like this talk of being able to taste her dreams. What else might the Meddler be able to do? What other of her dreams might he know?

"Don't worry," the Meddler said. "Don't you wolves have a saying: 'Like knows like best'?"

Firekeeper nodded.

"We're alike, you and I," the Meddler said. "Meddlers see the world in different ways, too, and often try and make changes."

"You are the Meddler," Firekeeper growled. "Not I."

"I am *a* Meddler," the Meddler said. "I am not the only one. None of those stories Plik and Harjeedian told that colored your view of me so unfairly were about things I personally did. I'd like to think I am capable of thinking about the ramifications of my actions."

"Like with Melina," Firekeeper said. "You think so well that now Citrine is missing a finger, and Peace is dying more quickly as the Dragon drinks his life."

The Meddler shrugged. "Melina proved a bit more volatile than I had imagined, but then I was hardly in the best position to research her life and inclinations, now, was I?"

"But you went ahead anyhow," Firekeeper said, "playing games with her and with Dantarahma and with Truth and with others, treating them all as if they really were those little crystal pieces that you carved."

"I've done my best to make amends," the Meddler said. "Didn't I help you when you went after Isende and Tiniel? Haven't I helped you since?"

"And I wonder," Firekeeper said, "why you have done this. Not the helping us with Isende and Tiniel; they were as much your problem as they were ours. But the help you have given us since, the prompting us to find a cure for querinalo and helping us learn about Virim. I do wonder."

The Meddler looked hurt and indignant.

"Can't you believe that I simply wish to help you?"

Firekeeper shook her head. "Why would you wish to do that?"

"Perhaps," the Meddler said, leaning closer to her and extending one hand as if he would stroke her cheek, "I like you. I do, you know, and not just because you're more of a Meddler than you care to admit. You're a very dynamic individual. When a man has lived as long as I have, an interesting personality is more beautiful than those physical qualities that fade and change all too rapidly in any case."

Firekeeper jerked back from the proffered caress, but her face burned as she remembered the one time the Meddler had kissed her. That kiss had been very different from the friendly pecks she had given to her friends, different from her kissing Blind Seer, for although the wolf might lick her in return, there was none of that interesting sensation as lip met lip and tongue touched tongue.

For a moment, just a moment, Firekeeper thought about inviting the Meddler close again. After all, this was just a dream. In a way it wasn't real at all, and so what would be the harm?

The Meddler seemed aware of her shift in mood, and leaned toward her again. His hand stroked her cheek lightly, tracing the line of her cheekbone, the silken curve of her eyebrow, trailing down to touch her lip.

Firekeeper trembled, realizing that this was the closest to human touch she could clearly remember. She must have been touched by her human parents, but she remembered her time with them only in dreams.

Oh, Derian had dressed and undressed her—but she had been indifferent to him as a male. He had been the one to grow embarrassed, especially as he grew to know her as a female who, to him, was human. Firekeeper's focus had been on the awkwardness of clothing. Doc had handled her as well, but always in a medical context.

This sensation of fingers against skin, touching for no reason but for the pleasure of touch, was heady, intoxicating as the time she had shared in a feast of overripe berries with some birds and become so dizzy that she had never touched the like again.

In that dizziness she started to lean toward the Meddler and felt him leaning toward her. In a moment his lips would touch hers, and they were so close to the soft greenness of the mossy ground. She could relax then, relax into warm, muscular arms, feeling skin touch skin, not fur. She could . . .

Firekeeper jerked back from the Meddler's touch, leaping back from him as quick as thought. Had she possessed fur, her hackles would have bristled. Had she possessed fangs, she would have bared them. As it was, she merely balanced on the balls of her feet, ready to run if the Meddler should come closer.

He, however, only looked up at her from where he had been, seated on the soft green, his hand where he had extended it to lightly touch her face.

"Second thoughts?" he asked with almost friendly mockery. "Pity. It was getting quite diverting. I don't think you can lose your virginity in a dream, but we could find out."

Firekeeper glowered at him.

"Maybe, but I have nothing to lose that I would wish for you to find. I remembered, just remembered, how that one kiss gave you this link to me. I think that is enough, more than enough."

"The choice is yours, Lady Firekeeper," the Meddler said. "When you consider our past encounters, I think you will realize I have never forced anything on you but an awareness of my presence."

Firekeeper was too light-headed to debate, but a new

thought came to her and she forced herself to focus, pursuing it as if it was a fat meal and she unfed for days. She cornered the idea and trapped it, and when she had examined it closely she turned and looked at the Meddler through narrowed eyes.

"I have thought of a reason," she said, "that you might want to be so helpful to us."

"Do you want to share it with me," he asked, "or will you leave it to fester in your heart?"

Firekeeper considered. Her first thought had been to hold the idea, to share it with Blind Seer when she awoke, but there was no reason she could not confront the Meddler and still share her insight with Blind Seer.

"I have been trying to think," she began, "why you are helping us, and could come to no thought but that you were being generous. Even in the tales that Plik and Harjeedian told, the Meddler had his share of generosity."

"Thank you for that, at least," the Meddler said sardonically. "But I take it that you have come up with a reason for me to assist you that does not involve my being generous."

Firekeeper ignored that jab, and continued as if he had not spoken.

"I just realized that I had been asking the wrong question. The question was not why would you help us, but 'What might you gain from what we are doing?' "

The Meddler's amber eyes widened slightly, as if in carefully hidden surprise, but he said nothing to either confirm or deny Firekeeper's suspicion. Still, she felt she was on the right track and spoke more quickly, with greater confidence.

"Once I asked myself that, then I began to understand. You showed me why we could not remain ignorant of the source of querinalo. Your reasoning was good, and as events have developed, quite accurate. So accurate, in fact, that I wonder if you might not have seen the first seeds of this invasion being planted, and decided to turn them to your benefit. After all, if there was indeed an invasion, we would pursue the cure for querinalo all the more stringently.

"Now I asked myself, why would you care for a cure? My first thought—which I do not think is completely right—was that you did not care for the cure. You cared, instead, for what we would find when we sought the cure. Virim. His pack. His fort. The last group of spellcasters in all the world untainted by the weakening and corrupting effects of querinalo, the last spellcasters who knew how to use magic as the art had been developed at its height, rather than as it has been rediscovered.

"And I asked myself why you would want these. After all, had it not been spellcasters who had locked you away? At first I thought you might wish to destroy them, or perhaps that you hoped that my allies and I would destroy them for you. Then I had another thought, one you yourself gave me, although you meant it to turn me away from Blind Seer."

"Ah?" the Meddler didn't quite ask.

"I thought you might have a use for these spellcasters, but as you showed me, you cannot get beyond the barriers they have put up against intrusion by bodiless spirits such as yourself. Now what use might you have for spellcasters? Were you not their equal or perhaps their superior? Superior, certainly, for humans rarely go to great lengths to harm those they can dominate. Those they use.

"But for all your knowledge and all your power, these spellcasters have one very important thing you do not. They have bodies. They live and breathe, whereas you, at least in physical terms, are dead."

The Meddler said nothing, and Firekeeper drew herself up and challenged him.

"Tell me!" she said. "Tell me the truth, or I swear that as soon as I awaken I will turn my feet from this place. Blind Seer and I have taken Bruck, and perhaps he has answers enough for us. We can bear him away to New Kelvin, then to the Nexus Islands. Perhaps when invasion threatens him as it threatens Derian and the others, Bruck will find a way to enable us to defeat the invasion."

"You mean that," the Meddler said in mild amazement. "You'd really turn back, just because you don't trust my motives."

"Yes," Firekeeper said. "And fight and probably die, because the stories say the Meddler acts from good thoughts, but does not think what they will bring. I would go to my death and even bring Blind Seer to his rather than be a little crystal figure you move about here and there."

The Meddler raised his hands in a theatrical gesture of surrender.

"Very well. I will confess, and I think in this place you can sniff truth from evasion. You are correct. I wanted you to come here. I suspected that at least some of Virim's cohort still lived. You are even correct in suspecting what I wanted from them. I want a living body. Spirit life is interesting, more versatile in many ways, but I need a body if I am to have even the slightest chance of gaining what I now realize I desire more than anything else."

"What?" Firekeeper asked. "Tell me. I cannot risk setting you free to do harm. I am sorry, for I do believe you when you say you have not meant much of the harm you have caused, but I must look out for my pack."

The Meddler looked at her and his gaze was sad.

"I'll tell you," he said. "You would learn soon enough in any case. You see, my darling little Meddler, I believe I have fallen in love with you. I want to live and breathe again so that I may try and win your love in return."

XXVII

BRYESSIDAN CONSIDERED WEARING his father's armor to his first meeting with the other men and women who would serve as generals of the gate forces, but decided against it. True, reminding them that he came from a line revered for proven military prowess would help with his campaign to be named commander in chief, but there were other ways to achieve this than marching in wearing the form and face of their old enemy.

Bryessidan's initial impulse toward wearing the armor had less to do with providing a reminder of his military lineage than with showing what might be done to enable a leader to be armored and yet provide minimal distortion for those nearby who must use magic. However, again there were other ways he could do this, although they would be more pedantic and less visually impressive.

So he arrived at the meeting in Hearthome clad in white and green as king of the Mires, nothing more. He rapidly learned that he was the only other reigning monarch leading a gate force, and considered this a good omen for his ambitions for overall command. Since King Hurwin was commanding the fleet, surely some parallel structure would be in order. It wasn't as if the other monarchs—or whatever title the allied ruler claimed—had been dissuaded from donning armor and carrying sword into battle in the name of the cause.

Perhaps not liking the possible consequences if they chose not to participate in the venture, all five nations on the Pelland continent had chosen to take part in the invasion of the Nexus Islands. In addition, two other nations—Tavetch to the north and u-Chival to the south—had chosen to participate. Several other nations had expressed a willingness to join in, but as they did not possess a working gate, and such was necessary to send in forces, they had been encouraged to either contribute to the fleet or train up forces against the unlikely eventuality that the Nexans would successfully resist the initial invasion.

So now Bryessidan and a few advisors took their seats in the council chamber Queen Iline of Hearthome had made available for this meeting. Perhaps in an effort to show her complete confidence in her chosen general—an older man who was not, contrary to popular speculation prior to the appointment, one of her sons—Queen Iline was not attending the meeting. She did, however, provide a lavish spread of refreshments, and no one doubted that any or even all of the bustling attendants present were her spies.

No matter, Bryessidan thought. *It's not like we're going to be discussing anything we don't want her—or any other of the monarchs—to hear.*

Given that Hearthome was the host for the meeting—a choice based on its relative geographical centrality and good harbors, nothing more at least according to Bryessidan's way of thinking—General Kynan of Hearthome took it upon himself to open the meeting. After a small speech of welcome, he offered each of the other generals an opportunity to introduce themselves and their attendants, then turned to the aridisdu from u-Chival who was head of that nation's contingent.

"Aridisdu Valdala," he said, "I believe you have recently read the omens regarding the progress of the fleet. Would you be so kind as to share a report with us?"

Aridisdu Valdala, a stocky, heavyset woman whose broad shoulders left no doubt that she could wield sword or spear as easily as she did whatever tools she used for divination, rose politely in acknowledgment of General Kynan's request. Before speaking she pressed her hands together in a gesture Bryessidan knew meant that she was replying as equal to equal, not acknowledging any authority on Kynan's part. Bryessidan wondered how many of the others here gathered caught that subtlety, and felt again how well suited he was to serve as commander in chief.

"The omens," Valdala said, "show the fleet to be on course and intact. They should arrive at their goal in approximately a moonspan, as was planned."

Since the fleet hadn't been gone much more than a couple handspans of days, Bryessidan might have made the same prediction himself, but Amelo Soapwort had assured him that the auguries of the u-Chival had been tested for accuracy, and were often astonishingly accurate.

Kynan acknowledged this report with gravity, then turned to the assembly as a whole.

"Before the fleet departed, the date set for the invasion was the second day of Bear Moon. Are there any objections to continuing with that date?"

Aurick of Pelland, a lean, red-haired man whose sharp gaze seemed to challenge anyone to say that he shared the reputed fondness of those of his nation for drug dreams, was the only one who did more than nod agreement.

"I have no objections, as long as the omens remain favorable. However, that raises an interesting question. What do we do if the omens are not favorable? What if they seem to show that all or most of the fleet has been destroyed? Do we press ahead or call off the venture entirely?"

Talianas of Tishiolo, the land that supplied the Pellanders with their drugs, smiled at Aurick in such a way that Bryessidan felt certain that the two men were old rivals. Not enemies, perhaps, but certainly they had butted heads in the past. Doubtless Aurick disliked what drug use had done to his people, while Talianas might feel it was a harmless form of amusement—and one that enriched his people besides.

Aurick frowned at Talianas and said, "Well? I'm sure someone other than myself must have thought about this."

Bryessidan decided that he had been silent long enough. He must seem decisive if he wanted command.

"I have considered the matter," he said, "and I think that we should go ahead, even if the omens for the fleet are not good. For one, what if the aridisdum reading the omens receive different replies?"

He glanced at Aridisdu Valdala and made the hand gesture that indicated he was not attempting to give offense, only saying what must be said. She nodded, dipping her head in acknowledgment of his courtesy.

Encouraged, Bryessidan went on. "The aridisdum are very skilled, my own Once Dead assure me of this, but errors do happen. Perhaps if only one or two nations had chosen to join King Hurwin and myself in this venture to regain control of the gates, I might feel less certain, but we are seven nations strong. Seven forces. Seven gates. From what the maps show, our gates do not open into one area of the gate complex, but are spread out."

He paused, not because he didn't have more to say, but because he wanted to see the reaction to what he had already said. Implying that the entire venture had been his and King Hurwin's idea had been daring, but he thought it merited.

Fromalf, King Hurwin's choice for leader of the land force, and one of Gidji's cousins, was nodding agreement with Bryessidan's opinion.

"I also agree that we should plan on making our assault, no matter what the omens are for the fleet. I firmly believe that King Hurwin will bring through most, if not all, of those vessels under his command. If they are not there before us, they will come soon after we have established our base. We owe the fleet our support. Also, we cannot forget that the fleet has taken far greater risks than have those of us who have remained behind. Although they are well provisioned, the intention was for many of the marines to return to their homelands through the gates, and for the ships to be reprovisioned via the gates before they began their voyage home. If we fail to make our assault and hold the land, then we will disappoint these brave men and women who are counting on us."

After Fromalf's speech, no one spoke for a long moment; then Merial of Azure Towers broke the silence she had kept to this point. She was a niece of the current queen, Anitra, and had fought and politicked in her aunt's service for many years.

"I agree," General Merial said. "We go ahead, even if the omens for the fleet are bad. I also agree with the chosen date of the second of Bear. I believe we need to refine other matters, such as the precise time to make the transition, and whether there is any way to assure that all of us will transition within a fairly close sequence."

"In the days before the Sorcerer's Bane," Bryessidan said, "there were ways of measuring time with close accuracy. However, even in those days the presence of arms and armor could skew the accuracy of such devices. Therefore, I suggest we work with the one accurate clock we all will have at our disposal."

"The sun," responded Fromalf, with a sailor's sensitivity for such things.

"The sun," Bryessidan agreed. "And as backup, because we cannot count on the second day of Bear Moon being clear, we should all burn watch candles. We should purchase them here in Hearthome, from the same chandler, and make certain they are poured from the same batch of wax, and wicked with the same material to make certain they are as close to each other as possible."

Kynan spoke up, quickly, as if aware that his dominance of the meeting was slipping. "I know just the shop. I will order both full-day and half-day candles for further accuracy."

"Good," Bryessidan said. "So, noon on the second of Bear is our target date. Now, I think we need to know precisely what type of forces each of us will be able to supply."

That took a while because, although for obvious reasons no one was supplying calvary—the advantages to be gained from mounted troops on a relatively small island whose surface was known to be rocky would be minimal—what the seven allied nations had to spare varied greatly.

The Mires, barred from anything but a local peacekeeping force by the terms of the treaty that had ended King Veztressidan's war, had managed to raise a small but sturdy force from the hunters and fishers who made their living from the swamps and marshes that made up the majority of the kingdom's terrain. For the rest, they were supplying healers of various types.

Hearthome and Azure Towers, as a result of their fairly continual border sparing, both had good-sized armies, but for that same reason they were unwilling to deplete those forces overmuch. A great deal of time was spent negotiating exactly how much of what type of troop either was willing to commit, and then balancing that against the forces offered by the other.

Pelland, which also shared a border with aggressive Hearthome, should have had a similar complaint but did not for two reasons. For one, Pelland's inherited status as a land ruled by those who could claim descent from the former rulers of the continent had made Hearthome less than enthusiastic about confronting her openly, at least until she had secured her other border. Pelland also had a highly regarded military tradition. If these days her soldiers were more likely to march in parades than go into battle, this did not mean they would not fight if the need arose.

That, at least, was what King Bryessidan assumed, based on reports sent to him by his own diplomatic corp. If Hearthome took Azure Towers, then subduing the relatively unarmed Kingdom of the Mires should be simple. Then, with almost half a continent's backing, Pelland would fall.

Except, Bryessidan thought, carefully hiding his amusement, *that Pelland has a second advantage, one that counts far more than her inherited prestige. Their king's drug-shaded dreams include those from a past where his ancestors ruled by strength of arms as well as magical lore. When magic became anathema, he and his ancestors chose to emphasize the martial virtues, as if by doing so they could make everyone forget how much they once relied on magic to hold their power. Of us all, General Aurick has the best and strongest army. I suspect he will be my rival for command.*

The last three of the allied nations were not as militarily powerful as the first three, but each had something to offer. Tishiolo, relatively isolated on the far side of the mountains on the eastern side of the continent, had little reason to maintain an army against her neighbor nations. However, the rough land gave haven to numerous ferocious beasts, and as a result even the most stolid farmer tended to have some skill with bow and spear. Additionally, Tishiolo's trade in drugs meant that she maintained a solid border guard against those who might decide to negotiate other than in the marketplace for her goods.

Tavetch had already provided much of the fleet, and many of the marines, but King Hurwin had left behind sufficient men and women with some military training that their gate could participate in the invasion. Moreover, like Pelland, Tavetch had a strong military tradition. Indeed, the less charitable said the Tavetchians followed the professions of pirates and raiders. Bryessidan, having learned something of the typical coming-of-age rituals practiced by the Tavetchian court, was not about to argue.

Finally, there was u-Chival. The powerful theocracy that reigned in that southern land had little need for a police force to control their people. In the five deities they worshipped, they had far more powerful means of influencing their people. However, although the u-Chivalum claimed to hold uncontested rule of the small continent on which they were situated, this was far from true. The name they gave their military body might translate as "Protectors," but Bryessidan's ambassadors had reported that the Protectors were quite capable of aggression as well.

But I don't think any of the others will want Aridisdu Valdala to hold overall command, Bryessidan thought a trace anxiously, for the u-Chivalum force as Valdala had described it in her report was impressive. *The majority of us are Pellanders in heritage, and would be uncomfortable being told to direct our troops according to the commands of strange deities.*

The discussion of who would supply what was finally settled and Bryessidan was wondering how he could raise the question of appointing a commander in chief when Fromalf of Tavetch, King Hurwin's representative, did so for him.

"That was onerous," Fromalf said, making as if to wipe sweat from his brow, "even if necessary. However, I think it raises one matter we have not yet addressed—that of who will command our joined forces once we have crossed through the gates and secured a foothold on the Nexus Islands."

"Do we need such a commander?" asked Talianas of Tishiolo somewhat predictably.

"I believe we do," cut in Aurick of Pelland, straightening and looking every inch a general. "In my experience, most battles are lost not because the soldiers are inept, but because troops are used unwisely."

"Still," Talianas protested, "what type of resistance can we expect? Our own Once Dead estimate that the local population cannot be more than a hundred or so. Based upon what we have already discussed, we will outnumber them ten to one—and that is without the fleet."

Aridisdu Valdala frowned. "The omens are very uncertain on the matter of numbers in the resistance. When some questions are asked—specifically about the number of adult humans we may face—the numbers are close to those you have named. However, when more general questions are asked, such as how strong a resistance we will face or do our enemies have allies we have not anticipated, then the deities do not reply nearly as clearly. We must take great care. I, for one, would rather report to my seniors that we had worried too much than apologize for the loss of life that will come from our planning too little."

"I agree," said Merial of Azure Towers and Kynan of Hearthome almost with one voice.

The two generals looked so surprised at finding themselves agreeing about anything that Bryessidan had to swallow a chuckle.

"I also agree," Bryessidan said with what he hoped wasn't too much eagerness. "In any case, no matter how greatly our forces will eventually outnumber those of the Nexans, initially we will be no more than fourteen—and no matter how closely we time our assault, the likelihood is that some pair will find themselves alone, even if only briefly."

"A good point," Fromalf said. "I believe that whoever is chosen as commander in chief should be willing to be among the first pair to cross through his or her gate, so that the commander will be present to coordinate the actions of all as they cross."

"The second pair, perhaps," countered Aurick. "My tactical simulations suggest that it would be best if the first pair to cross are both warriors armed with bows or some other distance weapon."

"The second pair, perhaps," Fromalf said affably. "Of course, there is no rule saying that the commander could not be an armed warrior."

"But who should hold this central command?" Kynan asked peevishly.

He must have already guessed it would not be him. Merial would refuse to take orders from him, as he would from her. Byressidan looked over at Aurick, and found himself being studied in turn.

Fromalf shifted deliberately in his seat, as if considering each of the seven generals in turn. Then he nodded seriously.

"I think that rather than asking ourselves who should hold this central command, we should be asking ourselves who can be spared from commanding his or her own forces, for that is what that general would need to do."

Aurick of Pelland frowned at this, but in thought rather than anger. He had spent a great deal of time detailing how well trained his forces were, how they frequently played war games against each other, and as a result had prearranged plans for almost any type of situation.

Is he wondering if he is willing to give over his carefully trained force to a subordinate? I suspect that he would find commanding a hodgepodge such as the invasion force very frustrating.

Aurick, however, said nothing, and Fromalf resumed.

"I, for one, would be reluctant to relinquish immediate control over those soldiers King Hurwin has entrusted to me. Frankly, as I noted before, our most skilled warriors are with the fleet. The men and women I have are technically good, but I think they will need a firm hand to keep them in line."

Aridisdu Valdala nodded. "Even without asking the deities for omens, I can see a candidate emerging for this difficult post. Let us be honest. Both myself and General Aurick have trained forces that will respond best to commands and tactics they know. For precisely the opposite reason, General Fromalf is reluctant to lose direct command of his forces.

"Honesty also forces us to recognize that neither General Aurick or General Merial will readily accept commands from one or the other. That leaves us with King Bryessidan or General Talianas of Tishiolo. King Bryessidan has never commanded an army, but he does come from a martial heritage. General Talianas also has not commanded an army."

"And I have no wish to command this one," Talianas said. "My soldiers, such as they are, are like those General Fromalf will command. My hill hunters and border guards will need a firm hand over them. Their ways are far different from the orderly carnage practiced by trained armies. They are fierce— none fiercer, I would dare boast—but they are likely to give way to looting and rapine if they are not aware they must answer to someone."

"Don't catch an arrow then," General Aurick said dryly, and Bryessidan thought the wry twist of his lip meant the opposite. "I should hate to have need to turn my troops against allies, and while it is important that we take the Nexus Islands, we cannot forget that their inhabitants—at least some of them—are valuable resources in turn."

Fromalf looked at Bryessidan, his gaze so level and so serious that had Bryessidan not half suspected that Fromalf was following orders left by King Hurwin, he would have thought the man genuinely regretted the request he was about to make.

"What of it, King Bryessidan? Are you willing to accept command of these seven allied forces? It will mean leaving direction of your forces to another."

Bryessidan schooled his features to seriousness, although in reality he wanted to grin in triumph at achieving what he had so intensely desired.

"I believe I can delegate," he said slowly, turning those arguments he had prepared when he thought he would need to debate his fitness before this body to another use. "Much of my force consists of medical personnel. As we have already discussed, they will also be of the most use holding the various gate points, rather than surging forth into battle. Therefore, they will remain under my eye."

"You have no real combat experience," General Merial said. Her mien was serious, but Bryessidan did not feel she doubted him. Rather she was asking him to consider this matter in case he had not. "I assure you. Real bloodshed is far different from war games."

"I know this," Bryessidan said. He decided that bringing up his father's war himself would be far better than letting another do so. "I was too young to serve as a soldier in the last war, but I tended the wounded when they were brought back to the Mires. I also toured battlefields, for my father thought this a necessary part of my education. Finally, I know all too well the price of failure. I will not let this venture fail!"

He thought his determination had impressed the others. Certainly, no one objected when Fromalf suggested the matter be put to a silent vote.

"We'll make it simple," Fromalf said, passing around sets of colored marbles. "Red if you favor King Bryessidan for the command; blue if you favor further debate."

Bryessidan appreciated Fromalf's tact, even as he wished the man had not had such foresight. He would have enjoyed an opportunity to have members of his staff analyze handwritten ballots, especially those that did not nominate him. In that way, he would have a fair idea who favored him and who did not.

But it turned out that such subtlety would have been wasted. When Fromalf spilled out the marbles, there was not a single blue among them.

"Very well, King Bryessidan," Fromalf said, rolling the marbles into the bag and tying it off with satisfaction. "You are elected commander in chief of the gate invasion force. Are there any matters of business you would like to discuss?"

Bryessidan recovered quickly from his momentary astonishment, surprised to find his goal so easily won.

"As a matter of fact," he said smoothly, turning to his secretary and accepting a sheaf of notes, "there is. We have discussed a great deal, but I think certain matters of tactics need to be refined, most particularly, how we will handle the presence of iron and its limiting factors on our Once Dead. Shall we begin there?"

"I have some thoughts," General Aurick said quickly.

Bryessidan listened to the man droning on, covering ground Bryessidan himself had already examined. He let his thoughts drift for one delightful moment.

I did it, Gidji! I did it, Father! With this invasion the prestige of the Mires will be redeemed, and then when we command the gates once more . . . and then . . .

He smiled and focused his attention on the discussion at hand, head held high, as if he already wore the crown of an emperor.

❧

FIREKEEPER AWOKE FROM what she knew was not a dream, wishing it had been a dream, and feeling just a bit cheated that apparently she was not to be permitted peace even when she was asleep.

Love! Who was the Meddler to speak of loving her? What did he know of her? This was hardly the first such declaration she had encountered. There had been her foster brother, Edlin, then the wolf Dark Death, each seeing in her not what she was, but what they idealized her to be. The one Firekeeper herself loved the most had spoken far less about his own feelings for her, but she knew he was with her, and wherever he was, her back was safe.

She looked over at the wolf, his blue eyes now closed in sleep. His nose was pointing toward her so that she could smell his breath and feel its soft caress. The scent was surprisingly sweet, for all that he dined on raw meat and fish. His were good teeth, young and strong, and his belly was sweet with resolution.

Blind Seer looked so completely at rest that for a moment Firekeeper felt a moment of resentment. *He* didn't have strange spirits declaring their love for him in his sleep! He wasn't denied the imaginary retreat of dreams!

Then she looked at Blind Seer more closely, noticed how his ears twitched and his paws moved just a little. She wondered if she really knew anything at all about what Blind Seer thought or dreamed. She remembered the vision the Meddler had shown her, and mused over what odd game Blind Seer might be pursuing.

She shifted herself upright. She could smell dawn, damp and not so far away. Here and there a songbird chirped a scattered note or two, not certain whether to welcome daylight or to tuck head under wing and sleep a bit more. For herself, Firekeeper knew. She was awake, and wouldn't be sleeping again.

Bruck's snoring came from the lean-to she had made for him from pine boughs and bent saplings. Elation drowsed on a tree branch above the lean-to. Firekeeper moved one foot and gently shoved a pile of tinder she had prepared earlier into the banked coals of her fire. She didn't need a fire, but she thought

Bruck might be sweeter if they offered him something hot to eat and drink when he woke.

They needed him sweet, for none of her other traps had been tripped. Bruck's capture apparently had served as warning enough to those who dwelled in this area—human and Royal Beast alike—not to go near the newcomers' handiwork. This meant that their camp had remained safe and secure, but Firekeeper knew well that she and her two allies could not remain in that relatively small space indefinitely, not if they hoped to achieve what they had come for.

Bruck had said quite frankly that he did not expect anyone to come to rescue him. He had not been firmly in any one faction, and time and too close quarters had, oddly to Firekeeper's way of thinking, distanced him from those who had once been his comrades. But humans were like that. They remembered the slights and offenses, the angers and indignations, and too easily forgot the kindnesses and sympathies.

She sighed and rubbed her face with her hands, wondering if she would ever fully understand these creatures who had given her body life, but who had not shaped her soul.

False dawn became true dawn, and Firekeeper's companions continued to sleep. The surrounding forest was quiet, but Firekeeper was not so unwise has to believe that meant it was untenanted. Rather, the reverse was true. Someone was out there, probably several someones, powerful enough to frighten the little songbirds, and to make the squirrels keep to the branches overhead.

Firekeeper slid a foot toward Blind Seer, and found the blue-eyed wolf already awake, his eyes narrowed almost shut, holding the position of sleep while ears and nose told him something of what had unsettled the surrounding woodland.

She took her lead from him, leaning to stir the fire, taking up her quiver and making as if she was inspecting the condition of the fletching on the arrows within. No casual observer, human or otherwise, would be certain as to how much she had noticed.

"Bear," Blind Seer breathed, "and wolves, many wolves. Boar and great cat. Puma and bobcat. Moose."

Firekeeper counted her arrows. A dozen. A bear alone could claim four or five. Bears were well known for being too stubborn to realize when they were dead. Boars, now that she considered the matter, were almost as bad. And pumas and bobcats . . . She knew less of moose, for they were northern creatures, but had heard that one angered made a bear seem mild. She had to struggle against an impulse to scan the trees.

Blind Seer no longer was pretending to be asleep, but leapt to his feet and shook off sleep with one enthusiastic motion that included bumping his head against Firekeeper and sloshing her with his tongue.

Had he been a human, his motions might have translated as "Darling, I believe there's someone at the door!" But of course there was no door, so that translation was fatally flawed.

Elation had also awakened, but as she did not take wing as would be her more usual course of action on such an occasion Firekeeper guessed that the peregrine had glimpsed motion in the skies above. Perhaps the golden eagle had returned.

The only member of their little encampment who had not awoken was the sorcerer Bruck. Firekeeper moved to inspect him, to make certain that he was not feigning sleep, but the man was soundly out. It was hard to tell in the pale dawn light that filtered through the pine boughs, but he didn't look well. Firekeeper suspected the contact with iron was taking a toll. She would need to make a decision about whether to keep it on him if he remained in her custody for many days longer.

She dropped her hand onto Blind Seer's head. They were in a difficult situation. The Beasts surrounding them could not approach without running afoul of the various traps and alarms—not to mention the assortment of arrows, fangs, and talons that would meet them if they brought their attack into the glade. However, Firekeeper and her allies could not remain indefinitely without food. Water they had, having made their camp near a small spring, but the falcon, at least, would need to eat fairly frequently.

Firekeeper could think of various ways that the three of them could be overwhelmed, and she figured a fight of some sort was in order. The only thing that puzzled her was why the

Beasts had waited for daylight. True, she saw better than most humans after dark, but darkness would have handicapped both her and Elation. Maybe the Beasts had felt they could better avoid her traps in daylight.

"We are the Bound," came a voice Firekeeper knew was a wolf's. "And we have come to honor our trust."

XXVIII

"COME THEN," GROWLED Blind Seer, "and tell us of this trust."

There was rustling among the surrounding greenery, and although the various alarms Firekeeper had strung crunched or snapped in warning not a single trap was triggered. Indeed, although the sounds were loud to Firekeeper's ears, they must have been soft enough, for Bruck did not even turn in his slumber.

Forth into the small glade came three wolves, a bear, a boar, a moose, and a puma. Firekeeper knew other Beasts waited out of sight, but these few were enough to set her blood pounding hotly in her ears. She rested her hand lightly on Blind Seer's shoulder, feeling as well as hearing the wolf's growl. Her hand was tickled by the brush of his fur as his hackles rose.

Firekeeper was oddly reminded of her first encounter with the wolves of Misheemnekuru. Then, too, had she and Blind Seer been challenged by guardians hidden deep within the greenery. Then, too, she and Blind Seer had wondered whether a battle must follow the challenge. Then words had been enough, and some of those wolves had become as dear as kin to Firekeeper and Blind Seer. So, she hoped, would it be now. However, the first words spoken by the Bound did not give much reason for hope.

"We have come to give you warning," said one wolf, who stood slightly to the fore of the others. His fur was black shading into grey, touched with a bit of white about his chest and shoulder. "The tale of our trust is an old one, and you three are young and may not know on what land you trespass—nor how closely you are courting death."

Firekeeper tossed her head to indicate the sleeping Bruck.

"I think we know," she said, "but we would hear your telling of how you came to call yourselves Bound."

The Bound did not react to her speaking as Beast to Beast, and by this the wolf-woman knew some form of her own tale had reached them. Their lack of curiosity was disheartening, but still she hoped that whatever version of their own history these Beasts might tell would provide her with some way to avoid fighting them.

The Royal Beasts were her people, those who had reared her and taught her what to value. Something in her revolted against fighting them as she had never felt restrained from fighting humans. She didn't know whether Blind Seer or Elation felt as she did, but both indicated their interest in listening.

The mostly black wolf was curt.

"This land is forbidden to any but the Bound and those we guard, unless we choose to admit them. Leave here or else your lives are ours by ancient rule."

Blind Seer flattened his ears, a posture that could indicate he was considering giving way—or that he was ready to fight.

"And what must one do to be admitted to your august company?"

The almost black wolf did not answer directly.

"From time to time one has come here, driven by rivals from territory he or she has held, dispersed from pack or herd too large. Those that have been willing to swear to share our ancient trust we have taken into our packs, given room within our hunting grounds. Thus, we have kept our numbers fresh and strong. We do not think you are such as these."

Elation cried high and shrill, "We most certainly are not! Even so, cannot you welcome us? We might bring you relief from this task to which you consider yourselves bound."

Firekeeper let hope touch her that the peregrine had found a solution. Surely, these Bound knew themselves more truly Tricked. They had taken on a task their ancestors must have thought would last no more than a generation or so, but that task had stretched to fill more than a hundred long years.

"We will not cheapen the fidelity of more than a century," the puma snarled. "There is no relief to our task but in the deaths of those we guard, and they will not come to death through any negligence of our own nor of our kits."

Firekeeper looked from puma to bear to boar to wolves, but in not the slightest twitch of ear or ruffling of fur did she see anything that indicated the least break in this shared resolution.

"So you have come to give us warning," Blind Seer said.

Now that it did not seem as if they faced immediate attack, his hackles had lowered. His ears and tail expressed interest, and not the least bit of fear. Seeing him, Firekeeper realized that she, too, was no longer afraid, merely ready for whatever would come.

The boar raised his head to catch their scent, wide, wet nose snuffling as he took in their resolution.

"Our warning is this," he grunted. "If you return as you came, leaving forever this territory we guard, we will not harm you. However, if you take step or flight into our lands, then we will offer no further warning and no mercy. You will be slain, not captured."

Blind Seer replied as calmly as if the boar had done nothing other than comment on the likelihood of rain ruining a planned hunt.

"Certainly, you do not think you can achieve this without dying yourselves? We are no roots to be grubbed out with your tusks, no fawns to fall beneath your claws, none of the half-blind, half-deaf creatures that must surely be your usual prey for you to be so confident."

The boar snorted in mingled indignation and amusement.

"You taunt well, pup. We have heard of you and your strange pack mate, even of the falcon. We do not doubt that in holding our trust one or more of us may be wounded or killed. That does not change our position."

A nearly white wolf who reminded Firekeeper somewhat of her mother Shining Coat snarled, showing excellent fangs.

"Were it not for us and for the trust we have borne so faithfully through the ages, you likely would have never been born. Indeed, Beasts might exist only within the custody of humans—if at all. Our ancestors made a pact that saved the lands that gave you birth. Neither they or we are the hunters of blind, spavined prey such as you imagine. The moon songs tell of you all as great hunters, battle-blooded warriors, but I tell you this—such is our heritage as well, and we will serve it with pride with our last breath and to our final drop of blood!"

Blind Seer's reply showed pity: "So you gave your own freedom that all other Beasts might be free. Surely, you can see the time for that is past. The great sorcerers are gone except for those you guard here."

The white wolf's snarl sneered afresh.

"Truly? This is not what we have dreamed. Magic contaminates the world afresh. We will not permit you—you who reek of the stuff—to spread it further. Indeed, were it not our law, laid down by those who came before us, to give warning before we attack, I would have fed your stringy flesh to the pups of my pack before now. Traitor!"

Firekeeper did not glance at Elation, but she thought the falcon could not have missed the import of the white wolf's accusation. Would this revelation that Blind Seer had magic of some sort rob them of their one ally here? They could scarce afford it.

The nearly black wolf bumped the white with his shoulder.

"Peace, daughter. We keep the law, as we have always kept the law. The warning is given. Now bloodshed may fairly begin."

"If we violate the terms," Blind Seer said.

"If you violate the terms," the nearly black wolf conceded.

Firekeeper spoke before the Bound could turn away.

"What of him?" she said, motioning to where the snarls and growls had finally awoken Bruck. "He is our prey, fairly caught. If we leave, must we relinquish the meat of our hunt?"

The bear, silent until now, gave a contemptuous grunt.

"That one? He strayed when his den mates told him stay. My people say if a solitary hunter cannot kill the wolves then he dies. I say the same as well."

The other Bound were similarly dismissive.

"Our trust is to guard those within the fortification," the white wolf said, "the ones who made the spell that burned away the magic. This one has separated himself from them. If they asked us to get him back, perhaps we would, but in breaking with them, he has broken with us as well. Such was the pact we made, otherwise we might have been split from our purpose as the humans split from their own."

Blind Seer's ears perked in astonishment.

"So you know that the humans have not kept faith with their task?"

"We do," the puma said, muscles rippling silken beneath her fur as she turned to depart.

"And this does not change your feelings about the suitability of being Bound to them?" Blind Seer protested.

The puma vanished without either sound or further comment, but the third wolf, one with a coat of shadow grey and eyes as pale as ice, said contemptuously, "They are faithless. Is that reason for us to be?"

"Our warning was meant," the bear grunted, lumbering away last. "Beware if you cross us or our kin again. There will be no more warnings."

Firekeeper watched, and felt that not only those who had crossed into the glade but those who had watched from out of sight were well and truly gone. She turned to Elation and Blind Seer.

The falcon was studying the blue-eyed wolf with interest.

"Did they accuse you of possessing a talent?" she asked without a trace of her usual mockery.

"Worse," Blind Seer said, holding his head high. "They knew me for being what I am, a wolf who might, if he dared try, learn to practice the art of spellcasting."

Elation shrieked, but it was with laughter, not indignation or anger.

"The pair of you! The pair of you! How dull life has been

without you turning what everyone believes inside out and upside down!"

"Then you will remain with us?" Firekeeper asked.

"Of course," Elation said. "I have not yet paid back that
golden eagle for chivying me like some fat duck. Moreover,
Blind Seer no more sought that ability than he chose the color
of his eyes."

Blind Seer looked up at Elation challengingly. "I may have.
I could have let it die within me when the fevers came."

"I have never known you to willingly lose a fight, wolf,"
Elation said. "Now, enough of that. What do we do about this
warning?"

"Take it, for now," Blind Seer said. "We will retreat a day or
so distant, back the way we came. Firekeeper, I saw you
counting your arrows earlier. Can you make more?"

"I have iron heads for another dozen or so," she said, patting the pouch on her belt, "and then there is always stone and
even sharpened and hardened wood. With Elation close, I do
not think I will want for fletching."

"Not my feathers surely!" the falcon shrieked.

"Definitely not," Firekeeper agreed. "But once we leave the
territory of these Bound Beasts, I think you will not begrudge
me the feathers from your prey."

"Then we do not give up the fight?" Elation said.

"Not in the least," Blind Seer agreed.

He had crossed to where Bruck huddled in his lean-to, and
now he nudged the spellcaster to his feet.

"This one can give us some information. He may be glad to
do so, since we have been assured no rescue is coming for
him. The Bound cannot be everywhere at once, nor do I think
they are as prepared as they imagine for what Firekeeper and
I can do."

"And me," Elation reminded. "And me."

Blind Seer grinned a wolf's grin, white-fanged with hunting joy.

"And you."

They broke camp—a simple enough task—and herded their
dazed prisoner back toward the Iron Mountains. He came will-

ingly enough, muttering that he had looked for help even in sleep, but none was coming. He didn't look at all well, and Firekeeper resolved that no matter what risk they took, she would remove the iron from contact with his flesh, for a while at least.

Safety was one thing, but torture she could not stomach—not without a greater reason than this.

With Bruck's stumbling to slow their progress, they did not make camp until many hours later than if they had traveled alone. Again Firekeeper built the spellcaster a lean-to, and after she was done, she removed the iron from around his wrists and ankles.

"But I thread it in the fasteners of your clothing," she said, doing so. "This maybe keep you less than magic."

Bruck stared at her. "So you don't trust me."

Firekeeper blinked at him. "Why should I?"

Later, after they had eaten, she sat with Blind Seer, staring away from the fire into the darkness.

"It's wrong," she said. "We must fight the Bound or betray Derian's trust, but still it's wrong."

"Wrong?" Blind Seer said. "Because they believe in what they are doing?"

Firekeeper nodded, resting her head against his.

"It would be easier if they were compelled, but they believe in the rightness of what they're doing. It seems wrong that we will kill them for keeping faith."

Blind Seer heaved a sigh.

"Sometimes, Firekeeper, right must be wrong. The deer wants to live, but the wolf still must eat. So it is here. The Bound must keep their trust, but we must keep ours. We are right. They are right. All of us are wrong."

Firekeeper sighed in turn. "It was easier when we were all just wolves," she said softly.

"I agree," the wolf answered without the least irony. "I agree."

Tiniel wondered, could only four days have passed since the town meeting? Tiniel could hardly believe the difference four days could make. Four days had been enough for Skea's drill sessions to begin to feel like routine, rather than the torture they had been initially. Four days had been enough for Tiniel to find himself assigned—in addition to his usual patrols on the gateway hills—to lessons in first aid. As if that wasn't enough, he was also expected to join Wort as the community quartermaster coordinated salvage operations in the heaps of debris concealed beneath those ruined buildings that had not yet been excavated.

Four days had been enough for Tiniel to decide that he would betray those he now trained with and labored beside. Four days could be an eternity.

Tiniel knew precisely what had pushed him over the edge. It had not been the degrading drill with sword and spear. True, Skea was not gentle with those he must train, but then the night-skinned warrior had excellent reason to push his trainees as hard as he could without wearing them out to such an extent that they would be useless when real battle came.

Too old to be of any help with military preparations, Urgana had pushed herself to long shifts among the papers in the archives. There she had found old records that indicated that the Nexans might have as little as half a moonspan before the fleet arrived. Apparently, even after the gateway installation was in place and fully operational, there had been things that were more efficiently transported by non-magical means: timber, large pieces of furniture, bulk foodstuffs.

Urgana had found records that showed when the ships bearing these supplies had arrived, and after coordinating the pre-querinalo calendars with the current ones, she had demonstrated fairly conclusively that Bear Moon began the shipping season.

Her announcement had brought momentary despair to the Nexans, despair relieved when two events gave them all reason to believe they had greater resources than they had dared imagine.

One of these events had been indirectly connected to Urgana's researches into the shipping schedules. Needless to say, iron was not welcome on the Nexus Islands, but that did not mean alternative metals—especially bronze, but also silver and copper—were not used in their place. Wort had reviewed the shipping manifests and come to the conclusion that one building, dismissed to this point as yet another residence, might have warehoused metal goods.

This supposition had proven correct. Tiniel's back and arms still ached from helping move aside the ruined timbers and shift heaps of masonry. Those aches were not eased by Tiniel's awareness that without Derian Carter's enhanced strength and the willingness of the Wise Horse Eshinarvash to cooperate with the horse-man hybrid, the clearance could not have been managed so quickly.

The storehouse had not merely collapsed from a century of neglect, but had been destroyed, probably by one of the last sorcerers during the days of chaos that followed the coming of querinalo in order to keep the resources stored within from being used against the rulers during their time of weakness.

After all, Tiniel thought, *they didn't know that those fevers were the end of everything for them. They probably thought it was a plague of some sort, that there would be deaths, but that their caste would recover. Until then, better keep the peasants from getting their hands on the means for making weapons and such.*

The materials within the destroyed warehouse had suffered from a century during which the ocean-borne weather had beaten its way through here and there, but the metal goods and bar stock stored within had been packed to resist those very forces. Although their arms and armor would be unconventional, the Nexans no longer needed to worry that they would need to go into battle armed only with spears of fire-hardened wood and shields made from chair seats.

Several of the Nexans were skilled in metalworking, and from the day the imminent invasion had been announced, the forges had not been permitted to grow cold.

But as heartening as Wort's discovery had been, Tiniel

thought that it had paled in comparison with what Ynamynet had coolly announced just the evening before at the conclusion of the community dinner. Tiniel had been there to hear it himself, for with the new crisis, luxuries such as private meals had been suspended. This was not because someone carrying off a tray made more work, but because the dinner hour had become a time when announcements and reports were made.

As Tiniel recalled the announcement of the night before, his vision darkened and anger surged to fuel his motions.

"Hey!" came an indignant yelp from his sparring partner. "Remember, we're just practicing. You're not really supposed to kill me!"

Tiniel blinked and saw the man staring at him with mingled admiration and annoyance.

"Oh . . . Sorry," Tiniel said. "I just got to thinking about everything."

The man dropped his spear shaft back into blocking position.

"Right. There's sure been enough to think about. Shall we take it from the start of the drill?"

Tiniel nodded, but as his hands rose and fell with the pattern of blocking and attacking moves that Skea had insisted they all learn, even though the newly appointed general was the first to admit that no real battle was ever so neatly choreographed, he ceased to see the man who stood opposite him. In his vision, Ynamynet was again rising from her place at the table at one end of the room, rapping her mug against the tabletop as a makeshift gavel.

"I HAVE AN announcement to make," Ynamynet said, her voice carrying with the ease of long practice. "Today, I confirmed something I have suspected for several days, something that may—just may—raise our chances for survival."

The small murmurs of lingering conversation dropped to an interested, listening silence.

"A few days ago," Ynamynet continued, "we gathered to discuss the danger we now face. In that meeting, we reviewed what resources we had, and how we could turn them to our best advantage. Even at that time, I thought of one resource that might be available to us, but until I could better investigate it, I decided it was best for me to remain mute.

"All of us know all too well that we will face opponents who have far greater resources than we do in all areas: military, supplies, and magical. Skea, with the enthusiastic cooperation of all the able-bodied of our community, has been making tremendous strides in equalizing the first. Wort, again with much willing and tremendous assistance, has worked miracles to rebalance the second. Unhappily, because of querinalo, not much could be done to help adjust the balance in our favor in the area of magical strength—or so we all thought.

"I, however, had my small hope. That hope had come to me when I reviewed how we had learned about this impending invasion. The news was brought to us in dreams and visions. Now, the visions came from a seer known to have great power—the jaguar Truth. What I allowed myself to consider was whether or not the other visionary might also have magical ability."

Like everyone else in the room, Tiniel had shifted to look at Isende. His sister was not sitting, as was usually the case these days, in the midst of a group of small children. Instead, she was sitting at the same table as Ynamynet. Derian, his expression grave, was sitting next to her. Tiniel had bitten into his lip with unguarded fury when he realized that they just might be holding hands.

Plik, seated across the table from Tiniel, had looked over at him in concern and said softly, "Don't worry. No one has hurt your sister."

Tiniel nodded and schooled his features to what he hoped was a more neutral expression.

Ynamynet had paused to allow the murmurs of surprise and interest to fade, but now continued.

"I asked Isende to spend some time with me so that I might do some tests. Kalyndra and True Star also joined us, sitting behind a screen and observing, so that I would not be tempted to see in my tests what I wished to see.

"I will not bore you with the details of those tests, but I do think a brief reminder of Isende's history would be in order, since many of you did not meet her until long after her arrival here and her bout with querinalo."

Not surprising, Tiniel thought sardonically. *After all, we were prisoners, kept under guard, and except for the Once Dead who studied us, and those like Zebel, Wort, and Skea who were assigned to guard or tend us, we really had very little contact with the community at large.*

"Isende has been termed Twice Dead, but the nature of her gift is not usually discussed. It manifested in the form of a close emotional link to her twin brother, Tiniel."

Tiniel found himself the momentary center of scrutiny, but as Ynamynet continued speaking without pause, attention shifted away with almost unbecoming haste. After all, the Once Dead was not speaking about him. He couldn't be very important.

"This link was so close that, while they could not read each other's minds, they were very aware each of how the other felt. They could channel those emotions into a form of communication, so that, for example, if the one was injured the other would know.

"However, querinalo ended this decisively. What the Spell Wielders did not suspect at the time—that no one but a very few intimates suspected until Isende experienced these highly detailed visions—was that Isende had protected a small reservoir of magical ability within herself."

A gem, Tiniel recalled in mingled anger and anguish. *She called it a "small gem of power." She barred me from her, but kept that for herself.*

Ynamynet smiled at the sensation her words had created.

"Please note, I said 'small.' Isende is not likely to be throwing around thunderbolts or calling up storms, at least not any time in the near future. We have too little time to research what she does have with anything like the leisure I would like. What she has may turn out to be more in the nature of a talent than the more adaptable ability of a spellcaster.

"However, I can state categorically that Isende is capable of true visions, and not just when she is asleep, but when she is waking. We have tested, and she can send these visions as well as receive them. This may greatly assist our ability to communicate at some crucial moment. We also hope to train her to use this ability to scout the seas in our immediate vicinity. Even a day's warning of the fleet's arrival could be crucial."

Excited babble arose, but Tiniel hardly heard it for the pounding of his heart in his ears. Ynamynet and Isende answered a few questions, but they seemed trivial to Tiniel in light of the revelation that while he was Twice Dead—a coward to be scorned for not being willing to protect his magical power—Isende had proven to be Once Dead.

Tiniel recalled how Derian Carter had become elevated in the eyes of the Nexans once they had learned of his triumph over querinalo—how they had honored him, even though Derian had become a monster. Superficially, Isende had remained her pretty self, and Tiniel doubted that any of these fools would realize that her willingness to sacrifice her bond to her twin revealed the monstrous nature that lurked within her pretty form.

"What about Isende's twin?"

The question captured Tiniel's attention, holding it quivering like an insect on a pin. What of him? Might he still have something to separate him from the horde?

Ynamynet's reply was cool.

"When I confirmed my suspicions about Isende, Kalyndra and I tested Tiniel without him being aware that we were doing so. He is Twice Dead. In fact, it is possible the talent was his sister's all along, and that he only shared it because of the peculiar nature of their birth."

There was no intentional cruelty in her reply. Ynamynet was merely being—as she always was—coolly factual. Nonetheless, Tiniel felt her reply as a personal affront, a painful rebuke.

It was at that moment, Tiniel knew, bringing his attention fully back to the spear drill when his partner's shaft dealt his gloved fingers a painful blow, that he had decided that the Nexus Islands and its preservation held nothing for him.

He would betray these pathetic souls, these fools who really believed they could resist the gathered might of nations. After all, they were doomed anyhow, so he wasn't doing anything but preserving himself against the inevitable.

Wasn't that what Isende had done? Preserved herself against the inevitable by sacrificing him?

High time for her to learn what it felt like. High time indeed.

XXIX

THE FOLLOWING DAY, Firekeeper and Blind Seer herded Bruck farther east. Elation scouted ahead, spoke with some of the local Royal Beasts, and found them willing to help the travelers.

"They know of the Bound," Elation reported, "and find them creepy, unnatural. That is why you have heard no wolf packs in the area. Those who were not of the Bound moved away from this area long ago, as have the Royal Elk and Deer. Those Beasts who are more solitary have maintained a presence on the fringes."

"They saw Blind Seer and me, then," Firekeeper said, "when we came this way before."

"They did, but chose not to intercept you, not knowing what sort of business you might have with the Bound and those they guard."

"But now it is different?" Firekeeper said. "They wish to help us now?"

"Let us say that they wish to keep an eye on you."

Seeing Blind Seer's hackles rise, Elation amended her statement.

"Not you particularly. Rather they wish to help you keep guard over what you have brought out from the Bound's keeping. They do not think we should bear such a burden ourselves, unaided."

Blind Seer let his fur lie flat, but a growl still rumbled in his speech.

"Kind of them. You are certain that none of these were Bound who concealed their alliance?"

Elation, who had been riding on Firekeeper's shoulder, ruffled her feathers and rutched her neck.

"I cannot be certain. How can I? It is not as if Beasts wear colors as do human armies. Still, I think I do trust them. They spoke to me freely of the Bound, and offered their help. They even apologized for not stepping forward sooner—and one of those who apologized was a puma, a *male* puma."

Firekeeper and Blind Seer both understood the import of Elation's statement. Unlike wolves, most of the great cats were solitary creatures, the males more so than the females, who, after all, must live in company when they raised their cubs. Solitary creatures did not cultivate the smoothing rituals that pack or flock or herd beasts did, so an apology from a puma was something to take seriously indeed.

A brown bear had offered them the use of the cave she and her cubs used for hibernation. The space was not large, but it had a single opening that would be easily guarded, and could be sealed with a rock or log barrier should Firekeeper and her allies all need to leave.

Bruck, wearied to stumbling silence by this second day of walking, entered this combination haven and prison without protest. He stripped off his boots and socks, even before accepting some berries Firekeeper had gathered along the way and the cup of water she dipped from a nearby spring.

"We give you more food later," the wolf-woman promised. "Better. Elation is already hunting."

Bruck looked around the cave. The bears had not been in residence for several moonspans now, and scavengers had rendered the space relatively clean. The cave mouth faced northeast, and although large enough to permit the brown bears entrance was not so wide that the day's heat had gotten in. Thus the interior was comfortably cool, especially in contrast to the summer day without.

"Are we camping here for long?" he asked, and Firekeeper heard the note of hope in his voice.

She wasn't surprised. Bruck's feet looked raw, and she didn't think the man had done much walking lately. Even if he had gone out into the forests near Virim's hold on a regular basis, the day-long march he had endured today would have been difficult.

"Perhaps we stay," Firekeeper said. "Much depend on what you tell us about those still back there."

Blind Seer added, *"Unless he can tell us how to eliminate querinalo without our having to bother those others. Then he and they can go about their lives untroubled."*

Firekeeper translated the gist of this, but even before she had finished Bruck was shaking his head.

"I can't do that," he said. "Can't, not won't. I simply do not have the skills. Tell me. What do you know of magic?"

Firekeeper considered how to reply. She didn't want to sound too ignorant, but there was a great deal she didn't know, not even in theory.

"Uses blood," she said, "and sometimes things—like gates and rings—to make easier to do. Usually is not simple as biting. Is more elaborate, like firing a bow or dancing."

Bruck tapped a blister on one foot and winced, then he nodded.

"Blood magic, then. I'm not surprised that's what you've encountered. In many ways it is the easiest form of magic, and the type best adapted to use by a group. I am not surprised that it would be the first to resurface."

Firekeeper thought about this. She had several questions, but decided to focus on one.

"So is more than one type of magic?"

"Oh, yes. However, I will be the first to admit that blood magic is probably both the most adaptable and the most powerful. You see, blood magic uses the life energy contained in blood to channel the user's magical power. The blood is not the power itself, any more than the bowstring is what makes an arrow pierce its target, but it is as indispensable as the string is to the bow. Without blood, the spells will not take form, just as without a bowstring, a bow and arrow are simply two pieces of wood."

Firekeeper heard the echoes of old lectures in Bruck's analogy. She wondered what his life had been like before he joined Virim. New World stories told how those colonists who were found to have magical ability were taken to the Old World and trained. Had Bruck been one of those so trained? Had he perhaps become a teacher in turn?

She forced herself to concentrate on the more immediate issue, although something deep within her hinted that knowing about Bruck himself and the things that motivated him was not such an idle indulgence as it might seem.

"Is querinalo a blood magic thing?" she asked, returning to her immediate focus.

"It is and it is not," Bruck said. He paused, staring at his feet as if they might explain for him. Firekeeper recognized the symptoms of overtiredness, and knew that overtired humans often said more than they intended.

She decided to push him. At the worst, he would fall asleep. Leaning back, Firekeeper scooped Bruck another cup of water from the spring. Then she tore a corner from his shirttail and began dabbing it on the broken blisters on his feet.

The pain brought Bruck back to the immediate moment, and he smiled at her wanly.

"That both hurts and feels good," he said. "Thanks."

"Tell me about how querinalo is and is not blood magic," she prompted. "While you talk, I make sure these feet not get sick and infected."

Bruck nodded and rested his back and shoulders against a jutting bit of rock.

"I can do that," he said. "Slow me down if I touch on matters you don't understand."

Firekeeper nodded agreement, and grunted for him to begin.

"Querinalo is more in the nature of a curse, rather than a sickness or fever or even an infection. Curses can be blood magic, but blood-magic curses work best if the ones who would create the curse have some of the subject's own blood to work into the spell."

"Make sense," Firekeeper said, partially translating a huff from Blind Seer.

The blue-eyed wolf lay in the shade of a nearby tree, cooling himself on a scrape of bare earth. Although the mountain air was cool compared with the temperatures they would have been encountering had they been on Misheemnekuru, or even in the lands where they had been born, still the wolf's coat was heavy. The Nexus Islands were a chill climate, and Blind Seer had not shed as much as he would have otherwise. Over the last few days, the situation had forced him to be out and about in the day's heat, and that, far more than the distance they had traveled, had worn at him.

Even so, Firekeeper was certain that Blind Seer was more interested than she in what Bruck had to tell them about the nature of magic and spells. Vivid in her memory was the vision the Meddler had shown her of Blind Seer pawing through scrolls and books, apparently trying to learn how to use the power that lay dormant within him.

"Now, when we designed querinalo," Bruck continued, his tone becoming animated, "obviously we could not get blood from every one of the sorcerers we hoped would fall victim to the curse. Therefore, Virim suggested another way of shaping the curse. Are you at all familiar with the other states of being one may enter? They might feel like dreams or seem like hallucinations, but you know they are real?"

Firekeeper nodded, but she took care not to give too much away. "When had querinalo. Saw things. Blind Seer, too. Others tell of such."

Bruck was obviously pleased. "That makes this easier to explain. There is a form of magic that is focused on those states of being. Most often it is used for divination, but sometimes it is useful for communication. In its most refined form, it can be used to influence the actions of another person."

As the Meddler did, Firekeeper thought, but neither she nor Blind Seer articulated this information.

"Virim suggested that we use this form of magic—the influential form—to create our curse. Our first anchor would be the gift or talent for any form of magic. Our second would be the use of blood magic by those we were cursing. In this way, two goals would be achieved. One, the curse would be more severe for those who persisted in using blood magic. Two, those who did not use blood magic would not be connected to the curse as forcefully. In this way, Virim sought to protect those with useful talents. Many would survive, but would be warned of the penalties existing for those who abused magic."

"How would they be warned?" Blind Seer asked. *"How would they know the difference between this sickness and any other?"*

"Simple," Bruck said when Firekeeper had translated the question.

He raised a finger and began counting off points, a habit to which Firekeeper had noted he was highly inclined.

"One, since you have experienced querinalo yourself, surely you noticed how the victim can feel what the curse wishes to destroy. This was deliberate on our part, a warning to those who did not fall in the first wave.

"Two, we created a dream vision of Virim himself—or rather Virim in his emblematic form—that would appear at some point to those in the throes of the curse. It was a sign and seal that those who had refused to cooperate with Virim's idealistic goals must suffer.

"Finally, since the curse did not strike each and all at once—beginning instead with the strongest, and moving to the less powerful—there was ample opportunity for the true nature of querinalo to be understood. That the sorcerers chose to persist in their adherence to magic—and to the pattern of domination and abuse that had come with it—sealed their fate. Those with less power might have survived, without magic, true, but alive."

Firekeeper, considering the general collapse of human society in both the Old World and the New, thought that Virim and his followers had been rather idealistic if they had believed that the sorcerers would relinquish what little hope they had of turning back chaos.

She said nothing, though. Bruck's feet had been treated, and Elation had brought a brace of wood fowl for the pot. As the wolf-woman began kindling a fire, she asked Bruck, "So is this blood magic and is this dream magic. What other magic is there?"

Bruck had reached that point of overtiredness where words came more easily than sleep. He spoke in great detail about various magical rites and traditions, of magic that could be used to commune with spirits that lived within the elements, of magic that was focused on potions or charms, of magic intimately tied to elaborate rituals or paintings.

However, no matter the type, each still required a spark of magical talent within the one who would learn it, else the rituals would not work.

"Effort is not enough," Bruck said. "Just as a deaf man cannot hear for wishing to do so or a blind man see even if he props his eyelids open with fingertips, so no matter how great the desire, one who is born without the gift for magic cannot simply follow the forms and expect them to work."

Another thing Firekeeper gathered was that all of these forms could be duplicated, often with greater ease and speed, by being hybridized with blood magic.

"That is why in the end blood magic came to dominate," Bruck explained.

He was yawning now, food and rest and a flood of talk having brought him around to true exhaustion.

Firekeeper felt that pressing him further would yield no good results. Instead, she asked her questions less frequently, watching the man fade into drowsiness and then into deep sleep.

She piled some timbers over the entry to the cave, and Elation perched nearby, eager as the human for some rest.

When Bruck was locked firmly away, Blind Seer came and nudged Firekeeper.

"Run with me, dear heart?"

"Gladly," she replied.

Together they let the night take them and give them for a few hours more the illusion that they were just wolves, and all the world a simple hunt.

❧

"LET ME TRY it on, Daddy! Let me!"

Four-year-old Neysa bounced from foot to foot, her hands raised toward the helmet Bryessidan had just lifted from his own head.

Indulgently, the king lowered the helmet over the little girl's head. Even with the new padding inside, it was so capacious that it covered her eyes. Nonetheless, the girl was ecstatic. Maybe she had imbibed something of the warrior spirit of her mother's people along with Gidji's milk.

"Do I look mean?" Neysa asked, tilting her head back so she could peer out through the eye slits. "Do I look fierce?"

Her voice came out muffled, but her enthusiasm was undimmed.

"I think she looks stupid," five-year-old Stave said sulkily.

"Don't let Neysa hear you say that," Gidji said. "She's quite likely to kick you. In any case, why quarrel when your father must leave us so soon?"

Stave looked unhappy, but nodded. The young prince had lost all his enthusiasm for the upcoming campaign when he had learned that his wartime duties included attending a series of formal events his father and mother were both too busy to attend.

His sister, Junal, the firstborn and presumed by most to be the heir apparent to the throne, had taken her similar duties much more seriously, but then she'd been serious ever since Gidji and Bryessidan had explained to her a moonspan before something of the risks Bryessidan would be taking, and what it might mean to her own future.

Neysa was struggling to remove the heavy helmet and Bryessidan assisted her.

"Did I look like a terrifying warrior?" Neysa asked.

"You looked terrifying," Bryessidan said tactfully. "But

then making the wearer look terrifying is one of the functions this armor was created to serve."

"Me next! Me next!" chirruped two-year-old Vahon.

Bryessidan shook his head. "It's a bit heavy for you, Vah."

Vahon began to scream in the manner of toddlers no matter how royal when thwarted and Gidji looked at him sternly.

"That's no way for a prince to behave when a king expresses his will. Behave yourself, Vahon!"

Vahon was so surprised at hearing himself spoken of as a prince by his mother—for usually Gidji felt that such reminders only gave children airs—that he stopped in midscreech.

"May I hold it?" asked Junal. "I want to look at it."

"Hold it where the others can see," Bryessidan said, extending it to her.

He imagined the armsman who had spent a good deal of time polishing the helmet after Bryessidan had worn it to practice wincing at the fingerprints on the gleaming brass and silver. Never mind, in a very short time they would be fortunate if fingerprints were all that marred the surface.

Junal reached one hand to take the helmet and Bryessidan frowned.

"Use two hands. I wasn't joking when I said it was heavy. When I wear it, my shoulders take part of the weight, but still it's not a light hat."

Junal accepted the helmet and studied it gravely.

"It looks different from the other soldiers' helmets," she said. "Is that because it's a king's helmet?"

"In part," Bryessidan said. "In part it's because it was a gift from the Alkya immigrants to the governor of the Mires in the days before the Plague."

Stave sought to redeem himself for his earlier sulk by displaying that he knew his lessons.

"The Alkya were the people who came here from halfway across the world to study our herbs and plants. A lot of them came because they were going to try a whole new type of farming there. Then when the Plague came, they were stranded. That's why people of the Mires—and maybe a few in Azure Towers—look different from the other Pellanders."

"Very good," Bryessidan said. "More than one of our ancestors came from that blending. Many of the Alkya had been in the Mires long enough to marry and start families, even before the Plague. That's why they blended so easily into our culture."

"The Mires," Gidji said, "has always been very accepting of different peoples and different gifts. I hadn't really considered that before. No wonder your father was prepared to welcome the Once Dead and Twice Dead into his service."

"The Mires," Bryessidan said, "have much to offer other nations. My father's enthusiasm for what we had to share led him astray, but while I see his means were flawed, I do not necessarily disagree with his goals."

Junal was still absorbed in the helmet, and now she glanced between it and the armor. The latter waited on its stand, every bit of trim polished. More importantly, the screws, hinges, straps, and suchlike had all been replaced, so the armor was as good as new.

"Why didn't they make the armor look like a person? Why did they make it look like a monster? Did they want to frighten people?"

"That was part of the reason," Bryessidan said. "But that isn't just any monster now, is it?"

Stave interrupted before his more methodical sister could reply. "It's not! It's a dragon, isn't it?"

"That's right. Today, dragons only exist in stories, but in the old days they were real. Kings rode on their backs when they went to war."

Bryessidan stared at the armor, wondering if that long-ago governor had ever ridden a dragon while wearing the armor.

"So they didn't just want to look frightening," Junal said thoughtfully. "I think they wanted to make sure that people were scared of them, not just of their animals. Could that be right?"

"Very right," Bryessidan said. "You've been thinking a lot, haven't you?"

She nodded, her lips tight, her eyes suddenly overflowing with tears.

"Don't go to war, Daddy! People don't need to be afraid of

you. You can just stay here and be king like before. You didn't need people to be afraid of you then."

Bryessidan gathered Junal onto his lap, wondering just when she had started losing baby fat and instead become this coltish creature, all arms and legs and knees. Neysa had stopped bouncing, and even Vahon was suddenly solemn, arrested by the sight of their big sister in tears.

Bryessidan started to look to Gidji for help, but realized that in this his wife could be no help. This was a matter for the king of the Mires and those who would be his heirs, those who would reign over the empire he dreamed of establishing.

"Junal," he said, keeping his words simple, but talking to her as he would to another adult, "the reality is, I need people to fear me. Kings can't be kings if people don't fear them."

"The Mires' folks don't fear you," Junal said. "I don't believe it. They love you."

"I'd like to think that I have earned that love," Bryessidan said, "but their love isn't enough. Even if that love would make every one of them fight and die to preserve me and to preserve the Mires over which I rule, that love wouldn't make other rulers love me. It might even make them hate me or fear me.

"And I'm going to be really honest with you, because someday you or one of the others is going to be king or queen after me. Lots of those who show a king or queen or prince or princess a smiling face don't do so from love. They do it from fear or greed or even from pleasure that they are in the presence of someone important.

"Even those who really do love me as their king love other people for some more personal reason. They would fight for me, but if their mother or father or children were threatened, then they might decide to go and fight to protect them instead. That's one of the reasons they need to fear me. They need to be just a little afraid of what I might do if they disobeyed. Do you understand?"

Four heads nodded, and even little Vahon, a beat behind the rest, seemed to understand.

"It's worse with the kingdoms near to us. Kingdoms are like greedy children, always wanting what someone else has.

The Mires has a lot, once you get to know her. She has intelligent, well-trained people, the plants in our wetlands, even good ports."

"And a gate," Junal said.

"And a gate," Bryessidan agreed, "and Once Dead who can make the gate work. Those Once Dead are another resource in which we have an advantage over other lands. Because my father welcomed them here, even when the Reprieve came, many remained with us rather than returning to their homelands or emigrating to the Nexus Islands."

"Do our Once Dead make people hate us?" Stave asked. "I know that lots of people are afraid of them. I was, when I was little."

"Fear us, certainly. Some probably hate us, because hate and fear can be close, just like love and fear."

"Or love and hate," Gidji said softly. "Bry, isn't this too much?"

"I'm going off to war in not very many more days," Bryessidan said, looking to where waning Lion Moon showed through the window. "If I am going to speak of these matters, perhaps now is the only time I'll have."

"Don't start thinking that way!" Gidji snapped. "You will win, and you will come home, and honors will be heaped upon your head in this land and in many others."

"I will do my best to earn those honors," Bryessidan said, "but I think the children also need to understand that even if I did not desire those honors, even if I decided that we of the Mires could do without a gate, even if I wanted to turn the days back to before those first emissaries arrived, I cannot. Choices have been made, choices that have shown the Kingdom of the Mires is strong and willing to fight. If I backed down now, they would decide I was weak, that I was afraid, and as soon as they finished with the Nexus Islands—as they will certainly finish—then they would come for us.

"The people of the Mires are brave—none braver—but we could not survive invasion. We only survived the last war intact as a kingdom because the Once Dead made that a provision of their treaty. Whatever exactly has happened in the

Nexus Islands we do not know, but whatever caused the Nexans to break their treaty with us, the result for the Mires is the same. Once again, perhaps as never before, we are vulnerable. I cannot turn back, because if I did within a few years there would be no Kingdom of the Mires any longer, just a gathering of low, wet lands whose people can claim an interesting and colorful heritage."

He concluded with a defiant glance at Gidji, but she no longer seemed angry that he was speaking so seriously. Instead, she was nodding agreement, rocking Vahon back and forth on her lap.

Junal pressed her head against Bryessidan's breastbone. He could feel her shudder as he stroked her hair. He wished he could reassure her that he would win, that he would always come back, that she would be queen only when she was ready, but he knew if he said those words he would be speaking lies.

Veztressidan had never weakened his son with the myth that his father was invincible. As much as Bryessidan might have wished for that reassurance during those long nights when he stared out into the darkness, wondering if the clattering hoofbeats he could hear in the courtyard below brought some routine bulletin or news that would change him from prince to king, he also knew that when the time had come, the lack of lies had made him ready to be a king.

"So," he said, setting Junal on her feet and carrying the helmet to join the armor on the stand, "you see why I will wear armor that inspires fear—not because I want to be feared for myself, but because fear of the King of the Mires will protect the Mires, will protect those I love . . ."

"I am sure the armor will protect you, too, Daddy," Junal said. She looked up at the polished silver and brass thoughtfully. "It's really very frightening armor. Certainly, it will protect you. I wonder if someday I will need to wear it to protect me, too."

Only if I win this war, Bryessidan thought, *for if I fail to do so, your wars will be lost before they begin.*

He straightened then, and placed the armor like a crown upon the stand.

But I will win, and you will wear that armor, as queen of the Mires, and perhaps of all Pelland as well, perhaps as empress of all the world, with your sister and brothers marching proudly as kings and queens in your train.

XXX

"SOMETHING DOESN'T SMELL right," Blind Seer said to Firekeeper.

Two days had passed since their retreat from the area held and guarded by the Bound, but those two days had not been wasted. For one, they had solidified their alliance with the local Royal Beasts, even managing to send word to their own pack where they were and what they were about. In this way, if they failed in their task, they would not simply vanish. Someone would know to look for them, and, if necessary, avenge them.

Another thing they had done was talk a great deal with Bruck—or rather they had listened while Bruck talked.

The spellcaster seemed almost pathetically eager to share what he knew about those who still held Virim's stronghold, going on at great length—even for a human—about those who remained within, about their factions, about their battles. Bruck had even sketched a diagram of the stronghold, apologizing for his lack of precision even as he drew the locations of doors and windows, and the likely placement of traps.

At first, Firekeeper had thought Bruck was talking so freely in an attempt to preserve his life—to show them how valuable he could be to them. As he talked more, she began to wonder if perhaps he—like the Meddler—intended to make them his tools. After all, the other spellcasters had forsaken him, even tried to kill him. Alone he could not win back his place, but perhaps with the help of Firekeeper and Blind Seer he hoped to win not only that place, but to make himself One now that Virim was gone.

Now, however, she shared Blind Seer's uneasy feeling that there was something off in Bruck's volubility, in the version of events he was giving them. Wolves trust those of their pack, but for all his groveling, Firekeeper did not think Bruck had truly subordinated himself to her and Blind Seer. Years ago, she had learned the painful lesson that humans can lie, and that they might see a wolf's honor as a wolf's weakness.

"I agree," Firekeeper said. "The trail has been muddled with too many tracks, but I cannot pick out the true course."

"Nor I," Blind Seer said, "but I do know where I began to lose my way. It was soon after we came to this place. I think soon after we first captured Bruck."

Firekeeper nodded. "He lies. I can smell that, but I don't know how we can sort the lies from the truth without going forward and learning for ourselves where the reality differs from his report."

Blind Seer huffed wolfish laughter.

"Impulsive, and likely to get us killed. Remember: 'Circling is not merely going in circles. The truth of the trail can be seen from either end.'"

Firekeeper rolled her eyes. Blind Seer was fond of quoting proverbs, and she no longer believed they all reflected the received wisdom of wolf-kind. Rather, she suspected he created them himself to serve his immediate purpose. Even so, there was sense to this one.

"So we circle," she said, "examining the trail to read its message before it becomes a hopeless mess. I will begin."

"Good."

"I have been thinking over all these tales Bruck has told us of Virim and his pack. At first I believed them, even to the smallest detail. Now I think they ring like the howls of a young wolf who wishes the pack to believe he has taken an elk when his prey is merely a rabbit. Big howl, little reason."

Blind Seer wriggled a little, as if he would pounce on her words, but he did not interrupt.

"Humans are like wolves," Firekeeper said, "in that the strong rule the rest. Just as the Ones are tested by the pack, so humans push at each other, vying for position over the most minor matters. I cannot believe that Virim's followers remained contentedly out in these isolated woodlands for over a hundred years when there were lands in the Old and New Worlds alike where they could make themselves One. Surely, someone would have become overwhelmed with frustration and sought to disperse. Bruck's tales tell nothing of this. All his tales are of rivalries within the group, rivalries to change the group's policy regarding the maintenance of querinalo. There is not a single tale of those who sought to disperse."

"Perhaps those who attempted to disperse were slain," Blind Seer suggested. "Remember what happened to Bruck when we captured him? Only a short time later, he was nearly killed by what he said was a warning from those pack mates who felt he had betrayed them."

"I have been remembering," Firekeeper said, "and that is why Bruck's tales stink! He has told us so much about his pack mates, even to their names and loves and rivalries. Why does he not mention those who sought to leave and failed? I think he tells us the tales that will draw us back there. The tales that will make us feel that we two—three with Elation—are enough to invade and take what we desire."

"I can think of many reasons why Bruck would want this," Blind Seer said, "from revenge to a desire to see those who attacked him attacked in turn to perhaps hoping that we would distract or weaken his opponents so that he could win back his position—or even take one that is higher. So shall we agree not to believe anything he has told us of that place and those people?"

"Except that the fortress has walls," Firekeeper agreed, "and only then because we have seen them ourselves, and possibly only after we have touched them."

"I can run with you on that trail," Blind Seer said. "Shall I tell you what has troubled me?"

"Tell."

"It is this matter of Virim's death. I know it matches neatly with my own visions when I ran after the fever, but could I really have slain one of Virim's power?"

Had Firekeeper possessed fur, she would have bristled at the suggestion that any battle held one on one could be beyond a wolf like Blind Seer. Instead, she had to settle for embracing him.

"I believed you when you told the tale, even though by then the Meddler had identified your mountain sheep as Virim."

"So did I," Blind Seer said, "because it mated tightly with my own desire to believe that although I had accepted this unforeseen ability, that I had taken it, hunted it, made it my own, rather than letting it make me its own."

"But you are less certain now?" Firekeeper said. "Why?"

"Bruck's tales again," the blue-eyed wolf admitted. "He has told us how a vision of Virim as the golden-hoofed mountain sheep went forth to each and every sorcerer who fell ill to querinalo. This was how Virim boasted of his achievement, making certain that each of his victims knew who was tearing out their lives."

Firekeeper was quick to sniff back along Blind Seer's reasoning. She thumped her hand on his shoulder and fought back an urge to howl in giddy triumph.

"And this is one tale we can believe," she said, "for we have it not only from Bruck, nor even from the Meddler, but from the records the maimalodalum discovered on Misheemnekuru. We know that Virim made his boast and how he made it."

"It is possible that somehow Bruck knew of my vision," Blind Seer said. "I suspect that anything that has happened in the fever dreams of querinalo are open to them. If I am right, then they know how the mountain sheep taunted me, and the penalty I exacted for his mockery."

"And used that vision to make us believe that Virim was dead—and not by the hand of any of his pack mates, but by your fangs. Why would Bruck do this?"

"To make us believe that we are stronger than those who hold what we desire?" Blind Seer suggested. "Perhaps to make us believe that Virim is dead? Remember, Virim is their One. If he has held them under his rule for more than a hundred years—without a single sorcerer succeeding in striking out on his or her own—then truly he is the greatest of them all. Would we dare challenge him if we believe him alive?"

"But if we believed him dead, and his pack reduced to snarling fragments," Firekeeper said, "then we might well go forward. Why not just come after us? Why have the Bound merely warned us when they could have slain us?"

"I don't know," Blind Seer said. "As I said, this entire situation doesn't smell right. Even now I think we only circle about the edges and so sniff out the outlines of the wrongness. I do not think we have picked up the straight trail that runs on the other side."

Firekeeper nodded, but another, deeply disturbing thought had come to her.

"I think you may be right when you say that Virim and his pack can run free in querinalo's mad dreams. Didn't you and Derian and Truth all speak within one of those visions? Didn't the Meddler join you there, and speak to you?"

"This is so," Blind Seer said. "I did not stay long, but strangely enough, it was the Meddler's urging that I do my best to survive that made me determined to do so only if I could do so as a wolf would. Strange, now that I think of it, but all three of us who met the Meddler in that glade not only survived, but survived with some vestige of our abilities. Was he meddling even then?"

"Probably," Firekeeper said, thinking of the Meddler's declaration of love and tightening her grip on Blind Seer as a barrier against the fascination she felt for the strange not-quite-man.

"I will need to consider," Blind Seer said, "whether I am grateful or not. I think I would have made my own choice nonetheless, but both Truth and Derian might have given way, and Derian, for all he denies it, is improved by the experience."

Firekeeper grinned, but a sudden thought wiped away thoughts of her friend.

"The Meddler has almost always spoken to me in dreams,"

she said. "What if Virim and his pack have had access to these?"

Blind Seer considered for a moment. "I don't think they could manage that. The Meddler is a canny fox not likely to forget to dig a channel to guide the rainwater from his den. I do not think he would speak freely to you if he did not believe his words reached you alone."

Firekeeper wasn't certain.

"What if he is allied with them? He is the one who set us to go after querinalo. He is the one who first warned us that the Nexus Islands were in danger."

"Neither of these," Blind Seer said, "seem to be to Virim's advantage. Besides, the Meddler was slain and his spirit locked away long before the coming of querinalo. He knew of Virim, true, but that hardly makes them allies. Surely if they were allied, Virim would have set the Meddler free."

"And we have seen evidence of the Meddler's long imprisonment ourselves," Firekeeper said, "and again the maimalodalum confirm his tales of the length of his confinement. Very well. I will hold my suspicions of the Meddler."

"As to being Virim's ally only," Blind Seer said, "we must not forget that he plays his own game and has a disturbing tendency to see living beings as toys he can tug at and gnaw for his own pleasure."

"I will not forget," Firekeeper said. "I won't even forget that I seem to be one of his favorite toys."

Blind Seer gave her a sloppy lick across one side of her face.

"Wise, Little Two-legs. Very wise. Now, tell me. We have decided that not one track or scent of the trail that has brought us to this point can be relied upon to lead us to our prey. Do we surrender? If we run hard, we might reach the gate in New Kelvin and be back to the Nexus Islands in time to fight at Derian's side."

"Only if we turned Bruck loose," Firekeeper said, "or killed him, and I am reluctant to do either. In any case, we two—three with Elation—may be great fighters, but I am not confident whether we would be enough to turn the balance of the battle. It seems too likely that we would be among the corpses on the battlefield, and that Lovable and Bitter would recite our praises as they ate our eyes. No, for Derian and for the Nexans and so the gates do not fall into the hands of those who would use them to justify invading the New World as they clearly have justified invading the Nexus Islands, we need to deal with Virim and find a cure for querinalo."

Blind Seer shifted from beneath her hold, and began pacing restlessly.

"Following the Meddler's lead," he said, "we have always spoken of finding a cure to querinalo. There is another course we could take, one that might be easier, especially since Bruck says Virim himself is uncertain about the newly weakened form of querinalo."

Firekeeper thought she knew where the blue-eyed wolf was leading, but she forced herself to state it aloud.

"We could go to the Bound and explain that we share their thinking and that of those first Bound. We could say that the reentry of magic to the world—even in the diminished form it now holds—is too much. We could then beseech Virim and his allies to hear our cries for rescue. We could ask him to bring back querinalo again, querinalo as it first was—terrible and deadly."

"That would certainly end the problem of the gates," Blind Seer said, "for none would be left with the ability to work them. We could beg for time to get the Nexans off the island so they would not be stranded."

"You say 'Virim,'" Firekeeper said. "Then you do not believe he is dead?"

"Let us say rather that if he is dead, I do not believe I killed him. Those who stand as Ones in his place could hear our plea."

Firekeeper considered. There was a certain comfort in the idea of returning the world to the one she had grown up believing existed: a world with no magic in it but the magic of little talents; a world safe from the distance-shrinking power of gates; a world where no one could make lightning do their bidding or take over the minds and wills of the helpless.

But she remembered, too, the pain and suffering of querinalo. She thought of those in whom magic almost certainly lay dormant—like Ynamynet and Skea's daughter, Sunshine. Reawakening querinalo to its full power would be sentencing her and others like her to a horrible and painful death.

And she thought of Blind Seer. Would a new querinalo leave him safe, or would the recrafted curse destroy even those who had survived it once?

She shook herself. Perhaps if she had never known querinalo's bite, and not seen those tormented by its fevers, she might have been seduced by this idea that they could go backward. But in her deepest heart she did not believe going backward was possible.

"Such begging should be our last answer," Firekeeper said at last. "I think it is time for us to return and confront the Bound."

"So we continue as before?" Blind Seer asked.

"Never as before," Firekeeper replied. "We go with eyes opened and teeth bared. We will walk into lies and fight our way to the end of querinalo."

"And if we make matters worse in the end?" Blind Seer said, not as one who doubts, but as one who accepts that no decision is without consequence.

"Then we will deal with that then," Firekeeper said. "Rabbits are caught when they freeze in terror. I no longer am sure what is right and what is wrong, but I am sure of one thing at least. You and I are not rabbits; we are wolves. Bruck and these others have long known only the Bound, and with their vow to Virim acting as a leash, these are more dogs than wolves. Let us remind him that a wolf is not a dog."

"And how fiercely wolves can bite," the blue-eyed wolf agreed. "And how fiercely wolves can bite."

❧

ISENDE WAS SLEEPING on the sheepskin rug in the front room of Derian's house when the knock came at the door. The young woman was so exhausted—or perhaps caught up in one of her visions—that she only stirred, then settled back into sleep.

Heading to answer the door, Derian stepped over her, leaving her to rest. Odd as it seemed, the discovery that Isende had some magical talent, might even have the capacity to cast spells, had not distanced them, but had brought them closer. Knowing that she, like he, carried the taint of magical ability had made Derian feel less like he was contaminating her with his very presence.

Derian opened to door to find Tiniel and Plik standing there. Plik's expression was neutral, but from the way Tiniel darted glances around Derian, both were aware that, despite the lateness of the hour, Isende had not returned to her own rooms.

Swinging the door open, Derian indicated his sleeping guest before lighting a candle lantern and stepping over the threshold to join them outside.

Summer had brought pleasant warmth with it. The same ocean breezes that in winter made going outside a challenge had mellowed so that they merely made his candle dance playfully, and kept the air from growing humid and heavy.

"Isende fell asleep while helping me review some of Wort's supply lists," Derian said. "Unless you need her, let her rest."

Tiniel shook his head. For the first time Derian noticed that he held a bone message tube.

"Let 'Sende rest," Tiniel said gruffly. "My business is with you. An osprey brought this through the gate from the Setting Sun stronghold earlier today. The tube is addressed in Pellish, I think. Since I couldn't read it, I went and asked Plik if he'd speak with the messenger. He did, and the osprey said the message was for you."

"If you're down here, who's in charge of the gateway hills?" Derian asked.

Tiniel looked insulted, as well he might, given that Derian had all but accused him of neglecting his duty.

"Enigma brought the osprey through, and I asked him to stay and watch. When I went to get Plik, I found Verul in the kitchens. He's up there now."

"Great," Derian said, trying to make his tone his apology.

He couldn't exactly apologize directly, after all, not without admitting that he'd suspected Tiniel of being careless because the message gave him an excuse to check up on what his sister might be doing in Derian's house so late.

Actually, Tiniel had made a good choice when asking Verul to cover the gate watch. Although Verul owed his crippling injury to Firekeeper's knife, the experience that had scarred his soul had come from having the very Spell Wielder he had been trying to defend view the wound Verul took in his service as nothing more than a convenient conduit from which to draw blood to power a spell. The callousness of the action had made Verul more determined than most to keep the gates from falling into the control of the remaining Old World Once Dead.

"I'll head back up," Tiniel said stiffly. "Verul was coming off his own watch when I asked him to cover for me."

"Thank you for bringing this," Derian said.

After Tiniel had departed, Derian looked down at the message capsule again. The handwriting on the outside was tiny, as it must be to fit, but he thought he recognized it.

Plik was making no move to depart, and Derian realized that whatever Plik had learned from the osprey had piqued his curiosity. He thought about sending Plik away, but the maimalodalu had given him good counsel before, and even without unrolling whatever missive the tube contained, Derian had a feeling he was going to need counsel.

"The osprey said," Plik commented casually, "that the message is from your friend Lady Archer. He also said to reassure you that he had seen the baby in her mother's arms, and—as best as he could judge, not knowing much of human infants—the child was fine."

Derian had not realized that he was delaying opening the message just from some such dread—usually he tore into messages from his absent friends and family with alacrity—but now he relaxed.

"Sometimes I think everyone knows me better than I do myself," he said. "Let's step into the stable to open this. I really don't want to wake Isende, but there's enough breeze to carry off a piece of paper."

Plik accepted Derian's invitation, glancing around the stable as if checking for friends.

"Eshinarvash is back on the mainland where the grazing is better," Derian said. "Enigma will open the gate for him in the morning. My father would never believe it—a horse actually letting a puma draw his blood, or a puma using a single claw more delicately than any surgeon does a scalpel."

Plik grinned, raccoon eyes twinkling above a very human mouth. As Derian hung the candle lantern from a copper bracket, he couldn't help but think that there was a lot about his current situation Colby Carter wouldn't believe.

My mother might, though, Derian thought, unscrolling the paper and bracing the top with a heavy-nailed hand that he no longer automatically winced at when his gaze chanced on it. *Vernita Carter taught me to look beyond our comfortable lives. I wonder what she'd think about this life I'm living now.*

Elise's letter managed to be both polite and direct, very like the lady herself. Her writing crowded the light paper with tiny but easily deciphered pen strokes.

> *Derian—I hope this finds you and Firekeeper well, wherever you are and whatever you've gotten yourself into now. I'm writing to tell you that Doc and myself (and Elexa) are traveling south of u-Seeheera now. We've been through u-Vreeheera, and through many of the towns on the road to the border with the city-states. In fact, I think you would recognize our route. It is quite similar to the one you and Firekeeper followed when going south.*

Derian looked up at Plik. "I have a bad feeling about this. You know already, don't you?"

Plik merely gestured to the letter. "I believe humans consider it bad form to keep a lady waiting. Finish your letter. Then we'll talk."

Grumbling mild protest, Derian obeyed.

> *Ostensibly, our task is diplomatic. Ambassador Sailor received suggestions from home that we not restrict our*

*southern contact to either the Liglimom in u-Seeheera or
to the Liglimom themselves. I have seen the documents
in question, and certainly he could have delayed until
winter made such travel more pleasant—I have never,
ever been so hot!—but he chose to use them as an excuse
for sending someone—me—to find out whether you are
absent without leave or really doing something that can
be argued as benefitting Bright Haven.*

*I am certain that you will be delighted to learn that I
am writing this from the city-state just north of Gak.
Gak, as you may recall, is the point where you, effectively, disappeared. Or, as Ambassador Sailor now believes more firmly than ever, went haring off after some
young woman.*

Disturbed as he was by the turn Elise's letter was taking, Derian found himself inadvertently grinning at Elise's phrasing.

"If she's not careful," he muttered, "she's going to turn out
just like her grandmother."

"What?" Plik said, perplexed. "Who?"

"Elise's grandmother is the Grand Duchess Rosene, King
Tedric's younger sister, a fine, upstanding woman in her sev-
enties, and a complete terror. Elise sounds just like the grand
duchess here."

"So the news isn't good?"

"I'm not sure. Let me finish."

*We will depart for Gak in a day or so. If we do not hear
from you otherwise, we will make enquiries in Gak. After all, asking after a long-absent friend is only natural.
Indeed, it might seem less natural if we did not query. If
you (or Firekeeper—I smell her muddy paws in this)
have nothing to hide, this will not trouble you, but if you
do not wish such enquiries to be made, then I suggest
you arrange to meet with us or at least get us a message
before that point.*

I know Firekeeper well enough to suspect that she will

*have done her best to have one or more of her friends
keep an eye on us. I think this especially so if we were to
travel. I even think I have spotted who might be the likely
party. Ravens are bold, but this one is particularly so—
and very inquisitive. I will trust this message to Firekeeper's friend, and hope that it permits you time to
prepare for guests.*

The letter was signed with a flourish, *Your loving friend,
Elise.* Beneath, in another, more square and yet less legible
hand was written: *I don't know if I approve, but I have absolutely no control over her. Have I ever? Doc.*

"Did the osprey get the letter from a raven?" Derian asked.

"Close enough. A raven was watching Lady Elise and her
entourage as a favor to Firekeeper. When the raven realized
what Elise wanted, he went and brought the osprey. Ospreys
can carry more weight and have greater range."

"Elise writes to say that she is coming here," Derian said,
"or rather to Gak, and my guess is that as soon as she talks to
Layo or Amira in Gak, she will head here. It would be bad
enough if she and Doc stumbled on this unwarned, but I cannot imagine that the senate of Gak would permit a visiting
diplomat to go off into the wilds without an escort. Did the
osprey give any idea how far ahead of them it was?"

"Not precisely," Plik said, "but it did mention it left immediately. My guess is that we have time to make plans."

"Great," Derian said. "I've got to consult with Ynamynet,
but there's going to be no turning Elise back. If the osprey is
willing, I'll send a return letter asking Elise to wait. Then perhaps Harjeedian or Tiniel can go and escort Elise and Doc. I
certainly can't go."

"I think the osprey would go," Plik said, "but the distances are
now within what a raven can cover easily. Send Bitter or Lovable. They know Gak from our earlier visits, and they'll attract
less attention than a seabird would. They also can act as guides
if Lady Elise insists on leaving before an escort can arrive."

"Sounds good," Derian said. "But first I'd better talk to

Ynamynet. I've heard a touch of grumbling about autocracy. This is not the time to generate more."

The stable door creaked on its metal hinges, and Isende came in, still sleepy-eyed and yawning.

"I'm sorry, Derian," she said. "I didn't mean to fall asleep and push you out here. Is there something wrong?"

Derian patted her shoulder. "No need to apologize, and I hope nothing is wrong. Certainly, it's going to be a complication. I need to go wake Ynamynet and consult her."

"At this hour?" Isende said. "It's awfully dark, must be late."

"Unfortunately, this is a matter in which hours may matter," Derian said. "Ynamynet has been working at least as hard as I have, but I think she'll understand."

"Is it the invasion?" Isende said, falling into step next to him.

"No," Derian replied, then laughed. "Or rather it is another invasion, one that has some nasty long-term consequences if I don't handle it right, but I think we can forestall the worst."

He told her about Elise's letter as they walked. He had to hold back lest he outdistance Plik and Isende, for neither had a trace of his height. Neither shared his sudden ebullience, either. Wondering at its source, Derian realized that in a strange way he was actually glad to know Elise and Doc were coming.

Unless Ynamynet had a good reason against it, he was going to tell his friends the truth, and ask that they withhold revealing what they had learned or acting upon it until the invasion was over—one way or another.

It would be good to confide in people he trusted, to know that should the Nexans fail in their effort to hold the gates, that the New World would not go unwarned as to the many and varied dangers the Old World still held. Derian thought he could die comforted, if not content, knowing that the New World would be warned that after a long dormancy the Old World was once again reaching out toward the New.

XXXI

WHEN BRUCK LEARNED they were returning to the area held by the Bound, he pleaded to be permitted to go with them. Firekeeper shook her head.

"You too slow," she said, "and another we must watch if trouble come."

"When trouble comes," Blind Seer said. *"I smell trouble as surely as I smell excitement in that man's sweat."*

Firekeeper felt no need to translate any of this, but went on addressing Bruck.

"You will stay here. If you give me your word you stay, you will be let go from this cave a little. If no, then you will stay within."

Bruck didn't ask how she could assure that. His gaze drifted to the array of boulders and logs Firekeeper had experimented with until she had found a combination that enabled the cave to be firmly sealed while leaving a gap through which light and fresh air could pass.

"What if you don't come back?" he asked. "I'll be locked in there for the rest of my life—and that won't be very long or very pleasant."

Firekeeper thought about telling him that by his own account he had lived a great deal longer than most humans, and this at the expense of who knew how many other lives. She didn't though. There was no need to be cruel.

She also contemplated telling Bruck that she had spoken with the local Royal Beasts about freeing Bruck if she, Blind Seer, and Elation did indeed fail, but decided against that as well. Best Bruck did not know how many watched him, nor how closely. Who knew what he might give away once he thought himself alone? Thus far he had been a model prisoner, even docile, but Firekeeper and Blind Seer alike were certain that at least some of the "bad smell" they had detected earlier came from Bruck himself.

"We come back," Firekeeper said.

She waited for Bruck to promise he wouldn't attempt to leave the area around the cave. When he did not, she set about sealing him into the cave, building her barrier mostly from stone, but with some thick greenwood as braces here and there.

Bruck himself was also secured with iron. The iron wire was no longer twisted about his wrists and ankles, but a few pieces fastened his clothing to him. Firekeeper also wove a few strands into the barrier, hiding her work beneath the thick, ropy vines she was using to anchor some of the logs. She didn't think Bruck would fail to realize the wire was there, but she thought the vines might make it harder for him to see it.

Perhaps the iron wire would not inhibit Bruck unless it was directly touching him. Firekeeper gave a mental shrug as she rolled another boulder into place. If Bruck showed no sign of the wire bothering him once they were gone, well, that would be something learned about him.

When the barrier was nearly complete, Firekeeper gave Bruck a supply of meat. She had already brought in a small supply of fuel for the cookfire. A seep at the back of the cave supplied water, although gathering it would be tedious work.

All the time she worked, Firekeeper kept expecting Bruck to speak to her, to try and convince her to change her mind, but the spellcaster said nothing. He simply watched her shifting rocks and moving logs, apparently as fascinated as if he had never seen anyone do physical labor before. Who knew? Perhaps he hadn't. The stories Firekeeper had heard about the world before the creation of querinalo made that seem possible.

Since Bruck was not speaking to them, Firekeeper felt no requirement to bid him farewell. Without a word, the three departed as twilight was falling.

Like Firekeeper herself, Elation was more accustomed to functioning after dark than was typical for her kind, and if there had been need she could have flown high watch for their group. However, a brace of Royal Screech Owls had offered to serve that role, and so Elation, better equipped in close-grown forest to ride than fly, had taken her perch on Fire-keeper's shoulder.

The peregrine was not light, nor was the leather pad they had rigged to keep her talons from destroying Firekeeper's shoulder particularly comfortable, but Firekeeper found Ela-tion a welcome burden. Somehow her presence seemed a promise that this journey—as had the first one they had made together—would turn out for the best.

Or am I thinking too like a human? Firekeeper thought. *Has that journey ever really ended?*

She grinned to herself in the darkness. That last really was human thinking. Beginning or end really didn't matter to wolves. What mattered was each step along the trail.

Concentrating on those steps, keeping the pace swift and steady, they crossed the intervening distance far more quickly than they had with Bruck. When midday brought heat, they rested, and resumed their journey again with the coolness of twilight. The owls left them when they departed the moun-tains, but even without those guides they traveled with confi-dence. The first time they had made this journey there had been need to scout the trail and learn where it might lead. This time they knew their destination.

And their destination knew they were coming.

Sometime in the flat, grey dark time that isn't yet dawn but is still not quite night, a hurtling form, mostly black-furred, that black touched with white, attacked Blind Seer without howl or growl of warning. Another wolf, this one a few shades greyer than the spreading sky above, launched itself onto Fire-keeper. However, although the Bound wolves did not an-nounce themselves or their attack, Firekeeper and Blind Seer were not without warning.

Blind Seer had caught the circling wolves' scent on the night breeze. When he had done so, he had alerted Firekeeper by pressing gently against her leg. Otherwise, he gave no sign, and even those who knew them well might have missed the message being passed. To those who stalked them, the pair must have seemed as indifferent to their danger as a rabbit overwhelmed by the desire to devour a thick patch of clover.

When the attack came, Firekeeper and Blind Seer were crossing one of a series of small deer meadows that increased in frequency the closer they came to the stronghold. Humans felt safer in open spaces, and Firekeeper did not doubt that they had something to do with these tidy, open patches. A wolf pack appreciated such areas as well, especially when many hoped to get in on the kill of a few.

Blind Seer fell back as the almost black wolf snapped at his apparently unguarded throat, causing his attacker to bite hard upon open air. There was a yelp that told Firekeeper's ears that Blind Seer had not missed his return strike. However, she was too busy to spare attention for admiring her pack mate's technique.

The wolf who had attacked her was probably the One Female, for Firekeeper could see that her teats had not fully shrunk back after nursing that spring's litter of pups. Her attack on Firekeeper came only a beat behind her mate's attack on Blind Seer.

Firekeeper's Fang was in her hand. She braced herself when the One Female came snapping at her face. With one hand, she blocked back the snarling, snapping fangs, with the other she brought up her blade. She knew she should go for a killing strike, but those teats and the pups to which they testified made Firekeeper bring the blade in a wide slash that carried across the wolf's narrow breastbone, then up and over the shoulder blade.

The One Female fell back, yelping in pain, and, quite probably, in astonishment. Firekeeper took advantage of the momentary pause to position herself so that Blind Seer was to her back. She longed to run for the apparent safety of the trees, but remembered all too well that the Bound were not only wolves, but counted pumas and bears and raccoons in their number. Wolves might find a stand of trees some slight hindrance; a raccoon or even a puma—if the trees were large enough—would find the same a gift.

Firekeeper didn't have time to shudder over the error her

impulse had nearly led her into. Elation had launched into the open sky as soon as the wolves attacked, but as soon as she had height enough, had stooped and dove in the manner for which peregrines were revered—even by humans, who only knew their Cousin-kind.

In the same way that Blind Seer had made a point of learning the best way to fight humans when he realized that his traveling with Firekeeper would make this a useful skill, so Elation had educated herself in the best ways she might contribute to battles where the prey was larger than the creatures she usually hunted. Peregrines were mighty hunters for their size, taking even fat ducks with ease, but once they left the air and struck, they were vulnerable until they could take wing again.

Elation had practiced striking not only with the weight of her body, but in long sweeps that enabled her to scrape her talons along exposed flesh or fur without giving up all her momentum. This is what she had done now, causing the white wolf that would have joined the One fighting Blind Seer to rear back in astonishment, wondering when the wind had grown sharp enough to draw blood.

But blood there was, dark blotches against the white of the wolf's coat. The white wolf hesitated, and her hesitation conveyed itself as a sign for the remaining members of the pack to hesitate, for none rushed forward to attack either Blind Seer or Firekeeper alongside their Ones.

Firekeeper was grateful for the breathing space. She was not at all certain she had her first opponent beaten. Confused, certainly, but perhaps not yet beaten.

Poised to bring her Fang into play if the One Female was to attack again, Firekeeper tried to see the fight as that One Female might and in this way understand how her opponent might react—and more importantly, how she herself might act.

Wolves usually aim for throat or flank when hunting, a tactic that allows them to strike at vulnerable areas while keeping their own hides clear of the horns and antlers of their more usual prey. When fighting wolf-to-wolf, their targets were similar, but as wolf-to-wolf battles—ferocious as they can be—have as their primary goal proving which contender is the better fighter, neither internal battles nor more standard hunts prepared the Bound for Firekeeper.

The Bound were Royal Wolves, larger and far more intelligent than the Cousins that humans knew and feared, but unlike Blind Seer and some of the yarimaimalom these Bound had not trained to fight humans. They were completely unprepared for an opponent who could move her Fang to wherever she needed it—and who knew their vulnerable spots all too well.

Perhaps their ancestors, those who bound them to their strange pact, knew something of how humans fight, Firekeeper thought as the One Female shrank back, yelping as much in astonishment as in pain. *These have viewed humans as weak things they must protect, and whatever moon songs they have heard sung of me, still they were not prepared.*

Firekeeper did not let her initial success go to her head. Some part of her still felt that she was doing something wrong in fighting Royal Wolves, especially when they were so confused as to where their loyalties should be. Moreover, she had promised Blind Seer that she would not hold back her blade's edge.

"I cannot defend you from a wolf pack and who knows what other creatures besides," Blind Seer had told her when they were making their plans. "That only means your death and mine as well. If we fight together, though, I think we can do far better than they believe."

Wolf's choice, she thought. *Blind Seer and I thought to offer such to those within Virim's fort, but what about these here? They will understand what a wolf's choice means far better than any human would.*

Howling a challenge cry, Firekeeper ran toward the injured One Female. Startled, the dawn-grey wolf began limping away, less in flight than in reflex. She had been attacking what must have seemed to her a naked, nearly defenseless creature. Now that creature was running at her, howling the cry that said, "You are weak. I am strong. I will rule in your place."

It was a situation any wolf pack would have witnessed time and again, for even in the packs of the Royal Wolves strength usually dominated wisdom and cunning in the selection of the Ones. The Ones were first to feast, first to fight, first in the hunt. Should antler or horn or even uneven ground make them unable to lead, they must show themselves capable of defending their privileges or lose them on the instant.

Nor was this wrong to Firekeeper's way of thinking. Were the Ones not strong enough to bring down the game, not powerful enough to break trail through the snow, then the pack would waste its blood and energy on futile ventures, and find itself too weak to survive a winter intact—or at all.

Challengers most often came from within the pack itself, for the pack members were the ones who were present when the Ones faltered. However, a powerful stranger, dispersed from his or her own pack, might decide that taking over an established pack was a better move than courting a mate and beginning the laborious task of winning territory and building a new pack.

So Firekeeper's howl of challenge was recognized by all the wolves, and changed not only the character of her own battle, but that of Blind Seer's as well. As her opponent had been the Bound's One Female, so his was the One Male. The males were well matched but Firekeeper had no doubt who would win. The question was, could she make good her own boast, and force the One Female to surrender.

If she did not, she would find little mercy from the Bound. *But then,* Firekeeper thought, *I expected none in any case.*

"You flee," Firekeeper howled after the fleeing mother wolf. "I see your tail trailing low and call that surrender. Turn and fight me, else here and now I claim your place, your mate, your pack, and your pups. Flee me and flee them. Surrender, and I may keep you in my pack."

The bloodied One Female staggered in midstride, clearly shocked to hear such a challenge coming forth in a wolf's voice from human lips.

She wheeled, limping still, blood catching and matting in fur above a leg she held a hand's breadth clear of the grass.

"What perverted notion is this?" was the sense of the half-whine, half-howl she sent to answer Firekeeper's challenge. "You are no wolf to rule a pack."

"Tell that to the wolves of Misheemnekuru," Firekeeper boasted as was the wolf's way. "Tell that to Dark Death and to Moon Frost. Tell that to those who have run under my leadership. But who are you to say what is perverted and what is not? From the tales I have heard, you are no wolf, but a lapdog, whining servant of human masters."

"The humans are not our masters!" the One Female growled. "We guard them to honor agreements our ancestors made."

"So say the dogs who sleep on the doorsteps outside of human houses," Firekeeper taunted. "They say they could leave any time, but they choose to remain. How does this differ from you?"

Peripherally, she was aware that the battle between Blind Seer and the One Male had faded into a circling, snapping draw, each wolf testing the other's reach, but neither attacking. Their ears had told them the battle had shifted in emphasis.

Firekeeper gave them little attention. She and Blind Seer had come here as invaders into territory held by the Bound for over a century. But she could feel that she had broken the wolves' certainty, shown them themselves in a manner they did not like in the least.

"Will you surrender, then," Firekeeper pressed, "and care for the pups you have borne as a wolf would, or will you fight for these humans and die as a dog?"

"I could fight as a wolf," the One Female growled, "and slice your naked hide to pulp."

"Try," Firekeeper suggested, shifting her Fang so the light glinted off the blade, "one-legged, bloodied, weak old fool. A wolf would know her limits and surrender. Only a dog would continue to fight and leave the pack to suffer."

The One Female trembled, her senses telling her to surrender, her pride urging her to fight. Tellingly, the members of her pack did not move in on Firekeeper as they might have. Firekeeper's talk of dogs and wolves had muddied the clarity of the matter to them. Then, too, there was the white wolf who trembled in the grass, licking blood from where Elation's talons had raked him, and Elation herself, poised to strike at the first wolf who moved.

Blind Seer broke the stalemate, darting forward, breaking his pattern of snap and circle, grabbing the One Male on the loose skin of his ruff and shaking the other hard, so that blood ran through the thick fur. The move was a threat, for Blind Seer had not bitten deeply enough to break vital muscles or bones, but it hurt and the angle of Blind Seer's hold made it nearly impossible for the One Male to bring his own jaws into play.

The One Female's trembling increased when she saw her mate grabbed and held. His eyes were narrowed, glazing in pain, and clearly every instinct in him yearned to surrender.

Firekeeper built on Blind Seer's move. She leapt as she had done once before, in another battle, landing so that she could straddle the injured One Female's back, and bring her own weight to bear. The position was one that wolves used in dominance fights, the hard play that establishes rank within the pack. But no wolf ever had knees with which to grip, and the familiar combined with the unfamiliar to overload the One Female's conditioning.

"Dog or wolf?" Firekeeper hissed, bringing her weight to bear, pressing her fingers in the gash left by her knife and reminding the other that she could bring fresh pain if she so wished. "Be a wolf . . ."

The One Female crumpled beneath the combined weights of confusion and pain.

"I surrender," she whimpered, "but if you are a wolf, then in the end, perhaps I am a dog."

Firekeeper rose, not trusting the One Female, but at the same time knowing that to the gathered pack the One Female's surrender would mean nothing if Firekeeper must continue to hold her down.

The One Female only rolled onto her back, exposing her throat, and as she did so, her mate went limp in Blind Seer's grip.

Firekeeper did not give the other wolves a chance to consider how they might turn this new situation to their own advantage. Every pack had at least one member who thought he or she should be One instead. The matter must be more complicated for these Bound, who must remain within a limited territory.

She had spoken of dogs and of wolves, but now as she considered this cage with its walls of promise, she wondered if she were not closer to the truth than she had imagined. The Bound Wolves had chained themselves, brought themselves to heel with the snapped command of an old promise—or was there something more? Was there some other hold Virim and his allies had over the Bound than an old pact, fulfilled in spirit if not in fact long before?

A high, shrill scream from Elation brought Firekeeper's attention away from the wolves.

"Trapped!" the peregrine shrieked. "We have been trapped."

Into the edges of the meadow, filling every gap, large or small, came members of the Bound. They showed themselves beneath shrubs or in the branches or trees. Wingéd folk laced the air with the intertwining net of their flight so that even Elation had no escape open to her.

An enormous bear, honey gold of coat, reared onto his hind legs. He was taller by a head and more than Derian, and seemed at least twice as wide, a living wall of fur, but fur that snarled to show solid white fangs, and spread paws to make clear the reach of the strong arms that terminated in long, curving black claws.

"Trapped," the bear growled complacently. "The wolves did their part in baiting that trap. I must say, you did better with them than any expected, but then they are only wolves and have odd thoughts about the value of surrender."

Firekeeper read the bear's contempt for those who would surrender in the bristling of his fur and the wrinkling of his wide black nose. She thought the One Female cringed a little under that contempt, and found herself angry on behalf of one who would have gladly slain her only moments before.

The wolf-woman watched the One Female carefully, all too aware that the arrival of the other Bound made the wounded wolf strong where she had been weak—that is, if she could count on the non-wolfish Bound to support her if she were to attack.

For his part, Blind Seer sat back on his haunches and scratched with a hind foot at one ear as if the actions of an errant summer flea were more interesting to him than the hostile attentions of the gathered Bound.

The bear did not like this at all, nor did the others. A puma hissed and lashed its long tail. Other creatures bristled or hunched or showed teeth after the manner of their kind. Blind Seer was unperturbed, and Firekeeper had never admired him more than for this foolish courage.

Almost imperceptibly, the Bound wolves drew back from the meadow's center, leaving the three intruders vulnerable in the center. Elation glided down from the tree limb on which she had been perched, taking a seat on Firekeeper's padded shoulder.

"Might as well see this through from here," she said. "The air above is full of shit, lice, and molting feathers."

Angry screeches and caws from above said that Elation's insult had been taken, but none of the many winged hunters dove to punish the peregrine as they might have easily done.

Firekeeper took her lead from her companions. Wiping onto the thick grass the worst of the One Female's blood from her Fang's blade, she made as if polishing off the remainder was the most important thing she could do. She would have liked to feel confident enough to sheath the weapon entirely, but there was a difference between a display of confidence and pure stupidity. Elation and Blind Seer could not be disarmed short of death, but without her tools Firekeeper knew she would be even more defeated than she felt already.

Blind Seer sniffed the air, as if scenting their many visitors for the first time.

"So, we have returned, and you have come as you have promised. Very nice. Very neat. Now, who dies first?"

The bear rumbled in admiring astonishment.

"I think you will die, wolf, you and the human wolf and the peregrine all. We will not die."

"Do you think we will simply lie down and let you have our throats?" Blind Seer asked. "I think not."

"I think," the bear said, "I could take you one and all, myself alone."

Firekeeper slid her Fang into its Mouth, and in the same motion pulled her bow from where it rested against her back. She leaned against the supple wood, stringing it and setting arrow to string.

"Still," she said, "my quills might sting a little even after I am gone. Will you have your masters pull them out for you?"

"I have no master but the promise I keep as it has been kept for over a hundred years," the bear growled, but his small eyes hardened as he studied the bow. Unfamiliar with humans these Bound might be, but apparently he knew enough about bows to take one seriously.

"Two-legged wolf, you have fewer quills than a porcupine," a lynx taunted from a tree branch, "and are soft all over, not merely underneath. Take care."

"Why?" Firekeeper asked, affecting innocence. "It is as my companion says, 'Who dies first?,' for we will not sit quietly and wait for you to take our lives."

There was an uncomfortable ripple through the gathered Bound, and Firekeeper was fairly certain that at least a few of those who had so confidently blocked the paths from the meadow had drawn back a pace or so. Even the aerial guard took their circles a little higher.

"It is true," Blind Seer said, pausing to lick beneath his tail. "No one goes into a hunt expecting death rather than hot meat at the trail's end. Here, though, this hunt will end in someone's death—and certainly many will limp or crawl before we die. But what is an eye or a limb to a promise, especially a promise that is empty and hollow?"

"Our promise is not empty!" bugled a stag with a stomp of one hoof for emphasis. "We have remained faithful to our promise for over a hundred years."

"But now you defend the very thing you thought to defeat," Blind Seer said. "I find that odd indeed."

"Defend what we thought to defeat?" croaked a raven. "What nonsense is that?"

Blind Seer replied, "My understanding was that you sought

to defeat the magic that would invade the New World and destroy the Beasts who made it their home. To do this, you allied yourself with this Virim, promising him that you would keep him safe if he used his art to defend the New World. Do I have the tale true?"

There was no one answer, but a moving of ears, lashing of tails gave answer that Blind Seer was correct, but that his listeners were suspicious of his approach.

"Now, when first we met you Bound," Blind Seer continued, "you told us that you were aware that the very humans you guarded had been faithless. By this we understood you to mean that you knew that magic—even spellcasting magic— had reemerged into the world, that querinalo no longer bit with a killing bite. Is this so?"

Again the Bound gave their wordless agreement, but the tension in their muscles warned that they were growing uneasy enough to forget the danger that Firekeeper's arrows offered.

She decided a reminder was in order. Dropping the arrows she had held ready to the turf, she pulled a headless shaft from her quiver and set it to string in one quick motion. Even without a head or fletching, the smooth stick flew true enough, burying half its length in the turf near a raccoon's tail.

Firekeeper grinned and reset a complete arrow to the string and pulled it back, ready to fire if any chose to answer her challenge.

None did. The tension among the Bound did not ebb, but none rushed forth, and Blind Seer again began his rambling discourse.

"Now, you know you have been betrayed," Blind Seer said, "but choose to redeem your foolishness with fidelity. Noble, I suppose, but what I want to know is how can you maintain this fidelity when the very reason for which you first sealed yourself to Virim's service is once again threatening."

"What?" a jay cried. "Threatening?"

"Old World humans are poised to invade the Nexus Islands, a place where there are gates that lead throughout the Old World and into the New," Blind Seer explained. "The invaders will surely win, for those who hold the Nexus Islands are few, weak, and noble. They might bring in reinforcements from the New World, but they will not. Why? Because they do not wish to risk any of these to be subjected to querinalo. Strangely, querinalo remains a curse of the Old World, not the New. I wonder why? Ah, but that little detail hardly matters. What matters is that by your stubborn defense you are making possible the very invasion that you originally sought to forestall."

The Bound remained motionless and silent, so Blind Seer glanced over at Firekeeper. "Interesting, yes?"

"Interesting," Firekeeper agreed, "that a hundred years and more of fidelity should be rewarded with the same invasion that these Bound tried to forestall. I think the New World will fall faster and harder, now. Before there would have been spellcasters who would have fought against invasion—if for no other reason than that they held land here. Now those are gone, and those who rule in their stead are without magic—indeed, they abhor it."

Elation keened, "The New World humans will be like fledglings when a weasel climbs to the nest. The Beasts? Naked, blind chicks. You taunted Blind Seer for the talent dormant within him. Odd to think that had someone been about who might have trained him—as I have heard a puma on the Nexus Islands has been trained—he might have been a spellcaster for the Beasts. Too late . . . Too late . . . And soon this meadow will be watered in blood."

The Bound were clearly unsettled. Postures were shifting from attack to guarded, angry defense. Firekeeper held her breath. The battle was not won, but would words be enough to unbind the Bound? What held them, after all, but words?

"Let us go through," she said. "We do not seek to harm Virim or any of his followers. We seek a solution to this problem. Walk with us if you hold doubts. You have promised to protect them from their enemies. What is there in that promise that forbids you to bring them supplicants?"

The Bound looked at each other, then the bear scraped at its chest with those long, black claws.

"Supplicants . . ." he mused. "Asking, perhaps, that things

be put right again. Yes. I can see my way to that. I will be among your escort."

The other Bound mostly seemed to agree with the bear, although one or two looked uneasy.

"I will go also," said a puma.

"And I, for my pack," said one of the wolves, a handsome silvery grey male with a ticking of black across back and shoulders.

"And we will fly as escort above," cried several of the raptors.

"And I will announce you," croaked a raven.

"Then we go," Firekeeper said.

She longed to place her hand on Blind Seer's shoulder, but she was not quite ready to give up her bow. Besides, the gesture might make them look weak, and undo all Blind Seer's careful stalking. She still wondered how he had found a path that would carry them to Virim while leaving the Bound's honor intact. Judging from a certain stiffness to his shoulders as he began to walk, Blind Seer was rather astonished himself. Clearly, he half expected the need to fight.

Elation launched herself skyward with a mocking shriek—probably meant for a certain golden eagle. She caught the wind with admirable ease.

"We go!" she cried. "We go!"

XXXII

 THE RAVENS SUCCEEDED in getting a message to Doc and Elise. Bitter reported that he felt fairly certain that nothing had happened to arouse too great an interest in what might be going on at the Setting Sun stronghold.

A date and place for a meeting was set up. Once he had

spoken to Ynamynet and others of the Nexus Islands informal ruling body and received their permission to confide in his friends, Derian impulsively invited both Isende and Tiniel to come with him.

"After all," he said, "finding you was what brought me out here. It would be good if Elise and Doc could see for themselves that you really exist."

Both twins accepted, although Derian felt that Tiniel's reasons had less to do with any interest in meeting the Bright Havenese and more with providing a chaperon for his sister. Even so, Derian didn't mind. If whatever was growing between himself and Isende developed, Tiniel would be a part of his life, whether or not Derian liked Isende's twin.

As they prepared for the gate to be opened, Derian promised Ynamynet that they wouldn't be gone long.

"I know we're taking away much needed hands," he apologized, "but I know Elise. She'll push and pry, and we'll find ourselves defending ourselves on yet another front. We need to have the New World mainland as a point of retreat if nothing more."

Ynamynet nodded. "I agree. I cannot imagine that anyone who would befriend not only you but Firekeeper as well would be easily dissuaded when she sets her mind to a purpose."

"In my message, I asked Elise and Doc to pick up some small supplies for us in Gak," Derian said, realizing that for all his pleasure at the prospect of seeing his friends he still felt guilty about leaving the Nexans. "I checked with Zebel and Harjeedian, learned what we needed for the hospital and sent along a list. Our bringing back those supplies, at least, should help. And Eshinarvash assures me that the riding animals haven't been let go completely wild. He has three waiting for us on the other side, so we'll go faster than on foot."

Ynamynet gave Derian a reassuring smile, a far cry from her usually cool expression.

"I can run things here for a few days. You will be missed, but I assure you, we can manage."

Impulsively, Derian reached out and grasped the Once Dead's slender hand in thanks. Her skin felt astonishingly cold. With a flash of insight, he thought he knew what queri-nalo had stolen from the Once Dead, and felt bone-deep pity.

"I'll be back," he promised. "We aren't going to abandon you."

Ynamynet's smile was the warmest he had ever seen from her.

"I never thought that for a moment—and I'll make certain that no one else does either."

THEY MET UP with Elise and Doc at the second ford along the almost invisible trail that connected the Setting Sun stronghold to the city-state of Gak. To Derian's complete sur-prise, the two adults were alone except for the infant Elexa.

Derian's sense of smell and his hearing were both improved since his transformation, and he knew no one was hiding in the shrubs or even close by, around the bend in the trail. Leaving his mount in Isende's care, he trotted out into the open, trying to act matter-of-fact even though self-consciousness about let-ting his friends see his new appearance in daylight burned along his nerves.

"You're alone?" he called, rather than any more standard greeting.

"We are," Elise assured him. "Our escort is made up of na-tives of Liglim. When I told them that we were crossing into lands held by the yarimaimalom, and that the yarimaimalom themselves would keep us safe, they remained hesitant about leaving important foreigners like us without protection, but when the ravens . . ."

Here, clearly having chosen the moment for dramatic ef-fect, Bitter and Lovable glided from the branches of an oak near the ford and strutted about importantly in front of Elise.

Elise grinned and shook her head in bemusement. "But when the ravens informed the Liglimom through appropriate signs and omens, as read by the aridisdu in our escort, that we would be safe, the Liglimom fell into line. It was rather dis-turbing to see such confident people taking orders from ravens."

"I can understand that," Derian said, "almost. For me, I'm getting used to being ordered around by almost anything with fur, fangs, or feathers. At least Bitter and Lovable didn't decide to talk. That would have probably created theological controversy."

Bitter fluffed out his feathers, while Lovable bounced and made little ears with her head feathers. Derian needed no translator to know that Lovable had wanted to show off her new skill, but that Bitter had dissuaded her.

Elise looked puzzled, but Derian didn't take time to explain. She'd probably learn soon enough.

"Well," Derian said, embracing Elise and clasping hands with Doc, and then motioning for Isende and Tiniel to join him, "welcome to the Setting Sun land grant. These are the formal holders of the land, by claim dating to before the coming of the Plague and still acknowledged in Gak. Isende, Tiniel, these are my good friends, Doc and Elise, more formally known as Sir Jared Surcliffe and Lady Elise Archer."

Elise dipped a curtsy and Doc, hampered somewhat by the fact that he held little Elexa in a sling across his chest, bowed. In turn, Isende and Tiniel made polite gestures of greeting after the fashion of the Liglimom.

Doc and Elise had established a small, comfortable camp, and invited their visitors to join them. When they were settled, Elise went for the heart of the matter with a directness worthy of Firekeeper.

"Derian, what's going on? Where are Firekeeper and Blind Seer? Why did you ask to meet us here rather than wherever it is you have been staying?"

Derian thought how to frame his reply. He and Ynamynet had discussed how much he should reveal, and Ynamynet had agreed that Derian might need to tell everything. She had asked that he try and swear the others to secrecy and he had agreed.

"I don't know where Firekeeper is," he began, "and I'm not being evasive. Truth says she believes they are still alive, but her ability to read the future is less than reliable."

"I remember," Elise said. "Truth went mad, didn't she?"

Derian snorted a humorless laugh. "It's worse than that now. The same 'curse' that changed me seized on her as well. I don't speak jaguar, but from what I understand Truth now sees all possible futures all at once. She does her best to filter through to those that are most likely, but it's difficult. However, she says that Firekeeper—or rather something that she refers to as 'Firekeeper's scent'—crops up frequently, so Truth believes this indicates that our wolf-woman is still alive."

"And Blind Seer with her," Doc said. "Or so we can hope. Where did she go?"

"To tell you that, I need to tell you a great deal more," Derian said, "and before I tell you that, I need to swear you to secrecy."

Doc was inclining his head as if to nod, but Elise looked guarded.

"Secrecy? From whom? From everyone or just from the locals? From our own government as well?"

"Everyone," Derian said. "Governments in particular. I can assure you we're not planning a revolt—far from it—but we've stumbled on things that are better not too widely shared."

Elise frowned, but her gaze rested on Derian's hands with their thick, hoof-like nails, on his mane-like hair, on his eyes, once hazel-green, now dark brown and almost without a white. She looked then at Isende and Tiniel, and her frown shifted to a look of deep concern.

"Derian, I need to know more before I can promise something like that. Not only am I an assistant to an ambassador—as you are, in case you've forgotten—but I am a future baron of Bright Haven. I need more than vague warnings of doom."

Derian had expected this, and when he felt Isende shifting and knew the younger woman was feeling indignant on his behalf, he reached out and patted her arm in reassurance.

"Very well, Elise. Do you remember what started the war between Bright Bay and Hawk Haven?"

"Of course I do," Elise said indignantly. "Queen Valora—Queen Gustin IV as she was then—started meddling in our local politics, trying to press her own candidate for the throne of Hawk Haven. Then rumors got out that Bright Bay still possessed magical artifacts. Suddenly, we found Stonehold and Waterland breaking their alliances with us and turning against us. New Kelvin wasn't far behind."

Derian nodded. "And all that was over the rumor of three magical artifacts whose very existence and powers were mere rumor. Had Allister Seagleam, as he was then, not allied himself with King Tedric, and had we not won that battle, not only wouldn't Bright Haven exist to make you and me assistant ambassadors, but Hawk Haven and Bright Bay might exist only as sections of other lands. And all of that was over the rumor of three magical artifacts."

"Is this about magical artifacts again?" Elise said.

"That," Derian said, "and worse."

Elise pressed her hands to the corners of her eyes, looking down into nothing, not even stirring when baby Elexa began to fuss. After a long moment, she reached out for the child.

"Can you promise me that these artifacts are not in danger of being turned against Bright Haven—or the Liglimom?"

"I wish I could," Derian said. "The honest fact is, if those with whom I am currently working and I fail, well, not only are those artifacts likely to be turned against those lands, but none of the New World will be safe."

Elise gasped and Doc gave a sharp cry of surprise.

"It's that bad," the knight said.

"It's that bad, and probably worse," Derian said. "Honestly, one of the reasons I want to tell you about this is so that if we do fail, someone will have warning."

"Derian, why haven't you asked for help before now?" Elise said.

"We can't," Derian said. "It's a very complicated story."

Elise looked at Doc, then down at the toothlessly smiling face of her baby, then back at Derian.

"So you found more than these fine twins when you went looking for them, didn't you? I think you'd better tell me. I'll keep silence, as long as I have your word that I can speak if danger threatens those lands to which I have sworn loyalty."

Doc nodded somberly. "That goes for me, too."

Derian felt relieved. "This is going to take a long time. Bitter, can you go back and have Enigma tell Ynamynet what we're doing?"

"Yes," croaked the raven. "Tell."

Elise jumped, jolting Elexa, who started fussing, and Doc laughed.

"So that's what you mean by them talking. That's startling."

"Good," said Lovable, bouncing up and down. "Go. Back. Soon."

The two ravens took wing and before the sound of their wings had faded, Derian had begun his tale. He began with the search for the twins, and the apparently deserted stronghold, and where that had led. He told of querinalo, and of what it did to those who had even the least magical talent. The twins helped him there, and when the discussion turned to the Once Dead and their powers.

He had to explain about the Meddler as well, and that was incredibly difficult, for although the people of Hawk Haven and Bright Bay paid great respect to their ancestors, ghosts and disembodied spirits were things that belonged to fireside stories. However, when he reminded them that giant wolves and talking ravens had belonged in the same category until Firekeeper and Blind Seer had crossed the Iron Mountains, they did their best to put disbelief aside.

After he explained how they had been forced to take the Nexus Islands, he did his best to explain why they had decided not only to hold them but to keep them a secret. Finally, he revealed the danger those islands were now in, and what the loss of the coming battle would mean to both the Old World and the New.

"And you're sure about this invasion?" Elise asked at last. "The word of an untrustworthy ghost, dreams, and visions seem very little to go on."

Derian spread out his hands so she could not ignore them, and looked her squarely in the eyes.

"So I might have said once," he agreed, "but no more. I believe an invasion is coming, and indeed, we dreaded as much even before the Meddler came troubling Firekeeper. Remember, the New World knew little of these gates, but the Old World not only knew of them, they have had use of them for at least the last ten years. Do you think they would give them up lightly?"

"No," Elise agreed. "They wouldn't. You are fortunate to have absolute proof of your suspicions. I am sorry for having spoken without thought."

Isende smiled. "It was hard for me to accept as well, Lady Archer. If Truth had not confirmed the validity of my dreams, speaking of certain things I had seen before I did, I might have doubted as well."

"So you've become some sort of warlord?" Doc said hesitantly. "That's hard to believe."

"Not a warlord," Derian said. "I leave the fighting to others. Rather I am something of a glorified administrator—a town mayor. We have very few adults, especially considering what we suspect we will face. All of us are doing two or three jobs, and when the time comes to fight, that will be all of our jobs—except for those who will be trying to save the lives of the injured."

"I wish I could get there!" Doc said, clenching his hands into fists.

"If Firekeeper and Blind Seer succeed in their mission," Derian said, "you could come across, but even the weakened form of querinalo can be deadly. I will not risk exposing anyone to it, especially one such as you who is certain to fall ill. You might help us for a few days, before the illness strikes you, but then . . ."

"Then I'd just be another invalid," Doc said, "and one for whom you likely couldn't spare the kind of careful tending that pulled you and Blind Seer and this 'Plik' you mentioned through the purely physical damage the fevers would have done."

"Knowing what you're up against," Elise said, "I can understand why Firekeeper went looking for this Virim, but Derian, is it wise? The Plague freed those without magic from domination by those who some chance of birth gave power. Is that right?"

Tiniel spoke for the first time other than to correct some point in Derian's account, and his voice trembled with barely suppressed fury.

"How can you say that, 'Lady' Archer? What did you do to earn your titles other than be born into the right family? What is the difference?"

Elise blinked at him, astonished by the violence of his attack.

"I suppose the difference is," she replied slowly, "that I have responsibilities that come with my social position. The sorcerers had nothing but competition between themselves to rein them in."

"You only have those responsibilities," Tiniel said, "because you find it convenient. I'm sure not every noble in your land is so ethical. I'm sure there are peasants and commoners who live pretty miserable lives because the ones who own the lands on which they labor think of them as nothing more than another resource to exploit."

"Tin . . ." Isende said, resting a hand on her brother's arm. "Calm down."

Tiniel did not. "It makes me want to spit, the way these northerners talk as if magical ability—especially spellcasting ability—makes a person automatically into a horror. You're not, 'Sende. I wouldn't have been. Our father told different stories, stories about how wonderful it was to live in a world where magic made all sorts of things possible. The hypocrisy of this woman makes me sick. Here she sits, cradling a baby that probably would be dead if she hadn't been lucky enough to have a husband with a powerful magical healing ability, and she has the gall to question the wisdom of letting magic return to the world."

Elise was aghast, Doc clearly furious. Derian tried to interrupt, but Tiniel turned his anger on to him.

"Don't try and tell me anything. Querinalo only improved you, refined you, and yet I've had to watch you moping about as if your transformation makes you some sort of monster. Do you think the Nexans would follow you like they are if you weren't Once Dead—blessed with many gifts? I promise you, they wouldn't. I wonder if Isende would be mooning after you like she's been if you weren't Once Dead—you and her both!"

A painful silence fell, broken by Elise speaking in proper drawing-room tones quite incongruous in a woodland camp.

"Well, I see there are many ways of viewing this matter, are there not? No matter. You have made your choice, Derian, but I think you should realize that not everyone is going to think you made the right choice."

"I will deal with that," Derian said, "if and when it becomes an issue. However, I think you now realize why I requested that you and Doc keep secret what we have confided in you. I actually have thought about the ramifications of our decision. However, when you see a flood coming, you don't usually sit around and worry how the pits from which you're digging the dirt and gravel with which to build a dam may breed mosquitoes after the spring rains."

"No," Elise said. "I can see that."

"So now you know what has kept me from my duties to Ambassador Sailor," Derian said. "I think I made the right choice."

"I think you made the only choice," Elise said, "given the options open to you."

"Thank you."

Doc looked at Elise. "How long before we must return to the city-states?"

"We have a moonspan or so," Elise said. "I told Ambassador Sailor not to expect us until Dog Moon, and, I can continue to send him letters so he won't fret too much."

"Then I'd like to stay here," Doc said, "or rather there, in the twins' stronghold, if they'll have me as a guest. I may not be able to cross to the Nexus Islands, but perhaps I can help from there. There must be herbs I can gather, medical preparations I can make."

Elise nodded. "That's a good idea. We might be able to help in other ways, too. You mentioned children and a few invalids. Before you feared to evacuate them because you could not spare those needed to watch them. Why not let Doc and I do so?"

"That's a lot to take on," Derian warned.

"Maybe some of the yarimaimalom would help," Elise said. "You mentioned that most of them cannot cross to the Nexus Islands because only those who were imprisoned there and survived know they can cross safely. However, some of the other yarimaimalom must feel a desire not to see the Nexus Islands fall to those who treated their kin with such cruelty."

"That's a thought," Derian admitted. "I can't imagine a single Nexan who wouldn't fight better and harder for knowing that their children were safe."

"What if everyone wants to retreat?" Tiniel said.

"No one has asked to yet," Derian said, "and the option has always been there. I think that all of us know retreat isn't really an option. What safety that could be won would only be an illusion, a long waiting for the day that the Once Dead break through some gate, somewhere."

"True," Tiniel said. "I keep forgetting. Short of destroying all the gates, that isn't an answer."

"And we can't destroy all the gates," Derian said. "The Nexus Islands are just that, a nexus, a crossroads, but there are other gates. We'd miss something, and then any advantage we have would be lost."

Elise said softly, "I can tell you have thought a great deal about this—not only about the present, but about the future as well. I'll remember that when the time comes to speak before whoever rules in Bright Haven."

Derian shrugged. "Thank you, but that future seems a long time away. Right now, I'm thinking I need to get back to the Nexans. For all we know, the invasion began while we sat here talking."

"Wait until morning," Doc suggested. "You've already had a long day."

Isende touched his arm. "Derian, you know that Enigma, at least, would manage to get you news. Trust Ynamynet. We'll go back tomorrow bringing very good news."

Derian allowed himself to be convinced. They spent the darkening hours in quiet conversation, and even Tiniel's mood brightened over good food and drink.

Derian slept that night in a roll of blankets near the fire, but although Isende slept just a few feet away, his thoughts were not of her, but rather of Firekeeper.

Hurry back, Firekeeper. Bring us what we need. Otherwise, I fear you will find no one left to come back to. I fear . . .

But his fears were so terrible and shapeless, Derian dared not give them shape, even in thought, and so Fear wearing charred bones and the sound of cracking stone followed Derian into sleep and twisted through his nightmares.

❦

FIREKEEPER KNEW SOMETHING of what to expect from a sorcerer's stronghold. Good Queen Elexa of Hawk Haven had told her many stories that featured this hero or that sturdy peasant or this valiant princess braving such places to win some treasure or honor or lover from the mysterious and powerful figure who dwelt within.

Then, too, Firekeeper had twice visited the far northern land of New Kelvin. As far as the wolf-woman knew, in all the New World, perhaps in all the Old World as well, New Kelvin was the one land in which the loss of magic had been mourned rather than celebrated.

New Kelvin had done its best to preserve not only the ways and manners of the sorcerers of old, but also their architectural styles and whims as well. From what she had seen there, Firekeeper had come to expect sorcerers to reside in high-jutting towers topped with sharp spiraling cones or jagged battlements or even both. She had come to expect heavy stone worked in elaborate and fanciful patterns, windows of brilliant, jewel-toned glass, and doors that seemed designed to encourage the idea that giants rather than mere humans dwelled within.

From the outside, Virim's stronghold fulfilled many of these expectations. It had towers of various heights, most topped with crenellated battlements rather than spires or cones. The door they approached was enormous, able to admit four or five humans on horseback, or a pack of wolves or a herd of elk. The windows were also large, set with heavy glass, clear central panes framed with deep borders of sky blue or forest green.

Yet for all the familiar elements, Virim's stronghold, studied now in the strong light of midday, rather than in the pale light of the Meddler's dream vision, seemed a bit peculiar.

For one, rather than being freestanding as was typical of human structures, it was built into the face of a granite cliff that served as the northeastern border of a tree-lined river meadow. The cliff itself was clearly a rough remnant of the mountains to the east, a massive mound of pale grey stone that was not quite a mountain, but was certainly far more than a hill.

The naked grey stone of the cliff was speckled with darker inclusions that Firekeeper realized were rough garnets running in erratic veins and clusters through the rock. These garnets were often in company with some mineral that gave back the sunlight in erratic sparkles. The effect was elegant, but distinctly muted.

"I wonder," she said aloud, "that this Virim did not make his lair more elaborate. I like the color of that stone well enough. It is good rock, solid and yet with interest for the eye. But the spellcasters we have heard of, whose relics we have seen, their tastes were like a raven's, favoring what was bright and shining."

The enormous honey-gold bear who headed the escort that now led them toward Virim's keep made a grumpy, grumbly sound that nonetheless sounded like pride.

"Virim made himself champion of the non-human world. Why would he share the spellcasters' tastes for gaudy display any more than he shared their other traits? He made his den as we Beasts do, a place for need, not display."

Blind Seer huffed soft laughter. "Need? I think you are

righter than you admit, bear. Mother wolves den when their pups are small and weak and need protection. Rabbits build elaborate dens, but not for show. Those many tunnels are meant to delay the weasel and the badger, not because they impress the mole. I think Virim built as a Beast would—for need, and his need was defense, not display."

Firekeeper nodded. "You're right, Blind Seer. I was distracted by my memories of New Kelvin, but in some ways this place reminds me of Eagle's Nest Castle in Hawk Haven. Queen Elexa told me that no force of arms could take that castle, but that she who would become the first ruler of Hawk Haven took it by stealth and trickery."

"So Virim was not quite certain his curse would work," Blind Seer mused, sitting down and scratching vigorously behind one ear while he studied the looming grey-stone structure. "Not only did he bind the Bound to protect him and his, he took the time to make these walls in case they failed."

The bear did not like this turn of the conversation at all. He had paused when Blind Seer sat—there was no Beast who did not know the discomfort of a difficult-to-reach flea—but now without signal or comment, he dropped to all fours and loped forward.

Those others of the Bound who had made themselves part of the escort followed the bear's lead, and rather than cause themselves any difficulty—after all, they wanted to go to the stronghold—Firekeeper and Blind Seer joined the group.

Elation had taken wing when they had come to open ground, and now she shrieked a question.

"Where are the creatures?" she asked. "There are no signs of them, not even the little ones even the poorest humans always keep for themselves: the chickens, ducks, and pigeons."

"The falcon thinks with her belly," Blind Seer said, breathing deeply as he scented the wind, "but she has a good point. If Virim and his people do not travel, I can understand why there would be no horses, but I don't even smell a pig or a cow. There are no sheep either. What do these humans do for clothing and food? Do you Bound hunt for them?"

The black-ticked wolf looked at Blind Seer in contempt.

"Of course we do not hunt for them. I thought you knew something of spellcasters and sorcerers. They have no need for hunting or for keeping animals such as you mention. Whatever they desire comes to them at their least whim. I remember seeing such when I was a pup."

"Oh?" The cant of Blind Seer's ears and tail expressed polite interest and mild doubt.

The wolf continued, a growl under-rumbling his account.

"I had been playing with one of my sisters in this very meadow. She stumbled and caught her leg in a twist of vine. Silly thing began whining and whimpering, and before the Ones could come and break her free, a human came forth. He cut the vines, and then to distract my sister while he felt along her leg, he created a little animal—I think it was gopher, some small rodent, in any case—from nothing but a wave of his hand. This startled her so that she forgot to snap when he felt her leg, even though it was badly sprained."

"Did he heal it?" Firekeeper asked.

"The gopher?" The wolf flattened his ears, clearly doubting her intelligence. "Not after she had eaten it. Greedy creature didn't even leave me a bit of fur."

"I meant your sister's sprain."

"I don't remember. Probably. She lived to grow strong, and possesses a very firm bite."

"A good ending to any tale," Blind Seer said politely.

Firekeeper appreciated his manners. The other wolf was beginning to bristle and raise his hackles, and this was not the time for a fight.

The bear's increased pace had brought him to the shadow of the enormous doors. Here he paused.

"We have escorted you to Virim's stronghold as you requested. This is as far as our trail takes us."

Firekeeper held up her arm in signal, and Elation dropped to take her place. Then Firekeeper addressed the gathered Bound.

"You are not coming in? Don't you wish to explain to Virim why you have let us through to his doorstep?"

The bear snorted. "As if you cannot talk for yourself! You

and your pack mates are very good at talking. I wish you well with it. Certainly, your bow and knife will mean little to Virim."

Firekeeper, remembering her iron arrowheads and steel blade, wondered otherwise, but thought nothing was to be gained by the mention.

Blind Seer glanced at her. "Shall we go?"

Firekeeper nodded. Elation made a derisive sound.

"Why else did we come this far?" the peregrine said.

The three went forward without a look back or a parting word for the gathered Bound.

For their part, the Bound watched in silence, waiting to see if the stronghold's doors would open to admit the strangers or if the portals would remain closed, thus signaling Virim's desire that the Bound carry out their sworn duty.

But even before the three had mounted the final step, the doors were swinging wide to admit them. Wolf and woman walked forward, pace matched by pace, the falcon watchful on the woman's shoulder.

"There is no scent of fear about them," the stag marveled.

"Are they then so brave?" asked the boar.

"No," grunted the bear, turning away. "It is because they are fools."

XXXIII

"I CANNOT CATCH the scent of whoever opened those doors," Blind Seer said as they paced forward.

The cant of his ears and tail showed alert interest, but Firekeeper, who knew him well, was aware of the tension that lay beneath the apparently confident attitude.

"I doubt your nose is at fault," Firekeeper replied. "I am

certain that people who could curse an entire world have ways of opening a door from a distance."

Without hesitation, they crossed the threshold that opened into an elongated ovoid chamber, whose shape recalled that of a human eye. A light, clear and brilliant, yet soft as the edge of a single candle flame, illuminated the vast space, showing floor and walls carved from stone the pale yellow-white of ivory.

Firekeeper did not need to look to know the illumination came from light blocks such as she had seen built into many structures constructed by the Old Country rulers. Most of these light blocks had been dead, but on Misheemnekuru she had seen a few of those blocks functioning. She had admired their effectiveness then, but now she realized that what she had seen there had been as a cloud-covered sky in contrast to the pure light of sunrise. Yet the pale stone of the walls glowed with none of the scorching brilliance of sunlight. The light remained soft and pleasant.

By this light, Firekeeper and her companions saw that the back edge of the ovoid entrance hall was lined with evenly spaced doors, each picked out in the palest of gold but otherwise undifferentiated from the walls around them. Even as Firekeeper studied those doors, wondering where they led, she contrasted this light-clad chamber to the grey-walled fortress they had entered.

"Perhaps Virim did wish to conceal his den," she said to Blind Seer and Elation. "Surely this place shows none of that humility and desire to be one with the natural world of which the bear spoke with such confidence."

Elation, who had been soaring about the upper reaches of the ovoid chamber, swept down and perched on Firekeeper's extended arm.

"The sky is as natural as any dark and messy forest tangle," she said, cocking her head to one side. "That is what this room reminds me of—the sky when you are flying, when nested in light and wind, with only the barest hints of color around you."

"Perhaps," Firekeeper said. "I know very little of the sky."

She turned to Blind Seer who had walked a few paces into the chamber and was inspecting it, nose to the polished stone of the floor.

"Can you catch any trails that might guide us to choose one door over the others? I have no great desire to chase a rabbit in and out of its warren. In those games, the rabbit ends up sleeping soundly somewhere and the wolf goes hungry."

"Think badger or weasel," Blind Seer cautioned, "or even fox. This is no rabbit we hunt. The rabbit relies on speed and caution alone. This Virim has teeth."

"I am warned," Firekeeper said, following the blue-eyed wolf deeper into the chamber.

She had kept some of her attention for the great doors through which they had entered, and now saw them begin to slide slowly shut. She made no move to stop them, but watched with equanimity.

"That," she commented, "I expected. Fox or badger this Virim, perhaps, but most certainly human."

Blind Seer and Elation, both all too aware that many humans equated caging with controlling, indicated their agreement.

"So," Firekeeper said, "no trail to any of these doors?"

"Not by scent," the blue-eyed wolf replied.

"Nor by sight," the peregrine added. "I scanned from above and these stones are pristine, without the least fleck of dirt or leaf mold much less any pattern of wear that would show one door has been more frequently used than another."

"All in keeping with our 'bad smell,' " Firekeeper said then.

She and Blind Seer had shared their suspicions with Elation during the return journey, and the falcon had admitted such made sense, although she herself had detected nothing more odd than was usual with humans.

"But then the days when I knew more about humans than did the two of you are long past," Elation had admitted, and Firekeeper had found herself both discomfited and pleased by this casual promotion.

So now Elation waited for direction, her gold-rimmed eyes

nonetheless watchful and alert. Firekeeper addressed both her companions.

"Humans are very strange creatures," Firekeeper said. "At first I thought them very like wolves in things that were important. Remember, Earl Kestrel went west of the Iron Mountains because the humans of Hawk Haven were circling and snarling over who would be their One. Lacking the fangs that would give him a solid bite in that battle, Earl Kestrel sought someone who could be those fangs for him. He hoped to find Prince Barden, but failing in that, he found me. I think he saw me as a tool, something he could hone and sharpen as humans do their swords and knives, then turn to his need."

Neither wolf nor falcon interrupted the wolf-woman's telling, although they knew this tale as well as did the teller. Perhaps they sensed she spoke to another audience.

"But I did not become some easily used edged blade, and Norvin Norwood did not find himself father to a princess waiting to be a queen. He accepted this with becoming grace, gave me home and name, even when I insisted I needed neither. Others who fought in that battle did not take their defeat so well. From the actions of two of these, brother and sister, I learned something very valuable, something that separates human from beasts more essentially than any matter of fang or claw or furred coat."

Blind Seer was studying her intently, more intently, Firekeeper thought, than her words merited, but she put that from her. One battle at once. This one, although joined so very quietly, must have her full attention.

"What did you learn, dear heart?" Blind Seer asked.

"I learned that while Beasts live in the world, humans live in two places simultaneously: that of the world and that which exists within their own minds. Sometimes these are close together. Sometimes they are not. Think on it, and you will catch the true scent of this trail."

Blind Seer did not disagree. Indeed, if anything the thoughtful expression on his features became more pronounced. Firekeeper looked at that expression of worry—

lines deepened between his eyes and head tilted slightly to one side—and thought how odd it was that a human head and a wolf's could show the same expression.

But perhaps it was not so odd, given how alike wolves and humans could be—and how very different.

She went on, speaking of that difference.

"Think of Melina," she said, "and all that she did because she came to believe that what she had imagined within her mind was as real—more real—than the events happening around her. Some might say she won that battle for who would rule after King Tedric in Hawk Haven, but because Princess Sapphire did not win in the fashion Melina had imagined, Melina could not accept this transformed world. She left it, burrowing deeper within herself, and what she did then, well . . . It is too much to tell, but Melina's end shows the danger of living too much inside the mind without adapting to the world without.

"But humans do this all the time. Beasts do not. Even Beasts like Truth who have the gift for seeing the future cannot be said to live within their minds as humans do. The many futures the diviners see are still rooted in reality. The diviners are seeing them, but not imagining them. In contrast, humans can live completely separated from the world around them, and yet believe themselves not only sane but even wise."

"This is true?" Elation said.

"This is true," Firekeeper replied. "And I think within this lies the answer to the riddle of these many doors—so alike, different only in their placing. In this, too, lies the answer to this strange stronghold, like but unlike any such place I have ever seen before."

"So which door?" Elation asked.

"You ask that as a Beast would," Firekeeper said with a laugh. "I will answer as a human. Any door will do, any and all. We are not within a place, rather we are within Virim's mind, within the palace built by his dreams, within the fortress built to protect those dreams, within the prison that has distorted those dreams into nightmares so twisted that even their creator does not recognize them, any more than he knows himself."

"Are we trapped then?" Elation asked, flapping her wings and taking ungainly flight.

"Virim is," Firekeeper said, "and our task is to find him and bring him to where he can see reality once more, and in that reality give us the answer we seek."

"Answer?" Blind Seer said, shaking as if he had run through a nest of dewdrop-soaked cobwebs and sought to clear them from his coat.

"Answer," Firekeeper said simply. "The one we have come here seeking, the answer to how the curse Virim laid upon the world may be lifted so that reality—good and bad, complex and simple—may move along its course once more."

"All well and good," Elation said, soaring higher, circling to inspect the doors, "but where do we begin our search?"

"We begin it with the Virim we have already met," Firekeeper said simply. "Bruck."

"Bruck? But we left him behind in the cave."

"Bruck," Firekeeper repeated. "He is Virim, and so no matter where we imprisoned him, he is here."

"Virim? I don't understand," Elation said.

"That is because you are a Beast and sane," Firekeeper replied. "Bruck is Virim, Virim seeking to know us and to escape himself. I know this because it is the only thing that makes sense—far more sense than to believe that a pack of humans would live in isolated harmony for over a hundred years. Bruck is Virim, the Virim who desperately wants to know us, and when he hears our call, he will not be able to resist coming forth."

Elation's shriek of disbelief was broken off in mid-cry.

Bruck had appeared, now standing a few feet away from Firekeeper and Blind Seer. He looked much as he had when they had first met him. The ravages of their journey did not mark him, nor did the burns left by the iron wire show on his wrists and ankles. His robes were clean and his feet shod in unworn slippers.

Only his gaze was changed from this first time they had met him. No longer was he hanging upside down, waiting for rescue from a trap; now he studied them with calm, inquisitive eyes.

Firekeeper did not wait for Bruck to speak, for she suspected that would be to allow herself to become trapped within the spirals of the fragment of Virim's personality that was Bruck.

"We are here to meet with Virim," she said.

"Virim is dead," Bruck replied. "I told you this."

"Then we would meet with the One who has taken over in his stead," Firekeeper replied.

"There is no One," Bruck protested. "Life is not as simple as you wolves seem to believe. There are ramifications, complications, issues, contingencies."

"Show me those then," Firekeeper said.

And he did.

Bruck fragmented. No longer did a single weedy, fair-haired man stand in front of them. Instead, they were surrounded by a crowd larger than Firekeeper could easily count.

There were old men with trailing beards and young men whose skin had never known the faintest fur. There were vital, warlike figures clad in glistening armor and bearing staffs topped with sharp blades, and bent aesthetes in robes so heavily embroidered that the thaumaturges of New Kelvin would have melted in envy. There were neat, scholarly figures, businesslike and professional, glancing into crystals set atop their polished staffs as they spoke. There were rough-clad woodsmen wearing buckskin trousers rather than robes, bows slung over their backs and their staffs shod in metal to protect the foot from wear.

There was even a mountain sheep, curved horns faceted like diamonds, and delicate hooves shining with gold.

Firekeeper immediately noted that for all the many, many differences between these men they all bore features in common. It was harder to tell with those who wore beards that covered their faces and trailed down their chests, but even in those whose eyebrows were so bushy as to be nearly another beard, she thought she saw something alike in the shape and pale greenish grey of the eyes.

Again, although the warriors and woodsmen were upright figures, carrying themselves with unconscious strength and health, they still shared something with the most attenuated of the aesthetes, with the most bent of the greybeards, even with the wicked, twinkling eyes of the mountain sheep.

"One and the same," Blind Seer said, "one and the same. This nose tells me if your eyes do not."

"My eyes see enough," Firekeeper confirmed. "So it is as we thought. Virim either never had a group of followers, or those followers are dead and dust now. All that is left is Virim."

"Virim," said Blind Seer, his hackles rising although otherwise he remained calm and controlled, "is quite enough."

Firekeeper nodded and pressed her hands to her ears. The many Virims had one other thing in common. They talked and talked and talked and talked. Old voices, cracked from too much use. Young voices, breaking high or low when they most desired gravitas. Bellowing voices, accustomed to command. Strong, clear voices that spoke softly yet carried, reminding Firekeeper somehow of the howling of a wolf. Intermixed with this babble of human voices was the bleating of the mountain sheep, the flat, animal noise still sharing something in common with all these shades and tones of human sound.

And they talked of ramifications, complications, issues, and contingencies.

"We must do something, else the New World will be lost, her uniqueness destroyed by the unbridled power of the Old World."

"Let the New World learn to find her own strength. If we intervene we will find ourselves weakening the very thing we seek to protect."

"There is no time, no time, no time!"

"The Beasts deserve protection, just as they deserve respect."

"What of humans? What of those who rely upon the magic you would eliminate?"

"Natural? What is more natural than magic?"

"We cannot give way. If we do, all we have invested in will vanish. Where will I be then?"

"Ebbing away, going who knows where . . . Why not use it? There is nothing wrong with that."

"Gain? Gain from what should be an act of the purest altruism? You are mad. It will corrupt the effort."

"Who wants to live forever?"

"Forever? Just long enough to make sure that the world is safe. Just long enough. Surely just long enough."

"Weaken the curse. Why not? Just a little. Surely those to survive those fever fires would not then abuse the gift they have been permitted to preserve. Surely not."

"They call themselves Once Dead. Many are as bad as any from whom they are descended. Perhaps the taint is in the talent."

"Then what of our talent, my talent, this talent we have turned to good, to death, to preservation, to death, to life, to live."

And the mountain sheep bleated and although Firekeeper knew the language of the Beasts she did not learn anything from what it said, for all it did was laugh.

"They argue out what brought them to this point," Blind Seer said. "It is as you said. Humans live within their heads. In Virim's mind, this is more real than the world without—the world he has clawed so deeply that it still bleeds from the wound."

Firekeeper nodded. "Virim argues with himself. They do. He does. How strange it is. Even they—or he—does not seem to know if he is one or many. Which is the truth?"

"Both," Blind Seer said simply. "Have you never seen a buck try to break both right and left, and so freeze in place? His body is holding still, but in his muscles he is running. So it is here."

"What can we do?" Elation shrieked over the clamor. (Not one head turned at the sound. It seemed that the Virims heard only themselves.) "We cannot ask these for an end to the curse or even for its intensification. We could argue until summer became winter and then summer again, and never reach resolution."

"Yet the answer we want is here," Firekeeper said, clenching her fists in frustration. "I know it."

She looked at Blind Seer for help, but the blue-eyed wolf only huffed his own confusion.

No wonder, Firekeeper thought with sudden insight. *Like them he is trapped within an unresolved conflict. Like them, he has taken one step down the trail and found the scent no more clear.*

She reached out and touched Blind Seer in sympathy, anchoring herself in the immediacy of the tickling guard hairs, in the denseness of the fur beneath. She could feel the warmth of his body, the rise and fall of his breath, the beating of his heart beneath.

And from this an idea came.

"Make Virim face reality," she said. "That is our only answer. For too long—maybe even from years before he created the curse of querinalo—he has lived mostly within his own mind. Let us drag him out, make him face what the world has become."

"How will we do that?" Elation cried.

"We will take him with us," Firekeeper said, "back to the Nexus Islands."

The clamor from the arguing Virims did not still one bit, but Firekeeper suddenly felt as if she, Blind Seer, and Elation were isolated in a pocket of silence. Almost instinctively she understood the nature of that silence. They had been trapped within the chaos of Virim's mind, and in that chaos there was no place for anything but what Virim thought. Her decisiveness had encapsulated them, as it were, within her own mind.

At that moment, she noticed a fourth, a man standing a step away as if waiting to be invited to join their little group. At first she thought this was one of the Virims come, perhaps, to speak for the rest. Then she recognized the long iron-grey hair, the amber eyes that always seemed to hold a trace of mocking laughter.

"Meddler! You are here?"

The Meddler bowed neatly from the waist.

"I am indeed, Lady Wolf. You know I have tried to remain close to advise and assist you. A place such as this is not really very hard for me to manifest within."

"I thought you said that Virim's stronghold was protected from intrusion by such as you," Firekeeper said sharply.

"It is," the Meddler replied. "But when you entered, I was given a way in as well."

Firekeeper felt rather than heard Blind Seer's growl. She had never quite gotten around to explaining to him the strange price the Meddler had extracted from her in exchange for his help back when their initial search for Tiniel and Isende had led them into some very dangerous places.

She hoped she would not be forced to do so now—and hoped even more intensely that the Meddler would not take it upon himself to explain. She had no desire to explain to the wolf that she had let the Meddler kiss her, and that if he had asked for more, she would have felt honor bound to grant that favor as well.

And with that on your conscience, she thought, *you had the temerity to criticize the Bound for their fidelity to Virim. It seems that you might be no wiser in your alliances.*

But Blind Seer did not press, nor did the Meddler confide, and Firekeeper hurried to fill the awkward moment with words.

"We are taking Virim back to the Nexus Islands with us," she said. "Perhaps he will find it harder to argue when he is among those who will die when the invaders come."

The Meddler threw back his head and howled with laughter.

"That is wonderful!" he said. "Tell me, how are you going to force a sorcerer of such power to do your bidding?"

"As before," Firekeeper said, reaching into the pouch at her belt. "With iron. I am not sure that it harmed Bruck who was Virim as much as he made it seem it did, but I must believe that he fears it."

"Good," the Meddler said, and Firekeeper thought that she saw him move back a pace or so, as if he, too, reflexively stayed clear of the metal. "And how will you get him back in time?"

Firekeeper frowned. "In time?"

"Before the invaders arrive," the Meddler said. "Summer is upon us. Remember the fleets that I showed you? They have set sail and will reach the Nexus Islands long before Bear Moon reaches her first quarter. You cannot hope to travel back to New Kelvin and use the gate there to arrive in time—especially if you are slowed by a captive and the Bound harry your heels."

Before Firekeeper could retort that Derian and the rest would not fall to the invaders without giving a good fight, Blind Seer interrupted.

"We will use the gate to return," he said in a rumbling growl.

"Gate?" the Meddler repeated.

"Gate?" Firekeeper echoed, almost in the same breath.

"Gate," Blind Seer repeated firmly. "There must be one here. The sorcerers of old relied upon them too greatly for Virim to have done without. We will find it, and if it does not go directly to the Nexus Islands, then I think it will take us to some point from which we can more easily reach the Nexus Islands."

She thought she saw annoyance flicker in the Meddler's amber eyes.

So he knew, she thought, *or at least suspected.*

The Meddler schooled his expression into one of admiration.

"I think you are right. There probably is a gate of some sort. However, how will you operate it?" He turned his attention wholly to Firekeeper. "I could operate the gate for you, Lady Wolf. You may recall that I have done such for you in the past."

And been paid with a kiss, she thought, *and apparently with access to my thoughts and dreams. That's a higher price to pay than I knew.*

Blind Seer huffed a laugh nearly as mocking as the Meddler's own. "We have no need for your services, Meddler. When we find the gate, I will operate it for us."

It was the blue-eyed wolf's first admission of his power and abilities that was not tinged with shame. Indeed, he held his head with the pride of a hunter who knows he can outdistance the pack and earn the honor of the kill.

The Meddler looked delighted, but Firekeeper suspected that delight was feigned. She had no doubt the Meddler would have opened a hundred gates for her. She thought his interest in her and her ventures was sincere, but that didn't mean it was an interest free from self-interest.

"Virim first," she said. "Only after we have him will all this else matter. Elation, you have the sharp eyes of your kind, tell me this. How many greybeards are there in that muddle?"

The falcon, who had never ceased to watch the throng of arguing Virims, replied without pause. "More than I have talons upon my feet."

"And beardless youths?"

"Some fewer, but still a good number."

"And warriors clad in armor?"

"Two feet of talons at least."

"And serious-eyed scholars?"

"More than that, of many ages and wearing countless styles of attire."

"And mountain sheep?"

"One."

"One only?"

"One."

"Then that one is our prey."

As Firekeeper reached into her pouch to find appropriate lengths of iron wire, the Meddler asked, "Why choose that one, simply because there is only one?"

"Not only," Firekeeper said.

She considered her bow, but she did not want to kill Virim or even risk wounding him severely. She would need to hunt without using either that or her Fang.

The Meddler was looking at her as if he still desired an explanation, and she could see no harm in giving him at least a partial one.

"Virim's resentment of the Old World and its power over

the New dates from his youngest years, perhaps to the very time he realized his inborn ability would mean separation from home and all he loved, so that his masters could train and control him. We know this not only from the stories, but from the fact that there are quite young Virims amid those in the crowd.

"I think that each of those figures represents a time that Virim doubted himself, each time he came up with a path he could or could not take, a course of action that might or might not bring him his goal. In the century and more since he created the curse that would create genocide among those who had been not only his enemies and his rivals, but his friends, confidants, teachers, and perhaps even family, Virim has had much time for guilt and to argue with himself over the rights and wrongs of his actions.

"But the one thing that never split was the identity of himself as spellcaster, sorcerer, a man with power enough to do what he had done. He might have doubted the actions, but unlike Blind Seer and Derian he has never doubted the rightness of his having that power."

The Meddler nodded. "And you think that Virim the Sorcerer, the Spellcaster, is emblemized by that mountain sheep."

"I know it is so," Firekeeper said, and her confidence was not mere bravado. She did know, as certainly as she knew the difference between the tracks of a deer and elk. "And more importantly, so does Virim."

Blind Seer looked up at her, his blue eyes shining. Hunting together was something they had done since he was a stumble-footed pup growing into strength and she a human girl, by wolf standards, hardly less stumble-footed than that pup.

"Shall I cut him from the herd?"

"Do," Firekeeper said, "and Elation, will you fly high and cry the course to me so that I may be where I am needed?"

"With joy," the peregrine said.

"And me," the Meddler asked. "What can I do?"

"Anything you wish," Firekeeper said, "except get in our way. That we would not forgive."

The Meddler nodded. "I understand."

And Firekeeper, hearing Blind Seer's hunting howl break apart both the silence that had held them and the chaotic babble of the many Virims, thought that she caught a hint of respectful fear in the Meddler's eyes.

XXXIV

WHEN DERIAN RETURNED to the Nexus Islands he was slightly surprised to find neither Ynamynet nor Skea coming to meet him.

As soon as she had finished closing the gate after him, Kalyndra explained, "There has been news. Ships have been seen by the wingéd folk who have been scouting offshore."

Derian dropped the pack he had been carrying.

"If you would have someone get that to Doctor Zebel," he said, "I'd better get down and hear the rest."

Plik was translating the seabirds' report when Derian arrived at headquarters.

"The wingéd folk think the ships are still two or three days distant, but they admit that they are not the best judges of how quickly such vessels can travel."

"What about the condition of those aboard?" asked Skea.

"Several of the ships carry with them the scent of sickness and death," Plik said, "but those are in the minority. Overall, the ships and their crews seem to be in good health. Although deck space on even the largest vessels is limited, the wingéd folk report that they observed military drill under way."

"Are they sure?" Derian asked.

Plik gave a sad smile. "They base their assessment on what they have seen Skea directing here on the Nexus Islands."

"Ah . . ." Derian said. "Well, then I guess they know what they're talking about."

Skea was already getting to his feet. Derian held up a hand to forestall him.

"Wait a moment. I have news of my own."

Quickly, he reported the offer Doc and Elise had made.

Skea gave a tight smile. "I'm not one of those who thinks my soldiers will fight harder if those they love are in danger. If anyone wants their small children evacuated, fine, but no adults, and none of the bigger children. We're going to need every one."

Ynamynet touched him on the arm. "What about Sunshine?"

Skea frowned. "Send her, by all means. She's too small to be of help."

"But what if people think we're protecting our child and not letting them protect their own?"

Skea growled. "If we don't hold this island, it won't matter what side of the gate the children are on. Doom will come soon enough."

Derian raised a placating hand. "If anyone feels so strongly that their child is too young to stay here, let that child go. Doc and Elise will need some help watching the younger children in any case."

"I'll sound the assembly horn," Skea said. "The news that the ships are close must be spread."

I wonder, Derian thought, *just how many of the Nexans are going to come up with excuses to follow the children through the gate to the Sunset grant? I wonder how many are going to suddenly fall ill?*

But neither his cynicism nor Ynamynet's proved justified. The Nexans greeted with relief the news that the smaller children and invalids could be cared for on the mainland without depleting the defending force. No one suggested that everyone make that retreat. Once again, Derian was forced to face that the Nexans understood the danger to themselves wherever they should go if they lost control over the gates.

He said as much to Isende as they left the meeting.

"I know," she said. "To those of us from the New World, the

Old World isn't quite real. No matter what we know intellectually, deep inside we can't believe that in a few days we're going to be facing people set on conquest. It's real to the Nexans. They know those people, those places."

Derian nodded somberly. "You're right. In my belly, this island is where the gates lead. That's the end."

"I guess," Isende said, slipping her hand into his and squeezing, "we'll be forced to believe in a few days. I'm off to the kitchens. If we do evacuate the children, they're going to need to be sent with at least some supplies. I told Ynamynet I'd speak with the head cook about what we can spare."

"Not too much," Derian cautioned. "They'll have access to the dairy animals we have grazing there, and to all the hunting the forests offer. I wouldn't be surprised if the yarimaimalom bring them more meat than they can use."

"No doubt," Isende said, "but some hard bread that could be soaked in milk and maybe some soft cheese would be best for small children. I don't know if your friend Lady Elise knows how to make cottage cheese."

"If she doesn't," Derian said, "I bet Doc does. Isende, one question."

"Yes?"

"You've told us about receiving visions. Is there any chance you could try and reach the Meddler, send him a message that if Firekeeper is bringing help she should hurry it up?"

Isende's expression tightened. "I've been trying, Derian. I've already been trying, but I really don't know if I'm getting through. I think we need to accept that we're going to have to face this on our own. Firekeeper may avenge us, but I don't think she can possibly do anything to save us."

Derian trapped her hand between his.

"Don't give up, Isende. Skea's done wonders with the training, and there are very few areas where invading troops can come ashore. We should be able to hold out, at least for a while."

"But for how long?" Isende said, disengaging herself and moving away toward the kitchen. "Just for how long?"

❧

AT THE FIRST note of Blind Seer's howl, Firekeeper turned from the Meddler. Elation had flown to mark where their chosen prey had fled, but Firekeeper did not need the peregrine's help. The mountain sheep's glittering diamond horns and the flash of its golden hooves gave the creature away even amid the brilliantly dressed throng of Virim's other selves.

Twists of iron wire in hand, Firekeeper ran to intercept the mountain sheep. The Virims did not precisely move to get in her way, but neither did they move to let her through. The mountain sheep darted between the oblivious human figures, using them for cover as a more usual animal of its type would have used the rocks and boulders of the rocky fastnesses that were its home.

But quick and swift as the mountain sheep was, Firekeeper was swifter and more lithe. Her skills had been honed where the cost of a misstep would be going hungry. Virim had been given no such incentive.

Moreover, Blind Seer was pressing from the front, anticipating the mountain sheep's frantic dashes and darts so that more and more frequently Virim found what had been an open way was filled with the lean grey form of the enormous wolf.

The mountain sheep's flanks began to heave with the effort, and plaintive noises somewhere in between a sheep's bleats and a human cry came to Firekeeper's ears. They were pitiable sounds, laments of desperation, but Firekeeper was not to be so easily swayed. A rabbit screamed with fear, so did a deer. You pitied them that, but to relent was to find yourself starved.

Between the three they drove the mountain sheep back and forth through the throng of arguing sorcerers. On their second pass—or perhaps their third—Firekeeper noticed something odd. The throng was thinning. It was still dense, but even as she watched she saw two arguing armor-clad sorcerers dissolve into one. This new one turned to begin arguing with one of the more scholarly types, one whose ornate robes were embellished with emblems than Firekeeper was certain she had not seen together before.

His internal argument is beginning to simplify beneath the pressure we are putting on him, the wolf-woman realized. *And with that simplification, no doubt he will soon be stronger. This is one hunt where we cannot hope to run the prey until it collapses. Time to end the chase before we find ourselves overwhelmed.*

She howled the high, clear note that would tell Blind Seer of her intent. Without question, Blind Seer pressed forward, blocking the mountain sheep, forcing it to dart to one side. When the sheep turned, Firekeeper was ready. She raced forward, leaping so that she knocked into the mountain sheep with all her weight. It stumbled, and Blind Seer made sure that it went down.

Firekeeper did not pause. Anchoring the mountain sheep with her body, she twisted the iron wire about its forelegs, hobbling it effectively even if the iron had no power against it. Blind Seer had moved to the creature's rear and was trying to get a hold on the hind legs, but the flashing of those kicking hooves warned him back.

"Elation!" Firekeeper cried. "Distract him."

The peregrine need no further instruction. She had already been flying overhead. Now she folded her long, sharp-edged wings, going into one of the magnificent stoops for which her kind were known. Lying on its side as it was, the mountain sheep saw her coming, and its wail of despair was almost human.

It flinched, squishing its eyes shut as if the delicate tissue of the lids could protect the orbs from the falcon's sharp talons. Its back legs thrashed blindly, as if it could run on the air.

Firekeeper used the moment of panic to shift her weight, pinning the hind legs near the hip so that the range and power of motion were diminished. Blind Seer darted in then, grabbing the legs and holding them firmly between his jaws. He wasn't trying to cause harm, but blood leak out nonetheless.

Elation had caught herself in mid-dive and risen to the

heights again, ready to dive if Virim showed signs of continued protest, but whether because of the iron wire that bound it
or from the firm grasp of Blind Seer's fangs on its vulnerable
hind legs, or merely from the overwhelming force of terror,
the mountain sheep had ceased to struggle.

Firekeeper wrapped several loops of iron wire around its
hind legs, and told Blind Seer he could release his prey.

"The blood tasted human," the wolf said, licking traces
from the fur around his mouth with his tongue. "I nearly let go
when the taste stung against my tongue."

"But you didn't," Firekeeper said, giving him an affectionate hug.

Then, tentatively, ready to pin her prey if it should stir
again, she rose to her feet. As she did so, she realized the
room was so quiet that the sound of Elation's wings echoed in
the ovoid chamber.

"The sorcerers are gone," she said.

"The prospect of death," Blind Seer said, "must make arguments over ethical considerations seem trivial."

Firekeeper glanced around the room. The Meddler seemed
to have vanished as well. She wondered if this meant that they
were back in something that more closely resembled the
"real" world, or whether he had taken her warning about the
consequences of his interfering so seriously that he had made
himself scarce.

She spared no further thought for the strange spirit, but
took a few steps back from the mountain sheep and hunkered
down to study it. It lay there, flanks heaving, eyes pressed
shut, the sorcerer showing as little sense as the creature whose
shape he had adopted would have done in a similar situation.

Firekeeper wasn't fooled for a moment. She reached out
and gently twitched one of the mountain sheep's ears.

"We can call you Bruck or we can call you Virim, or we can
call you Wooly Lamb or Twinkly Hooves," she said conversationally. "I admit, I would find the last rather ridiculous, but
perhaps such suits you best. We are no dogs to be fooled by
our prey playing dead—and you are no opossum."

"What if it is preparing some spell?" Blind Seer said, hackles rising and ears folding back. "I wish we had one of the maimalodalum with us. I cannot be sure I could tell if magic is being worked."

"The scent would probably be drowned out by all that surrounds us," Firekeeper said, stroking the wolf along his back. "I think we are still within Virim's mind, and that he is trying to decide how to present himself. He may have stopped arguing with himself, but the habit is an old one, and not easily relinquished I suspect. If he does not answer me soon . . ."

But the wolf-woman never had to voice what she would have done, and that was probably a good thing, as she was not completely certain.

The edges of the mountain sheep grew blurred, as if it was attempting to change into something else. Then the lines became hard and firm again. However, Firekeeper was certain she had not imagined what she had seen. For one, the thin trickle of blood from where Blind Seer had held the mountain sheep's hind legs between his jaws had stopped and the wound was healed.

Useful, she thought, but said nothing aloud.

"It hurts," the sheep bleated in that plaintive voice. "The iron hurts."

"Does it?" Firekeeper said. "I'd like to believe you so easily bound, Virim, but I note that your legs bear no sign of the blisters that Bruck carried upon him. Mother birds limp and flutter their wings to lead hunters away from their nests. I think you need to do better than that."

She had strung her bow as she spoke, and now she set an iron-headed arrow to the string.

"I do not know whether or not iron wire can harm you, but I feel certain that an iron arrowhead might provide a more serious inconvenience."

The mountain sheep's eyes flew open, and Firekeeper noted that they held a certain shrewdness of expression.

"But you want me alive," Virim said. "Would you shoot me?"

"I might," Firekeeper said, keeping her tone completely conversational. "I admit. There was a time I wanted you alive so that I might learn from you the solution to querinalo. Since then, I have learned a few things, and those have given me reason for thought."

"Oh?" the sheep said. "Do you mind if I move? It's difficult to see anything but the ceiling from this position."

"Move," Firekeeper said, "but I suggest you restrict your movements. I have had a long day, and if I am startled I think my arrow would loose."

The mountain sheep struggled awkwardly to lie upright, legs folded beneath as they would at rest, but whether because it took Firekeeper's threat seriously, or because of some ulterior motive, it did not attempt anything else.

As it settled itself, Firekeeper said, "Would you like to hear my new thoughts?"

"Certainly."

"Since coming here, we have confirmed that querinalo shares more in nature with a curse than with a true illness. Now, I know very little about curses, and most of what I know comes from the stories I have heard about the days before querinalo. I admit, my knowledge may be flawed. However, there was one thing about curses that stayed with me. Curses tend to have a focus of some sort. In some stories that focus is on a family, in others on an item, in others on a place. Querinalo is an impressive curse in that its focus is on a large group—so large that I nearly missed something important."

Virim said nothing, but Blind Seer answered her: "The focus of this curse has changed. Initially, it struck those in the New World as hard as it did those in the Old. Now it strikes only those in the Old World."

Firekeeper nodded. "From Bruck—a part of you who I think expresses a good number of your doubts about what you have done—we learned how the magical power the curse took from its victims was used to make Virim and his minions immortal. I didn't think of the obvious question at the time."

Again Blind Seer filled the gap left by Virim's stubborn silence. "What would happen to the immortality Virim had gained if powerful magic completely vanished from the world? Would he have the means to retain his life, or would he be condemned to death?"

Firekeeper smiled, and relaxed tension on her bow just a bit. It wouldn't do to stress the string so it would snap just when she needed it.

"Exactly. It seems to me very convenient that querinalo mutated to permit those with magical power to live, to breed. And to provide the next generation whose sufferings would give Virim his hold on life."

Virim stirred, and Firekeeper raised her arrow's tip. He hastened to reassure her.

"I am not going to do anything, but I want you to know, it wasn't like that. Not really. Not hardly. I wanted to see if a later generation would handle magic more responsibly than had those I had been forced to destroy. I hadn't counted on the reaction of the non-magical, nor the attitude of persecution and privilege that would create."

"I wish I believed that," Firekeeper said. She unstrung her bow and set it beside her. "I am strong, but my arms do get tired. However, I am very good at throwing a knife and I think a steel blade would do you no good."

She settled herself, her Fang held in a throwing grip.

"I wonder if managing querinalo was much the same for you. At first you could maintain your curse in all its horrid and glorious power. After a time, however, as the power that came to you from those you killed ebbed, you must have grown tired. You were caught between needs: to adhere to your ideals, to survive, to maintain your hold over those whose friends and families you had tormented and destroyed."

Virim did not protest. How could he, given that they had seen him deep in argument with himself? Firekeeper continued.

"So you changed the curse permitting it to give you those to prey upon while not letting them rise to such power that they could be a danger to you. Is that so?"

Virim did not reply, and Firekeeper gave a hard, dry laugh.

"Silence will serve you only so well," she said. "You see, I have a suspicion about your role in the curse. I think you remain integral to it, adapting it as you need so that it may serve you as you wish. That means that I don't need you to lift the curse. I can do it myself."

Virim's eyes widened and his nostrils flared in ovine panic. "How could you do that?"

"By killing you," Firekeeper said. "I think that would lift the curse. Therefore, you have a new dilemma. Rather than being a badger safe in a den constructed from my need for you, you now find yourself a grazing fawn caught in a thicket. There is a way out, but you must find it."

"Oh?" The word emerged as a flat bleat.

"That's right," Firekeeper said. "My needs will be served— or so I think—by your death. Now, you must convince me why I should leave you alive."

"Killing me will not end querinalo," Virim said.

"And why should I believe that?" Firekeeper replied. "But I have no desire to argue with you. You have spent a hundred years and more arguing with yourself. I noticed how danger to your life began to make the finer points of that argument seem unimportant. That makes me think my intention to take you with me to the Nexus Islands is a good one."

"Where?"

"The Nexus Islands," Firekeeper repeated with a degree of satisfaction. "I think that you deserve to experience some of the danger you have placed others in. Perhaps it will help you to concentrate your mind."

"You cannot pass the Bound," Virim said, but Firekeeper could tell this was only bluster.

"We will not need to do so," she said, but chose not to explain further. Instead she turned to Elation. "Can you guard him alone?"

In reply, the peregrine flew down and perched on one of the mountain sheep's great, curling horns.

"If this one values his eyes, I think I can."

Virim's involuntary pressing closed his eyelids was answer enough.

"If he does not behave," Firekeeper said, "Blind Seer and I will drag him after us. He will not be comfortable, but he will also not be in a position to do mischief."

"You are so cruel," Virim bleated.

"You have killed thousands," Firekeeper replied. "I am trying to save many lives. If that means you must bear a little rough handling, well, so it must be."

Without further comment, Firekeeper and Blind Seer moved to inspect the doors that lined the curving back wall. Even when viewed from up close, they seemed identical. Moreover, none showed evidence of lock or key. Firekeeper tried to pry one open with the tips of her fingers, then the point of her Fang, but she might as well have been trying to pry up a shaft of sunlight.

The wolf-woman was frustrated. She didn't want to resort to threatening Virim to gain everything she wanted. She knew that eventually one of those threats would need to be carried out, and she preferred to reserve such tactics.

Doors without handles or hinges, she thought. *If they are magical in nature there is nothing I can do, but such seems unnecessarily complex.*

"Firekeeper?"

The voice was the Meddler's. Firekeeper glanced around looking for him, then realized the voice was within her head.

"What?" she said aloud, then shaped a speaking thought: *"Why don't you show yourself?"*

"I would prefer not to," the Meddler said. *"You have left Virim's mind and are back within what you think of as reality. I do not wish to waste all my strength manifesting just so Blind Seer can growl at me."*

"What do you want?" she asked, trying not to be either too rude or too inviting.

"I have been searching this place. You were right. There is a gate here. You just need to get through the door at the far end of the wall."

Firekeeper felt encouraged. She also suspected that the Meddler was about to offer to open the door for her. Not wanting to be in his debt, she considered her options again. If the door was a magical door, could Blind Seer make some spell to open it? She doubted that. Neither of them had ever seen such done.

A locked door. She supposed she might be able to break it down, but she didn't know how long that would take, especially with the limited tools she had at hand.

A locked door. Humans usually made keys to open locks, but these doors lacked keyholes. Perhaps the key here was a spell of some sort rather than a physical key. She was turning away from thoughts of keys when an impulse made her return to consider it.

Spells took time and preparation. This wall with its many doors had not been constructed for decoration, certainly. More likely it was a defense. What good was a defense one could not pass through without all manner of dancing and chanting and smearing with blood? The defender might find himself trapped on the wrong side of his wall, and from what Firekeeper had seen of Virim, she did not think he would treat his own life so lightly.

An artifact, then. Something Virim could use quickly.

She padded over to look down at the mountain sheep. It looked up at her with the glazed placidity of a human who had seen too much change too quickly. Beasts got that look only when they had given up and were prepared to die. Somehow Firekeeper didn't thing Virim had given up. He was probably arguing with himself again.

Elation looked quizzically at the wolf-woman, but Firekeeper didn't offer an explanation for her return. Instead, she knelt next to the mountain sheep. Almost immediately, she felt Blind Seer warm beside her, ready to defend her should she do anything to make herself vulnerable.

"What are you doing?"

"The Meddler told me that there is a gate. It's at the end of the line of doors, over near where you were sniffing."

"I smelled nothing different there, but it is possible. How are we going to get through that door?"

"With the key," Firekeeper said.

She began patting the mountain sheep, starting near the head. Elation flapped to her shoulder, then returned to Virim's horn when Firekeeper moved further down the sheep's torso. She was very thorough, but in the end she had found nothing.

Blind Seer started to lick her in sympathy, then drew back. "You are smiling. What has the Meddler whispered now?"

"Nothing," Firekeeper said. "I was laughing at myself for

being stupid. I came to the decision that there must be a key to open the doors because I could not see Virim letting himself be trapped. But what good would a key do a mountain sheep?"

Blind Seer sat straight and scratched hard at one ear.

"Not much," he admitted.

"A sheep lacks hands," Firekeeper said. "It would open the door with its head. I think the key is there, perhaps in one of those sparkling horns."

She thought she saw Virim wilt slightly, but couldn't be sure. Impulsively, Firekeeper leapt to her feet.

"Off, Elation!" she said. "Time to go knocking on the door."

Firekeeper half expected Virim to change shape when she grasped him by the horns and began dragging him across the highly polished floor. He did not. Maybe the iron wire was inhibiting him. Maybe he was simply being stubborn.

Once they had reached the door, Firekeeper knelt and gripped the sheep firmly around its midsection. The sheep was quite heavy, and his barrel very round, but she adjusted her grip until she felt secure. Then, raising the sheep until its head was about level with where it would hit when the animal was standing, she tapped the horns against the door.

One tap was not enough. Nor was two, but on the third the door swung soundlessly open revealing a chamber carved from rock that matched the garnet-seamed granite of the exterior. The room was lit by glowing blocks. Their light revealed a deep, roughly square room. On the wall to their right were the signs and sigils that Firekeeper knew marked a gate.

"There!" she said with satisfaction.

Blind Seer was in before her, leaping over Virim and landing lightly on the stone floor. Elation flew in a bit more hesitantly and took a perch on the back of a chair that, along with a small table and a neat cabinet, was the room's only furnishing.

"Can you make the gate work?" Firekeeper asked.

"I believe so," Blind Seer said.

He had reared onto his hind legs and was sniffing the carvings on the wall. He lapped one with his tongue, highlighting its intricate workings with saliva.

"The marks seem like those," Blind Seer said, "I saw when

I watched Enigma work the ritual Ynamynet adapted for him. We will need blood to work the spell."

Firekeeper wrinkled her nose in distaste, but she knew the wolf was right.

"Watch Virim," she said. "I want to block the door open, then see what that cabinet contains. I recall Ynamynet used little pots to hold the blood and brushes to mark the wall. Such may be stored here."

"Good to have," Blind Seer said, "but not necessary."

The accessories were in the small cabinet, and Blind Seer directed her where to place them. The fat, round silver pots were miraculously untarnished, the bristles on the brushes unperished. Fleetingly, Firekeeper wondered if Virim had availed himself of the gate from time to time, or if some other means of preservation had been set on the tools.

If he had used the gate, where did it lead? Surely not to the Nexus Islands—or at least not to those gates they knew. Perhaps Virim had not used the gate for a long time. Ten or eleven years ago, no one would have been on the Nexus Islands to see him. Even after the first ventures had been made to reawaken the facility, the islands had not been inhabited until after King Veztressidan's fall. Perhaps Virim had kept the tools ready for use out of habit or boredom. Perhaps . . .

Firekeeper shook her head violently.

You're behaving like a human, Little Two-legs, she chided herself, *living within your head. Come out and deal with what is here before it bites and grabs hold.*

If Blind Seer noted her distress, he decided not to comment on it in front of Virim. The mountain sheep had lain passive since Firekeeper had dragged him into the room, but that didn't mean that any of them had forgotten him or failed to note how his ears twitched when they spoke.

"Now," the wolf said, "we will need blood to provide the power for the spell itself, and a small amount from each who will pass the gate."

Firekeeper looked over at Elation.

"Will you come with us? Travel in this way is not exactly pleasant, but I have experienced worse."

The peregrine flapped her wings nervously.

"You are going to work magic?"

"You heard us discuss the matter and did not seem distressed," Firekeeper reminded her.

"It is one thing," Elation said, "to hear such spoken of, another to see it done. Already this day I have seen more magical workings than I ever imagined."

Firekeeper remembered then that Elation had not been present during some of the more remarkable events in New Kelvin, nor had she been with them on Misheemnekuru when the Tower of Magic fell. Given this, her composure in the face of the magic her people—like Firekeeper's own—feared and abhorred had been remarkable. Indeed, Firekeeper wondered if the peregrine's relatively matter-of-fact acceptance of Blind Seer's claim to sorcerous ability had come from disbelief rather than otherwise.

With that memory, Firekeeper realized something else.

"We cannot take you with us," she said. "You would be as vulnerable to querinalo as any of those we seek to spare."

Elation fluffed her feathered and made a harsh, cakking noise of indignation.

"Are you saying that I am magical?"

"Do not take offense, Fierce Joy in Flight," Firekeeper said soothingly. "Likely you are free of taint. However, the ability may lie dormant within you, as we discovered it did in Blind Seer. We cannot risk you where we would not risk so many others."

Elation permitted herself to be soothed.

"I think I would know if I possessed some magic."

"So I believed," Blind Seer said, "but I did not, and I am still fighting disgust at what I have found myself to be. I know you are not one to turn from a fight, but from what I have learned from the yarimaimalom, the wingéd folk suffered more greatly from querinalo than did any other type of Beast. Your bodies, light as they must be to fly, do not take the fevers well."

Elation considered this. "So I must risk the gate, or I must risk the Bound. That eagle nearly had me last time, and this time I would need to avoid them when they are sure to be watching. Even if we found and opened one of those high towers we saw, I would be at a disadvantage."

Firekeeper frowned. "I had not considered that. You are endangered either way, then."

"And perhaps more certainly if I leave this fortress;" Elation said, "than if I go with you. I cannot believe I bear any magical taint, and you said you needed those who could fight for you. Besides, I have not seen Derian for a long time. I would like to see him again."

"He is much changed," Firekeeper warned, "and the fight you would join is far from certain. I know you are a strong flier, but the Nexus Islands are isolated, and even the seabirds say the winds are unfriendly to extended flight. If our efforts at defense fail, you may find yourself trapped there."

"I suspect," Elation said, "I would find myself dead. Living would mean surrendering to be enslaved by these descendants of the Old World rulers who are attacking the Nexans. Surely, death would be preferable to that."

"Surely?" Firekeeper said softly.

"Surely," Elation said. "Else why do you fight?"

And Firekeeper, having no reply for this, drew her Fang. Baring her left arm, she made a long, clean slice, then squeezed the flesh until the blood ran free to fill the fat silver pot that rested in the stained grooves on the polished stone floor.

XXXV

PLIK WAS SITTING by his little house, sharpening the points of sticks that Skea hoped could be turned into makeshift arrows, when a peregrine falcon he did not know dropped out of the sky and perched on one of the spreading limbs of the tree that grew nearby.

She was a lovely bird, an exemplar of her breed, but at that moment Plik had no attention to spare for the delicate mottled pattern of the feathers on her breast or the shining gold that ringed the otherwise dark brown eye she now fixed him with.

"You are Plik," she said. "I am Fierce Joy in Flight, usually called Elation."

"Firekeeper and Blind Seer's friend," Plik said, "and Derian's. They have spoken of you. Did you come to find them? If so, you have had a long flight . . ."

A terrifically long flight, when Plik considered where he currently was. The gates ruined one for any realistic assessment of distance. This peregrine had been born in the northern portion of the New World continent that held Liglim and Misheemnekuru. How had she reached the Old World?

". . . For nothing," Plik concluded. "They are not here."

"They are," the falcon said, "and I have come with them. However, they are in a bit of a difficulty."

Plik rose, dropping the partially sharpened stick into the heap beside his chair.

"Where are they?"

Elation seemed to approve of his decisiveness.

"Follow me," she cried. "I will explain."

Plik expected the peregrine to lead the way up the hillside to where the gates were, but instead she led him toward the rocky beach.

"Wait," he called, trotting after her as fast as his short legs would permit. "That isn't the way to the gates."

"It is the way to some gates," Elation corrected. "Look there. See that island? Not the closest one, nor the next, but the one beyond that, the one with the particularly sharp peak at its middle."

"I see," Plik assured her, shading his eyes with his hand.

"On that island," Elation said, "up near that peak, is a cave, and in that cave is a gate. Firekeeper is there, along with Blind Seer, and one other. . . . Do you know of Virim?"

"The spellcaster who created querinalo?"

"The same. They have him, or one they claim is him, although I wonder if that is not crediting an herbivore with too much ability."

Plik could tell there was a good story here, but he could also tell that the peregrine was agitated. The details could wait.

"You say there is a gate there," he repeated. "Is that how you came to the Nexus Islands?"

"I came here," Elation said, "from that island with the peak, by the strength of my own wings. We came there from the northwestern forests of the New World by means of a gate. However, Firekeeper does not think she and Blind Seer could swim from the peaked island to this one—or even to the next nearest island. They certainly could not do it with the mountain sheep in tow, and it is less than no help whatsoever."

"They need a boat sent to them," Plik said, pressing back the questions he longed to ask. "I believe the fishing boat is in port. Let us go there."

He went, trotting quickly, dropping to all fours from time to time to spare his feet. As he ran, Plik set about reconstructing what must—might?—have happened as he ran. Virim had used a mountain-sheep emblem. Firekeeper and Blind Seer had found his lair. The Meddler had said the old spellcasters could extend their lives.

Fine. He could accept that they had found something. They had apparently also found a gate, but not a gate that had come here, one that had brought them to a nearby island.

Plik could see the sense in that. Virim had known he was challenging all the might of his world. However, like all of his kind, he had grown accustomed to certain conveniences. Either he had been powerful and wealthy enough to build an unauthorized gate, or he had taken over a gate someone else had built for his own use.

That idea was both tantalizing and frightening. The Nexans had planned their defense around the idea that they knew where the gates opened. What if there were others of these unofficial gates?

Come to think of it, who had operated the gate for them? This mountain sheep? Virim? Someone else they had met?

Plik wrinkled his nose as he might have against an unusually strong scent. He longed to ask this Elation questions—starting with did the peregrine realize the danger she was in from querinalo—but Elation probably wouldn't want to stop to talk until the others were brought from their point of arrival, so Plik put the questions aside.

Happily, Chaker Torn, who captained the fishing vessel, was well acquainted with Plik, having appreciated Plik's willingness to take over much of the cleaning and sorting of his catch. Moreover, he was blessed both with a lack of imagination and an adaptable temperament, two elements of personality not usually found together, but qualities invaluable in one who must deal with both the ocean's unrelenting force and changeable temperament.

Chaker accepted without too many questions Plik's simple report that the peregrine had brought word that Firekeeper, Blind Seer, and at least one other needed to be taken off the peaked island. His crew—his half-grown son and daughter—was nearby, father and children having taken to sleeping in the rough fisherman's hut on the shore in case a vessel from the much dreaded invasion fleet should somehow escape the attention of those who watched it.

Plik wasn't quite certain what the humans thought they could do in such a circumstance, but for now he didn't care. It was enough that those he needed were there and ready.

"The falcon," he said, "is named Elation. She will let you know if you go astray."

"Don't see how we can miss," Chaker said laconically, his attention mostly for his ropes and sails. "Wind is with us. There's a cove where we can bring the boat close to shore."

There would be, Plik thought. *What would be the use of building a gate on an island that would trap you as soon as you arrived?*

"Then I'll be off to tell Derian and Ynamynet that our wanderers are returned," Plik said.

He found them both seated in the sunshine on the pillared front portico of the headquarters building, or rather Ynamynet was in the sun, while Derian sat back in the shade. Judging from the papers and rough maps spread between them, they were working on duty rosters.

"Firekeeper and Blind Seer are back," Plik said, "or they will be as soon as Chaker Torn fetches them from one of the lesser islands."

That got their attention, as Plik had intended it would, and rosters were set aside.

"Does Skea know?" Ynamynet asked.

"Not yet," Plik said. He bent and made a point of rubbing one foot with one hand.

He'd never had a problem with his bare feet feeling bruised or sore on Misheemnekuru, but the deep duff of those forests was far different from the pebbly footing of the Nexus Islands. One of the Nexans, a Never Lived who was the island's chief leatherworker and cobbler, had made Plik boots to protect his feet over the past winter. The cobbler had promised to make lighter shoes for summer, but that project, like so many others, had been put off under the threat of invasion.

Now the cobbler was crafting makeshift armor from leather and bits and pieces found in the ruins. His usually laughing countenance had become grim as he contemplated all those who would die because his work could not hope to hold up against the far from makeshift weapons their enemies were sure to be carrying.

Despite the alacrity with which they had put aside their paperwork, Derian and Ynamynet could not leave their posts immediately. One of the older children was sent to inform Skea of Firekeeper's arrival. Harjeedian was called from the archives and asked to handle any routine business that came up. A handful of questions, each a pending crisis to the one who brought it, came as soon as the mayors were seen leaving their posts. Thus it was that Plik, Derian, and Ynamynet arrived at the harbor as the fishing boat was returning with its unpredictable cargo.

The passengers were clustered on the front deck. Firekeeper was leaning against the rail, her set features a study in misery. Plik remembered that the wolf-woman suffered greatly from seasickness.

The falcon, Elation, was perched on the rail nearby, and Blind Seer sat near the middle of the deck. For a moment, Plik wondered if the crossing had been rougher than the relatively quiet waters would seem to indicate for none of the three passengers were looking toward the shore. Then he realized that was because they were keeping a careful watch on something that lay on the deck.

"Hey, Derian," called Chaker as he guided the vessel to the mooring and helped his son make it fast to the pilings. "Can you come aboard and help take this . . ."

He paused as if searching for some other word, then shrugged and settled for the most obvious. ". . . sheep ashore. Firekeeper carried it on, but I think she's going to have enough trouble getting herself off the boat."

Firekeeper didn't argue against this assessment, but only looked more miserable than before.

"Sheep?" Derian said, but he was already moving down the dock. He stopped as the peregrine took to the air and began gliding in circles over his head. "Elation?"

To Plik's surprise the young man's voice actually broke.

"Fierce Joy in Flight? That can't be you!"

The falcon gave a mocking cry, then an almost cooing mewling sound. Derian seemed to recognize a familiar voice. He beamed, then his face darkened with anger.

"What are you doing here? Don't you know the risks you're taking? Did those fool wolves forget to tell you?"

Plik took it upon himself to translate the falcon's reply, for Firekeeper was struggling to get off the fishing boat, and had no energy to spare.

"Elation says that they did tell her, but when she had the choice of golden eagles and gyrfalcons or an illness that she is certain will not dare touch her, she decided to choose to come. A good thing she did, too, or else those fool wolves would be howling on an island and hoping the wind would carry their cries."

Some of the anger faded from Derian's face to be replaced by worry. He nodded thanks to Plik for the translation.

"I see—or rather, I don't see, but I suspect I will. Here,

Firekeeper, let me get you to shore, then I'll come back for . . ."

He had reached the fishing boat by now and gotten his first clear look at what Blind Seer still guarded.

"It *is* a sheep. A mountain sheep. Look at those horns! Look at those hooves! Ynamynet, come look at this. It's just like Virim's emblem."

Ynamynet had been standing back from where the ocean water might splash her, but now she worked her way down the dock, sidestepping where Derian was half carrying a very seasick Firekeeper to shore.

The Once Dead bit down on one fingertip, drawing a drop of blood from a barely healed scab. Then she traced a pattern in the air with both her fingertips.

"I can see why you've bound this sheep with iron wire," she said to Firekeeper and Blind Seer. "Even so bound the power it radiates is blinding."

She apparently meant this literally, for Plik noted that she was pulling her head back and squinting as if to protect herself from glare. Plik found this interesting. Like most of the maimalodalum, he had possessed a talent for sensing magic, but in his case the sense most closely related had been sound.

Querinalo had robbed him of all that talent—or so he had thought. Now, as he reflexively opened those "ears" to try and hear what Ynamynet—very much a sight-oriented human— had "seen," he thought he heard a rhythmic pounding. If it wasn't simply wishful imaginings on his part, then the sheep must possess a considerable amount of power for Plik to be able to sense it at all.

Once on shore and collapsed on the prickly grass, Firekeeper continued to hold on to the ground as if feeling a latent tossing. Even so, she must have been feeling better, for she ventured her first comment since the boat's arrival.

"Is not just sheep, is Virim. Not Virim emblem. Virim. Take care."

Ynamynet glanced at Firekeeper, but there was not the least hint of disbelief in her assessing gaze.

"Is it then?" she said. "But from how you have him bound,

I do not think you have convinced him to be a member of your pack."

Firekeeper shook her head. From how her hand flew to her temple, she obviously regretted the motion.

"Not all of him, no. When Derian has on shore, Blind Seer and I try to tell. First, please, tell us. The invasion. How far?"

"How far?" Derian repeated, his voice showing none of the strain of the weight of the large creature he was now bearing to shore. "You sound like you know something about it. When you left, we didn't know for certain what would happen."

"Meddler tell," Firekeeper said tersely, and Plik didn't think the shortness of her speech was related to her nausea. There was a tenseness about both her and Blind Seer that hinted at something far more complex.

Ynamynet didn't seem to realize this, for she said, "The Meddler told you and you believed him?"

"Meddler show," Firekeeper said. "In dream. Ships. Troops. Is a lie?"

This last statement sounded so hopeful that Plik hated to reply.

"No," he said. "It's not a lie. There is a fleet coming. We expect it in a few days. It will probably try and land during the dark of early Bear Moon."

Blind Seer said, *"Then we have some time yet. Puma Moon was thin but visible when we went into Virim's fortress."*

Plik recalled the moon as he had seen it the night before. It had been so slim as to be the merest crescent. Tonight it would be dark. He said this, and Blind Seer, who was ashore now and sitting beside Firekeeper, wrinkled his brow in the expression for worry that canines shared so oddly with humans.

"I could swear that it was slim, but still giving light when we went into Virim's fort. Does the moon shine differently in different places?"

"I don't think so," Firekeeper said in Pellish. "I recall it was the same in New Kelvin when we arrived there as it had been here when we left."

Plik made a quick translation of Blind Seer's comments for

Derian and Ynamynet, both of whom had looked quite started at Firekeeper's—to them—strange comment.

"Strange indeed," Ynamynet agreed, "but perhaps we will find an answer when you have told your story. First, though, where do you think we should keep your guest?"

"Virim," Firekeeper said. She put her hand on Blind Seer's shoulder and pushed herself to her feet. "Virim. Do not forget. Virim. The Virim who make the Plague."

"I promise," Ynamynet said. "My spell is spent, but I saw the glow of his power with my own eyes. I will not forget and think him a mere mountain sheep."

Derian looked down at the limp creature he still held in his arms. "As if we could. I don't think I've ever seen a mountain sheep with horns of diamond and golden hooves."

"I don't think I've ever seen a mountain sheep," Plik said, "but I get your point."

Firekeeper had been considering Ynamynet's question, and now she spoke. "He is human as well as beast, but now he is mostly beast. Maybe open is better, and Blind Seer and I can watch him."

"Open is easier to run away from," Ynamynet reminded her.

"Is island," Firekeeper said with a shrug. "Where to he run?"

"Where can any of us run?" Derian said grimly. "That is the problem, isn't it?"

"Is maybe solution, too," Firekeeper said with confidence. "So I hope. Let us go to place by Derian's house. We can talk outside."

Derian agreed and turned his steps in that direction.

Firekeeper turned to Ynamynet. "You say you see Virim power with spell. Is iron wire really doing anything to stop this one?"

"It is hampering him some," Ynamynet said. "There were darker areas where the wire touched. However, I suspect the physical restriction is almost as much a difficulty."

"How much iron to really stop him?" Firekeeper asked.

Ynamynet gave an involuntary shudder. Plik recalled that she herself had experienced a probationary period where she wore iron to restrict her from easy use of her power.

"Really stop? I don't know. I have never seen such power."

"Would heavy collar do?" Firekeeper persisted, not permitting Ynamynet to avoid the distasteful subject. "I wish him to walk about with me and see these Nexans."

"A heavy collar might work," Ynamynet said, "but I think that much iron that close to the head might make him nauseous. It would certainly give him a throbbing headache. I would suggest if you want him at all alert that you employ bracelets and maybe a light necklace."

"We do this then," Firekeeper said, pulling loops of iron wire from a bag at her waist. "Will trouble you if I do with you near?"

"Not if it doesn't touch me," Ynamynet said.

They had reached Derian's house now. Derian set the mountain sheep down, then went inside and brought out chairs, setting one in the brightest patch of sunlight and motioning Ynamynet toward it.

When he took his own chair, the falcon Elation seated herself on the back and nuzzled his hair with gentle affection. Here, at least, was one old friend Derian didn't need to worry would be offended by his transformed appearance.

Firekeeper, now seemingly recovered from her seasickness, sat on the ground next to the sheep. As she altered the wire hobbles into the bracelets Ynamynet had suggested, she began to tell what had happened. Blind Seer interjected periodically, and Plik found himself translating automatically.

Sometime during Firekeeper's account, the jaguar Truth arrived. She seated herself without comment in the sun near Ynamynet. Zebel, the Twice Dead who was the Nexans' doctor, came soon after Truth. Like the jaguar, he did nothing to interrupt, only seated himself on a vacant chair and listened with rapt attention.

"So," Firekeeper concluded, "is how is. Think that Virim is not all happy with his making querinalo, but is not all unhappy either. One thing I do think. He likes living. So I bring him here. I think if he not help us, then he can die with us."

Plik saw the mountain sheep give a very human wince at this, but otherwise it offered no comment. From the expression on Ynamynet's face, she had seen the reaction as well, but she copied the old spellcaster's reticence, and commented on something else entirely.

"I think I know what happened to your missing days," Ynamynet said. "Time passes very strangely when one is thinking. I suspect that what you took for a few hours within Virim's stronghold were actually days—days of confused thought on his part while you worked yourselves through to some sort of clarity. Someone with a less determined nature might have been permanently trapped. I compliment you three on escaping at all."

"Escaping," Derian said, looking out over the ocean where the unseen fleet was inexorably approaching, "to die with us."

"To fight, then to die," Firekeeper said, as if that made a difference. Plik thought that to a wolf it probably did. "And maybe, just maybe, to live."

❦

As PLEASED as Derian was to have Firekeeper and Blind Seer back, what they had discovered on their journey had not precisely solved the near impossibility of how the Nexans could hold the islands against the invading fleet.

In the day or so since he had been brought to the Nexus Islands, the mountain sheep had wandered from place to place on the island. It was never alone. Two of the yarimaimalom wolves always were with it. During the day, True Star, an older woman who was one of the remaining Once Dead, joined Virim's escort. True Star possessed an unerring sense for which way north lay, a minor talent that might have been considered more important were she on the mainland, but was nearly useless on the restricted island where she had lived the latter part of her life.

However slight her talent, True Star was very familiar with the ways of spellcasters, and had assured them that should Virim attempt anything, she would know. Given that neither

Ynamynet nor Kalyndra could be spared, and that the talents of the remaining Once Dead, Frostweed and Arasan, could be used elsewhere, and that someone other than the wolves should be with Virim, True Star was delegated.

Certainly, Firekeeper could not be spared. Almost as soon as she arrived she was off again, this time to scour the forests on the mainland, bringing word to the remnants of the formerly captive yarimaimalom that their help would be needed to defend the Nexus Islands. Word had been sent earlier, but Derian did not doubt that Firekeeper and Blind Seer would succeed in using guilt and obligation to balance the fear those yarimaimalom would doubtless feel at the idea of returning where they had been so cruelly treated.

But even if Firekeeper brought back every wolf, puma, raccoon, and eagle, Derian feared it still wouldn't be enough.

"What we need," he said to Isende as they made what had now become their joint patrol of the gateway hilltop, "are those sea monsters I heard about when we first came here. Then the ships couldn't get safely to shore. I don't suppose you could find me one or two?"

Isende, who had proven very good at finding odds and ends stored in the various buildings, shook her head.

"I wish. I know Ynamynet has been trying to find out if there was ever any truth to those stories, but she has had no success. She's wearing herself out trying to decide what spells she and Kalyndra could work that might make a difference. The problem is, although they're our two most powerful spellcasters . . ."

"Our only two spellcasters . . ." Derian interrupted, trying to be playful. He was surprised to see a very odd look cross Isende's face.

"Actually," she said, then stopped. She took a deep breath and started again. "Actually, Kalyndra thinks I have a spellcaster's ability, not just some vague talent for seeing visions."

Derian felt an automatic protest rising to his lips. After all, where he'd been raised what Isende was admitting to would have been considered worse—or at least as bad—as admitting to a taste for cannibalism. He stilled the protest, thinking that now, when they needed whatever edge they could find, was not the time to make Isende nervous about exploring whatever potentials she possessed.

"Now that I think of it," he said, "there's a certain logic in what Kalyndra thinks. I tend to forget that you and Tiniel worked the spell that permitted you to open the gate back in the Setting Sun stronghold. At that time, we knew so little about how the gates worked—or about how magic works in general—it didn't occur to me to question that you and Tiniel could have simply followed some instructions you found cached beneath a floorboard."

"But now," Isende said, "you do know—and so do I. If one or both of us hadn't possessed a talent for spellcasting, then we could have followed those instructions letter-perfect until we'd bled ourselves dry and the gate would not have opened."

Derian grimaced at the image, but Isende didn't appear offended.

"And now you think—or Kalyndra does—that you are a spellcaster."

"That's right," Isende said. "She had me do some simple routines that her own people commonly used to test for ability. I didn't see anything spectacular, but she seemed confident that I had at least a trickle of ability. There isn't enough time to teach me anything complex, but there is some hope that I can help to relay spell effects."

Derian recalled with painful clarity the one time he had seen such a group spell being built—and what had happened to those who had attempted it when Firekeeper had barged in and ruined their concentration. It had not been at all pretty, and had been very fatal for those intertwined in the spell's power.

"You'll be careful?" he said, torn between his duty to find ways for the Nexans to defend themselves, and a strong desire to defend this one young lady.

"I will," Isende promised. "And I wouldn't worry too much. Ynamynet's best hopes are that we can come up with some defensive spells—mostly spells meant to counteract spells our opponents might use. Attack, apparently, involves forces she doesn't think either she or Kalyndra can handle."

"So we have three Once Dead spellcasters," Derian said, thinking back to what had been said when his flippant interruption had triggered Isende's startling revelation.

"Actually," she said, her grin taking the edge off her pedantry, "we have five."

"Enigma," Derian said. "I tend to forget him because all he seems interested in is working the gates—and he has become very good at that. Can he learn more?"

"Again," Isende said, "Ynamynet and Kalyndra don't think they have time to teach Enigma anything complex, but he has expressed a willingness to act as a relay for any spells they want to try."

"Good," Derian said. He couldn't say the news made him precisely hopeful, but it was nice to know they weren't quite as vulnerable to the other side's magic as he had thought. "But you said five. I've been trying, but I can't think of a fifth unless Frostweed or True Star or Arasan has shown more versatility than was initially thought."

"No," Isende said. She looked for a moment as if she might make him work out the answer himself, but perhaps how very tired he was showed. "Tell me. How did Firekeeper and Blind Seer and that falcon, Elation, get back here?"

"By gate," Derian said promptly. Then he repeated more slowly. "By gate . . . That's right. Someone would have had to work it. I guess I thought maybe they called on the Meddler, or Firekeeper found some way to force that Virim, but I don't think I really thought about it at all. Are you telling me that Firekeeper is a spellcaster?"

Isende shook her head. "Not Firekeeper. Her abilities seem to be talents related to the plant and animal worlds. No. Not Firekeeper. Blind Seer."

This time Derian gaped, letting his shock and momentary revulsion show plainly before he remembered to hide them. The thought that the wolf he had traveled with, had let guard his back, had trusted, was a spellcaster was almost more than he could accept.

"Blind Seer did have querinalo when I did," he managed weakly. "That wouldn't have happened if he didn't have any magical talent. I guess I never really worried about what he did have because no one ever mentioned what it was."

"No one mentioned it," Isende said, "because, as far as I can tell, Blind Seer never told anyone what lay at the root of his vulnerability to querinalo, even after he had survived.

"I don't know what your experience was, but when I had querinalo I could feel the nature of my abilities. For the first time, I realized that I had two distinct magical elements within me: my link to Tiniel, and something else that even then I suspected might be a more generalized ability—a spellcasting ability—although I didn't learn until later to think about it as that.

"Later, when I had learned more, I didn't want to accept that I could be a Once Dead spellcaster. I'd seen how terrible the Once Dead could become in their arrogance and their power. I didn't want to be in the least like them. I suspect Blind Seer felt the same as I did."

"Or even worse," Derian said. "I don't think the Royal Beasts even admit to the possibility of spellcasting Beasts. Talented Beasts, yes, but the ability to create and use spells seems to be something the Royal Beasts considered a solely human abomination."

"And they really may not have been aware that it was possible for a Beast to cast spells," Isende said. "Spellcasting is a very strange sort of talent. From what Kalyndra told me, if someone who has the talent goes untrained, it can remain unformed, a dormant force."

"I understand," Derian said. "At least I think I do. Spellcasters have the ability to work raw magical energy, but if no one tells them how to do it—if they have no idea even where to start—the ability might well stay dormant."

"Except for creating," Isende said, as if from experience, "a sort of restless feeling that you should be able to do something, but no idea even what that something is. I must say, you seem to understand this very well. Are you . . ."

Derian held up his hands in a defensive gesture before she could complete the question. "Oh, no. Don't start thinking I have a spellcaster's power, too. I'm sure I don't. But my profession back before I was sent off with Earl Kestrel and so started my wanderings gives me some odd insights."

"You worked at your family's stables," Isende said. "How would that help you to understand magic?"

"Have you ever bridled a horse?"

"Sure, and harnessed oxen. My family owned a farm, remember."

Derian grinned. "Well, you must have been preternaturally observant if you didn't find all those straps and buckles really confusing—especially the first couple of times you had to put on a harness."

Isende laughed. "I remember. I used to ride my pony with just a halter, but when my parents bought me my first horse, he had enough spirit that a bridle was needed rather than just a halter. I remember just staring at the thing when it was handed to me. I knew how it should go on. I'd seen the stable hands slip them on more times than I could count, but now that I was the one doing it I could hardly figure out which part went where."

"Right," Derian said. "Confused, with no way to figure out what goes where, that's how I figure a Royal Beast with a spellcasting talent might feel. Tangled. Even worse, coming from a culture that didn't even admit to the possibility of that type of magical ability manifesting, the Beast would need to be very, very clever to evolve the idea that his unformed power needed spells to give it shape."

Isende said, "I've talked to Plik about his own training. I understand from Harjeedian that Truth was given extensive training in how to read omens. What you're saying is that the Royal Beasts wouldn't have had any such tradition. They'd turn a blind eye to talents, especially useful ones, but they wouldn't give any training in how to use them."

"None," Derian agreed. "And after the Beasts lost the lands east of the Iron Mountains to humans during the early days when the Old World was colonizing the New, the Beasts blamed their loss on human sorcery."

"And so if any Royal Beast had received the faintest hint of what might dwell within him," Isende said, nodding in understanding, "he wouldn't have dared mention it. At best, admitting you suspected you were a spellcaster would be like admitting you had found a source of water after everyone had died of thirst. At worst, you might find yourself classified a traitor."

Derian walked for a bit, thinking this over.

"Well, I think we now have a fairly good idea why Blind Seer has been in such a very strange mood. Remember how he ran out of that one meeting? We were discussing spellcasting, and Virim."

"You told me." Isende colored a little. "At the time, I thought Blind Seer's edginess had more to do with the Meddler being the one who was prompting Firekeeper to go looking for a cure to querinalo. I can't get rid of the feeling that the Meddler is more than a little interested in Firekeeper—and not just in the way he was interested in me and Tiniel. I think the Meddler is interested in Firekeeper as a . . . well . . . woman . . ."

"Something your spellcasting talent is telling you?" Derian asked teasingly.

"I think more like woman's intuition," Isende replied, squeezing Derian's hand. "Or maybe I'm just seeing romance everywhere I look. They say that happens when you fall in love."

She looked up at him and smiled. Bending to kiss Isende gently on the lips, Derian was astonished to realize how that one smile could make his infinity of worries melt away—if only for a moment.

XXXVI

"I HAVE BEEN trying to decide," Blind Seer said to Firekeeper as they ran back toward the Setting Sun stronghold, "if we have ever tried quite so hard to get ourselves killed."

Firekeeper didn't slow as she reached out and stroked her hand along the soft fur on his back.

"We're not trying to get ourselves killed. Do you mean because we are voluntarily returning to an isolated island that is about to be attacked from the sea—with an attempt made via the gates as well—that we are trying to get ourselves killed?"

"Something like that," Blind Seer replied. His panting held laughter rather than fear or weariness.

"That's not trying to get ourselves killed," Firekeeper said. "It's only trying to keep those we care about from getting killed. What would a life preserved at the cost of Derian's or Plik's or even Harjeedian's life be worth? I have enough nightmares without creating more."

"I was wondering," Blind Seer said, "if those nightmares would be eased or enhanced if I were . . ."

Uncharacteristically, he paused in midthought. Firekeeper did not prod or probe, only kept on with her steady, easy pace. Her bow thumped lightly against her back. The summer sun was rising to the east. Soon these southern lands would be hot and sticky, but temperatures on the Nexus Islands would actually be pleasant.

Good weather for fighting, she thought, *if we must fight, as it seems we must. At least those of our company who are furred need not be concerned about collapsing from heat stroke.*

"Ynamynet," Blind Seer said, "and Kalyndra came to me soon after our return. They realized the implications of our arrival via gate, and were certain that Virim had not done the spell to send us through. They had already checked to see if you possessed any traces of a spellcaster's power, and had ruled that out. They did not take long to decide who must have made the gate work."

"And?"

"And they want me to join them in some complex of workings that they feel will give us a chance to not so much defeat as defuse most of the magics the invaders may turn against us."

"Ah?"

"The gates should be secure," Blind Seer went on, lengthening his stride a bit, as if chasing the idea he was articulating. "The iron that cages them is sound. However, even if one of those cages is broken, Ynamynet feels that the iron itself will warp the ability of any who cross into that area to work spells."

"I wish I were so confident," Firekeeper said, thinking that the Old World sorcerers who had attempted the gates earlier in the spring had been able to manage a return.

"I think Ynamynet wishes that she were so confident as well," Blind Seer laughed. "However, her point is well made. There are only two trained spellcasters in our number. Three others of us have some power, but we are like pups who have just shed our milk teeth. We can bite, but we know little about getting the most from our new fangs. So Ynamynet and Kalyndra must focus their efforts somewhere. They hope to discourage those spellcasters who might try and work magic against us from a distance while safe aboard ships at sea."

"Good thinking," Firekeeper said. "I had not considered that."

"Both of those ladies," Blind Seer replied, "know more about war and magic than either of them might wish."

"And you," Firekeeper said, "do you wish to learn more about war and magic?"

"Not really," the wolf said, "but I think I should do what I can. If querinalo had given me cat's claws, I would not like them much, but I would not hesitate to use them in defense of you and of our pack. Is this any different?"

"Only if you feel it is so," Firekeeper said.

"I did, once," Blind Seer admitted, "but when we returned I spoke with one of the ospreys who have been scouting the fleet. What he described made me shiver with fear as I have not shivered since I was a pup. When the osprey took wing, Truth came to me. She told me that the omens were not good, but that they were worse if magic were not used against our opponents. She did not say what magic, or whose magic, but I am no fool."

"Did you believe her?"

"How could I fail to do so when she stared directly at me, Ahmyn's fire blue and white in her eyes? There is no doubt that she sees omens, no doubt that she reads them with trepidation."

"Yet she has not fled," Firekeeper said. "So there must be some hope. A great cat has no fellow feeling. She would not stay if there was no hope."

"I think you are too harsh in your judgement of Truth," Blind Seer said.

They had reached the stronghold now, and slowed to a walk as they passed through the open gate and padded to where Doc and Elise had set up housekeeping with the evacuated children and infirm of the Nexus Islands.

"Think, rather," Firekeeper said, stroking him from shoulder to the base of his tail, "that I am willing to find hope anywhere I can, even if that means a friend would be faithless."

THE SETTING SUN stronghold had been well and strongly built. Even a century of neglect could not undo solid craft. The thick, high exterior wall still stood, weathered but with hardly a hint of crumbling. The shell of the house within that wall had its share of weathered shutters and broken windows, but was otherwise solid.

When Firekeeper and Blind Seer had first seen the Setting Sun stronghold, it had been so encased not only in the natural vines, grasses, shrubs, and brambles one might expect, but also in an illusion that had made it seem nothing but a copse of trees. That illusion was gone now, as was the bulk of the growth, pruned and browsed by deer, elk, and beaver until the stone wall was clearly visible.

In the moonspans that had passed since the Spell Wielders had fallen, another change had taken place in the area immediately around the stronghold. The blood briar that had made the region deadly to any unsuspecting travelers had been destroyed, herbivores proving themselves as adept at systematic hunting and killing as ever their carnivorous kin might be.

When the wolves rounded the corner of the large building, they saw what their ears had already told them. Doc and Elise were awake and about. They had taken their more rambunctious charges out into the rear yard of the house. While Elise nursed baby Elexa, Doc was working on some medical preparations over the newly rehabilitated stove of what had once been the stronghold's outdoor kitchen.

Neither of them were paying the least attention to the seemingly numberless swarm of small children who were darting here and there, happily absorbed in some noisy game. This was not, however, because they were indifferent to their responsibility. Rather it was because the children were being very well taken care of by an assortment of yarimaimalom nursemaids.

These mostly consisted of wolves, but also included a pair of does, and a mixture of noisy birds. The birds had assigned themselves the task of keeping the children away from the small pond and Doc's work area. The quadrupeds handled the rest.

Viewing the gathering of wild creatures and human young, Firekeeper felt a strange tugging on her heart. This was something like what her own childhood might have been, had her human parents survived and made truce with the Royal Beasts. From what she had been told, they had been on the way toward that accord, which was the reason that the wolves had cared for Firekeeper herself when the small settlement had been destroyed by a chance fire.

There were puppies in the mix as well as grown wolves, and it was hard to tell who was having more fun as they ran shrieking from each other in mad, tearing circles, always herded back from harm by the patiently watchful adults.

Elise, lifting Elexa to pat her against her shoulder, was the first to see the newcomers. She greeted them with a welcoming smile, but did not rise.

"So you're back," she said, "and ready to cross again? I think Enigma is waiting."

Doc turned. "He probably is, although you may need to call for him. I think he finds the noise the children make a bit intense. Last I saw him, he was on one of the roofs."

"Probably sunning," Firekeeper said. "Is cat."

"True enough," Elise said. "Ah, that's good . . ."

This last was addressed to baby Elexa, who had spit milk up all over the cloth Elise had spread over her shoulder. Firekeeper, who had done a little watching of human children, but never of an infant this small, found the entire procedure mystifying.

Was this some sort of offering from baby to mother? Wolves regurgitated their food, but that was at the pup's demand. Indeed, the impulse was so strong that the sound alone could trigger the reflex.

"Firekeeper," Doc called, "can you wait? I'm almost done with this batch of ointment, and you can take it with you."

"Is any news from other side that we is needed now?" Firekeeper asked.

"Not yet," Elise said. "But would they be able to get news out? I understand there is some fear that the gates themselves will be used for the invasion."

"Used," Firekeeper said, "maybe, but gates to New World is separate from those through Old World. Downhill a little, to one side. Should be safe, at least at first."

"And we have plans in place," Doc said, turning back to his pot and stirring a few more times before starting to pour the thick oily mass into a ceramic pot, "in case the wrong people come through. My understanding is that the invalids only agreed to be evacuated after they were given the assignment of watching the gate from this side. Their general is a young mother with a baby only a few moonspans old. She also wouldn't leave the Nexus Islands until she was given a way to be useful."

"Is what I hear, too," Firekeeper said. "Those Nexans is brave to a one."

Or frightened, she thought. *After all, they know better than Blind Seer and I do what will happen if the Once Dead rise to rulership again. Perhaps they are not brave, but have instead found something they fear more than death.*

⁕

WHEN THE WORD came that soldiers from the fleet were at last preparing to land on the Nexus Islands, Tiniel ran to his station on the gateway hilltop.

Although the inhabitants of the Nexus Islands tended to refer to it as "the" gateway hilltop, in reality there were a series of hills that crested in the middle of the rocky main island. The wedge-shaped buildings that held the gates had been constructed on these hilltops where they would be safe from all but the most violent storms.

Tiniel did not doubt that the Old Country sorcerers who had constructed the facility had possessed spells that moderated the weather in the vicinity of the Nexus Islands. After all, they would not have wanted all their difficult and expensive labor to have been swept away by a passing storm. Perhaps they had redirected the most violent of the weather elsewhere, and those storms were what had given rise to tales of monsters lurking beneath the ocean waters.

To Tiniel's way of thinking, that made more sense than that actual presence of monsters in the ocean waters. What ship captain would want to admit he feared a little bad weather? Monsters, however, especially in a world where things like griffins and dragons soaring in the skies were no more worthy of comment than would be cattle grazing in a field, monsters would be worthy of fear, and the sailors would be thought wise rather than cowardly for choosing to avoid them.

The wedge-shaped buildings that held the gates were arranged in clusters, rather like slices of pie from which the tips had been cut. From a distance, the clusters looked like solid, round buildings, since the areas between were roofed and the open areas between them usually continued the rounded line of the whole with a wall of some sort. These walls were rarely much higher than waist-high on Tiniel himself, although a few carried all the way to the roof, and a few were only knee height.

Although the roofing spoke of a certain amount of respect for the inclement weather, the walls suggested that those who had first used the gates, back before the coming of querinalo, might have given some thought to securing the gate complexes in case of emergency. Tiniel had looked at the records from the days before querinalo, and had noted that the first built of the gate complexes were the most likely to possess interstitial walls. Those that had come later were less likely to have them.

Like their worries eased over time, Tiniel thought, *or maybe they just got lazy.*

Tiniel's post was near the section of gates that came from a scattering of lands that included among them u-Chival. Only one of these gates, the one to the capital city, had been reactivated, and this not until following King Veztressidan's initial attempts at conquest. When various of those who opposed King Veztressidan had contacted their allies, the u-Chivalum had somehow managed to open one of their own abandoned gates, and had given Veztressidan a taste of his own tactics turned against him.

U-Chival was apparently the original homeland from which the Liglimom colonists had come. One of the reasons Tiniel had been given this station was that a form of the same language was still spoken there, and that those from the Old and New World could understand each other without much difficulty.

If any came through the gate they would find themselves in a cage built from heavy iron bars. Tiniel's orders were to keep back out of range of any weapons, warn the invaders that they should retreat immediately, before they found themselves unable to do so. If the invaders refused, then Tiniel was to call for assistance.

Skea had stationed a few groups of his soldiers up on the gateway hill against the possibility that would-be invaders would need more than verbal convincing. Verul, whose injured leg would not inconvenience him as greatly on this more limited field, was in command.

However, Tiniel had his own plans for what he would do if someone came through the gate from u-Chival, and it did not involve calling Verul, nor any of his troops, nor doing anything that would attract the attention of the wingéd folk who were serving as the defenders' messengers.

Although Tiniel's post was a solitary one, that was not the case for all of those who watched the gates. Much more attention was being given to the circle of gateways that originated in the continent of Pelland. King Veztressidan had been from Pelland. Reasonably, he had made his greatest efforts at conquest on his home continent. Therefore, the largest number of active gates were in that one complex.

That was where Derian was, armed with a sword and armored in something that covered his back and front. He wasn't wearing the helmet he'd been issued, but he'd tried it on earlier. Tiniel had noticed that someone had taken the time to ornament it with a bristling crest of what looked remarkably like Derian's own coarse red hair. No one had taken that much care with Tiniel's gear. The heavy leather fit well enough, but the helmet had a tendency to slide down and cover his eyes. He'd been experimenting with various ways to pad it the evening before, and thought he'd worked something out.

Tiniel didn't mind the relative solitude of his post. It proved to him that he had fooled the others into believing that he supported the defense of the Nexus Islands. He had certainly done everything he could to earn that trust: rising at dawn to drill, taking his watches as assigned, spending his spare time either in the archives helping Urgana (and gathering information he hoped would further his own goals), or in the kitchens peeling vegetables, carrying slop buckets, and humbly performing the most menial of menial labor.

Isende had openly rejoiced at her brother's choice to come out of his shell. If Tiniel had needed any proof that the bond between them was well and truly broken, her joy was that proof. Had Isende still been linked to him, there would have been no way Tiniel could have hidden the sliver of hatred and resentment that festered in his heart.

But no, Isende had sacrificed her brother and her closeness to him in favor of preserving instead a spellcasting ability that should have revolted her. Even now she was down on the lower slopes with Ynamynet, Kalyndra, Enigma, and Blind Seer. The word was that those five were going to attempt some magic that would keep the invaders from the fleet from making landfall.

The invader's white-sailed vessels hemmed the Nexus Islands in now, framing the rocky archipelago so entirely that Tiniel felt a trace claustrophobic. The ships were keeping well offshore. Channel markers had been removed, as had those that alerted sailors to rocks below the surface, but even Tiniel, who had never even glimpsed the ocean before his arrival at the Nexus, would have taken care not to get too close to those jagged, rocky shores.

"They'll need to come ashore in boats," said a familiar voice from behind Tiniel.

The young man spun and found Plik standing a short distance away, leaning against one of the walls and, like Tiniel himself, inspecting the fleet.

"Plik! I thought you were coordinating something with the yarimaimalom. What are you doing here?"

Tiniel tried to sound conversational, but he hoped Plik couldn't hear the hammering of his heart. Isende might have been fooled by Tiniel's apparent cooperation, but Tiniel had wondered from time to time if Plik had been as completely convinced. After all, the two of them had continued as neighbors in the pair of cottages. Plik had more opportunity than most to observe Tiniel when Tiniel might be unaware, and Tiniel had talked with Plik enough to know that while Plik might appear cute and cuddly, he was a wise old creature.

Moreover, the maimalodalum possessed a sense of smell as good as the raccoon he so much resembled. After hearing Firekeeper give a report in which information deduced from scent had appeared as essential as that which had been garnered from the more usual senses, Tiniel had worried that some element in his odor might give him away. He had taken to rubbing a scented ointment onto his body, claiming that the sea air was drying his skin. He didn't know if anyone even noticed his explanation, but he felt fairly certain that he would give himself away by something as normal as sweating.

"I'm looking at the fleet," Plik replied. "I am indeed translating the reports the wingéd folk are bringing. That's how I'm so certain landing boats are being readied for use."

"Ah," Tiniel said. "Sorry. I guess I'm jumpy."

"For good reason," Plik said. "I would guess this is your first battle. Gak seemed a very settled place, at least when I passed through there."

"It is," Tiniel said, and felt relieved to realize that even if Plik noticed anything odd about his behavior, he would pass it off to nerves.

Plik probably walked up here to see me because he had thought I'd need some comfort. Well, I guess I would, if I thought I'd be on the losing side. I'm going to have to do what I can to try and keep him safe. They'll owe me a few favors.

An osprey, doubtless coming in from a scouting run, landed in one of the wind-twisted evergreens that grew wherever they could find foothold on the slopes of the gateway hillside.

"Time for me to get back to work," Plik said. "I'll see you later."

He said the words as if they were a promise. Tiniel stared after the maimalodalu for a long moment before turning around and resuming his patrol of the silent circle of—at least for now—dormant gates.

❧

NEWS THAT THE ships of the invading fleet were readying landing craft came while Derian and Isende were in the dining hall sharing a late breakfast with some of the others who had been on late watch.

"I can't ask you to be careful," he said. "It's too late for that. I can only ask you to do your best."

Isende smiled up at him, and Derian wondered just when she had come to feel so right in the circle of his arms.

"I will. You do the same."

For a moment, Derian considered trying to convince Isende to retreat to the safety of the mainland, but he didn't let the words pass his lips. Too many people were listening, and hearing him trying to get his sweetheart away would certainly destroy morale. And, besides, Isende wouldn't do it, not even if he promised to join her—a thing he couldn't do. Both of them knew that should the defense of the Nexus Islands fail, the New World would soon be fighting for its freedom. Gak was the closest town to the Setting Sun stronghold, and would certainly be among the first to find itself immersed in war.

"Luck," Isende said, standing on her toes to kiss him, then she slipped out of his arms and hurried toward the door at the far end of the dining hall. Ynamynet would be assembling her spellcasters near the counsel building.

Derian gazed after Isende for a moment, then hurried to his cottage. He was struggling into his armor when he heard the door to the front room open. Only one person that could be.

"Firekeeper!" he called. "Come here, would you? I've got a strap twisted."

The wolf-woman padded in and reached up, straightening the offending strap. The armor fell into place quite neatly, and Derian got to work on tightening buckles and laces. Firekeeper reached to lace something at the back.

"This time, I dress you," she said, her voice husky. "Is long road since first you teach me about laces and buckles."

Derian turned and tried to find a smile for her.

"I knew those lessons would come in useful sometime. How come you're not wearing any armor? I know they were going to make you some."

"Not enough time to get used to wearing," Firekeeper said. "If we had comed back sooner, I would have tried, but now armor only make me too slow. I have taken other things—heavier shirt and pants be some armor, kit for fixing wounds and such."

Derian nodded. He wasn't about to argue, especially when what Firekeeper said did make sense. He knew that if he hadn't had opportunity to accustom himself to the weight and restriction of armor he would have been severely limited. As it was, he wished it wasn't necessary. Even though the morning was comparatively cool, he could feel sweat beginning to trickle down his neck and back. The discomfort would only get worse as the day went on.

As Derian settled his sword belt about his hips, he glanced over at the wolf-woman, thinking that something did look different about her. Quiver, knife, the little bag with her fire making gear, all were in their accustomed places. She held her unstrung bow in one hand. Maybe there were a few more pouches than usual on her belt, but that couldn't be it.

Then Derian realized what was missing. Blind Seer. In the years Derian had known them, the two had certainly spent time apart, but usually when any danger threatened, Blind Seer was there, the steady gaze of his blue eyes seeming to promise that no harm would come to Firekeeper.

Blind Seer would be with the spellcasters, with Isende. Derian wished this made him feel more secure about their safety, but he knew that should the invaders realize where the Nexans' magical support was coming from—and how very limited that support was—they would target that area immediately.

I wonder if that's why the sorcerers seemed to build so many towers, Derian thought, *or do their workings underground. They must have realized how vulnerable they were.*

A stomping of hooves and deep exhale announced Eshinarvash.

"You ride like a knight," Firekeeper said. "I think once, not so long ago, this is what you would want."

Derian tucked his helmet under his arm and went out. Eshinarvash wore a light saddle meant to protect his back and Derian's behind, but otherwise no gear.

"I think," Derian said, recalling the Battle of the Banks, "I was an idiot. I think you knew more about war and battle than I did, for all you'd never even imagined the like."

"Is still hard this imagining," Firekeeper said. "But soon we is not imagining, we is doing. That is always easier."

Derian put a foot into a stirrup and swung into the saddle. As he did so, Elation dropped from where she had been soaring above, and landed neatly on the perch set to the rear of Derian's saddle. She would be one of his scouts, and had agreed to relay messages at need. Various of the more sophisticated wingéd folk had agreed to do the same for the other commanders, while the wilder ones scouted and relayed their reports through Plik.

"I'd better get to my post," Derian said. "See you later."

Firekeeper nodded. "You will."

Eshinarvash had offered nothing but simple greeting, but as he began to carry Derian and Elation toward the gateway hill, he called to Firekeeper.

"And that mountain sheep? Has he said a word?"

"Not a word," Firekeeper said. "I go to him now, to see how he feels about being mutton for these sailors."

Derian grinned despite himself.

"Always the soul of tact, Firekeeper."

She gave him a casual wave. "Why change? Especially now when other have work so well."

With an almost playful bounce to her stride, she broke into a run. Derian gave her an answering wave, then forced himself to forget her. Firekeeper would be all right. They all would be.

He had to make himself believe that, or he was beaten before he laid hand to sword.

XXXVII

Firekeeper did her best to seem cheerful when she left Derian, but she felt far from confident that any of them would survive the next few days intact.

She had listened to the reports the yarimaimalom wingéd folk were bringing back from their examination of the fleet, and even though her grasp of precise numbers remained less than perfect, she had clearly understood that the number of armed soldiers boarding the various small boats that would bring them to shore outnumbered the Nexans and their yarimaimalom allies by many times many hands of fingers.

Nor were those who would come ashore all they had to fear. The wingéd folk had reported a number of strange devices being readied. Their descriptions were less than perfect, but Skea and some of the others had recognized them as weapons.

"They may only intend to use them to protect the ships in case we have aquatic allies," Skea had said, "but some of the more powerful catapults could be used to lob rocks or burning materials onto shore. Then, even the buildings would not be safe."

Virim is the answer, she thought, *but how do I make him do what I want?*

She found Virim standing alone but for a crippled lynx standing guard. The lynx had lost a forefoot to infection during his imprisonment, and that injury had made him determined to be among those who would try and keep the Nexus Islands from slipping from the control of those who had rescued him and his fellows.

"The human who was also watching this sheep," the lynx said, "left to join those who are preparing to fight the humans who will come on the boat. I have been watching in the human's place, but the sheep does little but graze. If it were not for those horns and those hooves, I would think it a completely usual sheep, and one more stupid than most."

Firekeeper examined Virim, and certainly he was doing a very good imitation of a particularly dull mountain sheep. A hank of the coarse, sharp-edged grass that managed to thrive in the island's sandy soil vanished into its mouth as she watched. The mountain sheep bent and took another bite, sunlight glinting erratic rainbows from its horns.

"Well, at least he won't be fainting from hunger," she said, "during what is to come."

The lynx sat back on its haunches and licked its remaining front paw. "What are you going to do with it?"

"Him," Firekeeper said firmly. "We all keep making the mistake to think of this one as a stupid thing. He—Virim—is very smart. Too smart. I would not be surprised if he has used some magic to keep us all thinking he is just a stupid sheep."

"Is that possible," the lynx said, "with the iron on him?"

Firekeeper gave a tight smile. "With this one I will believe anything is possible. I wish to take him to the shore, down there where the boats from the fleet will be landing. I have promised Skea my bow will help as it can, my Fang thereafter. I think I will bring this one. He can find if those big, curling horns can keep arrows from his fleece."

The lynx sniffed approval. "How will you drive him?"

Firekeeper uncoiled a length of rope. "I thought to lead him, but if you can keep a seat upon his back, you might prick him with your claws."

"It is a broad enough back," the lynx replied, "even with three legs I should have no problem staying on."

"Remember," Firekeeper warned, looping her rope about Virim's neck and through his horns, "this is no usual sheep."

"So we are trying to prove," the lynx said.

Firekeeper tugged at Virim's horns, but the ram refused to move. He dug in his front hooves and lowered his head. Firekeeper hid a smile within a scowl.

So he does not wish to go where the fighting is? Very good. Then maybe he will be convinced to help us.

The lynx needed no encouragement to dig in his claws, nor

did he see need to give warning. The mountain sheep gave an involuntary leap, and Firekeeper pulled, taking advantage of the transformed sorcerer's loss of stability. They moved down the slope, the mountain sheep stumbling as it tried to gain a solid foothold, the lynx yowling in feline amusement and challenge.

Few of those on the shore below turned to look. Their attention was for the long, narrow boats that were bringing the troops to shore. This particular group of defenders was under command of Wort. There was nothing of the quartermaster about the man now as he shouted for the archers in his group to fire.

"Any one of them who doesn't make it to shore is one fewer for us to deal with!" he yelled in encouragement. "Hold the gates! Hold the Nexus!"

To Firekeeper's ears, those were odd howls indeed, but the men and women kneeling on the sand seemed to take encouragement from them. Sadly, though, encouragement could not take the place of skill. Many of those shooting the bows had not so much as pulled back a bowstring before the emergency training had begun a few moonspans before. However, in their favor was the fact that the materials for making bows and arrows had been one of the few weapons that could be freely harvested from the forests near the Setting Sun stronghold, and several of the woodworkers had skill in that craft—skills learned when they served as manual laborers for King Veztressidan.

That Veztressidan has much to answer for, Firekeeper thought, continuing to haul Virim down the slope. *A pity he is dead.*

The soldiers on the landing craft were shooting at the group on the beach, but their arrows largely went wild, their aim thrown off by the erratic motion of their craft in the choppy waters near the shore. The boat had a war machine of some sort mounted in the bow, something like a large crossbow. The arrows from this carried with force and distance, and Firekeeper was glad when she realized that this weapon, at least, would lose its usefulness when the landing party was ashore.

Unless they don't mind shooting their own people, she

thought grimly as she continued to haul Virim toward where battle would certainly soon be joined.

The once great sorcerer was now bleating, but there was no coherent sense in the sound, only cries of mindless terror such as a Cousin would make.

Firekeeper kept pulling, but she felt increasingly uneasy. Virim's terror was more than playacting, surely. Yet she was certain that she was right about this creature being the "real" Virim and all of those others merely phantasms of his internal conflict. Could she have been wrong? If so, she had doomed them all.

A memory niggled in the corner of her mind, a tale told to her back when she had first sought the maimalodalum, believing that in the magic that had created them there was the answer to her own passionate desire to become a wolf in body as well as mind. Once she had realized the tales that were being told would not hold the answer, she had not listened as carefully as she might have done, but even so, the information was there.

There was something about the manner in which the Old World sorcerers had worked their magic, a problem that had made them eager to use the Wise Beasts when they had first encountered them. What was it?

She remembered then, and she used the despair that touched her heart to make her arms pull harder on the rope. Her pull was so violent that Virim stumbled into a run and the lynx nearly went flying off his back.

The spell the Old World sorcerers used involved killing a beast to take its form. Before they knew of the Royal Beasts, the Wise Beasts, the Beasts who were as intelligent as any human, they took the risk of losing their human intelligence in the merging with the animal. The risk was greater the longer they maintained the transformation. Could this have happened to Virim? Might I have caused it by forcing his mind into this one form, a form that could not hold his intelligence?

The more Firekeeper considered this, the more she felt dread that this might have been what had happened. Surely Virim, with all his longing to preserve the New World for the Beasts who were its natural inhabitants would not have used a

Royal Beast as a partner in his transformation. That said, then he must have used a Cousin, and even the most clever of Cousin-kind mountain sheep could not come close to holding the complexities of a human mind.

Firekeeper was giving way to despair when a glint of light from Virim's diamond horns reminded her that for all she was becoming accustomed to the creature, this was no normal mountain sheep. Virim had altered his vessel, but was the alternation an illusion, such as they had encountered in his fortress, or was it something more permanent? Would he have altered the body and left the mind untouched?

"And," said a sardonically familiar voice within her head, *"most importantly, what are you going to do about it? I will tell you one thing. You're right about part of your guess. Several of them, even. If you were going to pick a part of Virim to grab, this was the right one. And, you're right, Virim acquired this alternate form through a version of the same spell that would create the maimalodalum. However, in his kindness toward the creature he was using, Virim could not make himself destroy its mind completely. It remains, a thin shell that most of the time merely operates the body, but you rather surprised Virim. He took refuge beneath the mountain sheep's mind, and now he cannot—or will not—come out. You wanted him afraid, and he's very afraid—so afraid he even fears trying to save his own life."*

Firekeeper wanted to know how the Meddler knew all this, what price he would charge for his help, but there was no time for one of their leisurely debates. Screams were coming from the shoreline. The Nexans had not been the only ones with bows, and already a few of Wort's small command were injured or dead.

"I cannot reason with a sheep," she replied bluntly. "And I need this Virim's fear where I can reason with it. You are a spirit. He is spirit in hiding. Can you herd him out to where he must face what is going to happen?"

The Meddler's reply did not come immediately. In the distance, Firekeeper heard wolves howling and knew that the small pack that had joined the defenders elsewhere across the island was now racing in to meet the landing crafts. She hoped the humans would be intimidated enough to stay on their boats, that they would have shot all their arrows.

"If there was ever a time for you to meddle," Firekeeper cried to the continuing silence within her mind, "surely this is that time."

She had continued to drag the mountain sheep forward, and now they had come to a twisted pine heavy enough to anchor the rope. She wrapped the rope tightly around the tree trunk, then knotted it firm.

"Go," she said to the lynx. "Virim goes no further, and you are not equipped to fight this type of battle."

"I will go," the lynx said. "And climb a tree. If these soldiers think they will walk safely when darkness falls, they are much mistaken."

Firekeeper felt oddly encouraged by this parting promise. She strung her bow. As she set arrow to string, she listened for Blind Seer's voice among the chorus. It was not there, and again she took encouragement. If the efforts of the spellcasters had failed, then surely he would have joined the fight.

Wort's company had succeeded in slowing the landing craft, and now the chancy currents that made even the more open beaches insecure landing points were doing their part to unsettle an orderly debarking. Even so, there were knots of fighting here and there where a boat had made it to shore and the marines had jumped onto the beach, ready to meet the defenders.

Firekeeper sent an arrow into one marine, trying not to feel too bad about killing for something other than food or in immediate danger of her life. As she had said to Derian, the more abstract killing involved in war was hard for her to accept. Still, she was quick-witted enough to know that those who she did not kill from a distance she would face sooner or later.

But this is not the answer, Firekeeper thought desperately. *There are only so many arrows, only so many perfect shots. In the end, I might as well have killed none of them for all this will save the Nexans. And our resisting might well make the situation worse. Humans are terrible when they believe they have earned the right for revenge.*

Yet for all her despairing thoughts, Firekeeper kept fitting arrow to bowstring and finding targets. Her participation in the battle did not go unnoticed. The soldiers from the landing boats began to look around nervously for the source of the deadly arrows. Taking advantage of this distraction, several of Wort's soldiers managed to drive their opponents back so that they were fighting ankle deep in the dragging surf.

Firekeeper did not notice the strange war machine taking aim at her until after the huge arrow it fired sliced through the edge of the heavy sleeve protecting her upper arm. The arrow sliced flesh as well, carrying on until it anchored its quivering length in the tree to which she had tied Virim.

Automatically, Firekeeper dropped to the ground, trying to avoid any further fire. The archer, absorbed with reloading the machine, and cranking back the firing mechanism, had no attention for her.

Blood ran from Firekeeper's upper arm, coursing down the limb and spreading hot and wet between her fingers. The arrow had sliced cleanly, the sensation more like surprise than pain. That, though, would come.

Clapping her hand to the bleeding wound, Firekeeper rolled so that a rise in the ground was between her and the sight of those below. Her bow fell beside her, the string snapping, lashing against her face as if in reprimand for her carelessness.

Freely flowing blood from cuts to face and arm spattered the area with gore. Firekeeper probed the wounds, trying to evaluate the extent of the damage.

The diamond-horned mountain sheep, which to that moment had alternated staring dully with thudding its head against the trunk of the tree to which Firekeeper had bound it, now turned and stared at her with the first thing like intelligent regard she had seen in its eyes since they had come to the Nexus Islands.

"What did you expect?" she said to him. "To fight without bleeding?"

As Firekeeper spoke, her hands were busy, splashing water from her canteen onto the wound on her arm; if she lived, stitches would be a good idea. She smeared a liberal amount of an ointment made from blood briar on the cut. The ointment would slow infection and keep the skin from tightening, but most importantly it would numb the wound and the area surrounding it, enabling her to use her bow again almost immediately.

As Firekeeper bound a strip of clean cloth around the wound, she noticed that Virim was pulling at the rope, straining to sniff at a patch where her blood had soaked the surrounding earth. It was an unnatural reaction for an herbivore, and Firekeeper shivered involuntarily as she recalled what a spellcaster could do with fresh blood.

Could Virim work a spell, bound as he was with iron and half insane with terror? She couldn't spare the energy to worry about that. The large bow in the boat had not shot at her since she had fallen, but that would not last if they realized they had not taken her out of the fight.

She was in the process of retrieving her bow, and seeing if she could restring it without drawing attention to herself when she realized that Virim was talking to himself. He was using the speech of the Beasts, but although the sounds, scents, and gestures remained within the body of one creature, almost immediately she realized that there were two speakers.

Not pausing in her own labors, Firekeeper spared some attention for this peculiar exchange.

"Let me loose! Stop pushing me!"

"So the scent of blood was what it took to bring you back to the surface, huh? Think you can do anything to change what's about to happen?"

"Going to die here. Here. On this lousy scrap of rock."

"Gotta happen somewhere. Let me tell you, it doesn't matter where it happens. I died in a temple. Didn't change a thing. Well, now that I think about it, it probably did, but I'm sure you know what I mean."

"I don't want to die! Too much depends on me! I'm essential to the safety of the world."

"So we all like to think. I certainly did."

Initially, Firekeeper had thought that Virim was talking to himself again. With the mention of the temple, she began to wonder, and within a few more exchanges she was certain. The Meddler had not abandoned her when she had challenged him to help bring Virim back from wherever fear had driven him. Apparently, he had embraced the challenge, but it seemed that more had been needed to entice Virim to face the predicament he faced.

Blood—or, perhaps more truthfully, the power that he sensed dormant in the scent of her freshly shed blood—had given him some incentive to return.

Firekeeper glanced down the slope. Wort's forces, now augmented by oddly assorted yarimaimalom, seemed to have retained the upper hand—if only just. A few of the landing craft were backing oars, and Firekeeper saw that they held the wounded. That in itself was encouraging. If the invaders were completely confident they would win, they would have left the wounded ashore where they could be more easily treated.

But then, she thought, *this may have been a test on their part, an attempt to see how well prepared we were. Surely, they will regroup and try again. That is what a wolf pack would do. Wear down the herd until enough are wearied that the hunt is a success.*

And then there are the gates, she thought, her momentary pleasure at Wort's success fading as she considered the greater complexity of the situation. *They may expect support through those, and although that is not likely, as long as we must protect not only the landing points on the shore, but the gates as well . . . Yes. They are not cowardly to withdraw. They are very wise.*

Anger flared in her, anger at the situation, anger at herself for failing to do more, anger especially at the mountain sheep who even now continued to blather about his own importance and how he couldn't be permitted to die.

"So," she said, turning on Virim, the arrow she had put to string pulled back, and the hand that held the string quivering, not so much from strain, but from a mad desire to let it loose. "So, what will you do to preserve that life that is so important? I am sure the Meddler has told you what we want. Will you do it?"

Virim did not pretend not to understand.

"I cannot . . . cannot . . . You don't understand the complexities of the situation. I once thought things were simple, too. Believe me, a century of watching things go anything but the way I planned, the way I intended, that has taught me to be careful. Very, very careful."

Firekeeper snarled, as inarticulate as Virim himself had been a short time before.

The Meddler spoke and she heard him both in her head, and through the medium of the mountain sheep.

"Firekeeper! Give me a chance! I don't think killing him will break querinalo's hold. I've been—can you believe that I have gone into his mind enough to know something of his thoughts?"

"Harder to believe you are not," Firekeeper replied, deliberately not vocalizing her reply. She did let up the pull on her bowstring though, and she saw the mountain sheep's ears relax the slightest bit.

"I think the curse has its own momentum now," the Meddler continued. "I'm not saying that it can't ever be stopped, but doing so is not going to be as easy as ending this one pathetic life."

Firekeeper, who wondered if the Meddler himself might have reasons for wanting Virim kept alive, still had to admit that what he said had sense in it. Querinalo's range was too vast, its power too comprehensive for her to believe there could be as easy a solution as one death.

Still, no reason for Virim to know this.

"I have no choice," she said. "The fleet may win today, may come tomorrow. We must have others to fight for us. With querinalo we cannot recruit. Without it . . . Even then we would be sorely pressed. Humans are not wolves to quickly learn to hunt together, and even the best packs are those that have hunted together for a long time."

"A compromise, then." Virim spoke to her with remarkable lack of vacillation. "I will tell you where you can find others to fight for you."

"What?" Firekeeper said. "Who?"

"The Bound," Virim replied eagerly. "They have vowed themselves to me and my defense. They could be brought here through the gates."

"Too late," Firekeeper retorted.

She saw a marine about to attack Wort from behind and loosed an arrow to stop him. Wort, absorbed with the soldier he had been fighting, didn't even notice. One of the armed landing craft did, and a quickly aimed arrow shredded leaves from Virim's tree.

"Stop that!" Virim cried, and fell again to panicked ovine bleating that needed no translation. "You're putting us in danger!"

As Firekeeper fit another arrow to her bowstring, she heard the mountain sheep utter what had to be a profanity, although she recognized neither it nor the language in which it was spoken. Part of her brain did take idle note that whatever the word was, it could be shaped by a sheep's mouth.

She took careful aim, and the sailor behind the big bow on the landing craft fell back, bending over his thigh. Distance and the sounds of the sea and other battles drowned out his screams, but Firekeeper had no difficulty imagining them.

Something warm and wet hit her foot, and she noticed that using her bow had started her wounded arm bleeding again. The flow had completely soaked the bandage wrapped around arm, but the blood-briar ointment was doing its job and she felt no pain.

The Meddler's voice in her head said in the equivalent of a whisper, "Firekeeper, your blood. It's wasted. Give it to me, and I will owe you . . . serve you. Help you win this war. I promise."

"Promise," she demanded, as a counter to her revulsion, but she knew that was a frail enough demand. What could she do if the Meddler refused to honor his oath? "Promise or the blood in you will turn as sour and empty as your word."

Firekeeper was already moving closer to the bound mountain sheep when the Meddler's whispered voice in her head said, *"I promise, by the love I hold for you, by the blood you give to me, I promise."*

Firekeeper undid the sodden bandage on her upper arm, dropping it where the mountain sheep could reach. For good measure, she let some fresh blood run down her arm, between her fingers, into her cupped hand. This she flung directly at the mountain sheep. The wet mass landed between the creature's horns, seeping into the wool on the face, accenting the ornate patterns of the curling wool.

When the fresh blood touched the mountain sheep, Firekeeper felt a strange reverberation, a vibration of forces so powerful she staggered. Yet, not one of those fighting on the shore paused for the least instant, nor did the ravens and gulls falter in their flight.

Firekeeper drew her own conclusions from this. Rather than trying to see what she suspected was a purely internal battle, she drew her Fang and cut the rope that bound the diamond-horned mountain sheep to the tree.

She half expected the creature to run away or to collapse, but it did neither. Instead, the golden hooves remained rooted, the legs leading up to the heavy, compact body slightly splayed. The mountain sheep's curved-horned head swung back and forth, catching the sunlight and giving back rainbows in which sanguine hues dominated.

The reverberation faded, and Firekeeper stepped clear and methodically rebound her wounded arm. She felt light-headed, but that was only to be expected. Her canteen contained only a few swallows. Drinking these meant she had to leave her wound unwashed, but she smeared on more of the blood-briar ointment before binding the wound with a fresh bandage.

Her bow lay on the ground a few paces away. She picked it up and was setting an arrow to the string when the diamond-horned mountain sheep spoke in a purely human voice with the Meddler's familiar intonations.

"I've won, for now. Firekeeper, I can't do too much, but I can do a little. What do you want?"

Firekeeper checked down the slope. Wort's force had succeeded in its small battle, and the raven's cries told her that elsewhere on the Nexus Islands the landing parties were currently in retreat.

"I do not wish to waste what favors you owe me," she said bluntly. "Can you end querinalo?"

"I can and cannot. It is a complicated matter to explain."

"Save," Firekeeper said. "But remember, you are bound to me by blood. Do nothing to undo that binding. For now, I will go and help the others. Later, we will talk."

The mountain sheep's mouth should not have been able to shape the Meddler's sardonic smile, but somehow it did so.

"Ever trusting, dear Firekeeper. Ever trusting."

But Firekeeper had no words for him. A lean grey streak was racing toward her over the sands, up the rocky rise. Blind Seer, blue eyes glowing in triumph, checked himself in mid-leap when he caught the scent of her blood.

"We have won!" he howled. "The boats are leaving. And you, dear heart? I smell your blood, but you still stand."

"I stand," Firekeeper said, "barely. And I have much to tell."

"I am certain," Blind Seer said. "Ynamynet said she sensed great magics being worked here. Is there a tale?"

"A tale and again," Firekeeper replied. "Shouldn't it wait until we have helped the wounded?"

Blind Seer's ears flickered flat, then rose again.

"I spoke too quickly when I said we had won," he admitted. "Rather, we have respite. Others must pick up the wounded and gather the dead. We who live and lead are commanded to gather and plan the next stage of this hunt."

Firekeeper let her hand fall onto the wolf's strong back, taking comfort in his closeness. Then she turned to the diamond-horned mountain sheep.

"The Meddler has taken rulership of Virim," she said, "for now, at least. He is sworn to aide us."

Blind Seer did not look in the least surprised, and Firekeeper wondered what his newly attuned sense for magic had told him.

"Do you come with us," he said to the Meddler, a growl underlying his words, "or do I drive you as dogs drive the sheep?"

"I come," the Meddler replied, "most humbly. My word is given to Firekeeper, and although she may not believe me, I would not disappoint her for all the world."

Firekeeper, remembering confessions of love, knew she was blushing, but she ignored her skin's betrayal and struggled for composure.

"For all the world?" she challenged mockingly.

"Well," the Meddler admitted, falling into step beside her and Blind Seer as the blue-eyed wolf led the way to where the Nexan leaders were gathering, "perhaps for all the world. After all, wouldn't I then have everything—and everyone I desire?"

XXXVIII

PLIK DID NOT need his lost sense for magic to tell him that things had changed with the mountain sheep, nor that Firekeeper, blood-smeared and disheveled as she was, was coming to the hastily gathered conference with something other to report about than her small corner of the battle.

Yet she was not swaggering as Plik had seen the wolfwoman do when victorious. There was a tension about her that was at odds with the chattering energy displayed by most of the humans coming to the gathering that was being held on a sheltered section of open hillside.

Here is one, Plik thought, *who will not need to be convinced that this one small victory does not mean we have won the war.*

Firekeeper had borrowed a canteen from someone and was taking long swallows. She seated herself on the ground between the reclining mountain sheep and Blind Seer. Without comment, she had unbound her upper arm and pulled back the leather of her sleeve to expose a nasty slice.

Using the edge of the bandage, she wiped off the ointment covering the wound, then settled back. Blind Seer set to cleaning away the crusted blood, his tongue moving in rhythmic swipes, his ears making comment on the mingled taste of human blood and blood briar. When he finished there, he moved on to the side of her face.

None of those slowly settling in commented at this strange first aid. Plik thought you could tell who had been posted where by the degree of their injuries. Those who had been on the gateway hillside remained relatively pristine. Derian provided a marked exception. Plik knew that when the fighting had started and a group holding one of the main beaches had begun to fall back, Derian and Eshinarvash had come racing down to help.

Whether Derian's strange appearance had turned the tide of battle, or whether his orders had rallied the frightened amateur warriors, Plik didn't know. What he did know was that without Derian's action they would likely not be holding this meeting.

And if some force had come through the gate then? Plik thought. *If Derian had been needed there?*

He shook the thought from his mind. No one had come through the gates as of yet, but only the most optimistic among them believed this would not happen.

Derian and Ynamynet broke from their hurried conference, and glanced about the small circle of those they had summoned.

"We're holding," Derian began, "and more or less alive. Skea is reviewing his forces now, reassigning and redistributing troops to cover where bands were weakened. Kalyndra is going to be transporting the worst wounded to where Doc—Sir Jared Surcliffe—can hopefully pull them through. Don't expect miracles, though. Doc possesses a potent talent, but he can't do miracles, and the more he's drawn on, the less he'll be able to do later."

Ynamynet took over. "Let's have brief reports from each of you. Plik, what do our scouts say?"

"The wingéd folk report that, at least for now, the Nexus Islands remain ours. All of those who landed have either retreated, been captured, or are dead."

There was a small cheer at this. Plik smiled, knowing how much high morale was needed.

"However," he went on, "the invaders seem to have finally figured out who our scouts are. The gulls and ospreys report that the wind currents near the large vessels have become erratic. One gull was actually attacked by a little whirlwind and shredded to pieces before she could get away. This makes the rest of the wingéd folk hesitant about getting in too close."

"For good reason," Ynamynet replied. "Unhappily, there is nothing my small group of spellcasters can do to counter any protective magics that the fleet is using. We simply don't have the power to strike at that range."

Plik nodded. "That will be relayed to the wingéd folk immediately, and they will do their scouting from a distance."

Derian sighed heavily and ran his hands through his hair.

"We'll lose information, but that can't be helped. Better not to lose any of the wingéd folk. My report is fairly simple. There has been no significant action at the gates. Once or twice, watchers reported thinking they saw the beginnings of an activation glow, but that never developed. I know this has given rise to hopeful rumors that something is wrong with the gates—that perhaps the iron we've put around them has ruined their ability to transmit—but I'm not so optimistic."

Ynamynet shook her head. "Neither am I. I suspect instead that those were trial runs. My guess is that those who are using the gates have a coordinated time and date to activate them, but that some nervous or impatient Once Dead had to test."

"Is such coordination possible?" asked Xaha. The young man from Tey-yo had been assigned to attend in Skea's stead and bring the general a report.

"You came to the Nexus Islands after Veztressidan's wars, didn't you?" Ynamynet said. "Yes. It's possible. Simple, mundane logistics. They probably set a date a long time back, based on when the fleet should arrive."

"Right," Xaha said. "My report is pretty simple. We don't have a precise count of losses and inactives yet, but Skea thinks the shore forces can hold. He actually thinks some things—like coordination with the yarimaimalom—will work better if and when we are under attack a second time. That's the good side.

"The bad is that we spent a lot of arrows and throwing spears warding off the first attack. We have reserves enough to manage a second round, maybe even a third, but the marines on the landing craft are going to know what to expect. Many on the longboats were slow to realize that they needed to get shields up. That's not going to happen again."

Ynamynet nodded thanks to Xaha, then said, "I have one thing to add to Xaha's report. I think I know who is commanding the fleet and thus the naval assault. Some of us suspected this would be the case, but what we've seen today is confirmation."

"Who?" Derian asked.

"Hurwin the Hammer, king of the Tavetch."

"Tavetch," Derian said. "I think that Tavetch provided the Old World rulers for part of our Stonehold. The Stoneholders are pretty martial."

"So are the Tavetch," Ynamynet said. "Hurwin the Hammer fought against Veztressidan. His daughter, Gidji, is married to Veztressidan's son, Bryessidan, so we can make a pretty shrewd guess that the Mires also stands against us. Urgana has been doing what she can to identify the heraldry on the flags of various ships of the fleet, but she's been coming up mostly blank. Now I think I know why.

"Hurwin is not one to give away anything for nothing, not even for a brag. His ships have probably been sailing under alternate banners since they left Pelland or wherever. That's plenty long enough for the sailors to get used to the altered devices. And this way Hurwin could be sure we wouldn't be able to guess who was where and go after them."

"I'm not sure I understand," Plik said. "I'm sorry."

"No need to apologize," Ynamynet said. "Simply put, different lands have different reputations for military ability. The Tavetch are warlike, but they are also most skilled at naval warfare. The people of Azure Towers are skilled enough at war, but mostly from need rather than inclination. They have been involved in a long, ongoing feud with Hearthome and have had little choice but to learn how to fight."

"Hearthome," Derian said, "is aggressive then?"

"Very," Ynamynet said. "They faced Veztressidan first and lost. They have never forgotten that humiliation. Their queen would like to rule all of Pelland, but has to be careful how she expresses her ambitions lest she face an allied force similar to that which rose against Veztressidan."

"Got it," Derian said. "So this King Hurwin figures that if we knew who was on what ship, then we might target our attacks accordingly."

Firekeeper said, "Wolves take weak first, but humans might take strong and hope that herd goes to pieces. Either way, this Hurwin is wise. I have report, too, me and . . ."

She paused, looked at the mountain sheep, her head tilted in inquiry.

"I not know what to call. Is Virim. Is Meddler."

The mountain sheep spoke in a flat version of Liglimosh in which the plosives were almost missing.

"I am both, but mostly the Meddler. If you would take this wire off of me, I would be more comfortable, and might find it possible to return to a human form. That would be useful for many reasons."

Plik thought it was probably a good thing that Harjeedian was occupied with treating the wounded alongside Zebel. Surely the aridisdu would not have been able to resist expressing fear and revulsion at finding the Meddler even so strangely reembodied.

Firekeeper, however, seemed beyond revulsion. Her wounded arm was clean now, and she had anointed and wrapped it. Blind Seer, his ministering done, reserved his comment to raised hackles.

Wearily, the wolf-woman looked at Ynamynet.

"You is wise in magic. I leave this deciding to you. Blind Seer say where defending this place is considered, you is to be trusted. Do we unbind Meddler or no?"

Ynamynet's lips twisted in a wry smile at this mixed compliment, but said nothing. Instead she bit a drop of blood from the edge of her finger and traced a complex pattern in the air. When that was done, she addressed her attention to the mountain sheep.

"What do you have to offer us if we let you free of those wires? I can see considerable power, but arrayed in what I must—for lack of better words—call layers. The wire is keeping the topmost layer in check, and I think until that is released you would find doing any but elementary spells quite difficult, and even those would use impressive amounts of power."

The mountain sheep replied with disarming honestly.

"The few I have done I could not have done if Firekeeper had not let me have use of some of her shed blood. Without the wire, I can tap some of the power Virim has stored within him, but eventually I will need either another such source or access to blood."

"If we find ourselves fighting again," Ynamynet said, "blood should be readily available. What is this about stored power?"

The Meddler shifted restlessly. "This is neither time nor place for long lectures in magical theory. However, you do not think blood magic is the only form there is?"

"It is the only form—other than talents—I know how to use," Ynamynet replied. "But I have heard tales of other forms. Some of these use power sources worse than blood."

"And some do not," the Meddler countered. "Virim gathered a great deal of power to him, both through the medium of querinalo and through complex rituals that were once taught at places like Azure Towers. Do you wish me to waste time telling you more? I warn you. I agree with what has already been said. The invaders will attack again—when, I cannot say, but I do not think this King Hurwin will give us time to completely rebuild our losses."

Ynamynet looked as if she were at war with herself, but the immediacy of their need clearly won out over other considerations.

"Very well. You are right. This is not the time for theoretical discussions. What will you do if we unbind you?"

"Whatever Firekeeper commands, within the best of my ability to do so," the Meddler answered promptly. "I gave her my word that if she aided me, I would aid her. Her goal from the start has been the defeat of querinalo. I cannot do that, but I can do two things that will be of considerable help.

"First, I can tell you who does and does not possess magical ability. This will enable you to bring through reinforcements, if you so choose. Second, I can proof one or two who do possess talent against querinalo's curse. I wish I could lift the curse in its entirety, but even with Virim's memories to tap I would find this difficult to do without further study."

"Virim's memories?" Derian asked sharply. "Is he dead then and you have taken his place?"

"He is not dead," the Meddler replied. "He is hiding . . . again, this is a matter best left for later discussion. Suffice that I can help you, if you will let me help you."

Ynamynet looked at Firekeeper. "He says he will answer to you."

"And I follow you, in this," Firekeeper said. "Where is magic, you is One. I am pup. Even Blind Seer say this."

Ynamynet's smile this time was open and as warm as it ever became. Then she grew serious as she studied the mountain sheep.

"I cannot say I am exactly thrilled with working in compromise with the power that destroyed my people, that scarred myself and my family, but this is a time for compromises. Firekeeper, unbind the mountain sheep, and I will do my best to help you weigh the merits of whatever plan he suggests."

"Is all," the wolf-woman said, moving to untwist the wire about the diamond-horned mountain sheep's legs, "we can ask or hope."

❧

As firekeeper unbound the mountain sheep—or Virim—or the Meddler—Derian's head swam at the complexities of such a chaotic identity. He glanced up the gateway hillside, taking reassurance from seeing Eshinarvash standing calm and steady.

The Wise Horse had promised to warn Derian if the least thing went wrong up by the gates, and seeing him waiting, lipping the grass that thrust up from between the worn paving stones, Derian felt that here was a stability to balance the chaos a few steps away from him.

A gasp from someone—he thought perhaps Xaha—drew his attention back to the small gathering. Derian swung around, reaching for his sword, but before he could draw it, he saw that this was something for which no sword was needed—at least not yet.

The mountain sheep was blurred—there was no other term for it. Within that blurring, a gradual metamorphosis was under way. The figure was elongating, the limbs growing longer, the torso becoming more cylindrical, less barrel-like. As Derian watched, the mountain sheep turned into an elderly man with an unkempt grey beard that reached to the middle of his chest, lined skin, and pale, all too knowing eyes. He wore a tunic that strongly resembled the mountain sheep's wooly hide, dark brown woven trousers, and comfortable slippers. Last to vanish were the curling diamond horns, which remained jutting from the man's skull for a sparkling moment after the transition was complete.

"What you do, Meddler?" Firekeeper said, her voice dropping into a growl that matched Blind Seer's own.

"I am," the Meddler said, his voice thinner and quavering, as it was projected by the elderly chest and throat of his new form, but still somehow recognizably his own, "keeping my promise to you. I told you that Virim had hoarded power, and that I would turn that power to your cause. Some of that power was being used to keep him in the mountain sheep's form. By returning to this form, not only do I preserve that power, I gain the ability to communicate easily with all those here. That, too, should assist you."

Firekeeper studied him. "You look some like older Bruck."

"No great surprise there," the Meddler commented. "Bruck was an image of Virim when he was younger, before he committed to the course of action that would create querinalo."

The old man glanced from side to side, then moved with great care toward a large stone.

"If you don't mind, I'll just seat myself here. This body is in a bit better condition than it looks—but only a bit."

There was no comment as the Meddler settled himself onto the rock with some small grunts and a few popping joints. Then he looked around the gathered group and gave them a sunny smile.

He kept all his teeth, Derian thought. *And alive for what must be something like a hundred and fifty years—no, more. Amazing . . . and frightening.*

Ynamynet had turned to face the transformed Meddler, and now she spoke, her tone so matter-of-fact that it was a statement that she, at least, was not about to be impressed until something more had been done.

"I have been thinking about what you said before—about how you could check someone to see if they had any magical talent, and how if they did you could proof them against querinalo so they could come here without risking infection. You would need to see them in person to do this?"

"That is so."

Ynamynet nodded and turned her attention to the group at large. "I have a thought about who we might ask to aid us."

"Who?" Firekeeper asked.

"Grateful Peace of New Kelvin."

"Peace? What he do?"

Ynamynet's answer was indirect. "I have been thinking. One of our problems is that we face invasion from two points. We have already seen what the fleet can do. We suspect that our opponents will attempt an assault through the gates as well. Hopefully, they won't get through. Even if they do not, however, the fleet remains a threat. I have been wondering if Grateful Peace might not provide us with the means to stop that threat."

"How?" Derian asked. "New Kelvin is landlocked and possesses no navy. Even if it did, we could not get the ships through here. Do you think Peace might be able to recruit soldiers to fight for us? That's possible, and certainly the New Kelvinese would be less likely than any other New World nation to react negatively to the idea of magical gates, but Grateful Peace isn't their ruler. He does have the Healed One's favor, but still . . ."

Ynamynet raised one thin hand, and Derian realized that he'd been babbling, all his thoughts and worries flooding out as soon as Ynamynet raised the dam.

"Sorry," he said. "I've been thinking about this."

"I can tell," she replied. "Remember, I have visited with Grateful Peace several times after he requested opportunity to meet someone from the Old World. During one of these visits, I mentioned to him the research we were doing regarding the sea monsters that legend tells us once patrolled these waters. Grateful Peace's expression became distant, so distant that I thought I might have offended him.

"When I apologized, he shook himself slightly and said, 'I'm sorry. I was thinking about things I have . . . heard. I think you may indeed have a productive course of action there.' He would not say any more about it, but later Derian related something about the events surrounding what he called the Dragon of Despair. He mentioned that Grateful Peace was the one who ultimately rescued his land and his ruler from the creature. Combining these two things, I have wondered if Grateful Peace is what was called in my homeland a Dragon Speaker."

"Dragon Speaker?" Firekeeper said, startled. "That is the one who rules New Kelvin with Healed One. How did your land know him?"

Ynamynet looked puzzled for a moment, then she replied, "I suspect that the title, as with so much in New Kelvin, was adapted from one already in use in the Old World. The First Healed One seems to have been one who understood the power of words, especially words that resonate with former, potent usage."

Firekeeper shrugged. "If you so say, I believe. So you think that Peace can speak with dragons. I think he can. What is that to Nexus Islands?"

"What if Grateful Peace can speak to other creatures as well?" Ynamynet said eagerly. "What if those sea monsters are still here, still in these waters? What if they can be awakened to take up their duties as guardians once again? Not only would we no longer need to worry about the fleet, but we might be able to keep a channel clear so that the Bound could be brought through from that other gate."

Derian considered this, his initial excitement blending into apprehension. When he had told the tale of the Dragon of Despair, he had mentioned that Grateful Peace had won the victory, but Peace had not mentioned the price he had paid to do so. Surely, he could not be asked to take such a risk again. He was already an old man, and working as a Dragon Speaker of any sort would certainly be a risk.

From Firekeeper's expression, she, too, had thought of this, but her wolf-influenced attitude was different than Derian's own.

"We could ask Peace," she said. "If Nexus Islands fall, and New Kelvin is attacked, Peace will speak to dragons sure enough rather than see his pack be harmed. This might be a way to save him from that."

Ynamynet did not ask any of the many questions that were obviously begging to be answered, restricting herself to a simple, "Do we try this, or do we consider other ways that the Meddler's abilities may be turned to our advantage?"

"Reluctant as I am," Derian said, "I think I agree with Firekeeper. Grateful Peace must be given the opportunity to decide on which front he will defend his people. However, I want to ask him myself."

"You?" Ynamynet said. "You have refused to be seen by him to this point. Why would that change?"

"Because Peace has to see what he is risking," Derian said simply. "I am sure the Meddler will do his best to assure that querinalo doesn't get its claws into anyone we bring through the gates, but he himself admitted that he's only had a short time to digest Virim's lore."

"Fair," Ynamynet agreed. "Grateful Peace has regularly checked in at the gate. He is likely to be there at the assigned time today."

"Then," Derian glanced back up the hillside, "if nothing else happens today, I'll go through."

"Me, too!" Firekeeper said. "I would like to see Peace and Citrine."

"No," Derian said firmly. "You stay here and mind the Meddler."

Firekeeper looked at the old man sitting on the boulder, and frowned. He smiled back at her, all wise innocence.

"Yes," Firekeeper said, resting her hand on Blind Seer's back. "We watch the Meddler. Blind Seer and I."

NOTHING HAPPENED TO interrupt Derian's plans, so at midday, still armed and armored, he had Enigma take him through the gate into New Kelvin. The puma then curled up in a ball in front of the gate, and apparently fell instantly asleep.

A familiar voice greeted Derian before he had taken more than a few steps.

"Derian Counselor." There was a long pause; then, "Yes. Derian Counselor. You have changed, but I still know you."

Grateful Peace, lantern in hand, Citrine walking beside him, came from the sheltered alcove from which he had been watching.

"You," Derian said, giving Grateful Peace the New Kelvinese version of a formal greeting, perfect down to hand gestures, "have not."

He turned and smiled at Citrine. "You, however, have. You're taller, and quite a bit prettier. I'm glad you haven't gone all in for tattoos."

"I'm too young," Citrine said, "or so Grateful Peace says.

He says that tattoos are for when you know your own mind well enough to mark it on your skin. I have one, but it's little."

She pulled back her red-gold hair to show a small ornamental mark in the vicinity of her right temple.

"That says I'm Grateful Peace's daughter. He agreed with me that it wasn't too early to say so on my skin."

"What did Sapphire say when she saw that?" Derian asked, keeping up the small talk, knowing it was giving his friends a chance to adjust to his transformation.

"Crown Princess Sapphire said I should get one for Hawk Haven, then, too," Citrine said, with a giggle that sounded only a little forced, "since my birth land hasn't thrown me out. I said I would do it—but for Bright Haven, when that day came and I danced at her and Shad's joint coronation."

"Very politic," Derian said. "You are a credit to your father's famed diplomacy."

Citrine's smile this time was completely natural. She stepped forward and gave Derian a deliberate hug, flinching back not from his person but when she felt the armor he wore beneath his loose outer tunic.

"Armor? Certainly not because you were coming to see us!"

"Armor," Derian repeated, "because as we dreaded, the Nexus Islands are under attack."

"Tell us if we may help," Grateful Peace said.

Feeling a bit of a louse, Derian launched into an abbreviated account of what had happened, including the Meddler's enlarged role, and ending with Ynamynet's request.

"I had wondered if Firekeeper had managed to return without passing through this gate," Grateful Peace said when Derian concluded, "or if she had found another route. Well, it seems she has found an answer, if not the one for which you might have hoped."

Derian nodded, but said nothing. He would not push Peace to decide to join the Nexans in their defense. Peace might not be able to do anything in any case. The Dragon of Despair might have nothing to do with sea monsters.

He waited, and Peace's next words did not give him a great deal of reason for hope.

"Citrine, we brought some refreshments in case our wait was long. Why not pour us all drinks? I don't recall if Derian liked fruit tarts, but bring those as well."

Derian accepted the proffered drink and sincerely enjoyed the pastry. Peace had fallen into deep thought, so Citrine chatted politely with Derian, bringing him up to date on mutual friends. Several times she mentioned Edlin Norwood, and finally the import of these comments penetrated Derian's tension.

"Edlin? You say you saw Edlin yesterday? Is he in New Kelvin?"

Citrine laughed at his astonishment. "That's right. I guess we didn't tell anyone, did we? Firekeeper had so much to tell when she came through, and then we've only seen Ynamynet and the puma, and neither of them would really care. Yes. Edlin is here. He's the assistant to the ambassador from Hawk Haven to New Kelvin."

"Edlin? We're talking about Lord Edlin, son of Norvin Norwood?"

"People do change over time," Citrine said reprovingly. "Edlin went through a lot, and he came out of it . . . not really changed. He's still as goofy as ever, but his interests broadened. He and Peace stayed close, and so his New Kelvinese got better and better. He's been with the embassy for at least a year now. The ambassador doesn't mind. Edlin goes to all the formal affairs she doesn't want to bother with."

"Edlin," Derian repeated in wonder. "What does his father think?"

"Earl Kestrel is quite pleased," Citrine said. "Remember, the Norwood grant is just across the White Water River. Having his son and heir apparent intimate with the nation across the border is a good thing for all concerned."

"I can see that," Derian said.

"Borders," said Grateful Peace, speaking for the first time since he directed Citrine to get the refreshments. "That term certainly has changed with the discovery of the Nexus Islands. We never knew that we had a border in our basement. What other borders might there be?"

"I cannot say," Derian said honestly. "We think that each area in the New World probably had just one gate but we cannot know. We had no idea, for example, that the gate Firekeeper found to the northwest was there."

Grateful Peace nodded. "I see. It seems to me that my best choice would be to join the Nexans. At least there is a border we can see and defend."

Derian bowed his head and looked toward the gate. With a cat-like sense of timing, Enigma rose and stretched.

"I will go and speak with the Meddler," Derian said, "and we'll get the appropriate precautions in place before bringing you to the Nexus Islands."

"I need to make a few arrangements myself," Peace said. "I cannot simply disappear from Thendulla Lypella without raising comment. Shall we meet again in a few hours?"

Derian nodded. "I can't promise I'll be here myself, but if the fighting has not begun again, someone will be here for you. My guess is Firekeeper. She's the one to whom the Meddler made his promise."

"Then, if the fighting does not begin again," Grateful Peace agreed soberly, "I shall be waiting here for whoever comes. Good luck, my friend."

Derian smiled. "Thank you, but I cannot help but feel that luck is something you need to make, and I think by coming and speaking to you, I've added to our luck."

XXXIX

"EDLIN?" FIREKEEPER SAID, her voice alive with the purest astonishment. "Edlin? You here?"

Edlin Norwood, the young man eventually slated to be Duke Kestrel—but only after the deaths of his grandmother and father—stood in the lantern-lit darkness of the under tunnels of Thendulla Lypella.

The young man wore his hair pulled back in a queue, after the style of Hawk Haven, but his clothing showed the influence of New Kelvin's elaborate and expensive fabrics. Superficially, he looked much the same as he had when Firekeeper had last seen him three years before, at the festivities celebrating the naming of Prince Sun of Bright Haven, but she couldn't help but feel there was something different about him.

Edlin hadn't put on weight, and his shoulders might be marginally broader, but nonetheless there was a sense of steadiness, even a bit of gravity, that had not been there before. His smile, however, was as broad and open, and his manner of speech as uninhibited as ever she had heard.

All but bounding over to Firekeeper, Edlin gave her an enthusiastic embrace that reminded her of how young wolves fling themselves into their elders in the pack. Bending, he thumped Blind Seer resoundingly on the shoulder, to which the blue-eyed wolf responded with a long sloppy lick.

Even though Edlin once said he loved me and wanted to marry me, Firekeeper thought, *Blind Seer has never acted toward him as he does to the Meddler. Is it because he knew Edlin was never a threat to the primacy he holds in my heart? Does that mean I have given him reason to think the Meddler might be such a threat?*

The thought was uncomfortable, and Firekeeper shoved it from her mind by concentrating on Edlin. He had just completed giving Enigma a respectful bow after the fashion of Hawk Haven. The puma, torn between amusement and pleasure, was stretching his body in a long bow clearly modeled after the one Blind Seer had created to bridge the gap between human manners and those of wolves.

"You? Here? Why?" Firekeeper said.

"Not enough that I would want to see my sister, what?" Edlin said happily. "I'm working in the embassy here, don't you know. Still visit with Grateful Peace and Cousin Citrine whenever I can—almost every day. Happened to have come up to return some books when Grateful Peace returned. Didn't take too much to weasel out of him what was going on."

Grateful Peace, who had been silently studying the Meddler, looked at Edlin with a mixture of exasperation and genuine affection. Firekeeper knew that without Edlin, Grateful Peace would likely have been killed when the two men had been imprisoned together during the worst days of the reign of Melina as Consolor of the Healed One. Even so, Firekeeper suspected there were times that Peace wanted to thump the young man soundly between the ears.

"There was little 'weaseling' needed," Grateful Peace said with dignity. "It had already been agreed that the situation with the Nexus Islands was crucial enough that a few other people needed to know at least something. I had written a missive to be given to the Healed One if I did not return. I thought to give Edlin similar information, knowing that not even torture could make him relay the information prematurely."

Edlin beamed at the compliment.

"But what I did not expect," Grateful Peace said, "was that Edlin would insist on being permitted to come with me."

Edlin's cheerfulness faded. "Grateful Peace isn't a young man, and I'm not about to have him go into a war zone with no other bodyguard than Citrine. She can only look one way at a time, after all, and it sounded to me that if Peace does manage to pull off what Derian asked, then he's going to become a prime candidate for retaliation. I said I was coming, what?

"When Peace gave me the what-ho, come along, my boy, I dashed on down to the good old embassy, grabbed some of my gear, told Ambassador Redbriar that I was off to go hunting with some of the young bucks, and she sent me off with her blessings. Before I went, I scribbled her a version of the same patter the Healed One will get. My valet will give it to her if I don't come back, and he won't read it first, you can count on that. He's a younger brother of my father's man, and you know how reliable Valet is."

Firekeeper did indeed, and despite the seriousness of the situation, she smiled at the thought of Valet. Doubtless that esteemable man was still polishing the earl's boots and pressing his trousers, utterly content with his place in the pack. Then she gave Edlin an approving pat on the arm.

"I try and keep Peace safe. I would be in fighting, but I would have some of the yarimaimalom . . ."

She paused, but apparently in his new diplomatic capacity, Edlin had heard the Liglimosh term, for he signaled for her to continue.

"I think to have some of the yarimaimalom to watch him, but he cannot speak with them. A human would be better, and I know you is good with a bow."

"I've gotten better, too," Citrine said proudly. She was clad in simple but functional armor, probably meant more for practice than for actual warfare, but she bore its weight easily and moved in it without discomfort. "The New Kelvinese raise their armies from the citizens, so everyone is expected to know something about weapons. I've been training with the bow, and the New Kelvinese sword."

"I don't suppose I need to explain," Grateful Peace said, "that Citrine also refused to remain behind."

"Is good," Firekeeper said, "when the pack stand together."

She turned to the Meddler. "What you need to do?"

"I have been inspecting their auras," the old man with the Meddler's mannerisms said, "while you were exchanging your greetings, but I could assess their needs far better if each of them would permit me both to touch them, and to . . ."

He looked as apologetic as the Meddler ever could. "Give

me just the smallest drop of their blood, far less than they will need to give to the gate."

"Only a little," Firekeeper said, "and you keep none back."

"Not a fraction of a drop," the Meddler promised. "I assume you would prefer to do the deed?"

For answer, Firekeeper extracted a small leather folder from one of the pouches hanging from her belt. It contained a few small razors, a selection of needles, and several other items related to the extraction and storage of blood. Ynamynet had told her that such wallets had once been common, and that when those with a talent for spellcasting had begun to survive querinalo, they had been rediscovered and put to use again.

Firekeeper's Fang was perfectly suited for the task at hand, but she had learned that specialized tools were good as well. Besides, there was something about the deadly blade in her hand, no matter how steadily she held it, that made people tend to flinch away when she came toward them with it.

"I make just a little hole," she promised. "Who is first?"

Grateful Peace stepped forward. "I will go first. After all, if for some reason this Meddler says I should not go, then Citrine, at least, is going no farther than this point."

The girl—young woman now, Firekeeper reminded herself—looked for a moment very much like her older sister, Sapphire, for all that the two were so different in coloring and general personality. But Citrine knew her duty to her One as well, and raised no protest.

"Give me a hand," Firekeeper said to Grateful Peace.

He extended his left hand, and with complete disregard for the needle Firekeeper was about to put into his finger, turned to face the Meddler.

"Firekeeper does not think introductions are necessary," he said, flinching the slightest bit when the needle pricked his finger, "when everyone should be able to figure out who everyone else is, but I come from a more formal culture. My name is Grateful Peace. I have been Illuminator and Dragon's Eye, and now have the continued honor to serve Toriovico, the reigning Healed One of New Kelvin."

"And I," the Meddler said, "am commonly called the Meddler, although I sincerely believe that 'a meddler' is a more honest title. Certainly, there are others here who meddle."

He looked pointedly at Firekeeper as he said so, but she pretended to be absorbed in gently squeezing a single drop of Grateful Peace's blood onto a thin piece of glass her wallet held for just this purpose.

The Meddler continued, "I suppose I should also admit to a rather odd cohabitation with a spellcaster called Virim, and even with the faintest ghost of a mountain sheep whose name—if it ever possessed any—is long forgotten."

He extended his right hand and Grateful Peace brought his own to meet it. For a long moment, the two men stood that way, gazes locked in fierce assessment. Then the Meddler held his left hand out to Firekeeper.

"The blood?"

Firekeeper held out the piece of glass, and the Meddler squashed his fingertip into it. The shining red droplet hissed and turned into smoke.

"Interesting," the Meddler said. "You have no magic of your own, but there is a thread of another's power present. I do not think that querinalo could use it to get a grip on you, but it might travel the reverse of that road and find your . . . partner? Associate?"

"The dragon is what the dragon wishes to be," Grateful Peace said evenly. "But I will not bring harm to it. Can you protect it?"

"I can set a shield of sorts along that thread," the Meddler said. "But do you wish to protect this dragon? From what I can see, it does you no good."

"I made a pact," Grateful Peace said. "I will not violate what I promised, even by a technicality none of us could have envisioned at the time."

Firekeeper could not tell if the Meddler was impressed, but she knew she was. The Dragon of Despair had been a frightening creature, and the price it had exacted for its surrender had been brutal. She studied the Meddler. He was standing perfectly still, his eyes squeezed shut, the hand that was not interlocked with Peace's own making strange little gestures, moving to a music she could not hear.

After what seemed like a very long time, but she knew had not been long at all, the Meddler let Peace's hand free.

"Next?" he said, almost merrily.

The next two tests went more quickly, for neither Citrine nor Edlin proved to have any magical ability. Melina's long-ago use of Citrine had left scars the Meddler detected, but he assured them that she was in no more danger than "a pot was in danger of being mistaken for the soup cooked in it."

Citrine looked insulted by this assessment. Edlin was frankly relieved.

"Don't know what I would have done if I found out I had a talent, what? Heard what happened to Derian, though. Poor chap. Hear he's taking it hard."

"He is," Firekeeper said, "and you will not make worse. Nexans think very highly of Derian, even if he do look like a horse, and I always think highly of Derian, no matter what he look like."

Edlin grinned at her, then turned to retrieve various bundles from where they had been stowed in the shadowed spaces outside the bright circle of the lantern light.

"I wouldn't harm Derian for all the world, don't you know. He's a fine man, what? My father's always wishing I had a trace of Derian's stability of character."

Citrine had also retrieved a bundle of gear, and now she looked at Firekeeper with a trace of indecision.

"Do we need to give a lot more blood for the gate?"

"Not much," Firekeeper reassured her. "We need to go through two by two. First, I think, you and Blind Seer, then Grateful Peace and Edlin. I will come with the Meddler, and then Enigma will follow last."

They did this, and the passage went smoothly. However, as soon as they left the wedge-shaped building that housed the New Kelvinese gate, Firekeeper could scent a tightness to the air. Before she could howl a question, the raven Lovable glided down and perched on one of the nearby pylons.

"What is going on?" Firekeeper asked her. *"Has there been another attack?"*

"The gates are coming alive," Lovable said with none of her usual chattiness. *"All in the Pelland structure, so far. So far we have held, but Bitter says that we are being tested, as rash younglings will challenge the falcon."*

Firekeeper looked over her shoulder. The three new arrivals were looking from side to side, absorbing the miracle that they really had moved in a few steps from the cool, shadowed tunnels beneath Thendulla Lypella to the open air of a hilltop on the Nexus Islands. She wished she had time to give them a proper tour, but time was only one of the many resources that the Nexans lacked.

"Tell Derian," she said to Lovable, *"that we are here safely. I am going to take Grateful Peace to where he can see the waters, and learn what he can about sea monsters. Someone should tell Ynamynet, too."*

"I can manage that," Blind Seer said. *"For this battle, I am of her little pack, and she should know I am ready for the fight. Enigma is already gone."*

Firekeeper hated relinquishing the familiar security of having Blind Seer beside her, but she knew he was right. If they had been hunting elk or moose, he would have gone from her to drive the game. She would have found herself a place where she could best use her bow.

"Good hunting, then" was all she said as she knelt to embrace him.

"And to you," he replied; then he was gone, a grey streak vanished down the hillside.

Lovable had already flapped away, and so Firekeeper turned to her three humans and one Meddler—despite his current form, she was not in the least certain whether she considered him human.

"Lovable, that raven, told me that the other gates is coming active, but none have breaked through. Word goes to Derian and Ynamynet, but unless they cry other, I take you to where the water is so Peace can see if he can find these monsters."

Grateful Peace and Citrine nodded, but neither spoke. Firekeeper suspected they were both were still trying to accept their new surroundings. Edlin, however, beamed cheerfully and settled his bow on his shoulder.

"Righty-o," he said happily. "I say, do you think there will be a bush or someplace where I can change my clothes? I grabbed my fighting gear when I went by the embassy, but didn't take time to change."

"Bushes there is," Firekeeper assured him as she led the way down the hillside toward the shore. "Is good you have armor. Soon, I think, even if we all do our best, you will need it."

TINIEL WATCHED FROM his post as Firekeeper led the strangers from New Kelvin out of the gate complex containing the New World gates.

Compared to the attire worn by the Spell Wielders, the long, elaborately embroidered robes worn by the white-haired man who must be Grateful Peace were nothing unusual. The strange way he wore his hair, shaven across the front on his head, and the elaborate tattoos that ornamented the pale skin of his face were rather more startling.

Tiniel almost wished he could leave his post and get a closer look at them, but that would never do. Faithful unto death, that was he. Or at least that was what the others must think him to be.

His gate had experienced the same flickering of activity now being reported with increasing regularity at the Pelland complex. However, the stone surface had remained cold and dark for long enough now that he wondered if he had chosen the wrong post. He had finagled for the one leading to u-Chival because, since there were only one or two gates active there, the commanders of the defense had decided that it could be watched over by one human, as long as that human had the means to summon help when needed.

In Tiniel's case, that help took the form of a young, rather excitable merlin who had been hatched during the captivity of the yarimaimalom on the Nexus Islands. In appearance, Farborn resembled a miniature version of the much more impressive peregrine, Elation. Tiniel found himself wondering if they had been assigned together as a subtle insult.

The great commander accompanied by a falcon who was willing to risk querinalo to come to his side. Then there's me with the squirt. If I knew for sure they were making fun of me . . . But this isn't the time to draw attention to myself.

Farborn was as eager to prove himself as Tiniel was. Familiar with the merlin's motivations, Tiniel had found it astonishingly easy to prompt the diminutive falcon to take up his post outside the buildings housing the active gates.

"That way you'll see if trouble is coming our way," Tiniel said, "and can shriek the alert. If I see anything happening in the buildings, I'll call you, and you'll be that much closer to the Pelland gate so you can relay our warning to central command."

Farborn had agreed—not in words, of course. Tiniel could no more understand the speech of the yarimaimalom now than he could before. However, the fierce little merlin had bobbed in the fashion that was rapidly becoming bird talk for "yes," and had flown off to his current post.

He now sat on one of the taller stone pillars, scanning the area importantly, looking, to Tiniel's way of thinking, like a little boy dressed up to play soldier. Although one of the more senior wingéd folk periodically passed over the area, none of them challenged Farborn's territory, and so Tiniel thought he had done a fair job of securing himself from observation.

Tiniel thought that it was distinctly ironic that his status as a resident of the New World had automatically accorded him a greater degree of trust. The thinking that had granted this trust was that because Tiniel had no ties to the Old World, he would not be tempted to ally himself with any of those who came from there. That way of thinking certainly applied to Derian, Harjeedian, Plik, and even to Isende, but it certainly didn't apply to Tiniel himself. For his part, he was sick of both the New Worlders and the Nexans alike. His only hope for the honor and prestige and redemption he craved was with the Old World.

Now he watched with something like loathing as Firekeeper escorted the three who had arrived from New Kelvin down toward the island's main harbor. Earlier Isende had dropped by and happily told him that Derian had told her that this Grateful Peace fellow was supposed to be something called a Dragon Speaker, and that everyone hoped that he would be able to do something about the invasion by sea.

Another person with powers, Tiniel thought. *Everywhere I look, there are people just dripping with power. I wonder how Virim feels, learning what a lousy job he did getting rid of magic? Wait. This might be the best thing for me. An invasion by sea wouldn't do me much good. I need to have it come through the gates.*

He watched the receding figures with a new anxiousness, then turned back to the buildings containing "his" gates. They remained cold and dark.

What if I gambled wrong? I've gambled wrong my whole life. I failed with the senate in Gak. I failed trying to reestablish my family's stronghold. I failed miserably at the moment I thought we were finally successful—back when we opened the gates to this horrid place. I failed against querinalo. Everything I do is a failure. I can't fail this time. I can't!

He pressed his head against the iron bars that caged the gate, staring imploringly at the cold stone wall.

Hurry! he pleaded silently. *I can't bear to be a failure again.*

❧❦❧

THE AREA SURROUNDING the gate building in Bryessidan's capital was alive with the orderly confusion of soldiers preparing to march to battle.

Since the final planning meeting, time had alternately raced and dragged, but at last, unequivocally, the second day of Bear Moon had arrived, and the small but impeccably trained army of the Kingdom of the Mires was prepared to invade the Nexus Islands.

Only two uncertainties remained. Could they get through the gate? When they did, would they find the battle already over, the land already secured by the navy commanded by King Hurwin?

That night, safe in the quiet darkness of their shared bedchamber, Bryessidan had confided these two apprehensions to Gidji. She had laughed softly and snuggled next to his side. The way she rested her head on his shoulder was all loving wife, but her answer showed her mettle as a queen.

"You'll get through, Bryessidan," she said. "Maybe not on the first attempt, but certainly by the second or third. Don't despair. As for my father and his navy, we know they haven't won the battle already. If they had, they would have sent word through the gates. They didn't take a huge force of spellcasters with them, but they had enough that if the Nexus Islands had fallen, we would know before any but the Nexans themselves."

Her words had encouraged Bryessidan, but the hours of darkness stretched interminably, and every time he heard a sentry call or some other sound of activity, he wondered whether someone was coming to tell him that his labors had been for nothing. He had no idea when his listening passed into dreams and back again to wakefulness, but when morning finally released him to rise without seeming overly anxious, Bryessidan knew he must have slept at least some. Only in dreams could any world be as strange as the one he had experienced during that long vigil.

As he bathed and donned his armor, the king of the Mires reviewed the last minute reports brought to him by his various advisors. Essentially, they boiled down to one thing: No change. All is ready.

"At least here," Bryessidan added as he set the last one aside. "We can have no idea what our allies have done in the past several moonspans. If they were having difficulties, the written reports they have sent would not confess the truth lest they seem reluctant."

"And some places, like u-Chival," Gidji said, speaking as if reading his mind, "have not been able to report with any regularity. Still, the auguries show that my father and his navy have not suffered any undue disaster. I believe that you and King Hurwin alone could secure the Nexus Islands, so waste no thought on the actions of your allies."

Bryessidan kissed her, holding her face between his hands and taking care not to crush her against the brass and silver of his armor.

"You will receive reports as regularly as possible, my queen," he said. "I leave the Mires in your good hands."

Now, looking at the orderly movements of armed and armored soldiers, Bryessidan thought there was every reason for the confidence Gidji had expressed. Spontaneous cheers greeted him as he made his way toward the gate building, and he answered them with a wave before turning to greet Amelo Soapwort.

The Once Dead spellcaster was clad in all his gaudy regalia today, his long beard carefully plaited with strings of beads cut from what Bryessidan knew were gemstones that enhanced magical power. The two men publicly embraced, letting the enthusiastic roar of the gathered troops wash over them, then turned in to the shelter of the building, where they could converse in relative private—although what they said was readily heard by the gathered Once Dead and various military types already in the building.

"The gate?" Bryessidan asked, feeling like he was reciting lines from a play. He had read the report Amelo had sent earlier, and doubted anything could have changed in a short time. Still, it seemed impossible not to ask, not when the broad piece of stone stood across the building from him, polished and waiting within the elaborate carvings of its incised border.

"Is ready," Amelo replied. "We did the three-quarter cycle earlier today, shutting down the spell before sending anyone through. The gate is live, and has not been damaged in any way."

"Good."

"It is likely that the gate is still blockaded," Amelo said, "probably within the iron cage we encountered before. However, the Once Dead we are sending through on the initial passage is a fine archer. He has trained so that he is accustomed to the sensation of iron near him. His job will be to protect the soldier who is going through with him while that man breaks down the iron bars."

"And I will follow in the next group," Bryessidan said.

"The third," Amelo said with gentle firmness, "if Your Majesty will so permit. It is possible that in taking out the gate's defenses both our first two will be killed. The second group will be prepared to reconnoiter, and, if possible, hold the position."

Bryessidan had known this, but he hadn't thought it would hurt to seem a bit of a fire eater. Now he acceded to his advisor's position, but with a show of reluctance.

"I would not have any soldier take a risk I would not, but if you think this best, never let any say I was unreasonable."

"Never, Your Majesty," Amelo said, and Bryessidan thought that no one but himself saw the Once Dead's fleeting smile.

Bryessidan walked from group to group, speaking a few encouraging words to each. He spared a little extra time with the two pairs that would go through before him, letting them know he appreciated the risks they were taking. He might never have been a war leader like his father, but he well knew the value of praise, and it was so cheap to offer.

Then the high, sweet note of a horn signaled that the agreed-upon hour had arrived, and the first pair stepped up to the gate. Bryessidan stood to one side as the spells were recited, and blood donated on the spot from a crippled veteran of his father's war was spilled into the channels in the stone.

Two men heavily armored in hardened leather, not a scrap of iron on their persons, went to the gate. They watched impassively as their blood was smeared on the gate so it would know them, then stepped into the molten silver field. They did not so much vanish as seem to recede down a long tunnel, the edges of their shadowed images becoming wavery, until they were lost in the silver. The gate was then shut behind them, isolating the brave pioneers lest their enemy push back along that road.

Silence fell after their departure, a silence so absolute that Bryessidan could hear the flame sputtering on the tall candle that was being used to mark the passage of time. Almost transfixed, he watched as the wax retreated to the line.

Amelo called out "Next!" and two more, armed and armored much as the first pair, stepped forward. Again the taking of blood, the activating of the gate, the retreating into silver and shade. The wick sputtered, and Amelo cleared his throat.

"Your Majesty, it is time."

Bryessidan smiled and settled his dragon-visaged helmet upon his head. He said a few polite things that he immediately forgot to the young Once Dead who was to be his partner in this venture. Her job, he knew, was to leave her king, step back, and tell Amelo to start transporting the troops. If the previous pairs had failed, she was to make Bryessidan return to the relative safety of the Mires.

He didn't know how she could manage this if he didn't wish to go, but he suspected she had not been chosen for her role by lot.

Side by side they stepped through, feeling the familiar burning sensation. Then they were in a building somewhat more dimly lit than the one he had just left. Both close by and muffled by distance there was the sound of clashing metal, the shouts of soldiers interspersed with the weird cries and snarls of various hunting animals.

The iron cage that had enclosed this end of the gate was not gone, but the bolts that held it had been ripped from the wall on one edge, and it had been shoved aside, leaving a large enough gap that Bryessidan could easily push through into the building at large.

A dead man was sprawled on the ground, and in him Bryessidan recognized the Once Dead archer. His partner, however, was not at hand, nor were the other two. Looking ahead, his eyes adjusting to the dimmer light, Bryessidan saw them engaged in combat with what appeared to be a lynx and a soldier in armor cobbled together out of old boots.

The Once Dead spellcaster who had come through with him tugged at his arm, trying to draw him back, but Bryessidan jerked his arm free.

"We have a breach," he said. "Tell Amelo to bring through the others, or I will hang you from this iron cage myself."

She balked, but only for a moment. The living wall had not yet closed. Muttering some words, she slapped blood nicked from her finger onto the appropriate place, and vanished.

Bryessidan ran forward, his booted feet hitting the stone hard, his sword coming as easily from its sheath as if this was just another of the many practice sessions he had submitted to in the moonspans since this invasion had first been planned.

A limping, massy figure occluded the doorway at the narrow end of the building.

"More of them here!" it yelled. "We've got another break through here! Tell Skea! Tell Derian! The dam's broken!"

XL

WHEN THE FIRST of the iron cages went down at the Hearthome gate, Derian was there. Skea had given them a pretty thorough briefing about the temperaments of the peoples who held the lands on the other side of the gates.

"Hearthome and Tavetch are probably the most openly aggressive," Skea had said. "The Tavetch are, frankly, sea raiders, and in a weird way they could be said to cultivate the peoples they attack. Their king has been known to argue that if it weren't for his people's demands for tribute, the small settlements along the northern seaboard wouldn't be doing nearly so well. He might even be right.

"Hearthome is a different matter completely. Their queen, Iline, would like to argue that all she is doing is trying to unite Pelland, but the rest of the continent is having nothing to do with that. The usual target for her attacks is the kingdom of Azure Towers. That's ruled by a queen as well, and I recall rumors that there's some personal feud between them."

Since the Hearthome gate was in the Pelland cluster, and it was from Pelland that they expected the greater number of the attacks to come, Derian had positioned himself there. Nemeria, a level-headed young woman with a bellowing voice, had been given chief watch of the Tavetch gate, which was off in a cluster by itself, as was the u-Chival gate of which Tiniel had charge.

Skea would have liked to be up on the gateway hill, but for now the greater danger was offered by another sea attack. Moreover, the soldiers stationed there had already been through one nasty fight, and there was some concern their morale would break without strong leadership. By contrast, the group stationed in the vicinity of the gates was eager to prove itself the equal or better of their fellows.

The sun was climbing toward noon when the gates in various buildings began to flicker, but the stone never quite achieved the strange silvery sheen that indicated a transition was about to happen.

"Testing," Verul said, almost contemptuously. "They don't know if we've disabled the gates and don't want to risk anything."

Derian sent word to Skea and the stocky, dark-skinned general arrived almost immediately.

"Selecting noon would be a good way to time a coordinated action," he said, "since it occurs at about the same time everywhere."

"About?" Derian asked.

"There are differences," Skea said almost absently, "the farther apart places are. I guess the sun needs time to get across the sky or something. The Tavetch say we're moving, not the sun, but what does it matter if the result is the same?"

Skea moved to the center of the Pelland gate cluster, inspecting the positioning of the troops assigned there, and bringing in reinforcements from below.

"If they've somehow managed to coordinate the naval and gate attacks down to the hour," Skea said, "I'm playing right into their hands. However, I don't think they could have done that."

"Is there any indication of landing boats being prepared?" Derian asked, hoping the anxious note in his voice wasn't too obvious.

"Not that the wingéd folks have been able to see," Skea said. "A few of the ships are shrouded by a fog or mist of some sort, but whoever is raising it isn't powerful enough to cover the entire fleet. Still, we're unable to spy on the command craft, and ever since the sailors took to shooting at anything with wings, the yarimaimalom have limited their spying to what they can see from a distance."

"So if they're not getting landing craft ready," Derian said, "then the two forces aren't coordinated."

"Or they're even more organized than I think," Skea said, "and have coordinated for, say, an hour after noon, or two hours after noon. A candle is fairly accurate for that short a period of time, and we could wear ourselves out with guessing. Still, I think I'm right . . ."

Derian hoped Skea was, and surely this wasn't the time to start second-guessing the general. Even so, he could think of numerous alternate plans of attack. The attackers could have selected a day two or three days from now, but by flickering the gates they would force the Nexans to wear themselves out with watching. They could delay by a few hours, or come through in staggered waves, say a half-hour apart.

What if that mist could be spread? He knew that Ynamynet worried more about magics that would impede communication and ease of movement than she was about the destructive forces that had featured so frequently in the stories he'd been told as a boy. If the attackers could cover the island in mist, then the wingéd folk would be nearly useless, and even the yarimaimalom would be hampered.

But wouldn't the attackers be crippling themselves? Derian thought. *Mist or fog would be bad for everyone on both sides. Unless, that is, they have some means of seeing through the mist.*

With such suppositions and the fears they bred to fill his mind, Derian's primary reaction when the first gate transit occurred was a relief so intense that it astonished him.

The cry rose from those guarding the building holding the gate to the kingdom of Pelland, a land that Skea had described as possessing a powerful and well-trained warrior class, but in many ways weakened by its belief that it was sole heir to the continent's past glories.

Derian raced over in time to hear the excited report of the woman who had been stationed to watch that particular gate.

"They came through, two of them, both armored. One took a swing or so with a mallet or axe of some sort at the bars of the gate while the other started firing arrows at me. I was surprised, and I don't mind saying so, but I got my bow up and fired. They got out of there pretty quickly."

"Did the Once Dead seem to have any difficulty working the transit spell?"

"I don't think he had to do it all," the guard reported. "The gate stayed live, but sort of dimmed down."

"That will take power," Skea said with satisfaction. "Of course, I'm not too worried that the Pellanders will be using magic as one of their main attacks. I'm more worried about that from Tishiolo, Azure Towers, and, just maybe, the Mires."

Skea stationed extra soldiers to watch the Pelland gate, and sent for one of the stone workers to see if anything could be done to repair the damage already done to the cage anchors.

Derian returned to his post near the Hearthome gate, so he was there when the Hearthome force came through. Their tactics were similar to those used at the Pelland gate, but with two marked exceptions. Instead of a mallet, the invaders carried through something short, thick, and very heavy. When they began to swing it, Derian realized it was a battering ram of some sort. The pair using it had clearly prepared to operate the thing in a constricted space, and within moments the iron was bending beneath the short, thudding blows.

As Skea had trained them to do, the Nexans fired their bows, but the majority of their arrows clattered against the closely fit iron bars of the cage. The remainder struck the two within the cage on their armor and helmets. These, too, had been designed with this specific attack in mind, the joints covered, and the helmets coming down to cover the sides of the men's faces.

"The cage isn't going to hold!" someone yelled. "Tell Skea!"

Racing forward to see what he could do, Derian felt very strongly the irony that the Nexans had provided the invaders with their best shield.

We only thought about the cages protecting us from what would come in. Since iron weakens the powers of Once Dead, we didn't think about more prosaic forms of attack—even though those were what we were relying on ourselves.

But he didn't waste energy on recriminations. Instead, he grabbed a long spear from one of the Nexans.

"Poke them!" he shouted, demonstrating. "If they're busy with that thing, they can't fight back."

The archers dropped their bows and followed his example, but although they succeeded in killing the two with the ram, it was too late to save the integrity of the iron cage, and already, behind it, the gateway was beginning to glow, heralding the imminent arrival of reinforcements.

Derian felt a little sick. He'd never attacked anyone with such calculation before, but at the time it hadn't seemed calculated at all. He'd felt no more revulsion than if he'd been poking a pitchfork at a rat he found in the feed.

And those two men must have known they were doomed, he thought. *What incentive would make people go to their deaths like that?*

But he didn't have time to consider. Instead, he rallied the troops assigned to the Hearthome gate.

"They've weakened the bars," he reminded them, "and they'll break through eventually. That's certain, but remember. Two at a time. Just two at a time. Those are the odds in our favor."

The attacks that came through the other gates followed a similar pattern. The Mires proved to be the most coordinated, Tishiolo the least. There were some interesting variations to the ways the attackers sought to disable the iron cage.

Leaving the area near the Pelland gate, where a second or third attempt to break through had been thwarted, Derian heard excited cries from the soldiers stationed at the Azure Towers gate. This gate had shown less activity than some of the others, and they had even dared to hope that no attack would come from there. When it came, it carried surprises with it.

Two people came in through the silver wall. One was a slight woman, clearly marked as a Once Dead by the sigils and ornaments on her leather armor. Her companion was a tall man, also clad in leather armor, probably so he would not add interference of iron on his companion's abilities.

The soldier interposed a large shield between himself and the Once Dead. She, in turn, could just be glimpsed setting something dripping and amorphous directly on the iron bars.

Derian caught a whiff of blood, then the material hissed and steamed. As if this was a signal of some sort, the soldier wheeled around to interpose his shield between the hissing mass and himself, ignoring the arrows at his back. His companion shrunk back into the circle of his arms. Then, without warning, the hissing stuff exploded.

Despite the intervening shield, the explosion struck the two within the cage and they reeled back. The Once Dead was knocked from the protective circle of her companion's arms and into the iron bars. She screamed terribly before falling suddenly silent. Her companion had flung himself into the bars, synchronizing his backward thrust with the explosion's force and thus helping to further wrench the bars loose from their anchors in the stone.

The Nexan defenders had not stood idle during this carefully coordinated display. They fired as Skea had trained them to do, but as elsewhere most of their arrows clattered against the close-set bars of the iron cage.

Several of the Nexans were approaching with spears, ready to use the tactic that had worked so well at the Hearthome gate and elsewhere. They were caught in the blast and flung to the floor. This did not save them from being badly cut by clips of flying stone.

Derian ran forward and pulled the worst wounded back. The gate was glowing again, and he had no doubt that whoever would come through next would be as well prepared as these two had been.

Skea had come from somewhere and was shouting orders. Wolves were howling, the sound of their calls as they coordinated their own part in the defensive action ringing back and forth off the stone walls of the wedge-shaped gate building.

Derian had a headache but he knew he didn't have time for that. He shook his head to clear it and heard Pishtoolam, the head cook, yelling at the top of her lungs.

It took him a moment to translate as in her shock she had reverted to the oddly accented Liglimosh that was her first language.

"By all the elements! Where did they come from? It's an entire army!"

❦

TINIEL'S ANTICIPATION GREW when the gates began to come alive in the Pelland complex, followed shortly by those in the complex that held the Tavetchian gate. The gate to u-Chival, however, remained—other than a testing glow sometime earlier—ominously dark.

Have they lost their nerve? Was there some omen against their coming through? No matter what promises they made, if these u-Chivalum are anything like the Liglimom, they aren't going to go against the omens.

Repeatedly, Tiniel darted back and forth between the interior of the building holding the gate, and the door in the narrow end of the wedge. The fighting over at the Pelland complex must be fairly intense if the number of wounded he saw being borne away was any indication. Not all the faces of those he saw on the stretchers were familiar, so the Nexans must be holding their own.

Up on his high watch stand, Farborn was fluttering his wings with excitement. Tiniel had been told that merlins were relatively silent as hawks went, but Farborn was so distracted he was making shrill peeping sounds. It didn't take much imagination to hear these as "Let me come help! Let me!"

Part of Tiniel's job was to make periodic checks of the other buildings in this particular complex, just to assure that none of the supposedly "dead" gates had come live. The Nexans hadn't had the resources to cage all the gates, so they had settled on those they knew were active. The others had been booby-trapped and alarmed in a variety of clever ways, but these wouldn't stop anyone from coming through.

Tiniel returned to the building containing the live gate just as the wall between the intricately carved sigils began to glow silver. His heart gave a funny skipping beat, and for a moment he almost gave in to the impulse to call alert as he had been told. Then his resolution returned.

He'd done his best to learn how the other attacks had begun, and so he knew that the first pair through would probably concentrate on defending themselves and weakening the cage. Making sure his helmet was snug and that his armor didn't show any gaps—after all, the u-Chivalum wouldn't know he was a friend until he told them—Tiniel moved up next to the cage.

He stayed a spear's length back, but didn't dare go any farther. He had to count on the new arrivals needing a moment to adjust to the relatively dim light in the building to give him the time he needed.

The silver glow grew so intense that Tiniel feared it would shine right out through the door he hadn't dared shut lest that draw attention. Of course, it was only shortly passed noon and

the summer sun was high, bright, and hot, even on this ac-
cursed island, so he needn't worry, but fear made one a little
crazy.

The u-Chivalum proved to be a heavily armored pair of
men. One was so broad in the shoulder that he hardly fit into
the cage. The ornamentation on the other's armor suggested
that he was Once Dead, but Tiniel wasn't going to address him
by that title. The disdum also often wore elaborate attire, and
not all the disdum were Once Dead. Indeed, in u-Chival,
where magical talents were still highly distrusted, they were
more likely not to be. Calling a disdu "Once Dead" might be a
grave insult.

Not certain which of the two was in charge, Tiniel addressed himself to both.

"I'm a friend. I have a plan for how you can win this battle
where your allies are failing."

The man in the less ornamented armor had raised his hands
to grasp the iron bars of the cage as if he planned to rip them
free with nothing but the strength of his massive shoulders.
He paused in midmotion, as if noticing for the first time that
the building was empty but for Tiniel.

The man Tiniel presumed was the Once Dead spoke in
heavily accented Liglimosh, his tone controlled yet somehow
mincing, "What do you mean, you are a friend? Why should
we trust you?"

Tiniel moved a step closer. "Because I'm giving you this."

He reached up and worked loose a few of the shims and
wedges he had inserted to keep the bars of the cage in place
along one side. For over a moonspan, he had been using part
of his watch on the gateway hillside to unsecure the bars, hiding his work with considerable care. The Nexans' few stone-
masons and ironworkers were too busy to repeatedly check
their past work, and Tiniel's sabotage had gone undetected.

It had helped that everyone had been far more worried
about the Pelland gates.

"I've loosened the cage all along one side," he said. "It
won't be hard at all to squeeze by."

The Once Dead didn't look as if he trusted Tiniel, but he

was also not one to pass up an omen of good fortune. He turned to his companion.

"Get this cage down entirely. Do it, quietly, if you can. If you can't, leave it up, but bend it back so the rest of the army can get through."

The other man grunted, and began tugging at the bars to test their hold. Satisfied, he pulled out a lever and got to work. He was amazingly quiet, but then Tiniel thought he might have had practice.

The Once Dead slipped outside the cage into the open area and studied Tiniel. He was armed with a crossbow, sword, and a long, curve-bladed knife, but he didn't draw any of these.

"You have something of the look of my people, yet not. Nor do I remember seeing you before. Are you of the New World?"

"I am."

The man nodded as if some previous consideration had been confirmed. "And why do you betray your fellows?"

Tiniel answered promptly, "Because I believe they are the ones who have betrayed, not I. They have broken the trade agreement by which these islands were made independent. I only want to set things right."

The Once Dead twitched his lips in something between a sneer and a smile. "I see. An idealist. Perhaps I even believe you. What I most certainly believe is the evidence of my eyes. This building is unoccupied by defenders, therefore you are the watch and have not called them. How long do we have?"

"Possibly quite a while," Tiniel said. He hadn't expected this cool reaction. He'd envisioned being called an answer to their prayers or an omen of victory. This cool contempt wasn't at all to his taste, but he couldn't retreat now. "The Pelland cluster is very busy now. Most of the Nexan forces are there. If I don't call, they're probably going to be grateful for the reprieve."

"Then they must see you from time to time, I think," the Once Dead said, and Tiniel realized with shock that he'd been very close to dying right then. "Very well. Let them see you."

He dismissed Tiniel with a motion of his hand, and turned to his companion.

"Hahrahma, do you have the cage down?"

Hahrahma, who must have had a talent for strength to do what he was doing, replied by setting the entirety of the iron-barred cage gently down on the stone floor just to one side of the gate. He nodded jubilantly, and when he opened and shut his mouth as if replying, Tiniel saw to his horror that the man lacked a tongue.

Did they cut it out?

He didn't ask, but instead scampered toward the door in the narrow end of the building. He was nearly there when the Once Dead called after him, his tones low but penetrating.

"Oh, Idealist. Remember your ideals, or I will be forced to remember them for you."

He raised his crossbow, now fully loaded, and aimed it at Tiniel. Then he began to close the distance between them, so that even when Tiniel reached the doorway he would not be out of the line of fire.

"The quarrel will go through light armor such as that you are wearing, in case you wondered."

Tiniel didn't wonder. He also didn't doubt that if he were to go outside and start screaming for help, the Once Dead would punish his treachery either right then or when the battle was won; the u-Chivalum would win now. The heart of the gate was glowing silver again, and pairs of armed and armored soldiers were striding through. They seemed a bit surprised to find no immediate battle awaiting them, but not as surprised as Tiniel thought they should have been.

The first pair of soldiers to come through were assigned to finish moving the bars of the cage aside. Hahrahma was set to guard Tiniel, freeing "his" Once Dead, who he now learned was called Prarayan, to coordinate the troops as they filed out of the gate.

Watching and listening from his post by the main door, Tiniel learned why the u-Chivalum were so calm. In the fourth or fifth pair through the gate there came a woman whom

Prarayan immediately greeted with hand gestures indicating profound respect.

"Your auguries were perfect, Aridisdu Valdala," Prarayan said. "By waiting until the appointed time had gone by but a little, we found a perfect situation waiting for us. This young man," his tone dripped contempt, for all the words were polite, "favors our cause. Battle rages throughout the Pelland gate cluster, so that no one is likely to wonder what is happening here, especially as they can see their faithful guard going about his tasks, and looking with longing to join the fight."

"The Divine Five favor our action," Aridisdu Valdala said, "as the auguries told us they did. Shall we gather our force in strength, then strike?"

"That is what I would advise," Prarayan said. "However, we should not wait too long. Our allies will need us to provide a diversion so that they can make good the breaches they have doubtless established."

"True," Aridisdu Valdala said. "When we have a force of twenty safely arrived here, begin your attack. You recall where the Tavetch gate is located?"

"I do."

"Take that first. Then the Tavetch can join us in relieving the Pellanders."

"I will do as you command."

Tiniel listened to this with a distant sense of disbelief. He'd thought about what would happen when he allied himself with the Old World nations, and just about nothing was going according to his plans.

Sure the Old Worlders were through the gate, and were quietly augmenting their forces, but where was the appreciation? He'd imagined someone—someone he now realized looked rather like his deceased father—patting him warmly on the shoulder and then offering him a fine sword or even some magical artifact. He'd spent hours refining that moment in his imagination, finally deciding that a magical sword would be best, but he'd settle for an amulet.

Certainly, Isende was not the only one of the twins capable

of dreaming true dreams? And she did it without trying, and he was trying so hard.

Now here had come his big moment, and not only was no one asking him anything, they were practically ignoring him.

"Idealist," Prarayan called, his voice low but still managing to carry, "you've been seen for a few moments. Come here. Aridisdu Valdala has a few questions for you."

Tiniel moved to obey with alacrity, his heart beating fast within his chest. Now his dreams would come true. Now they would tell him that they had seen him in their auguries, that he was blessed by the Divine Five, the chosen of the deities.

Aridisdu Valdala looked him over critically. Tiniel felt his cheeks heat with a blush, and felt very glad that he was not as fair as Derian. He hoped they would not be able to tell how embarrassed he was of his mismatched armor and of the stout spear that was his main weapon for hand-to-hand fighting.

"Tell me, Idealist," Aridisdu Valdala said, "who might be the Horse, the Wolf, and the North Wind? Such figures have occurred again and again in our auguries, but I would know more."

Tiniel blinked at her. His cheeks were heating again, but this time from fury not from embarrassment.

Derian, again! Derian!

He wanted to press his lips close and tight rather than admitting that horse-faced outlander lout was anyone important, but from the way Aridisdu Valdala was looking at him, she was not accustomed to being kept waiting. He saw her fingering a sheathed knife at her waist and remembered that the Old World sorcerers had no reluctance to shed blood.

"The Horse," he said, and was pleased to find his voice steady, "may well be a young man named Derian Carter. He was among those who came from the New World and conquered the Nexus Islands."

Aridisdu Valdala exchanged a glance with Prarayan that said as eloquently as words that the idea was not a new one to them.

"Once Dead or Twice?" she asked. "Or Untainted?"

It took Tiniel a moment to remember that the u-Chivalum did not use the degrading term "Never Lived," but chose to view those without a touch of magical ability as marked by the blessing of the divine powers.

"Once Dead," Tiniel replied, and for once didn't feel bad about according to Derian what these people would certainly not see as an honor. "He had a mystic rapport with horses that querinalo has enhanced to the point of making him resemble a horse."

"Interesting," Aridisdu Valdala said. "You say he is from the New World. What is his native tongue?"

"Pellish, I believe, but he speaks Liglimosh fairly well, and what he calls New Kelvinese at least a little."

The aridisdu quirked an eyebrow at Tiniel's use of the slang term "Liglimosh," but did not mock him as Prarayan would certainly have done. Tiniel began to warm toward Aridisdu Valdala, and wonder if she would be the one to give him his honors.

"The Wolf," he said quickly, "is also from the New World. She is Once Dead as well—or so everyone thinks. However, she has been odd from the start. Her ability to communicate with the yarimaimalom could not be greater if she were one herself."

Aridisdu Valdala looked interested, but pairs of soldiers were filing from the gate, and clearly she was aware that this was not the time to ask many questions.

"And the last?"

"I am not sure," Tiniel admitted. "You said 'North Wind'?"

"Yes. That is the best title we could come up with. The impression was one of great power, but also of great cold."

Insight came to Tiniel. He remembered how Ynamynet always bundled up as if she were very cold, even in the heat of summer. He remembered a few lewd jokes, quickly stifled, about what Skea must do to manage making love to a woman that cold.

"I think I know who your North Wind must be," he said. "The magical forces are led by a Once Dead named Ynamynet. I believe she is originally from one of the Pelland countries, but I am not sure. She never speaks of her past, and as she spent many years in the forces of King Veztressidan, she had ample opportunity to learn Pellish."

"So this Ynamynet is not from the New World as are these others?"

"No. She was one of the Once Dead who took up residence here after the defeat of King Veztressidan. Her husband, Skea, a Twice Dead, is commanding the armed forces."

"I remember Skea," Aridisdu Valdala said. "A man with very dark skin and great military skills. I believe I remember Ynamynet as well, although we were never friendly. Very good. Where might we find these three? Our auguries indicate that our chances of success will increase if they are defeated early in the battle."

"I don't know about Firekeeper—that is the Wolf. She does not fit into any command structure. Derian Carter, the Horse, will be somewhere here on the gateway hillside. Ynamynet will be near the bottom of the hills, in the headquarters building with the other Once Dead."

"And how many are there of these?" the aridisdu asked.

"Very few," Tiniel said. "When the New Worlders came here, most of the reigning Spell Wielders were killed."

Aridisdu Valdala looked appalled. "These invaders from the New World must be formidable warriors and sorcerers."

"Not really," Tiniel said, shaping his envy into notes of scorn. "They really had little to do with the defeat of the Spell Wielders. The Spell Wielders mishandled a spell and slew themselves. Only a few who were not tied into a spell survived. Only one of these survivors—Ynamynet—is a spellcaster. She has since recruited a few others, but the force is small and untrained."

Aridisdu Valdala studied Tiniel for a long moment.

"Why are you telling me all of this, and so eagerly? You are from the New World yourself. You are betraying your own people."

Tiniel shook his head. "I am not. As I told Prarayan, I chose this side because I believe that Derian Carter and those who follow him are in the wrong. They violated an honorable treaty by sealing the gates and seeking to control them for their own benefit."

He tried very hard to look sincere, tried to keep the envy and jealousy that he felt for all the Once Dead—but most particularly for Derian Carter—to himself.

The aridisdu laughed and the sound wasn't in the least kind. She looked at massive Hahrahma who still hovered near Tiniel.

"Tie this man up and put him in a corner out of the way. We'll see how his ideals hold up later."

Prarayan glanced over from where he had been briefing his forces.

"Why not cut his throat?"

"He has information we may need," the aridisdu replied.

"Let me fight with you!" Tiniel pleaded, backing away from Harahma. "Let me prove myself to you!"

"You have betrayed your own people," Aridisdu Valdala said coldly. "I would not have you at my back even if you claimed to have been personally blessed by each of the Divine Five in turn."

Tiniel sought to find an argument that would make the u-Chivalum trust him, his voice breaking over the words as it had not done since he was much, much younger. Aridisdu Valdala did not listen, only glanced over her shoulder at mute Hahrahma.

"Gag him," she said.

Bound and gagged, then tossed into a corner like a disregarded heap of laundry, Tiniel watched helplessly as the u-Chivalum marched in near silence to the doorway that would take them into the gateway complex. The force contained more than the twenty Prarayan had originally specified, for Aridisdu Valdala's interrogation of Tiniel had delayed the force's departure, while the inexorable transfer through the gate had continued.

Seemingly timed to every ragged breath Tiniel took, more armed and armored soliders were coming through the gate. Two by two, obedient and silent, dark eyes shining in the light of the glowing blocks on the walls, the soldiers settled into their ranks.

Patiently, they awaited their orders, orders that would doubtless lead to the taking of the gateway hillside, to the defeat of the Nexans, and to the capture or death of all of those the Old World forces chose to view as rebels.

Including Isende.

Tiniel started to struggle.

XLI

THE TREMENDOUS HOPES with which Firekeeper had led Grateful Peace down to the water's edge had, by the day following his arrival, diminished. The lean thaumaturge had stood staring out over the ocean, the wind moving through his bone-white hair in its long braid the only motion he made. He didn't even seem to blink.

Firekeeper had waited impatiently at first, but there was that about the way Grateful Peace stood, the stillness of his entire body, that reminded her of something. When she realized that what he brought to mind was a great cat, crouched in hunting stillness, her impatience vanished, replaced by the deep, nearly infinite patience that any successful hunter knows must be brought to a hunt.

So had that day passed into evening, and with nightfall Firekeeper had escorted the three new arrivals to the public dining hall. Despite the fact that many of the Nexans were absent, standing watches or tending those who had been wounded in that morning's battle against the fleet's landing parties, the noise level was high and the pitch of the chatter so intense that had Firekeeper been able to fold down her ears she would have done so.

The arrival of the three strangers had caused a momentary ebb in the noise, an ebb that eddied to silence when Derian stood. In a very few words, these so well chosen that Firekeeper knew they must have been prepared in advance, Derian introduced Grateful Peace, Edlin, and Citrine.

They were greeted with cheers that, to Firekeeper's ear, sounded more tense and anxious than joyful.

That first set of introductions, however, had left out the Meddler. He stood there in his new human form surveying the gathered Nexans as if he had not seen them before, as indeed he might not have done. Firekeeper had no idea how many of the panicked mountain sheep's memories were the Meddler's to access, and certainly a sheep's eyes saw differently than did a human's.

After a slightly awkward pause, Derian introduced the Meddler as someone else brought from the New World to help. He was also greeted with enthusiastic cheers, but Firekeeper thought that a few of those gathered looked thoughtful. Doubtless they remembered that she had brought a mountain sheep, not a human back from the New World, and wondered at the change. However, being from the Old World, where such miracles might even be common, they kept their questions to themselves.

Following the meal, Derian and Ynamynet invited Grateful Peace and his entourage to come with them to the headquarters building. There they conferred at great length about what Peace might be able to do.

Grateful Peace sighed. "I sensed something there—or rather the part of me that is connected to the Dragon did so. However, what I know about dragons is what my 'companion' has taught me. I know nothing of sea monsters—not even if they are related in the least to dragons."

"We might be able to help with that," Ynamynet said. "Several of our older residents have been delving into the archives. Let me see if any are about."

Urgana was summoned, and offered to show Peace what had been located in the library and archives regarding sea monsters and dragons. He accepted graciously, and asked to be excused.

"Firekeeper," he said, pausing in the doorway on his way

out, "I know you are likely to be awake much of the night, but would you be willing to be my escort come dawn?"

Firekeeper gave a thin smile. "Tonight, I think I sleep. These Old Worlders is human in one way at least, they will prefer to fight in light, and I should be fresh then."

"Good, then unless you are helping with the defense, will you join me?"

"I will," Firekeeper promised.

"If I do contact one of these sea monsters," Peace continued, "I am not at all certain what language it might speak—or if it will speak any language at all. You, however limited your command of human tongues may be, are fluent in whatever is spoken by the Beasts. Moreover, I recall that you, like me, had no difficulty at all in communicating with the Dragon."

Remembering that strange conversation, and how close she had come to making choices she thought now she might deeply regret, Firekeeper hid a shudder, and nodded.

"I come with," she said, "and talk to anything if needed."

She slept that night between the Meddler and Blind Seer. She would have liked to be alone with the wolf, for lately they had not had much time to themselves, but she did not trust the Meddler out of her sight. He had been nothing but placid and cooperative, but Firekeeper, remembering the tales Harjeedian and Plik had regaled them with, did not trust lightly.

She was encouraged in her attitude of care by the arrival of Truth sometime in the night. In the days before the fleet's arrival, Truth had hardly left her watch stand overlooking the ocean. When the fleet had arrived, the jaguar had shifted her self-appointed watch to the gateway hills. Her presence there had stiffened the resolve of those who had been tempted to believe that the only attack would come from over the ocean. Whatever it was the jaguar saw—and her visions were so complex and confused that she could rarely articulate them—no one doubted that Truth's warnings were to be heeded.

So when Firekeeper awoke from restless sleep to find the burned-black jaguar with the flame-shaped spots lying in a comfortable sprawl, her white eyes with their blue slits fixed on the Meddler, she did not need Truth to articulate her warning.

"Stay with him," the jaguar said after a silence so long that Firekeeper might even have drowsed. "Staying with him may do no good, but if you do not, then he may do worse."

Firekeeper shook her head as if sleep were a physical thing she might banish. Sleeping as he was, wrapped in a blanket on the bare earth, the Meddler did not look in the least dangerous. If anything, he looked fragile and even a trace pathetic.

"What do you see, Truth?" she asked softly.

"More than I can say, and even as I say, I see that saying would shift the shapes of things, and these are contorted enough. Tomorrow will be less than kind. Try to sleep."

On those less than comforting words, the jaguar rose and padded away. When Firekeeper awakened again, shortly before dawn, she might have imagined it all a dream, but a tuft of fur the color of flame was caught on a shrub near where the jaguar had lain.

The ravens Bitter and Lovable were awake and about with the dawn, and Firekeeper enlisted them to watch the still sleeping Meddler.

"Blind Seer and I want to run up to the gateway hill," Firekeeper said, "and learn what has happened in the night."

"We could tell you," Lovable said brightly.

"I am sure you could," Blind Seer said, stretching and yawning so that the raven had a close look at every one of his magnificent white teeth, "but that would not shift the sleep from our bones and muscles. Don't tell me you can't mind a sleeping human for a short time!"

"We will mind him," Bitter said, tilting his head to bring his one eye to bear and studying the Meddler with interest.

"Watch him," Firekeeper said, "but do not converse with him. He is a dangerous creature, for all he looks so innocent."

"We remember the Meddler tales," Bitter reassured her. "Not only will we not speak with him, we will also not let him speak with any other. Now, run as you will."

Up to the gateway hill they went, and learned from Frost-weed, who had stood a watch all night, that the gates had fallen quiet with evening, but a few were beginning to show flickers of silver.

"Testing, again," he said, "and I feel in my bones that today there will be more than a test."

"You fight here or with Ynamynet?" Firekeeper asked.

"Wherever I am needed," Frostweed replied. "I can't cast spells, but I may be some help there even so. If Ynamynet does not need me, well . . ."

He thumped the butt of a spear on the ground.

They left the gateway hill, and before they reached where they had left the Meddler, Blind Seer paused.

"I should go to Ynamynet," he said, "so she knows I have not forgotten my post in this hunt."

"As if you would," Firekeeper retorted scornfully.

"Ynamynet is doing very well accepting what Enigma and I can do," Blind Seer said, "but she is not of the New World, and she has trouble with the idea that Beasts might think as well as she does."

"Or better," Firekeeper said.

She knelt and embraced the blue-eyed wolf, burying her head in his fur. Summer heat had thinned the density of his coat, but what remained was very, very soft.

"Good hunting," Blind Seer said, licking the side of her face and nipping gently at her ear.

"Good hunting to you," Firekeeper replied. "I'll let you know what Grateful Peace learns."

"Go and collect your humans," Blind Seer said. "Dawn is almost upon us."

Firekeeper collected the Meddler by unrolling him from his blanket and hauling him to his feet. Without complaint, comb-ing his beard with his fingers, he stumbled after her toward the headquarters building. Despite the earliness of the hour, there were people moving about the porch and going in and out the wide doors.

Doubtless, like Frostweed, many of the Nexans had stood a night watch and hoped to be able to function without sleep if the need arose come day. For how long could they continue to do so? Humans did not need as much sleep as did, say, great cats, but they did not do well when their sleep was repeatedly interrupted. A day or two of alarms, and the invaders would find their task made much easier.

To put this disturbing thought from her mind, Firekeeper considered instead how smoothly the Meddler had woken. Most humans did not sleep comfortably outside on what was close to bare ground. Nor did they roll easily to their feet without complaining at least a little about how uncomfortable they were. Was the Meddler's easy recovery simply because not long ago that body had belonged to a mountain sheep, or was it something else, a reminder that appearances could not be trusted where he was concerned?

Bitter and Lovable had flown escort, and as they closed with the headquarters building, Lovable squawked happily.

"Your outland friends are there," she said. "I thought I might need to go wake them. Rap on their windows. They stayed up late last night, studying papers. The younger one stayed up longer than the older two. I guess that's why she's yawning now."

And Citrine was indeed yawning, smothering the gulps of air behind the hand that did not hold a cup of what Firekeeper's nose told her was the strong tea that many of the Nexans loved to drink in the mornings.

"Breakfast?" she asked, eschewing the usual greetings. "Or do we go?"

Grateful Peace raised his eyebrows in the ironically amused fashion Firekeeper remembered quite well from the days when he had posed as Jalarios, and had guided them through New Kelvin.

"Unless we are under attack," he said, "then breakfast. Who knows whether the cooks will manage to serve any other hot meal today?"

Firekeeper agreed. The dining hall was quieter this morning, the people eating with measured intensity, talking softly to their closer neighbors.

Derian was sitting with Isende, and motioned for Firekeeper and the others to join him. Firekeeper thought he might have some orders for them, but the conversation avoided the fact that they might all find themselves fighting at any moment. She noticed that Derian ate with only one hand. She did not need to look to know that the other hand was locked with Isende's under the table's shelter. Isende, in turn, sat as close to Derian as was practical, periodically leaning her head against Derian's shoulder.

Blind Seer had told Firekeeper something of what Ynamynet and Kalyndra were doing in their attempts to protect the Nexus Islands from sorcerous attack. Much of what he had said to her meant as little as would a deer's excited discussion of the properties of various leaves and herbs when considered as forage, but Firekeeper had understood one crucial element.

The Once Dead who had taken over the Nexus Islands following King Veztressidan's war had reactivated the spells that had shielded the islands from magical spying. Ynamynet and Kalyndra had discovered that there were also components to those spells that, when activated, protected the islands from more direct magical attack. Keeping those up and running had been the small spellcaster's group's primary concern, and from what Firekeeper gathered, it had not been easy.

Unfurred as she was, Isende showed the costs of her labors more than did Blind Seer. Her warm brown skin was flat and sallow, her brown eyes bloodshot. Even her hair was limp. She ate steadily, without enthusiasm, and her usual flow of chatter was gone.

When the meal had been eaten, they parted with no more fuss than would have been shown if they were going about their usual day. Firekeeper approved. Maybe the presence of the many Beasts in the Nexus Islands force was showing the humans how little speculation and conjecture could do.

Maybe, though, they had faced what lay before them, and knew that today could not go as smoothly as had yesterday.

Grateful Peace asked that Firekeeper escort him to somewhere where he could be close to the water, but not invite attack from the ships in the blockading fleet. Firekeeper knew exactly where to take him, and led the way to a rocky spit overlooking the other islands in the archipelago.

"That one," she said, pointing to the peaked island, "is where Virim's gate is. When Chaker Torn came with fishing boat to take us off, he say the waters run over much rock. Big ship not get in, and even little one find bad if they not steered by one who knows."

"Not precisely clear," Grateful Peace said, "but I understand. What I need the three of you to do is to stand by and keep me from being interrupted. Based upon the research we did last night, I believe that the sea monsters—like the Dragon—are less Beasts as are creatures like Blind Seer or Elation, but are instead embodiments of elemental forces. Therefore, I think that they are still here, but when querinalo killed those who had summoned them to guard the waters, they faded out of contact with this plane of existence."

He looked at Firekeeper as if expecting her to ask what a plane of existence was, but she had seen a great deal since they had parted in New Kelvin.

When Firekeeper did not voice a question, Grateful Peace asked, "Firekeeper, could you ask the Meddler if my conjectures are accurate according to his far greater understanding of magical lore?"

Firekeeper did so, and if Peace was surprised that she could echo him so precisely, well, in these past years she been given more experience as a translator than he could ever dream.

The Meddler considered this with due thoughtfulness, then replied with the touch of theatricality that Firekeeper was coming to accept.

"Yes. As far as your knowledge goes, that is correct. I could give you a long lecture on how these creatures were first contacted and why they take the forms they do but—other than the fact that you wouldn't believe anything I said—we also don't have the time."

"One more question," Peace asked, "and answer me honestly, as you claim to value Firekeeper's life. The disaster caused when the Star Wizard summoned the Dragon of Despair is legend in my land, but I have reason to believe that these sea monsters might be amenable to logical, self-serving argument. Would you agree?"

The Meddler quirked the corner of his mouth in a smile.

"If you made a very good argument, then, yes, I believe they could agree. But it would need to be a very good argument."

Grateful Peace nodded. "I believe I have one."

He then seated himself on what looked like a bench coaxed from the living rock. Firekeeper remembered Urgana's tales of her sister, a Once Dead who could work rock, and wondered if this was a piece of Ellabrana's handiwork.

Grateful Peace motioned for Firekeeper to come to him.

"Have a seat," he said, patting a slim hand on the bench.

"I stand," she said. "But I listen."

Citrine and Edlin, armed and armored, weapons held at easy readiness, did not show the least offense at the favoritism given to Firekeeper. Rather, they reminded her of young wolves, knowing their place, and knowing that the hunt and the pack would be best served by their keeping to them.

The Meddler seated himself on the ground, leaning back against a comfortable backrest created by a granite upthrust. He had brought a mug of tea with him from the kitchen, and he sipped at it with such pleasure that Firekeeper was reminded again how long he had been without a body. What would he do to keep this one? She shifted her stance so that she could keep him in sight, even as she listened to Peace.

The Meddler noticed her watchfulness and gave her a wry smile. "I'll listen, too, but I won't do anything unless you tell me to."

She listened, and heard Grateful Peace's breathing move to a regular pattern, not overly slow, but measured and steady. Eventually, she heard him speak, softly, and could not say whether what she heard was New Kelvinese or Pellish or some language of her heart.

"I see you now. Lovely. Truly lovely. I suppose you enjoy your freedom. Slipping in and out of waves and worlds and water. What a pity your freedom is doomed. It's not going to be long before those who use magics akin to the magics that once bound you into time and space will rediscover that lore.

They'll touch you again, bind you again. How could they not? Why should they not? It's easier to set a hook the second time. Everyone knows that.

"I know that, and I only had a few hours to look at the old books. Oh, yes, much was destroyed, but knowledge once lost is found again more easily. You know that. That's how you swim as you do, knowledge rather than fins or scales or gills. Once you know someplace, somewhere, somehow, you know how to return. Why should it be any different for humans?

"Pity. The trap waits, and you cannot swim away from it. You live in all places, not just one place, and that makes getting away rather difficult, does it not? Humans know that, but then again they don't. It's easier to touch you in a familiar place. They'd need to rediscover the connections all over again in a new place, and that could take lifetimes—and you there are not you here. The hook there and then has not been set as it has in the here and now, the now and then. They might never find you again.

"But here. Here they would, unless . . . I've spoken to those who hold this land now, who hold this lore. They have told me to tell you this. Protect this place, these people, and they will vow not to set those bindings on you. They would instead make an agreement with you—your protection of them, their preservation of your freedom. It's worth considering. Those who are attempting to invade, those who ride those wooden ships and seek to force the gates, they might not make such a bargain. True, they might, they might take years and years to make the binding. They might do it tomorrow. Do you wish to exist with that hovering over your freedom? Is that truly freedom, or would it be a cage from which you could never escape?

"Yes. You could kill them all, all the humans on the ships and on the land and through the gates, but I know the price of that. You would bind yourselves then, for blood is binding, souls are binding. You would be free from those humans, but you would be forever bound to that course. Do you wish that?

"I thought not. How can you defend yourselves without incurring the bond of death and blood? Defend here without invoking it. You are mighty forces. I can sense that even through this thin thread of communication. Surely you have ways that are not those. I wonder if the mere sight of you might not be enough to frighten away those who thought to fight only a few isolated people they have convinced themselves are enemies. With your help, we can bring others who will join our battle here."

As Firekeeper listened she could hear faint echoes of voices: voices of the sea monsters. She could not make out what they said, and yet she could. They were almost frantic in their desire to keep their freedom, but they knew the truth of what Grateful Peace had said to them. They knew that were they to fight for that freedom and slay but a single one of the creatures they thought of as "blood bearers" they would be bound. So it had been in the days long, long ago when they had first been bound to protect the little interruptions in their eternity of swimming that were the Nexus Islands.

When Virim had created querinalo, he had slain all the "blood bearers," for only those whose blood held the ability to cast spells could bind the sea monsters. The sea monsters had returned to their freedom, but it could never be, as Peace had reminded them, a freedom such as they had known before, because the secret of how to bind them was no longer a secret.

Firekeeper was so locked into this wordless dialogue that she did not hear the commotions from the gateway hill, a commotion that announced that the long-awaited, long-dreaded attempt to invade through those carefully warded gates had begun.

She was unaware when the first probing attacks became breakthrough. She was unaware when her friends and allies began to die. Conversation between those who share the same form and the same language is difficult enough. When that conversation must span the gap between those with blood and those who are the elements embodied then it is slow, hard work indeed. Caught up in the fringes of that conversation, nothing could draw Firekeeper back into the world in which her body stood tense and unmoving, nothing, that is, but the fall and rise and rise and fall of the howling cry of one heart-beloved voice.

She snapped her head back so that she could listen more clearly and knew that she had stood motionless for long hours, for her neck was so stiff that the corded muscle within it felt like the cabled rope that held a tight-bound ship to the dock.

Blind Seer howled, "The hill! The hill! We have lost / are losing the hill! Retreat! Retreat! Else we will lose all and more! Else we will lose you as well."

Blind Seer's message was meant for the yarimaimalom, and with it rang, unheard until this moment, the blaring notes of trumpets giving the same warning signal to the human troops.

"Retreat?" Firekeeper said in dull shock, and she did not know what language she spoke. She looked around and saw that Edlin and Citrine stood out of earshot, bows drawn, attention riveted on the gateway hillside down the sides of which streamed the ragged ranks of the retreating Nexan army.

The raven Bitter, who sat haggard with feathers ruffled and beak red stained on the back of the bench where Grateful Peace still stared motionless over the crashing waves, gave the wolf-woman her answer. He spoke with measured cadence, as if he was speaking of something long ago and in another place.

"Our peoples fought well there on the hillside. The Mires gave us some trouble, for although their flock was small it fought like songbirds chasing the raven. Azure Towers gave us trouble, too, for if the Mires fought with its heart, the Towers fought with their minds, and clever minds they have there, quick in the ways and means of destruction.

"But we were betrayed, and that betrayal turned our hard-won victory to something more vile than mere defeat. From the gate leading to u-Chivalum marched in ranks of two trained soldiers armed and armored, well disciplined by their commander, and certain in the auguries."

"Betrayed?" Firekeeper interrupted. "As I recall, Tiniel held watch at that gate."

"Yes. Betrayed, by Tiniel, by the very youth for whom I gave an eye, in the pursuit of whose freedom my mate spent a night without wings and in purest pain. We were betrayed by

Tiniel. Rather than giving warning, he let in the invaders. We know this as fact, for their commander boasted of it, boasted loudly so that we could know the Divine Five were with the invaders and had sent them sure auguries of victory."

Firekeeper wanted to howl in despair and fury, but that would be wasted breath.

"Tell more," she said. "I heard retreat sounded, so we must still have some forces."

"We do," Bitter said, "but we have lost control of the gateway hillside, and with those gates freely at their disposal our enemies will be able to summon reinforcements where we cannot. When Derian realized what was happening he sent Enigma through the gate to the New World so that those there would know what had happened. My Lovable went with him, since she can speak just a little to humans. They, at least, will be warned, and Derian told Lovable to remind Doc and Elise that they could ruin the gate rather than make invasion of the New World too easy."

And we will be stranded here, Firekeeper thought. *Unless we recapture the gates, unless we . . .*

She looked to where Grateful Peace still conferred unhearing, unknowing with the sea monsters. She was about to go to the thaumaturge, to interrupt his trance so that he would know what had happened, when Blind Seer, running so hard and so fast that he was hardly more than a blur of grey, halted panting hard beside her.

"Firekeeper," the wolf said, "you know?"

"I know."

"Ynamynet believes she can create a wall around the gateway hill that will hold the invaders there a time. She came to ask me if you would lend us the Meddler for this."

Firekeeper glanced up at the Meddler, and saw from the frightened expression on his lined features that he had understood.

"Meddler? You are not mine to lend or order, no matter what Ynamynet believes. Do you join this fight or do you die with us all?"

"I could," the Meddler said, "follow Tiniel's example and join the other side."

"No," Firekeeper said. "You could not. I would kill you myself before that could happen."

The Meddler looked at her and smiled as if she had offered him her heart rather than a promise of his own death.

"I believe you would, and, more importantly, I believe you could. I have no desire to die, not at the hands of these invaders, nor at yours. I will help Ynamynet with her spells."

Firekeeper nodded. "I must tell Grateful Peace what has happened."

"Let Edlin and Citrine," Blind Seer replied. "They know enough."

Firekeeper nodded.

"Brother Edlin," she called.

The young man turned and beamed his wide, foolish smile. "What? I mean, I say. What?"

"Grateful Peace knows nothing of what has happened here. Bring him back and tell him what we face. I go, for just a little, with Blind Seer and the Meddler so that we may bind those invaders within their prize."

"Right. I say, this is a bad turn, isn't it?"

"Very bad," Firekeeper agreed. "Very bad, indeed."

XLII

MORE THAN ANYTHING in the world, Derian wanted to grab Isende and press her to him. Her skin was too brown for her to be pale, but she seemed so just the same. The knowledge of her brother's betrayal combined with the effort of raising the shield about the gateway hill had almost been more than she could bear.

Like an autumn leaf, washed to a skeleton by running water, he thought.

But he couldn't indulge himself. Isende was here not as his

sweetheart, not as the adaptable young woman she had proven herself to be these last few moonspans, but as Ynamynet's representative at this meeting to try to find some way the Nexans could continue to hold.

Ynamynet has sent Isende here to show everyone that the one twin should not be judged by what the other has done. My affection for her, ironically, could be held against her.

So he settled for squeezing her hand just for a moment, then moving to take a seat on one of worn stone benches that had been set some unimaginable time ago to make a rough circle in a protected copse of the island's twisted trees.

They had chosen to meet there rather than inside one of the buildings both for the convenience of the yarimaimalom, many of whom disliked going indoors, and because this way no precious moments would be lost if the invaders broke out of the shield that currently bound them on the gateway hillside.

When he looked back over his shoulder, Derian could see the shield shimmering pearlescent in the sunlight. When he looked out over the ocean he could see the towering masts of the blockading ships. Neither view was comforting, so he chose to concentrate on the faces of those gathered with him.

Skea sat one bench over, his helmet resting between his feet, his gauntlets beside him, but otherwise ready for action. Onion the wolf sat near, perhaps in conscious imitation of how Blind Seer would sit by Firekeeper, for as Derian understood it, Onion had become the yarimaimalom's war leader, much as Skea was for the humans.

Wort, one arm in a sling, sat on the ground where he could lean against a tree. His face was drawn with pain, but nonetheless he was reviewing the lists of supplies, crossing off items with an almost vicious stroke of the charcoal stick he held in his uninjured hand.

Isende sat across from Derian, and as he let his gaze rest on her for a moment, he saw Firekeeper coming up to join them. Once again, Blind Seer was not with her, but she had the Meddler in tow. The Meddler showed something of the same exhaustion as did Isende, but where she looked defeated, he seemed positively perky.

The last one to join them was Plik, who eased himself onto a seat on the ground near Wort with a deep sigh.

"I'm here to help Firekeeper with translating," he said.

Derian nodded thanks. Firekeeper looked pretty strained, and asking her to translate whatever the yarimaimalom had to say would probably not be a good idea.

No one was starting the meeting, so thinking wistfully of those days when before a major conference all anyone wanted from him was that he make certain Firekeeper showed up more or less clad, Derian cleared his throat. He didn't bother with speeches or with telling everyone how well they had done. This wasn't the time, any more than the time to admire a horse's gait was when it was running away with you toward a low-hanging tree branch.

"I have a report from Zebel on injuries and deaths. Most of you already know the worst. We've lost about a quarter of our number, either to death or to injuries bad enough that they can't help.

"The yarimaimalom may have lost even more—and they're the reason more humans didn't die. Many of the wolves are dead, as are several of the cats and a bear. Others are in bad shape, including a fox, without whose intervention I wouldn't be here. We've lost fewer of the wingéd folk because they did their best to stay out of arrow range. They're continuing to scout for us."

Plik interrupted, "Several want to know if they can do more than scout. They've heard about the exploding stuff Azure Towers used at their gate. They wonder if they could use something similar on the ships."

Skea frowned. "Possibly. We didn't have whatever that was during King Veztressidan's war, but it's possible we might manage something with oil."

He glanced at Wort. The quartermaster turned pages on one of his records.

"Possibly, but do we have time to design a delivery system light enough that birds could carry it?"

Derian decided it was time to rein this part of the conversation in.

"Later. It's a good idea, but later. Right now, let's hear what we have to work with. Isende?"

Isende brushed imaginary dirt off her trouser legs, and started talking fast, almost mechanically, her gaze fastened on a point somewhere near her toes.

"We have the gateway hill enclosed in a shield, and thanks to the Meddler, we're going to be able to keep it up at least through midday tomorrow. Even so, the shield needs to be supervised. Most of that is going to fall on Ynamynet and Kalyndra. The rest of us don't know enough."

She looked up now, her gaze holding a mingled defiance and shyness that ripped into Derian's heart.

"One good thing is that Ynamynet has discovered that if she—or Kalyndra—concentrates very hard, they can see what is going on inside the shield. The images are blurred, and there isn't any sound, but its something. Urgana is going through the archives, looking for more information about this element in the shield. It's not something we expected."

"But it is something that makes sense," Wort said excitedly. "I mean, the shield is something that would only be brought into operation if something dangerous came through the gates. Would you want to be kept from seeing in? I wouldn't. I mean, eventually, you're going to want to pull down the shield, and you'd better be prepared for what's on the inside."

Isende actually smiled, and Derian felt himself warmed by this return to her normally outgoing self.

"Another good thing," she continued, "is that Enigma managed to get back after carrying warning to Doc and Elise in the New World. That means we have his ability on our side, and the assurance that warning did get to them. If the invaders decide to push through, they're not going to have an easy time of it."

Plik interrupted again. "Absolutely not. Enigma reports that the yarimaimalom in the New World are gathered and willing to take on any who come through. They even have evolved a plan to bury the gate, if they believe that is necessary."

And even if it strands us here, Derian thought, but the thought came with an odd cheerfulness, for he knew that even if he never saw them again, his friends and family would be safe. *For now. Only for now. If we fail here, how long before the invaders open another of the New World gates? I hope Elise thinks to have some warning sent. At least the Liglimom would believe. I think my people would, too.*

He shook himself from these thoughts, knowing he had enough trouble without borrowing more. He forced himself to concentrate as Wort reported on their stores of weapons. It boiled down to what Derian had expected. They had hand weapons, but supplies of arrows were growing thin. Some bows would need to be retired for lack of appropriate-sized shafts.

When Wort finished, Skea nodded his thanks.

"My report has pretty much already been covered. We've done our best, and we might have held but for circumstances no one but Truth might have foreseen."

Skea didn't look at Isende as he said this, nor did anyone else, but the marked way they avoided reminding her that Tiniel's actions had given the battle to the invaders was almost as painful as a direct reminder would have been. Derian saw how her fingers dug into her skin through the loose fabric of her trousers, as if physical pain might somehow balance the agony of her heart.

To his surprise, he saw Firekeeper reach out and grasp the other woman's hand tightly in her own, stroking it as she might have the fur on Blind Seer's shoulders.

Pack animals, he thought. *They know there is no shame in offering comfort. I wish humans were so wise.*

Plik broke in again, and turning to give the new speaker his attention, Derian saw that Truth now sat on the ground alongside the maimalodalum.

"Truth asks me to apologize for her inability to predict what Tiniel would do. She says that she knew that his actions were key, but she could not see past what she calls 'swirling' to see exactly what he would do. From this, I gather that perhaps there was less certainty on Tiniel's part than we might imagine. Some force might have been applied to him about which we do not know."

Skea nodded. "Does Truth have any other advice for us?"

"She says that we should not do other than raise or lower the shield. Any futures where we attempt to penetrate it from this side—to send in a small force, for example—end in tragedy. Other than that, she says there are a few unpredictable elements that, until they resolve, create too much conflict for her to give good advice."

No one argued with this pronouncement, even though Derian was certain that he was not the only one who longed to be told what precise course of action would lead to them pulling a victory out of what seemed like—at best—a delayed defeat. They had all lived beside Truth long enough to know the risks the jaguar took in offering even this much counsel.

We risk our lives, Derian thought, *but she risks not only her life, but her sanity as well.*

He was about to ask Skea what tactical suggestions the general might have to offer when he felt a rhythmic rumbling. He looked around, thinking Eshinarvash might be galloping up with some message, then realized that the sound was not a sound at all, but a sensation felt in his bones and sinews, that vibrated in his very marrow.

The others were looking about now, too, glancing from side to side. He felt a mist or drizzle touch his skin, saw Wort bend over his notes to protect the writing. Then came a screeching roar, as might arise from the throat of some enormous bird of prey or from that of a hurricane suddenly gifted with thought.

Derian had risen to his feet, although he had no memory of doing so, and had both arms wrapped around one of the twisted tree trunks, but although there was a sound as of great wind, there was no wind. Instead, out in the ocean, there were now monsters.

They were sea foam and ice storm, waves crashing and sheeting rainfall. They were something like horses and something like cliffs, something like lizards and something like fish.

Derian's head hurt as he tried to make the shapes his eyes saw into something his mind could understand; then he ripped his gaze away. That was when he saw Grateful Peace staggering up the slope to join them.

Peace was soaked to the skin, his long robes clinging to his limbs as he walked. He leaned hard on Edlin's arm, and the expression in his pale eyes was haunted and haggard. Citrine walked on his other side, carrying both her and Edlin's gear. She studied Peace's face, and evidently what she saw there did not reassure her, for Derian saw the tears that splashed her cheeks.

"The fleet will not land," Grateful Peace said, sinking onto the bench Skea vacated for him. "Arisen once more are the sea monsters of which legend speaks. They will not attack the fleet—they have their reasons and I will not attempt to argue them away from them—but I have managed to make them understand that if they wish to maintain the freedom they lost when the Old World sorcerers bound them to protect these islands, then they must throw in their lot with us."

"In return for what?" Skea asked.

"Continued freedom," Grateful Peace said. "They are very unlike us, but they are enough alike to understand taking away of something they value."

Firekeeper's husky voice spoke for the first time.

"And you give?" she asked. "What?"

"Nothing but an explanation," Grateful Peace said, offering her a shadow of a smile. "These had more to lose than did the Dragon—and less to earn by taking."

"They fight only to maintain a freedom they already had?" Skea said, disbelief evident in his voice.

Edlin frowned at him. "Can't you understand that? I say! Is that any different from what the rest of us are doing? I mean, they may look a fright, but that doesn't make them any less human, don't you know."

Citrine punched Edlin, but Skea was nodding.

"Sometimes I forget," he said, "that shape matters very little. In the end, all that lives values similar things, and we will risk losing them to keep them. However, even without the fleet to fear, I do not see how those of us who remain can hope to defeat those who hold the gateway hill. Once the shield is down—and surely the invaders will find a way to bring it down—they can bring through reinforcements until there is not a one of us left standing."

Firekeeper surged to her feet in one lithe movement, hauling the Meddler up with her. He looked distinctly discomfited, as if he had some idea what Firekeeper was about to say.

"But if I bring more to fight for us," she said. "Is this enough?"

"Who? From where?" Skea said.

"They is called the Bound," Firekeeper said. "Yarimaimalom, but very fierce. Also, I think not risking querinalo, for Virim would have made sure those who serve him not get his sickness. I go through gate on little island—Meddler can open it for me. Peace, will the sea monsters let us go there?"

"I think they will," Grateful Peace said. "They have no desire to harm anyone, but they intend to make the waters sufficiently rough that passage over them would be fatal. I believe I could explain why you need safe passage."

"Then I go," Firekeeper said, "and the Meddler with. Peace, you need come with?"

"I can make my request from here," Grateful Peace said. "They thunder within my head, even now."

Derian wanted to draw Firekeeper aside, but this was not the time nor place to leave others wondering what secrets he might have, nor what he wished to say to her that he did not wish them to hear. Instead, he spoke his concern aloud.

"Firekeeper, can you trust him? The Meddler, I mean."

She shrugged. "What choice is there? Without help, we die. Even with help, maybe we die. Gate is fast, and I think the Bound will be close. Maybe we be coming back almost before we is gone."

"Why not bring someone else to work the gate?" Derian urged. "Enigma or Blind Seer."

"I wish much for that," Firekeeper said, "but Ynamynet needs them, and wherever I go, I must have this Meddler with me because—as you say—he is one who needs watching. He say he help me. Now I give him chance to do this."

Derian shrugged surrender.

The Meddler gave a wide smile. "Now I shall prove myself worthy of her," he declaimed.

Firekeeper tugged his arm, and as she trotted him off down the hill toward the water, Derian heard her raise her voice in a mournful howl and knew she was saying farewell to Blind Seer.

❀

KING BRYESSIDAN GLOWERED at the pearlescent white wall that stood between him and absolute conquest of the Nexus Islands.

Behind him, closer to the wedge-shaped buildings that held the gates, he was aware of the troops, their mood a dangerous mixture of restlessness and relief as they waited to learn whether their leaders would declare the battle won with the resumption of control of the gateway hilltop.

He had called a meeting of his associate commanders to discuss this very matter, and was waiting for them to join him in one of the small gardens laid out between the clusters of gates.

Bryessidan knew his own feelings without a doubt. For him, the battle would never be over until the entirety of the Nexus Islands were under the control of the allied forces.

"So close!" he grumbled. "So close! Amelo!"

His Once Dead advisor hurried up from where he had been consulting with others of his order.

"Any thoughts on how we can break through this thing?"

"I already have archivists in all the allied lands researching the problem, Your Majesty," Amelo replied briskly. "The Once Dead gathered here concur on one thing. This shield is not the result of a simple spell. Rather, it seems to be generated from an artifact built into this facility and dormant to this time. As none of our number knew of the existence of this shield, we conjecture that it must be a relatively new discovery to our enemies as well."

Bryessidan had thought of this already. "Else why go to all

the trouble of setting up the iron gates. Yes. I wonder how they discovered it? Doubtless they stumbled upon something in the records here. We can ask them—if any of them are alive to ask when we're done with them."

Aurick of Pelland strolled over from where he had been conferring with his subcommanders. Nodding casual greeting to Bryessidan, he reached out and poked at the opaque whiteness with one fingertip—or rather he tried to do so. The stuff had an unnerving trick of pulling away from you so that you felt like you were touching nothing. This led you to poke more deeply and was the prelude to another, nastier trick. For a moment Bryessidan was tempted to let Aurick discover that trick for himself, but such would be behavior unworthy of a commander in chief of such a large armed force.

"I wouldn't do that if I were you," Bryessidan said, hoping rather nastily that Aurick would persist. After all, Bryessidan had already issued an order forbidding anyone to touch the shield. The troops had the sense to obey, but Aurick might want to test his will against Bryessidan's and right now Bryessidan didn't mind if he chose this way to do it.

Aurick had conducted himself with great valor during the fighting, as had his troops. They had been the first to adapt to the attacks of the various beasts in the enemy forces, and Aurick himself had slain an absolutely enormous wolf in single combat.

Despite the protests of Aridisdu Valdala, who claimed the thing was intelligent, and therefore due the same civilized treatment that would be accorded to a human opponent, Aurick had instructed his personal guard to drag the brute's corpse back through the gate to Pelland so he could have it either stuffed or turned into a cloak.

However, Aurick decided to obey Bryessidan and pulled his finger away short of letting it penetrate the edge of the swirling whiteness.

"What does it do if you touch it?"

"It lets you get close, then surrounds whatever member you put into it and starts sucking the blood out, right through the skin. Amelo conjectures that's one of the ways the shield gets extra power to maintain itself."

"People will poke," Aurick agreed, "even if told they are not to do so. I now recall the order you sent around soon after this shield went up. Very wise."

"We learned what the shield could do when one of Queen Iline's nephews thought to show his valor by bashing into the shield," Bryessidan explained. "He flung himself into it shoulder first, like you would into a door. The shield let him in, then engulfed him. It still hasn't released him, though there's a bulge where he went in."

"Like a giant constrictor swallowed him," said Aridisdu Valdala, coming up to join them. "We learned about the blood draining ability when one of the man's comrades tried to pull him out and almost lost a hand."

"Nasty," Aurick agreed, obviously impressed. "Surely the design shows the work of our ancestors. They did not hesitate to be ruthless where such ruthlessness was needed."

Bryessidan didn't know whether to be repulsed or reassured by Aurick's attitude. They were at war, and so ruthlessness was a necessary quality, but this shield made his skin crawl just to look at it.

Or maybe I'm just offended at being thwarted, he thought, but he knew that revulsion rather than anger was at the heart of his reaction.

"Did we get any messages from the fleet before this shield cut us off?" asked Aridisdu Valdala.

Bryessidan shook his head. "None of my Once Dead have reported any such contact, nor did those from Tavetch. Amelo is questioning the others, just in case a quick mind-link was established, but I think any so contacted would have had the initiative to report."

"At least we know the fleet is here and in fighting trim," said Kynan of Hearthome, coming up to take his place in the circle. "I have been questioning one of the few prisoners we managed to take, and it seems that King Hurwin sent a force ashore yesterday. The Nexans took some injuries, but drove off the landing parties."

"Drove them off?" Bryessidan said in disbelief. "But surely they outnumbered the Nexans."

"The prisoner seemed to think the landing parties were more a test, rather than an actual attack. Doubtless, King Hurwin was waiting to see what we would do."

"I thought I saw ship's boats being readied," said Merial of Azure Towers, who had trailed up as Kynan was speaking. "Perhaps even now the Nexans are in combat with King Hurwin's marines."

The generals looked at each other, for a moment in perfect harmony as they shared the thought of their opponents being battered to a pulp just on the other side of that white wall. Then Aridisdu Valdala shook her head.

"The auguries are against such an action, at least not for the immediate future, although they are unclear why."

Fromalf of Tavetch arrived in time to hear this, and offered comment on Aridisdu Valdala's statement by way of greeting.

"King Hurwin certainly had long-glasses focused on the island. He could not have missed seeing when the fighting began on the hill here, but he would also have seen the shield go up. If I were him, I would have recalled any boats he had ready to launch until he had some idea of what was going on."

"I agree," Bryessidan said reluctantly. "King Hurwin is brave, but he is not impetuous. He wouldn't have lived to become a grandfather if he was. He'll attack, no doubt, but probably not until tomorrow at the earliest."

"But we don't need him, now, do we?" said Kynan of Hearthome with a mocking smile. "We have gates to seven different nations right here, and ample Once Dead to activate them. Whatever we desire is ours for the asking."

"What I'm asking," Bryessidan said, "is how to break this shield."

"And how to do it," Aridisdu Valdala added, "without unintentionally making it stronger."

Kynan, whose cousin was now the lump in the shield's otherwise uninterrupted smoothness, colored, but Bryessidan couldn't guess whether in embarrassment or indignation. Queen Iline's relatives—all of whom viewed themselves, unrealistically, as her prospective heir—did not tend to get along.

"Research is being done," Merial of Azure Towers said confidently. "Talianas of Tishiolo will not be joining us for that very reason. She has gone to her ruler to request access to archives that are normally kept sealed in the hope that they will contain the information we need."

Talianas was one of the few of the commanders who was also a Once Dead, although she was talented, rather than being a spellcaster. Her superior attitude continued to make Bryessidan's skin crawl, so he was just as glad not to have her there. Her second-in-command was much more tractable.

"Even if we do not find out how to break the shield," Kynan of Hearthome said, "surely the Nexans cannot maintain the shield indefinitely. Something must give: either their supplies or the concentration of their Once Dead."

"I agree," Bryessidan said.

But even as he tried to answer with appropriate confidence, the king wondered if it did. His youth had been spent surrounded by Once Dead, and although he did not have a trace of talent himself, he had learned a great deal of their lore.

If this shield was indeed artifact generated, rather than a spell, it might be possible for it to be maintained for quite a while with what had already been given to it. As for breaking down the shield, he wondered if that would be possible.

Surely those who had originally created the shield had taken into account that they would be enclosing one or more gates—and all the resources those gates could bring—within the shield.

We're lucky that they created a shield that permitted air to pass, he thought morosely, *but they wouldn't have wanted to risk suffocating those they might need to send in to deal with a problem. How long before we find ourselves being dealt with? We must find a way to take the initiative!*

He raged at himself for some timeless time, half listening as his allies articulated their own thoughts and frustrations. One thing was clear, even though it had never been openly discussed. He was not the only one to feel that their conquest would be incomplete until they held the entirety of the Nexus Islands.

"We'll do it!" he said aloud. "It may be a day or a week before we can join battle again, but we will do it, and this time we will win. For now let us quarter the troops here, and have food and drink brought to them. If the siege continues, we can rotate them back in groups."

"Siege," Aridisdu Valdala said thoughtfully. "Yes. That is precisely what this is, a siege. It is a very strange siege indeed, for each group holds a castle, and each stands without, yet it is a siege for all of that."

"Strange or not," Bryessidan said, and he took confidence from the sound of his own voice, "a siege is what we face. All of us understand the tactics of a siege. We know that the ones who win are the ones who have the better supply lines and higher morale among their troops. Who would that be?"

He had raised his voice, so that the nearest of the gathered troops could not fail to overhear him. A rushing murmur, a rough-edged wind rushing through a human meadow, carried his words to those out of earshot.

Someone began to cheer, and the cheering became general.

I've won, Bryessidan thought in satisfaction. *It's only a matter of time, now. Although the Nexans do not realize it, the battle is already joined, fought, and won.*

XLIII

CITRINE HAD GONE ahead to see how the sea monsters reacted to Grateful Peace's request. Now she came running to meet them, intercepting them on the path to the harbor where the fishing boat was anchored.

"I think . . . I mean. You've got to come here and see this."

Firekeeper blinked at her. The polished young woman Citrine had become had vanished, and she seemed closer to the eight-year-old Firekeeper had originally met. Citrine must have realized she had been less than clear, for she pulled herself up, literally straightening and squaring her shoulders, and met Firekeeper's gaze.

"The sea monsters," she said. "They have a message—for you, I think. Maybe for all of us."

Firekeeper didn't ask her to clarify. In her opinion, humans spent far too much time talking about things they could learn by running a few paces. She broke into a trot, glancing back to make certain the Meddler was following. He was, and she noticed that he looked a little younger than he had earlier. There was nothing definite; perhaps his beard was a bit more full. His skin was no less lined, but it seemed thicker, more supple.

Watch him, she thought. *He looks human, smells human, but he is less human even than you are. Though perhaps when it comes to being human he is even more so. Humans are not wolves. They cannot be trusted.*

But she turned her back on the Meddler, knowing that Elation and other of the wingéd folk soared overhead, and that the Meddler would not act against her under so many searching gazes. Retribution would come too quickly for him to benefit, and from the tales she had heard told, the Meddler understood personal benefit better than he did anything else.

They crested a rise overlooking the water, and what Firekeeper saw put all thoughts of the Meddler—or anything else—from her mind.

Even at their first manifestation, the sea monsters had not seemed like any creatures Firekeeper had seen before. Now their likeness to things with blood and bone, sinew and hide had vanished completely. They were sparkles in the water, flashes in the foam. They were crystal and mist-shimmer— and they were also a bridge. A bridge like no other Firekeeper had ever seen that stretched over the tossing ocean waves, one end anchored on the main island, the other on the shore of the peaked island that was their destination.

It was transparent and translucent, as if crafted from ice or pebbled glass, or water running over stones. It moved slightly, not from force of wind or tide, but because the creatures that had woven it from themselves were alive.

Firekeeper had the feeling that they were turning, looking at her, wondering what she thought of them and of this thing they had made, and she let a smile blossom on her face, a smile as bright as any she had ever shaped, a smile like the cry of the pack when the lone hunter returns.

"A bridge!" she said, and felt the words inadequate.

"I wonder," said a sardonic voice over her shoulder, "if Grateful Peace told them you get seasick."

Firekeeper turned to glower at the Meddler, but it was Grateful Peace, still leaning on Edlin's arm, although he seemed somewhat stronger than before, who gave reply.

"I did not," he said. "I simply asked that they give passage to those who would go and bring reinforcements, and passage to those reinforcements in turn. I thought they would simply still the sea so the fishing boat could pass safely. This marvelous creation is all their idea."

"They want us to move quickly," Firekeeper said. "This may not be easy for them to make. We go."

She paused to touch Grateful Peace lightly on one arm.

"Thank you. Now, I go so all your hunt not go to rot."

Grateful Peace nodded. "Thank you."

Firekeeper glanced at the Meddler.

"I'm ready if you are," he said with an engaging grin. "Off to the rescue."

The surface of the bridge the sea monsters had shaped was like nothing Firekeeper had ever felt before. She had expected it to be wet and slick, like walking on ice or rain-wet stone. It turned out to be perfectly dry. More startlingly, it moved under her feet, hastening her pace so that when she walked her hair blew back from her face as if she were running.

She grinned over at the Meddler.

"I tell you they want us to go fast. You can maybe run in that clothes?"

She indicated to his robes. They ended a finger's breadth above the tops of his soft leather shoes, but she wasn't sure he still might not get tangled in them.

"These are more natural to me than that mountain sheep's body ever could be," he replied, breaking into a jog. "And the footing is amazingly good."

They crossed to the peaked island in less time than even a swift boat could have carried them, and Firekeeper's stomach was much more steady. She watched the Meddler with care as he prepared the spell for opening the gate. For the two of them, they did not need a great deal of blood, and the Meddler supplied it from his own arm, neatly knotting up the wound with a bit of bandaging he produced from a little bag at his waist.

Despite all this evidence of cooperation, Firekeeper watched him carefully. By now, she knew the complex routine of the spell as well as she knew how to string her bow, and she was certain the Meddler neither omitted the least element, nor added any of his own.

For the final step, she and the Meddler each drew their own blood, and smeared the drops within the rounded form at the appropriate side of the gate.

The stone shimmered, and Firekeeper nodded to the Meddler. They stepped forward and were back in the small gate room in Virim's stronghold in the northwestern forests of the New World.

Firekeeper took two brisk steps in the direction of the doorway that would lead into the outer room and found that she could not take a third.

She tried again and found that while she could turn, blink, swallow, and breathe, she could not move a limb, not even her head upon her neck. She suspected that she could speak, but she did not. Instead she waited, immobile and increasingly furious.

There was no need to ask who had done this, no need to shout in anger and frustration, no one to whom she might howl for assistance. She was alone, alone with the creature who had made her captive, and she waited for him to cross into her line of sight.

He did so, reaching out and brushing her cheek with his

hand. The fingers were smooth and soft, too soft, without the least trace of callouses or weathering.

Why would they be? she asked herself. *That body is new, perhaps newer than Elise's new baby. It makes sense that the skin would be fresh.*

Nonetheless, she trembled at the unnaturalness of it, but the paralysis that kept her from moving hid her shame.

"You haven't asked any questions," the Meddler said, "but I'm going to tell you how I managed that. I'm rather proud of it, actually. Remember when you gave me some of your blood, back there when we were watching Wort and his soldiers fight?"

He paused as if expecting her to give him some light, conversational reply, but Firekeeper said nothing. The Meddler shook his head and looked just a little put upon.

"Most of the power in that blood went to subduing Virim, just as I had indicated it would. I held a bit back, though. You really were bleeding very freely, you know. Some went to help me reach through Virim's memories until I found the key to his human form. I hated being a mountain sheep. A wolf I could have borne—you might have even found me attractive—but never a sheep.

"I held a little in reserve though, and since you have never let me out of your sight for very long, I had ample opportunity to work a spell that would let me control your body."

He gave one of those annoyingly engaging smiles.

"Well, 'control' is probably overstating the matter just a bit. I can keep you from moving, even more than I am doing now. I could stop you from any motion at all."

Firekeeper didn't need him to explain what a deadly threat that was. There were insects and snakes whose venom paralyzed their prey. The creatures suffocated. Even if he let her continue breathing, he could rob her of the ability to swallow, and her spit would run from her mouth or maybe even choke her.

She blinked, and thought how soon her eyes would begin to burn if even that little motion was taken from her.

However, she couldn't bring herself to speak, and after a long and thoughtful pause the Meddler went on.

"It's for your own good. I hope you realize that. I can't bear the idea of you throwing yourself away leading the fight against the invaders. I want to save you, to protect you. Surely, you understand that I cannot let the woman I love go into such terrible danger—not when I have it in my power to prevent her."

"So," Firekeeper said, "what you do? Keep me like this forever? I tell you, if you free me, I go to them, even if I must run all the way to New Kelvin to find a gate."

"And what good would that do you?" the Meddler asked. "You could not open it."

"Maybe I run to Setting Sun stronghold," Firekeeper said. "Maybe among the yarimaimalom is one like Enigma or Blind Seer who can work the magic. I remember the spell."

"Stubborn," the Meddler said, "and in any case, you would be too late."

"I will not abandon my pack, not until I am sure."

"Don't wolves surrender when they are beaten?" the Meddler said in exasperation. "You keep claiming you are a wolf. Act like one."

"I am not beaten," Firekeeper said softly. "Why you think that I am?"

"You cannot move," the Meddler protested. "I could kill you with a gesture. How is it that you are not beaten?"

For a moment, Firekeeper wished that she had decided to pretend to be beaten. When the spell was broken and she could move again, then she could have attacked the Meddler. There was no law against attacking once one had surrendered, only that the surrender be true.

She suspected, though, that the Meddler would expect some such trick from her. Humans were full of them, so full that they had many, many words for them. Gambit, contrivance, trick, subterfuge, lie.

This creature standing before her in the shape of Virim was a master of tricks, but more than once his own tricks had turned against him. For now, she would not surrender, and she would find a way to win herself free.

"I not understand," she said into the silence that stretched between them, "why you do this. You promise to help me."

"I am helping you," the Meddler said. "What could be more helpful than preserving your life?"

Firekeeper blinked at him. There it was again, that insane human notion that preserving life justified any action—even the spending of the lives of others. A wolf pack would not survive a winter if the Ones thought that way. True, to a human observer, it might seem that the Ones benefitted from the pack more than the pack did from the Ones, but Firekeeper, who had seen how the strength of the Ones was the strength of the pack, who knew how weak a pack would be if every female bore pups every spring, knew that the Ones gave much for being first at every kill and the only ones to breed.

I have thought myself a One, she thought frantically. *I owe my pack for what they have given me.*

Her blood had done this, her blood and her own short-sighted impulsive desire to solve a problem. When they had first come to the Nexus Islands, she had witnessed how Tiniel and Isende had been controlled against their will by spells laid in their blood. She had frequently heard how reluctant the Nexans were to give blood to power spells that would otherwise benefit them from the fear that some would be held back to be used against them.

And then I give the Meddler access to my blood—lots of my blood—with no thought but that he could use it to solve an immediate problem.

Something in that thought rang less than true to her, and had Firekeeper already not been able to move, she would have frozen in her tracks to think the matter over.

Wait. Was I so foolish? I am not usually so foolish. The Meddler has control of my body. Might he have inserted a little bit of control into my thoughts as well?

She had seen this done before, and now that the idea had

come to her, it seemed very likely that the Meddler would not have robbed himself of such a useful tool.

What then does he not want me to remember? What little thought might betray all these careful plans?

She was oddly glad now that the Meddler had robbed her of motion, for she needed to be able to concentrate to work back through her memory. Had she been required to move about and speak and act like normal, he might have become suspicious, but now her silence would only be taken for anger.

As she might have worked through a game trail mostly obliterated by rain, the wolf-woman set herself to trail through her memories, back to that moment on the hillside when Virim had gone wild with fear for his life. He had gone wild with something else—the scent of her blood and the power it offered to work spells he might use to transform himself or defend himself.

The Meddler had spoken into her mind then, had whispered that if he had use of the blood she was so uselessly shedding he would be able to do something about Virim. She had given him that blood then, and . . .

Wait.

Firekeeper sniffed back along the trail. . . . Her memories felt as if they were engulfed in a thick rain, a rain that kept her from seeing clearly. She longed to go back to the relatively dry cave of her wrath at the Meddler.

How could he have trapped her? How could he have used her generosity against her? How could he claim to love her and do this to her?

But although that dry cave beckoned, Firekeeper had been driven out to hunt in the rain many, many times before. She was a wolf in her heart, but her human body could not go without eating for days on end as could that of a wolf. There was strength, then, in what her human body had forced her to do, and she drew on that strength now, pushing out into the driving rain, bending down to look to find the true thread of her memories.

She found it, almost obscured by puddles and mud. Now

she could follow the thread back, remember what had actually been said at that time.

She had not been such a fool as she had been led to believe. Now she could remember, and it was almost as if the scene played out again in front of her.

The Meddler's voice whispered within her mind, *"I will owe you . . . serve you. Help you win this war. I promise."*

Her reply, carefully thought through, despite the distraction of the battle raging on the beach below, of the pain in her arm, of the bowstring digging into her fingers.

"Promise or the blood in you will turn sour and empty as your word."

And the Meddler's reply, urgent, and holding a note of triumph she had not recognized then, but that rang high and true now that she knew to listen for it.

"I promise, by the love I hold for you, by the blood you give to me, I promise."

Firekeeper reviewed that exchange, and for a moment felt hopeless. What could she do with such words? She was no orator, never one to convince with the power of words alone. Her strengths were in action.

She felt a paralysis of spirit grip her, nearly as strong and solid as that which immobilized her limbs. Now, however, she knew the Meddler's touch, and knew this as a diversion. She was no fool. The pup who had come over the Iron Mountains might have thought all virtue was in a quick hard bite and the rest came after, but Firekeeper had learned a great deal in the intervening years. It was her own longing for days when things had been so simple—or she had believed them to be so—that the Meddler's magic was using to bind her into obedience.

Firekeeper snapped her teeth together, biting back a howl that would have mingled triumph and frustration, and so told the Meddler far more than she wanted him to know. Instead she shaped words and was pleased when they came out as clean and decisive as any thrust of her Fang could have been.

"Meddler," she said, "you gave me your promise."

"My promise to protect you," he said easily.

"No. This was your promise: to owe me, to serve me . . ."

He interrupted before she could finish. "And have I not paid what I owed? Didn't I spend my energies to help raise the shield? Haven't I served you by opening the gate and bringing you here? Haven't I served you by protecting you even when you would not protect yourself?"

Firekeeper felt the driving rain of confusion sheeting over her, but she was not to be diverted from the trail this time.

"You promised to owe me, to serve me, and to help me win this war. No matter what you say about having paid what you owed and having given good service, there is no way that you can say you have helped me to win the war. No. By taking me here as you have, you have, if anything, made the loss of the war all the more certain."

She realized that her words were far more articulate than those she usually managed to speak, and knew then that she was speaking not as much with her mouth as through the mental link the Meddler had established with her. He had meant it for his own benefit, and she had greatly resented it, but now she was glad for it, for she knew he could not escape her attack by the simple expedient of sealing her lips.

The Meddler looked startled, even shocked at this proof she had regained her memory, but when he replied, his voice held its usual sardonic confidence.

"And what if I did? You cannot hold me to that promise. What power do you have to bind me? You are no spellcaster. You are a confused young woman who is so rooted in her conviction that her heart and soul are a wolf's that she refuses to see what a very powerful and influential human she could be."

His tone turned pleading. "Listen to me. Come with me, Firekeeper. I will show you the many delights of being human. I will love you as you have only dreamed of being loved. I will show you potential you do not yet know you possess, potential that was robbed from you in the days when those who cared for you sought only to preserve your life.

"Had you been born in the days when I was young, someone would have recognized that part of you that forces the world around you to transform and change. You would have been inaugurated a Meddler, and found pleasure in that exclusive company. I might have been your teacher then. I can be your teacher now—your teacher and so much more.

"Come with me, and I will make you the first of a new generation of Meddlers. We will change this transformed world, and save it from the pains and sorrows that otherwise it will inflict upon itself. We will create a perfection that will benefit humans and Beasts and creatures whose existence you are only now beginning to suspect. Come with me, Firekeeper, and I will make you more than you can dream."

Despite the fluidity of his oratory, despite the tug that came from somewhere within the blood that he had taken from her, despite the love that shone in his eyes, Firekeeper was not tempted in the least.

"You promised me," she said levelly, "not only by the love you hold for me, but by the blood I gave to you. You promised twice, and to that promise I hold you. I do not know what this love is that you claim to have. It is like no love I have ever known, but I think it is a love I would be wise to fear. Yet although I know nothing of this love, I know my blood. You know my blood, and you have told me that it is what you have used not only to paralyze me, but to strengthen that body which you wear. Honor your promise or that blood will turn as sour and empty as your word."

She deliberately echoed her earlier words. Panic flickered through the Meddler's gaze, but when he spoke his voice held only a sneer.

"And how can you do this? You are no spellcaster."

"But you are," Firekeeper said, "and you made the promise, and that promise is linked to the magic for which you used my blood. One last time. Honor that promise and give me your aid as I choose to ask for it, not as you choose to tell me I need it. Honor that promise and set me free to live or die as I choose. Honor that promise or where my blood has mingled with your own and given fuel to the fire of your power, that power will turn to nothing, empty and hopeless as a belly filled with the acid of starvation."

Perhaps it was through the link that he had opened between

her mind and his own, but Firekeeper felt the tremor that ran through the Meddler when she raised her challenge. She knew then that, no matter how hard he might strive to deny it, she could do to him exactly what she had threatened. He had some power of his own, but she doubted that he had built too great a reserve in the few hours that he had controlled a corporeal form.

Most of his power must have its roots in what Virim had stored away and what he had taken from her. Since her power was what gave the Meddler access to Virim's, should he lose hers, he would lose what remained of Virim's as well. He would probably be a spirit once more, losing his tie to the body he so desperately wanted.

The Meddler stood tall and straight, gaze locked with her own, pale green-grey eyes meeting dark, and finding in that darkness no pity or irresolution.

Then Firekeeper felt her limbs returned to her own control, and her joy was so great that she longed to dance and howl as might a young wolf in all her strength. She did not though, but moved toward the door.

"We've wasted enough time," she said. "Come. We speak to the Bound, then hurry back."

The Meddler followed her, obedient now, and through the thread that connected them still she could feel that her defeat of him had only increased his admiration for her. She understood that. Wolves were much the same; they admired the strong and honored those who defeated them.

"How long," the Meddler whispered, "will you hold me to those words?"

"Why," Firekeeper replied, "should I ever set you free?"

❧

TINIEL HAD BEEN moved from the building that held the gate to u-Chival to one of the gardens between gateway clusters. When he was unbound and permitted to sit up and look around, he realized that he was in the same garden from which he and Isende had once been lured by the power of the now deceased Spell Wielders.

He tried to decide whether this was an omen that he would escape from here as well, but his head hurt too much for him to really care. The inside of his mouth, from which the gag had now been removed, was dry, sore, and slightly abraded. Nonetheless, when a stranger wearing a rich tunic and cloak over elaborate armor handed him a flask containing some liquid, Tiniel did not immediately swallow it, but looked up suspiciously at his benefactor.

"Don't worry," the man said in strangely accented but understandable Liglimosh. "You can drink it. It's just water. Water from astonishingly far away, now that I think about it, but no more extraordinary than that. I am Aurick, commander of the forces from Pelland."

Tiniel sipped from the flask and found it indeed held nothing but water, slightly warm from being kept in the flask but no worse for that. He inclined his head to Aurick in thanks, took another deep swallow before returning the much lighter flask.

"I am Tiniel," he said, "from not really anywhere."

Really not anywhere, Tiniel thought with despair. Before this he might have claimed some alliance with the Nexans, but they would never have him now. The Setting Sun stronghold had belonged to him and Isende, but he supposed he had forfeited any right to that as well. After all, how could he get back? And Gak? He'd rejected that city-state and his family there in favor of setting out on his own.

Aurick did not press Tiniel to say more, but took a seat on the bench across from the one Tiniel currently used as a backrest, being too sore and too stiff to sit comfortably upright. Aurick moved his sword easily to one side, and stretched his feet out in front of him in the manner of a man who knows to grab time off his feet when he can.

"So," Aurick said, "I understand from Aridisdu Valdala that you claim to have aided us for reasons of ideals. You think our rights to the use of the gates were being abused. Is that so?"

Tiniel shrugged just a little, then remembered that he really shouldn't be rude to a man who, after all, was the first person to be polite to him in hours.

"Yes, sir. That's right. I had heard about the agreement your people had made with the Spell Wielders here, and I thought that keeping you from using the gates wasn't fair."

"So you thought to help us conquer your own people."

"They aren't my own people!" Tiniel said, exhaustion and tension catching up with him and making him less than prudent. "The only one who might be said to be 'my' person is my sister, Isende, and she agreed with the others. The others aren't even from my own city-state, much less my own land. Most of them are like you, from the Old World."

"And you are from the New," Aurick said. "I think your situation is a great deal more complex than we have been led to imagine. Would you care to tell me something that will help me to understand?"

Tiniel looked at the older man and a thought occurred to him.

"You said you are from Pelland. That's a continent, right?"

"And a country," Aurick agreed. "You know of it?"

"Some of the Nexans came from Pelland," Tiniel said, "and some of the New Worlders speak a language I've heard called 'Pellish,' so I guess they might have come from your Old World."

"Quite possibly," Aurick said. "Pelland was—and is—a powerful land."

Tiniel felt a tantalizing hint in those words. Pelland was powerful, and Aurick of Pelland seemed to be more friendly in his attitude toward Tiniel than Prarayan or Valdala had been. Maybe it was because they viewed him as a mere colonist, and everyone knew that the Old World rulers hadn't exactly been kind to their colonists.

Aurick wouldn't have that prejudice. He might even view Tiniel with favor because Tiniel was foreign, and rulers knew they had to treat foreigners carefully.

Encouraged, Tiniel tried to sit up a little straighter, and found that some of the stiffness was leaving his muscles.

Aurick watched him and gave an encouraging smile.

"I don't suppose you'd like to explain something about the

Nexans. You see, they managed to put a shield up around the complex, and I'm a bit worried about what that might mean for my troops."

Tiniel knew about the shield. He couldn't have missed it, and, in any case, the shield had been repeatedly discussed in his hearing by those who were guarding him.

"Your troops?" he asked. "I've heard that it isn't wise to touch the shield, but you know that already."

"My troops," Aurick said, and smiled a touch sadly. "It's one thing to bring soldiers through a gate and ask them to risk their lives in a fair fight. It's another thing to leave them enclosed in some sort of magical bottle. We've been wondering what might happen next. Could the Nexans cause the air to become poisonous, or could they insert troops of their own? If this is going to become a deathtrap, I don't know if I can ask my soldiers to remain."

Tiniel felt warmed by Aurick's obvious concern for those who followed him. He also felt touched at being asked for information.

"You must have taken other prisoners," he said. "They might know more than I do."

"We have prisoners," Aurick agreed, placing a slight emphasis on the last word, "but that is all they are. They remain opposed to us, even though we have warned them that they might suffer the same fate as we would. You, however, chose to ally yourself with us. That is an entirely different situation."

Tiniel straightened further. He wasn't quite ready to get up on a bench, but he was feeling better every minute.

"I will help you as best I can," he said, "but I must be completely honest. I knew nothing of this shield—even though my sister is among the Nexan Once Dead."

Aurick managed to convey both sympathy and disappointment without speaking a word. Tiniel tried to explain.

"Isende and I both had talent—that is until querinalo came. After that, well, it turned out she had two talents and she sacrificed one to save the other."

"I see," Aurick looked impressed. "And so she is serving with the Once Dead. They must be delighted to have her."

"They," Tiniel said, finding that now he was talking he couldn't seem to stop, "are more delighted than you could imagine. You see, there really aren't that many Once Dead among the Nexans, not anymore."

He went on talking, telling Aurick about how he and Isende had come to the Nexus Islands, about their captivity, about their "rescue" and how it had been, for Tiniel, merely a new type of captivity. Aurick listened intently, leaning slightly forward, periodically offering Tiniel his flask. After a while, he motioned over one of the soldiers, and the woman took a seat to one side and began taking notes.

Tiniel had just finished detailing what he understood of the complex division of command between Ynamynet, Skea, and Derian, when a man wearing armor that made him resemble a bipedal dragon, even without the helmet he carried tucked under his arm, came striding into the little garden.

Aurick rose and bowed politely. The man glowered at him with what seemed like open dislike, but when he spoke his voice was polite enough.

"I only just learned you had gotten the prisoner to speak," he said. "Why didn't you send me a message?"

Aurick bowed, then gave Tiniel a reassuring glance.

"King Bryessidan, I feared the young man would be uncomfortable speaking before your august personage. I also knew that you were needed in many more places than this, and thought to spare you one chore."

King Bryessidan looked slightly mollified, but Tiniel didn't think he'd like to offend the king. He tried to look helpful, but didn't say anything lest it be misjudged.

"I see you have someone taking notes," the king said at last.

"I do, and copies were going to be sent to you as soon as I finished my chat with our young idealist here."

Aurick managed to say "idealist" in a manner that left Tiniel feeling quite good. He decided that sitting on the ground in front of a king was a bad idea, and pulled himself to his feet and managed a bow.

When he looked up, King Bryessidan was studying him with interest, but no apparent animosity.

"Very well," the king said to Aurick. "Does he have any information about the shield?"

"None," Aurick said promptly, "but a great many thoughts about those we will encounter on the other side."

"Report to me then," Bryessidan said, "as soon as is reasonable. You can brief me and the other commanders all at once. Ancestors know, we can't do much but talk for now."

"I will be at your command," Aurick said promptly.

When King Bryessidan left, Tiniel ventured to question Aurick.

"Is he like that because he's a king?"

Aurick grinned. "He's like that because he's commander in chief of this force, and I did act a little out of line."

Tiniel found this admission of guilt amazing and tantalizing.

"I thought you were the commander of the force. I mean, you said you were from Pelland."

"The country. I did mention that there is a country."

"You did," Tiniel looked down at his shoes.

He felt a big, warm hand on his shoulder.

"Don't worry, Tiniel. I'll look out for you. Talk to King Bryessidan if he asks you questions, but don't bother him otherwise. I'll keep an eye out for you."

He lowered his voice so that Tiniel felt fairly certain not even the nearest soldier could hear what he said.

"Between you and me, I think Bryessidan is eager to make up for his father's defeats. I'm not interested in having my soldiers used for another's glory. I'm sure you can understand."

Tiniel nodded. He did indeed understand what it felt like to be used. Looking at Aurick, he realized that here was another who would use him:

Visions passed through his head, visions of King Bryessidan conveniently dead, and Aurick now commanding and victorious. Aurick granting favors to Tiniel who had been of such great assistance to him.

Does it matter if Aurick wants to use me? No, especially if I can get what I want from the deal. Isende may see me as a hero yet, and the Nexans kneel before me and acknowledge me as their ruler.

XLIV

PLIK HAD GONE back to his cottage. The siege could go on without him, and he desperately needed to put up his feet and rest. Soon Firekeeper would come back from the New World with reinforcements, and doubtless he would be needed to help translate as tactics were evolved to accommodate the new force.

In the meantime, in addition to resting his feet, he needed quiet to work through a troubling thought that had been nibbling on the edges of his mind. It was something to do with war and the results of war, but he hadn't been able to make sense of it. Now that he had a few moments to think, perhaps he could puzzle it out.

He was leaning back in a chair that Diuric the carpenter had shortened the legs on so that Plik could sit at ease when he heard sounds of someone moving stealthily about in the adjoining cottage.

Tiniel's cottage.

Plik got to his feet and moved noiselessly toward the door, his mind racing with questions.

Had Tiniel somehow gotten out before the shield dropped? How? If he had, who might he have brought away with him? Might another invasion be being planned right next door?

Plik felt very inadequate to deal with such an eventuality, but he also knew that if there was trouble, he stood a better chance of talking Tiniel out of doing something foolish than just about anyone on the Nexus Islands. And if Tiniel did indeed have someone with him . . .

The door to the adjoining cottage was open, and Plik slipped to where he could peek inside. At first he thought that the person bending over the papers and books on the desk at the far end of the room was indeed Tiniel, then she moved, and he knew who it had to be—and how foolish he had been not to expect her all along.

Well, the maimalodalu thought, *I don't think I can be blamed for jumping to conclusions. Isende hasn't come down here for well over a moonspan, and I guess I'd like to see Tiniel. There are so many questions only he could answer.*

He cleared his throat. Isende turned, her motion slow and graceful, without a trace of nervousness or guilt.

"Plik," she said, not bothering with any more formal greeting, "why did Tiniel do it? I've just come from the infirmary. Rhul is dead. He was holding my hand. He was so far gone he thought I was Loxia, and she's not even five. He didn't seem to see Saeta, and she was right next to him crying her eyes out. Saeta's just lost her husband, and her babies are in the New World and now that we've lost the gates, she doesn't know if she'll ever see them again."

Plik couldn't think of anything to say. Rhul and Saeta were Isende's neighbors, the people whose children she had minded before the threat of invasion had turned her into an apprentice spellcaster and administrative assistant. In any case, Isende probably wouldn't have heard him. She continued speaking, her voice level despite the tears that rolled down her cheeks.

"Junco Torn will probably lose the use of his hand. Pishtoolam is directing the kitchens from a chair. She took an arrow in her leg and keeps boasting that being fat saved her from something worse than a limp. I've lost track of the bandages I've rolled. I can do that at least, but I can't do anything for the wounded, and I'm not sure it matters because when that shield comes down—and it will, even with what the Meddler did we don't have the power to keep it up—we're all going to be dead anyhow.

"And I keep wondering and wondering . . . How could Tiniel betray us like that? We might have held if he hadn't, especially with the navy unable to act. Was it something I did or something I didn't do? I know I haven't visited very much. It's been so busy, and I've been spending time with Derian, and I've been so happy and now . . ."

She gulped and wiped at the tears with an angry swipe of her sleeve. The motion didn't do much more than smear the tears into a smudge that lined one side of her face, but Plik didn't comment. Given how hard she was crying, the smudge would wash away of its own accord.

"I came here to look at Tin's stuff, to see if he wrote something, anything that would make me understand how he could do this, how he could put us all in danger. You think that's all right?"

The last question held a pathetic note, as if for the first time Isende questioned her being there in her twin's room, going through his private belongings.

"I think," Plik said, "that what you're doing is as useful as anything, but, Isende, tormenting yourself isn't going to change anything. Maybe you should just go get some sleep."

"I can't. I tried. I really did. Ynamynet and Kalyndra both have made clear how essential sleep is when you're working spells, but every time I put my head on the pillow I'd think of Tin and how before—when we still had that link—how I'd go to sleep at night and sometimes our dreams would get mixed up with each other."

She colored and Plik had some notion of what those dreams might have entailed. He wondered how their relatives could have let a young man and a young woman go off together like that without regard for what might develop. Maybe they were so accustomed to thinking of the twins as strange that they had forgotten to consider them as people.

He was fairly certain that no actual incest had occurred, but clearly Isende had been aware of her brother's impulses.

Plik didn't really understand human sexuality. In his heritage the raccoon dominated. However, some of the maimalodalum had taken after their human heritage, and he had observed—and felt grateful to be spared—the torments of being in heat all the year. Doubtless, if the twins had remained in Gak, Tiniel would have fastened his desire on someone other than his sister. Their powerful emotional bond would have made some things awkward, but that could have been handled. But alone together, bound to know what the other was feeling had put a strain on the siblings. Both had suffered, but Tiniel must have felt abandoned, first by the severance of the emotional bond to his sister. Later, when Isende turned first toward Rhul and Saeta's family, and then to Derian, that sense of abandonment would have been intensified.

Plik didn't think lying would help. Isende was too intelligent to be put off by a few soothing words—and matters were going to be worse for her long before they were better. If Tiniel was already dead, she was going to feel guilt and relief. If he was alive, and the Nexans recaptured him, then mere guilt would be a mercy indeed.

"Isende, Tiniel never discussed much with me. I know he was unhappy. I know he felt alienated and rather useless, but I had no suspicion that he was contemplating taking sides with the invaders. If I had, I would not have let him be given such a place of trust. As it was, I felt relief that he wanted to help."

"Me, too," Isende said. She had stopped crying now, and was mopping at her face, but no amount of tidying could hide her red and swollen eyes. "I thought he'd finally joined the community, realized he could be a part of something, even if our bond was gone. That bond . . . I was glad when we lost it, but for a while, it was everything we were. And if it had still been there, I might have felt something, might have guessed, might even have gotten an inkling from a dream."

Plik flicked his ears back and shook his head in reprimand.

"Tiniel made his choices. It must have been heady for him, to be able to plan and plot without your being able to get any sense of what he was about. My understanding was that you couldn't read each other's thoughts, is that right?"

"That's right," Isende said, "but we spent so much time together, and so much time feeling traces of what the other felt, that it was like there were times that I knew what he was thinking, even if he couldn't think messages at me. When he was thinking about how we should leave Gak and go to our ancestral lands, I knew something was up long before he actually told me. I bet I would have felt something this time, too."

Plik reached out and patted her.

"Isende, you couldn't and you didn't. That's that. Don't torment yourself with might-have-beens. Instead, maybe we should see if Tiniel left any notes. They might help us understand his intentions—and give us some idea how to speak with him when we see him again."

"If." Isende gulped around the start of another flood of tears, but she turned back to the desk and started sorting. "Tin isn't much of a writer, but he likes to draw. When we were planning on coming out to the stronghold, he drew all sorts of pictures about what we could expect."

She moved the books aside, now obviously looking for something specific. She found it a moment later.

"Tin's drawing portfolio. He stocked it up before we left Gak, saying he didn't know how long it would be before we could get such things again. I bet . . ."

She was untying the laces that held the leather folder closed as she spoke, and now she opened it at random. The topmost sheet showed the gates and a young man who was clearly an idealized Tiniel standing straight and talking to a lovely, curvaceous woman wearing the attire of an aridisdu. The aridisdu was handing Tiniel a sword, the details of which had been worked with loving care, from the gems on the pommel to the arcane inscriptions on the blade.

"Oh!" Isende said. "That's Conqueror."

"Conqueror?" Plik repeated.

"It's a magical sword that Tiniel sort of made up. You know, the way you tell yourself stories when you're still young enough to play make-believe? I was always coming up with magical jewels, but Tiniel liked the idea of swords and armor. Conqueror was his favorite, a weapon that could be wielded only by one whose purpose was firm and ideals were pure."

They leafed through the portfolio quickly now, and the pictures told a depressing story. Lost and confused, Tiniel had given himself over to fantasies. At first the pictures showed fragments of his unhappiness, and there was no doubt that Derian—looking more horsey than he did in reality—came in for a great deal of the young man's resentment.

Later, probably after the Nexans had faced the likelihood of the impending invasion, the pictures began to depict Tiniel doing heroic acts. At first these were in defense of the Nexans. Later, almost imperceptibly, they showed his belief that he would be a greater hero if he assisted the invaders.

"It's like he forgot everything we had learned about the Old World," Isende said. "These pictures show them as perfect heroes and the Nexans as grubs."

She didn't comment on the other recurring theme, that of Tiniel coming to his sister's rescue at some key moment. He rescued her from ravening wolves, brought a potion to her as she lay injured, chose her from a crowd of prisoners. The pictures were perfectly chaste, and Isende was drawn fairly accurately, but even so, Plik was sorry that Isende would be unable to deny that her rejection of her brother and his desire to redeem himself in her regard had led him to betrayal.

Hope always said that the truth was better than lies, he said, looking as Isende turned away from the portfolio, once again dissolved in tears. *I wonder . . . I do wonder.*

He was tying up the the ribbon that closed the portfolio when shouting and wolf howls from outside provided a welcome distraction.

"Is it attack?" Isende said, starting for the door at a run.

"No," Plik said, translating the glad cries of the wolves. "It's Firekeeper. She's back, and she's brought help."

◈

THE BOUND ARRIVED over the bridge of living water, flowing almost like the waves themselves, if waves could be furred and feathered, colored in tawny golds, silvery greys, clean whites, all shades of brown, and even, in the case of some loudly squawking jays, in brilliant blues.

There were far more of the Bound than Derian had imagined possible. Whatever else you might think of Virim, it was clear his minions had thrived in his service. Derian had expected wolves, bears, and assorted cats. He had heard how the eagles had pursued Elation, and so expected the wingéd folk.

What he did not expect were the strange assortment of other Beasts: fox, deer, and elk, even moose and raccoon. Apparently, Virim had taken no chances with his safety, and had recruited not only the great predators, but the watchful herbivores and the adaptable omnivores as well.

Firekeeper, catching her breath after a reunion with Blind Seer that seemed inordinately passionate given the short time that she had been gone, admitted to sharing Derian's astonishment.

"We go out and the Meddler—who they think is Virim—tell them what he wants. They come then, some then more, then many more, and more again. I think that we not be able to bring them all, but the Meddler do very well with working the spell, and the sea monsters made no complaint about letting these many feet cross the bridge."

Derian noticed that for once the Meddler did not preen over Firekeeper's compliment. In fact, he seemed distinctly deflated, the arrogant assurance that was more a part of him than any shape subdued. Perhaps maintaining the gate spell for that long had taken a toll, but Derian wondered if something else had happened.

If so, Firekeeper was not saying anything, and this was not the time to press her. With the arrival of the Bound, the battered Nexans had regained much of their confidence, and the more impulsive were already calling for the shield to be lowered so that they might assault the invaders before the invaders had an opportunity to similarly augment their forces.

"Those idiots don't seem to realize that they might have done so already," Skea growled. "We need to plan for more than rushing the gateway hillside. I, for one, would like to know just how far Virim's ability to control the Bound extends. If they'll only protect him, they're not going to be much good to the rest of us."

"Unless we deliberately put him in danger," Verul said, leaning on his cane and gazing at the shield, eyes narrowed in thoughtful speculation. "We'd need to pick an angle."

Derian interrupted before this tactical speculation could go too far.

"We're going to need to speak with the Meddler and the Bound. We should probably find out from Ynamynet just how far her control of the gate goes. Urgana and Arasan have been questioning the few prisoners we took, and we may learn something from them."

As before, they met in the open: Derian, Skea, Ynamynet, Urgana, Firekeeper, the Meddler, Plik, and Isende. Derian wondered a little about Isende's presence. As anger had grown about Tiniel's betrayal, she had become more and more hesitant to make herself conspicuous. Maybe her choosing to sit out in the open was her way of making clear that she was not going to hide because of her brother's guilt.

His heart warmed to her courage, but he couldn't single her out for anything other than a smile. There was too much to do.

The Bound were represented by an enormous moose with the ominous—or promising, depending on how you chose to view it—name Man Tosser. Firekeeper and the Meddler had assured Skea that the Bound would fight without the specific need to protect Virim.

"They think is like protecting from magic coming back," Firekeeper explained, "and this is why they help Virim in the start of this all."

Many of those Nexans who were not helping in the kitchens or hospital or with maintaining the shield stood within earshot.

Derian made no effort to clear them away. After all, their fate was being decided here. They were entitled to know what was being said. Still, he wished they had the sense demonstrated by the majority of the yarimaimalom. With a wild creature's sense of priority, most of these were either eating or sleeping, well aware that this would best prepare them for when the fighting began again.

Urgana was the only one with anything new to report. Not all the prisoners had spoken the same language, but most had been fairly eager to talk.

"The invaders are from seven different nations," she said. "Since each army had to come through its own gate, each has its own commander." She rattled off a list of names and places that Derian's tired brain could hardly register, then went on, "There is a central commander: Bryessidan of the Mires."

Ynamynet asked, "Is he then trying to recapture his father's glory?"

"That depends on who I spoke to. The one woman from the Mires—an herbalist, rather than a soldier—said that he was not, that because the Mires have been forbidden a large army since the days of Veztressidan, Bryessidan was the most logical choice for commander because his troops were mostly Once Dead and support personnel. However, the others—we had a couple from u-Chival, one from Pelland, and one from Tishiolo—seemed less certain. The one from Pelland was the least certain of all."

"Anything else?" Skea prompted. "Size of forces? How armed? Amount of magical support?"

Urgana passed several closely written sheets of paper over to him. "That's what I could get. We're hampered in that all of the prisoners were essentially infantry. We didn't get a single officer, not even a unit leader. Also, quite frankly, it is in the prisoners' best interests to lie rather than undermine our apprehension regarding the nature of the very forces they hope will rescue them.

"The one thing I was fairly certain about is that the forces from the Mires and from Tavetch are smaller than those from the other lands. The Mires didn't have an army, and Tavetch sent most of its troops with the navy. As we guessed, King Hurwin is in command there."

Discussion continued along those lines for some time. Then Skea turned to Ynamynet.

"I've been wondering about the shield. Is it possible for you to open just a single area? It would be so much easier to take one or two sections at a time."

Ynamynet was shaking her head even before he finished speaking.

"I wish we could, but we can't. It's quite possible that the shield contains that capacity, but if so we haven't figured out how to implement it. We were lucky Urgana and Harjeedian's research led us to the shield. We barely managed to work out how to raise and lower it. I'm not willing to attempt refinements."

Skea shrugged. "I'm not criticizing. I just thought I'd ask."

Ynamynet nodded wearily. "Believe me. We had the same thought, but right now it's all we can do to keep watch within the shield and to keep it solid. If this goes on much longer, we're going to have to ask for donations."

Derian didn't need to ask donations of what. Blood. It always came down to blood in matters of Old World magic. No wonder all the spellcasters looked so worn. They were probably using their own blood whenever they needed to watch within the shield.

To distract from the uncomfortable matter of donations, Derian asked, "What have you seen within the shield?"

"I recognized several of the people Urgana mentioned as commanders. They have had meetings much like this one, and I have seen Bryessidan speaking with various of the Once Dead. There is some traffic through the gates, but that mostly seems to involve transporting the wounded and bringing supplies. They're crowded in there, but as of now they haven't started rotating the troops back to their homelands."

Firekeeper asked, "New World gate. Have they used that?"

"No. They have guards on it, but no one has activated the portal."

There was an audible sigh of relief at this, and Derian thought the faces of the listening Nexans lightened a bit at the knowledge their children were safe.

For now, he thought.

"Our line of vision is less than complete," Ynamynet went on. "The shield has 'eyes' or patches of greater sensitivity at various points. There is also some sort of link to areas within the gate buildings themselves. This only makes sense, since otherwise the shield's designers would have badly crippled themselves. I will say, I have no idea how they managed it. The complexity of the spell is beyond anything we could do today. It's almost more than we can do to use it. My mind, at least, does not like sorting through so many simultaneously received images. That's why we've been taking turns."

There were other questions, about the Nexan prisoners, about the apparent morale of the troops trapped beneath the shield. Isende pointedly did not ask about Tiniel, and equally pointedly no one else did either, although there was a discussion of what the invaders might have learned from the captured Nexans.

Either that means everyone trusts Isende and is trying to spare her feelings, or they distrust her and don't want her reminded why.

Derian was about to suggest that they move to discussing specific tactics, when Plik indicated that he would like to speak. Most of the speakers had stood, but for Plik, perched up on one of the benches, that would be counterproductive, and there was a chuckle as those on the outside of the circle realized this.

"You all certainly realize by now that although Firekeeper has done something amazing in bringing the Bound to serve as reinforcements, and although we are five times blessed that Grateful Peace's communication with the sea monsters has eliminated the threat offered by King Hurwin's navy, we cannot win this war merely by force of arms."

Skea, who had been quietly reviewing the report Urgana had given him and making notations of his own along the bottom, looked up offended.

"I am afraid I don't realize that, Plik. By my calculation, we may indeed be able to win. We can encircle the gateway hillside and attack not only from all sides, but from above as well."

He drew in a deep breath and rose, clearly prepared to sketch details of his battle plan out on the smooth dirt at the center of the circled benches. Plik flicked his ears in an annoyed gesture that reminded Derian that boar raccoons were considered formidable fighters, even by creatures much larger than them.

No trace of annoyance or aggression showed in Plik's voice as he continued.

"I don't doubt you can come up with a plan that might let us win this battle. However, they can bring in reinforcements. We have reached our limits."

"We have other gates," Skea said. "There might be others on the lesser islands. There are the three blocked up ones in the basement of the headquarters building. We could open those."

"Even if we could," Plik said, "would we have time to open negotiations with potential allies? We were fortunate in that Firekeeper and Derian already had close ties to Grateful Peace. Those cellar gates open into the Old World, where we have no friends. If there are other island gates—and we cannot be at all certain there are—they might go to places as isolated as Virim's stronghold."

Skea, who for all his military ardor was still a reasonable man, nodded.

"Are you saying then that we should just surrender?"

"Not at all," Plik retorted. "I am saying that we must consider what will happen after we win this battle."

Derian liked how Plik did not say "if." Morale was shaky enough without it being undermined here.

Plik went on. "We win and recapture the gateway hillside and the gates themselves. Can we hold them? We know from the prisoners that we face an alliance of seven nations. Surely even if a few decided to withdraw from the alliance as a bad job, there would be others who would be equally stubborn about continuing. We did our best to defend the gates, and yet the iron cages were broken through."

Firekeeper said, "And if we break all the gates, is all that problem from before when we think about breaking them. We has learned that Virim made little gate. Who also do this? I want to run, but I know there is nowhere to run. But Plik, what can we do?"

"Seven," Plik said, "is a large number of nations to make trust each other. From what we have been told by the historians and scholars among us, these seven nations have rivalries among them. Only the suspicion that we were a worse threat brought them together. What if we gave them reason to believe that they could regain use of the gates, not as an alliance of seven, but as individual nations?"

"We might destroy the alliance," Skea said, his voice tight with eagerness at the possibility of an approach that might defeat their enemies for well and for good.

"Convincing them won't be easy," Plik warned. "It might not even be possible, but I think it's the only tactic that stands a chance if we want to continue to hold the gates."

"I'm willing to try," Skea said. "If we can manage a treaty that lasts for only a year we gain a chance to build new alliances of our own, bring in more troops."

Firekeeper nodded, then turned to Skea.

"Skea, I have idea on how we might beat army on hill—soon, even tonight. Will you listen?"

Skea, who had been about to draw some elaborate pattern on the smoothed dirt at the center of their circle, looked at the wolf-woman as if expecting some sort of challenge. However, her body language held only that curious mixture of humility and contained strength that Derian had noted before. It was a wolf thing.

She is saying in "wolf," "You are in charge, the One, but I have an idea that is valuable. Will you accept it without seeing me as a rival?"

Derian wondered if Skea would understand this nonverbal message. The dark-skinned man studied the wolf-woman for a long moment, then nodded.

"I'm interested, Firekeeper. What do you have in mind?"

"Night," Firekeeper said slowly, obviously searching for words, "is a friend to my kind. Let us make her our ally."

XLV

 BRYESSIDAN SLEPT FITFULLY on a cot set in a small tent in one of the small gardens between the wedge-shaped buildings that held the gates. That tent was a mark of respect due to his position—the other commanders had tents, too. Most of the troops slept on little more than a blanket spread out on the bare earth. Getting those through the gates, along with sufficient food and water, had been a logistical nightmare. They hadn't planned on having to camp.

Some of the troops had been sent back to their homelands and were standing by near the other end of the gate. Bryessidan hadn't wanted to do this, but there had been no other way. There simply wasn't room for seven armies to lodge on a cluster of hills, hills already crowded with buildings.

Night had been heralded by the shield fading from white, to grey, then to unbroken black. Encased within darkness, many of the soldiers had succumbed to claustrophobia. Several had flung themselves into the shield in a desperate attempt to get out of the enclosing darkness. It had been a near thing keeping the rest from following. Now, even those who remained, tended to face inward, where the light from small campfires and candle lanterns permitted them to deny the darkness that surrounded them.

Bryessidan's sleep was filled with nightmares wherein his army threw itself soldier by soldier into the shield, their blood adding to the artifact's power until it solidified into a shell of polished stone: smooth, slick, and unbreakable. The soldiers continued bashing themselves against that unbreakable wall. Their blood coursed down the sides, dripping and pooling at the base, rising in a flood that threatened to engulf them all.

He woke immediately, with an obscure sense of gratitude and relief, when something cool and sharp pricked the edge of his throat.

A husky voice speaking atrocious Pellish came from so close to his ear that he could feel the warm puffs of breath.

"Not move. Not call. Or you is dead."

Bryessidan had paid close attention to the reports garnered from the prisoners and from the traitor Tiniel. He knew at once who this must be: Firekeeper, the woman who thought she was a wolf, and who accepted by the wolves as one of their own.

Had Tiniel been the only one to speak of this Firekeeper with fear, Bryessidan might have taken his chances, but not a one had spoken of her but with an uneasiness that in some cases amounted to dread. Firekeeper was unpredictable, each and every one had agreed, not because she was chaotic by nature, but because she did not think as a human did. You thought you understood her, then she did something unthinkable.

And this was the creature who knelt at the side of his cot, holding a knife to his throat. Bryessidan could not think of a single cause that would be served by his dying bravely. He could think of a good many—including the happiness of his wife and children—that would be served by his coming away alive.

He let Firekeeper gag him with a length of clean cloth, then guide him through a neat slit cut in the back of his tent. Out of deference to their positions, the seven commanders had been allocated some open space around the edges of their tents. She led him through this open area as neatly as if she could see in the dark, tugging him after her. Then she walked directly to where Bryessidan knew the cold, black edge of the shield stood.

He balked, and Firekeeper pulled. She was stronger than he had thought, and he stumbled forward into and through a shield that was not there. They progressed down the hillside at a pace so fast he nearly fell.

Bryessidan was adjusting to the idea that his army was currently enclosed in nothing but night and their own fears when Firekeeper stopped. A male voice spoke very quietly from the darkness.

"What? Got one? I say!"

"Is king. Take."

Then the hand at his wrist was gone, but a different firm, strong hand grasped Bryessidan by the upper arm and started leading him down a pathway faintly marked by candle lanterns set so that their glow faced away from the gateway hillside.

"I say!" the young man said. "Your Majesty, and all that. Pleased to meet you. I am Edlin Norwood, Lord Kestrel, if you care for that unzoranic nonsense as King Tedric would say, and I suppose you must since you're a king. What I mean is, I'll be a duke someday, ancestors willing, so you're not to feel you're being mishandled, what?"

Despite the inanity of this Lord Edlin's speech, he was leading Bryessidan with great purpose and direction. Bryessidan glanced around and noticed that the night sky was heavily occluded by clouds, enough that the moon did not show. No wonder his soldiers had not noticed when the shield had been lowered. The sky was only slightly lighter than the area within the shield.

Bryessidan noticed a blacker darkness against the clouded sky and guessed they were approaching a large building. There were several still standing from the times before the coming of the Sorcerer's Bane, and he knew from the prisoners' reports that one in particular was being used as headquarters by the Nexans. He supposed that was where they were heading.

As they moved along the path, Bryessidan became aware of the glint of many pairs of eyes caught for just a moment in the dim light of the candle lanterns. He flinched from a particularly large and glimmering set that seemed to study him longer than had the rest.

Lord Edlin felt him move and spoke reassuringly, although not without forgetting to keep his voice low.

"Yarimaimalom, what? Strange word. Wise Beasts. Firekeeper calls them Royal. I say, though, magnificent creatures, especially when they're on your side, and these are most definitely on ours. If you're thinking about knocking into me and running, I wouldn't. The yarimaimalom like chasing things that run."

Lord Edlin sounded pleased, and for a moment not in the least foolish. They moved around the looming hulk of the building to where the opening of a door would not show light up to the gateway hillside.

Even as it doomed him, Bryessidan had to admire the planning that had gone into this operation. He and his fellow commanders had forgotten one key strength the Nexans had at their advantage—and the prisoners had not said anything to remind them.

They had overlooked the fact that Nexans' Beast allies could see in the dark, and therefore an attack by night was not as unlikely as it would have been against merely human opponents. Night was traditionally a time when battles ended and the troops retired from the field. With that in mind, Bryessidan and his allies had arranged themselves with the goal of getting through the long wait and hoping that their troops would be sane by morning.

The guards that had been posted had been meant mostly to keep order within the camp, not to worry about what might come from without, for why should the Nexans eliminate their greatest advantage when they could not take advantage of it? But they could, they could, and Bryessidan tasted the bitterness not only of defeat but of feeling distinctly foolish as he allowed Lord Edlin to move him toward their destination.

He tried to hearten himself with the thought that the chance of an overcast night had been in the Nexans' favor, for otherwise someone might have noted the shield going down, but that was slim enough comfort. Later, with added bitterness, Bryessidan would learn that the cloudy night had not been a matter of chance at all.

Lord Edlin conducted him inside the building. The entry foyer was so dimly lit that even if the door had faced the gateway hillside, Bryessidan wondered if the glow would have carried.

They're careful, so very careful, he thought with reluctant admiration mingled with dread. *I suppose it is because they have so little advantage.*

And he wondered if he and his fellow commanders hadn't been made a little heady, a little careless because their home bases and all the resources thereof were so close.

We are like children playing at camping out, he thought, remembering a game his own children loved to play when they visited their Tavetch relatives. *We settled onto our bedrolls, secure in the knowledge that no matter what the night brought, a safe haven was close by. That shield seemed so solid that we forgot that those who had raised it could lower it at any time—and that the choice was not ours to make.*

Lord Edlin was speaking to a young woman in armor who was clearly waiting to take over custody.

"Citrine, may I have the honor of introducing you to King Bryessidan of the Mires. King Bryessidan, Citrine, daughter of Grateful Peace, Dragon's Eye of New Kelvin."

The formality of these introductions was rather ruined when he added, "My cousin, too, what?"

Citrine, a young woman with reddish gold hair whose coltish lines showed she still had a good deal of growing to do, rolled her eyes and gave Edlin a gentle shove between his shoulder blades.

"Get out there. Firekeeper probably has someone else by now and she hates being kept waiting."

Then Citrine turned to Bryessidan.

"Your Majesty," she said politely, "please follow me, and don't cause any trouble. I'm not alone."

She gestured, and for the first time Bryessidan noted that a pair of ravens and a small falcon were perched on carved woodwork that ornamented the upper reaches of the entry hall.

"Bitter, Lovable, and Farborn. Farborn is feeling particularly angry tonight, so please don't give him any reason to go for you. Our doctors are too busy to bother with your injuries."

Lord Edlin had slipped out as Citrine was speaking, and Bryessidan decided to take the young man's confidence that his cousin was safe in the bird's care as the final proof that they would indeed attack him if they felt it was warranted.

Moreover, there was something cold in the young woman's tone when she alluded to the injured that chilled him more than the glittering eyes of the three birds. He went along the corridor she indicated with alacrity that he hoped would show his willingness to cooperate.

Citrine told him to stop in front of a pair of impressively carved double doors. Bryessidan recalled that the doors led into a large reception hall, and so it proved. The chamber was furnished with risers along the sides, and so was probably used for public meetings.

An odd choice for a prison, Bryessidan thought.

The room was well lit by blocks set in the walls. At first, he thought it was empty. Then he noted a restless, interested movement from higher up, and realized there were more birds up there. Large ones. More ravens, at least one eagle, hawks, and from a flash of blue, at least one jay. White bird droppings streaked the woodwork, so he guessed that this was not the first time the place had been used as a roost.

Citrine motioned the king to a table surrounded by a dozen chairs situated at the center of the vast space. It was furnished with a pitcher and a couple of drinking vessels and nothing else.

"You can sit there," she said, "and you can take off the gag. Edlin probably didn't knot it too tightly. He's good about that kind of thing, for all he seems a fool. There's water for you to drink and if you need to relieve yourself, you'll find a pot in that corner.

"Don't try to leave, please. Many of the yarimaimalom are out helping with the extraction, but there were others who couldn't be of much use, and they're patrolling the building. There are humans here, too, of course, and we'd hear an alarm. But, honestly, I'd worry more about the yarimaimalom."

She turned to go, and Bryessidan tugged off his gag and spoke quickly, his voice flat as it came through the cottony dryness of his mouth, "Lady Citrine, please. I know I am a prisoner, but what is intended for me?"

"Citrine," she replied. "I may have a New Kelvinese father, but I'm not interested in that unzoranic nonsense. Your Majesty, you are a prisoner, and soon you're going to have company. Then some of the Nexan leaders are going to talk to all of you and give you a choice. If you're smart, you'll take it. That's all I can tell you right now. I hope you'll be smart and wait patiently."

"Company?"

"Your other commanders," Citrine said. "Firekeeper went for you first, because we heard you were commander in chief. Derian and Plik are extracting others. We hope to get all of you, but that's probably not likely. Still, even four or five should be enough. Now, please be patient."

She left through the heavy door, and Bryessidan heard the

bolt shoot behind her. Dazed, he walked over to the table and poured himself some water. The drinking vessels and pitcher were all made from a lovely, light glass that would shatter if he tried to break it and use it as a weapon. Even the pitcher's handle was hollow and would likely shatter.

He wandered around the room. There were other doors, but all were locked. The birds made not a sound, not a squawk, but whenever he darted a glance upward, he saw the glitter of their watching eyes.

He tried to feel good that the Nexans had considered him the most important of the seven commanders, but he couldn't take much comfort in that importance. He wondered who they would bring next. He wondered if they would try to extract the prisoners. That would be harder. They'd been moved to the Mires, where Amelo and his associates could use magic to question them.

After what seemed like a very long time, the door opened. Citrine gestured in Kynan of Hearthome. Almost immediately after, a young man with very dark skin whom Bryessidan had not seen before brought in Merial of Azure Towers. She had scratches on her face, and would not admit where they had come from.

The young man, his voice still unbroken and holding great amusement, said in musically accented Pellish, "She think that because Plik is little and fat he is not ferocious. This is always a mistake to make. The little ones must be fierce. You should all remember. The little must be fierce."

It was a warning, and Bryessidan knew it, a warning that because the community on the Nexus Islands was not large, they should not be underestimated. It was a warning Bryessidan no longer needed, but from how Kynan and Merial both winced, he thought it was only now coming home to them.

I should have remembered, he thought, hiding his anger from the others by turning away to use the pot. *The Mires were not the largest of the Pelland nations, but my father used his mind and for a time everyone feared us. How could I have been so careless?*

Valdala of u-Chival came next, escorted by Citrine. With

them came a great cat of some sort. Its build was heavy and low-slung. Its coat was like nothing Bryessidan had ever seen before: the black of burned wood ornamented with spots shaped like living flame. The great cat's eyes were white, the slit pupils pale blue, but it seemed to have not the least trouble seeing.

When Citrine departed, the great cat remained, lounging on one of the raised benches that lined the edges of the room and studying them all with typically feline arrogance.

Aridisdu Valdala tugged the gag from her mouth, but what she said made little sense: "Ahmyn! Ahmyn!"

She would say nothing more, and huddled in a corner away from the others, obviously deep in prayer. As if silenced by her intensity, what little conversation that had occurred between the others died away into tense silence.

When Aurick of Pelland came in, his arms were twisted about his back and tightly bound. His ankles were hobbled, and his skin was bruised and scraped.

Citrine had been his escort, and in addition to Aurick, she also brought a carafe from which she refilled the pitcher.

"He was stupid," she said. "He fought. Derian is stronger, though. Some of his soldiers are fighting now. I wish they weren't. King Bryessidan, do you think you could make them surrender?"

Bryessidan looked at Aurick, remembering the prideful arrogance of the Pelland nobles, and their drug-addled minds.

"I think not," he said, and left it to Citrine to wonder if that was an admission of his inability to control the Pelland army, or his refusal to cooperate with the Nexans in any way. Let the others wonder, too.

Fromalf of Tavetch didn't walk in under his own power, but was dragged in by Firekeeper, unconscious, bleeding from his mouth, and with both eyes bruised and swelling. The wolf-woman looked unharmed, but her eyes shone with barely contained excitement.

"He not so smart," she said conversationally. "I think he let his One do all the thinking, and his One is on a boat. I hope you all is not the same. I hope you is Ones."

The wolf-woman straightened and surveyed them.

"In a little, we come, we come to talk." She looked over at Aurick. "Your people stop fighting now. Too many died. Is not smart to fight Beasts in darkness. Is not smart."

Aurick held his head up defiantly.

"Are we to understand that you hold the gateway hillside?"

Firekeeper shrugged. "You is to understand that we has always held it. You just stood on it for a time."

❧

WELL AFTER SUNRISE the next morning, Firekeeper helped move the tables and chairs, then settled into her usual position on the floor alongside the table where representatives of the informal ruling body of the Nexus Islands had taken their seats behind the table. Her bow was across her knees and her quiver near to hand, but she didn't really expect to need them. They were a warning, nothing more.

Blind Seer was with her, for once, sprawled on the floor, close enough that his fur brushed her arm. The Meddler sat in a chair off to one side where Firekeeper could keep an eye on him. He hadn't caused any trouble since his attempt in Virim's stronghold, but she was not taking any chances.

The seven captured commanders—the set had been completed when someone named Talianas had been taken as she was returning back through the gate to her homeland—were seated on comfortable, straight-backed chairs set in a line where they could easily see the Nexan leaders. Unlike the Nexan leaders, they did not have a table in front of them, and Firekeeper understood that this would leave them feeling more vulnerable.

The line in which the captured commanders sat was so straight that they could not see each other without craning their necks, and their chairs were spaced widely enough apart that they could not pass any sign by touch without being observed.

Those of the Nexans who were available to attend the meeting had taken seats in the risers at each side of the room, but these seats were not as full as they might have been. Despite their current ascendance in the struggle for control of the gates, the Nexans were stretched rather thin.

Formal introductions were made, and then Ynamynet cleared her throat.

"You seven must be wondering about the current status of your troops and of the Nexus Islands in general. This is how matters stand. Last night we succeeded in capturing most of the allied commanders with minimal losses to our own forces. In several cases, the troops were unaware that you were gone at all.

"When, with our attempt to extract Aurick of Pelland, the alarm was finally given, our attack moved into its second phase, that of securing the gates themselves. This was made rather easier because of several elements."

She held up a slim hand and began itemizing. "One, despite having dealt with the yarimaimalom earlier in the day, most of your troops still expected human opponents.

"Two, darkness was in our favor. In order to learn what the commotion was, many of the soldiers who were standing gate watch rushed from their posts. Our forces slipped in behind them, and the gates were secured. Darkness also helped, not only by limiting your soldiers' ability to see, but also by making them reluctant to use distance weapons.

"Third, the sea monsters who are currently making your vast fleet completely ineffective were kind enough to raise clouds that occluded the stars. Thus, when we did lower the shield, those who were on guard did not notice the change.

"I am not going to waste time on details. The gates have been taken, and we now hold them. Most of the injuries and loss of life during the active fighting was to your forces. Your armed forces were encouraged to surrender. Those who did not were killed. The injured are being treated by your own medical corp, under appropriate supervision."

Ynamynet paused, glanced down at her notes, and then said, "Any questions?"

King Bryessidan of the Mires, seated in the center of the row of chairs, said angrily, "I don't believe it!"

Ynamynet gave one of her wintry smiles. "We rather thought you would not. However, as we are not inclined to take you for a tour, you will have to settle for our word augmented by the testimony of one of your own. Talianas of Tishiolo, would you care to report what you saw when you came through the gate shortly before dawn?"

Talianas spoke Pellish, the language in which the meeting was being conducted, with an accent that reminded Firekeeper somewhat of what she had heard in New Kelvin.

"I made the transition," she said, her hands folded in her lap tightening so that the knuckles whitened, "and found myself faced by four soldiers in unmatched livery holding bows on me. Their leader, a dark-skinned man I have since learned is General Skea, demanded the surrender of myself and my companion. As it would have been foolish to do otherwise, I surrendered.

"General Skea took custody of myself and my companion, and after ascertaining that no one was expected to follow, took us on a short tour of the gateway hillside. What we saw was, to say the least, disheartening. All the gates were firmly in Nexan hands, each with its own group of archers standing ready. More troops patrolled the hillside itself, ready and at call. Birds of various sorts perched where they could maintain a ready line of sight between all points. General Skea demonstrated how an alarm could be raised and relayed within moments.

"Our own troops had been disarmed, and forced to relinquish their armor. They had then been ushered down to a beach where their only options for flight were rock-filled waters or the maws and claws of the Beasts that stood watch. These Beasts were augmented by a scattering of archers, so that should some contingent decide to take the chance of rushing forth, at least some would be picked off.

"General Skea told me that those in the beachside encampment were infantry. The infirmary was separate, and the Once

Dead are being held elsewhere as well, apart, not only from the troops at large, but from each other. Iron has been used to limit their magical abilities."

Talianas had delivered this report in something of a monotone, hands folded, but now she unlocked her hands to show that her own wrist was encompassed by an iron bracelet.

"The Nexans have not been unduly cruel," Talianas said. "There is fabric between the iron and my skin. Nonetheless, I would find performing even the slightest spell difficult, and I must assume the same is true for the other Once Dead."

Talianas signaled the conclusion of her report by settling back in her chair and lowering her hands.

Before Ynamynet could say any more, Kynan of Hearthome snarled, "What did they promise you to tell us all that? It can't be that bad! I refuse to believe it. My soldiers are trained warriors. Even roused from sleep, they could not be defeated by a handful of animals and makeshift soldiers."

Talianas did not deign to reply. Derian, his lips pressed tight to hide a smile at this first sign of dissension between the allies, rose and addressed Kynan.

"We have received reinforcements since you last saw our armies. Did you think you knew all the secrets of the Nexus Islands? You did not expect the shield. What else do we have at our disposal that you did not expect?"

Kynan bit his lip, but did not reply. Firekeeper permitted herself a lazy grin and rubbed the fur at the edge of Blind Seer's nearer ear.

"Kynan has been bragging that his soldiers, at least, would not be defeated, no matter what tricks were played on him. This news has bitten him hard."

"Now Ynamynet prepares to bite them again," Blind Seer said, angling his head so that Firekeeper could better reach an itchy spot. *"She smells of pleasure at the thought."*

"Many of you already know that General Skea, commander of our army, is my husband. He is coordinating our force, and has asked me to speak for him."

"Likely because you can't spare even a single man," Fromalf of Tavetch muttered through swollen lips.

Firekeeper doubted whether Fromalf thought anyone could overhear this little bit of defiance, but once again he had underestimated the yarimaimalom. She waited until Fromalf's gaze passed over her, and touched her bow in warning. Blind Seer panted a smile that showed all his teeth. Fromalf, fair-skinned after his kind, visibly paled.

Ynamynet, unaware of—or possibly ignoring—what Fromalf had said, continued to speak.

"Skea said you should be aware that our earlier precautions were meant to keep loss of life on your side to a minimum. If you consider those precautions, you will realize the truth in that. Why would we have caged those who came through the gates and then sent them back intact if we were your enemies? We refused you access to the gates, true, but we had our reasons, and as the Nexus Islands are ours, our reasons should have been enough."

Several of the commanders stirred at this, but they held their words until Ynamynet had finished speaking.

Already, Firekeeper thought gleefully, *they are learning who is One, and who is the least of the least.*

Ynamynet's expression, neutral to this point, became stern.

"Skea says to tell you that our tactics will no longer be geared toward keeping intruders alive. Any who come through the gates will be given one chance to surrender. After that, the arrows will fly. We have ample arrows, now, and ample bows, taken from your own forces. Doubtless, in a few hours, our appearance will not present the motley nature that so offended and confused Commander Talianas. We are in command of the Nexus Islands, and we will continue in command of the Nexus Islands. Your own actions have assured that this will be so."

Aurick of Pelland made sign that he would speak, but waited until Ynamynet acknowledged him.

"I believe all we have been told," he said. "Clearly, there has been a severe and life-wasting misunderstanding between our peoples. Might we know why we were refused the use of the gates?"

Ynamynet pressed her lips together, and Derian took over

speaking. Firekeeper knew this had been planned in advance, to make her seem the more stern, he the more lenient, and she was impressed by how well the two played their parts.

"As you must already know," Derian said, "I and several of my companions—including Plik, who sits here to my right, and Firekeeper down there on the floor—are from the New World. That is where the yarimaimalom come from as well. Since we know you have spoken with Tiniel, you probably have heard some version of how we came to the Nexus Islands and why.

"I will not waste time on finer points of that story. Suffice to say, we came here almost by accident, but when we had come, we realized we could not leave open a way into the New World without having some say in how it was used. Learning that querinalo, a legend in our own land, remained alive and dangerous in the Old World greatly influenced our choice.

"We did not know how querinalo spread, or if we permitted commerce between the New World and the Old whether we would also be trading in the Plague. We decided to work out the details of how to handle these matters, and that while we did so trade through the gates must be slowed."

Merial of Azure Towers said, "Why didn't you explain this?"

Derian gave her a long look. "Commander Merial, it is a great deal to explain. Moreover, why should we do so? Are you in the habit of explaining the policies of Azure Towers to, say, Hearthome, or of asking Tishiolo for permission to regulate your internal business?"

"Of course not!" Merial snapped, stung as Derian had intended her to be, by the reference to two of the lands with which Azure Towers shared a border.

"Then why should the Nexus Islands explain while regulating matters of its own internal trade?" Derian said reasonably.

"But," bellowed Bryessidan of the Mires, rising to his feet, "the Nexus Islands exists precisely because it agreed to provide trade through the gateways. If that trade is refused, then surely the Nexus Islands forfeited some of their rights."

Ynamynet cut in as Derian began to speak. "I was there

when those agreements were made, King Bryessidan. I knew your father, and served him in his war. Don't tell me about our right to exist. The Mires would not exist for you to lord over if we Once Dead had not agreed to support King Veztressidan. We have not forgotten that, but it seems that you may have done so."

She had risen to her feet as she spoke, her frosty coolness become a blast of wintery storm. Derian put a hand on her arm, and she took her seat with reluctance.

"That last," Blind Seer said, gnawing at the side of the pad on his right front paw, *"was not all performance. Ynamynet holds anger at the Mires that Bryessidan would take care not to forget. Nor should those of her homeland forget that they drove the Once Dead into exile in Veztressidan's court. She and the Old World Nexans have not forgotten, not for a moment."*

"I think they will not," Firekeeper replied, *"now."*

Indeed, King Bryessidan had retaken his seat with the haste of a pup rolling before the Ones. Merial of Azure Towers had gone motionless. Perhaps they were remembering what Tiniel must have related to them about how the Spell Wielders who had challenged Firekeeper and Derian had lost that challenge. Perhaps they were only remembering that, for all the courtesy the Nexans were showing them, they were prisoners.

Derian gave Ynamynet an anxious glance that was only partly show. Firekeeper caught the horsey scent of his sweat, and knew he was hoping that Ynamynet was willing to let old injuries be left out of new negotiations. Last night, when the Nexan leaders had conferred after the gates had been retaken, many of the Nexans had not been in the mood for forgiving.

Ynamynet gave him a thin-lipped smile and said, "You were explaining to the seven here the situation as it stands."

Derian nodded and turned to face the commanders.

"We of the Nexus Islands do plan to resume trade, and had been of a mind to recompense your rulers for losses that had originated from our refusing early spring transits. Needless to say, we are no longer interested in providing recompense, nor do we intend to do so. However, we are willing to resume transits—eventually and on our terms."

From the small side-to-side motions of the seven commanders' heads, Firekeeper knew that each wished to see how their associates were reacting, but that they were too proud to check.

She waited. Would they remember that the situation had changed, that the Nexans no longer needed the Old World now that they had contact with the New?

Seven faces stilled to immobility of which an owl might have been proud. Derian permitted himself a small smile.

"Of course, we would not expect you to agree without hearing what we intend, and having time to think about it. The matter is more complex than you might imagine. Indeed, it is more complex than I imagined until it was explained to me. My suggestion is this. We will take a short break to enable you to consider what you have learned, and to perhaps speak among yourselves. When we resume, I will have our senior statesman, Plik of the maimalodalum, explain the situation to you, and hopefully show you that our terms are to your own best advantage."

XLVI

PLIK STOOD ON his chair behind the table. He saw the seven commanders studying him, and knew from the expressions of interest but not shock that Tiniel had probably told them something about him.

He smoothed his chest fur with both his front hands, and began: "I am Plik of the maimalodalum—the beast-souled, for those of you who do not speak the language of Liglim. We are descended from creatures created by the mishandling of magic. Given what we are, you should not be in the least surprised to discover that one of the main topics of discussion among the adults of our community is the ethics and responsibilities that should ideally rule the use of magic. They were largely theoretical discussions, for we had no more magic in our community than is found generally.

"I realize that, strange as I am to your eyes, you have no idea how old I am. I am over seventy years old. In my early life I knew many, maimalodalum and Beast alike, who were alive in the days before querinalo removed magic as a ruling force in the world."

Plik paused, but the seven commanders were listening intently, and not a one, not even King Bryessidan of the Mires, who had shown himself so impulsive and temperamental, made a move to interrupt.

"In the days since I have come to the Nexus Islands," Plik continued, "I have often wished the maimalodalum were here so that I could talk with them about the gateway network, and what it means to both the Old Worlds and the New. You must remember that in the New World the existence of the gates was largely hidden from the common people. The only ones who were brought into the secret of the network's existence were those who were taken to the Old World to be trained in the use of magic, the potential spellcasters. Doubtless there were those here and there—lovers, special friends, a few valued advisors—who also learned of the gates, but these would not be likely to betray their knowledge to the common folks.

"I am not going to trouble you with a recapitulation of what happened when my associates came to the Nexus Islands except to ask you to accept that they had enough troubling them that they did not really think about the gates except to feel a certain vague gratitude that nothing was coming through to complicate an already complicated situation.

"I, however, perhaps as a result of my upbringing, did think about those implications. If there is anyone you can blame for those gates being closed against you, the person to blame is me. I showed my friends how traffic through the gates could unbalance what was already a precarious situation. I urged that the gates be sealed against use until our control of the Nexus Islands was secure."

Plik stopped now and deliberately surveyed the faces of the

seven arrayed before him. None of them seemed to find it in the least amusing that a creature resembling a raccoon was lecturing them. A couple—Kynan of Hearthome and Valdala of u-Chival—actually looked intimidated.

"Now we hold those gates again, and, as Derian and Ynamynet have made clear to you, we hold them more securely than before. Ironically, your invasion led us to discoveries we might not have otherwise made for years, if at all. Doubtless all of you but King Bryessidan, who rules his own land and therefore has no one to answer to, are wondering just how you will explain your loss to your rulers.

"What I am going to suggest is that you ask yourselves—and them—a completely different and more important question. Who, ultimately, is to have administration of the Nexus Islands and the gates?"

At last an interruption came, as Aurick of Pelland said sarcastically, "You have control, as we have been told repeatedly. Isn't asking who is in control redundant?"

Plik grinned at him, the teeth-bared smile of a Beast that is as much threat as expression of amusement.

"Commander Aurick, the alliance of you seven took the gates from us once. Surely, with what you have learned you might try again someday—next year, two years from now, two months from now. And would that attempt be made by an alliance of you seven nations or perhaps an alliance of just a few? How many of you took part in this venture less from resolution that the Nexus Islands should not be closed than from fear that your neighbors might get here first?"

Plik did not need to be wise old creature to know he had hit home. He pressed his advantage.

"Now, I ask you this. Would you rather deal with your alliance of seven—seven nations, any one of which has rather a lot to gain by violating the alliance—or with the single standing government of the Nexus Islands? Think about it. Seven or one? Seven, some of whom are friends, some of whom you wouldn't share a cup of tea with if fear hadn't driven you to this alliance, or one, the government of the Nexus Islands, a simple group who you now know were merely undergoing a bit of governmental reorganization and would like to reopen for business pretty much as usual."

Plik looked at Merial of Azure Towers.

"How about you, Commander Merial? Us or a continued alliance with Hearthome—and all the while wondering if Queen Iline might be borrowing a gate or two while her Once Dead were on watch?"

Merial stiffened, and Kynan glowered, but he also looked down at his boots.

"How about you, King Bryessidan?" Plik said, looking at the young king, who looked so much less martial without his armor of silver and brass. "How long before your allies are remembering your father's actions, and taking precautions so that the son does not act the same? How much fun would it be noting that the Once Dead who hold alliance to you are always being posted with those who will watch them carefully—and never with those from your father-in-law's land?"

Plik let his gaze shift to Talianas of Tishiolo. "And you? Your people, at least so I understand, live on the same continent as the rest of the Pellanders, but you have always been a people apart, holding to customs and languages that don't fit. Would your four continental neighbors tolerate giving you equal rights?

"How about u-Chival, Aridisdu Valdala? You are also from a culture apart. Your land is rather poor in Once Dead, a result of somewhat stringent policies regarding what were long viewed as those who were abominations in the eyes of the Deities. Could you keep your part in the alliance of seven, or would you find yourselves shouldered out?

"Fromalf of Tavetch . . ." Plik looked at the bruised and battled commander. "Your people have already found that the impulsive ways of sea raiders do not work so well in this complex situation. King Hurwin is becalmed, and has discovered that sea monsters are all too real. Will he want to devote the rest of his life to the intricate political maneuvering necessary to keep this alliance going, or would he be happier to have things—mostly—as they were?"

Merial of Azure Towers raised a graceful finger in indication that she would like to speak.

"Are you saying we could go back to the way things were before, that the Nexan government would overlook this invasion as a mere misunderstanding?"

"Hardly 'mere,'" Ynamynet said without standing. "All armies participating in the battles suffered loss of life, but proportionately, we suffered far more. That could not be forgotten. Our lands were invaded, the primary resource necessary for our survival ripped from our hands, yet, even so, we are willing to continue working with you. Terms, however, will need to be worked out in advance."

Bryessidan of the Mires interjected, "We already paid high fees for use of the gates. What more would you want?"

"For one," Derian said, "we want the prisoners taken from us returned, or at least their bodies. Nothing else will be acceptable. Remember. The Nexus Islands no longer need you. We have contact with the New World and can slowly open negotiations with those nations for the supplies we need. We have already begun such with Grateful Peace of New Kelvin."

"You can have your prisoners," Bryessidan said. "Most were removed to the Mires, and I assure you, I would not countenance them being treated poorly."

"Most?" Derian said.

"One—I don't know whether you would term him a prisoner—chose to go instead to Pelland under the protection of Aurick of Pelland."

Plik guessed from the tight whiteness around Bryessidan's lips as he said this, that this last decision had not been to the king's liking.

"Would that be Tiniel?" Plik said quickly. He didn't trust the others to manage to speak of the traitor kindly, but he held some small amount of pity for the young man.

"It is."

"We would like to talk to him," Plik said, "at the very least. His sister is of our company."

He gestured to where Isende sat to one side, her head bent over her notes.

"I believe she would like to speak with him," Plik concluded.

Aurick of Pelland said with a formality that did not hide some hidden emotion, "If your seeing Tiniel and speaking with him is a matter upon which our continued use of the gateway nexus rests, then stand assured, I will bring him here myself. However, I will tell you that Tiniel has thrown himself under my protection, and my honor would be in question if that protection were violated."

"Whatever that means," King Bryessidan said. "Your honor seems flexible enough when it come to taking orders."

He seemed to realize that he had been—to say the least—impolitic and drew in a deep breath. Then he fastened his gaze on Derian once more.

"What other terms do you have in mind?"

Derian consulted his notes. "When commerce is resumed, the gates are going to be used on a very tight schedule. There will be no more of this sending through a Once Dead and re-questing service. Each client will be given set days for service, and whether they choose to use their scheduled slots or not will be up to them."

"What about emergencies?" said Valdala of u-Chival. "These do happen."

"We might be open to address the matter of emergencies," Derian said with a slow smile.

Plik was reminded for all that he had met Derian in the capacity of Firekeeper's friend and a junior diplomat, Derian's upbringing had been as the heir apparent to a large concern involved with the carting and livery trades. Working out use of the gates might be second nature to him.

Plik slid down to sit on his chair, and listened as the negotiations began, watched as calculation took over from aimless resentment. Although they might not have acknowledged the fact aloud, the Alliance of Seven was ended, and each and every commander was now fighting for the best advantage for his or her nation alone.

Nothing was definite, but Plik thought he could see each of the seven commanders beginning to realize how onerous maintaining and operating the Nexus Islands could be—

especially since there was at least one nation within their precarious alliance that each did not trust.

Two, really, for as far as Plik could see, no one trusted Queen Iline of Hearthome, and she—and her representative—shared that tendency most heartily.

We might just have peace, he thought, *and a more secure hold on the Nexus Islands than ever before. That won't bring back the dead, but perhaps their spirits will rest more quietly.*

❧

KING BRYESSIDAN OF the Mires stood on the shore and watched as King Hurwin the Hammer was rowed ashore by two sailors so terrified that the normally ruddy hue of their skin appeared closer to a very pale green.

The reason for their fear was obvious. The small landing craft moved along a perfectly smooth and waveless channel in the waters surrounding the Nexus Islands, waters that everywhere else rippled and spat little foam-capped wavelets. Even the oars the sailors dutifully dipped into the water did not much mar the glass smooth surface of the channel.

Bryessidan suspected that the rowers were not necessary in the least, that the forces that now enlivened the ocean surrounding the Nexus Islands could have brought the boat to land themselves.

In contrast to his fearful sailors, King Hurwin appeared calm and even interested in his surroundings. Clad in a summer-weight tunic, leggings, sea boots, and a peaked cap, he looked well for someone who had served as admiral for a large, quite probably uncoordinated fleet.

Or am I letting my own failure to dominate my fellow generals color my assessment, Bryessidan thought. *Certainly, if the fleet had been mine to command, each ship would have sailed its own course, and at least a third would have ended up attacking each other.*

That, at least, had been the reaction when, following the

long meeting in which the Nexan government had stated its position, Bryessidan had attempted to reassume leadership of the Alliance of Seven. Fromalf of Tavetch had fallen into line, and Merial of Azure Towers had not seem particularly unhappy to let him take the lead. Aridisdu Valdala was still so shocked by the presence of the jaguar she kept referring to as "Ahmyn" that she could have been led in circles by the nose and probably would not have noticed.

The other three, however, had made quite clear that they were having no more of King Bryessidan's leadership. They still accorded him the respect appropriate to his crown, but as for the rest, they were so busy working out just how they would explain the situation to their respective rulers that they had no time for Bryessidan's attempts to salvage the alliance.

To Bryessidan's immense surprise, the Nexans were making no move to hold any of the commanders against their will. They weren't even trying to hold the troops, although they were refusing to return anything but personal equipment.

When the commanders were released following the meeting, each was given a mixed human and yarimaimalom "bodyguard," and then permitted to leave the building without further restriction. They emerged into a bright summer day, the sun already rising toward noon, and saw that the gateway hillside was aswarm with organized activity.

Derian Carter—or Counselor, Bryessidan had heard him called both—had sauntered out with them, and now he gestured toward the hillside.

"We're sending your troops back," he said, "or rather, we're permitting your Once Dead to send them back. Supervised, of course, and any who didn't want to leave for whatever reason has not been forced."

Bryessidan was pleased to learn that the troops from the Mires had been among those to refuse to leave the Nexus Islands. Perhaps knowing their monarch's eye was directly on them had led to this valor, but he thought that the fact that the best healers were in this group also had something to do with their determination to stay.

Unsurprisingly, the majority of the Pellanders, especially

the elite units, had been the other group to resist departing their captivity. The u-Chivalum, their morale undermined by the ill omen of their commander's mental collapse—and the prevalence of the yarimaimalom in the Nexan force—had been the most eager to leave. The troops from Hearthome had been quick to depart, and when they began to go, those from Azure Towers had decided they could not remain and leave their land vulnerable.

With that, there had been little to keep the soldiers from Tishiolo and Tavetch from joining the general exodus, and all of this had begun while each army's supreme commander was being lectured on the changed situation.

Little did we know how changed it was, Bryessidan thought. *All the while they were talking to us so reasonably, encouraging us to ask questions, making sure we understood just how bad matters were for us, they knew matters were infinitely worse.*

He toyed with angry imaginings in which, at the sight of him the armies had rallied, surged out of the detention camps, and beaten every Nexan, whether traveling on two feet or four or flying about, to a bloody pulp.

"But it wouldn't have happened that way," he muttered.

"Excuse me?" asked the polite voice of Grateful Peace of New Kelvin. "I did not quite follow what you said."

King Bryessidan tried not to feel annoyed that this graceful man with his bone-colored hair and odd facial ornamentation did not give him his appropriate titles.

"I was saying," Bryessidan said, "that I wonder how they make the water look that way."

"As I understand it," Grateful Peace said, "the boat is actually not traveling on the water's surface, but on the 'backs'— if such creatures can be thought to have backs—of the sea monsters."

Bryessidan had just a moment to absorb this strange and unsettling idea; then the landing craft was grating ashore on the rocky beach and the sailors were leaping out to drag it above the tideline. King Hurwin leapt out with them and splashed to the shore.

"Bryessidan!" he said, greeting his son-in-law with a bear's hug. "So things certainly did not work as we had planned. Trust me to discount tales of monsters again. I certainly have something to tell the grandchildren."

King Hurwin gave an affable nod to Grateful Peace. "I have no idea who you are, who any of you are, but I saw you through my long glass staring out to sea, and the sea monsters came soon after. Are you some form of Once Dead?"

"I am not," Grateful Peace said, "not as you mean the term. I am Grateful Peace, of the New World nation of New Kelvin."

Bryessidan listened with half an ear as King Hurwin asked Grateful Peace who this one or that one was. The Tavetchian king had seen a great deal through his glass, and now desperately desired to know what had actually happened.

Grateful Peace complied, providing information in a sparse and efficient manner that made Bryessidan feel fairly certain that the rumors he had heard that this "Peace" was or had been a spy master in his own land were probably correct.

Grateful Peace escorted the two monarchs to a smaller room in the headquarters building and went to inform the Nexan rulers of King Hurwin's arrival. The two monarchs were left alone—or relatively so, since their bodyguards only drew back a few polite steps. King Hurwin had been speaking Pellish, but now he switched to Tavetchian.

"So, son. I received a long scroll outlining the situation and initialed by you as being an accurate description of what had occurred. I don't suppose it was, by any chance, a fabrication?"

Bryessidan recalled the document. "I fear not, Father Hurwin. There was a bias to the presentation—these Nexans do not seem to see that they brought our actions upon themselves by refusing us use of the gates—but where matters of sequence are concerned, it was accurate."

"I thought it probably was," King Hurwin said, "when I saw you waiting on the shore looking so sour. Before then, I admit, I had rather hoped it was a ploy of some sort. Ah, well. I suppose we must negotiate with them."

Judging from the expressions on the bodyguard's faces,

few—if any—spoke Tavetchian, so Bryessidan spoke rather more freely than he might have otherwise.

"What I don't understand is why they are willing to continue doing business with us. Surely it is not all a matter of profit."

King Hurwin smiled sadly. "It might help you understand if you had ever been a raider. Year after year, Tavetchian ships go to the same lands and raid the farmsteads. We don't hit the same farms every year, but it is a rare region that goes untouched. Every year some young sailor asks, 'Why don't they just leave? They know we're coming. They know we'll win.' The answer is, they can't leave. The land is what they have and what they know. Our raids are just another of the trials of working those lands, and are probably far less annoying than creatures that cannot be fought, like weevils and birds."

"You're saying that is the situation here?" Bryessidan said. "These islands are all they have?"

"That, and the fact that they would rather work with us and keep control of these gates than risk any one of us taking over. Don't for a minute think that for all their good manners they think of us as friends. Your heir might someday earn their trust, but those of us who have shown our willingness to invade will never be trusted. It's part of the risk of raiding. Really, if we had to lose, we came away better than we might have done."

"I hate what they're doing," Bryessidan said. "They've turned us against each other. We had an alliance. Now, from the way the others have been treating me it's as if they expected me to try and usurp the nexus, and that they're glad to give it back to its 'rightful' owners."

"We would have ended up having to watch each other," King Hurwin said, thoughtfully. "I realized that. Would you want Queen Iline having a door into your land?"

"Not really."

"So, you see, the Nexans have only anticipated what we ourselves would have had to deal with sooner or later. Clever of them, really. Not only will we police ourselves, we'll police the others as well, just in case anyone gets any bright ideas.

Yes. These Nexans will be a force to reckon with in the years to come, don't you ever forget that."

"So you're going to accept their terms?"

"What choice do I have? All the reasons I stated back in your counsel hall moonspans ago still hold. My kingdom is sea-girt and isolated. The gates make it less so. As long as the Nexans don't ask anything unreasonable—such as tithing in blood or slaves—then I will make treaty with them."

"And what is to keep them from breaking this one as they broke the last?" Bryessidan asked, his voice tight with frustration.

"I dare say that these Nexans do not feel that the former treaty—made, remember, with those they conquered—was precisely binding on them. There is even some merit in that line of thought—especially for those who arrived here from the New World."

"I cannot believe you are taking this so calmly!"

"What else is there to do?" Hurwin said, reaching for a pitcher and pouring himself some water. "We lost, yet most of my ships will go back with most of the gear and crews intact."

"Most?"

"Ah, they didn't have you read that extra sheet, did they?" Hurwin's formerly placid smile became a little bitter. "Each nation must give one ship—one small ship, admittedly—loaded with the arms and armor of the sailors of the other vessels over to the Nexans. They know they won't get everything, not even with their aerial spies supervising, but they'll get quite a lot."

"But not the crews," Bryessidan said.

"No. They don't want the crews. They're smart enough to know slaves are a bad idea. My guess is that the ships will be dry-docked somewhere or other, and that they'll raise the crews themselves, perhaps from the New World, more likely from the Old."

"On that free day," Bryessidan said angrily, "they insisted upon. That was a term that stuck in my craw. One day out of every season, agreed upon in advance when those who wish to be considered for residence on the Nexus Islands must be permitted access to the gates."

"They're smart," Hurwin said, "and we'd be smart to take them up on it. Malcontents in all our lands will end up as their problem, not ours, and, who knows . . . Someday . . ."

Someday we might just sneak in a spy or two, Bryessidan thought.

The thought gave him some feeling that he was retaining a small measure of control. Until King Hurwin's arrival, Bryessidan had balked against signing the treaty with the Nexans, even though Gidji, to whom Amelo had recited the terms, had sent him a letter urging him to do so.

Now, seeing that even the monarch of the seas saw no alternative but to give in, Bryessidan felt there was less shame in making peace with the Nexans.

Where there is life, there is hope, he thought when the next day he signed the formally prepared document in the presence of witnesses both of the Nexans and of the former seven allies.

He knew that his signing—and King Hurwin's—would be used to pressure those monarchs, such as Queen Iline and the disdum of u-Chival, who for their own reasons were still arguing terms. He no longer cared. There were even rumors that the u-Chivalum were considering withdrawing into isolation once again, to protect themselves from the contaminating influences of other lands.

Let them, Bryessidan thought, signing his name with a flourish, then pressing his thumbprint in his own blood over the words. *Running away doesn't solve anything, but you need to learn that for yourself.*

Now that he had decided to sign the treaty, Bryessidan felt curiously free, freer, in fact, than he had since he had been crowned king. It was as if in making his own peace with the Nexus Islands, he was also making peace with his father's wars and the mark they had left on the Mires.

Bryessidan supervised the evacuation of each and every one of the denizens of the Mires, and he himself was the last to turn toward the gate. Before he did, he turned to Derian Counselor and Once Dead Ynamynet.

"I am certain we will meet again. May it be the beginning of friendship, as well as peace."

Ynamynet gave him a wintery smile that could have meant anything, but tall Derian flicked his horse ears and said with what seemed like genuine warmth, "I hope so, Your Majesty. There are always far too many enemies, and far too few friends. I've seen enough to treasure even those met in the strangest circumstances."

And Bryessidan, bowing with the courtesy of monarch to monarch before he stepped through the gate, thought of the wolf-woman Firekeeper, of the yarimaimalom, of the maimalodalum, and realized with a certain amount of surprise that he would be pleased to someday be among those strange creatures Derian Counselor named friends.

He was met on the other side of the gate by his wife and queen. Gidji's face was alight with real joy, and she hugged him as if he was nothing more than a man, and she a woman, not him a king and her a queen, and their marriage arranged besides.

"I worried about you, Bry," she said softly, so softly that only he could hear. "I worried from the moment you donned your armor and left the palace. I worried that my foolish talk of empire might end up robbing me of riches I never knew I had until I watched them walk away from me."

And Bryessidan, loosening his wife's embrace only enough that he could look at her with wonder, thought that even in defeat there might be victory, if you were wise enough to know when it was offered.

XLVII

 TINIEL LISTENED, BUT his ears almost refused to hear as Aurick of Pelland told him that he must return to the Nexus Islands.

"I told them that you had thrown yourself on my protection," Aurick said, "but whether that will mean anything to them or not, I cannot say. I only wish you to know that as important as my honor is to me, my first duty is to the service of my rulers. They have ordered that you be surrendered. If the Nexans release you, and you wish, you may return. I should be able to find some place for you in my household."

He wheeled on his booted heel and left the room. Tiniel watched him leave, and when the guards came for him, let them escort him to the Pelland gate without word or protest.

One person and one person only was waiting for him when he came through the gate: Isende.

Tiniel looked at his sister, his twin, and saw a stranger. He wondered what she saw when she looked at him. His garments were very fine, the tightly woven brown cloth of the Pellander-style tunic and breeches was shot with a trace of something that made the fabric shimmer. His laced boots were in the Pellander style as well, high and tightly fit to his calf. His hair, freshly cut, was topped with a round cap that held a pheasant's feather.

The outfit would have been dreadfully hot and confining back in Gak, but in the cooler climate of the Nexus Islands, it suited him just fine.

By contrast, Isende wore something halfway between a smock and a loose dress made from some coarse fabric. It was belted at the waist with a strip of cloth cut from an entirely different weave. The garment fell below Isende's knees, stopping at a ragged hem at the middle of her calf. Her feet were clad in rope sandals. Her hair was tied back from her face. She looked very tired.

"We had little warning you were coming," she said, "but I had arranged to see you alone. Oh, Tin . . . How could you have done that?"

He blinked at her, and drew himself up as tall as he could.

"I did what I thought was right."

"You did . . ."

Isende thrust something that she had held tucked beneath her arm at him. Tiniel took it, only realizing after he held it that it was his drawing pad. His face grew hot as he thought of the dreams and imaginings he had committed to those pages, but he held on to his dignity.

"I found this in your rooms," Isende said. "I went there, trying to understand how you could have done what you did."

"I did what I thought was right," Tiniel repeated sternly.

"Were any of the people here ever real to you?" his twin asked him. "Did you ever really get to know them?"

He frowned. "I knew them as well as was necessary."

"Well, then," Isende said, reaching out and grabbing his free hand above the wrist. "I think it's about time you got to know them a little better."

He thought she would take him to the dining hall, where the Nexan community tended to gather even when meals were not being served, but she headed instead to the headquarters. They met remarkably few people along the pathway down, and those they did pass acted as if Isende were alone. These few also all seemed to be armed, and Tiniel thought with a certain amount of pride that he was apparently feared.

Isende led him up through the main portico and in through the front door. Once they were inside, Tiniel could hear more stirring. Isende led him toward what he vaguely recalled—he hadn't had much business here—were a series of large rooms that had probably been used as offices or reception parlors back in the days when the Nexus Islands had been a flourishing crossroads for trade.

Now they had been converted into a series of infirmaries. The scent of alcohol stung Tiniel's nostrils. This, strong as it was, could not cover the sweeter, sickly scent of infection and rot, of stale urine, and of bowels out of control.

Isende paused outside one of the open doors.

"Doctor Zebel. I've brought him. Is it all right to come in?"

"As I said," came Zebel's familiar voice, "but if he causes any trouble, I won't answer for him."

Tiniel had always thought of Zebel as a friend. Certainly, the doctor, along with a few of the guards, had been the only ones to show him and Isende any kindness during their first captivity. Zebel's voice was without inflection now, and when the twins entered he deliberately turned his back.

Isende said, "This is where the worst of the wounded are. Do you remember Junco Torn? He sailed with his father and sister on the fishing boat, but since she was grounded, he begged to be assigned to fight ashore."

Tiniel looked down at the young man on the bed. The man was obviously awake, but his eyes were shut. He moved his shoulder as if to put his hand on the outside of the blankets, but although the muscles twitched, no hand appeared.

"One of the u-Chivalum swords smashed Junco's upper arm. Doc—he's in the next room—tried his best, but there was no saving the limb. We had to amputate. It was very nasty."

Isende moved on before Tiniel could fully adjust to that "we." He knew her too well to suspect that she was giving herself airs. Had she been forced to be part of the medical staff? Was that a punishment for her being related to him?

Anger rose in his breast at the unfairness of it all. Isende should not be punished for his choices. Besides, if he had made a peace, the Nexans might now be thanking him for it.

He wanted to ask Isende, but she was moving over to another bed. On it lay a woman Tiniel vaguely recognized.

"This is Yornisaya," Isende said. "You might remember her. She was one of those who went to Gak with you. She also worked in the kitchens. She's also an apothecary, and we owe her a great deal for blending many of the medicines we had to treat the injured. When the u-Chivalum army emerged, she ran up to the hillside to help bring away the wounded.

"A solider did not approve and cut her across the head with the blunt edge of his sword. I suppose he thought he was being merciful. However, where the edge would have cut and might have glided off the bone, the solid impact of the metal knocked her out. There are bones cracked in her skull. We have done our best to relieve the internal pressure."

As if cued, Yorinsaya turned her head to one side and Tiniel saw her scalp had been shaved and what looked like a triangular piece of bone cut away. The wound had been patched with something—maybe metal?—but was ugly nonetheless.

"We think she will live," Isende said, reaching down and

squeezing Yornisaya's hand, "but we don't know if she will ever see again."

"See?" Tiniel said.

"Oh, didn't I tell you? The blow robbed her of her sight. As we do not know what was broken, we do not know how to fix it."

Isende moved on to the next bed.

"Do you remember little Eteo?" she said, indicating a dark-skinned boy too old to be a child, but certainly not a man. "He was running messages between Skea and the various subcommanders. One of the Pelland archers saw him and shot at him. Eteo took an arrow to his back and one to his leg before he fell."

Isende peeled back the blankets. Tiniel turned his gaze away. To his astonishment, he felt Isende's hand grab his hair and pull his head around so he could not help but see.

"Look!" she said, and her voice sounded as harsh as Firekeeper's did. "You did what you felt was right. You should see what happened."

Tiniel did look then, and saw the long line of stitches going over Eteo's back and down his leg.

"He sprained his 'good' leg when he fell," Isende said, "and so it is going to be quite a while before he walks at all. By the time he can, muscles are going to have atrophied. It's going to be a long time before he can run again, but he's a brave boy, and I believe he will."

She patted Eteo's shoulder and pulled up the covers.

Humiliated by the memory of her tugging his hair, Tiniel did not try and turn away again, although the injuries he was forced to view sickened him. Isende seemed to know each and every person, and how they were injured. Gradually, it dawned on him that she had been working in the infirmary voluntarily.

Most of the patients either ignored him or pretended he wasn't there. Some, though, stared at him with hatred so intense that Tiniel longed to flee.

I only did what I thought was right! he longed to explain, but he didn't think anyone here cared to listen.

When they left that first room, Tiniel learned that those patients—grim as their injuries had been—were the hopeful cases. The next room held those for whom the chance of recovery was slim—and who would have had no choice at all but that Doc, who like Grateful Peace had been temporarily protected against querinalo, was helping with their treatment.

Here were those who had taken injuries to the gut or lungs, those who had lost so much blood that their bodies had retreated into an unbreakable sleep.

Once again, Isende insisted on introducing each and every one, telling Tiniel who they were, what they had done, and how they had received their injuries.

Time and again, he heard the refrain, "an u-Chivalum solider," "an u-Chivalum archer," "an u-Chivalum spear," and knew that he, rather than the man or woman who had actually wielded the weapon, was being blamed.

The final room was in some ways the worst, for none of the injured spared him by turning away their gaze, and all suffered without words, for they had no words—at least that humans could understand.

Here were the injured and dying yarimaimalom, the Wise Beasts of the southern woodlands in the New World, the Bound of the north. Administering their care was Harjeedian of Liglim, and serving as his translator was Plik. Harjeedian gave Tiniel a look so hard and so full of anger that Tiniel wondered if the aridisdu would curse him, but he only turned away and stalked from the room.

Tiniel thought he could not bear it if Plik, too, denied him, but when the maimalodalu looked at him, he saw only pity.

Isende was continuing her litany, telling Tiniel about this wolf, that fox, this wildcat, and Tiniel listened with increasing impatience.

Hadn't she realized she's made her point? She blamed him. Fine. She could just be that way. Those animals should have known that human weapons were too much for them.

Plik interrupted, placing a small hand gently on Isende's arm.

"Save your throat, Isende. You've told him, and I fear he does not understand."

Isende flinched at the gentle touch, and looked at her brother. "You don't, do you?"

Tiniel straightened his shoulders. "In war, choices must be made. I made mine. Each of these made their own."

Anger flared in Isende's eyes, eyes that Tiniel had once thought so like his own.

"You are to be brought before the council," she said. "But I have one more thing to show you."

Tiniel looked at her, then sighed in what he thought was dignified resignation.

"Lead on."

She did, taking him to the back of the large building and down a short flight of stairs. The room was lit with glow blocks, and cold wafted up so that Tiniel wondered that his sister in her light shift did not shiver.

"Ynamynet," Isende said, as if explaining, "is proving to have a gift for cold. She used it here, so that we could have time to prepare a proper funeral."

The cellar had been converted into a morgue, and the dead of the Nexus Islands were arrayed in neat lines upon the floor.

"I'm sure you remember my friend Rhul," she said, choking up as she looked down at one of the closer bodies. "His wife is nearly paralyzed with grief over his death. His little children don't yet know they are fatherless."

Before Tiniel could say anything, Isende moved over to stand by a man of middle years, and began, "This was Ollaris. You may recall him as a cobbler. He died when an u-Chivalum spear took him in the stomach and ripped him through. He leaves . . ."

Tiniel did not want to hear any more. They were alone here, and he did not hesitate to raise his voice.

"Isende! I have had quite enough of this. People were injured. People died. Fine. I understand. I even understand that you blame me. I don't know why. I did not plan the invasion. I did not close the gates to legal traffic."

Isende gasped and Tiniel thought she might hit him, and wondered what he would do if she did. Surely no one could blame him for defending himself, and he had really put up with quite enough.

Isende held her hand, though, standing trembling for what seemed like an eternity. When she finally brought herself to speak, her voice was level and hard.

"You let in an army. Without the u-Chivalum army, our forces might have held. Haven't you heard me tell you how many of the injuries were due to the u-Chivalum?"

"I heard," Tiniel said impatiently, "but haven't you heard me? I didn't start this war. I simply took what I thought was the right side. No matter what I did, people would have died. People would have been hurt. I didn't cause it. If anyone did, it was Derian Carter and his crazy insistence that a handful of refugees could hold something as valuable as the gates."

Isende didn't rise to this attack on her lover. Instead she looked Tiniel eye to eye and hissed, "People! After all I've said, after all I've shown you, you can still simply say 'people'? People didn't die here. Fathers and mothers died. Husbands and wives. Brothers and sisters. Son and daughters. Cousins. Nieces. Nephews. Beloved friends, some of whom had known each other for years, who had suffered exile, war, and privation and were closer than you and I ever were."

"Closer!" Tiniel was stung. "You knew my heart!"

"I had an occasional glimpse of your soul," Isende said. "I knew you were troubled, but I never imagined how far into fantasy you had gone."

She pointed to the man at her feet and continued as if Tiniel had not said a word.

"Ollaris leaves behind his wife and three children, all of whom were born on the Nexus Islands and for whom it is the only home they know. Because of this, when their eldest child, a girl, asked to remain rather than go to sanctuary in the New World, they permitted her to do so. Laria worked as a runner, and was coming in with a message when her father was carried in on a stretcher. She stayed with her father, held him while he coughed up blood and cried for his parents—the grandparents she had never known. He died in her arms, and then do you know what she did?"

Mesmerized by Isende's passion, Tiniel asked, "What?"

"Laria took off the shirt soaked with his blood, put on one somewhat more clean. Then she went out and ran more messages. During the day, she seems fine, but at night she screams, begging for her daddy to sing her to sleep. The doctors don't know how to treat a wounded mind. She may never recover."

Tiniel looked around the morgue. In the clear, pale light of the glow blocks, the faces were looking more and more familiar. He'd eaten beside that woman. She was always knitting something. Socks, usually. She'd say you couldn't have enough socks, and then laugh.

That man had sung loud songs while mucking out the stalls or pigsties. He'd dug the smelly stuff into raised garden beds and talked endlessly about his plans for importing worms and making covers for some beds so he could grow some hardy greens come winter.

That boy over there . . . he'd been good at ball games, and very proud of how quickly he learned to use a bow. Judging from the hole gaping on the side of his neck, he hadn't been good enough.

Tiniel began to shake.

"Get me out of here!" he said, turning to Isende, barely keeping from shouting his demand. "They're looking at me."

"No," she said sadly. "They'll never look at anyone again. You're finally looking at them."

❧

TINIEL WAS EXECUTED later that day, up on the gateway hillside, in front of witnesses from each of the seven formerly allied nations, Elise and Doc, Grateful Peace, Citrine, Edlin, and any of those Nexans who cared to attend.

Before Skea took the axe to Tiniel's neck, Derian read a prepared statement explaining why the execution was occurring. He, Urgana, Ynamynet, Harjeedian, and a drifting cast of others had composed it the night before, well aware that this execution was one of the first public acts of the new government of the Nexus Islands.

"We do not do this for vengeance," he said, and his voice, hard and cold, didn't even sound like his own. "Vengeance will not bring back the dead. We do not do this for punishment, because punishment is intended to correct, and the only correction that can happen after death is in the hands of others than those who breathe the air of this world.

"We do not do this because a law was broken, because it cannot be fairly said that those of us here on the Nexus Islands had any laws. We sentence this man, Tiniel, born of Gak in the New World, to death because he broke something far more vital than mere law. He broke trust.

"Breaking that trust led to many deaths, to sorrows that will always remain. At the heart of any community is trust, and in violating that trust, Tiniel has violated the right to remain within the community.

"We cannot pass such a betrayer of trust on to any other land, so we take the responsibility for him unto ourselves. If any message is to be taken from this execution, we hope that it will be this: We shall bear responsibility for our own. We expect that all who live on these islands and have commerce with them will recognize the high value we place upon the ability to trust."

Derian looked up from the paper to see Firekeeper's dark, dark gaze studying him. Blind Seer was beside her, leaning slightly against her leg, his blue-eyed gaze fixed also on Derian. Together, almost as one mind, wolf and woman nodded their approval.

Then Skea, who as the general of the Nexus Island forces claimed that his trust had been most violated of all those violated trusts, stepped forward. He held a large axe, the blade honed so sharp that the edge seemed to cut light.

Up went that shining blade, then down. Tiniel was dead. The nation of the Nexus Islands had sent its message to worlds both Old and New.

* * *

LATER, IN THE security of his cottage, Derian held Isende in his arms while she wept, the sobs coming from her in ragged gasps that seemed to leave her nearly suffocated from lack of breath.

"I'm sorry," she gasped, for what seemed like the hundredth time.

Derian bent and kissed the top of her head, noting, incongruously, that somehow she had found time to wash her hair and that it smelled of lavender.

"It's all right," he said, as he had over and over before. "Cry it out. You've had a terrible time."

"We've all had a terrible time," Isende said, her voice ragged. "Saeta lost Rhul. Frostweed lost his sister. Everyone here has lost friends. Why am I crying? Crying for him?"

"He was your brother, your twin," Derian said helplessly. "Isende, I don't think I could love you as much as I do if you couldn't cry for your brother, no matter how crazy he became in the end."

Isende looked up at him, and although tears still streamed from her eyes, Derian thought something he had said must have reached through her horrible pain.

"I don't have a brother anymore," she said. She held up her hand so he could see the little white scar along one side, the scar that marked where she had been physically joined to Tiniel at their birth. "I always had a brother. I knew that, I think, even before I knew there was an 'I.' First, I knew there was a 'we,' and from that I had to learn what 'I' was."

Derian didn't know what to say, so he kept his mouth shut and listened.

"I thought I wanted to be rid of him," Isende went on. "I was glad when I let querinalo burn through the bond. Now, though, now that I know what came of that, I wonder . . . Did I kill all those people? Did my selfish desire to be rid of Tiniel, to be free from that bond, did it make him into what he became?"

She looked up at him, and Derian knew he had to find something to say.

"That's the type of thinking that drove Truth insane," he

said. "We always wonder about might-have-beens, but in the end, what we must deal with is what is. I know that doesn't help. It doesn't answer your questions, but it's all I have."

Isende wiped ineffectually at her teary face. Derian tugged a not too unclean handkerchief from his shirt pocket, and she scrubbed at her cheeks.

"I must look a wreck," she said.

Derian was wise enough not to answer. Ballads were the only place where weeping women were heart-tuggingly lovely. He was happy to settle for simply heart-tugging, especially with someone who trusted him enough to cry in his arms.

"So," Isende said, "how are you going to deal with your helping of 'what if'?"

In case Derian might think he might evade her point, she reached and stroked the long, hairy line of his horse's ears.

"I can't bear the thought of never seeing my family again," Derian said simply. "What you've gone through with Tiniel, learning how quickly family and friends can be taken from you, made me realize that I can't wait forever—or forever might not be there. I've talked to Elise, and she's going to help prepare the way."

"Doc and Elise are going to have a lot of ways to prepare," Isende said. "First back in Liglim, then all the way to Hawk Haven. I wonder if anyone will believe them?"

"Anyone and everyone is not going to have much choice," Derian said. "Grateful Peace has promised to coordinate with Elise, and they're working out how best to have him serve as witness without making her seem as if her loyalties might be compromised."

Isende looked shocked at this, and Derian stroked her cheek in reassurance.

"Don't fret. Elise has a great deal of standing with King Tedric, and even if she didn't, Crown Princess Sapphire is her first cousin, and knows very well how firmly Elise believes in the dream that is Bright Haven. No one will be able to accuse Elise and Doc of withholding information about the existence of the gates. Whether Bright Haven decides to request that the gates within its borders be opened, that is someone else's decision."

"If they did," Isende said shyly, nestling up against him, but not looking up into his face, "that would certainly make it easier for you to visit your family."

"And to bring you to meet them," Derian said softly, kissing the top of her head again. "Would you go with me?"

"I would."

XLVIII

PLIK HEARD WINGBEATS outside the window of his cottage, and looked up just as the raven Lovable landed on the wide stone sill.

"There's a meeting!" Lovable said, "And you are requested to attend, and even if you had lived all the years since Earth and Air created life between them, you would not believe who has called this meeting."

Plik thought of the most unlikely person he could imagine, and one sharp-featured face immediately rose to mind.

"Firekeeper?"

"Firekeeper!" Lovable replied. "She asks that all gather at the patio behind Derian's cottage. She asked me and Bitter if we would carry the messages. We're racing!"

Lovable looked ready to take flight again, and Plik called out to her.

"When is this meeting?"

"Why, as soon as all can be gathered," Lovable said. "Firekeeper may have changed enough to ask for a meeting, but she is as impatient about waiting as ever before."

Plik decided that he would not miss this event even for a fresh bucket of fish guts. That the meeting was being held out-of-doors argued that Firekeeper did not care if everyone on the Nexus Islands heard her business. However, that did not mean her business was not serious. The wolf-woman had a marked dislike of secrets.

Doubtless because so many have been kept from her by those who thought they knew better, Plik thought.

As he made his way to the appointed place, he hoped that Firekeeper had thought to warn Derian in advance. A few days ago, Isende had moved her belongings into the young man's cottage, and if Plik's nose hadn't lost its sharpness—and he knew it hadn't—the young lovers were often involved in activities at which they would be rather embarrassed to be interrupted.

As if all the Nexans do not know, Plik thought with fond amusement. *And as if each and every one does not give the two their blessings.*

When the raccoon man arrived at Derian's cottage, he found Derian out and about, preparing for his guests.

"We asked Firekeeper," Derian said, shyly proud of that "we," "whether it would not be as well to hold this meeting in the big hall at headquarters, but she said that we'd all been inside enough. So we've rustled up chairs and some blankets for those who would prefer a seat on the ground. Isende's filling some pitchers with water."

"Can I do anything?"

"Translate for the yarimaimalom," Derian said. "I have no idea what Firekeeper is about, but Truth certainly had an inkling long before I did. She's been sleeping in a patch of sun out by the back wall since midmorning."

Plik promised to translate, and went to claim a seat on one of the blankets. Truth was still dozing, and Eshinarvash was cropping some grass off to one side. Before Plik had finished settling himself, Bitter and Lovable arrived, followed almost immediately by Grateful Peace, Citrine, and Edlin. Lady Archer came next, bouncing a drowsy infant Elexa. She gave Plik a polite curtsey and greeted Grateful Peace's contingent like the old friends—and in two cases, cousins—that they were.

"Doc wouldn't come," she said. "He said that he's going to

spend as much time in the infirmary as he can. We're planning to leave tomorrow through the Setting Sun stronghold gate, and then journey with Harjeedian to u-Seeheera."

She gave a gusty sigh, as if already feeling the jounce of the saddle, and continued on.

"From there, it's close counsel with Ambassador Sailor, and then, I suspect, back to Port Haven to report to King Tedric and his heirs. I'm going to suggest our ship puts in at Silver Whale Cove so we can brief King Allister first. It's strange to think that you will have been home in Thendulla Lypella for moonspans before we even reach Eagle's Nest."

"Strange indeed," Grateful Peace agreed. "I have no difficulty in the least understanding why the Old World nations were reluctant to give up the gates once King Veztressidan had reminded them of the network's usefulness. In my own land, I suspect there will be considerable debate, but in the end, since the gate is there and active, I think we will choose to use it."

"Querinalo," Elise said, "remains the problem. I have been watching Doc closely, but so far the Meddler's—or Virim's or whoever that strange man Firekeeper has trailing after her really is—protection has held."

"I have also felt no ill effects," Grateful Peace said, "and we must not forget that those with no touch of magic about them would not be vulnerable to querinalo."

Elise nodded. "But I can't forget what we were told about Blind Seer. He had no idea he had a talent, and nearly died. I've talked to many of the Nexans, and they have quite freely described the injuries many of those 'Once Dead' took to preserve their power. Some were horrific."

Plik interjected, "They could always choose to let their power go. I did."

Derian, coming out with two more chairs, had clearly been listening. "Sometimes it's not so simple, even for those of us from the north who are absolutely certain we'd rather have nothing to do with magic."

He twitched his long horse's ears as he said this, but didn't shy away from their gaze as he would have only a few moonspans before.

Skea and Ynamynet arrived at that moment, followed by Zebel and Harjeedian. The doctor looked rather surprised to find himself there.

"Doc said he would cover for us both. He said I am a pillar of the Nexan community, and soon enough Harjeedian is going to return to being a disdu and diplomat rather than an apprentice physician. Then he said that for all my skin is brown that I was looking pale, and needed sun."

"You do," came a blunt comment that could only have come from one person.

Firekeeper and Blind Seer had arrived unheralded. Now the wolf-woman carried a chair over for Zebel, then turned to get one for Harjeedian.

"The war is over for all of us but you healers, you still fight and fight."

Plik noted that the Meddler—or Virim—had arrived with Firekeeper and Blind Seer, and that Blind Seer was directing the Meddler to a chair toward the front. Firekeeper crossed to join them, and with some deliberation picked a ladder-backed chair for herself. She put this at the front, and then ruined the effect by turning it backward and straddling it, resting her chin on her folded arms over the back.

"I take chair so you can see me," she explained, "but I not think is comfortable."

"You're young yet," Grateful Peace said. "Remind yourself of this arrogance when you are my age and your joints are punishing you for all the abuse you are giving them now."

This stirred a general chuckle, and Firekeeper used the pause after it to call the meeting to order.

"Is Derian done running back and forth? And Isende?"

Derian came out the back door of his small house holding a pitcher with water. Isende came with him, and as if that was a signal, the falcon Elation soared down from the sky and took a perch in one of the trees that shaded the patio.

Looking around, Plik saw that several more of the Nexans—Urgana, Pishtoolam the cook, Wort, and Frostweed among them—had joined the group. A fair number of the yarimaimalom who remained had drifted to the edges of the gathering. Firekeeper did not seem surprised or annoyed, and so Plik guessed that all of these had been invited.

"I have a problem," Firekeeper began, "and I cannot think how to make it right. I think and think, and I talk with Blind Seer, but he is too close to me to be able to come up with answer. I am wishing to myself that I had a pack and could draw on their wisdom, then I think: I have a pack, and that pack is here."

Plik knew he was not the only one present to feel honored by those words. Firekeeper had always made such a point of being a wolf and nothing but a wolf that learning she had broadened her alliance to include such a motley group astonished and warmed him.

But why I should be astonished, I don't know. If this group is not a pack in the best and finest sense of the term, then never did a wolf pack run.

"My problem," Firekeeper said, turning and pointing as if her words would not provide enough identification, "is the Meddler, or Virim, or maybe even a mountain sheep."

"The Meddler foremost," said that one with a certain insouciance, "but Virim is here as well, and even the sheep, although I must admit that I have just about defeated the urge to graze."

"A pity," Eshinarvash said. *"It is a useful ability."*

The Meddler did not respond or react, but Plik did not doubt he had heard and understood. Plik decided that translation was not needed.

"I have no wish," Firekeeper went on, "to have this one running at my heels for all my days, even if he could keep up. But he is too much to leave without being . . ."

She paused, clearly struggling for a word.

"Controlled?" Derian suggested. "Restricted? Limited?"

"Bound," Firekeeper agreed, nodding her head in thanks. "But I not know how to make this binding or to make the promises he has made to me protect all. So I come to you, to ask. What do we do about the Meddler?"

"And how," Derian added, "do we deal with the fact that the Meddler seems to have taken over someone else's body. I'm not forgetting that he did us all a favor when he did so, but I'm not really comfortable with the idea."

"Can they be separated?" Wort asked.

The Meddler faced the group and offered one of his smiles.

"If you want an insane spellcaster on your hands, yes, we can probably be separated."

"Iron," Skea said, "might make Virim—or you—less dangerous."

"True," the Meddler said, "but prolonged contact with iron is painful. Ask your wife. . . ."

Implicit in those last words was a warning that if one spellcaster was so chained, how long before all spellcasters were chained. It would be so easy to argue that it was a precaution for the good of the community, for the safety of the Nexans at large.

Plik saw Firekeeper rest her hand on Blind Seer's shoulder. Here was one spellcaster who would never wear an iron collar. Who would chain Enigma? And was it fair to do to a human what one would not—or could not—do to a Beast?

Skea added, "The wearing of iron would only be for a limited time, until appropriate guidelines could be put in place."

"Of course," the Meddler said, lowering his eyelids and leaning back in a lazy stretch. "Of course. Until you needed a shield raised or a gate opened or some other spell worked. What you are proposing is slavery, Skea. Slavery, pure and simple."

"What I am proposing," Skea replied, "is defense. I do not consider myself a permanent general to these islands, but of late my thoughts have been much occupied with the question of dangers coming from outside. In the end . . ."

Skea paused to give Isende a look meant to reassure her that she was not to consider herself in the least to blame.

"In the end we learned that our greatest danger came from within our ranks. That same problem is what Firekeeper has brought before us today. You, Meddler, are permitting your actions to be guided by Firekeeper. How long will that last?"

"Forever, if she wishes," the Meddler said. "Of course, she

would need to give me some indication that she would return similar fidelity to me."

Plik saw Firekeeper glower, and she looked at the Meddler.

"My blood," she reminded him, "gave you access to Virim, but not so you could control him forever, only because he was going to get himself killed."

"And you wanted him alive," the Meddler said, "because he alone holds the answer to the elimination of querinalo. And I have kept him alive for you, and I have drawn on his skills for you, and now, suddenly, now that the danger is passed, everyone is thinking about poor Virim, and no one seems to feel anything but fear of the poor Meddler."

Plik had not removed his gaze from Firekeeper, so he saw her features tighten, but she did not say a single word. It was left for Derian to ask the difficult question.

"What would happen if we asked you to leave Virim's body?"

"Most likely," the Meddler said, "I would continue as the sort of spirit I have been since my own body was killed. However, there is a chance that I would fade away."

"Die?" Derian said.

"More or less," the Meddler said. "Lose contact with this plane of existence, at least."

"Good," Harjeedian said, and several others who shared his religious beliefs, and who Plik knew had spent a great deal of prayer on this matter, nodded.

Plik practiced a variation of the religion of Liglim, but perhaps because he was a maimalodalu, and accustomed to tolerance of strangeness, he was less fearful of the Meddler than were his co-religionists.

"Might you," Grateful Peace said, "find yourself trying to locate another body you might inhabit?"

"I might indeed," the Meddler said. "I do not like being bodiless."

"Even though as a bodiless entity you are effectively immortal?"

"Even so. Immortality is very dull when there are few with

whom you can talk, and fewer who will enjoy that communication. I would rather be mortal and enjoy good meals, sleep, and even the delights of love."

The Meddler gazed over at Firekeeper, and she visibly tensed. Blind Seer's hackles rose, but beyond that there was no response.

Plik wondered what attracted the Meddler to Firekeeper. She was not particularly beautiful, her skin was knit with scars, and she was notoriously hard to understand. Moreover, her devotion to Blind Seer was obvious. Perhaps that was part of her attraction to the Meddler. Perhaps, though, there was something else, something Plik could never understand.

An awkward silence had followed the Meddler's last statement, but Ynamynet's cool voice finally broke it.

"So we have a series of problems. The matter is not only what we should do about the Meddler/Virim, it is also whether we should deal with them as one entity or two. Moreover, if we choose to deal with them as two separate people, we have two separate problems: one a spellcaster of immense ability and knowledge far beyond our modern students of the art, the other a spirit with a reputation for involving himself in the lives of others—often with the best intentions in the world, but with a tendency to overlook some complexity and so create a potential for disaster."

Her little speech ended, she smiled a tight smile that nonetheless held more humor in it than Plik had seen for a long, long time.

"That is it, isn't it?" Ynamynet concluded.

"Is it," Firekeeper agreed with open admiration. "Now I know why I not figure out what to do. This is not a problem, is a nest of hibernating snakes."

Firekeeper looked over at the Meddler/Virim. "I want to talk to Virim. I heared you and him talk before. You say he is still there. Let him come up and tell us he like where he is with you."

The Meddler glowered at Firekeeper.

"He's crazy, I tell you."

"I think," Firekeeper said, "that he is not, else you would

have been quickest to let us talk to him so you could show us how much good you is doing for us. Now, let him up to talk, or by my blood that let you . . ."

The Meddler interrupted the wolf-woman, throwing his hand into the air with what Plik mused might just be a universal gesture of defeat.

"I know, or that blood that you gave me will sour. You charge a high price for your help, Firekeeper."

"Is how should be," Firekeeper said seriously. "Now, let us speak with Virim and see if he as crazy as you say."

"Fine!" the Meddler said, and leaned back in his chair, throwing his head back to rest against the topmost slat.

There was a long, long pause, during which time Plik noted that all of the Once Dead were alert to the moving of forces which he—and most of the rest of those there assembled— was unable to sense.

He saw Ynamynet moving her hands in a slight pattern, and wondered if she was preparing some defense, just in case the Meddler had been telling the truth.

Truth had risen to her feet and stood staring at the man in the chair, her white eyes so dilated that they seemed nearly as blue as Blind Seer's. But these were the only signs that anything was happening. The man in the chair remained so still that were it not for the signs of his breathing, Plik would have thought he had died.

At last the man in the chair stirred, then shook his head slightly as if trying to clear a mild headache. He raised a hand and stroked his beard, adjusted his posture so that he was sitting upright, and opened his eyes. They were the same eyes out of which the Meddler had looked, but somehow they were different.

Plik struggled to define why, and decided that where the Meddler's gaze always held a trace of humor—ironic as that humor might be—these eyes, Virim's eyes, were defined by sorrow mingled with regret and seasoned with more than a little fear. Those were the eyes that studied the assembled Nexans, closed for a moment as if needing to register the visual image, and then slowly opened again.

"You can't really blame him," said Virim.

His voice was very much like the Meddler's in tone and pitch, but utterly unlike as well. It was as if a different man played the same instrument, and transformed it by the tunes he chose.

"The Meddler, I mean," Virim continued. "He so very much wants to live, so very much wants to have a chance to interact with the world again, that even I can hardly blame him for maligning me. And his maligning was not so very much off course. He said I was crazy, implied that I was violently so. I am not violent. Despite all the deaths I have caused, I do not think I have ever been dreadfully violent. However, I think I have spent much of the last hundred years, ever since I permitted myself to contaminate what you call querinalo for my own benefit, more than a bit insane. That, however, is not what you are gathered here to decide. You are gathered here to decide what to do about two dangerous individuals: the Meddler and me."

Firekeeper had been leaning forward as she listened, her Fang drawn and ready in her hand. Plik did not doubt that Blind Seer would alert her if Virim attempted anything magical. More important, he was certain that Virim had noticed as well.

"Would you Nexans, you who have fought so hard in these last days to preserve your homes and your lives, would you blame me if I told you that what I want—and what the Meddler wants—is very much the same as you? For me, I want a chance to live and to perhaps make amends for what I have done. As for the Meddler, he has told several of you himself that he wants to live again in a physical form, even with all the restrictions that implies."

Derian spoke from the back of the gathered group.

"We're not looking to kill you, Virim, not you or the Meddler, but you have to admit, both of you provide a problem too much like the gates for us to overlook it. We don't want to put an end to you, but we sure don't want to set you loose and find out what others would do with you—or what you would do yourself."

Virim nodded solemnly and stroked his beard.

"I can understand this. I'm not even going to ask what you would do if I protested that you had no right to make such choices for others—that we are not gates to be administered. I don't think the young woman with the knife would agree."

He sighed, and seemed to grow smaller as he hunched forward and looked at the ground.

"And to be honest, I'm not sure that I would agree either. The days when I thought I knew the answer to life's problems are long past. The Meddler still thinks he knows, but maybe he could benefit from an education. So I have a question for you all. Would you like to give the two of us that education?"

"Two as one?" Firekeeper said. "Or would you sit on the Meddler as he sit on you?"

Virim straightened. "Actually, I think I might be able to give the Meddler what he wants—a living body—and still keep my own intact. However, I would need your permission to do so."

He looked over to where Zebel and Harjeedian sat.

"Doctors, do you have in your care one who, despite all your best efforts, will die?"

Zebel and Harjeedian exchanged startled glances, and then Zebel said, "We do. Arasan the Once Dead. He's one reason Doc isn't here with us. Arasan is fading away, sleeping more and more, and soon he's going to simply stop breathing."

"I could," Virim said, "let the Meddler move into this man's body, and then between us we could try and lure that man back into life. He would need to accept cohabiting with the Meddler, but he would be alive."

"But his body is broken," Zebel protested, "beyond our ability to repair it. Are you saying you could fix it?"

"I might be able to help," Virim said. "The Meddler would actually do more. He could take knowledge he has learned from me about the preservation of life, then employ it to helping this man heal. However, this is not something that can be done from the outside in or I assure you we would have offered before. It is something that only can be done from the inside out."

Bitter croaked from where he sat beside Lovable on the eaves of Derian's house. *"When I was near death, the Meddler came and gave me reason to live. His persuasiveness might be up to the task."*

Plik translated, and there was excited if apprehensive stirring among those gathered. Despite having been Once Dead, Arasan had been very popular with the Nexans in his quiet way. His talent had been a gift for song—not beguiling or enticing song, simply songs that gladdened the heart. To win Arasan back from death, even in this odd way, would seem like the best omen for the success of the Nexan enterprise.

Derian said, "I remember his persuasiveness myself, but would Arasan want to live with the Meddler sharing his body? What if after he was healed he regretted the choice?"

Virim shook his head. "Those of you who have been near the edge of death know that there is no room for the personal evasions we the living manage on a daily basis. If Arasan does not wish to accept the Meddler's offer, then he will not, and he will go into death."

"And the Meddler?" Harjeedian's voice sounded very tight, and no wonder, given his mixed feelings about the Meddler.

"He would be in a position to resume the life—the existence rather—that he had before he came into my body. He would be no worse off than before. I would be free of a tenant whom I did not invite. You would be free of the problem of a meddler with all my abilities. It is not a perfect solution, but it is one that would permit us both—and Arasan—to go on living."

The debate that followed was all the more intense for the awareness that Arasan might be slipping into his final sleep even as they tried to decide whether they could handle the consequences of letting him have a chance at life.

Finally, Firekeeper broke in. "You speak of us giving you 'education.' You mean by this you stay on Nexus Islands?"

"I will stay here," Virim said. "That I promise, and I will swear it on anything you would like. There were some very binding oaths in the old days. I could even teach you a few. Firekeeper, once I thought I knew all the answers, and I had the arrogance to act on those answers. Now I know that I do not, and that actions I thought would save those I valued from pain and suffering did so in the short term, but may have made matters far worse in the end. I no longer want to change the world. I want to make amends."

Firekeeper wasn't about to accept this humble statement without further pressing, "And the Meddler? How do he feel?"

Virim's beard twitched as he smiled. "Ask him yourself."

This time the transition went more quickly, and from something in the eyes that were now the Meddler's, Plik suspected that Virim had kept some sort of control of the body. Even so, he thought they could trust whatever the Meddler said.

After all, Plik thought, *once the Meddler is free from Virim's control, he could—and certainly would—say whatever he likes.*

Firekeeper also seemed aware of the transformation.

"So, Meddler," she said. "What think you?"

"I think," the Meddler said, "I am willing to take up the challenge Virim has offered, especially since the alternatives seems to be either remaining under his control or risking having us both slain as a threat to the safety of the Nexus Islands."

Ynamynet commented, "You would not be immune to such a penalty, Meddler. We will expect you to live by the same rules as the rest of the community, even if you are some sort of deity."

The Meddler gave a tight smile. "I have never claimed to be a deity, only a meddler, and as such I am hardly unique."

He gave Firekeeper a particularly stern look, but the wolf-woman did not seem in the least perturbed.

Firekeeper glanced at Blind Seer. Then, despite her awkward sprawl across the chair, she rose to her feet in one lithe motion. It was noticeable that her Fang was still in her hand, sunlight glinting both off the blade and the cabochon-cut garnet in the hilt, one bright, the other bloody.

Rather like the decision we must make, Plik thought.

"So," Firekeeper said, "what is this we do? I bring this to you, my pack, and I will do as my pack decides."

Derian gave her an approving smile. "If we are to vote on this, no one should feel pressured by what his or her neighbor thinks. Isende, do we still have the pieces of that cup I broke?"

"I can get them," she said, hurrying into the house and emerging a moment later with pieces of a clay mug and a deep ceramic jar.

Plik watched her carefully for any sign of resentment that the Meddler/Virim was to be given a chance at life, when Tiniel, who had, after all, done his harm and would be unlikely to do any more, had been executed without debate. Not the least bit of anger showed on her features, only worry.

And given the choice we have to make, Plik thought, *I cannot blame her in the least.*

When Isende went into the house, Derian had begun picking up pebbles from the ground. Now each person was given both a pebble and a piece of pottery.

"Pebble says you favor giving Virim's plan a chance. Pottery says you do not favor it, and believe we need further discussion."

Wort looked at the two items in his hand. "Shouldn't we assemble all the community?"

Zebel spoke before Derian or Ynamynet could reply.

"Arasan may not last out the hour, much less the time it would take to assemble, explain the matter, and then vote. If you feel that this issue needs to be brought before the community as a whole, then by all means, you should vote in favor of a delay."

"But that delay could be fatal for Arasan," Wort said.

"Quite possibly," Zebel said, "but remember, what Virim has suggested may not save Arasan—he may choose against it—so you must choose what you feel is best with the larger, not the smaller, picture in mind."

Wort nodded, the serious, thoughtful expression on his face replicated over and over again among the group.

"I offer my hands to help those of the yarimaimalom who need someone to drop in their piece," Plik said.

Derian colored. "I forgot about that. Thanks, Plik."

The voting went quickly enough. Isende had thoughtfully

lined the bottom of the jar with a dishcloth so that sound would not give away who voted what way. When the jar had gone around the circle, Derian and Ynamynet moved to the front and spilled out the contents onto one of the blankets where everyone could see.

Neither pottery nor pebbles dominated, but as the count progressed a clear majority was shown in favor of letting Virim's odd experiment be tried.

"We'll keep an eye on you both," Wort said, his voice hard and tough. "We've had enough of being shoved around by powerful spellcasters, just you remember that."

"We will," Virim said. "I assure you. We will."

XLIX

TWO DAYS AFTER she had called the meeting that had ultimately freed her from sole responsibility for Virim and the Meddler, Firekeeper and Blind Seer walked into the infirmary.

The rooms were a great deal more empty than they had been. A few of the more severely injured who still needed bandages changed or help getting to and from the pot or whose residences were, for one reason or another, ill equipped for one with their particular injury remained in one room. Even the few yarimaimalom who were accepting human aid were here.

Another room held but one tenant, and it was to that room, after greeting her friends in the common room, that Firekeeper and Blind Seer went.

Zebel was bending over the bed in which Arasan lay, propped up against a heap of pillows and breathing hoarsely. Derian stood nearby, holding a pot containing something that smelled foul. He looked very worried. Ynamynet, Sunshine in her lap, sat to one side, and her own expression of concern lightened when she saw Firekeeper and Blind Seer.

"Zebel," she said softly. "They're here."

Zebel glanced up, then back down at the man on the bed.

"Arasan," he said, "Firekeeper is here. Now, calm down before you do yourself an injury. Firekeeper, come over here so he can see you."

As Firekeeper moved to obey, Derian explained, "The Meddler heard you were leaving the Nexus Islands, and insisted he had to see you. When we didn't find you right away, and someone said they thought you might have already gated out, he grew so agitated we thought he might cause himself—themselves, him and Arasan—irreparable harm."

"Blind Seer and I were talking with Truth," Firekeeper said, "by the rocks she likes. We went into little cave, so she not get so distracted by every little thing that moves. You know how she is."

"That explains why even Elation couldn't find you," Derian said.

"You should have howled," Firekeeper said. "We would have heared."

Derian gave her a look that said as clearly as words that not everyone cared for the sound of wolf howls, and Firekeeper twitched her mouth in a small smile.

"What he want?" she asked.

From the bed, the Meddler spoke in Arasan's musical voice. The words came faint and weakly, for the injuries that had nearly killed Arasan's body were slow to heal, even with the Meddler's meddling. That they were healing at all was what Zebel called a miracle, and Firekeeper, far more practical in her outlook, took as proof that the Meddler did indeed want to continue living.

"I wanted a chance to tell you that I haven't given up on someday winning your love, Firekeeper."

Ynamynet's eyebrows rose, and her arms tightened around Sunshine so that the little girl squirmed. Derian looked startled. He glanced over at Blind Seer, but although the blue-eyed wolf had stiffened and his hackles had risen, he did not growl.

Firekeeper had long ago confided all that had happened between her and the Meddler to Blind Seer—even the Meddler's confessions of love and her own early reactions to that interest.

When she had told Blind Seer what the Meddler had tried to do to her in the name of that love, the blue-eyed wolf had not been pleased. Wolf-like, he had wanted to rip out the Meddler's throat, but Firekeeper had dissuaded him on the grounds that since that throat also belonged to Arasan, the situation could become awkward.

And she had said more, and now she tried to share those thoughts with the Meddler.

"I not understand what this is you call love," she said.

"I adore you," the Meddler began. "You fascinate me. I want you with me always. I want . . ."

"You want," Firekeeper interrupted. "You not seem to care what I want. I not want you. I know who I want, and he is not you."

She laid a hand on Blind Seer's head, just in case the Meddler retained the least bit of confusion about who she meant.

"But, Firekeeper, can't you understand?" the Meddler's voice had risen with the force of his protest, and now he began to cough.

Zebel made him sip something that smelled strongly of honey, but when he suggested the sick man lay back, the Meddler refused.

"I need to talk to her," he said peevishly. "I need to explain that she's making a horrible error."

Firekeeper tilted her head to one side in a wolfish query.

"What error?"

"How can you let yourself believe you love a wolf?" the Meddler said. "You are human, no matter what you choose to think. You are not a wolf. You must give your love to another human, not to a Beast, no matter how noble and intelligent and talented that Beast may be."

Blind Seer growled, *"I am glad you think so highly of me, Meddler, but take care."*

Firekeeper did not translate, for she knew the Meddler

would understand, but she saw the three humans stiffen and realized they thought Blind Seer was about to attack. Zebel, indeed, had, with more courage than wisdom, moved to insinuate his body between the wolf and his patient.

Firekeeper hastened to reassure them.

"Blind Seer not hurt the Meddler. He remember is Arasan, too."

She returned her attention to the man on the bed. He was— or would be, when the healing was completed—a handsome figure of a man, but she felt not the least stirring in her heart or her body when she looked at him.

"Meddler, I have thinked . . ."

"Thought," Derian muttered reflexively.

"Thought a great deal about this," Firekeeper continued, choosing her words with care.

A long time ago, Derian had told her a poorly chosen word was like tainted water and could create sickness. Then she had not believed him, but now she had seen enough that she knew her friend had been right.

"In my thinking," she went on, "I have tried to understand what is meant by love. First, I thought about mating, but I think that love is more than mating. Humans are different than wolves in this, because they are in season almost all the time and so their heads confuse desire and love. I think this is one way the wolf way is wiser. Wolves are only in season for a short time each year, and even then, for the good of the pack, only the Ones breed."

She drew in a deep breath, knowing she was oversimplifying, but knowing this must be said, even if this talk of mating was making Derian's face turn a little red.

"Wolves understand," Firekeeper continued, "that love is for more. Love is trusting someone will guard your back. Love is knowing that when you are wounded, that your loved one will drag food to where you are fallen. Love is knowing that you would do this for the other, even if doing that means going hungry for yourself. Love is knowing that when you die, someone will care enough to sing of you to the moon."

The Meddler was staring at her in such complete silence

and with such profound attention that Firekeeper wondered if Arasan was making him listen rather than think about what clever thing he would say next. She hurried her words along lest the moment be lost.

"You, and not just you, some others who think they mean well for me—and for Blind Seer—have spoken about how our hearts loving means nothing because our shapes are different. For a time, I let this confuse me. Then I came to know more and more people who loved, and I realized that this matter of shape was all a twisting, turning mass of vines, something that seemed more massive than it was.

"When Bitter was mutilated by the blood briar, Lovable did not stop loving him. She nearly died trying to save him. Afterwards, he was ugly, but no one said, 'Lovable, find yourself a strong young mate. This hurt bird cannot fly well.' I think, even, that if Lovable had left Bitter, then everyone would have thought her weak."

"But they are both ravens," the Meddler said softly, "not a raven and a deer."

"Or a human and a wolf," Firekeeper said. "I know. But what does human and human or wolf and wolf matter? I think that matching only matter for mating and for bearing children. Yet not all humans have children, and you do not condemn those like Urgana who have not become mothers, or like Arasan who are not fathers. As I said before, in a wolf pack, not all the pack members are parents to pups. Indeed, if every member of a pack tried to have pups, then that would be the wrongness, not the other.

"Humans love their mates even when the time for having young is over. They care for each other even when they grow old and ill. To me, when you say you love what you are saying is you desire, you want . . . You want what you see now. What you desire now. There is no strength in that feeling to carry you where change will take you. That is not love. That thing you are calling love is something my wolf's heart does not understand."

Firekeeper looked at Ynamynet. "You and Skea have just one child. Would you have put Skea from you if in the fighting he had been so wounded that there would be no others?"

"Never!" Ynamynet said so fiercely that Sunshine looked about to cry. Ynamynet went on more quietly. "You speak closer to the truth than you know, Firekeeper. For a long time, because of what querinalo did to me, I did not think I could have children. Skea told me that didn't matter, and he could love me even though my body is like ice to hold. I thought he would soon tire of me, but you know this is not the way it is with us."

Firekeeper looked at Derian, but she would not embarrass her friend by pointing out his own physical changes made him as much unlike Isende as like. He, however, spoke his own thoughts.

"I thought I was a monster, yet no one has told me that I should not love Isende, and she herself told me that shape and the bearing of children—I mean . . ." His face grew as red as his hair, "I mean, we don't know if we can, but no one has told us that we cannot love."

The Meddler was restless and wild-eyed. "But Firekeeper is a human and she says she loves a wolf! Ynamynet and Derian—you at least started out human, and just changed a little."

Firekeeper shook her head.

"I started out wolf, and have learned a little to be human. In my heart, though, I do not think I could love a human, or love after the best of the human way. I am a wolf, and a wolf is who I love. Shape does not matter. Heart and soul is what loves, as Ynamynet and Skea, and Doc and Elise, and Bitter and Lovable, and all those who have fought to hold on to their love even when others and even their own hearts have told them to doubt."

She knelt and put her arms around Blind Seer.

"He is who I love. If you love me, Meddler, then wish us well. That would be true love, to feel joy that I have found one to trust and who I wish to run beside for as long as I have life and breath."

The Meddler stared for a long, long moment.

"I see. I don't know what I have to live for. I wanted a body so I could be with you."

Firekeeper looked at him and grinned. "That is nonsense. There is so much more to live for than something that silly."

Blind Seer forced the Meddler to meet his gaze. *"Will you leave her be?"*

"It seems," the Meddler said, "I am being given no choice."

Firekeeper nodded and turned to leave, Blind Seer beside her. The Meddler called after them.

"Wait! I realize you're leaving. Where are you going?"

Firekeeper looked back over her shoulder. "First through the gate to Virim's place to visit the Bound, and make sure their wounded are well. From there . . ."

She paused and looked at Blind Seer. The great grey wolf panted one of his laughing smiles, and she grinned in return.

"Who knows? The world is so very large, and in these years we have seen so little. We go to see more."

"Together," Blind Seer added.

"Together," Firekeeper repeated. Her hand lightly brushing the wolf's back, she walked from the room.

She didn't bother to look back, because she knew that someday they would return. Instead, she looked ahead because ahead was where the footing was less than sure.

She heard Derian murmur, affection in his voice, "Wolves!"

And she answered silently, her heart filled with contentment, "Yes. Wolves."

GLOSSARY OF CHARACTERS

Agneta[1] Norwood: (H.H.) daughter of Norvin Norwood and Luella Stanbrook; sister of Edlin, Tait, and Lillis Norwood; adopted sister of Blysse Norwood (Firekeeper).

Aksel Trueheart: (Lord, H.H.) scholar of Hawk Haven; spouse of Zorana Archer; father of Purcel, Nydia, Deste, and Kenre Trueheart.[2]

Alben Eagle: (H.H.) son of Princess Marras and Lorimer Stanbrook. In keeping with principles of Zorana I, given no title as died in infancy.

Alin Brave: (H.H.) husband of Grace Trueheart; father of Baxter Trueheart.

Allister I: (King, B.B.) called King Allister of the Pledge, sometimes the Pledge Child; formerly Allister Seagleam. Son of Tavis Seagleam (B.B.) and Caryl Eagle (H.H.); spouse of Pearl Oyster; father of Shad, Tavis, Anemone, and Minnow.

Alt Rosen: (Opulence, Waterland) ambassador to Bright Bay.

Amery Pelican: (King, B.B.) Spouse of Gustin II; father of

---

[1] Characters are detailed under first name or best-known name. The initials B.B. (Bright Bay), H.H. (Hawk Haven), N.K. (New Kelvin), or L. (Liglim) in parenthesis following a character's name indicate nationality. Titles are indicated in parentheses.

[2] Hawk Haven and Bright Bay noble houses both follow a naming system where the children take the surname of the higher-ranking parent, with the exception that only the immediate royal family bear the name of that house. If the parents are of the same rank, then rank is designated from the birth house, greater over lesser, lesser by seniority. The Great Houses are ranked in the following order: Eagle, Shield, Wellward, Trueheart, Redbriar, Stanbrook, Norwood.

Basil, Seastar, and Tavis Seagleam. Deceased.

Amiri: (city-state of Gak); aridisdu.

Anemone: (Princess, B.B.) formerly Anemone Oyster. Daughter of Allister I and Pearl Oyster; sister of Shad and Tavis; twin of Minnow.

Anitra: (Queen, Azure Towers) a respected ruler.

Apheros: (Dragon Speaker, N.K.) long-time elected official of New Kelvin, effectively head of government.

Arasan: (Nexus Islands) Once Dead.

Aurella Wellward: (Lady, H.H.) confidante of Queen Elexa; spouse of Ivon Archer; mother of Elise Archer.

Aurick: (Pelland) a popular general.

Barden Eagle: (Prince, H.H.) third son of Tedric I and Elexa Wellward. Disowned. Spouse of Eirene Norwood; father of Blysse Eagle. Presumed deceased.

Barnet Lobster: (Isles) sailor on the *Explorer.*

Basil Seagleam: see Gustin III.

Baxter Trueheart: (Earl, H.H.) infant son of Grace Trueheart and Alin Brave. Technically not a title holder until he has safely survived his first two years.

Beachcomber: a Wise Wolf.

Bee Biter: Royal Kestrel; guide and messenger.

Bevan Seal: see Calico.

Bibimalenu: (L.) member of u-Liall, representative for Air.

Bitter: a Wise Raven.

Blind Seer: Royal Wolf; companion to Firekeeper.

Blysse Eagle: (Lady, H.H.) daughter of Prince Barden and Eirene Kestrel.

Blysse Kestrel: see Firekeeper.

Bold: Royal Crow; eastern agent; sometime companion to Firekeeper.

Bright-Eyes-Fast-Paws: a Wise Jaguar.

Brina Dolphin: (Lady or Queen, B.B.) first spouse of Gustin III, divorced as barren.

Brock Carter: (H.H.) son of Colby and Vernita Carter; brother of Derian and Damita Carter.

Brotius: (N.K., Captain) soldier in New Kelvin.

Bruck: a sorcerer.

Bryessidan: (King, Mires) son of Veztressidan; husband of Gidji; father of Junal, Stave, Neysa, and Vahon.

Calico: (B.B.) proper name, Bevan Seal. Confidential secretary to Allister I. Member of a cadet branch of House Seal.

Caryl Eagle: (Princess, H.H.) daughter of King Chalmer I; married to Prince Tavis Seagleam; mother of Allister Seagleam. Deceased.

Ceece Dolphin: (Lady, B.B.) sister to current Duke Dolphin.

Chaker Torn: (Nexus Islands) captain of fishing boats; father of Juneo and a daughter.

Chalmer I: (King, H.H.) born Chalmer Elkwood; son of Queen Zorana the Great; spouse of Rose Rosewood; father of Marras, Tedric, Caryl Gadman, and Rosene Eagle. Deceased.

Chalmer Eagle: (Crown Prince, H.H.) son of Tedric Eagle and Elexa Wellward. Deceased.

Chelm Charlock: (Mires) minister for International Trade.

Chetuk Meadows: (Pelland) an emissary.

Chutia: (N.K.) Illuminator. Wife of Grateful Peace. Deceased.

Cishanol: (L.) assistant to Meiyal, disdu in training.

Citrine Shield: (H.H.) daughter of Melina Shield and Rolfston Redbriar; sister of Sapphire, Jet, Opal, and Ruby Shield; adopted daughter of Grateful Peace.

Colby Carter: (H.H.) livery stable owner and carter; spouse of Vernita Carter; father of Derian, Damita, and Brock.

Columi: (N.K.) retired Prime of the Sodality of Lapidaries.

Comb Ripper: a Wise Bear cub.

Cricket: a Wise Wolf.

Culver Pelican: (Lord, B.B.) son of Seastar Seagleam; brother of Dillon Pelican. Merchant ship captain.

Daisy: (H.H.) steward of West Keep, in employ of Earl Kestrel.

Damita Carter: (H.H.) daughter of Colby and Vernita Carter; sister of Derian and Brock Carter.

Dantarahma: (L.) member of

u-Liall, representative for Water. Deceased.

Dark Death: a Wise Wolf.

Dawn Brooks: (H.H.) wife of Ewen Brooks, mother of several small children. Deceased.

Dayle: (H.H.) steward for the Archer Manse in Eagle's Nest.

Derian Carter: (H.H.) also called Derian Counselor; son of Colby and Vernita Carter; brother of Damita and Brock Carter.

Deste Trueheart: (H.H.) daughter of Aksel Trueheart and Zorana Archer; sister of Purcel, Nydia, and Kenre Trueheart.

Dia Trueheart: see Nydia Trueheart.

Dillon Pelican: (Lord, B.B.) son of Seastar Seagleam; brother of Culver Pelican.

Dimiria: (N.K.) Prime, Sodality of Stargazers.

Dirkin Eastbranch: (knight, H.H.) King Tedric's personal bodyguard.

Diuric: (Nexus Islands) a carpenter.

Donal Hunter: (H.H.) member of Barden Eagle's expedition; spouse of Sarena; father of Tamara. Deceased.

Edlin Norwood: (Lord, H.H.) son of Norvin Norwood and Luella Kite; brother of Tait, Lillis, and Agneta Norwood; adopted brother of Blysse Kestrel (Firekeeper).

Eirene Norwood: (Lady, H.H.) spouse of Barden Eagle; mother of Blysse Eagle; sister of Norvin Norwood. Presumed deceased.

Elation: Royal Falcon, companion to Firekeeper.

Elexa Archer: (Lady, H.H.) daughter of Elise Archer and Jared Surcliffe.

Elexa Wellward: (Queen, H.H.) spouse of Tedric I; mother of Chalmer, Lovells, and Barden.

Elise Archer: (Lady, H.H.) daughter of Ivon Archer and Aurella Wellward; heir to Archer Grant; spouse of Jared Surcliffe; mother of Elexa.

Elwyn: (Isles) also called "Lucky Elwyn"; a sailor on the *Explorer.*

Enigma: a Wise Puma.

Eshinarvash: a Wise Horse.

Eteo: (Nexus Islands) a young boy.

Evaglayn: (N.K.) senior apprentice in the Beast Lore sodality.

Evie Cook: (H.H.) servant in the Carter household.

Ewen Brooks: (N.K.) spouse of Dawn Brooks, father of several children.

Faelene Lobster: (Duchess, B.B.) head of House Lobster; sister of Marek, duke of Half-Moon Island; aunt of King Harwill.

Fairwind Sailor: (B.B.) ambassador to Liglim from Bright Haven.

Farand Briarcott: (Lady, H.H.) assistant to Tedric I, former military commander.

Farborn: a Wise Merlin.

Feeshaguyu: (L.) member of u-Liall; representative for Earth.

Fess Bones: a pirate with some medical skills.

Firekeeper: (Lady, H.H.) feral child raised by wolves, adopted by Norvin Norwood and given the name Blysse Kestrel.

Fleet Herald: a pirate messenger.

Fox Driver: (H.H.) given name, Orin. Skilled driver in the employ of Waln Endbrook. Deceased.

Freckles: a Wise Wolf.

Fromalf: (Tavetch) a general.

Gadman Eagle: (Grand Duke, H.H.) fourth child of King Chalmer and Queen Rose; brother to Marras, Caryl, Tedric, Rosene; spouse of Riki Redbriar; father of Rolfston and Nydia.

Gardener: a maimalodalu.

Garrik Carpenter: (H.H.) a skilled woodworker. Deceased.

Gayl Minter: see Gayl Seagleam.

Gayl Seagleam: (Queen, B.B.) spouse of Gustin I; first queen of Bright Bay; mother of Gustin, Merry (later Gustin II), and Lyra. Note: Gayl was the only queen to assume the name "Seagleam." Later tradition paralleled that of Hawk Haven where the name of the birth house was retained even after marriage to the monarch. Deceased.

Gidji: (Queen, Mires) called "Daughter of the Hammer." Daughter of King Hurwin of Tavetch; spouse of Bryessidan; mother of Junal, Stave, Neysa, and Vahon.

Glynn: (H.H.) a soldier.

Golden Feather: a Wise Owl; mate to Night's Terror.

Grateful Peace: (Dragon's Eye, N.K.) also, Trausholo. Illuminator; Prime of New Kelvin; member of the Dragon's Three. A very influential person. Husband to Chutia; brother of Idalia; uncle of Varcasiol, Kistlio, Linatha, and others; adopted father of Citrine.

Grey Thunder: a Wise Wolf.

Grub Digger: a Wise Bear cub.

Gustin I: (King, B.B.) born Gustin Sailor, assumed the name Seagleam upon his coronation; first monarch of Bright Bay; spouse of Gayl Minter, later Gayl Seagleam; father of Gustin, Merry, and Lyra Seagleam. Deceased.

Gustin II: (Queen, B.B.) born Merry Seagleam, assumed the name Gustin upon her coronation; second monarch of Bright Bay; spouse of Amery Pelican; mother of Basil, Seastar, and Tavis Seagleam. Deceased.

Gustin III: (King, B.B.) born Basil Seagleam, assumed the name Gustin upon his coronation; third monarch of Bright Bay; spouse of Brina Dolphin, later of Viona Seal; father of Valora Seagleam. Deceased.

Gustin IV: (Queen, B.B.) see Valora I.

Gustin Sailor: see Gustin I.

Half-Ear: a Wise Wolf.

Half-Snarl: a Wise Wolf.

Hard Biter: a Wise Wolf.

Harjeedian: (L.) aridisdu serving the Temple of the Cold Bloods; brother of Rahniseeta.

Hart: (H.H.) a young hunter.

Harwill Lobster: (King, the Isles) spouse of Valora I, during her reign as Gustin IV, also king of Bright Bay. Son of Marek.

Hasamemorri: (N.K.) a landlady.

Hazel Healer: (H.H.) apothecary, herbalist, perfumer resident in the town of Hope.

Healer: a Wise Wolf.

Heather Baker: (H.H.) baker in Eagle's Nest; former sweetheart of Derian Carter.

High Howler: a Wise Wolf.

Holly Gardener: (H.H.) former Master Gardener for Eagle's Nest Castle, possessor of the Green Thumb, a talent for the growing of plants. Mother of Timin and Sarena.

Honey Endbrook: (Isles) mother of Waln Endbrook.

Hope: a maimalodalu.

Hurwin: (King, Tavetch) called "the Hammer"; father of Gidji.

Hya Grimsel: (General, Stonehold) commander of Stonehold troops.

Idalia: (N.K.) assistant to Melina. Sister of Grateful Peace, spouse of Pichero; mother of Kistlio, Varcasiol, Linatha, and others.

Iline: (Queen, Hearthome) renowned for intrigue.

Indatius: (N.K.) young member of the Sodality of Artificers.

Integrity: a Wise Wolf.

Isende: (Nexus Islands) twin sister of Tiniel.

Ivon Archer: (Baron, H.H.) master of the Archer Grant; son of Purcel Archer and Rosene Eagle; brother of Zorana Archer; spouse of Aurella Wellward; father of Elise Archer.

Ivory Pelican: (Lord, B.B.) Keeper of the Keys, an honored post in Bright Bay.

Jalarios: see Grateful Peace.

Jared Surcliffe: (knight, H.H.) knight of the Order of the White Eagle; possessor of the healing talent; distant cousin of Norvin Norwood who serves as his patron. Spouse of Elise Archer; father of Elexa.

Jem: (B.B.) deserter from Bright Bay's army.

Jet Shield: (H.H.) son of Melina Shield and Rolfston Redbriar; brother of Sapphire, Opal, Ruby, and Citrine. Heir apparent to his parents' properties upon the adoption of his sister Sapphire by Tedric I.

Joy Spinner: (H.H.) scout in the service of Earle Kite. Deceased.

Junal: (Princess, Mires) daughter of Bryessidan and Gidji; sister of Stave, Neysa, and Vahon.

Junco Torn: (Nexus Islands) a sailor; son of Chaker.

Kalvinia: (Prime, N.K.) thaumaturge, Sodality of Sericulturalists.

Kalyndra: (Nexus Islands) Once Dead; mother of Skea.

Keen: (H.H.) servant to Newell Shield.

Kenre Trueheart: (H.H.) son of Zorana Archer and Aksel Trueheart; brother of Purcel, Nydia, and Deste Trueheart.

Kiero: (N.K.): spy in the service of the Healed One. Deceased.

Kistlio: (N.K.) clerk in Thendulla Lypella; nephew of Grateful Peace; son of Idalia and Pichero; brother of Varcasiol, Linatha, and others. Deceased.

Kynan: (Hearthome) a general.

Lachen: a Once Dead.

Laloreezo: (u-Chival) a kidisdu; an emissary.

Laria: (Nexus Islands) a young woman; daughter of Ollaris.

Layozirate: an important citizen of Gak; mother of Petulia.

Lillis Norwood: (H.H.) daughter of Norvin Norwood and Luella Stanbrook; sister of Edlin, Tait, and Agneta Norwood; adopted sister of Blysse Norwood (Firekeeper).

Linatha: (N.K.) niece of Grateful Peace; daughter of Idalia and Pichero; sister of Kistlio, Varcasiol, and others.

Longsight Scrounger: pirate, leader of those at Smuggler's Light.

Lorimer Stanbrook: (Lord, H.H.) spouse of Marras Eagle; father of Marigolde and Alben Eagle. Deceased.

Lovable: a Wise Raven; mate of Bitter.

Lovella Eagle: (Crown Princess, H.H.) military commander; daughter of Tedric Eagle and Elexa Wellward; spouse of Newell Shield. Deceased.

Loxia: (Nexus Islands) young girl; daughter of Rhul and Saeta.

Lucho: (N.K.) a thug.

Lucky Shortleg: a pirate.

Luella Stanbrook: (Lady, H.H.) spouse of Norvin Norwood; mother of Edlin, Tait, Lillis, and Agneta Norwood.

Man Tosser: a Wise Moose.

Marek: (Duke, Half-Moon Island) formerly Duke Lobster of Bright Bay but chose to follow the fate of his son, Harwill. Brother of Faelene, the current Duchess Lobster.

Marigolde Eagle: (H.H.) daughter of Marras Eagle and Lorimer Stanbrook. In keeping with principles of Zorana I, given no title as died in infancy.

Marras Eagle: (Crown Princess, H.H.) daughter of Chalmer Eagle and Rose Rosewood; sister of Tedric, Caryl, Gadman, and Rosene; spouse of Lorimer Stanbrook; mother of Marigolde and Alben Eagle. Deceased.

Meddler: a spirit.

Meiyal: (L.) iaridisdu of the Horse.

Melina: (H.H.; N.K.) formerly entitled "lady," with affiliation to House Gyrfalcon; reputed sorceress; spouse of Rolfston Redbriar; mother of Sapphire, Jet, Opal, Ruby, and Citrine Shield. Later spouse of Torovico of New Kelvin, given title of Consolor of the Healed One. Deceased.

Merial: (Azure Towers) a general, Anitra's niece.

Merri Jay: (H.H.) daughter of Wendee Jay.

Merry Seagleam: see Gustin II.

Minnow: (Princess, B.B.) formerly Minnow Oyster. Daughter of Allister I and Pearl Oyster; sister of Shad and Tavis; twin of Anemone.

Moon Frost: a Wise Wolf.

Nanny: (H.H.) attendant to Melina Shield.

Neck Breaker: a Wise Wolf.

Nelm: (N.K.) member of the Sodality of Herbalists.

Nemeria: (Nexus Islands) a young woman with a loud voice.

Newell Shield: (Prince, H.H.) commander of marines; spouse of Lovella Eagle; brother of Melina Shield. Deceased.

Neysa: (Princess, Mires) daughter of Bryessidan and Gidji; sister of Junal, Stave, and Vahon.

Night's Terror: a Wise Owl; mate of Golden Feather.

Ninette Farmer: (H.H.) relative of Ivon Archer; attendant of Elise Archer.

Nipper: a Wise Wolf.

Nolan: a sailor on the *Explorer*. Deceased.

Noonafaruma: (L.) member of u-Liall; representative for Magic.

Northwest: Royal Wolf, not of Firekeeper's pack. Called Sharp Fang by his own pack.

Norvin Norwood: (Earl Kestrel, H.H.) heir to Kestrel Grant; son of Saedee Norwood; brother of Eirene Norwood; spouse of

Luella Stanbrook; father of Edlin, Tait, Lillis, and Agneta; adopted father of Blysse (Firekeeper).

Nstasius: (Prime, N.K.) member of the Sodality of Sericultural-ists, sympathetic to the Progres-sive Party.

Nydia Trueheart: (H.H.) often called Dia; daughter of Aksel Trueheart and Zorana Archer; sister of Purcel, Deste, and Kenre Trueheart.

Oculios: (N.K.) apothecary; mem-ber of the Sodality of Alchemists.

Ollaris: (Nexus Islands) a cob-bler; father of Laria.

One Female: also Shining Coat; ruling female wolf of Firekeeper and Blind Seer's pack.

One Male: also Rip; ruling male wolf of Firekeeper and Blind Seer's pack.

Onion: a Wise Wolf.

Opal Shield: (H.H.) daughter of Melina Shield and Rolfston Redbriar; sister of Sapphire, Jet, Ruby, and Citrine.

Oralia: (Isles) wife of Waln En-drook; mother of three children.

Ox: (H.H.) born Malvin Hogge; bodyguard to Norvin Norwood; renowned for his strength and good temper.

Paliama: (L.) a kidisdu.

Pearl Oyster: (Queen, B.B.) spouse of Allister I; mother of Shad, Tavis, Anemone, and Min-now.

Perce Potterford: (B.B.) guard to Allister I.

Perr: (H.H.) body servant to Ivon Archer.

Petulia: (city-state of Gak) trai-nee kidisdu.

Pichero: (N.K.) spouse of Idalia; father of Kistlio, Varcasiol, Linatha, and others.

Pishtoolam: (Nexus Islands) chief cook.

Plik: a maimalodalu.

Polr: (Lord, H.H.) military com-mander; brother of Tab, Rein, Newell, and Melina.

Posa: (Prime, N.K.) member of the Sodality of Illuminators.

Postuvanu: (L.) a kidisdu of the Horse, son of Varjuna and Zira.

Powerful Tenderness: a maimalo-dalu.

Puma Killer: a Wise Wolf.

Purcel Archer: (Baron Archer, H.H.) first Baron Archer, born Purcel Farmer, elevated to the title for his prowess in battle; spouse of Rosene Eagle; father of Ivon and Zorana. Deceased.

Purcel Trueheart: (H.H.) lieutenant Hawk Haven army; son of Aksel Trueheart and Zorana Archer; brother of Nydia, Deste, and Kenre Trueheart. Deceased.

Questioner: a maimalodalu. Deceased.

Race Forester: (H.H.) scout under the patronage of Norvin Norwood; regarded by many as one of the best in his calling.

Rafalias: (N.K.) member of the Sodality of Lapidaries.

Rahniseeta: (L.) representative for water; sister of Harjeedian.

Rarby: a sailor on the *Explorer.* Deceased.

Rascal: a Wise Wolf.

Red Stripe: also called Cime; a pirate.

Reed Oyster: (Duke, B.B.) father of Queen Pearl. Among the strongest supporters of Allister I.

Rein Shield: (Lord, H.H.) brother of Tab, Newell, Polr, and Melina.

Rhul: (Nexus Islands) spouse of Saeta; father of Loxia and others.

Riki Redbriar: (Lady, H.H.) spouse of Gadman Eagle; mother of Rolfston and Nydia Redbriar. Deceased.

Rillon: (N.K.) a maid in the Cloud Touching Spire; a slave.

Rios: see Citrine Shield.

Rip: see the One Male.

Rolfston Redbriar: (Lord, H.H.) son of Gadman Eagle and Riki Redbriar; spouse of Melina Shield; father of Sapphire, Jet, Opal, Ruby, and Citrine Shield. Deceased.

Rook: (H.H.) servant to Newell Shield.

Rory Seal: (Lord, B.B.) holds the title Royal Physician.

Rose Rosewood: (Queen, H.H.) common-born wife of Chalmer I; also called Rose Dawn; his marriage to her was the reason Hawk Haven Great Houses received what Queen Zorana the Great would doubtless have seen as unnecessary and frivolous titles. Deceased.

Rosene: (Grand Duchess, H.H.) fifth child of King Chalmer and Queen Rose; spouse of Purcel Archer; mother of Ivon and Zorana Archer.

Ruby Shield: (H.H.) daughter of Melina Shield and Rolfston Redbriar; sister of Sapphire, Jet, Opal, and Citrine Shield.

Saedee Norwood: (Duchess Kestrel, H.H.) mother of Norvin and Eirene Norwood.

Saeta: (Nexus Islands) spouse of Rhul; mother of Loxia and others.

Sapphire: (Crown Princess, H.H.) adopted daughter of Tedric I; birth daughter of Melina Shield and Rolfston Redbriar; sister of Jet, Opal, Ruby, and Citrine Shield; spouse of Shad.

Sarena Gàrdener: (H.H.) member of Prince Barden's expedition; spouse of Donal Hunter; mother of Tamara. Deceased.

Seastar Seagleam: (Grand Duchess, B.B.) sister of Gustin III; mother of Culver and Dillon Pelican.

Shad: (Crown Prince, B.B.) son of Allister I and Pearl Oyster; brother of Tavis, Anemone, and Minnow Oyster; spouse of Sapphire.

Sharp Fang: a common name among the Royal Wolves; see Northwest and Whiner.

Shelby: a sailor on the *Explorer*. Deceased.

Shervanu: (u-Chival) an aridisu; ambassador to the Mires.

Shivadtmon: (L.) an aridisdu.

Siyago: (Dragon's Fire, N.K.) a prominent member of the Sodality of Artificers.

Skea: (Nexus Islands) a Twice Dead; spouse of Ynamynet; father of Sunshine.

Sky: also Sky-Dreaming-Earth-Bound, a maimalodalu. Deceased.

Stave: (Prince, Mires) son of Bryessidan and Gidji; brother of Junal, Neysa, and Vahon.

Steady Runner: a Royal Elk.

Steward Silver: (H.H.) long-time steward of Eagle's Nest Castle. Her birth-name and origin have been forgotten as no one, not even Silver herself, thinks of her as anything but the steward.

Sun of Bright Haven: first born of Sapphire and Shad.

Sunshine: (Nexus Islands) daughter of Skea and Ynamynet.

Surf Hands: a maimalodalu.

Tab Shield: (Duke Gyrfalcon, H.H.) brother of Rein, Newell, Polr, and Melina.

Tait Norwood: (H.H.) son of Norvin Norwood and Luella Stanbrook; brother of Edlin, Lillis, and Agneta Norwood.

Talianas: (Tishiolo) a general.

Tallus: (Prime, N.K.) member of the Sodality of Alchemists.

Tangler: a Wise Wolf.

Tavis Oyster: (Prince, B.B.) son of Allister I and Pearl Oyster; brother of Shad, Anemone, and Minnow Oyster.

Tavis Seagleam: (Prince, B.B.) third child of Gustin II and Amery Pelican; spouse of Caryl Eagle; father of Allister Seagleam.

Tedgewinn: a sailor on the *Explorer*.

Tedric I: (King, H.H.) third king of Hawk Haven; son of King Chalmer and Queen Rose; spouse of Elexa Wellward; father of Chalmer, Lovella, and Barden; adopted father of Sapphire.

Tenacity: a Wise Wolf.

Tench: (Lord, B.B.) born Tench Clark; right hand to Queen Gustin IV; knighted for his services; later made Lord of the Pen. Deceased.

Thyme: (H.H.) a scout in the service of Hawk Haven.

Timin Gardener: (H.H.) Master Gardener for Eagle's Nest Castle, possessor of the Green Thumb, a talent involving the growing of plants; son of Holly Gardener; brother of Sarena; father of Dan and Robyn.

Tiniel: (Nexus Islands) twin brother of Isende.

Tipi: (N.K.) slave, born in Stonehold.

Tiridanti: (L.) member of u-Liall; representative for Fire.

Toad: (H.H.) pensioner of the Carter family.

Tollius: (N.K.) member of the Sodality of Smiths.

Toriovico: (Healed One, N.K.) hereditary ruler of New Kelvin; spouse of Melina; brother to Vanviko (deceased) and several sisters.

Tris Stone: a pirate.

Truth: a Wise Jaguar.

Tymia: (N.K.) a guard.

Ulia: (N.K.) a judge.

Urgana: (Nexus Islands) Never Lived.

Vahon: (Prince, Mires) son of Bryessidan and Gidji; brother of Junal, Stave, and Neysa.

Valet: (H.H.) eponymous servant of Norvin Norwood; known for his fidelity and surprising wealth of useful skills.

Valora I: (Queen, the Isles) born Valora Seagleam, assumed the name Gustin upon her coronation as fourth monarch of Bright Bay. Resigned her position to Allister I and became queen of the Isles. Spouse of Harwill Lobster.

Valora Seagleam: see Valora I.

Vanviko: (heir to the Healed One, N.K.) elder brother of Toriovico; killed in avalanche.

Varcasiol: (N.K.) nephew of Grateful Peace; son of Idalia and Pichero; brother of Kistlio, Linatha, and others.

Varjuna: (L.) ikidisdu of the Horse; husband of Zira; father of Poshtuvanu and others.

Vernita Carter: (H.H.) born Vernita Painter, an acknowledged beauty of her day, Vernita became associated with the business she and her husband, Colby, transformed from a simple carting business to a group of associated livery stables and carting service; spouse of Colby Carter; mother of Derian, Damita, and Brock Carter.

Verul: (Nexus Islands) a Twice Dead.

Violet Redbriar: (Ambassador, H.H.) ambassador from Hawk Haven to New Kelvin; translator and author, with great interest in New Kelvinese culture.

Viona Seal: (Queen, B.B.) second wife of King Gustin III; mother of Valora, later Gustin IV.

Virim: a mystery.

Wain Cutter: (H.H.) skilled lapidary and gem cutter working out of the town of Hope.

Waln Endbrook: (the Isles) formerly Baron Endbrook; also, Walnut Endbrook. A prosperous merchant, Waln found rapid promotion in the service of Valora I. Spouse of Oralia, father of two daughters and a son. Deceased.

Wendee Jay: (H.H.) retainer in service of Duchess Kestrel. Lady's maid to Firekeeper. Divorced. Mother of two daughters.

Wheeler: (H.H.) scout captain.

Whiner: a wolf of Blind Seer and Firekeeper's pack, later named Sharp Fang.

Whyte Steel: (knight, B.B.) captain of the guard for Allister I.

Wiatt: a sailor on the *Explorer*.

Wind Whisper: Royal Wolf, formerly of Firekeeper's pack, now member of another pack.

Wort: (Nexus Islands) a Twice Dead.

Xarxius: (Dragon's Claw, N.K.) member of the Dragon's Three, former Stargazer.

Yaree Yuci: (General, Stonehold) commander of Stonehold troops.

Ynamynet: (Nexus Islands) Once Dead; spouse of Skea; mother of Sunshine.

Zahlia: (N.K.) member of the Sodality of Smiths. Specialist in silver.

Zebel: (Nexus Islands) a Twice Dead; a doctor.

Zira: (L.) kidisdu of the Horse; wife of Varjuna; mother of Poshtuvanu and others.

Zorana I: (Queen, H.H.) also called Zorana the Great, born Zorana Shield. First monarch of Hawk Haven; responsible for a reduction of titles—so associated with this program that overemphasis of titles is considered "unzoranic." Spouse of Clive Elkwood; mother of Chalmer I.

Zorana Archer: (Lady, H.H.) daughter of Rosene Eagle and Purcel Archer; sister of Ivon Archer; spouse of Aksel Trueheart; mother of Purcel, Nydia, Deste, and Kenre Trueheart.